T0368774

Merlion and the Bay

a novel

Karyn R. Workman

iUniverse, Inc.
New York Bloomington

Merlion and the Bay
a novel

iUniverse books may be ordered through booksellers or by contacting:

iUniverse
1663 Liberty Drive
Bloomington, IN 47403
www.iuniverse.com
1-800-Authors (1-800-288-4677)

ISBN: 978-1-4502-6045-9 (sc)
ISBN: 978-1-4502-6046-6 (dj)
ISBN: 978-1-4502-6047-3 (ebook)

Printed in the United States of America

iUniverse rev. date: 09/30/2010

To my husband, Mark, and children, Gillian & Sam, who spent many evenings alone while I wrote.

Journey and Arnel Pineda who inspired me to 'Don't Stop Believin'

Chapter 1

THE WEATHER WAS warm in downtown San Francisco, warmer than normal for early September. The skies were clear and a vibrant shade of lazuli. The fog of the early morning burned off and it looked to be a beautiful day. As Laramie walked through the doors of the former Bank of America building, she looked up to see the reflection of the skyscrapers bounce off the windows of its' cubic form, put on her sunglasses, let out a deep sigh and smiled. These streets between the Embarcadero and Montgomery, known as the Financial District, were her security blanket, this was where she felt most comfortable.

Heads of men, all ages, turned to watch her stroll along the concrete, even the women did a double take, with a cringe of envy. With each stride, Laramie remained completely unaware of their glances. She was fortunate to have stunning good looks and brains, outwardly the model of perfection. Her long blonde hair wisped back in the wind. She was born with her mother's sky blue eyes and flawless olive complexion and her father's leanness. She looked taller than the five-foot-eight frame she carried. Underneath her Lauren jacket, she wore a short sleeve turtleneck dress, nude hose and platform pumps. She sauntered gracefully across the plaza, her jacket blowing open, heading for the sleek black limousine parked on the street.

A medium height Asian man, dressed impeccably in a black suit with a starched white collared shirt, walked around the rear of the limo and opened the door. His shoes, flawlessly shined, reflected the same buildings of the skyline. His hair was jet black, short and slightly spiked to the side, a mild imperfection. His black wrap-around sunglasses masked his eyes. His smile was as perfect as his clothing.

"Good morning, Miss Holden," he replied with a smirk. He firmly closed her door while gliding his glove across the chrome handle to remove any fingerprints. He walked toward the driver's door, opened it and sat. He adjusted himself back into his leather seat and looked into the rear view mirror, noticing the center privacy window was down and the sunroof was open.

"What a beautiful day we are having in the city," he said in a gleeful way. "Where can I take you today?"

"Thank you for the formalities, Mr. Tién," she said as she leaned forward to the privacy window. "But, to answer your question, *you* can take me home," she responded with a flirtatious sound.

"Yes, Ma'am," he answered with a growl. "However, until we're out of sight, I'm strictly Mr. Professional. You never know whose eyes are upon you."

Laramie laughed along and settled back into her seat. *So much space in these cars and all for one person to sit. With inflation and gas prices high, why not be more economical?* She could have easily taken a cab or ridden the BART, however with further thought, that would leave her friend of eight years, Manchu Tién, without a job. The driver put the car into gear and proceeded along California Street.

Manchu Tién was fourth generation Chinese-American. His family owned a small market on Grant Avenue in Chinatown. Above the market, Manchu lived in a small flat with his wife, Lian, his parents and his grandparents. Manchu and Lian were the only family members who spoke English or for that matter spoke anything. On many occasions, Laramie received a bow and a smile with giggles that followed, causing her to speculate on their knowledge of English. Lian, graceful as her name, was petite and demure. She had silky black hair that she tied neatly behind her head. She was attractive with porcelain-like skin that resembled the dolls found in the Chinatown shops. Her clothes were very plain but cleanly pressed. Her mannerisms seemed formal with tradition; one would never guess she lived here all her life. Lian worked at the market with her in-laws and seemed comfortable with her life and position in the Chinese community.

Manchu, or Manny to his friends, drove the company limousine for the law firm, Graham, Mathers and Holden. In the evenings, Manny started classes at San Francisco State University; he hoped to earn his degree in finance. As much as he loved his parents and grandparents, he was more Americanized and less fond of old Chinese traditions.

"*Just a small town girl, livin' in a lonely world. She took the midnight train going anywhere…*" played on the stereo up front. Manny lip-synched to the music.

"Turn it up, turn it up. I love old Journey," Laramie sang. "*...A singer in a smoky room. A smell of wine and cheap perfume. For a smile they can share the night. It goes on and on and on and on ...*"

"You know the rules, Laramie. The screen goes up first. But, nothing beats the classics."

"My parents used to play this all the time when I was growing up," Laramie said feeling nostalgic.

"Yeah, but do you know any contemporary musicians?"

"Why, yes I do. I just can't name one since you put me on the spot. You act as though I never do anything besides work."

"Ha. That's all you do is work. You only leave there to go home and sleep. I bet if they let you have a bed there, you'd never leave," Manny remarked as he amused himself. "Let's face it Laramie, you are a true workaholic. The consummate professional."

"Well, not today Mr. Know-it-all. Today I am packing for a vacation. So, that proves you wrong," Laramie retorted, almost defensively.

"I'm surprised. Where you going? And with who?" Before he continued, his sarcasm appeared. "No, wait. Let me guess. You're going to Chicago with Graham for a Monday conference and you are taking Saturday and Sunday off as vacation days."

"Wrong, wrong, and wrong. It is an actual vacation of sorts. I'm flying to Singapore for three weeks. I'm planning to be relaxed poolside and frequenting the spa." Laramie stretched out as though she was on the lounge chair already.

"C'mon, what's the catch?"

"That's the *of sorts* part. I have to meet with a bank for the DemCorp project, an old client friend of Edward's. Pardon me, Mr. Graham." Laramie spoke. "Anyway, all the negotiations have to run like clockwork. We're facilitating the contracts and construction for a new luxury hotel in Singapore. Hence, the vacation plans. I have really been brushing up on my international laws and customs for this one. Mr. Graham is sending me, specifically."

"Any of your partners could have handled this, Lara. Did you ever think the old man is sending you because he wants you to have a life?" Manny smirked as he looked into the rearview mirror for a response.

"Oh, *please*, Manny. What is with men that you think women should be married with children? If I were a man, no one would say a thing. It would be expected to have face time on the evenings and weekends. You would be telling me that I have dues to pay in order to climb that corporate ladder. Do you know what it took to be the first woman partner at Graham, Mathers and Holden, and still be under thirty?" Laramie ranted.

"Whoa, cowgirl, pull back on the reins." Manny cut her off. "I know you're brilliant in law. I know you have credentials most men would die for, but you are lacking a social life. It is possible to have both." Manny paused for a moment. "You know, let's stop this conversation. I'm sorry I brought up the subject." In a relaxed tone, Manny said, "So, you're going to Singapore, eh? I've never gotten farther than Hong Kong."

"Oh, damn, sandals!" Laramie blurted. "I don't think I even own a pair. Where am I going to find them on short notice and at this time of year?"

"No problem, Miss Holden. I know a guy," Manny said as he cracked a smile. "It'll only take a quick phone call."

Manny picked up his cell phone and hit a number he had on speed-dial. The conversation was completely in Chinese, and impossible for Laramie to understand.

"Done," Manny replied. "We just need to make a quick stop in Chinatown."

The limousine made a quick turn left and headed back toward Chinatown. As they drove down Washington Street, Manny pulled over in front an old four-story building. Manny and Laramie entered through a side door, next to the gift shop on the ground floor, and climbed stairs.

"Please just tell me it isn't on the fourth floor." Laramie said, almost breathless.

Manny knocked on a third floor door. A voice, from behind the door, muttered something in Chinese to which Manny answered. After the door unlocked and opened, an old Asian man, about seventy years old, stood in the entryway. Manny held his hands in front and bowed to this gentleman, as Laramie watched carefully and repeated the same act of respect. The old man shuffled his feet in baby steps to another room, motioning them to follow.

As they entered the back room, Laramie cried, "I think I have died and gone to heaven!"

Boxes of shoes piled up along each wall, some reaching to the ceiling. Tables were set up in the middle with even more boxes stacked upon them and underneath. *There must be hundreds of styles and sizes.*

Laramie turned in amazement. "Wow, I never knew God was Jimmy Choo."

Laramie spied a flat sandal, white with Swarovski crystals. She looked below to if the gracious man had her size. *Bingo, a size 8!* Along another wall, she found a gold gladiator style, also in her size. She looked around for something a bit more formal. *Aha! A beautiful pair of metallic peep toes with a stiletto heel.* In less than fifteen minutes, Laramie found three pairs of shoes that would normally take her all day. She asked Manny to find out what she owed the gentleman.

In a broken English accent, the old man replied, "Seven hun-wed, fifty dolla'. Take Visa."

Laramie could hardly believe the bargain and grabbed her Hermés bag from Manny. She pulled out her Visa card and handed it to the old man. She bowed, then leaned over and kissed him on his forehead.

"Xiè Xie," Laramie spoke, thanking the man in the limited Chinese that she learned. When the old man began to leave the room, he turned back, smiled and nodded at Laramie. Laramie bowed again, and then the old man was gone.

"*Holy cow!* Manchu Tién, why have you kept this place a secret?"

"Lara, you'd be broke with your addiction to shoes. And, *do not* tell my wife this place exists or we'll never move out of Chinatown."

A few moments later, the old man returned with Laramie's card and receipt, and a shopping bag to carry her shoes. As they proceeded to leave, Laramie turned to the old man, waved and said, "Zài jiàn."

Once again, he smiled and shook his head in disbelief, then closed the door. Laramie and Manny raced down the stairs and headed back to the limo.

As they drove out of Chinatown, Laramie tried to think of all the things she needed to pack. *Make a list.* She couldn't even remember the last time she wore a swimsuit, maybe in undergrad. *Short sleeved blouses, linen slacks, a few summer dresses, maybe a pair of shorts, bras, panties, and toiletries. That should do it. The hotel should have a laundry service and anything else I forget, I can just buy.* Laramie loved to shop. If law hadn't intrigued her so much, she could have easily been a buyer for a large department store. She looked great in anything she wore.

As the limo turned down Broadway Street, Laramie saw that she was close to home. Her stomach began to growl. She forgot it was after ten o'clock and she skipped breakfast.

"Manny, let's stop at Asqew Grill for a quick lunch after I pack. I *cannot* eat at the airport. The food is awful. If I fill up enough then maybe I won't eat the airplane food either. Unless… I become desperate."

"As long as you have time to make your flight, it's cool with me. I don't want to be blamed for any mistakes in getting the boss' package shipped off on time." Manny continued, "What's this place serve? And, don't say Chinese."

Laramie smirked at his response. She always found Manny to have a great sense of humor. No matter what time the firm called him, whether he was in class or not, Manny was always professional and reliable. He was the same in his friendships, though Laramie often viewed him more as a brother than a friend. Without siblings of her own, Laramie sewed together a small faction of true friends. Her girlfriends, Liz and Gillian, she met in college. The boyfriends rarely made the grade to be anything more than a casual acquaintance. They became controlling, demanding or completely self-absorbed. She often questioned how she continued to find the same types of guys.

"Here we go, Ma'am, 1708 North Point Street."

"You might as well come on up and watch TV, since it'll take a bit for me to pack."

Laramie found her flat on a complete streak of luck. A couple got divorced since the newborn son looked nothing like either parents, especially the father. The young wife sprung the happy news before she learned her new older husband was sterile. In an attempt to screw the ex-wife, the new bachelor decided to sell the flat below market value. Of course, the scorned man was a client at the firm. This made the move a lot easier since there wasn't any costs in marketing the place.

Built in the late forties, the building reflected the designs of the Art Deco style, especially around the windows. The new, light coral trim painting showed this detail clearly. As they walked to the entry, Laramie slid her access card through the reader, pushed the door open and held it for Manny to grab. They walked down the hallway toward the elevator. The white marble floor glistened, reflecting the light from the gold wall sconces. The molding work was exquisite and maintained impeccably. Laramie pressed the elevator button and the door opened immediately. As they entered, she selected the fourth floor, also the top floor. The car lifted with a slight shake in the movement, reminiscent of the building's age. Though the mechanisms were modern, the elevator car was original. The only original trace of the Deco design was in the cast iron work around the midsection. *Ding.* Laramie and Manny exited the car and walked toward her apartment. The fourth floor had the same flooring and woodwork as the first floor however, there was a tufted wool rug that ran the length of the hall.

Laramie's flat was completely different from the lines of the building though it still had the same marble floor. Off-white was the color of choice for Laramie. As you entered the flat, your view was a narrow hallway with cream walls and a row of framed prints, each highlighted a different flower in a subdued color. If you looked closer at each painting, one would notice that Laramie painted them herself. The atmosphere surrounding the entry gave the impression of being in a gallery without the stark, cold feeling. Opposite the paintings, a door led to a half bath.

Laramie walked inside, passing the bath, to the next opening on the left, and entered her kitchen. Once again, the off-white color was continual throughout except for the countertop, which was dazzling granite in various shades of tan. Her cabinets were a raised panel with fluting between each unit. Wall cabinets had a bubble glass that appeared to be oozing down and left distorted shapes of the objects that were stored inside. They gave the feel of a traditional European kitchen. Laramie placed her purse on the counter and walked over to the phone.

"Help yourself to anything, Manny," she said. "I have to change my voice mail and have all my calls forwarded to the office."

As Laramie continued with her phone set up, Manny walked past her and opened the refrigerator. When he looked inside, he saw only a door full of condiments; some cheese, butter and restaurant take-home containers on the shelves, along with bottled water and a few bottles of Chardonnay.

"Man, Laramie, did you ever hear of grocery shopping? You know they do sell food in San Francisco," Manny said back. "Stop by the store when you get back and Lian will set you up with all the essentials."

"No thanks! I don't even know what some of things are that you sell. I can pass on all the bug parts and hanging dead ducks," Laramie shuddered as she spoke, thinking about the gross visuals of the market. "Believe me, I'll shop as soon as I get back. I've been at the office a lot lately and I just haven't had time to shop."

Manny grabbed a bottle of water, shut the door and walked around the breakfast bar, past the dining room table, and into the living room. Laramie had a few silk Persian style rugs on the floor that were originally her parents. Her sofa was an over-stuffed camelback design in a rich caramel hue. Atop the cushions, she had a few hand-embroidered pillows she bought while on various business trips. Across from the sofa were two spider-back mahogany chairs with Dupioni silk seats and a table between them. As you looked beyond the chairs, the shutters gave you a slatted peek of the bay, the real artwork. Manny sat down on the sofa and picked up the TV remote off one of the glass and wood tables. He turned on the large black Plasma TV on the wall over the fireplace and looked for a coaster to set his water.

"Don't you have coasters or anything?" Manny asked quizzically.

"Just put it on the table. It's just glass and it won't leave a mark," Laramie answered as she walked past Manny on her way toward her bedroom.

With shopping bag in hand, Laramie entered her bedroom. The feel of her room was far more feminine than the rest of the flat. Her carpeted floor was a plush off white. Her walls, painted in cream vertical stripes, gave the room visual height. Against the far wall was her bed, with a velvet-upholstered headboard, also in a hue of white. The bedding was a blue on white toile fabric with solid navy blue silk pillows. Sharing the wall to the living room was her dresser, a bent oak antique painted in a shabby chic flare. Many of the things in Laramie's room she brought with her when she moved to San Francisco. On her dresser was a photo of Laramie as a child with her parents, along with pictures of her friends and Edward. Her bedroom shared the same great bay view as the living room.

Laramie walked into her closet and dug for her suitcase. In every other arena, she was a very organized person, meticulous as she chose each item she bought, but not in her closet. This was a danger zone. Laramie couldn't decide whether this was her one area to let loose and go crazy, or if the lack of storage prohibited neatness all together. She found her suitcase buried behind shoeboxes and lugged it onto her bed. *Now the fun begins.*

"Lara, do you really think you'll take the time to enjoy your travel or you just kidding me?" Manny asked.

"No, really. I plan on a real vacation and sightseeing," she answered. *Pack the shoes first.* "This is going to be an adventure I want to take full advantage of since I don't know when the opportunity will come again." She gently folded her clothes inside the suitcase. She walked into the Master bath and opened the medicine cabinet, she pulled her toiletry items from the shelves and packed them into a travel bag.

"I hope you're right and remember to follow that thought once you get there," Manny shouted, while he tried to follow the news on TV. "Get out and meet people. See what the locals do. Really experience the culture."

"I never realized you were such the travel aficionado." Laramie laughed. "I will, I promise." Laramie walked back into her closet toward a small safe and removed her passport and some cash for the unexpected. "Manny, can you give me a hand?"

"Did you over pack *again*? Did you ever think about investing in a larger suitcase?"

Laramie just couldn't part with her suitcase. She had it ever since she went to college. The corners saw a lot of moving in the last nine years, the soft leather skin darkened and had scratches from all the travel it saw. The wheels still moved freely despite the way Laramie always over packed.

"All right, Lara, you sit and I'll zip." Manny grunted and strained to get the zipper around the corners. "Damn, is all this really necessary?"

"I know but wait until you try to lift it." Laramie winced. "I hope your medical insurance is current."

Manny slid the suitcase off the bed and rolled it into the foyer. "Is there anything else you need before we leave?"

Laramie looked around her bedroom, turned off her alarm clock and closed her window shutters. She walked into the kitchen, unplugged the coffee pot, and grabbed her purse off the counter. *I think I have everything.* She glanced back one more time before she walked out the door.

As Manny walked down the hallway to the elevator, he held the door open for her, letting out a deep sigh. He knew things wouldn't be the same without seeing her for three weeks. Laramie brightened his day with her good moods. Their lunches always drew a good debate over politics or relationships. They always had a great friendship but it is more than that; she was family to him.

"What's with the heavy sigh?" she needlessly asked. She could tell by his expression that they felt the same. She would miss his stories regarding Lian, his parents, and the old people that came in to buy herbs for homemade teas. Some of the items grossed out them both.

"You know, the same old thing. I always miss you when you leave. Lunch with Edward isn't the same when you're not there. Three weeks is a long time."

"Please don't start Manny. I'll miss you too. You know that. I think this trip will really help me decompress. I need a fresh breath. A break." Losing her melancholy feeling, she smiled and returned to her upbeat manner. She placed an arm around Manny, kissed him on the cheek, and said, "Let's get some lunch!"

"Okay, where is this place?" Manny replied with a slight smile. They passed the restaurant and parked a few buildings further down Steiner Street, which wasn't easy in San Francisco for a small car let alone a limousine. They walked arm in arm down the street to their destination.

Manny opened the door to Asqew and allowed Laramie in first. The restaurant was a small chain in the Bay area. The décor was simple but hip. It was the perfect place for a quick lunch, without frills. A young woman named Sierra, by her nametag, greeted them at the door. She had dyed black hair and a few piercings in her brow and wore the standard black t-shirt and black pants. Without missing the rhythm of chewing her gum, she asked, "Is it just the two of you?"

Laramie smiled and said, "Yes." Laramie was polite that way, rarely judgmental. However, Manny eyed her up and down.

As the hostess walked them to their table, Manny whispered to Laramie, "Just where do you think they found Vampira?"

"Shhh. Stop it or she'll hear you." Laramie giggled.

They sat mid-section at a table for four. A young brunette, in a chipper voice, asked, "What can I get you two to drink?"

Laramie answered first, "I'd like water with a twist of lemon."

Manny quickly added, "Make it two. Thanks." He turned to Laramie and said, "Is there anything on this menu that looks familiar?"

"Why don't you try something new?"

"You know, I would but so many of these fancy dishes have stuff in them that I don't like. See, look there, cranberries in a salad, that's Thanksgiving food. Yuk, forget about that one too," Manny said as he browsed his way down the menu. "Here, right here. I'll have the Santa Fe Chicken salad."

The young waitress came back with their drinks and set them on the table. "Are you ready to order" she asked.

After they ordered, the waitress thanked them and proceeded to the back of the restaurant where the kitchen was located. Manny looked around the place and noticed many of the customers dressed the same conservative way, oxford shirt and khakis. Laramie sipped her water and followed Manny's eyes around the place. "What exactly are you searching for? Am I missing something?"

He laughed. "No, but you can sure tell the difference between the customers and the hired help. You have Goth Girl and Chipper Cheerleader working, and Tad the Republican, wearing khaki's, *of course,* reading the financial page."

"Quit it," she said, smacking his hand. "So, when do you and Lian plan to move? I couldn't wait until I moved away from home. Have you even started house hunting yet?"

"We started to look in the Noe Valley and the Glen Park neighborhood. We have just enough for a great down payment. Of course, my parents expect everything should be paid for cash. So, I really don't bring price up at home. We're just looking for a nice three bedroom so we can have an office and baby's room too."

"Baby's room? Are you trying to tell me something?" she asked inquisitively.

"*NO*, and let it rest. We're hoping to buy after this next semester is over. I still want to be close to work and school."

The waitress walked up to the table with their order, mistakenly placing them in front of the wrong person. Laramie and Manny picked up their plates and exchanged them as they smiled off the mistake.

"I don't mean to be rude but we have to eat quickly so you can take me to the airport. I guess I'll just order something to go at one of the airport restaurants before boarding. It looks like business is picking up here and I don't want to have to wait for another item."

"Can't blame you there. I've known you too long for pretenses, so chow down."

Laramie ate about half of her meal and looked up at Manny. "Am I that difficult a person?"

"No, not that I think so. Where did that come from? Oh man, you're not going to ask me all that chick stuff. I am not telling you whether your butt is big or if you look fat in that dress. Forget it." Manny rolled his eyes; he didn't want to see where this conversation was going. He learned his lesson in answering that type of question from Lian. "Remember you said we have to be quick."

"I know, I know. It just seems like everyone has someone. Sometimes I feel alone. Like, it would be great to vacation in Singapore and share it with someone. That's all. I rarely date. No one at the office would even consider it because of Edward."

"It's called a social life. Hello? We were just talking about this an hour ago in Chinatown. Do you ever listen? Do something for yourself for once. Put Laramie ahead of the firm. Take a Saturday off. Please, would you do it for all of us? No more chick questions either."

They finished their meals and waited for the waitress to bring their check. Laramie grabbed it quickly. "Thank you but this time I am doing something for you. Thank you for the advice, though." She grabbed her wallet and laid the money on top. As the waitress walked by again she grabbed the check and money and asked whether change was needed. Laramie nodded her head no.

"Well Mr. Manchu Tién, take me to the airport if you will," Laramie said smiling.

As the long sleek limousine cruised down Highway 101, Laramie sat back and stared out the window. She looked forward to arriving but never the preflight and flight. She detested the thought of going through airport security. *All these years and still no one has been able to come up with a better system.* She was thankful her flight went out midday. Most families had children still in school and opted for later flights in hopes that they would sleep. Laramie remembered vividly her night flight with an obnoxious boy that kicked her seat all the way to New York. As she became a more seasoned traveler, she realized the importance of flying business class versus coach. She softly sang along with the music on the CD player.

Manny pulled off the exit for San Francisco International Airport. He followed the signs for international departures. He pulled the limo in front of the skycap's station for Singapore Air. He ran around to Laramie's side and opened her door. As she stepped out, she looked behind to make sure she hadn't left anything. Manny retrieved her suitcase from the trunk and rolled it around carefully, since he knew how much she packed inside and feared an explosion. He handed the suitcase off to the skycap and hugged her goodbye.

"Have a great trip, Laramie. We'll miss you here."

"Thanks a bunch, Manny. I will miss you all, too. But, I'm off on a wild adventure, right?"

The lines at the security point weren't as long as she thought they'd be. She took off her shoes and jacket and placed them in the bin. As she walked through the station, it sounded the alarm. *Oh great, now what? It figures it did it to me.* The screening agent pointed her to the side where an older woman, in uniform, passed a wand all around her. *No beep.* She was free to pick up her things and redress. *Just how much plastic explosive do they think I can fit in my high heel? Simply ridiculous.*

She slowly walked down to Concourse G for international flights. Of course, her flight left out of the very last gate, Gate 101A. She slowly sauntered into the Gucci store. *This may not have been my best choice. One great outfit and I can really damage my American Express. Buying one pair of sunglasses wouldn't hurt, would it?* She stepped over to the counter and tried on a few pairs. *Which frame do I choose, black or tortoise?* She asked the clerk her opinion. They both agreed the black was more versatile. *Of course, I'll need a case to carry them too.* She justified her purchase as she reminded herself that she would be at a beach, a pool and sightseeing.

Laramie looked at her watch; she still had another hour before boarding. *Argh.* She looked around and saw the usual news stores and tourist shops. This reminded her to buy a large bottle of water for the flight. She walked into Pacific Gateway Gifts & News and picked up her water and the latest issue of Cosmopolitan magazine. The headline always grabbed her attention only to read that the content did not.

"*Ten ways to drive your man crazy in bed,*" Laramie read aloud. "Didn't the ten from last month work?"

After browsing the shops, Laramie strolled to her gate when she overheard her name on the speaker. After she waited behind a few people, it was her turn to speak to the gate agent. She identified herself and showed her boarding pass.

"Well, Miss Holden, we have some good news for you. It seems a gentleman by the name of Edward Graham has upgraded your ticket to First Class, both ways," informed the gate agent.

"*Really?* You're not kidding. This just must be my lucky day." She let out a small squeal of delight. Laramie exchanged her boarding pass as she beamed the whole time. She had a few minutes before they called First Class to board. She pulled out her cell phone and hit the speed dial.

"Hello? Is that you Laramie?" Edward pretended as if her name didn't just show up on caller ID.

"Yes, and you know it's me. Thank for my seat upgrade. You didn't have to do that."

"I know, Dear. That's what makes it so nice. Please have a wonderful trip. Make sure you find time for Laramie. Relax. This isn't all about business, so I don't want any reports until your first two weeks end. Do you understand me?" Edward specifically made a point that did not go unnoticed.

"Yes, I do understand; no business for two weeks. I got it. I love you and I will miss you." Laramie blew a kiss into the phone.

"Love you and miss you too. Bye, Dear." Edward hung up his phone.

"Bye."

Laramie hadn't really been away from Edward since she graduated Law School. It felt so awkward to be going on a business trip without him. How quiet her days would be without him.

Laramie boarded the plane and walked to the front where First Class was located. She was amazed at the difference in space between Business Class and First Class. *So this is how the other half live?* As soon as she sat, a flight attendant walked to her and offered her a beverage or cocktail. Laramie politely declined the beverage. However, the beauty of this young Asian woman captivated her. The young attendant was just stunning. Her mannerisms were so modest compared to the American flight attendants. She had gracious sounding words as though she chose them carefully, a trait completely unlike Americans in general. Her uniform fit her exquisitely, with a flattering scoop neck top, ever so reserved. The print on the fabric was a beautiful floral on a navy background. Her black straight hair pulled back into a chignon. Her skin was flawless like fine china. This woman epitomized grace and beauty.

Next stop, Seoul, Korea in thirteen hours.

Chapter 2

LARAMIE LILA HOLDEN was born on April Fool's Day in 1978, just seven months after the wedding. Contrary to Audrey's hinting, no one bought the story that Laramie was premature. She was a long, skinny, bald baby and perfect in her parents' eyes. Audrey decided to name her after the town of her conception, Laramie, Wyoming. Oddly enough, the named seemed to fit her, so Tom agreed to it.

After Audrey's maternity break, she brought the baby to the office with her daily. At first, the men thought this was a bad choice, however, Laramie was an exceptional baby. Being a newborn, she mainly slept and ate. As long as those items were addressed, she remained silent. As she grew, Audrey placed her in her bouncer, where Laramie happily stayed and watched everyone walk by the office. Eventually, Audrey purchased a small television with a VCR in the bottom for Laramie's favorite, Disney videos. As everyone took their breaks, they played with the baby. It was as though Laramie had four parents.

After her first year, Laramie's pale blonde locks grew slowly. Audrey felt she would be bald forever. Her mother wanted to put the cute little clips in her hair or make a whale spout. However, their bigger concern was Laramie's mobility in the office. She dumped file folders off the desks in an attempt to see what was on top. It only took a few times before the men told Audrey that Laramie needed to be confined to certain areas in the office. Audrey gave in and placed a safety gate at her office door. The little princess was not pleased, not at all.

In that year, the group pulled their financial resources together and bought out the senior attorney as planned. When that took place, they renamed the firm to Graham, Mathers and Holden. Some of Tom and Edward's early networking paid off. They had a slow but steady stream of clients recommended by friends at the courthouse. Most of their clients were Chinese immigrants that were misinformed of their rights in the city. With the large migration of Asians, many of the established Caucasian families saw them as a threat to their community. There was enough tension among the gay community already with the double murders of Mayor George Moscone and Supervisor Harvey Milk. Attorneys needed to be cautious on who they represented.

The firm agreed to litigate a case for a Chinese family that lost their only son. He was in his mid-twenties when he jumped onto a cable car going down Powell Street. Unfortunately, a cable split, shorted on the car and electrocuted him, due to his lack of grounding. At first, the city claimed there was no accident, since the young man had needle marks on his body. Their claim was that a drug overdose caused the death since heroin use was prevalent. In the trial, his physician confirmed the needle marks were from his illness with Diabetes and self-administering insulin. Tom argued the case, since he had better skills for that, while Edward co-chaired since he appeared intimidating. Audrey and Andrew intensively researched the case law. The city saw a loss coming and tried to settle with the family, which they declined. Tom knew they would win the jury trial and they did. The family won the original judgment and punitive damages in the millions. The city planned to appeal but protests suggested they reconsider. The firm collected a hefty percentage of the money for their role in the trial.

That case opened the firm to a huge amount of clients. They moved their office from Turk Street, near the courthouse, to the Bank of America building on California Street. The four Harvard Law graduates became the hot ticket in town. They each had offers to join other firms but refused the invitation. Their new cases carried weight in the city but not to the degree of the first. They were invited to parties and golf dates with other prominent attorneys and judges. When Audrey saw their photos in the society pages, she knew they 'arrived'.

Later that year, Andrew Mathers married Violet, his college sweetheart. The others were cordial to her but she never fit in the group. No one saw in her what Andrew did nor did they want to. Violet made innuendoes toward Audrey about her own pregnancy and delivery coming long *after* the wedding night. Audrey understood what she meant and ignored her for Andrew's sake. She knew Violet was jealous of Laramie because of the attention their daughter received.

The Holden's parties became the place to be seen. They moved to a beautiful Victorian house on Clay Street in Pacific Heights. It was larger than

Tom's parents but obviously smaller than Audrey's parents home. The rooms were few but large. As their income increased, so did the scale of the parties. Laramie loved to have her friends over and play. The house was alive with laughter and friendship.

As the years passed, Laramie grew up with the other children of San Francisco's most prominent families. She was a beautiful and well-mannered child. Audrey paid strict attention to proper behavior. Laramie's wit and humor was a reflection of her father's. Tom spent countless hours with Laramie on the weekends at the park. The sportiest thing they did together was play Frisbee since neither were athletically inclined. Tom took the family for hot air balloon rides over Napa Valley. Laramie was afraid of heights but went with the safety of her father nearby. She was a daredevil as long as Daddy was there. The family hiked and tobogganed at Lake Tahoe over long weekends. Though, holidays were still spent with family.

Laramie excelled in school with her studies. It was then that her parents saw her photographic memory. She gained some of their best characteristics. Unfortunately, she needed braces like her parents and inherited Audrey's dreadful singing voice. She participated in school clubs and activities. She was her parent's pride. She loved people and felt a duty to welcome a stranger like her mother. She knew her parents had money but that didn't stop her from befriending anyone who didn't.

Her mother taught her to give back to society for the blessings they received. Every Sunday morning the Holden family went to the missions in the Tenderloin neighborhood to serve meals to the homeless who had become a significant problem in the city. Laramie felt she needed to help these people and started a fundraiser for a shelter at school. Her endeavors didn't go unnoticed. Soon, a local television network spotlighted the cause. In the following year, the Holden House opened. It offered clean beds and showers for the poor of society.

Chapter 3

LARAMIE SAT IN her best friend's room as they listened to the new Mariah Carey songs on the CD player. She stayed at her girlfriend's house all weekend while her parent's went to Carmel for an anniversary getaway. When Laramie looked up, she found it strange to see Edward in the doorway. He asked to speak to Laramie alone. As he sat next to her on the bed, he explained that there was a terrible auto accident with her parents. Laramie asked if she could visit them in the hospital. Edward explained she couldn't, they both died at the scene. Laramie sat stunned, unable to cry. *No, he must be wrong. My parents would never leave me. They love me. They love me.*

As Audrey and Tom made their way back from Big Sur, a logging truck pulled out in front of their car. They could've possibly survived that, however, the logs broke free and crushed the car. The driver of the truck sustained minor injuries. When the police arrived, so did the attorney for the paper company that owned the truck. Television helicopters flew overhead and took video of the crushed car and the covered bodies along the roadside. The police contacted Edward first. He had the awful task of telling Laramie and her grandparents.

Laramie's grandparents flew in immediately. Both sets remained so traumatized by the event; Tom and Audrey were their only children. They stayed at the house with Laramie in hopes of helping her cope with the loss. Laramie stayed quiet as she listened to the older folks talk about her care. Audrey's parents agreed to take her home with them after the funeral. This way she was near both families.

News crews camped outside the house and at the funeral home. Andrew and Edward found the loss tragic and beyond words when asked for an interview. Lines formed around the building with people paying condolences to the family at the wake. The event remained front-page news in the city due to the Holden's celebrity status. At the cemetery, the cameramen and reporters took pictures of Laramie as she stood between the two caskets. She looked at the metal containers without emotion only a single tear. *Mommy, Daddy, I never got to say goodbye.* Everyone told her things would be better over time.

After Laramie moved to her grandparents, Edward brought a lawsuit against the paper company, their subsidiary trucking company, insurance company and the driver. He and Andrew were determined to fight on behalf of their friends and Laramie. He claimed wrongful death and negligence. The paper company claimed the accident was due to Tom's driving skills, not their driver.

The trial brought national coverage. Edward argued the case personally even though he was the most intimidating person in the court room. The paper company tried to get a change of venue due to the popularity of the case, the judge denied it. Edward proved the paper company falsified equipment records, replaced faulty material on the logging truck after the accident, and hid documents that showed the alcohol content of the driver. The jury sympathized with the family since a few jurors knew of the Holden's by their generosity to the city. Near the end of the trial, Laramie came with her grandparents to listen to closing arguments. As her family cried around her, Laramie stayed reserved.

The jury remained sequestered while they deliberated. During that time, the paper company offered to pay all damages without filing an appeal as long as the amount remained sealed. Their goal was to keep the company in business without dropping their stock prices. Without the agreement, they would file bankruptcy, which would result in mass unemployment for their workers and no collectible assets. Edward and Andrew knew it wasn't about the money but vindication for their friends. However, they wanted to provide a future for Laramie without financial constraints. They agreed to the deal after they spoke with both families. The Holden's and Cummings' didn't want to be responsible for other families' financial losses. The original amount of the suit was twenty million dollars, and as promised the punitive damages remained sealed with only Edward, Andrew and Laramie's family knowing the true amount. The firm didn't collect one dime from the trial. Edward and Andrew refused to make a profit off the death of their best friends.

Chapter 4

LARAMIE SPENT A year away from San Francisco. She lived with Audrey's parents during that time and went to a local private school. On an outward appearance, she seemed like a well-adjusted twelve-year-old girl. Her grades excelled as usual. Her activities at school kept her busy. However, her grandparents worried since she never fully grieved over her parent's death.

On the last day of the 1990 school year, Laramie attended an academic awards banquet. Her archrival was there. This girl was vicious. Though Laramie harbored no grudges, this other girl didn't like the new girl getting the class' attention. In the back of the auditorium, Laramie spoke and laughed with her friends as her enemy walked up behind her.

"So, Laramie, where are *your* parents?" she asked snottily.

Laramie refused to answer and tried to continue her conversation but the nasty girl refused to end it.

"Oh that's right, you don't have any. They died in San Francisco, queer capitol of the world. Are you sure it was an accident and not AIDS? Maybe they were queer too and never told you. You're probably just a part of the city's filth."

The other girls stood horrified. Laramie remained calm and kept her dignity. She wanted to strangle this girl but knew it would be the wrong way to handle things. She didn't need the adverse effects of the confrontation. She could not allow her enemy to see her emotional weakness. She politely excused herself and walked away. A few of her girlfriends followed her, a few stood up for her and the rest remained quiet, fearing further retaliation.

Internally, Laramie vowed to never step foot in that school again. Her grandparents didn't understand the sudden change in her behavior. They spoke with her several times, however, Laramie refused to discuss it. Over the summer, she became reclusive. She remained at home and read most of the time. A few girls stopped by and she greeted them happily but she wouldn't leave the yard. She found her peace in the pages of books.

At the end of summer, her paternal grandfather became seriously ill with heart complications. Everyone knew he would die shortly and he wanted to spend his remaining days in Charleston. Lila asked Tom's parents if they could care for Laramie but they had their own health problems. They contacted Edward and asked for him to care for Laramie. They felt if she went back to the city then she might feel better among old friends again. He was reluctant to take on a teenager being a single man but he finally agreed.

Early September, Laramie moved into Edward's home in Cow Hollow. She transferred back to Presidio Hill School in her old neighborhood and rekindled old friendships. Edward noticed the change in her disposition as well. She was happy yet reserved. She participated in conversations but really shared any insight to herself. He didn't know what to do being a single man in his late thirties. He barely kept a steady girlfriend let alone a teenager. Slowly, they worked through the awkwardness. The never really developed a parent-child relationship at that time, it was mainly an adult friendship.

In her high school years at Drew School, Laramie spent her time after school reading any book she got her hands on. Unfortunately in Edward's home, that was mainly law books. They had discussions at dinnertime regarding the cases Laramie read. He was aware of her keen ability to remember specific facts regarding the cases. Her AP classes kept her challenged and occupied. However, she looked forward to Fridays because they were the extracurricular days. She loved to paint, take photographs, anything to do with art. She found those classes therapeutic for her self-expression.

By graduation time, both her choice universities, Vanderbilt and Rice, accepted her application. She eventually settled on Vanderbilt in Tennessee, partly because it was her grandparents' alma mater. She felt it gave her a connection to her family. She planned to major in Public Policy Studies. She volunteered so much in the Bay area and felt she could do more by working for the city. Edward found her choice admirable but not lucrative. He felt the program lacked a challenge for someone with her intelligence. Since it gave her a tranquility internally, he supported the decision in hopes she would blossom socially.

When she arrived at Edwards five years ago, she was a new teenager. However by the summer after graduation, Laramie became an elegant young woman. She remained well mannered and selfless. Her braces came off and her smiled dazzled everyone. Edward saw a lot of Audrey in her. Though, over those years she still hid her emotions. She didn't lose her temper or cry when frustrated like many young girls. She had many friends but lacked anyone as a special friend. He knew she needed to be away from the safety of his home. She needed to flourish on her own, even though that meant he'd miss her terribly.

Chapter 5

DURING HER FLIGHT to Nashville, Laramie wondered whether her choice of university was a smart one. She thought that she needed to stay closer to Edward. *I could've gone to UC Berkley and commuted instead.* However, Edward wanted her to get out and be among people of her own age. He refused to indulge her reclusive behavior. After she landed, she took a commuter bus to the campus. *I guess Nashville isn't so bad after all. I don't know any country songs but I can learn.* She loved the greenery of the city and the small town feel compared to San Francisco.

The bus dropped her off at Barnard Hall where she went to find her room and new roommate, Elizabeth Wellesley. They spoke briefly on the phone and Laramie found her to be friendly. *I don't know about living with a stranger though. What if we don't get along? What if she doesn't like me?* She entered the dormitory and went to the second floor. A resident pointed her in the right direction down the hall. As she entered her dorm room, the small size shocked her. *My bedroom at Edward's is larger than this. How are we supposed to fit two people in here?*

"Welcome, Sugar. You must be Laramie Holden. I'm Elizabeth Wellesley but you can call me Liz. Actually, I prefer if you call me Liz," she spoke in her heavy Southern drawl. She held her hand out for Laramie to shake.

"It's nice to meet you, Liz."

Laramie wasn't sure how to continue the conversation. Elizabeth exercised her southern hospitality immediately.

"Make yourself at home. That isn't all you brought, is it?"

"Oh, no. My other things are being shipped here. Have you unpacked already?"

"Absolutely, Darlin'. You have the closet here and this dresser. Do you need help with anythin'? I have a ton of extras. My Momma over packed everythin'." Liz sat on her bed and watched Laramie empty her leather suitcase, a graduation present from Edward.

"I'm good. Thank you."

Laramie didn't know how to react. Her new roommate's extrovert personality intimidated her. *Why did I listen to Edward and sign up for a double room?* Laramie longed to be home in her comfort zone already. Liz commented on each article of clothing Laramie placed in her closet.

"Oh, I just adore those shoes. Where on Earth did you find them? I must say you have great taste in clothin' as well." Laramie smiled at her comment.

"Bloomingdales. They're my favorite. We have a lot of specialty shops in the city and I find most of my things there. So, Liz, where exactly is Aiken, South Carolina?"

Liz described her home about half way up the Georgia border. Aiken was a charming town, home to many thoroughbred horse breeders like her parents. She chose Vanderbilt since her family had lineage there as well. She was the same height as Laramie but with a cheerleader's build, trim but athletic. With her golden blonde hair was styled in a shoulder length bob, she looked like the epitome of a southern sorority girl. She told Laramie about her parents and her older brother, who was a fourth year cadet at Annapolis. Her family was rich in southern history.

Liz offered to walk around campus with her so they could become more acquainted with their surroundings. As they walked down 24th Avenue, they received a load of catcalls by the fraternity brothers looking at the next wave of new girls on campus. Afterwards, they headed to Rand Hall for lunch. Liz appeared to chat without inhaling which Laramie found humorous.

When they arrived back to their room, Laramie had a message from Edward inquiring about her first day. She quickly called him back and told him she was fine and not to worry. His house was quiet with Laramie gone, and he called because *he* missed her. He missed their conversations. He missed her company. He had her there for the past five years and now the house was his empty bachelor pad again.

The evening continued with twenty questions from Liz. She wanted to know absolutely everything about Laramie and the West Coast. They discussed their course list and their intended majors. They talked about boyfriends. Liz found it difficult to believe that Laramie never had a steady beau and that she was still a virgin. Laramie learned quickly that Liz was far worldlier.

The school year began without a hitch. Laramie quickly delved into her studies but not without comment from Liz. She forced Laramie to attend the Friday night football games. She was determined to make her roommate have a few activities on her social calendar as well. They went to fraternity parties later in the fall where Liz met a sophomore named Randy Beresford, a brother in Kappa. He liked Liz from the start. Even though Liz teased at him, Laramie knew she felt the same about Randy. Laramie watched their relationship blossom with a hint of envy. Liz could make Randy eat out of her hand with ease. *How does she do that?* The roommates became best friends easily. They respected each other's space and opinions. Laramie learned to accept Liz's criticism on dating. She had a few upper classmen ask her out and she reluctantly went on the dates, however, outside of doing beer shots together there wasn't any real connection on other levels. Laramie quickly learned that her virginal virtue was a magnet for some of her dates, a trophy to win. Needless to say, few ever had a repeat date.

Laramie went home on holiday and worked at the firm. She did some mindless duties, mail delivery, answer the phones, and occasionally, research for Edward. He continued to see a natural ability in her to recite the law. He encouraged her to pursue that field after she finished her bachelor's degree. She hadn't given it much thought until he mentioned it.

Soon, their first year ended. Laramie and Liz agreed to be roommates for their sophomore year. They stayed in contact over the summer. Liz told her Randy came to visit a few times which surprised her but not Laramie. Laramie's sociology and psychology classes taught her well in observing others and their behavior. She recognized her own fault in avoiding confrontation. She didn't want the emotional display that came attached. For her, it was easier to run and deal with her problems by herself. She didn't want anyone see her emotions since it showed a weakness.

Chapter 6

IN THEIR SECOND year, the girls decided to pledge a sorority. In reality, Liz wanted to do it and made Laramie join her. Greek life was huge on campus. They were accepted into Chi Omega and decided to move into the sorority house since there was space available. They met another girl, named Gillian O'Malley, in the house. She was from Essex Fells, New Jersey. Her father was a Circuit Court judge and her mother stayed at home. She had two younger siblings who idolized her. Anything Gillian involved herself in, her siblings followed whether it was sports or theater.

Gillian was a fan of anything Irish, Notre Dame, Boston Celtics, U2, accents and a good Irish lager. She had long dark auburn hair, fair skin, green eyes and stood the same height as Laramie. Gillian's fuller bust line brought on unsolicited comments and stares. This forced her to be outspoken and quell the solicitations. She was a force just as strong as Liz. Laramie didn't stand a chance against her friends, something Edward relished. The trio became inseparable.

Liz continued to date Randy. Laramie and Gillian knew he would ask Liz to marry eventually. He was from Charleston, about four hours from Aiken. He was a good ole' southern boy and Liz's family adored him. Randy reminded Laramie of a young Tom Selleck with the ruggedness but still polished in his mannerisms. Laramie wished she had the same control over men as Liz but felt it must be a inherited gene.

Laramie put more effort into her studies than her friends who found the social scene a bit more important. Laramie continued to make the Dean's list every semester. She felt guilty since her coursework seemed easy to her, interesting but easy. On breaks, she flew home to work and see Edward. She began to question the relationship between Linda, the receptionist, and him. Nothing ever seemed inappropriate at the office but Laramie knew there was more to it even though she couldn't pinpoint it.

Over the summer, Liz and Gillian came to vacation for a week. Before then, neither girls traveled that far. They loved Edward's house and Edward as well. He became this old flirt but not in a creepy old man way. This was the first Laramie saw him behave that way and now understood why he never married. Laramie's personal interest in the law developed that summer. This didn't come without hints and shoves from Edward and Andrew. They knew she was a natural.

Chapter 7

AS THE THIRD year began, Laramie took more legal related classes. She felt the progression in her parent's footsteps and embraced it. She defined her career path. Her GPA remained above a 3.85, something that gave her a sense of pride.

The beginning of the year brought on fundraisers for the sorority's sponsored charity, Make A Wish Foundation. She loved anything that helped the less fortunate. During the fundraiser with a fraternity, Phi Kappa Sigma, Laramie met the second string quarterback, Sam Anderson. *Cute. Very cute.* He was tall and very muscular with wavy sandy blonde hair and brown eyes, a handsome combination. His perfect smile hooked her, in addition to his well polished charm. He had a slight arrogance that Laramie found attractive though unsure as to why.

Sam asked her out for a date which Liz and Gillian forced her to accept. She was nervous, yet she went. She listened to him talk about sports even though she knew nothing about them. Occasionally, he asked her something about herself or her interests. They hung out at a sports bar, just off campus. By the end of the date, he kissed her goodnight at the door. Laramie felt the rush of her attraction for the first time and blushed.

He continued to ask her out and she accepted. Their dates consisted of heavy petting but Laramie stopped it there. It wasn't as though she wanted to remain a virgin; she wanted it to be special. Just after exams, she and the girls went to Sam's frat house for a party. Laramie drank more than she should've and Sam saw a golden opportunity. He persuaded her to follow him to his room. He said all the right words, how much he loved her and wanted to take their relationship to the next level. She gave in due to a clouded judgment.

Sadly, he wasn't in it for the both of them. She took the initial pain and received nothing more than his selfishness. Her first time left no desire to do it again. There was no magic moment, no bond between them. Afterwards, he seemed callous that she didn't participate more.

Laramie, devastated by his actions, left the party while he continued with the celebration. When she broke into tears in her room, her friends knew something went horribly wrong. It was the first time in two years that Liz saw her cry. Laramie explained what happened and how awful she felt. Liz consoled her and tried to explain it away on the alcohol. Laramie appeared to accept that reason for now.

Laramie didn't hear from Sam over Christmas break and didn't expect to either. Edward asked her directly what her problem was since he knew she wouldn't offer it. Nothing prepared him for what came next.

"I felt so used. I wanted it to be special. I wanted it to mean something. Please tell me it won't always be like that."

Initially, Edward's mouth hung open. "Laramie, wouldn't you feel better discussing this with Linda? I'm not sure I'm the best person to answer you." *Damn, I thought the problem was her classes.*

"No. I want *you* to tell me. I want it from *your* perspective."

He cleared his throat before he continued. "Sometimes men aren't as caring as women. Sometimes, men think about sex and only sex." He continued his speech as he slowly tried to disassociate himself from the group. "Now, that's not to say men don't have feelings. They can be buried in the scheme of things. Not all men are selfish. Perhaps if drinking hadn't been involved, it would've been better. I can't speak for this young man nor can I speak for you. This is something between the two of you and can only be resolved by you. Give it time is all I can say."

"Well, what about the other areas of sex? When does that happen?"

"Oh, for the love of God, Laramie. I can't do this." He slammed his hands down on the table. She was in a dangerous area. "I don't feel comfortable discussing this with you at all. I thought you'd learn this through your girlfriends. I am sorry, Dear, but you really need to seek a woman's perspective."

Edward became too flustered by her questions to continue. He called Linda in his office and made her discuss it with Laramie. Linda did her best to inform Laramie about the different aspects of sex and recommended she read a book for further information.

"Laramie, it's not always like what you experienced. When you meet the right person, the experience *is* special. You won't second-guess yourself when that happens. Sex is sex, an act between two consenting adults. Making love shares the emotional attachment between two people acting selflessly, there to please the other beyond the act itself. Do you understand me?"

"I think I do. Thanks Linda. You cleared it up far better than Edward." They shared a good laugh over that.

When Laramie arrived back to school, she gave Sam another chance. He apologized for the event and vowed to make it up to her. She soon found he placed a lot more in his words than in his actions. Anytime he wanted to mess around, he professed his love for her and questioned her love for him without proof. She felt guilted into the act and found no pleasure. He girlfriends tried to talk her into dumping him but Laramie didn't have the courage or self-esteem to confront him on that.

"I would just leave his sad ass at the curb. Ignore him. Don't take his calls. You are such a beautiful young woman to be wasting yourself over *him*. He doesn't deserve you, Lara," declared Gillian flatly.

Gillian detested Sam, as did Liz. Laramie tried to justify his actions to her friends but in reality, she justified his actions to herself. They dated for the remainder of the year with a break over the summer as suggested by Sam.

Laramie went back to the firm for the summer. Edward continued to request difficult work from her. He tested her knowledge continually. Her life revolved around the law with an occasional lesson in business. She was the firm's prodigy. *She is far more brilliant than her parents and she hasn't even started law school yet. Hmmm… I wonder.* Edward wasn't sure whether facts and organization disciplined her or if her memory recalled information better. However, even with the facts, her ability to interpret the law and defend her position was what impressed them the most. She had a maturity in that realm far beyond her years.

Chapter 8

"I CAN'T BELIEVE WE are in our senior year. It all went so fast and so will this year," Gillian said sadly.

"I don't know what I'm going to do without y'all," Liz added.

Laramie replied smiling, "We haven't even gone to our first class and you're already talking about the end. We're going to make this one better than last year. You both know that. Liz, has Randy hinted at any future plans yet?"

"Not one bit. And, it's not as though I haven't given him the incentive or the opportunity. I'm afraid I'll have to buy my own ring and put into his hands. He needs my direction somethin' awful."

Laramie laughed knowing the statement wouldn't be too far from the truth. He adored her and followed her like a lost puppy; she loved it that way. Gillian dated with some regularity but nothing steady. Most men didn't appreciate her directness and honesty, especially in bed. Laramie didn't know whether she even had a relationship with Sam anymore. He didn't bother to call her once over the summer to say hello. All of her attempts were met with message taking.

When she met up with Sam a few days later, she asked why he never called. He explained they were on "two a days" for football and just too tired to call. When he showed up at the sorority house, her friends realized Laramie fell back into his trap. As Gillian walked past him, she pretended to sneeze but in reality she said 'asshole' to which Liz replied with a southern 'bless you.' Laramie rolled her eyes and bit her tongue to not laugh. *Oh, they are so bad! Funny, but bad.*

Their nights together frustrated Laramie. Sex meant when he was done, they were done. She wondered whether or not he was aware of the other parts of her anatomy.

For her Public Policy class, she began her senior thesis on the Asian community in San Francisco since she was so familiar with it. The paper caused many late nights at the library and on the internet. She wanted it to be perfect so when Sam called for a date she had to decline a few times. He wasn't very sympathetic to her cause. When she finally finished her paper, she went to the frat house to visit him. The guys said he was in his room. As she neared the door, she heard noises that could not be misconstrued for anything but a woman's moan. She wanted to walk in on him but her lack of confidence stopped that. She was furious and deeply hurt. She told Gillian and Liz what happened. It wasn't a surprise to them. Actually, the surprise was that it didn't happen earlier. They supported Laramie and her choice to end the relationship.

After the holiday break, Sam came to call on Laramie. His actions surprised her since she felt he moved on. She told him what happened and he denied it. He claimed it had to be a gag by his frat buddies because he wasn't even there. Laramie couldn't prove it was him since she only heard a female voice. *Well, since he never did anything to make me moan...there might be truth in his statement.* Gillian and Liz were furious with her and her inability to end things.

By the time Spring Break came, her dating relationship became strained. Sam went to Florida with his friends while Laramie went home. Liz planned to be with her family at Rosemary Beach, Florida. It was a small town down the coast from Panama City where Sam was. Imagine her surprise when she saw him in Coyote Ugly with some freshman tramp on his lap doing things shy of needing a hotel room. *That's the final straw. If she won't break it off after this, I'm doin' it for her.* Liz pulled out her cell phone, walked up in front of him and snapped the picture. *Busted. You good for nothin'... oh, I'm too much of a lady to say it.* She emailed it to herself before he could grab the phone out of her hand. She gave him her best southern haughty grin before she walked away.

When the girls arrived back at school, Liz sat Laramie down and explained the situation before she showed her the picture. Laramie seethed at the sight. *That no good S.O.B. He does nothing but lie. Now it's over.* When he came to see her, he was full of excuses about the timing, drunkenness, goofing in good fun, everything but the truth.

"Let me tell you something, Sam. You have screwed me for the last time and it took you two years to do it decently. It's just too bad it was never in bed. It's over. Find someone else to believe your lies."

Half the sorority house stood there applauding and whistling. Laramie

Holden became a strong woman that day. She wasn't sure what she wanted but she knew she didn't want him.

"We are so proud of you, Sugar," Liz cheered.

"The liar. The cheat. What a jerk. It's about time you dumped the rotten son of a bitch. Such a jackass..." Gillian looked over to her friends. "What? Oh sorry, I got carried away," Gillian smiled and answered sheepishly.

Laramie felt a sense of relief from the experience. *I feel pretty damn good. Ha.* Later in the week when she spoke to Edward, she told him of her actions. He, too, expressed his pride in her actions.

Laramie finished her fourth year on the dean's list as always. Her senior thesis caused a debate among some of the professors. They felt her observations of the Asian community in San Francisco weren't completely accurate. However, not one lived in the area, *ever.* She didn't care since she would be at Harvard in the fall anyway. Her recommendation letters from Edward, Andrew and Judge O'Malley, along with perfect score on her LSAT, sealed that fate.

In the summer after graduation, Randy finally proposed to Liz. They planned to marry the following June. Liz worked in a small gallery in Aiken, hoping to utilize her Art History degree. Gillian went back to New Jersey with her degree in Communications and landed a job at a radio station in Manhattan. Outside of a few stolen weeks, their lives went separate courses. They maintained contact weekly via phone and email. They supported Laramie's desire to go into law, knowing she would be an awesome attorney.

Chapter 9

LARAMIE MADE HER move to Boston but not without some discussions with Edward. His father, Walter, kept the house on Beacon Hill but spent most of his time in Boca Raton, Florida. Laramie thought she'd live on campus to be close but Edward judiciously suggested she move into his father's home. His reasons were twofold, assist Walter when he was in town and keep the house secure without being empty. She saw his perspective but the downside from her view was she had to commute daily. The traffic in Boston was heavy even outside of rush hour. The Big Dig lessened some of the traffic but not where Laramie drove.

As she walked through the halls of the Law School, it felt surreal to be in the same place as her parents. As with San Francisco, the ambiance of the area gave her a sense of comfort. The course of study hadn't changed much either. She still had the same mandatory classes set for all first year students, such as Contracts, Torts, Property, Criminal Procedure and Civil Procedure. Laramie looked forward to her writing class but felt the legal research class was a waste of her time. *I've researched for the past seven years for Edward. What exactly do they think I'm going to learn at this point? Please.*

Once accustomed to her class and reading schedule, she joined a few specialized reading groups led by the faculty. She gained a lot of insight and offered her opinions as well. Some of her professors witnessed her natural ability to recite case law when she hit her stride. She decided to take on one social club per year. In her first year, she joined the California Club, naturally. She didn't view issues the same as her liberal counterparts. As long as she didn't have to come face to face, she presented her case thoroughly. Without the benefit of her girlfriends to push her, she avoided the confrontation. It was clear that she would never make a tough trial attorney.

She maintained impeccable outlines, which became in demand from other first year students. She participated in weekend study groups. During the week when not in class, she read constantly. Occasionally, she took her books to Boston Commons around the corner if the weather was decent. She visited the same pubs and restaurants as her parents and Edward. When she felt melancholy, she drove past the house on Walker Street where her parents and Edward lived during their time at Harvard. *The new owners must think I'm some sort of stalker when I drive by so slow.*

She missed her girlfriends terribly. She sporadically called to check in with them and receive the latest news. Laramie didn't travel home for Christmas the first year and regretted that choice. She missed seeing friendly faces. However, on Spring Break, she drove down and spent a few days with Gillian. She got a first hand tour of Manhattan. She loved the garment district and the Lower East Side for the bars and restaurants.

After the first year exams were over, she flew back home to see Edward and intern for the summer. She could run circles around the new associates but stayed silent. It wasn't her position to correct anyone in the firm. When her grades finally posted, she had a 3.95 GPA. Astounded by the news, Edward took her out for a shopping spree to her favorite stores. Clothing was her weakness, especially shoes.

She met Manchu Tién in the mailroom that year. Of course, they became fast friends. His humor was quick and she loved it mainly because it humored himself. By the end of summer, she met his girlfriend Lian. Laramie was happily jealous over their relationship. She missed having a boyfriend but not if it meant someone like Sam. Imagine Manny's shock when he learned she wasn't just another intern but one of *the* Holden's of GMH. It intimidated him at first but Laramie put him at ease about her position and influence.

At the end of June, Laramie flew to Charleston for Liz and Randy's wedding. She was in the wedding along with Gillian. It was the first time they were all together since graduation.

"Laramie, you cried more than I, and I'm the bride. Don't tell me you've been pinin' after Randy behind my back," Liz said jokingly.

"I don't know what came over me. I think it was because poor Randy is stuck with you for life. Talk about a prison sentence." Good thing no one was in front of Gillian when she spewed her drink.

"Laramie. I am a lady today so please refrain from makin' comments that may cause me to change my disposition. I would hate to have your demise captured on film."

"*Lady?*" Gillian choked out. "As if the *white* dress wasn't already pushing the envelope."

Their time together was limited but well spent. They had a special bond that even Randy knew better than to get in between them. The women remained true to each other and themselves. No subject was off limits or too embarrassing to ask. However, if you asked their opinion be prepared to hear anything. They knew the truth hurt initially but it was far better to hear that than lie and suffer further down the line.

* * *

Her second year proved more interesting than the first since she had elected specific classes directed toward Contract Law and International Law. She wanted to do Corporate Contract Law for the firm. She loved research as well, and the fact it didn't require direct confrontation. When a trial occurred, she could sit second chair with the seasoned litigator. Her focus this year socially became the International Law Society. She co-chaired that year, not common for a second year student.

She loved the challenges the law presented to her. It gave her focus on other things besides a social life. She did manage to go on a single date, which turned into a legal debate more than a social occasion. She was among some of the brightest young legal minds and many came with oversized egos. She politely begged off when asked out again. *How do they pass through a doorway with a head that large?* She felt the date didn't go far enough to spur any romantic thoughts when the male perspective lacked any female equality. *Jerk. How do I always find them in a crowd? I must be a magnet. Laramie. The big "L" for loser.*

She went home for Christmas and worked at the firm as usual. However, this season she spent more time with Manny and Lian. She loved their company and their acceptance for who she was, not for what she had. She began to hear the rumors of her childhood settlement and that angered her immensely. She didn't speak about that with anyone and most didn't pry.

Once again came the final exams. Laramie studied in time blocks. She learned from last year that after a certain saturation point, she wasn't absorbing any more information. This new approach kept her rested and focused. She exited the building afterwards with a sense of relief. *Only one more year to go!*

Manny and Lian picked her up at the airport. She adored them and felt like they were more family than friends. She put in her daily hours at work but the weekends were hers. Manny tried to fix her up on a few dates but they ended in disaster, not because of Laramie but because he played the over protective brother. They bickered like regular siblings and Lian refereed many times.

"Why don't you just have them fill out applications to date me? If the guy why so bad then why'd you fix me up in the first place? Geez, Manny, you're worse than Edward."

"Dressing cheap didn't help, Lara. You were asking for trouble."

"Maybe that's what I wanted. Maybe I just wanted to sleep with him. I should've worn a shirt that said 'fondle me'. For crying out loud, I feel like my virginity is growing back. I didn't think it was possible to reverse it. From now on, I'll pick my own dates."

"Fine," Manny retorted.

Laramie slammed back, "Fine."

"You both are at extremes, opposite extremes. You just don't realize how much alike you are. Come in from your corners and apologize. *Now.*"

They knew better than to argue with Lian and did as they were told. Manny made a dirty look, which caused Laramie to lunge at him. Luckily for Manny, Lian caught her before she tore him to shreds.

* * *

In the past year while Laramie was in school, Manny asked to marry Lian. However, they followed the traditional Chinese wedding customs known as the Three Letter and Six Etiquette. Since they stayed traditional, Manny submitted his letter to Lian's family for his request to marry. After the long process, the matchmaker viewed their birthdates for compatibility. As they explained this to Laramie, she thought it was a joke at first. She never grew up with such cultural customs.

When the wedding day arrived at the end of another summer, Laramie was excited to see Lian in each of her three wedding dresses. The ceremony was spectacular at every stage. She stood with a cousin of Lian's that explained each stage to her. By the end of the day, it was the best wedding Laramie witnessed. She congratulated her best friends repeatedly she was so moved by the occasion. *Always the bridesmaid and never the bride. How I loath that saying.*

Chapter 10

YES, MY LAST year! By the time Laramie entered her third year, she just wanted to be out of school. She looked forward to beginning a career. *I have no idea how physicians tolerate all the schooling.* This year was much like her second, she picked most of her classes by the subject matter for her electives. Since she opted to work the corporate business sector, she enrolled in a business course at the university. The background she had in undergrad wasn't enough knowledge to support her goal. Edward felt she overextended herself by doing that, as did Andrew. She actually viewed the course as light reading compared to her law books.

She became involved in the Legal Aid Bureau, in addition to the International Law Society. This time she spread herself thin but couldn't give up anything; both activities held importance to her. She maintained the values taught by her mother. She had to make compensations in other areas, meaning her social life. She backed out of party invitations and all dates. It was the first time she returned to her reclusive behavior. This worried Edward.

He came to Boston for Christmas to keep an eye on her. He wanted to be sure she changed her behavior for the right reasons. She was excited to see him and have company in the house besides his father visiting in the Spring and Fall. *I know he's here to watch me. I'm fine, really. Doesn't he see that? I'm not hiding. I'm just busy.* During this time, she started to get offers by other firms interested in hiring her. She had no intention in accepting any of them. Some just wanted to use her intellect strictly for research. Yes, she would have a hefty salary but at the cost of huge billing hours and weekend face time. She wanted to work at the firm with Edward and Andrew. She missed her friends and San Francisco. She wanted to enjoy her life.

Her final exams were over the first week of May 2003. Laramie graduated, Summa Cum Laude, as one of the top ten students at Harvard that year, an amazing feat. She performed far better on her exams than she even thought. *I am done, done, done! Well except for the bar exam.* Edward, Andrew and Violet flew in for commencement and even ran into a few old alumni. As a graduation gift, Edward bought her a Patek Philippe watch. Laramie never really wore jewelry but it carried a huge sentimental value to her. Edward's speech regarding the pride of her parents sent her into rarely seen tears. So badly she missed them that day. It was one of the few times they witnessed her cry. Special occasions made her realize the loss she had in her heart for them.

Laramie had her clothes packed ready for her move back to the Bay. She sent her books and personal belongings ahead. *My things should already be at Edwards when I get there.* She began to think about her housing arrangements. She thought about dating again as well. *I can't exactly bring anyone home if Edward's there, too awkward. Though I need to make it to a second date, first. That should really be my focus. Let's hope the dating pool in San Francisco has improved.*

* * *

Laramie flew in on the weekend. After she unpacked her things, she called Manny and Lian. Lian began her work at Manny's family market. She wasn't thrilled by the idea but since they provided their housing, she couldn't say no. Manny continued his studies in Finance but happily took summer off. He worked at the firm fulltime now as their limo driver and did odd jobs that Edward asked. Manny didn't complain since they remained flexible during his school year.

Laramie sat the bar exam in July and worked at the firm as an intern. She looked forward to becoming an Associate. She went to the courthouse and did filings for the firm, just as her parents did. She had her own dues to pay. She met some good-looking guys along the way and dated a few but without regularity. They were interested until they realized she was a *Holden*. She tried to get past that, even thought of using her mother's maiden name. Eventually, she realized any man who wanted to be with her needed to be self-confident and not intimidated by her or her family name.

The news of her passing score on the bar exam brought cheers among her friends and family. Outside of Continuing Legal Education credits, her education was done. She became an official associate at Graham, Mathers and Holden the week after Thanksgiving. *Yes!* She waited for her first paycheck before she initiated the housing subject with Edward; she really wanted a place that was hers. Somewhere if she wanted to walk around naked, she could. Edward understood her reasons and asked her to wait for the right property and not rush. She agreed.

* * *

Laramie worked hard during her first year, honing her skills as a Corporate Contract Attorney. She went to additional seminars for specialized learning. Her career continued at a rapid progression. She undertook more cases than the seasoned associate. She gave her face time after hours and on the weekends. She knew she wasn't above anyone working there though sometimes the sentiment wasn't mutual. She felt some odd stares at times and noticed the whispers in the lunchroom. She did her best and felt that was enough.

In early 2005, Edward had a client filing for a divorce. As part of the agreement, his place in the Marina District had to be sold. Laramie was familiar with the area and loved the resurgence it was making for people in her age group. She spoke to Edward about the flat and expressed an interest in buying it. Edward played mediator with his client who wanted to sell it below market value to lessen the equity his cheating ex-wife would collect. Eight weeks later, Laramie had a moving truck hauling her belongings to her home on North Point Street. *Home!*

She loved having a place of her own, decorated in her style with things she purchased. Her biggest downfall was the fact that she didn't know how to cook. Of course, she learned to make a few college staples but nothing of substance. Up to that point, Edward and she had his cook at the house and she dined out for everything else. She called Liz for a few recipes, which brought on comical hysteria.

"Lara, darlin', even if I gave you a recipe, you probably don't own enough of the gadgets to prepare it. My first bit of advice would be to take a cookin' class. I'm sure somewhere in that city there has to be a culinary school."

"I'm not asking to be the next Emeril. I just want to make simple dinners on occasion. You don't think I can do it, do you?" Laramie challenged.

"No, I do not. Honey, you are brilliant when it comes to books, however, I've seen you burn microwave popcorn in the dorms so bad we had to remove the batteries out of the smoke detectors. Do you recall that event?"

"I do not. It must've been someone else named Laramie." *Of course she forgets nothing.* Laramie stuck her tongue out to the phone.

"And if you make one more face at me, I will reach through that phone and—"

"And what?"

"Well, I'm too much of a Southern lady to speak such foul words."

Laramie cried with laughter to the point of choking. She had the privilege to see Elizabeth's temper. When provoked, she could make a truck driver blush. She missed her friend especially at humorous times since she only had Manny around to make her laugh.

Laramie took Liz's advice and signed up for a few basic cooking classes taught by a local restaurant, determined to prove Liz wrong on her domestic abilities. Her first lesson consisted of making a Southwestern stew. *How hard could this be?* Laramie wasn't sure what she did wrong in browning the meat but it created a grease fire that set off the sprinklers. The owner felt awful but asked her to quit the course. She suggested a local community college where they had better insurance for those type of accidents. *Perfect, just perfect.*

As she relayed her story to her friend, Elizabeth, pregnant at the time, laughed so hard that she peed her pants. Manny told everyone he knew her story and heard it featured on the local radio station as one of the Darwin winners. *I never should have told Manny. Traitor.* Fortunately, they omitted Laramie's name. Lian assisted her in buying the basics for the kitchen. She suggested Laramie begin with minute rice, pasta and precooked dinners in a bag.

Chapter 11

WHEN LARAMIE MADE partner, most of her male coworkers slowly excluded her on the Friday bar nights. Until then, she was always one of the gang. However, opinions differed among the women. Some idolized her for her accomplishments and knowledge of the law while others felt she had obtained her status through family channels. She obviously didn't sleep her way to the top, the thought alone made her cringe. *What a horrible visual. Yuk.* The other partners had some choice in who achieved the illustrious promotion. However, it was her own merits that brought her to her present level.

"Power can and does bring out the worst in people," warned Edward speaking from experience.

"I understand that but why can't they see the client base I've established and revenue I've brought in? Some of the associates here haven't generated the same revenue in the last five years combined."

"Laramie, you're asking me to fight this battle for you. First, it is not my position to do so. Second, it is not a battle to be won. Is it fair? No. Life isn't fair. The partners here know how and why you were promoted. Many got their promotion on less merit. You need to distance yourself from office gossip and concentrate on your work. You will not win over everyone. It is impossible."

"But it is so infuriating. I just want to be viewed for my work."

"Let me explain it this way. There are many golfers that play the Master's every year. They have been professional golfers for years. You are Tiger Woods. You are young and confident. You earn a spot to play with the veterans and you come in only to beat them all. How many of those golfers feel Tiger earned that title? The smart ones see his natural talent being rewarded. The angry ones feel he didn't deserve the win because he didn't pay his dues. It's the same thing here. The attorneys that are of lower caliber will always view you as getting special treatment. They will never admit their own inadequacies as the problem for their position." *Edward, once again, the voice of reason.*

Laramie understood his view but it didn't make it any easier to accept. *I thought these people were my friends.* She went out of her way to show the disbelievers the reasons for her promotion but it didn't change anything. She no longer had the free time to prove herself. Edward made her take on more responsibility for her own financial gains. She was Chairwoman on Cummings Corporation, inherited through her maternal grandfather, even though Edward oversaw the business on a fulltime basis. On top of that, she was asked to join the Board of Directors of a few Dotcom businesses in the area. Andrew checked the books for the firm and the corporation. Laramie mostly remained the figurehead.

Laramie felt she reached many of her goals, except the social ones. Once again she put herself out in the dating world. She attempted to meet men employed outside of the legal field. Her association with the Internet companies provided men who were comfortable with her success however no one she found attractive. She tried the five minute bar musical chairs kind of dating but that only brought out men trying to get laid quickly. She wanted to call them all 'Sam.' *I give up.*

She put herself out there with no valid takers and as a result, she poured herself into her work once again. Edward watched from the outside, unable to figure out her social problem. *She's a beautiful and intelligent woman. So what's the problem? What happens that stops her from a second date? This isn't the life her parents wanted for her. She's missing out on real happiness and I don't know how to show her what she's missing.*

Chapter 12

AFTER A BRIEF layover, Laramie boarded the plane and situated herself back into her seat. *Only six more hours. I know so little about this country.* She pulled out her travel guide and read about the history. It was interesting to see so many cultures living together under one government with such little conflict. Each religion celebrated their holidays in relative safety. *Ha, no protesters? That's hard to believe. Apparently, they haven't been to the U.S.* Laramie was happy to note she would be in country during the Chinese Moon Festival. It sounded so exciting. She went to many festivals in Chinatown and wondered how they compared. She thought about her contracts and decided to review them while she sat near the pool. *No, Laramie! You promised yourself no work until the business meeting. I don't even know whether I'm capable of relaxing enough for a vacation.*

She tried to put all work related thoughts behind her with the help of a cocktail. The flight attendant brought her a white wine as she asked. Laramie knew her tolerance for liquor was lower than most of her friends, except for maybe Lian. *If I have at least four cocktails between now and landing, I should tired enough to sleep and get onto a normal time schedule.* Singapore was eight hours ahead of San Francisco, just enough to confuse her sleeping habits. With every drink, her tour book became harder to read. Obviously, reading the same paragraph three times was enough to convince her to end that insanity. She grabbed her pillow and blanket and fell into her reclined seat. It wasn't long before she fell asleep.

Just as the airline scheduled, wheels down was at five minutes past one, in the morning. Laramie rose from her seat after an awakening from the flight attendant. Still feeling a bit groggy from her drinks, she slowly grabbed her bags and walked off the plane, not without thanking the staff first. As she made her way to luggage claim, she was disappointed to see all the stores closed, as if she had the energy for shopping. She stood by the carousel waiting for her suitcase to appear. In its present state, the suitcase was hard to miss. Seeing the poor condition, Laramie realized it was time to find a new replacement. *I'm almost embarrassed to be seen with that suitcase. What was I thinking?* This was one more thing to add to her list of shopping while there.

Laramie walked over to the wall of house phones and looked for her hotel, The Tanjong Beach Hotel & Spa. The photo next to it had a concrete patio, surrounded with chairs, tables and tropical pants, overlooking the beach at sunset. It looked so relaxing that she was ready to pour herself into the picture. Regardless of how much time she napped on the plane, she needed a bed to completely rest. She picked up the phone and waited for a voice on the other end.

"Good evening, Tanjong Beach Hotel and Spa. May I help you?" a soft voice spoke on the other end.

"Hello. This is Laramie Holden. I have a reservation with your hotel and my plane *just* arrived. How do I get from here to there? Is there a shuttle?"

"Welcome Miss Holden. There is no shuttle. Please exit the airport from your location and take any limousine to our hotel. All the drivers know the location and procedure. Is there anything we can do for you before you get here? Run a lotus flower bath? Or perhaps you are hungry?" Laramie thought her suggestions were wonderful but she really wanted to crash until noon.

"No thank you, that won't be necessary. It was a wonderful thought."

After they exchanged good byes, Laramie strode outside to the first limousine. The driver eyed her up and down and seemed eager to take her wherever she wanted to go. However, at the mention of the Tanjong Beach Hotel, he became completely professional and very accommodating. *Hmm... I wonder what got into him?*

As the limo drove away from the airport, Laramie struggled to see the landscape. It was far too dark for anything to be visible aside from the Singapore Flyer, and all the wine didn't help her vision either. She could see the street signs that pointed to Sentosa Island and she knew that was where the hotel was located. The slow melody playing inside the vehicle relaxed her, almost too much. As the limo made its way over the bridge, Laramie saw the monorail track as well as the wires for the cable cars. She hoped to have a better look around but the lighting down the road wasn't bright enough and anything resembling a shop closed quite some time ago.

As the limo pulled up in covered entry of the hotel, Laramie saw through the glass doors to the lobby. The driver startled her when he opened her door. The hotel was a lot smaller than she expected, which was fine. Laramie expected something more on the lines of a Four Seasons or a Ritz, but this was… *quaint*. The architecture reminded her of a tropical island with large wood columns supporting most of the structure. The front entry was mainly glass which exposed the seating area and upper loft. The tan color scheme was neutral and serene. She walked to the left where a young Malaysian girl worked the front desk.

"You must be Miss Holden. Welcome to our hotel. We hope you had a relaxing flight. Is this your first time to Singapore?" she kindly said as she checked in Laramie.

"Yes, this is my first time here. I'm really looking forward to my stay. Thank you."

"If there is anything we can arrange for you such as guides or tours, please call the front desk. We are all knowledgeable in the many things Singapore has to offer. Most people speak English so you should not expect any difficulty there. Samad will show you to your bungalow. Once again, if there is anything we can do for you, please call us. Have a wonderful evening and thank you for choosing the Tanjong Beach Hotel and Spa."

Laramie noticed how polite the staff was, everyone came around the desk bowed and smiled. Not used to these customs, it was a gracious feeling. It wasn't the sterile feel of traveling to the big hotels chains in the U.S. Whether the staff was sincere or not, it felt as though they were to Laramie.

Laramie followed the bellhop, Samad, out of the rear of the building. The gardens had lush greenery that grew over the hardness of the stone paved area surrounding the pool. Off to her left, Laramie noticed a wooden bar in the same architecture of the main building but in a smaller scale. Lounge chairs and umbrellas flanked the pool which had beautiful mosaic tile work on the bottom and sides, that glowed with the night light shining in it. Laramie looked up to see the gentle surf creeping up the sand. It was far more peaceful than she expected. She envisioned herself on the powdery sand for the next two weeks. *I can't wait until I can dig my toes into the sand and surf.*

Laramie trailed Samad to the last bungalow on the right, closest to the beach. The bungalow's wooden planked roof softened the hardness of the stucco walls. The plants and palms were at a height that provided much privacy. Samad unlocked the heavy wooden door and motioned for her to enter first. He walked in behind her and placed her suitcase upon her bed but not without a struggle. Laramie offered a hand but Samad smiled and declined. She felt guilty packing so much into her bag especially when he tried to lift it. Laramie tried to tip Samad but he politely refused her money, since tipping wasn't customary in Singapore.

Laramie investigated each area of her new home. The floral arrangement was exquisite but not made too high to block the view of your guest or the flat screen TV on the wall. The woven furniture was dark with cushions showing exotic leaves and birds. Off to the left corner, a small kitchen and bar area with matching rattan table and chairs, upholstered in the same fabric as the living room, filled the area. Between the living area and breakfast area were French doors that led outdoors. As Laramie passed through the doors, she stood beneath a covered lanai area with another table and chairs. *Wow!* Two steps down was a magnificent soaking pool. The pool, not as detailed in the tile work as the main pool, looked tranquil. The lushness of the plants and sweet scent of the flowers, that surrounded the pool, were glorious.

Laramie walked into her bungalow and through the French doors that separated the bedroom from the living area. In the center of the room was a massive carved wood king size poster bead. It was dressed in beautiful cotton and crocheted linens with over stuffed down pillows. The bed, already turned down, invited Laramie to crawl inside and sleep. *A real bed! My body is screaming for you.*

After unzipping her suitcase, she unpacked into the massive wall closet and carved wooden dressers. She grabbed her toiletry bag and walked outside her room to the bathroom, just left of her room. She turned the light on and stood surprised. *This is gorgeous.* The bathroom walls had various textured tiles reaching the vaulted wooden ceiling. The wooden vanity held two hand-painted porcelain basins. Above the basins were two beautifully carved wooden mirrors with a fresh floral arrangement hanging on the wall between them. In the back of the room sat the tiled water-jet soaking tub enclosed by glass to accompany the showerhead and wall jets. *Now why would anyone ever leave this room?*

As she looked around, she noted this hotel was not showy or overdone but it was painstakingly detailed and elegantly furnished. *Whoever designed this place has great taste. I wonder whether she is local or international. Bottom-line… will she come to San Francisco?*

Chapter 13

"KAT, WHEN YOU have a minute, please come here. I have a list of things to be done this week," said Akihiro as he sat behind the dark mahogany desk.

He spun in his chair and looked out the rear of his office where a wall of reflective glass aided his ability to watch the guests unnoticed. It was important to Akihiro that the staff treat everyone with the best possible attitude and congeniality, after all this was *his* hotel.

In the four years since its building, Akihiro Amori's hotel became the standard for small hotels in Malaysia, Indonesia and Singapore. He spent many weekends training the staff himself in the early days. Akihiro wooed a local chef to work for him and paid for the classes to teach him international cuisine. Many of the signature dishes on the menu were inspired by his mother and grandmother, European but with an Asian twist. He sought out the artisans in Jakarta for the furniture in the hotel. He purchased his bamboo linens from the best weavers in Brunei. This labor of love had his touch all over it. He dreamed about this project for a long time and spared no cost in bringing it to fruition. His hotel employed the locals as well taught them how to insist on making things better. Akihiro wanted his hotel to be the best for the staff, the best for the guests and the best for the environment. His passion paid off.

"Akihiro, we have two new guests this week. The first is a gentleman, a software salesman, from Bangkok. He will be staying a week. The second guest is a woman, an attorney from the United States, who will be here for three weeks."

"Are there any specialty items requested? Has the staff been updated on our guests? Has Ahmed submitted this week's restaurant specials? If he has, could you oversee the tasting to make sure they are acceptable? Is there anything I forgot?"

"No. I believe you have covered everything. I will check with Ahmed once I leave here." Kat walked out of the office and returned to her desk outside the door.

Mei Hui Tan, known as "Kat" to everyone, began working for Akihiro Amori when the hotel opened in early 2005. She could run the business almost as well as Akihiro, maybe even better. Kat researched all of the guests that stayed at The Tanjong, trying to find their likes and dislikes. Everyone at the hotel received the highest level of service. In doing that, many of the guests were repeat customers or friends of previous guests. Word of mouth was their advertising, which allowed more money for luxuries in the guest rooms.

Kat lived in the city with her two girlfriends. They shared an apartment by Clarke Quay, on the river. She rode the MRT back and forth to work thus eliminating the need for a car. Living in Singapore could be expensive depending on the area where you lived. Many of the twenty-something's lived in the city to be close to work and the clubs. The cost of an auto was high but adding in the license auction, taxes, fuel, and insurance made it prohibitive for the average citizen to afford. The subway and bus system were affordable, easily accessible and very reliable.

Kat went to the University and earned her degree in hotel management. She had Akihiro in a few classes thus resulting in their meeting. Both students were sharp and very business savvy. Both also came from diverse backgrounds. Kat grew up in a middleclass environment as the only child to Chinese parents. Both her parents worked for the banking industry in the city center.

Her petite frame and softened appearance left a new acquaintance surprised to find she was shrewd and outgoing. Kat learned a long time ago that it didn't pay to always be polite, sometimes honestly wasn't polite at all. This was one of many reasons Akihiro hired her. She told her thoughts as they were whether she thought the person needed to know or not. She was loyal but sometimes she could be fierce. She protected Akihiro much like a cantankerous sibling. Their relationship was always as friends. They saw each other as attractive but in a 'still not my type' point of view.

Akihiro Amori, now in his early thirties, was the eldest son of Tadashi Amori, a Japanese realtor, and Lucia Rodriguez Amori, a traditional stay-at-home mother. His parents met when Tadashi studied at Oxford University. Lucia, the daughter of a Spanish father and English mother, worked at a local pub across from the campus. After a soccer match, Tadashi and friends went over to the pub to celebrate their win. He fell in love with Lucia immediately. However, the feeling was not mutual. He chased her for many months before she finally agreed to go out with him. After long courtship, Tadashi won her heart. Following his graduation from Oxford, they married and went to live in Singapore.

Tadashi owned a large real estate company in Singapore. His hope was to have both of his sons work in the family business. Shinji, the youngest of both sons, worked for his father in the city. His father wanted Akihiro to join the company but Aki always wanted something of his own. Akihiro was smart like his father but bullheaded like his mother. Lucia finally settled the argument one night after dinner. Akihiro would follow his dream and open his own hotel but if it did not run a profit after the first year then he would quit and join his father and brother in the family business. This idea seemed to please all involved.

Akihiro was always headstrong, especially in sports. Many times as a youth, he sat on the bench during a soccer game for pushing on the field. His father felt Karate was a better alternative to teach his son discipline and respect. Akihiro excelled in Karate, spending many weekends in tournaments. He gained the discipline his father sought. Karate made Akihiro a more controlled person, it made him think before reacting. By the time Akihiro finished high school, he ranked number one in Karate in Singapore. In those years, Akihiro focused more on his studies. Despite his good looks, he didn't date much in school due to his shyness. Yet, the girls called and sent notes asking for a date with regularity.

After high school, Akihiro went to England to attend Oxford University as his father did. He loved the sports and the friends he made but he was homesick for Singapore and his family. After his second year, he transferred to the National University of Singapore. While studying Marketing and Hotel Management, he worked throughout college, then after gradation for the Bank of Singapore. His work experience was invaluable when he decided to build the Tanjong Beach Hotel and Spa. After working for the bank for six years, Akihiro had a sufficient down payment and a few investors among his friends. Akihiro called on a few coworkers in the mortgage sector and corporate officers his father knew when it was time for financing.

In the early Spring of 2004, a groundbreaking ceremony took place with Akihiro making the first dig. Within months, the first timbers were set in place. Akihiro spent weeks inspecting the construction as well the materials going in the hotel. Begrudgingly, his father, Tadashi spent weekends on site assisting his son; he wanted Akihiro to succeed. He knew his first priority was his son's happiness. Lucia, his mother, assisted Akihiro in the décor. While Akihiro picked out each item, Lucia narrowed the choices for her son. Her invaluable taste in décor resulted in the cohesiveness of the hotel.

By the following spring, Akihiro held the grand opening of his hotel, feeling such pride in his commitment. This new structure was a piece of him and his first love. Every employee at the Tanjong realized the dedication required for his or her position. No task was beneath anyone, even Akihiro. The newspaper reviews were stellar, which brought the first guests of the season. There were few problems at first, such as the pump not working properly in the pool and the spa did not open as scheduled due a lack of products for use. However, guests, locals and friends heavily utilized the outdoor bar.

By summer, the operation ran smoothly. The hotel had a steady stream of guests, each passing on the word of their new find. Akihiro's hotel was a success. He spent many nights on the sofa in his office to make sure each guest had their proper attention. The service at the Tanjong quickly preceded the guests. Employees had competitive compensation and soon a list began for any potential vacancies. Throughout the startup, Kat assisted Akihiro as though the hotel was her own. They knew they had a superb business and their friendship complimented the place.

Chapter 14

WHAT TIME IS *it?* Laramie turned over to view the clock on the nightstand. *Oh geez, it's already 10:30 am.* She slowly poured herself out of bed, hit the light switch in the bathroom to get a good look at her face. *Well, no real puffiness under my eyes. That's a good start.* She brushed her teeth and washed her face of any remaining makeup. Laramie grabbed a clip and twisted her hair up, letting a few tendrils flow down. She rummaged through her drawers until she found her bikini and pareo. After she changed, she looked in the mirror one last time, just in case. She ran the checklist: sunglasses, room key, cell phone and money. *Now... how do I carry all of this? Well, looks like my phone and money stay here. I'll just write off my breakfast to my room. Done.*

Akihiro stood at the outside bar checking through the register receipts from the preceding night. He wore his usual uniform: a pair of khaki slacks, a white, short sleeve, button down oxford shirt and leather sandals. He felt looking casual made the guests feel more relaxed around him and the grounds. He was correct. Behind him, he heard the sound of the chair moving across the stone.

"I'll be with you in one moment." He wanted every guest to feel acknowledged. He just needed one more receipt to print off before he turned. Laramie noticed he spoke impeccable English with a slight Asian accent, not what she expected.

"That's quite all right. Take your time," Laramie answered back nonchalantly, double checking her appearance.

He quickly caught her American accent. Without turning his back, he replied, "Miss Holden, welcome to The Tanjong Beach Hotel and Spa. What can I get you this morning?"

"Wow, that's a great trick. Though, just Laramie is fine. Unfortunately, I don't have the benefit of knowing your name, Mr. …"

"Call me, Akihiro." He turned and faced this woman sitting at the bar. Stunned by her natural beauty for a moment, he stumbled with his words, and then cleared his throat. "Pardon me, what is it that I can get for you?"

"Well… I'm not too sure. I would love an ice water first. The plane was dehydrating. What do you recommend?" *Holy cow, this guy is hot. Come on Laramie, keep your wits about you. I wonder if I can fit him in my suitcase. Now , THAT would be a wonderful souvenir.* She sat there looking at his deep black eyes and thick black hair. His cheekbones and chin had a chiseled look to them. The sun warmly kissed Akihiro's skin, though with his parents' heritage, a tan wasn't necessary. Laramie hoped she wasn't drooling or doing anything the least bit embarrassing.

"If you're looking for something light, I would suggest the coconut pineapple juice with ginseng. To eat…" Akihiro grabbed a menu from the bar and briefly reviewed it. "… I would choose the fresh fruit and lychee tofu. After such a long flight, you really need to acclimatize yourself with our food and environment."

Akihiro handed Laramie the menu. As she reviewed her choices, he placed her water on the bar. He couldn't help but stare at her. There was something about her that caught his attention. *What is it? Is it her eyes? Is it her smile?* Laramie decided to go with Akihiro's suggestion.

"I'll trust you on this since I'm not a tofu eater. This is a stretch for me." Laramie watched him work behind to bar. She measured him up and down, and found all of him attractive. *Unbelievable. He's seems to have the whole package. Well… so to speak.*

"Tell me, is this your first time to Singapore?" Akihiro picked up the house phone to call in her breakfast; he ordered and then hung up.

"Actually, yes. I bought a few travel books to read on the plane. I saw a few things that interested me but if you have any suggestions, I'd love to hear them."

"You are here for pleasure then?"

"Well, partly. I have two weeks for vacation then I have a week for business at the end. However, after seeing the beautiful beach this morning, I wish it were all vacation." She shyly smiled.

"Is that legal business?" *My attorney never looked that good. Damn.*

"Yes… how did you know?" Laramie felt a bit uncomfortable with this man knowing so much about her and she knew nothing of him.

"The hotel tries to know as much as possible about the clients. It helps us cater to your needs better."

"Oh, okay. Well, the firm I work for has sent me to oversee a property deal for a new hotel in the city. Actually, the contracts are finished but I need to review them and report the steps we need to have in place before the hotel opens. You know, construction, permits, management, staff … Anyway, I don't want to bore you with the details." *Stop rambling. I sound like an idiot.* After she finished speaking, a waiter placed her breakfast in front of her at the bar. The plate looked delicious covered with carved shapes of pineapple, half peeled longan berries, rambutan, and mangosteen. In the center was a small bowl with white cubes, which Laramie assumed was the tofu.

"Don't let me keep you from eating, please," he stated as he motioned his hand toward her plate.

"It looks beautiful. I almost hate to touch it." Laramie started with the fruit first, the pineapple being the safest. *Great, now what? I've never seen anything that remotely resembled this fruit. At least I think it's fruit. I should've stuck with eggs and toast.* She seemed perplexed by the other fruits and looked at Akihiro for guidance. He picked up the longan berry and peeled off the rest of the rind.

"You can eat the flesh off the seed or put the whole thing in your mouth and do it."

"Thanks, because I had no clue. What about the other ones?"

"You eat the rambutan the same as the longan, but don't bite into the seed, eat around it or pull it away from the seed. As for the mangosteen, you need to use a spoon and scoop the fruit out of the skin. Try the tofu. Please tell me what you think."

Laramie placed a spoonful in her mouth and chewed it. Quickly, her face changed. *Oh, I have to swallow this. It's awful. I hate tofu. Can I keep it down once I do? Only one way to find out. You got lucky with one bite, don't be stupid and try another.* Akihiro studied her expression and began to laugh as he watched her.

"What are you doing? Is it that bad to you? Why do you not spit it out?" he said handing her a napkin.

"Oh God, that was awful. And I didn't spit it out because I didn't want to be rude." Laramie still felt a bit embarrassed. Akihiro thought she was humorous. She looked at him and began to laugh herself. "Whatever you may say, you can't say I wasn't willing to try something new."

As they conversed for a while at the bar, a young Chinese man, looking in his early twenties, walked behind the counter next to Akihiro. He raised his hand to high-five then low five his boss. He was dressed in the standard uniform of the hotel, a white polo shirt and khaki chinos.

"Good morning, Miss Holden. I hope you are enjoying your breakfast. The lychee tofu is one of my favorites," Huan said.

Laramie and Akihiro looked at one another, laughing all over again.

"Laramie, would you like a tour of the city this afternoon? That is if you don't mind me being your tour guide," Akihiro asked, truly leaving his comfort zone.

Caught by surprise, Laramie responded, "Oh, I would love it. Your boss wouldn't have a problem with that, would he?" Huan laughed. It was apparent to everyone but Laramie, that Akihiro was the boss. "Okay, what's so funny?"

"Mr. Amori *is* the boss."

She swung her head back to Akihiro. "What? You're not the bartender? I feel so stupid. I am so sorry, Akihiro."

"No, no, no. There was no way for you to know that. I should have introduced myself better. My full name is Akihiro Amori and I own the Tanjong. I will say I am impressed at the courtesy you show my staff, or who you think is my staff."

"Well, Mr. Amori, I would still love a tour of the city. Just let me know what time to be ready."

"I have some business to take care of this early afternoon, so why don't we plan on five o'clock? We could have dinner out after, if you don't mind."

Laramie wasn't sure whether this was a friendly gesture or a date. It was better to error on the side of caution and view it as a nice gesture. "Five o'clock is perfect. I'll just meet you in the lobby at that time."

"Perfect. Enjoy your day." Akihiro turned away smiling and patted Huan on the back before walking into the main building.

"Okay Huan, what's the low down on everyone knowing my name?"

"Don't tell anyone I told you," he said as he winked, "but when you make a reservation, you give us your name, address, phone, etc. Kat, she's Mr. Amori's assistant manager, she searches you on the Internet or calls your office to talk with personnel. Mr. Amori wants everyone's visit to his hotel perfect and tailored to their tastes." Clearly impressed by the degree of personal attention given to the guests, Laramie wondered if a tour guide was Akihiro's idea or a part of the hotel plan.

Laramie chatted with Huan for a while. She learned about his family and his friends. He taught her a few slang terms in Singlish, a mix of Chinese, Malay and English. Huan spoke very highly of the staff and Akihiro as well. She assumed the working atmosphere was a pleasurable one based on the stories and expressions of the workers. After a short while, Laramie realized she was extremely comfortable talking with everyone who came to the bar. It was dual fold, every one of the staff enjoyed meeting and speaking with her, too.

After her morning conversation, which extended into the afternoon, Laramie lounged at the pool. The weather was very humid, despite their claim that it was the dry season. She drank an iced tea that she found unbelievably spectacular. She wanted to know what was in it but, after the tofu incident, she changed her mind. Occasionally she dipped her body in the pool to cool off. During this time, her thoughts came back her clothes for the evening. She wanted to dress simple but nice since she had a dinner later. *What to wear, what to wear… no ideas.* She didn't know what time they would be out until so she wasn't sure whether a sweater was necessary. The more flustered she became thinking about it, the more she felt like it was a date. It had been a long time since Laramie felt giddy.

By three o'clock, Laramie returned to her bungalow. She quickly plugged in her laptop and instant messaged Liz.

> Liz, got a date. What to wear? Nothing trampy. Please help.

She waited anxiously for her reply. Liz was online but Laramie wondered whether she was too busy to see the message.

> Hey Lara! No idea what you packed. Dress party casual.
> A date, huh? Who's the guy?

Laramie quickly typed back, stumbling on the keys. She was never a good typist and being flustered didn't help.

> Owns hotel. Very hot and sexy. Will not share, get your own. LOL.
> Will chat later.
> Love U. Miss U.

Suddenly, Laramie hated everything she packed. It was too late to shop so her choices were in front of her. *Party casual, yeah right.* Eventually she opted for her white and tan halter dress, a good choice due to the humidity. She quickly showered and dressed. She had a faint pink glow all over from sunbathing, which looked radiant against the light colors of her dress. The humid air caused her long hair to wave. It looked nice and natural. *Oh sure, it never looks this good at home, but I'll take it.* She sprayed some perfume on all the hot spots, primped her hair a little more, and then took a final look in the mirror. *This is as good as it gets.*

Akihiro stood in the bathroom attached to his office. He was nervous. He wondered when the last time he felt like this was. Generally, on a personal level, he was shy. Through years of business, he overcame his fear of public speaking but a beautiful woman was a completely new matter. However, Laramie made him feel comfortable, as though they knew each other for years. *But why am I so tense now? I've met beautiful women many times.* When he asked her out, he meant it as a courtesy but then it began to feel like a date to him as well. He looked at his watch and knew it was time to go. He hadn't any game plan, ideas for dinner, nothing. *Do I hold her hand? Kiss her hello? No, no contact. That could be uncomfortable for her.*

Kat looked at Akihiro leaving his office and smiled a devilish grin. She knew he was jittery and preyed on it.

"What? What is that smile for? Is something wrong?" Akihiro looked over himself as he checked to make sure all was well.

"Nothing. Nothing at all. I was just wondering when you were going to show Mr. Chareunchit, from Bangkok, around the city too." She couldn't stop laughing. Her shoulders shook with the hilarity of the situation. She did not best Akihiro too many times but this was one time when she nailed him. He knew it and called her juvenile.

Laramie stood as Akihiro entered the lobby and walked toward her. The staff's eyes were on them both. As Akihiro looked at his workers, they smiled and nodded. The bellhop pulled up with Akihiro's black Mercedes SL500 convertible. Samad sat in the driver's seat until Aki cleared his throat to get out. Laramie was glad he owned a car and not a motorcycle like many people in Singapore; she wasn't dressed for a motor bike.

After they quickly departed for the city, Laramie viewed all the beautiful trees and flowers along the road. She never realized how beautiful Singapore was considering she saw very little the previous night. *The whole country looks landscaped. Just beautiful.* This ride was a delightful departure.

"I hope you like boats. I thought a river cruise would be a great start. We can pick it up by Clarke Quay."

"That sounds great. I'll follow your lead." Then the awkward silence appeared. Laramie tried to think of something besides the weather. "So, what made you start your own hotel?"

He smiled at her, feeling the same discomfort. "It was something I always wanted to do. My father wanted me to join him in real estate but it was not my interest. My younger brother, Shinji, works for him and they argue all the time. This way, I don't report to anyone, so there is no argument. What made you study law?"

"That's easy. It's in my blood. Both my parents were attorneys."

"Were? Are they retired now?"

"Oh, no. They died in a car accident when I was twelve," she replied factually.

"I am so sorry, I didn't know."

"It's okay. I'm surprised you didn't know that too." She grinned. "Anyway, I lived with my grandparents for awhile until I moved in with Edward."

"Edward? Your boyfriend?"

"Oh God, no! Edward was my parents' best friend and my legal guardian. He is one of the partners at the firm, along with Andrew Mathers and well, now you know who the Holden's are."

The news regarding Edward was a relief to Akihiro though he wasn't sure why he felt that way. He found everything about her attractive, her ability to make him feel relaxed. He watched her smile and talk about her friends. Laramie had a great sense of openness. She wasn't afraid to tell her stories whether they portrayed her silly or not.

"Oh geez. I'm sorry. I don't mean to talk about myself so much. You must think I'm crazy."

"No, not at all. The stories are really comical. We have such different cultures but such similar childhood stories. Keep going." Occasionally, she stopped to ask him about a building or park she saw. She was similar to watching a child experiencing something new.

"Your accent… it sounds different. I can't seem to place it. If I'm being too forward please tell me."

"I'm surprised you caught that. It is slightly different. My mother is Spanish and British, though raised in England, which explains most of the sound. With my father being Japanese, I tend to speak slower. Though I think your accent is far more noticeable." *That explains his looks. That's why I couldn't place him. Still, I find his accent sexy, very sexy.*

Laramie laughed. "I suppose I do sound strange compared to everyone else here."

Akihiro parked along the river. They walked down to the dock where the bumboats were. Bumboats were open hulled boats with benches and a small covered area in the center to escape the sun. Akihiro helped Laramie onto the boat and they walked up front to have a better view. The sun started to lower in the sky, which shaded half the river making the stores and restaurants easier to see. Akihiro pointed out the G-max bungy jump, Riverside Point shopping complex and Singapore's very own Hooters. The street vendors started to prepare their grills for the evenings patrons. Surprised by the ornate architecture, Laramie thought the area would be more modern like the skyscrapers across the river. *Just amazing.* She was in awe of the beauty of the city and could not wait to see the lights of the evening.

Further down the river was Boat Quay, Akihiro stated that they would probably dine over there. Each restaurant had tables and umbrellas set up along the river. The smells of the cuisine filled the air, making them both hungry. Laramie hoped dinner would be more successful than the tofu. Akihiro pointed out the statue of Sir Thomas Stamford Raffles, founder of the city, and gave a brief history lesson. *Just keep talking Akihiro so I have a reason to stare.* Soon the boat passed under Cavenagh Bridge, a walking bridge. Laramie watched the people standing above them, waving, and waved back. Occasionally, she turned and smiled at Akihiro. On the other side, in front of the Fullerton Hotel, was an adorable bronze of children jumping toward the river. As the boat approached the Esplanade, Aki told her of the many concerts and theatrical performances he attended there. He explained why locals called it The Durian, after the spiky pungent fruit. Laramie stated quickly she was not going to try it.

Soon they came in front of the Merlion, the national symbol of Singapore. He explained the story behind the mythical beast, half lion and half fish. Laramie listened so intently that she didn't notice another boat coming toward them. The other boat, swerving quickly, created a sharp wake that hit the bow and splashed across Laramie's dress, soaking the top portion. She quickly gasped and looked for anything as a cover. *Oh my God. No. This can't be happening. No.* She found nothing in sight and rapidly folded her arms. Her dress became transparent when wet. She was so embarrassed that she wanted to cry. Akihiro felt horrible looking at the anguish in her face. He swiftly removed his shirt and placed it over her. Initially unaware of the situation, the owner of the boat apologized and refused to accept payment for the ride. However, he did have an extra shirt on board which he tossed to Akihiro. On the return, Laramie sat quiet on the boat and tried to think of a way to salvage the evening. Her eyes welled up but she refused to cry. *Damn it! Isn't this just perfect. I feel like such an fool. What do I do now?*

Akihiro helped the captain dock the boat and walked over to Laramie to assist her off the boat. No one spoke a word until they reached the car.

Akihiro felt he should take the first step. "Laramie, if you want to go back to the hotel I would completely understand. I cannot apologize enough."

She didn't want the evening to end, at least not in this manner. *Can anything be worse than this?* Trying to make light of the circumstances, she shrugged her shoulders, cracked a smile and replied, "You don't happen to know of any wet t-shirt contests, do you?"

She began to laugh. She didn't know what else to do. Akihiro looked at her in astonishment. *This poor woman is completely humiliated in public, in front of strangers, and she has the ability to laugh at the situation.* He was awestruck by her response.

"You are amazing, you know that, don't you? Keep my shirt on and we'll run into one of the shops. I'm sure we can find something else for you to wear."

After she changed her dress, they walked along the riverbank. Eventually they sat down at Hot Stones Restaurant. They opted for dining along the river rather than inside the building. By now, they both were very hungry and the sizzling stones that passed them made them hungrier. Laramie ordered a glass of house chardonnay, a safe move. Akihiro asked for a Grey Goose straight up. The evening seemed to be getting back to normal until they looked each other in the eyes and laughed all over again. They took turns eating while the other talked. Laramie ordered a steak and found it to be larger than she could finish. Akihiro finished his meal and occasionally helped her eat the steak. Not something he would normally do, but he lost himself in his relaxation with her. *Oh, he is so funny. Good thing I wasn't really hungry.* Laramie never had anyone eat off her plate and found it amusing.

After dinner, they continued their walk along the river. Akihiro told stories of his youth with his brother. *His poor mother, she must be a saint by now.* It was pleasant to hear of sibling rivalries and antics. She held onto every word he said. Conservatively animated when he spoke, she felt as though she was there when the story happened. At the halfway point of their walk, Akihiro reached over for her hand, which caught her off guard. It felt soft and warm. He kept talking without missing a beat, as though it were commonplace. Laramie smiled to herself. She liked it. *Very nice.*

Soon it was after eleven o'clock and they both were tired. Laramie held on wonderfully despite the time change. As they entered the hotel laughing aloud, the staff watched them walk out toward the pool. Akihiro and Laramie were so engrossed in their conversation that they missed the stares and giggles by the workers. However, the females noticed at once that Laramie's clothes were different, causing much speculation.

When they reached Laramie's bungalow, they stood in uncomfortable silence again. Akihiro wasn't sure how to end this scene. He wanted to kiss her but felt that would be too forward. Laramie hoped he would kiss her but didn't want to appear trampy. Eventually, he leaned in and kissed her lightly on the cheek. Laramie felt a rush of warmth flow through her and wondered how she would react to an actual kiss.

"Would you care to have lunch tomorrow? That is if you haven't made any plans." Akihiro hoped she would see him again.

"Are we going to be on a boat?" she asked smiling.

"No."

"Then yes, I would love to have lunch with you tomorrow." *As if I would say no.*

Her response brought a smile to his face. He found her an amazing woman.

"Wonderful, then it's a date."

Chapter 15

LARAMIE WOKE UP and rushed to her laptop. It was already late in the evening back in the States. She had such an incredible evening despite the boat incident that she had to share it with her girlfriends. As soon she fired up her laptop, she typed away at her email. She went into detail regarding the boat and felt proud in saving the night. She told the girls all about Akihiro, his hotel, car, smile, and even eating from her plate. She described the goodnight kiss, wishing it was more. Laramie tended to be reserved when it came to men so this revelation in wanting more was a departure for her. She wished she could just do a conference call with the girls but being overseas made it pointless, not to mention expensive. She typed a full page of details she only shared with her closest friends. She signed off by saying 'if I'm dreaming, never wake me.'

Laramie called the front desk to inquire about the lotus flower bath they offered. She decided to stay in for the morning and slowly prepare for lunch. The voice from the front desk said someone would be there shortly to run her bath. After a knock at the door, it surprised Laramie to see Kat standing there with a basket full of items.

"Come in, please. I'm surprised to see you here. I just thought one of the other girls would've done this."

"Normally they would be here, but Akihiro asked me to come. He has to cancel lunch." Kat saw the disappointment in Laramie's face immediately and watched her mood turn somber. "Although, he would like to make it up to by having dinner again. Is that all right for you, Miss Holden?"

Laramie perked up quickly. She smiled and nodded in the affirmative. *They both are like kids first dating. I wonder whether I ever looked as ridiculous?*

"I assume you wanted the bath before meeting for lunch. We can still prepare it for you for the evening. I'm going to put all the ingredients in the tub and when you get ready just add the hot water."

Laramie watched her pour in coconut milk, sea salts, some kind of oil, and lastly, three lotus flower blossoms. The flowers smelled fabulous.

"Miss Holden, the hot water will cause the blossom to wilt. This is perfectly fine. After you finish your bath, open up the flower and rub the softened oils over your skin like a perfume. Men go crazy for this scent." Laramie looked at her and wondered whether she implicated Akihiro in that conclusion. "Yes, Mr. Amori, too."

Slightly embarrassed for being transparent, Laramie smiled. "Thank you, Kat. I'll keep that in mind."

As Kat walked out of the bungalow, she turned to say. "Miss Holden, he has quickly become smitten with you. You both need to smile less and talk more. Good day."

Laramie closed the door. *Wow! That was quite direct. He said she held nothing back. I thought Asian people were more reserved. She must be the anomaly. Smitten… really?* Laramie suddenly had more time on her hands than she thought. She dressed in her bathing suit and walked down to the beach area. She found a chair placed partly under a breezy palm tree. *This is as good a spot as any. Let's just get situated first. Yes, there we go. Perfect.* It wasn't too long before she fell asleep to the sounds of the gentle surf rolling on the sand.

From inside Akihiro's office, he saw Laramie down on the beach. He wished he could join her but his business came first. He wanted his meeting with the banks over; he wanted to play. Concentrating on his phone call was hard with sweet temptation just outside his window.

"Akihiro? Are you still there?" Rhys inquired in his heavy British accent.

"Yes, Rhys, I'm here. I lost my thought for a moment. With the refinancing of the hotel approved, how long until I have approval on the loan to buy the Cheung property next door?"

"A few weeks at best. Your longest time will be spent in underwriting. The only document I need from you is your three-year business plan. After I get that, I'll send the papers over via courier for your signature."

"I have the plan; I can drop it off in the city later. Wait. I'll have Kat bring the plan over and pick up your docs so cancel the courier. "

"Great, that works for me, chum. Do you want to grab a pint later?"

"Sorry, made plans but another time. Bye Rhys."

Akihiro met Rhys Davis while he attended Oxford. They hit it off immediately one evening as they sat at a bar watching a Manchester United game against Chelsea. The pub supported Chelsea while Akihiro and Rhys cheered for Manchester. A few of the patrons, less than amused, called the men out to the street. Being a handful of beers into the night, the duo walked outside to end this disagreement. When the fists flew, Akihiro blocked, turned and kicked. Apparently, no one told the fine British gents that Akihiro was a national titleholder in Karate. Lucky for Rhys, his fighting mate was far more skilled than he was, otherwise, the results could have landed them in the hospital. Since that night, they remained like brothers. When Akihiro left England to return home, Rhys finished at Oxford and moved to Singapore. They even worked together at the bank for a few years. Knowing their history, Rhys was Aki's first choice for lending to build the hotel.

Akihiro sat in his chair and looked across the pool at Laramie. She stood on the sand, gazing across the water, and watched the waves curl past the break wall. Occasionally, she looked back at the hotel and wondered whether Akihiro was in his office. Most of her thoughts were about him. She wondered if he was attracted to her. He certainly made her heart race. Common sense tried to prevail in both of them. *This dating won't last more than three weeks, is it worth pursuing?* Laramie came to the belief this was all in fun and vacations are supposed to be fun. She walked back to the patio area and stared at her reflection in the office window. Akihiro felt as though she looked right through him.

As she soaked in the tub, she carefully planned her wardrobe for the evening and made sure her options were *not* transparent when wet. The lotus flowers smelled heavenly. Her skin felt so soft. *If only it were Akihiro's hands caressing my arms.* She knew she wanted him and that surprised her. She never thought so boldly about a man. Sure, she fantasized about different men and wondered how they would be in bed. This time she wanted to experience it, feel every sensation.

Akihiro knocked on Laramie's door shortly after five. He wore a black and white knit shirt that clung tightly to his muscular build and black slacks. *Damn, he looks hot. Let's just skip the dinner and go right for dessert. Right here. Right now.* She smiled and told him to come inside a moment; she needed to get her purse and sunglasses before they left. Akihiro watched her walk away and let his mind wander. Laramie was very attractive in her linen shorts and cutaway sweater. The back of her legs looked long and sexy in high heels. She smelled sweet and knew it was one of his favorite scents, a lotus flower. *Why does she have to stand next to the bed of all places? Do we really need to eat? Do we really need to be wearing clothes? Do I really have this much restraint?*

"I was not sure whether you wanted to attempt Boat Quay again. If you're willing, I know a nice Italian restaurant there," Akihiro suggested.

"I'm up for it. But tonight, it's my treat, okay? If this is going to be a regular thing then we have to split it." When she realized what she said, she hoped she didn't really say it aloud. She didn't mean to presume they were a couple. "Oh no, that's not what I meant. I didn't—"

"It's all right. Don't apologize."

Laramie wanted to kick herself. *Why am I constantly putting my foot in my mouth around him? He must think I'm idiot once again.* She sat quietly in the car as they left the island. As they passed the cable cars, she asked about them. Akihiro explained people use them for crossing over to Sentosa Island or going to Mount Faber. He said the views were spectacular and if she wanted a thrill he would take her on a glass-bottomed car. Laramie laughed the offer off without disclosing her extreme fear of heights. *Not on your life! Will never happen.*

Akihiro managed to park on Circular Drive even though cars lined both sides of the streets. Laramie thought this part of the city had a great vibe for the locals and the tourists alike. He held his hand out to help her out of the car but never let go. They walked along the sidewalk and pointed in the windows of the shops. Sometimes Laramie went inside to check out a painting or a souvenir, as Akihiro waited patiently. When they arrived in front of the restaurant, he pulled out a chair for her. However, tonight he sat beside her instead of across from her. He pointed out the passing bumboats and they laughed about the previous night's incident. The waiters at Al Dente's were very attentive and polite, however not very Italian looking. Looking around, Laramie noticed that Singapore was similar to San Francisco with the shop buildings side by side and skyscrapers around the city. She sipped on her wine as she listened to Akihiro tell stories about the guy's nights. His friends sounded similar to hers, loyal and supportive, yet humorous.

"How did your meeting go today? Kat mentioned that you were talking with your bank."

"It went better than I hoped. My dream has been to expand the Tanjong. The only way to do that is to buy the land next door. I've been talking to Mr. Cheung for almost a year and we have finally agreed on a price. I now have to wait for the bank to approve the loan. I still want to keep it a small hotel so I'm debating on the number and size of bungalows. Or do I make it a single building with larger rooms and suites?"

She saw his face light up when he spoke of the expansion. His plan was a great idea and it made good business sense. She asked many questions about the details, which impressed him. She had a sincere interest in his ideas. He leaned back in his chair and placed his arm along the back of her chair. He leaned in close and held his other arm out to describe his vision. Laramie followed his hand, listening to every word. When he stopped, she turned to face him and found they were very close to each other. Akihiro moved forward and kissed her lightly on the lips. Quickly, she felt a sensation of warmth through her. She didn't want this kiss to end. She didn't want the evening to end. When he pulled away, he stared in her eyes, he needed to know whether he made the right move. Laramie blushed as though it were her first kiss and turned away with a grin.

"Let's go. I want to show you something."

They held hands back to the car until he backed up against the building and pulled her in close to him. He cupped his hands around her face and kissed her repeatedly. She wanted to melt right there in his arms. When he stopped, she stood there breathless, slowly opening her eyes. *Please don't end it there. This is becoming torture.*

With her breathing still rapid, she whispered, "Is that what you wanted to show me?" He nodded no and smirked.

They took a short car ride down Raffles Avenue until they parked in front of the Singapore Flyer, the huge air-conditioned Ferris wheel. Laramie saw it from the limo ride to the hotel, but standing up close she realized just how high it was. She knew this was the 'something.' *I have to walk in there. I have to get inside the car. Oh crap, I can't breathe. Come on, you can do this, Lara. Inhale slowly. Oh God, no I can't.*

"Are you ready? It has spectacular views of the city. Wait until you see it from the top."

Laramie held his hand and hoped he didn't notice the shear panic in her face or the clamminess of her hand. She wanted to stop him but he seemed excited to show her.

"How long does it take to make a full circle?" *I won't be alone. I can do this. Look out and not down.*

"About thirty minutes."

"Oh really, that's not long at all." *Breathe in. Count to five. Now out. Count to five. I know I'm going to hyperventilate and pass out. How will I explain that?*

"Just how high it that?" Laramie asked trying to cover her nervousness.

"One hundred and sixty five meters. That's about… five hundred and forty feet."

Once they entered the capsule, Laramie sat with her back to the center support, the only area that wasn't glass. When the door shut, she felt her heart race. She did notice they were the only people in the capsule. *Keep smiling, Lara. You can do this. Oh geez, this would be so romantic if I wasn't afraid of heights. I can feel my arms burning. Panic attack, I know I'm having a panic attack.* Akihiro stood against the glass and called her over to see the city. Laramie wanted to but she froze. He looked over at her and saw her face was completely white. He knelt in front of her to calm her.

"Laramie, are you afraid of heights?" She nodded. "Why didn't you tell me?"

She started to cry, mainly out of fear, as she fanned her eyes. She was so embarrassed, even more so than the previous night.

"I wanted to but you were so excited to show me. I thought I could do it. I tried to stay calm but when they shut the door, I freaked. I'm so sorry."

He wiped her tears off her face. It was hard for him to see her cry, see her afraid.

"No, no. Don't be sorry. It's fine. Look, we'll get through this together. I'm going to sit right next to you and hold you, all right?"

Laramie seemed to accept that solution. Akihiro straddled the bench, pulled her close to him, and held his arms around her. He rubbed her back and stroked her hair as he tried to calm her. He wanted this to be romantic to see whether there was any real chemistry between them. Laramie looked into his eyes and placed her arms around him. *Oh those eyes. They pull me right in.* He pressed his lips against hers softly, starting with small pecks. Laramie opened her mouth slightly and kissed him back harder. Quickly, he grabbed her waist with one hand and held the back of her head with the other. His kissing grew more intense this time, deeper and longer. He felt her breathing change. He wanted her but this wasn't the time or place. Her body ached to be with him; she wanted his touch.

"The cars are stopping. I think we're next. See, Laramie, you made it after all."

She smiled at him. He got her through it just as he said. However, neither wanted the moment to end. *That was the shortest thirty minutes I ever experienced.*

The drive back to the Tanjong was quiet. He held her hand the entire way back. They glanced and smiled despite the tension in the air. Neither knew how to break the silence. He walked her to her bungalow door just as the night prior. *Do I invite him in my room? How will that make me look? I need to keep some virtues, right? I'm not going to be able to push him away if he kisses me again. What do I do?* Akihiro fought his own conscious at the same time. *Damn, she drives me wild. Would holding her be enough? How do I kiss her goodnight and walk away? Can I walk away?* After Laramie unlocked the door, she turned to face him not knowing what to expect. She looked into his eyes for a clue but couldn't read him. Akihiro held her face, kissed her solidly, and stopped. He puzzled her with this move.

"Laramie, if I don't stop now, I won't stop at all. That would not be fair to either of us. I'm not going to push you into something you might not want. We'll have more time to work that out. Will I see you tomorrow?"

"Yes," she whispered back. *Doesn't tomorrow start in another hour?*

As he walked away, he ran his hand through his hair, surprised by his own chivalry. Laramie entered her bungalow, shocked by his response. She didn't know how to explain her feelings at that moment. She knew if he pressed the issue, he would be beside her in bed. Now, she had all night to think of what might have been.

Chapter 16

AKIHIRO SAT IN his chair with his legs propped on the desk. He tapped a pencil in his hand, so deep in thought that Kat entered the office unnoticed. She eventually cleared her throat to make her presence known.

"Tell me how your evening went with Miss Holden."

"It was great in the beginning. I took her on the Flyer thinking it would be a fun way to see the city..."

"What's wrong with that?"

"She's afraid of heights. She went on to make me happy and panicked. She turned white with fear. I felt horrible."

"Don't beat up yourself. You didn't know and she didn't tell you. Neither of you are mind readers. I'm going to tell you the same thing I told her, 'you both need to smile less and talk more.' By that I mean, you would've learned she was afraid of heights if you both talked. You both are like teenagers on a first date. You're adults."

"I can not stop thinking about her, Kat. I don't even know what that means to me."

"I can tell you what that means. It means you better be honest. You say I'm too honest but it never got me in trouble like a white lie can."

"I will. It just isn't the right time."

* * *

Laramie stayed in bed late and ordered room service. She was too nervous to go out and run into Akihiro. She didn't know how to slow down her feelings. She thought some space between them might make things easier, calm the passion. The thought of sightseeing this afternoon did appeal to her. In the meantime, she took her travel book and lay next to the soaking pool. It was the first time she used it since she arrived in Singapore. The gardens around the pool were green and lush. The flowering vines that climbed the wall had a subtle fragrance, similar to jasmine. The palm fronds blew in the light breeze causing the light passing through to flicker upon the water. Since she was alone, wearing a bathing suit top was needless. She set an alarm on her cell phone to signal the turn over time. The last thing she wanted was the discomfort of a sunburn. She wasn't hungry but the heat and humidity dried her out. She never experienced weather like this. She knew the humidity of South Carolina but this was so much heavier, denser. She walked inside to the refrigerator, grabbed a bottled water then continued to tan.

She tried to keep her head clear but thoughts of Akihiro kept coming back. Every time she relived their kiss, the same rush of warmth went through her. It was love at first sight for her, despite how cliché the sound was. She knew it and didn't deny it. *Love? Lust? Love with lust? What am I going to do? Did I push him too far? Am I being too easy? Does he want to sleep with me? Or any woman? I know this should be simple and I'm probably complicating things myself. I wish had my friends with me. What could come from this anyway? We are thousands of miles apart. Maybe I should beg off any further dates, which would be the responsible thing to do. Visually the temptation would be gone. But one touch sends me over the edge.*

A short while later she heard a knock on her door. Laramie assumed it was the housekeeper. She yelled out the door was open and continued to tan her back.

"How are you today, Laramie?" asked the voice in a familiar accent.

Oh crap, it's him. I can't get up. I don't have a top or a towel. Maybe he won't notice. Yeah, right. What a stupid statement.

Akihiro sounded quieter than normal, not as upbeat. *That's it. He's going to call off the dating. I put him in an uncomfortable position being the owner here.* Akihiro walked onto the lanai and sat on the stairs. Laramie knew that the vacation break-up was next. Trying to be ignorant of the mood, she offered him a water or soda out of the refrigerator.

"Thanks, but no. About last night, I apologize for pushing myself onto you. I don't know what came over me. I just wanted to say I'm sorry."

I knew it. Why does this happen to me? What am I doing that pushes them away?

"You don't have to apologize. Maybe we both got a bit carried away."

Laramie swallowed hard. "Does this mean I won't see you anymore? Because I don't think I'd like that." *I am not giving up. Not this time.*

She is really making this hard. I don't want to walk away. He looked into her eyes and was about to speak when Laramie interrupted.

"Akihiro, I was hoping to go in town tonight and have some fun. But, I don't have an escort and I don't know my way around. I don't think I would trust anyone else besides you. Would you do this for me?"

She followed her heart this time and took a chance. Akihiro looked to the sky and contemplated his answer. She called him on his bluff. *I can't look at her face and say no, I can't.*

"Yes, but only as your tour guide. Understand?" She nodded yes. "I'll meet you in the lobby at eight."

Whew! The Gods are smiling on me now. This was a lucky break for Laramie. She had another chance to change things around. She needed a plan and had zero ideas. *Not good. What's open on Tuesday nights? Some clubs and bars. Alcohol will lessen the anxiety. There has to be moments when we will be alone, right?*

Laramie looked elegant in her fitted sundress. The blues and teals in the fabric accentuated her suntan and blonde hair. She felt relatively secure tonight despite her streak of late. She sat in the lobby and leafed through a local magazine. She was about to read the society pages when Akihiro and Kat arrived.

"Are you ready to go? You don't mind if Kat comes with us, do you? I told her some of my ideas and we believe we found one that we can do as a group. We will also be meeting some of her friends in the city. Is that acceptable?"

"Yeah, that sounds great. The more the merrier." *Damn. There goes that plan. Make the best of it now.*

Kat sat cramped in the back seat of Akihiro's car. There was no more room for that of a small child but it kept everyone to himself or herself. They drove to the Tanjong Pagan area, just outside the financial district. When Akihiro parked the car on the road, he announced they were there. Laramie looked around and saw a few clubs but nothing out of the ordinary.

"What are we doing?" she asked.

"Karaoke!" exclaimed Kat.

"Oh no, really, because you don't want to hear me sing. I know I have character flaws and singing is the biggest." Laramie felt the horror internally.

Akihiro laughed and asked, "How bad could you be?"

Laramie knew she was outsmarted. First, any ideas of being alone were a past issue. Second, she knew she had to make the best of the situation. Third, no one sang worse than Laramie Holden and these unsuspecting people would pay for this idea.

The trio walked inside, passing a few rooms before they met up with Kat's friends. A waitress walked in for drink orders and Laramie asked for an extra shot in her rum and Coke. Everyone exchanged pleasantries and proceeded to inform Laramie of Akihiro and Kat stories from college. They asked her questions about the United States and whether she knew any movie stars. *No, I've never met Brad Pitt or Tom Cruise.* She listened and tried to understand while they spoke Singlish. She looked to Aki and Kat for translations a few times. She quickly learned they ended their sentences with 'leh' or 'lah' which was similar to the Canadian's 'eh.' A lot of drinking and laughing occurred, with that Laramie hoped everyone would forget about singing. Akihiro ordered some appetizers, which Laramie appreciated. She skipped dinner and stayed at her bungalow. She didn't want to eat alone since she always ate alone.

One of the girls fired up the backdrop screen while another started the music and machine. Kat's friends sang first. The girls did a few duets and sounded pretty good. Of course, Akihiro sang perfectly. *Is he bad at anything?* The two guys attempted to play air guitars with their music. Sporadically, Laramie glanced in Akihiro's direction, unable to catch his eye. She did admit she was having a great time. Then came her turn. The group decided the song each person sang and Laramie's was *My Way* by Frank Sinatra, the number one karaoke song played in Asia.

"I am making this disclaimer right now, I can't sing at all. You have been warned. Also, my sincerest apologies to Frank Sinatra and the rest of the Rat Pack."

As the music started, the backdrop showed scenes of the 70's decade, mainly American. When Laramie belted out her song, everyone covered their ears. Some held their stomachs from the pain of laughter. She was honest about her lack of talent. Toward the end of the song, the group laughed uncontrollably. Laramie turned to view the backdrop and saw a line a Japanese soldiers committing hara-kiri. Laramie followed the soldiers lead. That encompassed it all.

"Who wants me to sing another?"

Kat yelled for someone to take the microphone, quickly. Akihiro's tears rolled down his cheek. Laramie sat back in her spot on the sofa, across from Akihiro, trying not to show her embarrassment. She downed the rest of her drink and ordered another. Laramie liked these people. They were a lot like Manny and Lian. Of course, they knew Laramie couldn't sing. One of the young guys asked Laramie to do a duet with him. She tried to push him off but he didn't give up. She let him pick the song since this was new to her. Big mistake. He chose *Summer Nights* from *Grease. How the hell am I supposed to do this one? Why couldn't it have been Grease Lightnin'? Lara, look at your partner and the screen and you'll be fine. Besides, everyone will be laughing at your voice.*

Just as the music started, the waitress walked in with her drink. Laramie grabbed it off the tray and held it for security. Her partner was really nice and made jokes with her to put her at ease. The duo added some dance moves to their song, stood close and shared a mic, then hugged at the end. Once again, the room was in an uproar. People from other rooms now stood at their door to hear the American sing. However, this time when Laramie sat down, Akihiro stared at her. She tried to read his expression but his dark features and the dark lighting of the room made it difficult. He seemed angry to her. *Did I do something wrong? This was his idea. I'm having fun and he is not going to spoil this.*

Akihiro turned his head away and chatted with the girl on his left. He listened in body only. *Damn, she blends in with everyone. She's not afraid of being foolish. She's amazing. How do I maintain this front? How can I walk away from this?* Just then, Kat pulled him out of the room.

"I know I'm going to regret this but Aki, she's great. She certainly can't sing but she's a great sport. I know I'm usually over protective but go for it, lah." Kat's speech slurred a bit, as did everyone's.

Akihiro hated to cut the night short but it was a weeknight and they had work in the morning. He walked into the room and said his goodbyes, which drew boo's from the crowd. Laramie stood up, hugged her new friends, and thanked them for a wonderful time. Surprisingly, they invited her back anytime. *Are they that desperate for comic relief?* Akihiro said they would take Kat home first then head back. She was fine with that and squeezed sideways into the back seat so Kat could get out easier.

When they arrived outside Kat's apartment, she turned to Laramie and said, "You know Laramie, I was wrong about you. You're a lot of fun. I like you."

Akihiro helped her inside, as she needed it. He returned quickly and Laramie took her place in the passenger seat.

"You know, I was skeptical about being with a group of people I've never met. Karaoke would *never* have been a choice of mine but I really had fun. Thanks."

When she touched his hand on the shifter, he moved it to the steering wheel. Besides 'your welcome,' Akihiro didn't say another word all the way back. *I don't understand. Was spending time with me that terrible? Did I say something wrong? Did I do something wrong? Damn it. He really didn't want to be out with me, did he?* He pulled up in front of the hotel and was about to get out and walk her to her bungalow when she turned and angrily said, "Don't bother."

"What is that supposed to mean?"

She was so mad and hurt. She tried not to cry but too many drinks made that impossible. "It means, I'm a big girl and I don't need your charity. If you didn't want to be with me, you could have said so. I can take it."

"Laramie, it's not like that."

"I see exactly what it's like and you don't have to worry about me. I can occupy my own time from here on out. Good night, Mr. Amori."

She slammed the car door and walked off, holding in her tears. When she got to the other side of the lobby, she swiftly walked to her bungalow. *How humiliating! Why do I put myself in these situations only to set myself up for the fall? Will I ever learn?* She was hurt and heartbroken. Now she spent her evening crying herself to sleep.

At first, Akihiro thought to chase her down, then he felt it was safer to let her go. He slammed his hands on his steering wheel in anger. *She asks me to take her out, so I do. I try to be neutral and that's wrong. I avoid contact so she isn't pressured into anything and that's wrong too. What was the right move?* He drove around the corner to his condo at Sentosa Cove, still angry. When he walked inside, he grabbed a glass out of the cupboard and poured himself a drink. He opened the sliding door and stood on the deck over looking the marina. He played back the scenes of the evening and did not see one thing out of line. *Why did she have to cry?*

Chapter 17

KAT STROLLED INTO Akihiro's office. He sat in his chair facing the window and didn't notice that she entered.

"Outside of a slight headache, that was a great night. Laramie was correct in the fact she can't sing. What a good sport." Akihiro turned around in his chair and shook his head.

"What did you do this time?"

"Did you ever think maybe it was her and not me? I didn't do anything. I kept my distance. I left her alone. She touched my hand and I just pulled it away so I was not initiating anything," Akihiro defended his position.

"You rejected her. Is that what you're saying? Then I don't blame her for being mad."

"*Why?*" he replied with much aggravation.

"Let me make this as clear as I can. You asked her out the first day. She is humiliated and left standing almost naked and wet. Instead of calling the evening, she laughs it off and continues. Then the second day, you take her to the Flyer and she gets on it despite her fear of heights. You spend your evening intimately and when you get back, you push her away. She asks you out and you set her up with a group outing. She goes along with it. She has to be the worst singer in America, for sure Singapore, yet she still gets up and humiliates herself for you."

"I didn't ask her to sing."

"Aki, you brought her to a *karaoke* bar. What else was she supposed to do? Then she tries to thank you and you snub her. Now you wonder why she became upset. She's disgraced herself three days in row for you and you sent so many mixed signals. The woman probably has no self-esteem left. Now do you understand it?"

"I never saw it from that perspective." Akihiro threw his head back into his chair. "How do I make it up to her?"

"That depends on you. You better make it good."

Akihiro arrived at Laramie's bungalow just as housekeeping was leaving.

"Sir, she's not in her room. I think someone said she went into town to shop."

Akihiro walked into the main building and instructed the front desk to notify him as soon as Laramie returned.

Laramie decided she needed to do more things on her own. From her perspective, any chance of spending more time with Akihiro was gone. He made it clear last night. *Maybe some shopping will make me feel better, always does.* She had a driver drop her off on Orchard Street. She knew the first thing on her list was a suitcase. The battered condition of her suitcase left no other options. She stopped at Uncle Sims and purchased a new leather luggage set complete with a train case. He agreed to hold it for her until she returned later. She walked along the street and stopped in any shop that caught her eye. It was similar to Union Square back home. She went into the OG Complex, browsed around, and felt content to find items in her size. It at least offset her mood from the previous evening. Laramie perused the tables, outside some of the stores, loaded with electronic items and gifts, very similar to Chinatown.

Eventually, Laramie made it to the Paragon Shopping Center. She decided to go to the Ralph Lauren store first. She loved his fashions since they remained classics and she was a semi-conservative dresser. She spotted a flirty black organza dress. It was lovely with spaghetti straps, a pleated bodice with a ribbon trim, and then it flowed below the empire waist. She tried it on and fell in love with it. She purchased a tight navy pencil skirt and sheer blouse with a matching camisole from Versace. The ensemble looked tailored specifically for her. Very eye catching. She continued to Miss Sixty and bought a tailored shirtdress. She thought it would be perfect for business in a few weeks. In addition to the dress, she also purchased a deep v-neck shirt with a baby doll bottom, and an open back black cocktail dress. *With a blazer over it, I can wear this to work and right out at night. Oh this is great.* She looked at her watch and remembered she needed to return to Uncle Sim's to pick up her luggage. Her day for shopping was over.

Laramie quickly found a cab to take her back to the hotel. She wondered if she would pass Akihiro, which caused her to get emotional all over again. *Stop it, Laramie. You are not a crier. Stop giving in to your emotions.* Luckily,

Samad worked this shift and helped her unload the taxi's trunk. As soon as she passed through the lobby, the front desk called Akihiro to inform him of Laramie's return.

Her bungalow door was open as Akihiro stood silently against the frame. Laramie, too busy to notice him, jumped when he called her name.

"What can I help you with, Mr. Amori? How else have I offended you" The sarcasm was obvious.

"Laramie, I'm sorry."

She quickly interrupted, "It seems you've said that a few times already. Today you like me and tomorrow you'll reject me. This roller coaster has to end. What exactly is it that you want from me because I honestly don't know?"

She tried to remain calm but the more she spoke the more her voice cracked.

When he walked through the door, his other hand held a bouquet of flowers. She accepted them and placed them on the dining table.

"I didn't realize how confusing I have been. I never meant to hurt you, really. Please, let me take you out tonight and make it up to you. *Please?*"

Shaking her head, Laramie replied, "I don't think that's a good idea."

She wanted to remain strong but her feelings hurt so bad. *Don't cry, Lara. What is the matter with me? I never cry like this. I'm Laramie Holden, unwavering lawyer. Now I look like this blubbering child. I want to believe him but this has happened two days in a row.* She turned her back to him and stared out at the pool. He came up behind her and placed his hands on her shoulders, rubbing them slowly. Then he slowly turned her around and lifted her chin to see her face. She tried to avoid eye contact but he held her face still.

"Please, go out with me tonight. I promise I won't hurt you anymore," he whispered.

"There are no more chances after this. I mean it."

She wanted to say no but knew she couldn't. He bent over and kissed her lightly on the mouth, teasing her with his lips until she would smile.

"I will pick you up here at seven. And dress formal." With that, he left.

Laramie showered and was ready by six thirty. She decided to wear the new Versace outfit, a pencil skirt and sheer blouse. She fired one last email off the Liz.

> I know I must be crazy but I am giving him another chance.
> I hate to lose this, at least as far as vacation companion.
> I'll let you know. And yes, I am a sap.

She heard his knock and opened the door. Both were pleasantly surprised to see the other dressed up.

"Wow, Laramie, you look amazing," he replied astounded.

"Thank you. You look quite handsome yourself."

He held her hand to the car and opened the door for her. He sensed her reservations and hoped to erase them throughout the night.

"Before we pull out, I need to know your choice. We can go to Equinox in the city which is on the sixty-ninth floor or somewhere closer to the ground."

"Equinox is fine if we don't sit near the window, okay?"

It was another quiet drive. She wanted to believe him but she remained unsure. They pulled into the valet parking at The Stamford, Swissôtel. Many heads turned to view the beautiful couple as they entered the building. Akihiro was sharp in a dark suit with a light striped tie. Laramie's outfit hugged every curve and Akihiro definitely noticed. They rode up the elevator to the sixty-ninth floor. The hostess sat them in a semi-circle booth with a clear view of the city. Quickly their waiter came, asked for their cocktail order and left them menus.

Laramie smiled at Akihiro. "This is beautiful. Thank you."

"I'm going to say this one last time, then let's put it behind us. I apologize for hurting your feelings. It was never my intention. I hope you know that."

His apology meant a lot to Laramie. She wanted to be sure that they could move past these mistakes. They sat close together in the center of the booth and Akihiro pointed out some landmarks that were illuminated. The city looked spectacular at night. Shortly the waiter brought their drinks. Laramie decided to play it safe with a chardonnay while Aki drank his usual, Grey Goose straight up. They ordered their dinners and slowly reached a fair level of comfort. Laramie told him about the sorority parties she had in college with Gillian and Liz. She disclosed many embarrassing stunts they pulled during rush week. She admitted she lived a bolder life outside of Edward's view. However, much of the discussion ended when their food arrived.

Laramie was never a shy eater on dates. She just hated when the wait staff asked about the service with a full mouth. As she ate, Akihiro spoke. They continued with their cocktails. As Laramie spoke of Manny, Akihiro dined on his entrée. They had one last cocktail before they left the restaurant. Akihiro explained the night wasn't over, they still had one more stop.

"Does it involve a boat, a Ferris wheel or Karaoke?"

"No, none of the above," he grinned.

They stood hand in hand until his car appeared. He drove back toward Sentosa and turned left just before the causeway. They pulled into the lot at St. James Power Station.

"The place opened last year. The complex has just about everything inside, all kinds of music. I hope you feel like dancing."

"I *love* dancing. Is this another one of your many talents too?"

"Actually no, but I manage."

They held hands as the entered the Powerhouse. The black walls of the place contained bright scenes from what appeared like a comic book but still maintained an industrial vibe. They practically yelled everything to each other to hear over the blaring speakers. They found a table for two next to a support beam and Laramie sat. Akihiro went to the bar and came back with more drinks. Laramie was completely unfamiliar with Asian music. She did not understand the lyrics or language for that matter, but the beat was similar to American Pop and Rock music.

They danced to a song with almost a hip-hop beat, after which came a slow song. Akihiro held her close with his arm tight around her waist. Laramie had one hand in his and the other on his shoulder. Occasionally, she brushed her cheek against his to see him. She lost herself on those smoldering black eyes. He would brush his lips across hers, teasing her. Very appropriately, the next song was Santana's *Smooth*. Their bodies, pressed close, merengued to the Latin rhythm. Laramie held her arms above her head while Akihiro ran his hands down her sides. Many of the bystanders noticed the sexual tension on the dance floor. She slowly turned around, making eye contact. There was no one else in that club as far as they were concerned. When the song was over, they walked to their table. Before Laramie could sit, Akihiro spun her in his arms and kissed her with such passion it astounded her.

"Do you want another drink?" he said with a grin.

"Yes, if you don't mind. All the dancing made me thirsty." *Watch yourself Laramie, the more you drink the more clouded your judgment becomes. But, I can stay in his arms forever.*

After a few more dances, Akihiro asked whether she was ready to go back to the hotel, and she was. When they neared his car in the parking lot, he kissed her again just as hard as inside the bar but longer. Laramie's breathing began to increase. This deep passion was new to her and she didn't know how to handle it. As they followed the road down the coast, she wondered what to do when they arrived at her door. She was so torn. She wanted him to share her bed but she still had reservations from the previous nights. *Can I make him wait a few more days? What if he asks me directly? How do I answer?*

As they stood outside, Laramie's back was against the door. Akihiro moved in closer and held her face for a moment, looked in her eyes and wondered about her passion. He kissed her open mouth with his tongue searching for hers until he found it. He ran his hands down her sides and rested them on her rear. He held her tight and pressed her hips into him. She felt the hardness against her and panicked. She stopped him.

"I can't. I can't do this."

"Yes you can, Laramie. Don't be afraid, just go with it," he continued in a deep voice.

"I can't." She pushed him away. "I'm just not ready. I'm sorry." She wanted to sleep with him but she was afraid. "Can we talk in the morning?"

She knew she upset him. She didn't mean it. He nodded yes, kissed her on the cheek and walked back to the hotel.

She sat on her bed stunned that she rebuffed his advances. She wanted to be with him. Surely, he knew that. She slept with only one other man and that was so long ago. She lacked confidence in bed and refused to be humiliated there. She slowly undressed and went to soak in a hot tub.

Akihiro drove home and once again had a drink out on the deck. Akihiro tried to make sense of what happened but found none. *How does she do this? Why does she do this? Does she want me or not? Everything is okay publicly but nothing in private. What goes through this woman's head? She's been with a man before so what's the problem?* Then it hits him. *She was afraid. When was the last time she's been with a man? That's the problem.* He tried to walk off the steam and put the evening to rest, however it wasn't possible. He couldn't get her out of his head. He threw on shorts and a t-shirt and drove back to the hotel.

Laramie just finished her bath when she heard a knock on the door. *Who on Earth is that?* She unlocked the door and Akihiro barged in without even a hello.

"Laramie, I can't do this. I have to tell you, you have intoxicated me beyond any sane reasoning. I can't stop thinking of you. I hate being away from you. You may think you're not ready but you are. I won't make you do anything you don't want, but you need to think about this."

He turned his back, running his hands through his hair, looking out at the pool and moonlight. Had he looked, she blushed from his declaration. She slowly walked up behind him and dropped her robe where she stood.

"Lara, I want you. But, I want you to want me too."

She placed her hands on his shoulders and whispered, "I want you, too."

Akihiro turned and looked down to see Laramie standing bare.

"Oh, are you beautiful."

He removed his shirt and held her close, his skin against hers. He kissed the side of her neck and along the front of her collarbone to the other side. She ran her hands up and down his back. She knew she could not turn back anymore, she didn't want to either. He picked her up and she wrapped her legs around him. He carried her to the bedroom and slowly laid her on the bed. His eyes and hands explored her body, every curve, every valley. Akihiro kissed her, teasing her with his tongue, biting on her lip. When his hand caressed her thighs, outside and inside, she jumped. He knew the pleasure was just starting. She watched him remove his shorts and lay back next to her. As his kiss occupied her mouth, his hand cupped and rubbed her breasts. Slowly his hand went past her navel, and then between her legs, which caused Laramie to jump again. He began the foreplay, causing her to moan. The more intense it became, the more she fidgeted in place.

"Stop it. Please don't," she whispered.

"What's the matter? Doesn't it feel good?" he replied in a deep moaning tone.

"Yes. I mean no. I just… I mean… I've never…" she tried to say more but stopped.

Akihiro looked in her eyes. He didn't understand her at first. *What's wrong? What is she trying to say? Oh, she's never had an orgasm.*

"Laramie, do you trust me?" She nodded yes. "Then trust me now."

He placed her arm above and around her head and held it in place. Her other arm was beneath him. He returned to his foreplay, not taking his eyes off hers. His face was intense, his eyebrows furrowed. The faster his hand moved up and down, in and out, the more she tried to pull her arm away. Her legs began to spasm but still she maintained her eyes on his. Her body shook and she tried to move away but he held her in place. She whispered and begged him not to stop. The closer she got, the more his smile grew. This was unlike anything she ever felt. She moaned loudly and cried out. When her body became rigid, he climbed between her legs and entered her, which caused her to gasp for air. She squeezed her fingers into his arms and met every thrust. Laramie never felt anything like this before. He kept his rhythm for a while, longer than she imagined, until he pushed hard into her and shook. While still on top, he kissed her for a moment until he turned off to her side. Laramie had tears running from her eyes. She never felt something so powerful. It consumed her emotions.

As he wiped her tears, he said, "Lara, you were amazing." He continued to place kisses over her face.

"No, I think that goes to you more. I was afraid because I never had … never been…"

"Shhh. You've been there now and you were so beautiful."

"Akihiro, will you stay with me tonight?"

"I didn't plan on leaving. Our night isn't over yet."

The sexual escapade continued late into the night, each time more relaxed and slightly different. She gave everything she had, no longer did she hold back. He erased her fear but not her shyness. She didn't want the morning to come and end this tempest. Eventually, exhaustion settled in and they required sleep.

Sometime before dawn, Akihiro awoke to a noise he couldn't believe. There was another vice Laramie had besides singing; she occasionally snored like a drunken sailor. He tried to turn her head, that didn't work. He rolled her over, that too, didn't work. Eventually, he had to wake her. She mumbled first before she opened her eyes.

Akihiro whispered to her, "Lara, I think there is someone else in the bungalow."

Startled by this statement, she replied, "Did you hear a noise outside? "

"No, I think it came from in here."

She became afraid and asked, "Could it be an animal?"

"No, I think it was some old man snoring and he was in this bed."

"Very funny. You woke me to tell me I snore. I already know that."

"Yes, but I didn't. It scared the hell out of me."

Akihiro started to laugh. Laramie grabbed her pillow in an attempt to beat him with it. She forgot he was a Karate champion, and he easily climbed on top and pinned her down. He stared at her lying nude in bed with her hair flowing over the sheets. *Damn, she is stunning.* He bent forward and started to kiss her again. It was impossible to pull himself away from her. Eventually, he let go of her wrists and wrapped her in his arms.

She knew she fell in love with him the first time they met. She tried not to think about going home to the States, but it was the cruel reality. She decided to make the next two weeks the best she could. Akihiro was unsure what he felt but he knew he didn't want her to leave Singapore.

Chapter 18

WHEN LARAMIE WOKE in bed, she found herself alone. A note was left of the nightstand.

> *Dear Laramie,*
> *I wanted to be there when you woke up but I had to get to work. Stop by my office when you are able. Last night was spectacular. You are a remarkable woman.*
> *Fondly,*
> *Akihiro*

She smiled after reading it and placed it in her suitcase. Indeed, the previous night was spectacular, so much so, Laramie smiled all morning. She quickly showered. As she dressed, she glanced at the bed and let out a deep sigh. *Wow.*

As Laramie passed the lobby, Kat greeted her.

"Good morning, Laramie. How was your evening?"

"Good morning to you. Um… I have to say last night was… impressive. Is Akihiro in his office? He asked me to stop when I awakened."

"He is but he is on a phone call. I will let him know you are here when he hangs up. Where did you go for dinner?

"Equinox. The views were stunning. I don't know whether Akihiro told you I'm afraid of heights but our table was far enough away from the window. Then we went dancing at the Powerhouse. I had such a great time."

"Aki went dancing? Really? Now, that is amazing. Oh wait, he just hung up the phone. Mr. Amori, Miss Holden is here to see you. Go on in, Laramie."

This was the first time Laramie saw his office. The walls had grass cloth covering them with wooden masks hanging in a group. Two upholstered chairs, matching the lobby furniture, faced the massive wooden desk. To the left was a wooden door that led to a restroom. *Very nice, not too masculine.* Akihiro sat in his leather chair behind the desk. Behind him, a wall of glass stood overlooking the pool area and beach. Laramie noticed he did not have any personal photos or mementos in his office. Nonetheless, the office had a Zen-like feel just like the rest of the hotel.

Akihiro stood from his chair and walked to Laramie. She was nervous about the previous night and what type of reaction to expect. He embraced and kissed her good morning. That was the reassurance she needed.

"Good morning. I see you've finally awaken," he said smiling.

"Well, I had so many distractions during the night that interrupted my sleep."

"Really? What kind of distractions?" said Akihiro, as he randomly placed kisses all over her face.

"Why are you torturing me? You shouldn't start something you can't finish."

"Who said I can't finish?" *Oh, please never finish.*

His kisses ran down her neck and across each shoulder. As she moved in synch with him, her breathes became deeper and quicker. He knew he excited her.

"Is this why you wanted me to come here?"

"No, but this is a better idea. I asked you to come here to see what your plans were for the afternoon."

"I haven't made plans since I got here. I've been leaving that up to my tour guide."

"Which tours have you enjoyed the most? Public or private?"

She laughed, not at his question but he happened upon a ticklish spot. She winced and tried to push him away. She begged him not to tickle her but he didn't listen. The screams and hollers were so loud that Kat banged on the door outside.

"Here are my thoughts. I have some papers that need signed at the bank. What if I drop you off on Orchard Road so you can shop? When I'm done, I will pick you up and we can go stroll around the Botanic Gardens."

"Botanic gardens, huh? I'm just trying to think of how this can backfire on me. Hmm, bees… locust… snakes… the plague. What could go wrong? No really, that sounds fine."

Akihiro asked her to return in an hour. After he kissed her goodbye, Kat rung in to tell him *someone* was on the phone.

The ride into the city was comfortable. Laramie, with sunglasses on, basked in the warmth of the sun. Back on Orchard Road, Akihiro dropped her off at the Palais Renaissance, an upscale designer shopping complex. They agreed to meet at the entrance in an hour. Soon, he was on his way to the Bank of Singapore to meet Rhys.

As he walked into Rhys' office the two men shook hands, hugged, and slapped each other on the back. Rhys stood the same six foot height as Akihiro. They were photo negatives of each other. Rhys had blonde wavy locks and was fair complexioned. His eyes were a very light blue and almost glowed when his pupils narrowed. He dressed properly in a suit and tie, a standard for the banking industry.

"Blimey, mate, every time I call you for a pint, Kat tells me you're out."

"I've been playing tour guide at the hotel for a client. Doing all the standard tourist things. All the things you hate to do."

"Yes, well for how long? I was going to ask whether you wanted to see Home United play Tampines Rovers. Maybe afterwards we can patron some clubs."

"I would really like to go but not this time. Let me give you these documents, the last year's detailed financials for the hotel. What did you need me to sign?"

Rhys handed a short stack of papers each highlighted where to sign. It took a few minutes to get through all of them.

"Well mate, I will send this off to underwriting. I should hear for your approval in a week or two. I'll speed it up where I can. Give me a bell, when you're free."

Quickly the men shook hands and Akihiro departed.

Laramie sat patiently outside the shopping center, without any bags. She perked up when Akihiro pulled up then she ran to the car. The drive was longer than she anticipated. Laramie counted three name changes for Orchard Road before they arrived at the Botanic Gardens.

As they passed through the visitor's center, Laramie heard the sound of the cascading falls ahead. The lush greenery crept right to the water with the flanking beds stuffed with pink cannas. They started their walk past the heliconias with their pink, orange and yellow blossoms. They passed an island in Symphony Lake that reminded Laramie of a giant mushroom. Aki explained it was the stage for the symphony when they perform concerts in the garden. He told her that he attended them when time away from the hotel was available. He pointed out the bromeliad collection, which Laramie knew as tropical houseplants at home. They stopped in the mist house to see the rare orchids. The humidity inside surpassed anything she felt in Singapore yet she loved the exotic flowers. After the outdoor orchid garden, they stopped for drinks.

"This place is magnificent. I only wish I would've remembered my camera." Laramie continued, "I don't know if can handle another building like the mist house. *Whew!* Now that was humid."

They walked to a bench and sat close together. Akihiro held her hand as he sipped water. He told her they were near his favorite part, the Bonsai garden. That didn't surprise her since he was part Japanese and the décor of the hotel was reminiscent of the same influence. They stood and continued their walk. When they arrived at the Bonsai garden, Laramie looked with amazement at the dozen or so hefty trees, each in a stone container, with gnarled roots and twisted trunks. *What are the ages of these things? I thought Bonsai were small.* She watched as Akihiro studied every curve of the tree. He ran his hand over the mass then onto the leafy tops. She listened as he told her his philosophies on the creation of the trees. *He really does love this area.*

They continued to the old bandstand area. It reminded Laramie of an old gazebo in the center of small southern towns, painted in white with wooden details. They walked up the stairs to the middle and took in the panorama. The yellow-green leaves of the rain trees surrounded them. He intently watched her take in the beauty and serenity of the area. He knew she truly enjoyed being there. *How many other things do we have in common? She is unbelievable trying new things, meeting new people. Is there anything she isn't wonderful at doing? Well, besides singing. Ha.* When she looked and smiled at him, he kissed her lightly at first. The passion elevated the kisses to a harder and faster level. They forgot their surroundings only for a minute before they stopped. Laramie's eyes remained closed, as she wanted to savor every moment.

"Are you hungry? Are you ready for a late lunch?"

Yes, Akihiro, I am hungry but not for lunch.

They walked hand in hand to Au Jardin, a plantation styled house on the grounds. They opted for a table on the terrace that looked over the gardens, even though it was on the second floor. Laramie informed him that small heights like this one didn't bother her. The glass windows kept the humidity out and enabled unobstructed views. The tables, dressed in white linens with flower and candle arrangements, made her feel underdressed. She looked around and felt more at ease since many of the guests were dressed the same.

"This place is beautiful with a picture perfect setting. You have amazed me with every place you've taken me," she said glancing around the room and out the window. She noticed he grinned at her when she looked back. It took her a moment to realize why he smiled. "What? That's not what I meant." Her cheeks blushed. "That was amazing too, but I meant the sights of Singapore."

He laughed as she tried to back out of her statements. Laramie was hilarious to watch because each attempt to correct herself resulted in further innuendoes. Eventually, she realized it was better just to stop talking. During lunch, they shared their political views, spoke of jobs they held during college, and discussed differences in religious holidays.

"Well, I believe we have solved the world's problems in one lunch. I just need to stop at home before we go back. You don't mind, do you?"

"I didn't realize you had a home. With the hours you've been keeping, I figured you worked when you weren't with me. So you do find time to sleep." She continued, "They say a home tells a story about the owner."

"When we get there you can tell me my story."

They made their way back onto the island. Instead of turning right to the hotel, Akihiro turned left. They drove past a few golf courses before they reached the front of Sentosa Cove. The entrance had two stucco and brick towers surrounded by flowers. In the center was a roundabout with a fountain containing bronze dolphins playing in a make believe sea. The greenery along Ocean Drive remained lush despite the new construction. Laramie sensed he didn't live in any area; he lived in *the* area. When they approached the condominium complex, the guard opened the gate. They passed by a large fountain in a base resembling a giant Chinese soup bowl. They parked beneath a six story contemporary building made of stucco and glass. Laramie followed Akihiro to the elevator as she tried to take in her surroundings. When the elevator doors opened, they stepped into a small glass encased foyer. To the left was the living room with an overstuffed tan sofa. A large watercolor of a dragon boat race hung over the sofa. However, the real view was outside on the terrace, the Straits of Singapore.

"That is magnificent. How do you leave that view every morning?"

He walked behind her and placed his arms across her breasts and waist, and then he nibbled at her neck.

"I leave that view for this view." *Oh, right answer. How does find the right thing to say?* "Follow me and I'll give you the tour."

She trailed him out of the living room, viewing the wall art and furniture design. It was more traditional than she expected but still masculine. Off the dining room was a long galley kitchen with stainless appliances. The few items on the counters were neat and orderly. Further down the main hall was a full bath with raised fixtures, all white porcelain. The monochromatic color scheme carried through to each room. The guest room had a simple dark wood sleigh bed and white linens, similar to the hotel. In the rear of the condominium was the study or third bedroom. The room had an upholstered bench in coarse linen, which sat behind the wooden desk against the wall. Laramie noticed a theme in the artwork, though each seemed to be a different medium, they all were of boats.

"Did the same person decorate the hotel as well as your home? They have great taste. I mean this place is stunning. I can't believe the views from each room."

"Actually, I picked everything for the hotel. However, I have to give some credit to my mother. She narrowed down the choices. Now, the best room for last."

He held her hand as he led her to the master bedroom. When they entered the room, he gently pushed her onto the bed and climbed on top. She had no intentions to stop him. *I've waited all day for this. How does he know just what I need? Actually, want.* She lay with her eyes closed and waited to be surprised as he traveled to different parts of her body. He removed her shirt, which was far easier than her shorts. After he stopped a moment, she opened her eyes to see him stare at her with his dark eyes. He took off his shirt and shorts and climbed next to her.

"Akihiro, is something wrong? Tell me, is it me? Did I do something?"

"No, nothing is wrong. Put any of those thoughts out of your head. Everything is perfect," he smiled half heartily.

"Really? Your eyes told another story."

"Sometimes the way you see things isn't always the way they are."

Laramie decided to leave it at that, though his comment was mysterious. Soon he made her forget everything but the moment. He did things in ways she never knew. Their bodies completely entangled in such a manner to bring absolute pleasure. Not until they reached their peaks did they stop and lay quietly together. Laramie stared out the window, losing her thoughts in the mesmerizing waves. Akihiro spooned behind her with his head near her hair. It was peaceful. There were no distractions, no people, and no work to interrupt them.

"Tell me my story. Do you think you know me?"

She thought carefully before she spoke, "Well, you are very stringent on your thoughts and designs because you find beauty in simple treasures. You desire things at their most basic level. I think you want to live your life with the same creativity you imagine but are too apprehensive. You hide the things you love and the people you love for fear someone will see it as your weakness. You also hide the things that clutter your mind behind a hardened façade. You don't want to give up that which you control. The more you control, the safer you feel. I think that is your story."

He was speechless. The more he thought about it, the more he realized how accurate she was. *How can she know this? Is she some kind of psychic?*

"You were very honest in your thoughts and descriptions. I never knew I was that transparent."

"You're not. You hold secrets and I can't see past them," she whispered.

Bam! He swallowed hard after that statement. He was unsure what to say next. *Should I open myself to her? Will she stay if I do? I can't take the chance she would leave. It will only be harder the longer I wait. No harm can come from that which you don't know, right?*

"One secret is you will never know how accurate you may have been."

"Can we lie here for a while? It feels good in your arms. Besides, the view is so relaxing."

Laramie slowly dozed off to the sound of the waves. Akihiro let her sleep as he reflected on the things she said. He knew his honesty was what she sought but it all seemed early in the relationship to disclose everything. After all, only five days have passed but it felt like so much longer. Somehow, he managed to keep her at his side over this time. He knew he wanted her to stay there. He didn't know whether he was falling in love with her or the idea of her. He noticed her interaction with his staff, Kat, Kat's friends and even strangers. She was at ease with everyone. She treated everyone as her best friend. She was above no one. He smiled thinking of her streak of bad luck but still she persevered through it all with a smile. *What drives this woman? How is she so in tune with her surroundings? Does she work at this or is it a natural gift?*

"Laramie? Come on Omae, it's time to wake up."

She stretched her arms out and smiled. "Did you just call me *omae*? Would that be someone else's name?" He smiled and nodded no.

"No, actually, it is a Japanese term of endearment. It slipped. I hope you're not offended by it."

"Oh no. It's nice. I was just surprised, that's all. You'll have to give me time to think of one for you."

"No rush. But you do need to wake up."

"Why?" she whined.

"What do you mean *why*? It's already passed dinner. Don't you want to eat?"

"Eat? That's all we've done is eat. I'll never fit into my clothes at home."

"I like what you are wearing now."

"Ha, that's funny. I can't exactly wear this to the office. Human Resources would have my job. Too bad they don't have your sense of humor." She paused moment and continued, "If I wasn't here right now, what would you be doing with your time?"

He sat on the edge of his bed. "You want to know my routine? It is far from exciting. I would have discussed next week's business with Kat. Then I would go food shopping and prep the cooler for the boat."

"*Boat*? You didn't tell me you had a boat too. Wow, you have all the toys, don't you? Where is your boat? No wait, first, what's the name of your boat?" She sat up quickly in bed.

"Kisaki. It means *Empress* in Japanese. And, my boat is down below in a berth."

"Empress, huh? Fitting since ships are women. Would you take me for a ride sometime? The closest I've ever been is the ferry to Sausalito and Alcatraz."

"In fact, I was going to see if you wanted to go for a ride over to one of the islands on Sunday. There's a hotel over there I want to check out, the competition. Now, get your clothes on and let's go."

Laramie dressed as she questioned him more regarding his routine. He spent many hours at the hotel, just as she did at the firm.

"By the way, what did you have in mind for dinner? You can't possibly eat full dinners every night. How about pizza and beer? We can eat it at the bungalow and watch TV. Are you game for a quiet night?" Laramie posed.

Her idea wasn't bad. In reality, it was a great way to start a relaxing weekend. He agreed since Ahmed made a great chicken and leek pizza. He was unsure whether Laramie would eat it but there was only one way to find out. When they arrived back at the hotel, she walked to the bungalow while he ordered the pie and picked up the beer. *It's hard to believe this has only been five days. It feels so much longer. Lara, plan for today. Don't think too far ahead and ruin the time.*

When Akihiro arrived at the bungalow, Laramie, already in her pajamas, watched the local TV channel.

"... these are today's top picks for things to see and do in Hong Kong. This is Christina Ling, Channel 5 News, reporting live from Hong Kong."

The station listed upcoming events for Singapore as well as a weather guide. Akihiro took two bottles and placed them on the coffee table with the pizza box. He placed the other beers in the refrigerator, grabbed a few napkins and the remote before he sat next to Laramie. *Just like a guy, stealing the remote.*

"Have you ever been to Hong Kong?" Laramie inquired.

"Yes, it's like Singapore only on a larger scale. It can be crazy during the New Year, but still not to be missed."

"I suppose we are limited to English speaking movies since I don't understand Singlish or Chinese. What kind of pizza did you get? Nothing with strange looking bugs on it, I hope."

"Not unless you think chicken and leeks look like bugs. Move over, you're taking all the room on the sofa."

"Not my fault, blame the owner. He's the one who put in small sofas. How do you find the movie listings?" Laramie attempted to grab the remote but found his grip unable to break. "What kind of movies do you like? Action? Suspense? Drama? I already nixed the chick flicks and horror. I can't watch horror, it gives me nightmares."

"How about Mission Impossible III?"

"Seen it."

"What's the DaVinci Code about?"

"That's about the search for the heir of Christ through the work of the Knights Templar. Not big for a Buddhist I suppose." She winced. "Seen it anyway."

"What haven't you seen? Would that be the short list?"

"I haven't seen Pirates of the Caribbean. Is that okay?"

"Perfect." Akihiro set the remote to start the movie. In reality, it was a great idea to stay indoors. The normal work stress and hiatus with Laramie wore him for the week. He tried to remember the last time he spent an evening this way and couldn't, let alone have the date suggest it. He watched her as the movie began; she sat so intently with her legs crossed Indian style, as she ate her slice of pizza. There were no pretenses; she was truly comfortable there with him. Occasionally, he rose for another beer but they both mainly stayed on the sofa. He lounged back against the sofa arm as she lay between his legs, using his abs for a pillow. She was asleep by the end of the movie. He slowly crawled out from under her and then carried her to bed. He bent over her and kissed her goodnight.

"You're not going to stay?" she whispered.

"No, not tonight. I have errands to run in the early morning. You sleep. I'll call you when I get back. Good night."

Chapter 19

WHEN HE ENTERED the house, he heard the voices already loud. He walked into the kitchen to find his father and brother at the table. He walked over to his mother and kissed her hello as he grabbed a cup of espresso.

"How long have they been fighting today?"

"Only a few minutes. Where have you been lately? I called the hotel a few times this week and Kat said you were gone. I've never known you to be away so much."

"I know. I've been busy with a guest and at the bank. Rhys thought the wait on the loan should only be a week or two, then I can begin plans for expansion." Akihiro looked over at the table, where his father and Shinji argued, and continued, "Will they ever agree on anything?"

"They both live to disagree. That is where they find their bond. Hmm, you have been with a guest. Is she beautiful?" Lucia eyed her son, waiting for a reaction.

"What makes you think it's a woman?" he scoffed.

"Akihiro, you are my son. What else would distract you from your work? I assume you have put to rest the other issues."

"Not exactly but I'm working on it." His mother rolled her eyes. "What? I will resolve it this week. Now, what did you make for breakfast? It smells great."

It was a typical morning in the Amori house. The lemon scent of the fresh baked Magdalenas and freshly pressed espresso filled the kitchen. Akihiro walked to his father first, as a sign of respect, hugged him, and then he went on to shake hands with his brother. Each opponent tried to recruit Aki to his side. He knew better than to get involved in the politics. He felt his mother's eye still upon him. She knew the intricacies of each son and knew this woman was more than a guest. *Please Mum, stop staring.*

Eventually the argument subsided long enough for Tadashi to hear his eldest son's business news. Akihiro updated him on the loan, design ideas and construction. He knew his son worked hard to achieve his goals, and Tadashi supported him.

"Who's the woman, Aki? Didn't think we could hear Mum and you?" Shinji poked.

Shinji was the typical antagonizing younger brother. He looked more Japanese that Akihiro but they both had their mother's deep dark eyes. Shinji idolized his brother. When he was younger, Aki taught him soccer when Tadashi lost patience. He taught Shinji to ride a bike, then a motorbike. However, Shinji was not shy with the girls as Akihiro was. The boys were the best of friends as well. They held similar interests in sports and business. Shinji often wished he was strong like his brother and went into business for himself.

"I said she is just a guest. Can we leave this subject?"

"It is a woman. I knew it. I can see it in your face. Is she from Singapore or elsewhere?" Lucia felt vindicated in her thoughts.

"She's from the United States. But I'm not going into this any further, so stop." He was uncomfortable talking about his relationships. It was easier to redirect the conversation back to the family real estate business. After Akihiro finished his coffee and roll, he excused himself from the table. He hugged his father and kissed his mother good-bye.

"You're leaving so soon? You just got here. She must be special to have you on the move so quickly," Lucia spoke factually.

Akihiro smiled at his mother but refused to respond.

* * *

When Akihiro returned to the hotel, he read his messages from Kat, who took off the weekends. He made his phone calls and cleaned the loose papers off his desk. As he spun in his chair, he saw Laramie seated on the beach alone, but moreover, she looked lonely. She ran her fingers in the sand then looked out to the sea. He wanted to join her but knew he had business to finish first.

Laramie loved to watch the water ripple onto itself. She loved to see the ships out at sea and wonder where they were headed. She looked at the sea, searching for the answers to the questions in her heart. Usually she wasn't so emotional, so indecisive, but Singapore changed everything. *What makes him so different? Why am I so drawn to him? Besides the obvious. Is he what I've been missing? It has been a long time since I was on a real date. Could it be the attention? Maybe I'm just channeling all his good points to the forefront. Am I aware of any bad? Am I making him bigger than he is? More perfect? Though, when I'm with him, I'm happy. I haven't felt happy like this since my parents were with me. What could possibly come of this? I'm so confused.* She was so engrossed in her thoughts that she didn't hear Akihiro walk up behind her.

"What are you thinking?"

She sighed heavily. "Just about my parents. Sometimes I really miss them. I have so many questions and no one to ask, no one to answer. I miss all the laughing we did. I miss having them tell me how wonderful and talented I was even when I wasn't. I miss having someone to cry to when I'm hurt."

His heart crumbled for her. He tried to imagine her predicament but that was beyond his comprehension, especially after his morning. That part of her heart was still twelve, still unable to heal. He wiped the tears off her cheek then kissed it.

"I'm sorry. You must think all I do is cry. In reality, I rarely ever do. This shocks me much more than anything. Such a departure from my normal self."

"Maybe you just needed to be somewhere else. I mean without the distractions of work and friends."

"I suppose you're right." She pushed her feelings back in her mind. "So, how was your morning? Did you do the things you needed?"

He didn't bring up the fact he was with family. "Yes. I am ahead on paperwork so the weekend is completely open. Let's see… what haven't we done?"

"I'm glad you mentioned that. Don't misunderstand me, I love being with you but I don't want to take you away from your friends and family either."

"You're not. I am where I want to be. I will let you know otherwise, all right? Anyway, this weekend starts the Autumn Moon Festival. I thought we would walk around Chinatown."

"Oh, great idea. I forgot about that being away from home. I usually go with Manny and Lian. Let me run and get cleaned up and I'll meet you in the lobby."

"Well… maybe you need help. Sometimes the middle of your back is hard to reach." He strummed his index finger down her back.

She smiled at his slyness, took his hand and strolled to the bungalow. She undressed and turned on the shower. She felt rather modest since she never showered with a man. She tried to hide her nervousness but the blush in her cheeks gave her away. Akihiro went inside first and held his hand out for hers.

"Come here. I have seen every inch of your body. Now you're shy about this? Relax. I mean it, just relax."

Obviously, he was more experienced in the art of sexual pleasure and less inhibited. Internally, she fought to overcome her fears, especially with him. They stood embraced under the showerhead. The warm water puddled between their bodies. He slowly gathered her hair back and ran his fingers through until all of it was wet. He poured the shampoo in his hands and rubbed them together before he spread it in her hair. He slowly massaged her scalp. *Oh my, who knew having your hair washed could be so sensual?* Laramie happily moaned it felt so good. He rinsed her hair and then gathered the washcloth and lathered it with the lotus flower soap. He started with her face as he made small circles barely touching her skin then he moved the cloth down and around her neck. He tilted her head back as the water flowed across her face like a rain shower. He placed the cloth on her arms, and ran it gently from the finger tips to the underarm, which caused Laramie to giggle. He repositioned himself behind her, pressing harder with the cloth along her back and following her body to the floor. She giggled again when he reached her feet though she tried to suppress it. Akihiro circled to her front, started the same pattern only with a lighter touch across her breasts, then again making his way to the floor. On the way back up, his hand moved between her legs. He finished with a rinse but not with her. He kissed her softly. Then his kisses became harder, crushing her lips, as the water flowed over them. He stopped quickly to prepare for the next step.

"That was amazing. I have never felt anything like that."

"It's not over yet," he grinned slyly.

Akihiro pulled her close as he turned on the body jets. *What could be next? What is he thinking?* He tilted the jets just so. She followed his lead unable to decipher what was next, the confusion showed in her face. He placed her foot on the tub edge, twisted her body to face the jet until it landed between her legs. Laramie jumped at first but she now was aware of his direction. He stepped behind her, held onto her hips and plunged inside her. He moved at a slow rhythm as she squeezed his hands.

"Don't move. Stay perfectly still," he said with such seduction. She tried to balance herself by holding her hands against the walls. The rhythm continued at a slow pace then began to quicken. Her breathing became faster and deeper until she screamed out his name. Akihiro held her up as her knees began to buckle beneath her. His speed increased until he stopped and squeezed his arms around her, her body shaking inside his. Laramie never felt anything so explosive. He stopped the jets and sat with her in his lap. She had her arms wrapped around his neck, her face turned on his shoulder before she opened her eyes and looked him in the face. Initially, her eyes slowly encircled his face and then moved her gaze back to his eyes. She wanted to tell him she was in love with him but she couldn't. She was truly speechless.

Laramie remained quiet as they dressed. She searched for the right words to say but was unable to find them, still astounded by the experience. All her thoughts were single words. *Wow. Unbelievable. Incredible. Again.* Akihiro sat on the sofa, unphased, and watched sports as he waited for her to finish. She hurried to put on makeup. She was ready within minutes. She joined him in the living room and shut everything down before they left.

As they drove into the city center, she caught his eye and smiled back. It wasn't until they parked when the conversation began.

"Laramie, say something. You've been quiet the whole ride."

At first, she just shook her head and grinned. "I have to tell you that I can never look at a showerhead and wall jets in the same manner ever again. Am I the only adult who didn't know about that?" He laughed at her comment. Flustered by the whole experience, she continued, "Now I see why they sell so well."

He leaned over to her and kissed her cheek. He really adored her inexperience maybe because it was so genuine and honest. She had a natural way of building his ego.

They parked on South Bridge Road and walked a few blocks before they reached Pagoda Street. The Hindu temple on the corner was ornate with carved human figures and animals, painted in vibrant colors, which ascended to the top of the tower. It was unlike anything Laramie witnessed. The pagoda style architecture blended with the old colonial style originally in Singapore. Some buildings reminded Laramie so much of home with the Chinese characters on the signs. Every store had racks on the brick road with paper lanterns and cultural items. The restaurants had tables set up outside their entrance. The lanterns, strung above their heads, waited for evening to come. Akihiro stopped at the Buddhist temple on Sago Street. He quickly entered, lit a candle and said his prayer to Buddha as Laramie watched. She wore a sleeveless shirt and felt too disrespectful to enter the building. Though, she marveled at the beauty and craftsmanship of its interior. As they walked back toward the Chinatown Complex holding hands, Laramie heard someone call Akihiro's name. He didn't want to stop and with good reason.

"Akihiro, you have to stop. Someone is calling you."

"I know someone is calling me and no, I don't want to stop." His pace picked up.

"But why?"

His actions confused her. Laramie could hear the calling voice become louder. He finally stopped and turned to the person who called him.

"Laramie, this is my younger brother, Shinji. Shinji, meet Laramie Holden. Okay, now we must be going so I'll call you later."

"No way, Aki, I don't think so." Shinji kissed Laramie's hand and continued, "You're the woman who has kept my brother from work and family. He has tried to keep you a secret and I can see why. You are a beautiful woman." *Oooh, isn't he charming.*

"Thank you. It's a pleasure to meet you as well. Your brother has told me a great deal about you. I wondered if we'd meet."

Akihiro attempted to step in the conversation but Shinji cut him off.

"Why don't we walk down to Riverside Point and have lunch? It's quieter there and I can tell you if the stories are true."

Laramie definitely noticed the difference in personalities. Shinji was not shy at all. Laramie looked at Akihiro before she answered. She was in an awkward position and didn't want to be there. Akihiro was reluctant since he knew his brother and his reputation around women. Laramie looked away to play it safe. *This one is all on you Aki. I'm not getting involved.*

"Actually Shinji, that's fine but I want to pull my car up closer."

"Great, then Laramie will walk with me and we'll meet you there. Whoever gets there first grabs a table."

This completely went against Akihiro's better judgment. He didn't want Shinji to slip and say the wrong thing but he also didn't want to appear suspect. He was first to arrive at Brewerkz, a restaurant and microbrewery. He sat at an outside table and waited for the others to arrive. His patience faded as the time passed. A few minutes later, Laramie and Shinji arrived. Akihiro stood to pull out her chair and kissed her after she sat.

"That walk was longer than I expected. Have you ordered drinks yet?" she asked.

"No, not yet but I ordered appetizers so the waitress should be back soon. What do you want? Wine? Beer?"

Shinji shot in, "Let's do the draft sampler. No one's in a hurry right?"

Laramie looked at Akihiro for direction; none came. *Come on. Don't put me on the spot.*

"Isn't that where you get glasses of all the beers they make?" Aki nodded yes. "Well, I'm game if you all are." *She doesn't have a clue of what is in store for her.*

When the waitress arrived with the food, Akihiro ordered three draft samplers.

"Laramie, how long have you been in Singapore? Is it all vacation or work too? I hear the States have the worst reputation for vacation time."

It was twenty questions from Shinji but Laramie was happy to answer him. It wasn't long before the beer arrived. They all started with the same variety first, the Hopback Ale. The men seemed to be fine with it but Laramie thought it was awful and placed her vial on Akihiro's placemat. After the fourth sample, she felt a bit of a buzz. Her last glass was the India Pale Ale, her favorite of them all. She decided to stick with that choice as the men continued to try the special reserve samples.

The conversation rolled around the table with subjects safe to discuss. Shinji broke the trend when he told stories of their youth. His perspective was slightly different from Akihiro's.

"... so Aki tells me this girl really likes me and he knows I like her. All I have to do is sing her a song outside her classroom and she promised to go out with me. So I start to sing *Girl You Know It's True* by Milli Vanilli. The classroom was roaring because none of it was true."

At that point, Laramie laughed so hard she had beer coming out of her nose and mouth. She tried to grab the napkin as fast as she could but to no avail. Beer dripped between her fingers. Shinji laughed so hard he couldn't breathe. Akihiro covered his face to avoid the spray and handed his napkin to Laramie to dry her hands.

"Well, isn't that just perfect. I had a good streak going until now. Two whole days without any accidents."

He proceeded to tell Shinji of Laramie's unfortunate events with the night of Karaoke as the apex. Shinji begged her to sing for him but she refused. Akihiro handed him a knife in case she changed her mind. They laughed like three fools as patrons at other tables watched. Some strangers listened in on the conversation, laughing with them. Two older gentlemen that sat beside them offered to pay to hear her sing, of course, she refused. As the afternoon progressed so did the beers. At one point, Shinji leaned back on his chair to get the waitress' attention and fell backwards. *Finally, my turn to laugh. Oh geez, I hope he's not hurt.* They tabbed out and decided to walk along the river in search of a new bar. They crossed the bridge to Clarke Quay and opted for another table by the water. They still had time for dinner before nightfall when the floats ran for the festival.

"Laramie, do you want to eat now or later?"

"You know, I'm so stuffed from the other place that I'm going to pass. But, I do need to use a restroom."

The server pointed to the path between the bar and dining tables inside. Within seconds, Laramie was out of view.

"Aki, it wasn't my intention to interrupt your date. But, I see why you haven't been around. She is beautiful... and funny. I don't know why she's with you when she could have me instead." Shinji amused himself with his statement.

"I really don't care that you're here. I just didn't want anything said ... well, just no mistakes. I've been with her every day. She's perfect, even her mistakes are perfect. Last night we stayed in for beer and pizza and that was amazing."

"It sounds like you're falling for this one. Too bad she lives in the States."

"Yes, my thoughts too."

As Laramie walked through the restaurant, she slipped on the tile. She grabbed a man's arm to stop her fall. After she caught her balance, she apologized. The man, already quite inebriated, blocked her way and proceeded to tell her to stay awhile. Laramie kindly declined and tried to leave. The drunk held her arm and said he really wanted her to stay. She tried to be polite but that didn't work. She demanded he let go. He laughed at her and pulled her closer. Her voice became elevated and angry which caught Akihiro's attention. He walked over to the drunkard and asked him kindly to let go of his date. He told the stranger he didn't want trouble. The belligerent man finally let go of Laramie. Akihiro asked him to apologize to Laramie but the man refused. Laramie said it wasn't necessary, she just wanted to leave and she didn't want Akihiro in any trouble either. He gave in to her request for peace. As they walked out of the building, the man jumped up and trailed them. He took a swing at Akihiro, who bobbed away, but landed the punch across Laramie's face, sending her to the ground. As Shinji ran over to help Laramie, Akihiro's fist busted the man's nose. As the man tried to throw another punch, Akihiro blocked it and kicked his opponent's knee in. Within seconds, the police were there. Witnesses at the restaurant told the police the man started the fight and hit Laramie in the face. As the officers took the drunk away, Akihiro ran over to Laramie who sat on a chair with her head back and an ice pack on her face.

"Akihiro? Did you hit the man who hit me?" Laramie spoke in a slow groan.

"Yes I did, Laramie." He was so worried about her.

"Good. That makes two for the day. Does this mean I will be accident free tomorrow?"

Akihiro and Shinji laughed at this insane American woman who continued to plow through all her misfortune. Akihiro removed the ice pack off to get a better look at her injury. Fortunately, all she had was a little swelling on the cheekbone and a slight bloody nose. Akihiro wiped her face clean as she sat there.

"Do I look okay or hideous?"

"You look fine. Why does it matter?"

"Well, if I look hideous, then we need to back to the hotel but if I look okay we can stay out and drink more."

Akihiro took her face gently into his hands and kissed her passionately. *Damn, she is the most remarkable woman I've ever met.*

"I think the hotel would be safer for you," Akihiro advised.

"Come on Shinji, side with me. We haven't even seen the floats yet."

Shinji held both hands in the air to avoid a battle as he backed his way out of their dispute.

"I'll make you a deal, Lara. As soon as the parade is over, we go back, okay?"

"Thank you, Aki. And Shinji…" she called his attention just to stick her tongue out.

The longer they sat, the more they laughed. The more they laughed, the more they drank. Laramie attempted to tell a few jokes only to forget the punch lines. Luckily, she was a funny drunk. When asked a response, her every answer was *what?* She thought this covered her from memory lapse. It was unclear, based on the company, whether this worked or not.

Nightfall came quickly and the floats with Chinese characters came down the river. It was a breathtaking sight. There was a tall pagoda with sea coral and waves around the base, all illuminated internally. Next, individual floats appeared each with a sign of the zodiac. Laramie never saw anything like this. *This is so spectacular.* Her favorite float by far was the dragon float. The city came alive for this celebration. The bridge back over to Riverside Point, already decorated, now lit up brightly. The red lanterns between the buildings glowed. All the tourists awed over the spectacle.

After the parade, Akihiro reminded Laramie it was time to go. She almost hated to leave the festivities, but she did make a deal. She stood up, hugged Shinji goodbye, and told him to visit her anytime. He agreed and kissed her on the cheek. Akihiro held her hand all the way back to the car so she couldn't wander.

Once inside the bungalow, Akihiro looked in Laramie's travel bag for Tylenol. He figured the swelling might hurt in the morning. After taking the medicine, she began to undress. He tried to help but she insisted she could do it herself. Once she was bare, she called him to lie on the bed with her. He told her that she should go to sleep but that wasn't what she wanted.

"Don't you want me?"

"Of course I want you but —"

"Then come here."

He walked over to the side and she pulled at his pants and unzipped them. Once he was undressed, he climbed next to her. She started to kiss him on the neck as her hand moved lower on his body. She took him in her hand and rubbed with a firm grip. Her kisses slowly descended on his body. When she reached his waist, he grabbed her arms and pulled her up to him. *I can't let her do this.* Confused by his move, she looked him in the eyes. He told her no. He didn't want her to do anything that she may not choose to do sober.

"Stay here, sleep with me, anything but just don't go."

She was more emotional in her speech than normal, due to the alcohol. He couldn't say no to her. He tried before without success.

"Here… move up closer to me and just sleep, okay?"

"Okay. Thank you for rescuing me. You're my knight in shining armor. Hmm… do they know what a knight is in Singapore? Not the kind in the sky but the ones on a horse."

He chuckled. "Yes, we also studied European history."

She moved in closer and rested her head on his chest.

"Close your eyes, Lara and sleep. Good night."

He could feel her breathing become shallower. He rubbed her arms and kissed her forehead. He knew it wasn't long before her night ended.

Laramie took a deep breath and said, "I love you." She was asleep.

Chapter 20

WHEN LARAMIE WOKE up, her head hurt slightly. *Ouch!* She couldn't tell whether it was from the punch or the beer. Either way, she knew it all could be worse. She heard the water running in the shower and assumed that was where Akihiro was. She knocked on the door before entering. He stepped out of the shower and wrapped himself in a towel. She wiped her hand on the mirror to get a better look at her cheek. It was a little red and sore to the touch but overall, she faired well.

"I guess it could be worse, right?"

Akihiro moved her face from side to side for inspection. "It could've been a lot worse."

"It all took place so fast. I can hardly remember what happened. Most of the night seems like a blur. I remember coming back here." She looked at them standing naked. "Did we… last night?"

"No, we didn't." He was not about to go through the details of the prior night. Nor was he going to bring up anything she said and did not mean. "Are you up for boating? I thought we'd take a run over to Bintan and check out a similar hotel. Afterwards, we can swim and snorkel."

"That sounds fun. I've never been snorkeling. Heck for that matter, I've never been on a speedboat either."

Laramie packed a tote bag with her bathing suit, pareo and sunscreen. She tossed her hair up in a clip and threw on sunglasses. She was ready.

They drove back to Sentosa Cove and parked underneath Akihiro's unit. He quickly ran inside the condo, packed a cooler and changed into his swim trunks. He met her down at the docks and walked her to his boat. Laramie knew nothing about boats other than some were motor and some were sail.

She saw large ships in the neighboring docks, similar the yachts in the Bay. He helped her step on and handed her the cooler. He went to the bow, untied the ropes and repeated the task in the stern. He hopped on quickly and started the engines. Slowly he backed into the channel and began their trip.

He saved a long time for this boat; this was his baby. The Kisaki was a thirty-eight foot Sea Ray Sundancer. Everyone assumed he'd want something more high performance, like a Cigarette or Itama, but he wanted a place to escape and relax. She had everything he needed.

Laramie was very inquisitive regarding this new adventure. She watched Akihiro pull the throttles back slightly.

"So, it's like driving a car and that is the accelerator, right?"

"Come here. Stand in front of me and I'll show you."

He waved for her to stand in front of him. Unknown to Laramie, this was a huge step for Akihiro. He never let anyone touch his boat, not even Shinji. He placed her hands on the throttle and let her feel the lunge in power as she pulled back. *Whoa.* She felt the loss of thrust as she pushed the throttle forward. He explained the reason for the dual throttles, and how each can work independently based on your need. She figured out the gauges until she saw the one marked *Hours.* He explained boats don't track mileage; they measure the hours a motor runs. *That makes sense. I never really thought about it.* Once they cleared the buoys, he pulled her hands back on the throttle and felt the bow lift in the water as the speed increased.

The ride was bumpier than the ferries in the bay. *I think it's time to leave this to the experts.* She looked at all the other boats around them and watched them fade in the distance. The water was shades of azul, aqua and turquoise depending on the depth. As The Kisaki cut through the waves, some of the hits were hard on her hull. This startled Laramie but when she looked at Akihiro, his face was calm. *This must be normal. This is so loud though. I wonder how fast we are going. I wonder how long until we reach Bintan. This isn't so bad. I guess I don't get seasick. Whew!* Akihiro motioned for a drink and pointed down to the cabin. She hadn't gone down there yet. *Hmm, this could be interesting.*

She went through the tinted door and down the four teak stairs. *This is amazing.* This was nothing like what she imagined; it was luxurious. There were high lacquered wood cabinets along the portside, a table for dining and a long bench seat. On her starboard side, a bank of cabinets held a small refrigerator, microwave and sink. *Wow, running water. This is unbelievable.* She grabbed a bottle of water for him and continued her tour. She opened the door immediately to her left, which was the head with a sink and showerhead. *Gee, look at that, an adjustable showerhead no less.* In the bow, wooden cabinets surrounded a huge bed. She jumped up on the bed and to get a different perspective. *This is comfortable. Oh, a built in flat screen TV. Why would you want to watch TV when you have the whole ocean to view?* When she sat up, she noticed another bench seat in the back with another TV. *Oh, I better get back with his water.*

Laramie handed the bottle to him and told him how beautiful she thought his boat was. He smiled and kissed her. She wanted to stay next to him and watch the water. Occasionally, they passed another watercraft and waved to the captain. Laramie watched everything he did and absorbed it all. *Is there anything this man can't do? He runs a great hotel, he's funny, a great dancer, phenomenal in bed, extremely handsome, tasteful, polite. Did I say phenomenal in bed?*

After a few hours, they arrived at Bintan. The island was lush, tropical and rocky. It was noticeably larger than Sentosa Island. They rode the coastline until they reached the Banyan Tree Resort. It slightly resembled the Tanjong with villas placed around the main building. It had a stunning infinity edge pool overlooking the water that caught Laramie's eye. However, she preferred the beach at the Tanjong better since the waves were smaller. As they pulled up to the dock, a young boy took the ropes and tied them to the posts. Akihiro helped Laramie off the boat and they walked up to the hotel lobby.

Akihiro picked up some brochures and spoke with the staff. She browsed around looking at the art and the furniture. It was a lovely place with its own charm. *Something's missing? What is it? The people. His staff makes The Tanjong feel like home. They know your name, your interests, and your reason for being there. They seem to have a genuine interest in your stay.*

They went upstairs to the Treetops for lunch. The view was stunning. She saw the striations in the water colors better than from the boat. They decided to sit outside and enjoy the breeze flowing along the coast.

"Akihiro, I think this place is beautiful, but it's not the Tanjong. I'm not saying that because you own it. Really, my honest opinion is that this has many of the same features but your staff makes the difference."

"Thank you. I would have to agree with you. Look around and tell me what you see."

Akihiro sat back in his chair, sipping on his water. Laramie looked around the hotel. Everything was very beautiful. The men all wore pressed polo shirts, shorts and sandals. Some of the women had beachwear on. Though, their bathing suits were not the type to get wet. *This is all show.*

"I don't feel as relaxed here as I do at the Tanjong. You have a calmer feel, less pretentious."

"Exactly."

Laramie had a light lunch even though she didn't eat breakfast. Aki ate healthy, as always. They both stuck with water to drink. Coming across the salt water left them parched. From the deck, Laramie saw The Kisaki and the boy that helped them dock. He was rinsing off the side of the boat near the fuel cap.

"I love the boat. She really is a beautiful machine. Despite the bumpy ride, it is tranquil being out on the water. I understand why you do this. Are you able to get away often?"

"I try every weekend unless I'm out with friends, sometimes I even cancel that to be out on her."

"Friends. You don't speak much of them. I mean I know Kat is your friend but besides that. Where as I rant on about Manny, Lian, Liz and Gillian."

"I don't spend too much time with the guys. Men aren't like women, we don't feel the need to be in touch all the time. We hang out when we can. Besides, the guys work during the week and those who aren't dating are mainly at football games."

"Speaking of dating, I know it's none of my business and cut me off if you want to but you haven't spoken about anyone there either."

I need to change this subject. This isn't the place or time. "You're right I haven't and I am going to cut you off there because I don't believe it's polite to bring up other women."

"Well I'm glad you said *women* not that I thought you were otherwise but it's good to have it confirmed." He raised his eyebrow at her comment. It was obviously a joke on her part.

"Let's finish up here and we can head back to Pulau Hantu for swimming. We'll get the ride behind us first."

They brought the boat slowly along the coast before leaving. Over the island, Laramie noticed the houses, colorfully painted, all sat on stilts. It was hard to determine the economy of the place seeing these homes and then the resorts. She assumed the rich stayed rich and the poor stayed poor. This was the way of many places in Indonesia. Howcver, she thought the children were all the same. Their ideas of fun were to swim, jump and play; something money can't buy.

After they left the coast, Laramie lay down on the rear cushion of the boat. This blocked some of the wind and still let her feel the sun. *I can't remember the last time I had this much fun. I can watch him stand there all day doing nothing just as long as he stood there. So much has happened in one week. I can't believe I feel this way. Love at first sight? I guess it's not the joke I thought it was. Eat your own words, Lara.*

They arrived outside Pulau Hantu with the sun high in the sky. The heat and humidity soared, making it uncomfortable when they were still. At that point, swimming was an excellent choice. The coast was rocky and shallow so Akihiro anchored away from the reefs. He pulled out snorkels, masks and flippers from under one of the seats. She put on the flippers and picked up the mask when Akihiro grabbed it from her hands. He spat inside and rubbed it around the eyepiece. *Yuk.*

"If you think I'm not going to ask about that, you're crazy. Why did you spit in my mask?" Her face contorted with a look of disgust.

"You spit in the mask because it will keep it from fogging up while you're underwater. Give me a minute and we'll jump in together."

After they splashed and came up, Akihiro placed the mouthpiece in her mouth and had her bite down. He told her to put her face in first to get used to breathing through the tube. *This is an odd feeling, unnatural. Whoa, I can see so clearly under here.* After she was comfortable with breathing, they swam up closer to the reef. The visibility of the water was extremely clear. Laramie encountered a starfish lying on a rock. It was striped in browns and blacks, completely different that those at the Monterrey Aquarium. *What a beautiful world under here!* She examined the different species coral before a cuttlefish moved in the sand and scared her. The fish raced by as she came close to them. However, as she lay still on the water's surface, a few of the clown fish and butterfly fish returned. The water was so peaceful and quiet. She felt as though she was in a National Geographic episode. When Akihiro tapped her shoulder, she jumped and broke the seal on her tube, sucking in saltwater.

"You scared the heck out of me," she said still coughing intermittently.

"I'm sorry I thought you saw me coming by you."

"No. I couldn't hear anything under there. It was so awesome seeing all the fish and coral. Though some squid looking thing moved in the sand, making me jump."

"We've been out here for awhile and I thought I better get you back on the boat before you burn your back." *Gee, I never even thought about that.*

"Okay, I'll follow you." She looked around and tried to find her bearings. The boat seemed so far away not realizing the power of the currents. Akihiro held out his hand to help her onto the swim platform. Just as she stood, he pushed her back in the water. She swam back not without a dirty look. He apologized for playing and held his hand out again. As she stood, she took his hand and pushed off the boat with her foot, which placed them both in the water. She swam faster and boarded but then realized she had nowhere to get away. *Crap, I'm stranded. Now, I'm screwed.*

"Where are you going to run now, Lara?"

"No, you can't do anything. We're even now," she pleaded.

Akihiro grabbed her, picked her up, and held her over the side of the boat. Laramie screamed and begged him not to throw her. He laughed as he started to swing and count, one, two… before he stopped and kissed her. He slowly set her feet on the deck, holding her shoulders and plunged his tongue inside her mouth. She missed his kiss and touch today. She pulled him closer to her, running her finger through his hair. She wanted him. They raced to the cabin below, shed their suits and jumped on the bed. Laramie climbed on top of Akihiro and continued to kiss him. As she began to move, she sat up too quickly and hit her head on the corner of the ceiling and front hatch. It was too late to recover and yes, he caught it. Akihiro began to laugh as she held the back of her head.

"I have never seen anyone with the luck you have. I am just glad it doesn't spread to those around you."

"You realize these things only happen around you. I don't know whether it's Singapore or you specifically."

He pulled her down and rolled on top her, still laughing. For some reason it really struck him funny. Laramie threw her arms and legs out to the side, waiting for his laughter to subside.

"Hello? Are you done yet?"

"I'm sorry but it hit me funny. I'll stop laughing. And no, I'm not done yet."

After their lovemaking, they dressed and headed back to Sentosa Cove.

Laramie helped him clean the boat, gathering the brochures and towels. He carried off the cooler. They made their way to the condo to unload.

"Laramie, why don't you get something to drink while I get these things put away?"

She was happy to oblige. She opened the refrigerator and unlike hers, there was actual food and drinks inside. In the door, she found a Tiger beer. She yelled out to Akihiro for a bottle opener, which he responded with 'in a drawer by the sink.' She walked out on the terrace and took in the view. *I love this place. I never thought I'd like anywhere more than San Francisco but I could get lost here.* She began to think of Akihiro. *I don't even know what he feels about me or if he feels anything at all. Yeah, sure, he's been great taking me everywhere but I'm sure he does that with more of his guests. Of course, I hope he doesn't sleep with all of them. Geez, I sound like a schoolgirl. I'm a mature adult, right? I should be able to just come out and ask him what he feels. But what if its not what I want hear? Then what? Could I still continue?*

As Laramie contemplated her future, Akihiro watched her from the kitchen. *Look at her out there. She is so easily pleased. I don't think I've ever looked out there the way she does. I wonder whether she really loves me or was that the beer talking? I know I could ask her but what if it was a mistake. I'd look like a fool. But what if it were true? Then what? She leaves here in less than two weeks. Should I just follow this to the end and say goodbye? Can I say goodbye? What if I'm in love with her? San Francisco is so far away.*

"What are your thoughts? About the evening I mean," he clarified.

"Hmm, well, I haven't given it any thought. I'm actually pretty worn from the day. Why do you ask? What are you thinking?"

"I didn't have anything in particular."

"What if we have a quiet night in my bungalow? Maybe you could stay with me and we could go to bed early? I know you have to work tomorrow but you could pack a bag with some clothes." She wondered whether that question demanded too much time from him. She started to rethink her statement. "You know what, never mind. I have to stop monopolizing your time."

"Listen to me. I spend my time where and with whom I choose. Your offer is tempting and we can go back to the bungalow however, I am not staying the night. If I stay with you, I won't want to work in the morning and I have to work. Do you understand?"

"Aye, Captain." She saluted him.

They spent the evening watching American sitcoms on the television and eating takeout. True to his word, Akihiro left shortly after ten o'clock. Laramie tossed in bed, unable to sleep. She missed having him next to her. She missed his smell, his touch. She knew the coming week would be more of the same loneliness.

Chapter 21

"WHAT DID YOU and Laramie do this weekend?"

"What makes you think I spent the weekend with her, Kat?"

"Ha. You don't think I hear the gossip from the girls at the front desk? Or housekeeping?

He told Kat about meeting up with Shinji, the beer through the nose incident, Shinji falling over his chair and lastly the fight.

"Was Laramie okay? She doesn't have a black eye or anything? She has the worst luck of anyone I know." Kat tried to retain her composure but the stories were too funny,

"No, just a little swelling but that was gone by yesterday. We went to the Banyan Tree yesterday and looked around. I think we are fine in our market. We cater to some of the same types of clients but they are lacking in customer service. Besides, Bintan is still emerging as an island whereas we have the city close to us. That leaves them strictly to tourists where we can serve the business industry as well."

"Did you tell her?" Kat poised.

"No."

"Are you seow or what? It's not right, Aki."

"Han na, Kat. It's not like I haven't tried." *Enough already.*

* * *

Laramie looked at the list of services at the spa, and decided to have the seaweed wrap, facial and full body massage on the beach. The sound of waves breaking on the beach seemed to fit the mood and relaxation of the massage. The girl working at the desk asked for her preference, male or female. Laramie chose male because she thought he could do a deeper massage. After she undressed and wrapped herself in a towel, she walked into the hydrotherapy room and reclined on the table. Within minutes, an average sized man came in with a tray of oils and a small bucket and paintbrush. *Oh, this is going to feel so good.* First, he placed cool cotton pads scented with lavender over her eyes. Then, he began to paint her body with the seaweed mix. *Oh gross. Try not to think of how slimy this feels.* Afterward, he wrapped her body in clear cellophane, then warm moist towels and finally plastic sheeting. Just before he left, he moved an arm covered in jets over her body positioning them at various locations and started the warm water. *Now this feels excellent. I'm going to be so relaxed how am I to stand after this?*

A short while later, the man returned, removed all the coverings and wiped down her body. *Heavenly.* He asked to follow him to another room where a young girl waited for Laramie to sit in the dentist looking chair. It was far more comfortable than it appeared. The young girl began the facial treatment. She massaged creams on her skin that seemed to follow almost the same pattern as her shower with Akihiro. *Hmm… now THAT was a shower.* She wiped off the creams and placed a moist towel over Laramie's face. *Yes, this was the right choice for today. It's been months since I treated myself. I need to do this more often.* She dressed for lunch and hoped to see Akihiro.

Laramie decided to eat in the dining room today because she didn't want to be in the humidity and get sweaty before her massage. The server brought a menu and she perused her choices, finally she decided on a light salad and iced tea. Laramie sat alone at the table, which made her feel a bit melancholy.

"Do you mind if I sit with you?" Kat asked.

"No, Kat, not at all," answered Laramie, surprised.

"How are you enjoying your trip so far? The country isn't too big so it makes it easy to see a lot in a short time."

"Actually I am having a great time, more so than I thought. Though I have to say, I never planned to meet anyone. Every day has been another surprise for me."

"Despite your run in minor tragedies, we love having you here. You've been a positive influence on Akihiro. He's usually a workaholic but you've managed to get him out and have him relax. Besides, I don't think I've ever had a better time at Karaoke."

"Please, I am never singing again. I tried to warn you but —"

"Laramie, what do you think is going to happen in two weeks when you leave?" *Damn, she is direct. No punches pulled here.*

"Honestly Kat, I don't know. I assume Akihiro will go back to his normal routine and just put this behind him."

"What about you? Can you put this behind you?"

"No. No, I can't but I don't have a choice. My family and friends are San Francisco, so is my career."

"Laramie, are you in love with him?" *Why are you doing this to me?*

"Yes, but please don't tell him. Please, Kat. Everything is already difficult for me and I don't want to have any false hopes. I'm just going to continue with things as they are."

"I won't say anything, I promise. But, I will say he has some confusion inside that he is working through and I don't know how it will end."

"That's rather mysterious. Can you elaborate on that?"

"No, I can't. I don't want to speak for Akihiro. He needs to tell you his own feelings whatever they may be. Anyway, I need to get back to work. Maybe we can all go out again. It was really fun but no singing."

After Kat left, her statement puzzled Laramie. *What does she mean? What kind of confusion?* She replayed the last week over in her head. *Did I miss something?* She rehashed those questions through her head all through lunch, still unable to find an answer.

Laramie walked down to the last bungalow looking building near the beach. The masseuse waited for her patiently. Laramie apologized for being late. He assured her she was right on time. She climbed onto the table and faced the ocean. *Such a beautiful sight. So serene.* He began with her front, starting at her shoulders. Every pressure point ached, as though they waited for this release. He lifter her arms and massaged her from her shoulders to her finger tips. When he reached her knees and feet, she jerked slightly. He smiled at her embarrassment of being ticklish. She slowly turned onto her stomach and the masseuse began with her calves, working up her leg. *This is so perfect. I'll give him about five hours to stop.* When he reached her back, he slowly rolled her towel to her waist. Once the massage was over, he placed hot stones down her spine. The heat felt so therapeutic. Laramie closed her eyes and listened to the waves. They gently began to lull her to sleep.

As the man returned and removed the stones, she knew it was Akihiro. She smelled his cologne. She decided to play along with his game. He proceeded to massage her back.

"Oh, that felt so wonderful. Those stones were great. Oh, could you go lower? Yes, right there. Now a little harder. Harder. Harder. Perfect. If I roll over can I have a *Happy Ending*?"

Akihiro smacked her on the ass. "The *Happy Endings* are done in the bungalows. How did you know it was me?"

"I smelled your cologne." Laramie pulled her towel up and rolled onto her back. "Hello and how are you today?"

He leaned over her and kissed her hello. This is what she needed. She missed seeing him this morning.

"Busy, but I wanted to see you. Are you enjoying your day?"

"Well, not completely. Do you think you can send someone to my bungalow to finish my massage later?" she grinned.

"Sure, do you want them to bring dinner too?"

"Oh, I like your way of thinking. Yes, that would be perfect."

She smiled as he kissed her goodbye and returned to his office. She felt so much better now that she saw him.

Laramie stretched out on the lounge chair near the soaking pool at her bungalow. The late afternoon sun wasn't nearly as hot so she decided to tan a bit more. *Mmm... a massage later. I can't wait, especially for his touch. Don't forget the happy ending either.* Laramie was at the foot of the pool, closest to the beach. The sun stayed bright in the sky as she soaked it in. Still, Kat's words made her think of the possibilities it meant. She said things pointedly for a reason. *What kind of confusion? What does that mean? She was so vague. Whatever it is, it doesn't seem to affect him presently, at least what I notice.* She dismissed the comments to something less pertinent. She would have fallen asleep if it weren't for the noise from the main pool. Laramie heard a knock on her door and yelled that it was open and to come in.

Akihiro walked inside the bungalow and headed for the pool area where Laramie sunbathed.

"Are you ready to eat? I brought some Chinese in from town." He walked out beside her and bent his knees to a squatting position to kiss her hello.

"Now that's better than anything you brought." She stood from the lounge chair and followed closely behind Akihiro.

"Oh, one other thing." He turned around to face Laramie. "How was the water?"

He caught her by surprise and casually pushed her into the pool. A devilish smirk escaped his mouth. His move completely caught Laramie off guard. After she rose to the surface of the water, she looked at him with daggers in her eyes. It was evident his quick move was not appreciated by the recipient.

"Why don't you come in and find out for yourself?" She asked angrily.

He chuckled to himself as he walked into the bungalow. He grabbed a towel for her before he returned. He stood by the pool with towel in hand offering it to her.

"Come on, Laramie, let's eat before the food gets cold."

Laramie pulled off her top and threw it at him, soaking his shirt.

"If you want me, come in and get me," she posed back to him.

"Okay, you made your point. Come on."

She threw her bottoms at him this time. "No, I don't believe I did. Which option has you hungrier?"

Her statement brought a smile to his face. He debated his options before he removed his watch and shoes. Laramie smiled as she watched him undress.

"Does this mean I get my *Happy Ending* now? I mean I need something to build my hunger for dinner."

"I guess we will see."

Slowly, Akihiro walked into the pool as he made his way toward Laramie. She remained at the back wall of the pool and waited for him to come to her, still smiling.

"You realize that since I had to put forth this effort in getting you that the scenario may have changed."

"What scenario? And from what to what?" she toyed. Laramie tried to contain her laughter. "Besides, aren't you forgetting you put me in here?"

"Don't you remember Pulau Hantu?" he questioned with a smirk.

"Yes, I do. As a matter of fact, we are even on that. You can't change the rules midstream. Please remember my luck, it's never good. Besides, you pushed me in here."

He moved directly in front of Laramie and pulled her forward to him. She tried to maintain a grasp on the pool edge fearing what might come next but her wet fingers slid off the side.

"Lara, you're remembering the wrong part of the trip. I'm talking about the part after we were both onboard." His tone was even. He knew she would catch on in a second.

"Now that you mention that part, I am recalling it more clearly now," she replied with a smile. She moved her arms around his neck and her legs around his waist. "What exactly has changed?"

"The location, just the location."

He pulled her close and tight as he stared into her eyes. She glanced back and forth looking all around his face before she moved in to kiss him. Tonight, Laramie decided to stake her claim and Akihiro was more than happy to oblige. Neither were in a position to oppose the other nor did they want to do so. It took a while, but inevitably Laramie received her *Happy Ending.*

Chapter 22

DEAR LIZ AND Gillian:

My email will be short. I wish I could call you, it would be so much easier. Anyway, I'm having a great time in Singapore. I've been out with Akihiro everyday. He is amazing. So handsome, brilliant, polite, funny and … I have the rest of the week for fun then back to work. I have so many stories when I get back.

Miss you both! Laramie

Laramie wished she were closer to home for the simple reason to speak with her friends. Her morning was empty so it seemed like a good time to go through her email. Edward sent a few emails, as did a couple paralegals. It appeared everyone at the firm felt the need to 'cc' Laramie on whatever the news was for the day. She spent at least an hour as she sifted through each letter and tried to condense what was important. As much as she enjoyed her time in Singapore, she missed being involved in the business. She eagerly waited for Friday when she had her first business meeting. It was time for Laramie to be back in the saddle. She thought it would give her more to talk about with Akihiro than listening to him all the time. She wanted to be an active part of the conversation.

After she ate lunch inside her bungalow, she was inspired to surprise Akihiro. She dressed and headed for his office. She asked Kat if he was busy.

"Actually, no. He went to the kitchen to see Ahmed. You can go in and wait for him if you want."

Laramie shut the door behind her. She quickly undressed and neatly placed her clothes on the chair in front of his desk. She sat naked on his chair, turned around and faced the glass panels. She heard his voice as he came closer. *I can't believe I am doing this. This is so out of character for me. Talk about leaving your comfort zone. Come on Lara, be adventurous. I've never been the seductress. Ooh, this is kind of fun.* Akihiro opened his office door as he continued on the phone. Something angered him but Laramie was unable to tell what from the conversation. When she turned to surprise him in his chair, he grabbed her clothes and threw them at her. He snapped his fingers, made the motion to get up with his thumb and continued his heated conversation. Not so much as a smile or a wink, Laramie felt humiliated. She took her clothes and dressed in his bathroom. She took a deep breathe before she opened the door and walked out. She made it as far as the lobby before she started to choke up. She walked out in the street and hailed a cab. She asked the driver to take her to Clarke Quay.

Oh my God, I have never felt so embarrassed in my life. What was I thinking? I should've never done this. Learn from this Lara. Am I imagining he dismissed me like a common tramp? Crap, Monica Lewinsky was treated better than this. I don't understand how this backfired. I just wanted to add a spark to his day. Apparently, I have overstepped my place. The driver dropped her off and she walked down the river before she decided to go into a bar and drink away her embarrassment. The more she drank the angrier she became. *Most men would've welcomed my plan. They would jump at a naked woman offering sex. No, not him. Apparently, he is the only one to make the rules, the times, the places. How could he have reacted so cruelly? Is that how he values me? I didn't deserve that. I deserve better.*

Akihiro finished his call and asked Kat where Laramie went. She told him she didn't know. He walked to her bungalow and no one answered. When he got back to the lobby, the desk clerk told she left upset and hailed a cab. Kat happened to be at the front desk during the conversation.

"What happened? Why was she upset?"

"I have no idea, Kat. I think she wanted to surprise me and I couldn't be bothered at the time. I had Ahmed on the phone trying to salvage food in the freezer. I asked her to get out of my chair. She went into the bathroom, got dressed and seemed fine when she walked out."

"Wait a minute. Did you say *got dressed*? Was she naked?"

"Yes. I don't know what she had in mind. It didn't matter; it wasn't the time, or the place. I have to worry about more important things right now." Akihiro still agitated by the scene.

"For the record, I am staying out of this. Not another word."

"I'm sure she'll get over it. Anyway, ring me when she gets back."

By dinnertime, Laramie was still gone. Akihiro paced in and out of his office. He tried to make it look like work but Kat knew better. She asked him whether he needed her help with anything but Akihiro told her everything was fine. Dinnertime passed and the sun set. Akihiro sat in his office and waited for her to call. Nothing. He worried something might have happened so he called Shinji.

"Hey, I think I may have made Laramie mad. She went into the city after lunch and hasn't come back yet. Could you do me a favor? I'm going to check the bars on the west bank, could you check the east?"

"Sure, no problem. If I find her first, I'll call you."

Akihiro started at Riverside Point. He figured she had to be somewhere they had been together. *What the hell is her problem? Just like a woman to get emotional over nothing. She knew I was working. Why would she do that? She's a professional, she should know better. What if someone was with me?* By the time he searched half of Clarke Quay, his phone rang.

"Aki, I found her. She's at the Clinic and she's pretty drunk."

Akihiro walked into the club and Laramie sat at the bar. She was completely intoxicated with slurred speech as well. Laramie was never a big drinker, which was evident from the Moon Festival.

"Come on Laramie, let's go. You've had enough."

"Oh look it's my... what are you anyway? The boss. The rule maker. Oh, hi Sh-sh-shinji. Sorry, I'm not into two men at once. And… and, I don't do the brother thing either. These are my new friends though I don't remember their names." She waved her arms around.

"I said it's time to go, Lara," he reiterated firmly.

"Uh oh. That's right, you're the boss." Laramie began to unbutton her blouse and unfasten her shorts. "That's right. We do it only when *you* decide. How could I forget? I'm just the stupid American tramp… or whore, whatever. Well, just stupid American." She could barely stand let alone walk.

"Stop it, Lara, just stop it."

"Stop it, Lara, just stop it. Ha, ha, ha. Now I sound like the boss. Wait. I have to say goodbye. It's not right to be rude. Ha. Ha. You wouldn't know what that means."

Shinji volunteered to get the car since the conversation sounded personal. After he arrived back near the bar, he helped Akihiro load Laramie into the car. Akihiro thanked him for the help. They made a few stops along the way for Laramie to vomit. It was unknown what and how much she drank. When they arrived back at the hotel, Samad helped Akihiro carry her to the bungalow.

"Oh look, I'm home," she yelled. "Thanks for nothing and good night."

"Let's go, Laramie. Get in bed. Give me your shoes first. You can leave your clothes on."

"Are you sure? Isn't it easier to screw me without clothes? Oh wait, you must know another way to do it 'cause you know everything. How much do I owe you for the lessons? I should've asked the rate first or was it on the house? On the house. Ha. Another place you must've done it."

"Goodnight."

Akihiro closed her doors and lay down on the sofa. *If she gets sick, it's going to be a long night. Morning should be interesting.*

Chapter 23

LARAMIE'S ROOM WAS dark when she woke. Her stomach felt sour but not enough to be sick. Her head pounded pretty well too. She remembered leaving the hotel for the city but everything after that was a mystery. She opened her bedroom doors and took some Tylenol out of her bag. She went to the kitchen to get a glass of water. When she turned around, she found Akihiro awake on the sofa. It was apparent he drove her back and slept there all night.

"How are you feeling?" he asked testing the waters.

"I've been better. I assume you brought me back last night?"

"Yes."

"Well, thank you. That makes us even, now get out," she replied coldly.

"What is your problem?"

"Oh, that's rich. My problem. Why don't you click your fingers and ask me to fetch your paper? You probably treat a dog better."

"Are you mad about yesterday? Why?"

"Granted, I should not have been so forward in my actions in your office. Believe me that was *completely* unlike me to be so unprofessional in a work place. But… oh my God, was I the only person in your office? I remember sitting there naked to surprise you and you threw my clothes at me, snapped your fingers and kicked me out. Either that or I was hallucinating."

"I apologize, I didn't mean to come off like that but I was under a lot of stress."

"Tell me, through out my unfortunate series of events, namely, soaked naked by a boat, scared to death, laughed at singing, and punched in the face, was I not stressed?" Laramie said like a true litigator.

"I guess you were."

"Oh, you bet your ass I was. Did I take it out on you? Even once?"

"No."

"Thank you, you made my point, now *GET OUT*."

"Laramie, you're being unreasonable."

Laramie contained her emotions long enough to walk back into the bedroom and lock the door. *I'm being unreasonable! Deep breathes, Lara. He doesn't see where he was wrong. I thought it was obvious. Don't cry. It's not worth it.* She attempted to hold her emotions in but she faltered. *Damn, I'm not even a good whore. I hate men.* She lay on her bed and silently cried. Akihiro pulled at the doors, asking her to unlock them. She was deeply embarrassed and hurt.

"You promised you wouldn't hurt me and you lied, so just leave."

"Lara, I said I'm sorry. What more do you want from me?"

Laramie refused to answer anymore. *Don't waste the tears. He doesn't get it. Jerk.* After a few minutes, she heard the door close. Akihiro left. Eventually, she slept with hopes of feeling better when she would awaken.

Akihiro stormed through the hotel to his office. *Forget her. I apologized. What does she want? My blood? I don't need this garbage. I have a business to run.*

"Hey Kat, could you come in here?"

"Is it safe? Samad told me she was drunk when you found her. Is she okay?"

"I don't want to talk about her. She's on her own. I have a business to run and need to focus on that. Ahmed was able to salvage the produce and most of the meats could be cooked this week. We lost our inventory of fish so we need to reorder that. Did they leave an invoice on the freezer repair?"

"Yes, here it is. The technician said that pipe from the condensing unit burst and caused the freezer to warm. Luckily enough, the temperature was under five Celsius when they caught it."

"I'm waiting on a fax from the architect with preliminary figures for the addition next door. Has it come in yet?"

"Let me check." Kat ran into her area and grabbed all the papers off the machine. "This is everything off the fax this morning."

As Akihiro sifted through the papers, he came across four pages for Laramie from her firm. He pulled them aside and handed them to Kat. "Could you deliver these for me?"

Kat nodded and left the office. When she knocked on Laramie's bungalow door, no one answered. The second time, Kat struck harder. Laramie flung open the door.

"What more do you—Oh, I'm sorry Kat. I thought you were someone else. What can I do for you?"

"How are you feeling? I heard you really tied one on."

"Is that what *he* said? Because, I'm fine."

"No. Samad told me. He helped Akihiro carry you. Anyway, these faxes came in for you. I thought I'd bring them by. Are you sure you're all right?"

"You didn't mention anything about our conversation, did you? It would be waste at this point. I don't know what was thinking yesterday. I just wanted to surprise him. It all went horribly wrong. Now, I find I'm horrible at relationships too. I should've known better than to get involved, especially with someone so chauvinistic."

Why are Americans are so open with their personal lives?

"Chauvinistic? Really? I never thought that of Akihiro. I'm going to regret this, but how so?"

Laramie proceeded to describe the incident at the office, snapped fingers and all. Then, she continued with that morning's conversation. Kat knew she was in the middle and wanted to find a way out of their problems. Kat told her that Akihiro was better with Laramie than without her. Unfortunately, Laramie reached her saturation point.

"Let me try an experiment in the office. I won't say a word but he may see what he did wrong. Laramie, he's just as new at this as you are. I told you both 'you both need to smile less and talk more.' It wasn't some kind of proverb, it's communication. When one of you talks, the other needs to listen." *Am I the only adult around here?*

Kat sat at her desk and worked on a stack of files. When the phone rang, she answered it. A few minutes later, Akihiro walked out to talk with her. Kat, still on the phone, looked up at him, handed him a file, snapped her fingers and gestured for him to leave. Akihiro went into his office miffed at her behavior. *Damn Kat, you don't have to be rude.* It took him a few minutes to discover her scheme. He knew she talked with Laramie. He walked back to the doorway and smiled.

"I get it."

"Get what? What are you meaning, Mr. Amori?"

"Laramie told you what happened. You made your point. Did she say anything else?"

"No, all I did was hand her a fax. I told you I wasn't getting involved."

Akihiro sat in his office and wondered how to fix the problem. *I've already given her flowers, dinner and dancing. Drinking is out. She was sick enough yesterday. Dinner on the beach? No, she may not show. I have it.* Akihiro called Kat and gave her a list of stuff he needed quickly. After an hour, Kat returned with a bag full of items.

"Kat, I need your help. I need you to get her out of the bungalow and keep her out for about a half hour. I know you're not getting involved but you wouldn't be if you should just want to talk, right?"

Reluctantly, Kat agreed. She called Laramie shortly after four o'clock. She asked if all the pages of the fax came in because they had more come. Laramie counted them and said it looked fine. Kat asked if she would come up to the office just verify they had everything. Kat explained she would go there but Akihiro left for the day and she couldn't really leave the phones until later. Laramie agreed.

"Kat, are you sure you had more pages? I counted all of them and they're in order."

"Well, let me see. Some could be duplicates. Hey, by the way, are you feeling any better?"

"I guess so. My hangover is mostly gone. I should know better than to drink. I have a low tolerance for alcohol. Was that it?"

"Can I ask a personal question? Is it hard to be the only female partner in a large firm? Do they ask for things they'd never ask another man?"

Laramie smiled and took a seat across from Kat. "In the beginning it was hard. Edward was used to asking me to get things at home and that it rolled into the office too, like coffee. It was okay at first, then the others started to ask and I finally was fed up. They felt so bad, it reversed. I had so many offers of coffee it was crazy. Now, we take care of ourselves."

"If you want to stay and chat, that's fine. As much as we are all family here, I am still a supervisor and we don't have girl talk like back at the University."

Their conversation continued for a while. Kat hated to deceive Laramie but she did really enjoy the conversation. They had many things in common at work. Laramie liked Kat quite a bit, although, Kat's personality was stronger than Laramie's.

"Laramie, thanks for coming up here. I know you weren't feeling well. I appreciate it. One more thing, it will work out, somehow they always do."

Laramie opened her door to her bungalow and found candles, in all sizes, lit all over the room. As she stepped inside, she noticed the pink flower petals on the floor. She heard soft music as it played throughout the room. When she walked out on the lanai, she saw more candles and petals floating in the soaking pool. *Where is he? I know he's here. So this is why Kat called me up front. It's not going to work.* Laramie walked inside toward the bedroom and opened the French doors. Strewn across the bed were more flowers. Even more lit candles were on the furniture. A chilling bucket with champagne sat next to the bed with two flutes, fruit and chocolates on the nightstand. In the middle of the bed, Akihiro sat with his legs extended and crossed.

"I am so sorry. I know I broke my promise. Believe me, I never meant to hurt you. You had every right to be furious. What I did was cruel and rude. Will you forgive me?"

Laramie stood there calmly, unable to find her next move. *What do I say? Can I stay mad? This is the most romantic thing I've ever seen.* She held her fist over her mouth and contemplated her options. Her eyes moved side to side as she searched for an answer. *If I give in now, what's down the line? How many times can this happen? How many times do I want to be hurt?* The more she thought about it the more her anger faded. She tried to hold in the tears. *Don't cry. Stay strong.* Akihiro saw the struggle in her face. He wanted to reach for her but she had to decide on her own. She sat on the edge of the bed, contemplating her next move. *What do I do? God, I am so in love with him. What should I do? I only have ten days left. Is it better to give in than to lose that time with him? If this was the last day I would ever see him, is this how I would spend it? Would I walk away or stay?* She carefully stood up and walked toward the doors. She held the handles in her hands, paused a long moment and then shut them inside the room. He stood in front of her after she turned.

"Laramie, will you forgive me?"

"It's not about forgiveness. It's about being true to your word, true to yourself. I would always regret it if I walked away."

"I have never met a woman like you. I don't think another even exists. You are so beautiful but beautiful doesn't even capture you. I can't imagine a day without you."

He placed his hands gently on her face and behind her head. Slowly, he lifted her head to face him. Her eyes, wet with tears, met his gaze. *Please don't do this to me again. I don't think I could take having my heart break anymore.* He kissed her lightly at first and the passion started to build. Laramie met his kisses with the same desire. He helped her out of her clothes and carried her to the bed. They kissed for a long time before they fueled the rest of their passions.

Chapter 24

IT WAS STILL dark outside when Laramie awoke in his arms. As she laid there, she questioned her decisions of the previous night. *I hope I did the right thing. We seem so good together but is that just in bed? Would we survive anything long-term? That's assuming there would be a relationship. Laramie- you have become too involved in something that could be just a fling. But, is it wrong to fall in love? Sure, there can be only two outcomes. Is opening myself up to him too big a risk?*

"Good morning. You're up early. Come here and lie closer." Akihiro pulled her to him and wrapped his arm over her. He wanted to feel her skin next to his.

"Good morning to you. I guess I am up early. It must be the thoughts of getting back to work. This is actually my last day of vacation. Tomorrow starts the meetings, power lunches and dinners. You almost made me forget why I came here."

"I'm going to miss seeing you throughout the day."

"Really? Are you really?" She honestly meant the question. *Please give me some validation.*

"Of course I am. I have a great time with you. You should know that by now." Akihiro propped himself up against the headboard. "Tell me Laramie, where do you see this going? Think about it. You live in San Francisco. That's thousands of miles away. You have your firm and I have my hotel." He felt the need to define their priorities.

"You're right. I don't know what I was thinking. I guess we just make the best with the time we have." *There's my answer. We don't view things the same.*

They stayed in bed, in each other's arms, for a while longer. *Does she want some kind of commitment from me? It's not realistic.* Laramie realized she fell for a man that didn't feel the same way. She knew he cared for her but his feelings were not the same and that was painful.

The silence in bed was awkward. They had different perspectives, neither of which were wrong. Laramie rose first and threw on her robe. She called for coffee and toast. She asked Akihiro if he wanted anything in particular. He said no. When he showered, he asked if she wanted to join him. She said no. They spoke one-word responses. They didn't have to say what they felt, the other already knew. After he dressed, he kissed her goodbye and told her he would call later.

After Akihiro arrived in his office, he changed his clothes. He sat in his chair and stared out the window. *There is no way possible to make this anything more than what it is. Doesn't she see that?* He spun around and buried himself in his work. He had to catch up since he spent so much time with Laramie.

Laramie finished her breakfast and dressed in her bathing suit. Today seemed like a good day for a walk. She reflected on many things; work, family, friends, relationships. *His wants don't match mine. That is the reality. This would be easier if I didn't care so much. Then I could go home without any regrets or false promises.* She walked further down the beach, wondering about the past two weeks. *Do I have any regrets? No, not really. Look at the positive. Is there a positive? Be objective. Look at all the time spent together. He has been a great guy. I've seen so many beautiful places. He has been a wonderful lover. I've enjoyed talking and laughing with him. Tried many things I never would have done. Think about how lonely I would've been if we hadn't met.* She smiled as her spirits picked up. After her walk, she sat on the sand in front of her bungalow, out of sight.

When the sun became too hot, the air-conditioning beckoned her. She perused through her faxes and emails. She gathered her file and read through her documents. She made notes in the margins of questions had for the bank. She hoped her contact was current on the project and knew foreign corporation policy. *Ahhh. It feels good to do something familiar. I needed to get back on track.* She emailed the office for information. Due to the time change, only the associates worked the late hours so many answers had to wait for morning. The owner of DemCorp, Frank Paradise, was a huge client and Edward's friend. Laramie knew perfection was the only outcome. She organized the papers and her notes. She placed them inside her laptop bag. *Ready for tomorrow!*

She pulled out the navy shirtdress she purchased up on Orchard Street, and readied her wardrobe for morning. She placed her navy pumps underneath the dress with her stockings in the toe. She loved to be prepared. *Finished. Now what?*

As she sat in her bungalow, she wanted their last official night together to be special. *What about dinner inside here? I can have them dress the table. I'm sure Ahmed knows Akihiro's favorite foods. Besides, this is a lot safer than getting naked.* She called Kat for assistance.

"Remember, I am not involved but how did last night go?"

"It went fine Kat. Thank you. Anyway, the setup worked. I am having dinner sent to my bungalow tonight. Could you check with Akihiro and see what time will be good for him? Thanks." *Looks like six o'clock is it.*

She called Ahmed as he had many of Mrs. Amori's recipes. Ahmed told her Akihiro's favorite dish was Paella. However, he wasn't sure if they had enough time to prepare it. Laramie asked if she helped him in the kitchen could they do it on time. He was very reluctant to allow her in the kitchen since she wasn't a trained chef and had no idea where anything was located. *Please. Please. Please. It's for Akihiro.* After she begged, he gave in.

Laramie was more helpful than Ahmed thought, than she thought. He sent her to the refrigerator a few times when they heard Akihiro coming. She finished cutting the meat and vegetables. She placed the rice in the steamer. *Stick to the simple things Laramie.* Ahmed cooked the meat and prepared the spices. All the aromas and flavors started to meld. *This smells glorious.* When they finished, Laramie hugged and thanked him.

She went back to the bungalow and showered quickly. After she dressed, she flipped through the stations on the television until she found the music channels. *Okay, I can't do anything foreign. God only knows what they are saying. Nix the AC/DC. Disco, ha, definitely out. Ooh, this sounds romantic. Contemporary Mix, that's perfect.*

Shortly after six, Akihiro knocked on the door. She welcomed him with a kiss and a Grey Goose, straight up with a twist.

"Thank you." He looked around the room and saw the candlelit table for two. "Wow, what's the occasion?"

"I told you this morning. It's the last night of vacation. I wanted to thank you for all the wonderful things you've done. Are you okay with that?"

"You realize there isn't any food on the table. Not that it doesn't look great but I'm a little hungry."

"Oh sarcasm. You're going to eat those words."

"Good pun, but I'm still hungry."

A knock on the door interrupted the playful conversation. Laramie opened it, letting the staff enter. They set up a tray on the counter and placed covered entrees, bread and butter on the table. They filled the wine glasses with an aromatic merlot. One staff member pulled the chair out for Laramie to sit and placed her napkin on her lap. Akihiro sat across from her. Quickly, the staff removed the plate covers and then left.

"Paella? Who told you? How did you do this?"

"Do you like it?" He nodded yes, still surprised. "Good. No one told me. No, that's not true. I went to Ahmed. We went through your mother's cookbook. She had it marked as your favorite. So, I became the Sous chef for the afternoon. It was a lot of fun."

"And Ahmed agreed? In *his* kitchen? Wait, I was in the kitchen today. I didn't see you."

"Yeah, I know, I had to hide in the cooler. Had you looked inside, that could've been hard to explain."

"Thank you. This was a wonderful surprise."

They sat at the table and conversed intermittently throughout the dinner. After they finished, they continued the conversation for a long while. Laramie sipped on the wine. Akihiro went back to his Grey Goose. Laramie heard *Iris* by the Goo Goo Dolls play across the speakers, one of her favorite songs.

"I love this song. Would dance with me?"

"Are you going to sing?"

"Why?" Akihiro grabbed the knife off the table and simulated the hara-kiri motion from Karaoke. "Very funny. No, I won't sing."

He stood up and pulled her in at her waist. He held her hand in his and they swayed to the music. She felt so good in his arms. She loved his touch and his smell. *What could be better than this?* She lifted her head and admired the magnificence of his face. Her eyes darted back and forth, as she gazed into his eyes.

"Akihiro, would you make love to me? Please?"

His movement stopped as he just stared into her eyes. Laramie chose her words specifically. This was her attempt to reach out to him. He knew exactly what she meant and wasn't sure how to respond. *If I continue, it would be an admission that I care for her more than I have committed. If I stop, it would be over and she'd be gone. Which decision can I live with?* The longer he paused the more she regretted her words. She knew she put him on the spot.

"Don't answer that. It wasn't a fair question. I —"

He firmly pressed his lips against hers, holding her shoulders tight in his hands. He gently bit at her lips before he plunged his tongue in her mouth again. The adrenal rush burned through her body. His kisses became deeper. His breathing became harder. His lips traced down her neck. Her fingers touched his sides ever so slightly. She felt her knees weaken. He undressed as he kissed her, and then helped her remove her clothes. He pulled her in tight and lifted her. He sat her on the back of the sofa and entered her. Laramie let out a deep breath and concentrated on the feeling of his movement. He pulled her off the sofa and pressed her back against the wall as she locked her legs around him, still moving to the same rhythm. He was rougher this time and Laramie gladly accepted that. When his arms became weak, he carried her to the bed. Laramie pleaded with him to keep going. He sat her on top and moved her hips with his. His moved one hand to the top of her bud and pressed it with his thumb to the same movement as her hips. The more he moved his thumb the more irregular her hips moved. Until finally, she placed her hands behind her on his legs, her body shook as she moaned. When she stopped, he sat up pulling her into him. When he stopped, she thought he had finished, he hadn't. He rolled her on her back and climbed on top. He brought her to another orgasm before he finally finished.

They stayed in bed quietly. Laramie rubbed her fingertips across his arm and he lay behind her. She tried to think of how she felt. *Fulfilled? Happy? Natural? Sensual? All of the above.*

"Akihiro, I — "

"Hush. Just lay here next to me." He knew what she wanted to say. He committed to deeply caring for her but he wasn't sure if he was in love with her. *What do those words mean anyway? I find her unbelievably attractive. She is funny, considerate, and honest. However, she can be childish, stubborn and emotional. Sure, I can't wait to see her and spend time together. I want her not just in bed but also around me. But, does that mean in love?*

Laramie agreed that silence was perhaps the best idea. She wondered what happens next. *What if he does love me? What am I prepared to do about it? Is there anything I can do? Very possibly this could be as far as it goes. Am I okay with that? Do I have a choice?* She turned and faced him. She pecked and teased at his lips. She regained her strength and wanted more. He pretended to be too tired to continue. Every time she came closer to him, he backed away and eventually rolled over. *Damn! I guess an early night is the best idea for an early morning.* When she rolled to her other side, Akihiro pulled her shoulders back. He moved quickly and pinned her beneath him. He held her arms out and kissed her a few times at first. His kisses became more frequent and more intense.

"Did you think we were done?" He smiled with a devilish grin.

She smiled. "I had my doubts."

"Not tonight, Laramie."

Chapter 25

ONCE AGAIN, LARAMIE was the first person awake. She showered as quickly as she could. She bent over to dry her hair and screamed when she stood.

"You scared the hell out of me. You need to knock or yell, anything." She continued after she caught her breath. "Did you sleep good?"

"It's ironic how the positions have changed. Wasn't it you that got to take the mornings slow? Now you're ready to shoot out the door." He embraced her and ran his hands across her body. "Are you sure you need to leave so early?"

"You are so tempting. However, I can't imagine you as the 'quickie' type. Unfortunately, I am in charge of the meeting and need to set the example of being on time."

"Wow, this is the first time I get to see the corporate version of Laramie Holden. I'm not sure I like the strong businesswoman. You're very intimidating."

She rolled her eyes. "I hardly view myself as intimidating. Follow me. We can talk while I get dressed. The meeting will probably run most of the day. Do you want me to call you for dinner?"

"You're casting me aside already? I didn't expect that."

"Stop it. I am not blowing you off. If things run late, I don't want you to wait on me. That's all I'm saying." He watched her with a grin. "What is so funny?"

"Usually I am watching you take your clothes off, not put them on. Though the pantyhose… not so sexy." Again, she rolled her eyes.

"Why don't you put clothes on and drive me into the city so I don't have to take a cab? This was we can talk on the way there. What do you say?"

"Do you have ten minutes so I can run through the shower?"

She looked and her wristwatch and yelled, "Go!" *He is impossible.* She walked into the living room, collected her purse, laptop, and bottled water. "Six minutes and counting."

The ride into the city brought more anxiety as Laramie thought about her day. Laramie tapped her fingers on the center console. Akihiro stomped on the accelerator, which pushed her back into her seat. She continued to tap her fingers, unphased by the speed. She looked into space for answers to her thoughts. He watched in amazement. *She has no idea what's going on around her. She has blocked out everything.*

"Laramie. *Laramie.*"

"I'm sorry, did you say something?"

"Yes, I called you twice. I've stomped the accelerator and been weaving through cars. And you sat through all of it, completely unaware of what has been going on around you."

She placed her hands over her face and took a deep breath. "I apologize. I get on a thought and it consumes me. I didn't mean to ignore you." She leaned over and kissed his cheek. "I'm horrible at names and everyone's will be new. The last thing I need is to insult someone."

"You'll be great. This is your specialty, remember?"

"Yeah, you say that but… You know where the building is right?" He looked at her with an 'are you joking' sort of look.

As they parked in front of the Tong Eng Building, she gathered her belongings. She leaned over the console and kissed him. He held her face and kissed her again.

She shut the car door and leaned into the window.

"Thank you for driving me. As soon as I know what the schedule is, I'll call you. Love you. Bye."

She closed her eyes as she stood and turned to the building. As she walked toward the door, she waved her arm in the air. *Damn it. How could you slip like that you fool? Cross your fingers. Maybe he didn't hear you.* He clearly heard her. He knew she slipped and tried to cover it. On one hand, Akihiro felt good to hear her say how she felt without being drunk. On the other hand, he wasn't sure how that statement affected their relationship.

* * *

Laramie walked into the building and into the Bank of Singapore. The receptionist, who expected her, politely greeted her. She didn't have time to sit before a good-looking young man, around thirty, came out to see her. He was wearing a charcoal suit with a white shirt and red tie. What surprised Laramie was the man wasn't Asian. He held his hand out to shake hers.

"Miss Holden, what a pleasure to meet you. My name is Rhys Davis. I know you expected James Cheow. However, he was called away unexpectedly. I have familiarized myself with your project and will assist you in every way possible." *Nice British accent. Bond, James Bond. Love accents.*

"It's very nice to meet you, Rhys. As long as we are ready to work, I don't have any problems."

She followed him to a corridor adjacent to the tellers. As they walked past the cubicles, Laramie noticed the similarity in their work environments. *What's different? They're quiet. Everyone works quietly.* She entered the conference room, which had people seated and ready to start. She greeted everyone in the room. When Laramie sat down, she drew a key plan that had all the names and their positions in the room. She pulled out her laptop and connected it to the WiFi network. She unpacked her documents and set them in specific piles based on her list of questions.

"Please bear with me a moment and we'll get started. Have all cell phones been set to silent or vibrate? Thank you. We won't need the additional disruptions. Do you have scheduled breaks or do you want to take a break based on our progress?"

"Miss Holden, we are here to assist you. We can break whenever you see fit," Rhys replied cordially.

"Call me Laramie, please. Let's get started. Who has the updated lease agreement?"

Laramie compared her notes with the document and redlined certain points in the terms. She asked for the survey and questioned the listed easements. She asked if anyone had the latest search record for liens. She asked to see which permits they had from the Singapore Land Authority. She asked for the time schedule for construction noise and for the locations of entry and exit for the vehicles. She asked for the latest documentation for weight limitation on the roads and repairs. Confused by the last request, Rhys questioned the necessity.

Laramie explained, "I realize heavy equipment will be in and out, and the roads are marked and rated for weight. I don't want my client paying for road repair because the street was not structurally sound in the beginning. That is why I want to know the last time repairs were made on the roads."

She continued her investigation into every document. She amazed Rhys with her tenacity. He rarely worked with any Americans let alone a female.

He looked at her face and listened to her voice, which seemed an unlikely marriage, brains and beauty.

"By the way, Rhys, I thought Tuesday would be the best choice for meeting the construction manager. I want to know his concerns prior to commencement. Also, we need to have the owner here to review the redlines on the lease. What day do you suggest for that?"

"Monday morning. It's best to review the documents with a fresh eye. Are you ready for a break?"

Laramie looked at her watch. It was past noon. She thought they were only a few hours into the day. *Where did all the time go?*

"I apologize. I didn't realize time. Let's break for lunch and meet back in an hour and a half. This way you can catch up on email and voice messages before returning." Laramie checked off a few lines on her notepad. She knew there was more to cover.

"Laramie, where would like to dine for lunch?" Rhys asked.

"Oh, you choose. You know the area so much better. Can I trouble you a moment? I have a personal phone call to make before we go."

Laramie called the hotel and reached Kat. She hoped Akihiro was available, no such luck. She asked Kat to leave him a message that she would call back on her next break. She walked out and met Rhys in the lobby.

"We can walk if you don't mind. The restaurant is a block away, just the far side of this building."

"I will follow your lead." Laramie smiled.

Laramie and Rhys walked to the restaurant and made small talk until they entered Rogues. It was a lovely circular building framed in glass windows. It really highlighted the view of the local area and people. After they seated and ordered, Laramie broke the tension.

"Rhys, how long have you lived in Singapore?"

"Almost six years. Hard to believe I've been away from London that long. I came here after I finished college. Laramie, I believe somewhere in my papers it says you are staying at the Tanjong Beach Hotel on Sentosa. I would've thought you'd have stayed in the city center."

"Actually, I spent the last few weeks on vacation there and felt it was worth staying for the duration."

"Well, you picked well. Akihiro Amori, the owner, is a fine chap. Have you met him? I understand he socializes among his guests."

"Yes, I have met him on several occasions. I have to agree with you." Laramie smiled slightly. *Oh boy, have I met him.*

"Before I forget, the bank president and some of the board member have asked if you would attend a dinner tonight at The Fullerton around six o'clock.

It is a rather formal event and I would be honored to accompany you. I hope that doesn't cause any problems."

"In reality, I would have to juggle a few things around. You said formal too." Logistically, Laramie tossed some ideas around. "Let me think. I can call the hotel and see if I could have a change of clothes delivered. If that works, then I would be delighted to attend."

Laramie wanted to say no but she knew her first priority was this deal. She really wanted to spend the entire weekend with Akihiro. *How am I going to tell him I won't be there? I know he'll understand but that doesn't make me feel any better.*

When she returned to the bank, she called Kat.

"I hate to ask this but I have a huge favor."

"Is it business or personal?"

"Business but a little personal too. I have a dinner tonight that requires formal wear and what I have on won't work. Could you send someone to the Tong Eng building with a change of clothes?" She proceeded to list what she needed and where to find it in the room. "Also, can you tell Akihiro I won't be back in time for dinner? I feel so awful but I have to put business ahead today."

"I'll pack up your things and have them sent to you. I'll pass on your message too. Enjoy yourself." Laramie thanked her dearly.

Laramie continued her meeting with Rhys. They discussed the insurance coverage and amounts, DemCorp's financials, as well as the types of privately owned shops acceptable to have on the main floor.

"Laramie, isn't some of this out of the legal realm? The construction manager, shops, etc.?"

"Yes, some of it is. However, my client is also a friend to the senior partner at my firm. Because of that, we are doing more than we normally would. Construction isn't my area at all, outside of the legal contracts and Singapore employment restrictions. Speaking of that, before I leave to go back to the States, I will need a list of candidates and their resumes for the General Manager and CFO positions. They have been prescreened, correct?" He agreed.

"Again, we have let time slip past us. We best prepare for the party. I hope this isn't too inconvenient for you. I will await you in my office. No rush."

* * *

Shortly after lunch, Kat told Akihiro that Laramie had to cancel dinner for an unexpected business dinner. He wasn't happy about it but he understood.

He missed seeing her, whether she was at the pool or beach, she was still close by. *She can be so great one minute and so frustrating another. When she talks, everything is larger than life. When she smiles, she lights up the room. And when she snores, she wakes up the entire hotel.*

"Aki, you have a call on line one. Christina."

"Thanks, Kat." He closed his office door before he picked up his call. "How are you doing? Still out of town?"

"Actually, I got back last night. I left you a message at the condo but when I didn't hear back, I assumed you were at the hotel. Anyway, I have a huge favor to ask. I have a charity dinner tonight at The Fullerton and no escort. I know you hate those types of events but I really need you to do this. Will you?"

Akihiro detested going to formal events. However, he knew he had a lot to discuss with Christina. He figured since Laramie wasn't going to back until late, he actually had the opportunity to finish some unresolved business.

"All right, but I need to talk with you as well. It's important."

"Pick me up at five thirty. I owe you!"

* * *

Laramie looked stunning in her black dress. She wore her hair down in soft curls with a bit more makeup due to an evening event. She was used to social parties since she and Edward attended them regularly in San Francisco. She had natural poise and a keen ability to make conversation with about anyone.

As she and Rhys entered the banquet room at The Fullerton, a spokesman announced their arrival. This was more formal than Laramie expected. She wasn't worried; she just thought it was to be a smaller gathering. Rhys introduced her to the bank president and his wife. Laramie thanked them for their cooperation in her business transaction and complimented them on their country. It wasn't often you saw a gorgeous tall blonde, let alone on the arm of Rhys. His preference was for brunettes. Nonetheless, they made an attractive couple. Every so often they heard names announced and every politely applauded the new guests. She and Rhys stood near the bar in the back of the room. She enjoyed meeting new people and seeing the diversity in the city.

Shortly before seven, the spokesman said, "We would like to welcome Channel 5's beautiful anchorwoman, Christina Ting and her fiancé Akihiro Amori."

Laramie shot her head around in disbelief. *No, there must be two of them.*

He has to be mistaken. She looked at the door and there was no mistake, he said the correct name and fiancé in the same sentence. She saw Akihiro lean over and kiss the woman on his arm. *Oh dear God, NO! This has to be a cruel joke. He can't be engaged to her.* Suddenly the room seemed to spin. Everything appeared to move in slow motion. She saw clearly but felt numb.

"Laramie, are you all right? You look awfully pale," Rhys asked her.

"Actually, I don't feel well. I hope you would excuse me while I use the restroom."

Laramie felt the anxiety build in her system. Her heart raced and her senses burned. She left through the rear hall doors and quickly made her way to the restroom. She entered the stall in enough time to vomit. Her body shuddered as she experienced a full panic attack. *This can't be happening. It can't be real. Please let me think this has been some terrible dream. This has all been a lie? Why? Why did he do this to me? God – I loved him.* Her tears streamed down her face. *Damn. I have to get out of here. I can't go back in that room. I can't face these people anymore. Especially not looking like this. This is awful. No, this is beyond awful. What am I going to do? Come on, think Laramie, think.* She asked the restroom attendant for a piece of paper.

Rhys,
My sincerest apologies. I'm afraid I've taken ill and must leave. Please give all concerned my most gracious thanks.
Regards, Laramie

She pulled herself together the best she could. As she entered the hallway, she stopped a young girl and handed her the note. Laramie described Rhys and she asked that the girl wait ten minutes before she delivered it. After the young girl agreed, Laramie ran through the lobby and entered a cab.

Shortly after Akihiro and Christina entered the room, they slowly made their separate paths. Christina spoke with friends of hers and Akihiro went to the bar. He noticed Rhys at the other end of the bar.

"How are you, Rhys? I'm surprised to see you here. This isn't your game."

"Your bloody right. Where have you been of late? Better yet, you're here with Christina? I thought the two of you cancelled your engagement. You back on again?"

"No, it's over. I'm just doing her a favor. I guess we should make it official for the press. I've just been busy with other things." Akihiro ordered a drink from the bar.

"Well, you don't mind if I have a go at her, do you? Just kidding."

"How did you end up here?" asked Akihiro standing with his back against the bar.

"Hoodwinked, I tell you. I was reassigned a new project and the bank execs decided we needed to be here. You know me, I'd rather be down at the pub drinking a pint."

"*We*? Who's with you? Anyone I know?" asked Akihiro nonchalantly as he sipped on his cocktail.

"As a matter of fact, I believe she is a guest at your hotel" Akihiro felt a deep lump in his throat. "Her name is Laramie Holden. Have you met her? Beautiful blonde, not my type though."

Akihiro's heart raced. "Laramie's here? Where is she right now? How long has she been here?"

"For God's sake, man, calm yourself. We arrived earlier. Then she suddenly became ill. Poor girl, she looked awful. She went off to the restroom."

"Tell me Rhys, was she here when Christina and I entered? Think clearly."

"Well yes." Just then, the young girl from the hall handed Rhys the note. "Oh right. Just my luck, I'm on my own. It seems Miss Holden has decided to leave due to an illness. I'm afraid I'll have to make apologies for her."

"Do me a favor. I don't have time to explain. Please take Christina home. I have to go."

* * *

Laramie sobbed all the way back to the hotel. Overcome with emotion, she knew more than anything she needed to checkout quickly. As she passed through the lobby, she asked for a final bill and for a bellhop at her room in fifteen minutes. When she got to her bungalow, she started to pack her things. *Oh my God — I was the only one who didn't know. Now all the things Kat said make sense. His turmoil regarded his fiancé. That's why he didn't spend time with his friends. That's why he avoided his brother in Chinatown. They all knew. How did I miss this? How could I have been so blind? Why did I have to fall in love with him of all people?* She sat outside on the lanai and wept the most painful tears. Her ache went deeper than she imagined.

Akihiro raced back to the hotel. He asked if Laramie had returned and the front desk said she was in her bungalow. He ran through the lobby to her bungalow door. He rapped on the door and Laramie, who thought he was the bellhop, yelled for him to enter.

She wiped her tears away, said her bags were on the bed and she would be inside in a moment. She stood up, wiped her tears and walked into the bungalow. She gasped when she looked up to see Akihiro standing in the room.

"Laramie, it's not what you think."

"How would you know what I think? Or what I feel? Or anything at all?" she replied seething.

"I didn't know you were going to be there. I would never have gone. I didn't want you to find out this way."

"You apparently didn't want me to find out in *any* way. You certainly went out of your way to hide it all. That's okay because I'm leaving and your fiancé won't need to know your ignorant American whore was here."

He reached out to grab her hand and she pulled it back.

"Don't touch me. I already feel dirty enough." Laramie sobbed again. "Why did you do this to me? What did I ever do to you to deserve this? Tell me. What did I do?" She trembled as she placed her hand over her eyes. He tried to reach out for her again. "I said don't touch me."

"Lara, please let me explain. I tried to tell you but I didn't know how you would react."

"Well, now you know. Damn it, you had ample opportunity. You sat right here when she was on the news, and then again when we were at Bintan. You're nothing but a liar and a cheat."

"Look, Christina and I *were* engaged but we stopped our relationship long ago. We just never made it official. When she called today, she was just asking for a favor. I thought since you were going to be out 'where was the harm?' I told her it was finally over and that we need to part ways."

"*Really*? Because your faces at the benefit didn't say 'parting ways.' It doesn't matter what you say now, I can't tell the lies from the truths. I can't trust you."

"Don't say that, Lara. Everything we've felt for each other has been real."

"No, no it hasn't. All I know is how *I* feel. I fell in love with you. I was willing to give up everything for you."

"I never asked you to—"

"You never had to ask."

"Stay here, we can work this out. Don't do this to us."

Angered by that statement, Laramie glowered, "Don't you dare put this on me. At least be man enough to take responsibility."

"That's not what I meant. Believe me, I wish I would've done this differently."

"I wish I'd never come here." Samad knocked at the open door with the luggage cart. "Come in, the suitcases are in the bedroom."

"Just wait, Samad." Akihiro tried to buy more time.

"That's fine. I'll carry my own bags."

Akihiro grabbed her wrists and pulled her into him. He kissed her passionately. Laramie wouldn't respond. "Tell me you don't feel something for me."

"Oh, I feel something. *Contempt.* Now let me go."

She pulled her wrists away and pulled her suitcases behind her. Akihiro tried to continue the dialogue. As they passed through the lobby, he pleaded with her to listen to reason. Laramie refused to discuss it anymore. She handed over her luggage to the cab driver.

As she was about to sit in the cab, he placed his hand on her arm and said, "Laramie, I don't want you to leave."

She looked him dead in the eye and replied, "You don't have a choice."

Chapter 26

LARAMIE WOKE UP in her room at Raffles. She wished it were all a bad dream. *I'm alone… again. Just when I think I've found happiness, it's stolen away. Would I have stayed if he was honest? Did seeing him with her make it worse? Doesn't he see my humiliation? My hurt? Why did he put me in that position? All those people knew about her. What kind of man seduces a woman whiles he's engaged to another? What a fool I must look like.* She cried all morning. She wanted to forget him but she couldn't, she still loved him. Anywhere she went in the hotel, she saw couples. The flowers reminded her of the Botanic Gardens. The umbrellas in cocktails reminded her of Chinatown. The candles reminded her of their nights together.

She knew she needed to snap out of it. The depression and self-pity had to stop. *Come on, Laramie. You're a senior executive at a prestigious firm. You didn't get there from being emotional. View this as a contract that was broken. What would you do? What would you seek as compensation?* Her thoughts started to spark. She knew what she wanted. She wanted Akihiro to feel the same way. *But how?*

She looked around her room for her laptop. *Where's my laptop? Damn it, it's at the bank. I wonder if I could pick it up?* She called the bank and they were to close in thirty minutes. Luckily, she stayed in the city. The ride to the office building was short. The receptionist asked if she felt better. Laramie almost forgot her reason for leaving the party. She said it must've been something she ate and thanked her for her concern. The receptionist handed over her laptop and the change of clothes. Laramie thanked her again.

When she got back to the hotel, she typed out a list of the people she accepted as visitors and callers, no exceptions. No coincidence, Akihiro's name was not on the list. She sat in her room as she worked all afternoon. She *googled* Akihiro's name. When the results came on the screen, one of the first articles had an engagement picture of Christina and him. *That hurts for now. Do what you do best. Don't get emotional. Stay strong. Keep focused.*

In the evening, she took a break and walked around the city. Her eyes welled with tears when she approached The Stamford Hotel, remembering the dinner at Equinox. *Why did this go wrong? Maybe it wasn't meant to be. Though it felt so right. Should I call him and hear his explanation? Either choice I make, there is no going back*. Laramie needed to clear her head of her confusion and the only way she knew how was through work.

* * *

Akihiro sat on his deck overlooking the water. He wasn't sure what his next step should be. He wanted to go to Laramie and make her listen, understand and accept his apology. *Why won't she be sensible about this? She is acting childish. If she can't be adult enough to listen to me, then I don't need her. Forget her. This was ending soon anyway.*

After he dressed, he drove to his parent's home. Lucia sat in the kitchen at the breakfast table as she read the newspaper and sipped on a cappuccino. Tadashi was at work already. Shinji already dressed for work, sat next to his mother eating a roll and coffee.

"Akihiro, you look awful. Another night on the town?" his mother asked.

He leaned over and kissed his mother hello. "No Mum, it was just a long night."

"Why didn't you bring Laramie with you? Or is she still mad from the other day?" Shinji asked.

"Who is this Laramie? Is she the woman you have been seeing?" inquired Lucia.

"She was. It's over, all over."

"What happened? The two of you seemed perfect together. She's a great person. One of the best sports I've ever met for a woman," Shinji added throwing punches in the air. "She took that right hook like a pro."

Akihiro sat down and explained the night before with Christina and him. He continued to tell of the fight at the hotel afterwards. When he reached the point where Laramie entered the cab, he covered his emotions with a cough.

His mother replied first. "Akihiro, I told many months ago to end that relationship. You thought I was just moaning needlessly. Now you see the trouble that could've been avoided. No woman wants to find out there is another. How long have you known this woman?" Aki tells her two weeks. "You tell me how you feel about her and then I will tell you how you really feel."

Akihiro described meeting her the first day, their boat trip, the Singapore Flyer, Karaoke, the Moon Cake Festival, boating to Bintan and the quiet nights.

"No, you have told me what you have done together but how do you feel about her? Are you in love with her?"

"I don't know. I love having her near, listening to her stories, watching her laugh at herself. She's funny, smart, … and beautiful."

Shinji jumped in between bites of breakfast, "If you don't love her, I do."

Lucia smacked him upside his head and told him to be quiet.

"Let me tell you what I see. I see my son completely blinded by love for a woman and he can't admit it to himself. Knowing someone for years doesn't make them a match, it makes them a friend. I cannot tell you she will listen, but she deserves to know."

Akihiro kissed his mothers cheek and thanked her. He knew she was right. He needed to see Laramie and tell her he loved her.

While Laramie was at the bank, Akihiro went to the Raffles Hotel. He walked up to the front desk and asked if they would call Laramie's room for him. The young female desk clerk felt horrible when she told him that she could only put through calls by people on an approved list. He understood and walked outside of the hotel. He sat on the bench along the driveway and wondered his next move. *What do I do now? How do I reach her? I can't go to the bank that would put Rhys in an awkward position. She has to leave here sometime. I'm just going to have to be waiting.*

Chapter 27

AFTER SHE SHOWERED, Laramie went to the front desk to check for messages. The desk clerk told her that a man was there yesterday but he was not on her list and asked if she wanted to add him. Her heart began to race. She knew it was Akihiro. Laramie asked if there was a note or anything. The clerk said no. Once again, the heartache returned. She told the clerk the list remained the same.

Laramie went into the Empire Café for breakfast. She wasn't very hungry. In fact, she didn't eat much the day before either. She sat at a table for two and admired the period looking pieces around the room. The dark antiques and formal fabrics were very different from the Zen feeling of the Tanjong. *Now I see how lonely this vacation would've been without him. I admit it. I'm lost without him. Do I listen to what he has to say? Maybe he does deserve a chance before I try to get even.* She decided to give this love one last try. *If he can't find an outstanding explanation for any of this, at least I've have made the last effort.*

Laramie took a cab to the Tanjong. The staff were delighted to see her. They heard rumors of the fight through Samad but no one had any concrete information. When she asked if Akihiro was in, they said he called to say he would be at home in case of emergency. They offered to call him for her but she didn't want him to have advance notice.

She caught a cab and asked the driver to take her to Sentosa Cove. She assumed she would find him in his condo or on his boat. When she arrived at The Berth, she forgot about the gate guard so she decided to walk back to the condo. She asked the cab driver to wait for her in case Akihiro was gone. When she arrived at the doorway, she pressed the doorbell, no answer.

She tried again, still no answer. *Maybe he's on the boat.* She walked around the complex and saw the Kisaki was in her berth. As she walked down the pathway toward his condo, she looked up and saw him standing on the deck. She was about to yell out to him when Christina walked onto the deck. While there wasn't any physical contact, *she* was there. Laramie stood frozen in her tracks. *That damn liar. It's not over. No more chances.* Laramie turned around and headed for the cab. *I am such an idiot. Now I have confirmation. How do you explain this one?*

Akihiro stood on his deck looking over the water when Christina walked out to join him.

"We let this go too far anyway. It was time to end everything and move on. I don't know why we were waiting. I'm sorry my presence got you in trouble with your girlfriend. You should've told me you started seeing someone."

"It's not your fault. I should've told her from the start and I should've told you. I had no idea she would be there. It was all bad timing. Now I have to find a way to see her."

"You really love her, don't you?" asked Christina.

"Yes, I really do. I don't want her to leave. I just need to talk to her before she does."

"Well, I believe I have all my things. If I forgot something, just send it to my place. Good luck to you Aki, and call me if you need anything."

Akihiro turned and hugged Christina goodbye. Another chapter in his life ended. He needed to reconcile with Laramie, he just didn't know how.

Laramie started to cry but stopped. The more she thought about her latest revelation, she angrier she became. There was no turning back now. She definitely wanted compensation for this; she wanted revenge.

When she arrived at her hotel, she walked directly to her room. She opened her laptop and began to cut and paste legal templates. When she finished, Laramie had a generous leasing contract. *This should make anyone want to sign. It's a big pill to swallow but it has to work.* Laramie set her alarm for five o'clock in the afternoon. She needed to contact Andrew Mathers for access to her trust account. *How am I going to explain the need for money? How do I get him to wire the money without Edward knowing? This is going to be a stretch.* She had to give that some thought. One benefit was her account was accessible in Singapore since Bank of America had an office there.

The phone rang sharply at nine o'clock in the morning in San Francisco.

"Hello, Mather's residence."

"Hello, Violet. It's Laramie. Is Andrew at home? I need to talk to him."

"Good morning Laramie. How are you dear? How is Singapore?"

"Actually, quite nice. I have had a great time. But I do need to speak with Andrew."

Andrew answered his call. "Laramie, how are you? Is anything wrong with the DemCorp deal?"

"No, nothing is wrong. Actually, another opportunity opened up for them and we need to react faster than normal. I've already cleared this with Edward last night and he said to call you first thing this morning." She knew this was a lie but there was no other way. "As you know, due to the banks and their restrictions here in Singapore, there is a beachfront property here for lease and it will only be available for a few days. Anyway, that isn't enough time for DemCorp to establish further credit in any bank. Therefore, what we came up with was to take money out of my trust and put into my Bank of America account. They have an office here and I can transfer funds easier. This enables DemCorp to complete the transaction and they can reimburse funds in the U.S."

The phone went silent a moment. Laramie started to worry Andy that didn't believe her. *This could be awful. What if he calls Edward to verify this information?*

"You realize Laramie, when you move the funds into your account you are responsible for the taxes. When you're reimbursed, you are responsible once again. From a tax viewpoint, it becomes a terrible financial move. Didn't Edward see that?"

"Yes, he did as a matter of fact. However, you know he and Frank Paradise have a long friendship and great business sense. I'm sure he views the return on the investment to be of a higher gain."

"Well, how much money are you talking? You said it was a lease contract correct?"

"Two million dollars."

Andrew choked after her response. "*What*? For a lease?"

"I understand what you are thinking and quite frankly it is a large sum of money but I have seen this land and the views. It is paradise, no pun intended. I calculated the amount based on the current land value if a Singaporean purchased it. Since we don't have citizenship, we can't buy land without a special permit front the Singapore Land Authority. Those permits could take months. In that time we lose any options of gaining it."

"Well, yes, I understand but —"

"Well then, you know why this has to be done quickly to gain the sellers interest. I have the lease agreement all ready for his signature. We plan to hold the meeting on Tuesday. Therefore, the money has to wire into my account today to compensate for the time change and all."

"I understand. I will transfer the funds when we hang up. I don't want to hear any complaining whatsoever when the IRS slams you with a large bill."

"Thank you so much, Andrew. Everyone involved appreciates the hard work you do for the firm. If they don't, I sure do. Thank you."

Who knows how I pulled that off that one! I hated to lie and I'm sure I'll pay for that. Thank God, he doesn't know anything about international business and Singapore Law. Now all I have to do is set up the meeting. I don't know how well Rhys knows Akihiro and I don't want anyone to be tipped off. I will have to set this up myself.

Laramie seemed to back to herself. She was a sly attorney and a scorned woman, a very evil combination. However, revenge was not in her character. She loved to win but she always played by the rules. She knew she needed to confirm the money transfer in about an hour. In the meantime, she decided to grab a bite to eat and lounge on the rooftop pool.

* * *

Akihiro still had a hard time without her. He hoped when he turned around she would be there. The silence of the day grated on him. He knew Kat was correct, everyone was correct. He thought there was plenty of time to discuss things with Laramie. He never imagined this would happen. However, sitting at home only made him feel worse. He called Rhys to meet him for a pint at the Highlander.

Rhys sat at the bar and waited for Akihiro to show. It wasn't long before that happened.

"I have to say mate, the other night was quite odd. I missed something completely."

"Yes, I'm sorry I didn't have time to explain things to you. It's been a crazy two weeks." Akihiro ordered a beer and began to tell Rhys of the previous two weeks. He told him that Christina picked up all of her belongings and that relationship officially ended. He was on track to fix everything.

"You realize I cannot be a party to this. I have to maintain a personal silence due to the nature of the business. If you had told me this a week ago, I could've excused myself from managing her account."

"No, I know that. I am not asking you to get involved. All that I ask you to do is keep me informed on her whereabouts. I need to speak with her and I am restricted from that at Raffles."

"Well there's nothing proprietary about that. Let's get another pint and toast to a resolution to your love life."

* * *

Laramie checked her bank account online. *Yes, the money is there! I am in business now.* She also received an email from Frank Paradise of DemCorp thanking her for the real estate proposal. Even though they mainly did large-scale hotels, he knew there was a niche for the small boutique hotels. He was onboard as long as it didn't interfere with the original hotel construction.

Chapter 28

AKIHIRO WALKED INTO the Tanjong later than normal. He woke with a slight headache after his night with Rhys. Beer was never his drink of choice and now he remembered why. As he passed the front desk, the clerk asked if everything was resolved with Laramie. He thought it was odd and asked her to clarify. She told him that Laramie came there yesterday morning to see him. They told her Akihiro was at home and she decided to go there herself. *Why didn't she call or ring the bell?* He remembered he was on the deck most of the morning. *No. Oh no. This couldn't have happened twice. Christina was there picking up her things but that doesn't mean Laramie saw her. We could've just missed each other. I'm sure that's what happened.* Akihiro tried to reassure himself with some sliver of hope. He knew it was too late to reach her at the hotel. She wouldn't be back there until evening and he would be waiting.

Kat walked into Akihiro's office and sat down for her usual weekly guest review.

"I see Laramie has checked out. Not only that, the gossip going around has something to do with Christina. I am not going to say 'I told you so', it's too late for that. Then, I hear she was here yesterday looking for you. Does this mean you worked out your problems?"

"No. It has not been worked out yet. She came by the condo yesterday around the same time Christina packed her stuff and left. I didn't see her but that doesn't mean she saw Christina either. I have Rhys keeping tabs for me."

"Rhys? What does he have to do with this?" asked Kat, somewhat confused.

Akihiro started the story from Friday morning to present time. Kat shook her head in disbelief when he finished.

"I'm going to tell you right now that your plan to confront her isn't a safe one. You may not like the results if you put her on the spot. You have no idea why she came here yesterday. And, involving Rhys can be detrimental to his career. You might want to rethink this."

"I don't have a choice. She won't see or talk to me any other way."

* * *

Laramie and Rhys met with the property owner first thing in the morning to discuss amendments to the original lease agreement. The owner was reluctant to sign but Laramie assured him without the lease, DemCorp was free to back out of the deal. After the owner signed the document, he left.

"Tell me Laramie, how are you feeling? We worried over you this weekend. I hope it wasn't anything too serious. Though I have to believe recovery at the Tanjong must've been relaxing."

"Thank you for asking, Rhys. I feel much better. It must've been some sort of bug. I can tell you I am rid of it permanently. As for the Tanjong, I was mistaken. While it was wonderful for vacation, it isn't suitable for business. Actually, I have taken a room at Raffles."

Rhys knew she was at Raffles but felt if he brought it up Laramie was too smart not to catch a connection. He continued that the evening was a loss without her presence and that the execs greatly admired her graciousness. They continued their pleasantries and chose their words cleverly. *She is brilliant. I'm not going to get her to slip on much at all.*

After lunch, Laramie informed Rhys she had another meeting set up with a different property owner for Tuesday. Since the bank would also be party to the deal, she required complete nondisclosure of the transaction. He assured his discretion and assistance. They continued their meeting regarding the first property. He gave her the list of screened resumes. He provided permits, an updated lien search and insurance requirements. She reviewed the construction loan documents and found them in order. Rhys handed her the papers on the road improvements including repair dates as she asked, as well as construction noise time limitations.

"Rhys, would ever consider moving to the U.S.? You have been a tremendous help on this deal." Laramie smiled for the first time in the past two days.

"Thank you but I have to pass. You have far too many loopholes in your country. Singapore's very straightforward and difficult to misinterpret. By the way, who are we meeting tomorrow?"

"Oh that's not important. I'm sure it will go my way. We have an expression in the U.S. 'money talks and …' Actually, that's not important either."

"Can I give you a lift to your hotel?"

"Thank you but I think I may do some shopping first."

Rhys enjoyed spending time and working with Laramie. She made him feel comfortable. She didn't ridicule or belittle anyone. When one of the secretaries spilled some coffee on Laramie's papers, Laramie asked for towels to clean it up stating she should have left room for the cup. Many of the bank employees found her pleasant as well.

After Laramie left for the day, Rhys called Akihiro. He told Aki that she wasn't any different that day than on Friday except she had changed meeting plans for Tuesday. Rhys said how he asked her questions regarding her weekend and well-being, all her answers were nice.

"You have your work cut out for you. If this woman is heartbroken, she doesn't show it. She has complete focus. I want to say you've met your match but I do believe she is smarter than you thought. As for information, she isn't going back to the hotel directly. She plans to shop first. "

"That's great news. If she is going shopping then I have time to get to the hotel before she does. Thanks, Rhys."

* * *

When Laramie arrived back at the hotel, she stopped at the front desk to check for messages. She had one that confirmed her meeting the next morning. *Yes, that is what I was looking for today. Ah, for the sweet victories.*

She walked thru the lobby and stopped in front of the Writer's Bar when she dropped one of the messages. She bent over and picked up the paper. When she stood, Akihiro stood in front of her. She met his gaze and remained calm.

"What do you want? I thought I made it clear to stay away from me."

"Sometimes you don't get what you want. I came here to talk to you. Will you at least sit with me?" asked Akihiro.

"No, but I will give you two minutes which is two minutes more than you deserve."

"I know you stopped at the hotel and then the condo. I spent the morning on the deck and never heard you. Believe me, I wish I did. I want to make this work. I miss you. I am so lonely without you."

"*Really*? Was that before or after Christina was there? Did you forget that part? Though, I'm damn amazed at my timing. I felt guilty not giving you a chance to talk. Now I find that was my own stupidity. Not a mistake I'm likely to make again."

"Yes, Christina was there but to pick up the last of her belongings, nothing more. We both said goodbye."

"How convenient and yes, I do believe you. Your two minutes are up. Goodbye, Akihiro."

"Don't leave. I can't let you go. *I love you, Laramie.*" He stared into her eyes and waited for a response.

He caught her off guard. She never expected to hear him say that. Her eyes glassed over with tears.

"You bastard, how dare you say that to me now. *Now,* you find you miss me, need me and love me. What happens a week from now when I'm back in San Francisco? You won't miss me, need me, or love me. You'll continue just as you did before. I'm sorry it's all too little, too late."

"Why are you being so obstinate? Why are you acting like some immature child? Those were the words you wanted to hear and now I've said them. Why isn't this enough for you? What do you want from me?"

"I'll answer you then I'm leaving. I gave you every part of me, every part. I exposed my thoughts and feelings completely. I was petrified to have sex with you. I was inexperienced and embarrassed but I wanted to be with you so I pushed aside my own fears. You asked me to trust you and I did. All I ever expected was the same honesty and trust. What did you do? You hid behind lies. Even now, you come here and omit facts from the story. You had no intention of saying Christina was at the condo, regardless of the reason. You waited to see what I knew first. You don't trust me enough to be honest. You want to control the situation by what you're willing to disclose. So now, you come here to tell me you love me but you still aren't honest. That isn't love, Akihiro."

He spoke without thinking it through, retaliating in anger. "You're wrong Laramie. I do love you. I'm just not perfection like you are. I just don't know what to say to make you happy. I don't think you want to be happy. I think you were a sad little girl who grew up to be a sad woman and you don't know anything else. I think happiness scares you."

Those words stung and stunned Laramie. For a moment, she fought for words but found none.

"You're right. Okay? You're right. Do you feel better now?" She pushed him aside. "Then let me just wallow in my world of unhappiness."

"If you walk away now, it's over. I'm not coming back."

Akihiro was firm in his decision. He didn't want her to leave but he no longer wanted to throw barbs at each other either. It was obvious they both hurt. Laramie stood frozen at the ultimatum. She wanted the bickering to end but didn't see a resolution in sight. Both were headstrong individuals. She turned back to face him.

"Akihiro, I… I…" She wanted to say I love you but felt it wouldn't change a thing. They would continue to tear at each other over the next week. He hoped she would finish with the words he wanted to hear. "… I can't do this. Goodbye."

His chest sank. *No. Please change your mind Laramie. That wasn't the answer you were supposed to say.* He wanted to chase after her and not allow her to leave. He knew he couldn't force her to be with him. They each turned and walked away from the greatest love they ever felt.

Chapter 29

LARAMIE AND RHYS worked together most of the morning as they reviewed their documents. The receptionist knocked on the conference room door to say Laramie's guest arrived. Laramie walked with her back to the lobby to greet her guest.

"Good morning Mr. Cheung. I am so glad you were able to come on such short notice. Please follow me. I have everything prepared in the conference room."

"It is a pleasure to meet you, Miss Holden. I have to say your offer has intrigued me."

The elderly Chinese man walked behind Laramie to the room. Laramie asked if she could get him a tea or water. He declined politely. Rhys stood up when they entered the room.

"Mr. Cheung, this is my banker Rhys Davis. He is here to witness the contract and verify funds. Rhys, this is Mr. Ong Cheung. He is the owner of the property next to the Tanjong Hotel."

Both men shook hands and sat at the table. *What is she doing? Akihiro is in process to buy that property from him.* Laramie pulled out a lease agreement and wanted to review the terms.

"As we discussed on the phone, you have no written contract of sale or lease on your property, correct?" Mr. Cheung nodded in agreement. "I must tell you I have admired your property. The location is perfect for what I am looking to build. I represent a corporation in the United States that builds hotels. Normally, we construct large capacity chains. However, I have convinced them this is a golden opportunity to venture into a different area and they agreed."

"Miss Holden, I don't know if this is a good idea. I feel as though I have promised this land to another."

"Yes, I am aware of Mr. Amori's interest in the property but how long can you wait to see that come to fruition?" Rhys coughed on her statement. *She knows Akihiro wants it. Now by placing me in the room, she knows the business can't be disclosed. She is more clever than I thought. I have to think of a way to terminate this.*

"May I review this contract?" Rhys asked.

"Understand we are not buying the property, we are leasing it. You still maintain ownership," continued Laramie.

Laramie explained each section to Mr. Cheung. Rhys sat by unable to do a thing. Laramie had him locked. The terms were beyond normal compensation. Mr. Cheung was a fool not to sign the agreement since everything was in his favor.

"Let's just recap. The terms are for ninety-nine years, which is standard. However, this clause is extremely important. DemCorp has one year in which to begin construction if they fail to comply all monies of good faith are nonrefundable."

"What monies of good faith? That isn't standard in a lease agreement," Rhys stated, confused by her statement. Mr. Cheung looked at Laramie for an explanation.

"Yes, I am aware of that. I am so confident this is the right deal for Mr. Cheung that I am putting up the initial capital personally."

"May I ask how much money, Miss Holden?" Mr. Cheung questioned.

"Absolutely, I have a bank check from Bank of America in the amount of two million U.S. dollars." Rhys looked at her in disbelief. *She is pressuring him with the money. He doesn't stand to lose anything. I'd even take that deal.*

Mr. Cheung was quite surprised. He knew the property was worth six million dollars at most. *Why does she put this money up personally? Is this a trick?*

"Miss Holden, that is a sizeable amount of money even for my property. Am I to understand you want a ninety-nine year lease with a payment of two million dollars? If you do not build within a year, the land remains mine and so does the money. Is that correct?"

"Yes that is correct. Rhys, can you confirm the terms for Mr. Cheung?"

Rhys reviewed the terms of the contract and confirmed the answer to Mr. Cheung.

"There is one stipulation." Laramie continued. "The lease has to be signed *today.* I leave for the States in a few days and I have to bring the documents home with me. I realize this puts added pressure on you and for that I truly apologize."

Mr. Cheung knew that Rhys acted on the behalf of the bank. He knew the terms were accurate. He knew Miss Holden was a beautiful woman and intelligent. Still he was unsure about the contract. He felt a responsibility to Akihiro. Laramie saw the unrest in his eyes. She knew she had to do something to persuade him.

Laramie spoke in a very calm manner, "Mr. Cheung, I can sense you are uneasy about this deal. I am willing to let you take the contract to your family and attorney for discussion. Please remember this has to be signed today or I must withdraw the contract."

"Yes, I understand Miss Holden. I appreciate you tolerance and will return with an answer later today. Thank you very much. Mr. Davis, a pleasure meeting you."

Laramie walked Mr. Cheung to the door and then returned to the conference room.

"You have puzzled me, Laramie. I don't understand why a woman of your brilliance would make such a foolish contract. You offer of good faith monies in an amount that is thirty percent of the actual value of the land if you were able to purchase it. It appears that you are giving him two million dollars to sign the contract. Can you explain the logic?"

"No." She looked through her papers to finish their discussion from earlier in the morning. "Let's take a quick break and then we can pick up where we left off. Is that all right with you?"

Rhys agreed. He wanted to ask her not to go through with the Cheung property but knew she was resolute. He wanted to call Akihiro and inform him of the meeting. However, Laramie now controlled the situation. Rhys entered his office and picked up the phone.

"Kat, I have a tremendous problem. Mr. Cheung was here this morning and Laramie Holden offered him a sizeable amount of money to lease his property."

"You have to stop her. That is Akihiro's dream. He's worked hard to buy that land. How much money are we talking? Is it possible to buy her out?"

"I don't think so. She offered two million dollars on a bank check."

"Two million dollars for a lease? We can't compete with that. She knew how to out bid him. What is the status on Akihiro's business loan? Can you find an answer today? Did he sign the contract?"

"No, not yet. He has until the end of the business day. Akihiro's loan is still in underwriting."

"Would it help if I talked to her? Do you think she would listen?"

"Kat, you can't say a word. She would know immediately that I called you. I can be fired for disclosing any of this."

"We can't win this. I know she is hurt but I never thought she would go this far. She doesn't understand what that land means to him, not completely. I won't be the one to tell him. I can't do it."

"Look, I have to run. I'm only on a break. I will tell you more later. Bye."

Laramie passed the reception desk and commented on the lovely flowers. The receptionist informed her that the flowers arrived for her. Laramie cautiously picked up the card and read it.

> Dear Laramie,
> I was wrong. I am extremely sorry. Let's talk this over, please.
>
> I love you, Akihiro

A pang of guilt passed through Laramie's body. It didn't matter how he felt; it was too late. She knew Mr. Cheung would be back to sign the contracts. She had no way to back out. *Even if I talked to him, he would hate me for destroying his dream. I should have thought this through better. I didn't leave any room to reverse things. What was I thinking? How did I become this malicious woman? He was right. I create my own unhappiness.* Laramie left the flowers on the counter. When she reached the conference room, she had a message to immediately call Edward. *He knows. I'm afraid to hear the trouble. I wonder if I could avoid him a day or two?*

When Rhys entered the room, he informed Laramie that she had additional messages from Edward since the break. He told her she could use his phone if she needed privacy.

She dialed Edward at home and cringed when he picked up the phone.

"Laramie, what the *hell* do you think you are doing? I received a call from Frank Paradise thanking me for your astute real estate skills. You are not there to be buying property."

"I know that Edward but I thought I was a tremendous opportunity. And we didn't buy the land, we are just leasing it."

"Leasing the land? Then tell me why you lied to Andrew and had him wire two million dollars out of your trust?"

"It's for good faith and so the owner would sign the contract."

"*What?* Are you out of your mind? What is going on over there? This isn't like you to lose judgment. This was a simple assignment. Close the deal on the hotel, rest and relax. Have you screwed up the original deal as well?" he yelled into the phone.

"No, Edward, that deal is almost finished. Actually, I have to go back to the meetings. I will call you later."

"Laramie, do not hang up this phone. We are not ..." *Click.*

Laramie never heard Edward so angry. She was sorry she started this and sorry she lied to the people she loved. *I am no better than Akihiro. I stood there and preached honesty and trust and I have compromised both. I have hurt everyone I love by this. What have I become?*

When she arrived in the conference room, Rhys sat beside Mr. Cheung, who returned. Laramie knew she had to finish what she started. It was too late for her to back out. She greeted him and slid the documents across the table. Rhys knew something was wrong by her face even though she tried to hide it. After Mr. Cheung finished, Laramie handed him the bank check. She thanked him profusely and accompanied him to the lobby. She called the sign company regarding the posting, as it was required for all DemCorp properties. She specifically asked them to wait until the Thursday afternoon to install it. They agreed it was no trouble at all. She then contacted the Graphics Department at DemCorp to send the files for printing.

Rhys sat in the room numb over what transacted. He desperately wanted to call Akihiro and Kat. However, Laramie's sudden disposition worried him.

"Laramie, are you all right? What is upsetting you? I noticed it when you arrived back from break. Is something wrong at home?"

"Rhys, I have never made such a poor choice than right now. I did something I regret and now must live with it. Have you ever done that?"

"We all make mistakes Laramie, some are larger than others. Do you want to discuss it?"

She shook her head no and began to tear. Rhys handed her a tissue and tried to get her to sit.

"I hope you don't mind if we end things here today. I'm afraid I wouldn't be able to concentrate like I should. I apologize for my lack of professionalism, truly."

"At least let me drive you to the hotel, please."

Along the way to Raffles, Rhys tried to comfort her. He knew she regretted the lease of the Cheung property. She wanted to confess to someone how awful she felt but she knew she didn't deserve a sympathetic ear. She thanked Rhys for the ride and entered the hotel. Immediately, Rhys called Kat.

"I have terrible news. Mr. Cheung signed the contract. While that is most distressing, Laramie wanted to cancel the offer but it was too late. I just dropped her off at the hotel and she is completely distraught. I'm afraid it is all too late."

"Akihiro will be devastated. I suppose we should remain silent and wait for the fallout to come. I hope she's not around when that happens."

* * *

The front desk at Raffles informed Laramie she had several phone calls from Edward stating that it required her immediate attention. After she entered her room, she called Edward.

"Hi Edward. I'm sorry I'm just getting back to you now."

"Laramie, I just don't understand what has gotten into you. Have you lost all your senses? You do realize this business deal you entered into was a financial disaster. We have raised you better than this. You are smarter than this so my anger must come as no surprise to you. On top of all of that, you lied to me and to Andrew. You have never lied to us in your life. What the hell is happening?"

"Edward, I am so sorry. I never meant to lie to you and Andrew and I feel awful about that. I let my anger the best of me and entered into that deal out of revenge. I don't know what I was thinking. I have never felt so bad than right now."

Laramie cried profusely into the phone. This display of emotion was a rarity for Edward to witness. Even at the death of her parents, Laramie cried very little.

"Laramie, Laramie dear, stop crying and tell me what happened. There must be some way I can help. Calm yourself and tell me what is happening there."

Laramie started from the beginning, omitting the sex, which Edward did not need to hear. She told him how she saw him at the party. She told him about the ultimatum at the hotel. She told him about the Cheung property. She regretted that she went to that extreme. She told him how Akihiro wanted to talk. She told Edward it was too late; the deal was complete.

"Edward, I just want to come home. I can't be here when he learns what I did. I can't bear to see his face."

"Laramie dear, I wish you would have called me. I cannot help you at this point. You have to face your actions even if it means you may see him again. Besides, you aren't finished with the DemCorp documents. This was a costly mistake, I don't mean the money, I mean your heart. Remember we all make poor choices. You're certainly not the first. Your parents could have told many stories about me when I was younger. We will discuss this new property deal when you come back. In the meantime, think clearly and act cautiously."

"I understand. You're absolutely right. I brought this on myself and I will deal with it. I love you and miss you. I'm truly sorry, Edward."

"Don't worry about Andrew and me. We could never stay mad with you. We love you too much. Try to get some sleep. Goodnight, Laramie."

Chapter 30

ANOTHER DAY WITHOUT *her. I miss her face, her smile. I can't stand this. I never should have made her choose. I should've given her more time. Kat was right all along. Why did I lash out like that? How did I allow her to set me off so quickly? I've become just as emotional as her. This isn't like me.* Akihiro sat at his desk with his hands clasped together. He knew he spoke harshly. He let his temper go at her expense. Depressed by the past few days, his concentration on business was negligible. Everything around him felt empty. He felt empty.

Kat watched him from her chair. In all the years of friendship, she never witnessed his moods like this. She knew it would worsen when the leasing contract became public. She hoped for Laramie's sake, she was back in the States when that occurred.

* * *

Laramie struggled to get through the meetings. She was sharp and organized but the expression on her face spoke of sadness. Everyone in the room noticed it. She remained focused until they finished. She thanked everyone for their patience and persistence. After everyone cleared the conference room, Laramie cleaned up her papers. Rhys watched her from the other end of the table.

"Well Laramie, I suppose this is the end of your trip. You fly back tomorrow, don't you? Any last wishes before you leave?"

"If only that were possible. This was a difficult week for me personally and

I leave with many regrets. I've made irrational choices and I have to accept the consequences. This probably sounds like mass confusion to you. I just want you to know the real Laramie Holden was the person you met on Friday. I wasn't myself this week."

"Laramie, I don't know what troubles you but I can't imagine it can't be fixed somehow. You may not find a solution this week or next but you will find a way to set your life straight. I have every confidence in you."

She stood up and walked toward him. She thanked him and hugged him. He was a wonderful asset to her the past week. She gathered her things and left for her hotel to pack.

After she arrived back in her room, she packed up her clothes and shoes. She left out her change of clothes for tomorrow. She sat on her bed unsure what to do next. *How will I ever tell him I'm sorry? Even if I could, would he believe me? Why should he? I have never felt so much pain. I never thought so much love could hurt so bad. How will I get through the days anymore? What about the nights? They will be just as lonely. I'm sure once I'm back home everything will go back to normal. Someday I'll look back on this and laugh. Right?* She laid in bed unable to sleep most of the night. She wanted to stay awake in hopes tomorrow would not come.

Chapter 31

IT WAS EARLY in the morning when Akihiro drove to the hotel. The past week was miserable without Laramie. He called her several times at Raffles but the staff would only take messages. He wished he hadn't given her an ultimatum. Kat was correct; it did backfire. Akihiro knew Laramie was leaving for the States today and tried not to think about it, about her. He knew it was useless. His best thought was to pour himself into his work and let time heal the wounds.

As he drove around Mr. Cheung's property, he noticed two men posting a sign. The side posts and backing were up and they were getting ready to paste the cover text. Akihiro pulled off the road in front of the men and asked what they were doing. A thin Malaysian man explained that someone leased the property and planned to build on it. They were there to assemble the marquee announcing the new hotel. *Lease to build? That can't be. Mr. Cheung agreed to hold the property while we waited for the bank documents..*

"Well, can you tell me who's leasing the property?" Akihiro couldn't understand why his neighbor would do such a thing. *We had an agreement.*

"Yes, it's some company called DemCorp," stated the worker.

"NO, no, she wouldn't do that to me. I can't believe it. That bitch." Akihiro shook his head in disbelief.

"Excuse me, sir?" asked the worker.

"No… nothing. Thanks for the information."

Akihiro turned his car around and headed for the city. He knew he had to reach Laramie before she left for the airport. This time he wasn't going to listen to the staff or anyone else. This time he had something to say and she was going to listen. As he crossed into the city, he had to deal with the traffic of everyone else going to work. He pulled onto the East-West Parkway to try to circumvent the bustling traffic. At least traffic was moving at a steady pace. As the hotels became closer in view, he stepped on the gas and started passing the slower drivers. He received a few honks but made it through quickly. He started to lose patience dealing with one-way traffic. The closer he got to the hotel the more agitated he became. *I just can't believe she did this. She knew that owning property was my dream. What sort of woman would go to this trouble over a broken romance? Three days ago, I was there to speak with her. I confessed my love and ask forgiveness. Where is the sanity in any of this? Now… now, I want to strangle her.*

Akihiro raced his car to the entrance of the hotel. He stopped long enough to place the gear in park but not long enough for the valet to greet him. He wasn't thinking rationally, clouded by his anger.

A lovely young woman greeted him at the reception counter. "May I help you, Sir?"

"Yes, I need to see Laramie Holden. I know she is a guest here. I do not care what restrictions she has imposed on visitors. I need to see her *now*." Akihiro stood firm.

"Sir…" she tried to respond.

"I don't care about your rules. I demand to see her immediately. I will knock on every room if I have to until I find her," demanded Akihiro pounding his fist on the granite counter.

"Sir, if I may? Miss Holden has checked out. She left about fifteen minutes ago. The driver took her to the airport," she explained.

"Great, thanks. I apologize too."

Akihiro ran out the doors and jumped into his car. He barely made it out of the parking area without running down any innocent bystanders. As he pulled onto the street, surrounding people looked to see where the screeching of tires originated. *This is going to be close. I may make it in time and catch her at check-in.* Akihiro continued his weaving through traffic. He hoped Buddha was on his side and all the police were elsewhere in town.

In the distance, Akihiro could see the entrance for the airport. He knew he had to park his car in the short-term parking lot and run for the building. As the stress mounted, he began to sweat. His movements were agitated and his patience wore thin. He tried to think what he would say to her but he was bewildered.

Laramie rolled her luggage into Changi Airport. She was sad to leave Singapore but more afraid to face the trouble she caused. She followed the signs to checkout number three. The long rows of ticketing agents made the process more efficient than at home. Since she traveled first class, she didn't have to wait in any lines. The agent placed the stickers on her luggage handle and directed her to Immigration.

She fumbled through her purse until she found her passport. Other than a few items of clothing and souvenirs, she really didn't have anything to declare. Normally, she would pass through the station without a care but she wanted to get home. She wanted to be in her safety blanket and surround herself with friends and family again. After she walked through Immigration, she sat on a nearby chair to get her things reorganized to pass through the security checkpoint. As she walked toward her next stop, she heard her name. Thinking it a mistake, she continued to walk. *No, I'm sure I heard my name.*

"Laramie, wait," Akihiro shouted.

The immigration guards asked him to step away from the desk area unless he was a passenger. He called out to her again, however this time she turned. She just stared plain faced in his direction, almost hypnotized. *Oh my God, he knows.* Akihiro stepped back to avoid arrest but was still in plain sight through the glass panels.

"*Please*, do not get on that plane. Come out here and talk to me... *Laramie*." Travelers around them turned to see what the commotion regarded.

In her eyes, pools of tears welled up. She looked at the ground and slowly raised her head back up as tears trailed down her cheeks. She knew he had read the sign and that was what brought him there. She felt shame, the shame of destroying his dream out of revenge. She thought they would be even by hurting him but it was clear her deed only brought guilt and sorrow not vindication. It seemed all too unreal the events of the past three weeks.

"Laramie, don't do this. I am pleading you." Akihiro turned in a circle with his hands in his hair. His disbelief of the situation became emotional. He wasn't sure why he wanted her to stay. He could see the emotion in her face. It was not a smile for the victor but sorrow. *Why does she confuse me like this? We've both been hurt.* Did he still love her or did he hate her? Where did it go from there?

Laramie shook her head slowly, wiped her eyes and turned back toward her gate. She didn't want the last thing she saw to be his face, at least not under this circumstance. As she took a deep breath, she walked away and didn't turn back once. *How will I ever look at myself in a mirror? Who is the person I'll see?* She heard Akihiro call her name a few more times but Laramie continued to walk away, she could no longer look him in the eye. Her cell phone rang. She knew it was Akihiro but did not answer. Shortly, she would board her plane and this would end.

Akihiro was befuddled. *She just can't get away like this. I can't let her leave.* As he walked toward the parking lot, he had one last thought. *Maybe, I can talk to a ticket agent and get a pass to the gate.* He has seen this regularly with people picking up teenage children or the elderly flying alone. He darted between people to get to the Singapore Airline counter. There was a short line but luckily, there was no line for First Class passengers.

"Pardon me, Madam. It is very important that I get a pass to your gate. My fiancé just went through security and I missed her. We had a fight and I can't let her fly home without the chance to correct things. Please, can you help me?" Akihiro lied to play on her sympathies.

"I am so sorry, Sir. We can't let anyone continue as a guest to the gates." The ticket agent sincerely apologized. "It is the policy of the airport and the airlines."

"Can't you say I am assisting a passenger? Please this is extremely important. Haven't you ever been in love? Had a fight? I can't let it go like this. *Please.*"

Akihiro was about to beg her when she said, "Sir, even if I can give you a pass to enter, I do not believe you have your passport with you to pass through Immigration." She was correct. It was heart wrenching to be this close and not be able to catch Laramie. Akihiro started his walk back to his car. It was over. That which seemed to him to be some of the best weeks of his life quickly turned to one of the worst. He was upset at losing the property next door, upset at Laramie for not seeing him, and upset with himself for not stating the truth from the very beginning. *How could I have made so many poor choices? How did I let this stranger affect my life so quickly?* Akihiro had plenty of time to reflect on his thoughts on his drive back to the hotel.

Laramie sat on the stool at Harry's Bar. Still visibly shaken at seeing Akihiro, she asked the bartender to make her a rum and coke, heavy on the rum. The bartender tried to make polite conversation especially since the place was nearly empty for so early in the morning. Laramie smiled at his attempt but declined to chat as he set her drink down on the bar. *That was a close call. Too close.* She knew the sign had posted earlier than the time she specified. Her attempt to sneak quietly out of the country almost met with close disaster. She knew she was safe on this side of the terminal.

As Laramie sat back in her chair, she spent her remaining time reflecting on the events of the last three weeks. She accomplished her business right as she planned. As much as she wanted to forget Akihiro, she couldn't. She knew she was in love with him despite the shouting match and avoidance. She tried to talk herself out of her feelings. *Laramie, you will be home shortly and life will get back to normal. Of course, I still have to face Edward and Andrew. I hope I have the good sense to learn from this. Now I know how anger and pain can cloud my judgment. I know I will never forget him but I hope the pain passes quickly. I never want to feel pain like this again.*

She realized she learned quite a bit about him in the thirteen days they spent together. In the dating world that would be equivalent to about two months. It was also the longest she had been with a man since her relationship in college. She reflected on the first day she met Akihiro and chuckled at thinking he was the bartender. He was so handsome and funny. She was comfortable around him, which was difficult for the controlling attorney in her. Laramie loved the places he took her sightseeing, especially the Botanical Gardens. She thought of their first night together, his touch, and his kiss, the feel of his body and the warmth of his embrace. He made her feel like a woman, not an insecure college student taking whatever her boyfriend gave. That night set a completely new standard in that genre. Laramie reflected on their last night together, dancing in her bungalow and making love, at least what she felt was love. *Why couldn't he just be honest? Why couldn't I be honest?* She knew the answer would have prevented the best few weeks of her life from ever happening.

It didn't matter how strong her drink was, she wasn't going to forget him for a long time. The pain of her heartache was something that would linger long after she returned home. She placed her empty glass on the bar and walked slowly to her gate. She was in no frame of mind to shop or look at souvenirs that might remind her of places they had been. Unknowingly, her depression started to take hold.

Laramie waited at the gate for the boarding announcement. When the gate attendant called First Class passengers, Laramie sauntered down the ramp to board her plane. She settled in her seat and pulled out the monthly airline magazine. The flight attendant noticed her from the arriving flight of three weeks ago. Not wanting to reveal her personal woes, Laramie smiled and told the attendant how much she loved the country. She really did love Singapore.

As the plane lifted off the runway, Laramie knew it was really over. She quietly sat looking out the window and silently cried. She was alone… again.

*   *   *

Akihiro arrived at his office. After he walked in and slammed the door, he sat at his desk unable to decipher his emotions. *Why? Why of all things did she go after the Cheung property? I can't believe she did this. As much as I hate her right now, I still want her here. I just can't let go of her. How did we let it get this far?* Kat knocked on the door and asked if she could come in. Akihiro agreed.

"I saw the sign next door. You want to talk about it?"

"I don't think it will do any good. That was my future, the hotel's future. Now it's gone. How can I expand without the land?"

"Well, all hope may not be lost. I spoke to Rhys yesterday and he told me what happened."

"*You knew?* And you didn't tell me? Why?" Akihiro replied angrily.

"Because, she had Rhys in the meeting. He was subject to nondisclosure of the deal until it was public record which now it is. He would have lost his job if you or I contacted her or Mr. Cheung."

"Wasn't there any way to stop her?"

"No. But wait until I tell you the terms of the contract. Apparently, the lease term is ninety-nine years, normal. However, if that company doesn't break ground in one year, the contract is void, not normal. In essence, we have to wait a year and it may be possible to purchase the land."

"One year? Why would she do that? It doesn't make sense. Even if the lease becomes void, I will still have to negotiate with Mr. Cheung again. I am disappointed and shocked he would break our agreement."

"I agree with you. But, you need to hear the rest of the story. Laramie paid him a two million dollar signing bonus. The money came from her *personal* account."

"Signing bonus? She had *two* million dollars? Kat, this doesn't make any sense."

"Oh, I know. It gets worse. When the one-year mark is reached, and construction has not commenced, not only is the contract void but Laramie loses the two million dollars as well. The money was nonrefundable. So, who could blame Mr. Cheung for signing?"

"That has to be the worst financial deal I've ever heard. The property was only worth six million. Didn't she see that? So, her brilliance ends at the boardroom. Kat, how could a woman say she was so in love yet turn around and do something so vicious?"

"The same way you went to the airport to stop her. Sure, you were livid but part of you wanted her to stay, part of you still loves her. Besides, she almost cancelled the deal. Rhys said after the break when she returned to the conference room, she wanted to back out but Mr. Cheung had come back to sign the papers. The deal almost didn't happen. I don't believe she entered the deal for financial gain, only to hurt you. Rhys said she was depressed and left for the day afterwards. It sounds to me like she is still in love with you."

Akihiro sat forward in his chair as he rested his elbows on the desk. He covered his face with his hands and sighed.

"Despite all of this, I do still love her and want her. It's too late. It was over the minute she walked on that plane."

"Aki, I saw some really explosive emotions from her and you. I hardly believe it's over. Anyway, you have a pile of work that needs reviewed and signed. I can't order supplies until you sign off so, get moving."

Kat shut the door behind her and went back to her desk. Akihiro leaned back in his chair and kicked up his heels on the desk. *This isn't over Laramie Holden. I'm not finished with you and I'm certainly not ready to let go. We will meet up again. I don't know when or where but it will happen.*

Chapter 32

LARAMIE UNPACKED HER suitcase and put her things away in her bathroom. She felt so lonely in her apartment. Everything felt different, empty. She had no desire to go out or call her friends. She knew eventually that Liz or Gillian would call her for a love update. *How am I going to respond now? Oh yes, I'm still in love with him and he says he's in love with me. Well… until I screwed him out of his dream by being a bitch. Oh yeah, that sounds like a great vacation.* Many times on the flight, she teetered on calling him when she arrived home. However, her fears and guilt prevented her.

She thought about the week ahead with regret. She knew she had to face Edward and Andrew ultimately. She hoped news of her real estate venture was not public in the firm. She feared the story would compromise her reputation. *I hope my desk is stacked with files. The more work I can bury myself in the better.*

Laramie tried to watch television but of course, every show had a connection to Singapore. She turned on her stereo but the music made her cry over Akihiro. *I don't think I can ever hear 'Iris' again. How am I going to get through this? It's only been two days since I left. Should I call him and tell him I sorry? Would he even take my call? I wouldn't. How can I be so smart and yet so stupid? Why did I have to go for the most drastic item? Why didn't I just walk away?*

Shortly after six, Laramie's phone rang. Edward wanted to make sure she arrived home safely. More importantly, he wanted to be sure that Laramie was fine. Her crying left him uneasy. He remembered when her parents died, Laramie remained stoic for quite a while before she showed any emotion.

Many of the family thought she tried to find a logical reason. When there was not an answer to her quest, she finally expressed her sorrow.

"How was the flight back, Laramie?" he asked calmly, testing the waters.

"It was smooth. I didn't expect anything less."

"What about you? How are you feeling? You had me quite worried while you were away."

"I know and I am deeply sorry Edward. Apparently, I'm not the smart person I thought I was. I made foolish decisions without any thought. I allowed that to cloud my judgment. Now I need to keep that from happening again."

"Laramie, you will do it again. We all have been there. Of course, for me it was a younger age. Falling in love makes people do the craziest things. But when you are there, it all seems normal. Ask me stories about your parents some time. You will find you are just like they were."

"Really, my parents did irrational things? I always thought they were smart people."

"Being smart has nothing to do with being in love. Your mother could run your father ragged and he loved every minute of it. They even saved me from a crazy woman more than a few times."

"I'm glad you said something. I feel better knowing I'm not the only person. I'm glad I have you, Edward."

"I'm glad I have you, too, Laramie. I will see you on Monday morning. We can talk more then. Bye, Dear."

Hearing Edward tell stories made Laramie feel better. She remained frustrated with her emotions and unable to find a solution.

* * *

Another weekend has passed without Laramie. I don't feel any better and I don't see an end to this. I should have given her space and time to think. Maybe if I hadn't pressured her, the outcome would've been different. On the other hand, the future of my hotel rests in her hands. She has the ability to push or delay DemCorp from building. How can I change the events? She was hurt but she was sad too. Rhys believes she wanted out. Could that be true? Does that mean she still loves me? Do I care if she loves me? She ranted on being truthful and honest. Where was the honesty in stealing my land?

Akihiro visited his parents as he normally did on weekends. He knew his mother would question him about Laramie. He wasn't sure how to answer her. He knew his father would ask about the loan for the Cheung property. He wasn't sure how to answer that either.

As he entered the home, he saw Shinji first.

"Hey, tell me what happened. Did you and Laramie work it out or did she leave you standing?" Shinji teased.

"She not only left me standing, she buried me along the way."

"What does that mean?"

"I mean before she left, she leased the Cheung property out from under me."

"What? No way. I can't believe she would do that." Shinji stood in complete shock.

Lucia entered the living room where the boys stood. She caught the last part of the conversation and questions. She asked, "What do you mean she leased the property? She took your dream from you? This same woman who loved you? I cannot believe what I am hearing."

"Mum, there is no one angrier than me. In some distorted way, I pushed her to that point. I said some rough things to her in anger. I didn't mean to but she made me so furious when she wouldn't listen to reason. I gave her an ultimatum and it backfired. No lectures, I've already gotten one from Kat. When I found out, I drove to her hotel and wanted to strangler her but she already checked out. I tried to track her down at the airport and was blocked. I saw her but she wouldn't come back through Immigration to talk."

"What has gotten into you, Akihiro? That is not like to you to be so emotional and rash in your decisions."

Shinji chimed in, "Yes, but you haven't met Laramie Holden either."

"Akihiro, what do you do now for land? Your plans to expand are over. Could you build at new location? I mean construct a second hotel? Perhaps on one of the islands?"

"I've thought about that. The lease on the land expires if they don't break ground in a year. In the mean time, I will look for additional land for a second location. Bintan is out. While they have the Banyan Tree already, I think the location is too remote. I was thinking about Batam. It has an airport and ferry transportation from here. Besides, I know a few people in real estate who can research that for me."

Shinji knew Akihiro directed the comment to him. "I will look into it on Monday. I just never thought she would do something like that. I was totally wrong about her."

"No, you weren't. You are men and you have no idea what a woman is capable of if you push her into a corner. The fault lies with you and her. You both acted irrationally when you were hurt. I'm sure she thinks the same thing about you."

Akihiro knew his mother was correct. She had such insight to relationships that it amazed her sons. They didn't understand that with her years came wisdom and experience.

* * *

"Laramie, it's great to have you back. Mr. Graham is waiting for you in his office," said the receptionist, Linda.

"Thank you. It's good to be home," Laramie half smiled.

Laramie walked along the corridor to the furthest office. When she arrived, she knocked on the door.

"Come in Laramie. I've been waiting for you. Right now, I want to talk to you alone then we will call in Andrew. Sit down."

Get ready because here it comes. Laramie sat in an oversized tufted wingback chair. Edward's office was reminiscent of an old English manor. She knew some of the furniture was his fathers that had no other place besides Edward's home. The dark paneling on the walls had a cold feel and made the room feel even more formal. She felt as though she was at the Principal's office whenever she entered.

"How much damage control have you had to do? I really hope this hasn't gotten around the office," Laramie inquired.

"Lucky for you, this has stayed between Andrew and me. Your credibility would be floundering at this point. Anyway, you already know I am executor of your parents' estate and trustee of your trust. However, as you approach thirty years of age, I will no longer be in charge of your financial planning. You will be responsible for yourself. We thought you had a level head until now and quite frankly we worry about handing over the reins."

"I know I made a mistake. Yes, it was very costly but I hope the return will make up for the down stroke."

"Laramie, this has nothing to do with the amount of money, it has to do with your thought process. You went into that deal with complete disregard for anything or anybody. Just how many times do you think you could afford to do that? DemCorp stood to lose nothing. All the capital was yours."

"I know and I am terribly sorry. If I could reverse it, I would." Laramie became emotional but quickly regained her composure.

"When you turn thirty, you have the option of leaving the money in the trust or making your own investments. My suggestion is to leave it and add the provision of two signatures to release funds for the first year. Once you have proven yourself to Andrew and me, we will release you the entire amount. Do you understand what I am saying?"

"Yes, you want me to have Andrew or you cosign any release of funds for an additional year. I haven't any problems with that since I haven't any plans to withdraw from there again. Is that why you wanted Andrew to join us?"

"No. You owe him an apology for lying over the phone. He went out of his way to help you. He trusted your word because he trusted you. You have a lot to prove to fill those shoes again."

Laramie knew Edward was correct. She needed to apologize to Andrew. Both Edward and Andrew reared Laramie since her high school years and initial years at the firm. In essence, she was their child, their protégé. Edward picked up the telephone and called Andrew to join them. Andrew was still the short round man from her parents' youth. Of course, his face aged and his weight went up but still one of the best numbers guy in the city. He waddled into Edward's office and sat in the chair beside Laramie.

"Andrew, I'm so sorry I lied to you. I can't even give you a good reason for it. I made a poor choice and compromised my relationship with you and Edward. I hope you will forgive me." Her sincerity was evident.

"Laramie. Dear, all we want is what is best for you. If you wanted revenge on a boyfriend, we could've helped you for nothing. Two million dollars, even for a great land purchase, is not the way to handle it. Not even Violet spent that much money when mad at me. I'm sure Edward has told you that news of that deal will not leave this office. I hope you have learned from this."

"I truly have. I am actually looking forward to getting back to work and putting the past behind me. I love you both." Laramie walked over, kissed and hugged her mentors and pseudo-fathers. Edward gestured for her to leave and she left.

Laramie walked into her office. *Ah, this is more like it.* Pictures of her friends dotted her view as she spun in her chair. *I missed my office, my personal sanctuary. Holy cow! Didn't anyone work while I was gone*? The stacks of folders on her desk teetered on each side. *Well, I suppose its best to start at the top.* She leafed through each folder and divided them by date received then importance of client. Some folders went into a separate pile for the associates and paralegals to work on. She pulled the first folder down and opened it. *Hmm… a no compete contract was breached. Who are the parties? This could be a fun one.* By the end of her first day back at work, Laramie found her groove.

Chapter 33

LARAMIE WENT OUT of her way to make up for Singapore. She regained her status with Edward and Andrew. On Saturday mornings, she spent many hours working to clear files off her desk. The more face time Laramie put in, the more face time the associates had. This created an uneasy feeling among the associates. They were unsure whether she was there for herself or as a commandant for them. It didn't matter to Laramie; the more she concentrated on business the less time she reflected on Singapore. She picked up the phone many times and dialed the number for the Tanjong, then quickly hung up. *What would I say at this point? I wonder if he has forgotten me? Though, the land deal probably has my picture on a dartboard in his office. I can hardly blame him. I have to find a way to forget this. Forget him.*

Laramie had one week to shop before Christmas. Normally, she loved to shop but lately she worked so many hours that it exhausted her. However, she promised Lian lunch and a day of shopping. They agreed to meet at noon at Daily Grill on Geary Street, just off Union Square.

Laramie entered the restaurant to see that Lian arrived first. She waved off the hostess and walked directly to the rear of the place. Lian stood up and hugged her friend.

"It is so good to see you. We wish you'd take a break from work and visit more. I can't imagine being there all the time is healthy. You need to rest."

"I know and I agree. With the days getting shorter, it's dark when I get up and when I get home. I am so tired but I need to prove to Edward that I'm back on my game."

"You look pale. You're probably not eating well either. All carry out food at work? You need a break from work, Laramie. Go out. Have fun. Date even."

"*Date?* I don't think so. I'm just not good at relationships. Besides most men feel threatened by me."

"Those are excuses. I know a few really nice Chinese guys that are single..."

"No. I appreciate it but no thanks."

"You're still carrying a torch for him aren't you? That's why you spend your time at work and why you won't date. If that's the way you feel, have you tried calling him?"

"Oh please. Would you talk to me if you were him? I wouldn't. I can't believe I was such a bitch. I replay that in my head and see so many different scenarios. Why didn't I choose something less drastic?"

"How does the saying go? 'Hell hath no fury like a woman scorned.' You should see me with P.M.S. I become this horrible monster. I feel sorry for Manny at least once a month."

Laramie laughed with Lian. She needed this break from work. She needed the company of another woman who understood her problems. "Let's order so we can get shopping."

The waitress brought both ladies their salads. Lian dove right in however Laramie stared at hers first. For some reason, it no longer looked appetizing. She took a few bites and headed for the restroom. She bent over the toilet and vomited. *Great, just what I need is a virus with Christmas one week away and no other time to shop.* She cleaned herself up and walked slowly back to the table.

"Are you okay?"

"Yes. This is what I get for a stomach full of coffee and no food. You are right I do need to eat better. God knows how old some of the food is in refrigerator. Yuck."

"Go for the yogurt, that's always to safest bet."

The ladies finished their lunch and headed to Macy's first. Laramie needed to cram a lot of shopping in this weekend. During the week, it was impossible to get away from the office. She pulled out her list of gifts. Edward's was always the hardest gift; he had everything he wanted already. Andrew and Violet were second on her list. They were equally as hard to buy a gift. Manny and Lian were the easiest. They both were clotheshorses. In the middle, she had Liz and Gillian, though their gifts were always something small but personal. Lian and Laramie agreed to call each other via cell phone to locate each other in the store. As Laramie's hands became full, she needed to rethink the amount of shopping that a person could accomplish in a day.

"Hey, Lian, where are you? My hands are full and I don't think I can carry one more package."

"I'm in Menswear but I'm just finishing up. Where are you?"

"Well, I'm in Ladies Fragrance. You just want to meet me there?"

"That's fine. Bye."

Their afternoon was great therapy for Laramie. The last time she shopped was in Singapore. She missed walking down Orchard Street. She loved being there to discover new stores and designers. With those thoughts, Laramie daydreamed of Akihiro. She missed him and still loved him. *Date? Is Lian crazy? In my head I will always compare him to Akihiro. That's not really fair but I can't help it. Everyone says I will forget him with time but it seems everything around me is a reflection of those days. My brain wants to say goodbye but my heart won't let go.*

"You're thinking about him again, aren't you?"

"Is it that obvious?" replied Laramie, feeling quite melancholy.

"Transparent, doll."

"It has to stop. I can't go through each day like this. But, for some reason I just can't let go. Stop me if I go on like a fool. Anyway, I see your hands are just as full. You want to stop for the day and pick up again tomorrow? I only have a few people left on my list, ooh, plus an exchange gift for the firm."

"That works for me. If I quit now, I'll be home before Manny and I can hide the gifts. Can you believe he still tries to peek? A grown man?"

The women exchanged their air kisses and departed for their homes. By the time Laramie entered her flat, her fingers were numb. *I should've called a cab. I'll remember that for tomorrow.* It neared dinner time and she looked into the refrigerator for anything to eat. *I don't even want to know how old that it. Gross. I really need to be organized at home.* As Laramie opened another food carton, the smell was so awful it caused her to run for the bathroom again. *Great, vomiting twice today. Maybe I am working too much. I hope I'm not getting some intestinal flu. I better make an appointment for meds on Monday. It would be awful to be sick over the holidays.*

The next morning Laramie felt so awful she had to cancel shopping with Lian. Her stomach felt queasy most of the morning. Around ten, she finally ate some dry cereal.

Later in the afternoon, when she felt better, she finished her shopping on the Internet. She hated to pay the high shipping cost for overnight delivery but she had no choice. *Super, my shopping is finished and I got to do it in my pajamas.* Lian called to check on her and Laramie told her it was probably some type of stomach virus. She promised to see the doctor in the morning.

Laramie walked into Dr. Grant's office at nine o'clock. She was a bit early but that also meant an early exit too. She sat patiently until the receptionist called her name. She entered one of the examination rooms and proceeded to tell her past life history, or at least it seemed so. They drew a vial of blood and asked for a urine sample. Laramie complied. She returned to her exam room and waited for the doctor.

"Good morning, Laramie. I haven't seen you in a long while. So you think it's a stomach virus? Your blood pressure is fine and you don't have a temperature. When was your last cycle?"

"Gee, I don't know. It has always been irregular. A couple months I think but I have been under a lot of stress so that affects it sometimes."

A medical technician knocked on the door and handed a sheet of paper to the doctor. He read her test results and made a few notes in the margin for his use.

"Well, you do not have a virus or mono. It seems you are pregnant."

The news completely shocked Laramie.

"*Pregnant*? That can't be. *No, no, no.* It has to be something else. Maybe the tests are wrong. Are you sure those are my results and not another patients?" The more time she thought about it, she knew it was quite possible. She began to sob. "No, that has to be wrong. I cannot be pregnant."

The doctor saw she was very emotional over the news. He placed his hand on her back and tried to comfort her. It didn't do any good. She was unable to fully grasp the news. She thanked the doctor for seeing her on such short notice. She asked him what she should do next. He said she had a few options, raise the baby or place the baby up for adoption. She was about seventeen weeks along, also too late to abort the pregnancy. After he left, she began to dress. She cried in the office before she was able to gain her composure. *Pregnant? What am I going to do?*

She walked to her office. Normally, she took a cab but she needed the time to think. She thought about her options. *A baby? But I'm alone. I know other people do it but they're not me. What am I going to tell Edward? How will this impact the firm? I can't hide it that's obvious. Damn it. What was I thinking to be unprotected? The bigger question is what about Akihiro? I can't call him and say 'hey, remember me? I'm pregnant.' That's the last thing a single man wants to hear from a woman, especially one who screwed him over.* She cried on and off along the way. *On the other hand, I'm not getting any younger and I don't have any prospects that I'd consider dating. Is this a blessing in disguise? It would mean my family, my real family. Of course, that would mean lifestyle changes. Dear God, what am I going to do?*

When she arrived on her floor, she asked if Edward was in his office. Linda said he was and she was free to enter. She walked inside the room and shut the door. She sat in the chair for a minute before Edward looked up from his papers.

"So, just a stomach virus? Nothing that's contagious I hope."

"No, not contagious. Not a virus either."

"Well go on. What is it?"

"I'm pregnant, about four months along." She began to sob again. She cried into her hands as her shoulders shook. Edward came around the desk and pulled up the other chair next to her. "What am I going to do, Edward? I feel like a kid myself. How am I going to get through this? How bad will this affect the firm? I'm just at a loss."

"Oh Laramie, I don't give a damn about the firm. Are you okay? I know this had to be devastating news. Look at me. Come on, look up. I am here to help you get through this. Do you understand me?" She nodded yes. "Your family and friends will support you through this and you'll be fine."

"I knew I was irresponsible with the land and money but I never expected this. It's supposed to happen to other people, not me. I don't know if I'm ready to be a single parent."

Edward chuckled, "You're never ready for parenthood. That job is impossible to plan. I remember you coming to me as a teenager. Remember I was a single man. We had some ups and downs but we made it okay, didn't we? Now you will do the same thing. Have you decided to keep the baby?"

"Yes, I thought about adoption but I don't think I could do it."

"Have you decided when you are going to tell Akihiro?"

"I'm not. I thought about it and I have done so much damage already. I am not going to add this to his misery. No, he has no reason to know."

"Laramie, I think you are making a terrible mistake. He is the father and don't you think he has a right to know?"

"No. Besides, he lives in Singapore and I live here. I don't want him back in my life out of guilt or servitude. No one is going to tell him. I seriously mean it Edward, promise me."

"I have learned long ago to stay out of other peoples affairs. I can only express my own opinions. I will respect your wishes but I feel he has the right to know. What's your next step?"

"Geez, I have no idea. I guess find a obstetrician. I don't even know any. Liz is the only one with kids and she's out of state."

"Let's call Violet and find out who she recommends."

Laramie spoke with Violet. However, she told Laramie how blessed she was to have a child. Her quick support caught Laramie off guard, usually Violet was judgmental. Violet gave her the name of her daughter's doctor, a leading Ob-Gyn at San Francisco Medical Center. Laramie thanked her and decided to call the physician from her office. She had many phone calls to make, namely to her friends.

She sat quietly in her office and stared out her window. She began to overcome the original shock and started to embrace the idea. *Wow! I'm going to be a mom. I can't believe it but it's true. This certainly explains why I keep getting sick.* She ran her hand softly over her belly and wondered when she would show. She thought about how her life would change and that scared her a bit. She thought about Akihiro. *Well, you gave me a gift I will always love.* She called the doctor and set up an appointment for the following week. *This is some kind of Christmas present.* She picked up the phone and called Liz first.

"Well, how y'all doing Lara? I haven't heard from you in a while and I was getting' worried." Laramie adored her southern accent. It made everything sound happy and inviting. "Are you ready for Christmas? I am not. I still haven't bought a thing for Randy and I only have a few days left. It has been crazy here with my in-laws coming to visit. Please tell me something good."

"Let me think. Are you sitting or running around?"

"I'm sittin'. Why?"

"I'm still in shock and I know you will be too. It seems that I am four months pregnant."

"*What*? Did you just say pregnant?"

"Yes. I thought I had some kind of intestinal flu so I went to the doctor. I cried at first. I was not prepared for that bit of news. However, the more I think about it, the better I feel."

"Oh darlin', a baby can never be bad news. It is truly a gift from God. Believe me, I know, I have two of them. How did Akihiro take the news?"

"I haven't told him. I'm not going to and neither is anyone else."

"Lara, that is not the right thing to do. He is the father and he should know. I know things ended badly but this is one way to make amends."

"Or make things worse. No one has thought of the idea that maybe he is happy with his life the way it is. There hasn't been one phone call of interest since then. Not that I expected anything differently. I'm not going to drop news of a baby. I don't think I could take the rejection of him not wanting either of us. I can't face that again. It was too painful to get over the first time." Laramie started to choke up as she spoke.

"Lara, you still are not over him. This could be your chance to reconnect. Have you ever thought of that, Sugar?"

"I will tell him, just not right now."

"Promise me you will tell him. I mean on a stack of bibles."

"I promise when the time is right. Anyway I have my doctor appointment next week and I'm curious how that will go."

"Well at four months you should start to show some belly. I remember with Amanda I didn't show until my sixth month. However, with Billy, I was huge the whole time. Have you told Gillian yet?"

"No, I called you first. As soon as we hang up, I'm calling her."

"I am so excited for you. After all that mess, something beautiful came out of it after all. Love you, Sweetie. Call me after the doctor appointment. Remember if you need anything or just want to talk, I am here for you."

Laramie hung up with Liz. She had always been a stable force in Laramie's life. She made her call to Gillian next. It was almost the same conversation verbatim. It amazed Laramie how identical her girlfriends were. *So far, no one has agreed with me regarding Akihiro. They would feel different if it were them.* She called Manny and Lian and asked to meet out for dinner. Lian was more than happy not to cook. Manny left school early on Wednesdays so that made it easier to get a table.

Laramie arrived at the San Francisco Soup Company first and grabbed a table for four. It wasn't long before Lian was there. They went through the line instead of waiting on Manny.

"So are you feeling better? You looked awful last week shopping. It wasn't something going around the office was it?"

"Actually I feel okay, some days better than others." The women sat at their table and Laramie continued the conversation. "The doctor recommended a specialist and I have an appointment set up for next week."

"Oh my God, Laramie, are you okay?"

"Yes, it's nothing that won't be gone in five months."

"What?"

"I'm pregnant, about seventeen weeks to be exact." Lian jumped up and hugged her. "I have an appointment next week with the obstetrician."

"Are you okay with this? You know the whole Akihiro thing again?" Lian tried to ask without stepping in a sensitive area.

"I was upset when the doctor first old me but after talking to Edward and the girls, I feel a lot better. As for Akihiro, I have decided to not tell him and do this on my own."

"Oh. Okay."

"You don't agree either. No one does. Look, if I called him right now, two things would happen; either he would want to be a part of it or nothing to do with me. I've had enough problems and I don't want to subject myself to that unknown."

"I don't agree but that's my opinion."

"What's your opinion?" asked Manny as he neared the table.

"Laramie is going to be a mommy."

"Are you kidding? Really? I guess that's cool if that's what you want. Congrats. So what's with the opinion?" He leaned in and kissed his wife hello.

"She has chosen to not tell Akihiro about the baby," Lian added.

"Whoa! Not tell him? Why? It's his, isn't it?" Laramie punched him in the shoulder.

"Yes, it's his. Thank you for the extra dose of immorality."

Chapter 34

LARAMIE SAT NERVOUSLY in the examination room, waiting for Dr. Post. This was her first visit to an obstetrician and didn't know what to expect. On top of the fact, she never met the doctor before. She hoped her bedside manner was pleasant. After a rap on the door, a slender woman around fifty-five years old appeared. She wore her blonde and gray hair short and layered. She was quiet spoken, which had a calming effect. She smiled at Laramie when she entered the room.

"It's a pleasure to meet you, Laramie. I understand you just found out you were pregnant. Nothing to worry about, I have been through this hundreds of times. We'll set up a schedule for visits and ultrasound dates to monitor your progress. Before we start the exam, do you have any questions?" Laramie said no.

The doctor performed her exam, pushing and pressing around Laramie's abdomen. Laramie didn't know what to expect and it wasn't bad. After the doctor finished, she patted her on the leg and told her to sit up.

"Everything feels normal, and yes, you are about eighteen weeks along. Do you want to hear the heartbeat?" Laramie nodded yes. Dr. Post put the stethoscope in her ears and began to place it over her small belly. "Can you hear it? It beats at a faster pace than ours, very normal."

"Oh my God, I can hear it. I can hear the baby's heart." She became teary as she heard the rapid thumps. "I'm sorry. I didn't realize I was going to be this emotional. This is just amazing."

"Well, you will become very emotional as your hormones change, as well as tired. I'm sending you home with some booklets, which will answer many questions for you and prenatal vitamins. If you have any concerns, call the office. Okay? You're doing fine, Laramie."

Laramie left the doctor with a renewed feeling of optimism. She had many questions and hurried home to read her literature. She wanted to know what happens at every stage of the pregnancy. She walked into the guest bedroom and looked around. *This all has to change.* She needed a nursery now.

Lian was the first to call.

"Well, how did it go? What did the doctor say?"

"She said the baby is about the right size for eighteen weeks and everything looked normal. I was a little nervous at first. Oh, Lian, I was able to hear the heartbeat. It was so amazing that I cried. This tiny little beat rapidly pulsing. I know I'm pregnant but hearing that made it all real. There really is this tiny person inside."

"I am so excited for you. What else did she say?"

"That was about it. I will have my first ultrasound in a few weeks. I can't wait for that. I wasn't sure how I felt about it all, scared I guess, but now I feel … womanly. Does that sound goofy?"

"Not at all. It is perfectly natural. At least that's what I hear."

"Hey listen, let me run. I have another call on the line and I still have to call the girls."

After they exchanged goodbyes, Laramie spoke with Liz and repeated the story again. She was happy she had the support base of her friends. However, it was a time like this when she really wished her parents were alive. She picked up the picture of her parents off her nightstand and gleamed at it. *I know this isn't exactly the way to go about things but I am excited.* She wanted so much to share this with them as well as her grandparents.

The next morning at work, Laramie went into Edward's office. He was on the phone but motioned for her to sit down. She sat patiently. She was in such a good mood for once since it seemed the morning sickness finally lightened.

"Good, I'm glad you're here. I need to talk with you but first tell me about the doctor. I need all the prep I can get to be a grandparent."

"Everything is great. The baby is growing like normal and in a few weeks is my first ultrasound. Oh, oh, oh… I was able to hear the heartbeat. Edward, it was so amazing and inspiring. We'll need to get a stethoscope so you can hear it too."

"Keep the positive note going since I just spoke with Frank and there seems to be a problem with disbursements from the bank. Some of the trades are behind in payment and threaten to walk off the site. They are already a month behind and they can't afford to lag further. Therefore, you need to pack for Singapore and leave tomorrow afternoon. You won't need to stay more than a few days."

"*What?* I can't go to Singapore. Can't this be handled over the phone?" Laramie pleaded.

"No Laramie, it can't. They have tried that and still nothing is moving forward. This is your case and *you* are the person to correct it."

"But Edward, I can't go. I'm pregnant."

"Yes, a lot of women are pregnant and they still travel. I'm sure you will be fine in that capacity. I would advise you to put together your files and make copies so you have everything you need."

"No. I can't go back. Can't you send an associate?" Laramie answered defiantly.

Edward sat back in his chair, surprised by her boldness. She behaved like a child having a tantrum.

"No. I thought I made this clear. Laramie, I understand your predicament. However, you put yourself there, not me or the firm. We had this conversation when you came home. You claimed to be responsible for your actions, and this is one of them. I'm sorry dear but you are going. You can decide whom you choose to see and from whom you choose to hide. This would be an excellent time to tell Akihiro. Don't you think?"

This sudden news angered Laramie. "No, I don't think. I told you my plans on that. Fine, I will gladly go to Singapore because it's my responsibility."

"Laramie, I can't show you any special treatment. You understand that don't you?"

Reluctantly, she answered, "Yes, I know that. I'll be in my office packing up my files if you need me then I'll be at home."

Chapter 35

LARAMIE HAD MIXED feelings when the plane landed. She loved how vibrant and alive the city was. She had so many great memories there but also the memories that hurt her the most. She grew paranoid that she would see someone she met or knew, especially Akihiro. She knew discretion was the key this trip. She knew she had to stay away from areas like Clarke Quay and Boat Quay at night.

She felt lucky that she had a tall frame and stayed slender for being in her fifth month. She planned her wardrobe very carefully, lots of flowing tops and pleated skirts. Her regular clothes became too tight at this point. Yet, she didn't want to buy any maternity clothes until after the ultrasound appointment.

She decided to stay at Raffles since it was familiar. It was very difficult to walk through the lobby and not remember the conversation with Akihiro. *Is it possible to see him without him seeing me? No. Why chance it.*

She knew a few places he would be if in fact his schedule was the same. Usually on Thursday mornings, he went to the market with Ahmed looking for the perfect cuts of meat and fish. *I wish I could see someone to pass on my apologies. What about Kat? She would have to be at the hotel while he is at the market. I guess I don't need that added risk either. I'll be seeing Rhys and he is sure to pass on the info that I was in town. You know what? I don't know if Rhys knows I'm here. That may work to my advantage.*

Later that afternoon, Laramie received a call from Frank Paradise. She thought it odd he would call her in Singapore and not speak to Edward locally first.

"Good Afternoon, Laramie. I hope you are adjusting to the time change again. I wanted to contact you before you left though I never expected Edward to have you there so quick."

"It was unexpected but I try and stay flexible. I have my files with me so this really shouldn't take much time at all. I do apologize that there was a discrepancy on the disbursement of funds in the first place. I should have been more thorough."

"Actually, I wanted to talk to you while you were in Singapore. It's regarding the leased property venture on the beach. I'm not sure if Edward has talked to you but… the real estate market isn't thriving as it once had. As a result, we have decided to make some changes in our holdings, namely the beach property. Before you say anything, I know you put up your own money as collateral for the contracts. What we have offered to do is compensate you for half the amount."

"Frank, you really don't need to do that. It was a judgment call on my behalf and not a responsible one at that. I cannot allow you to be party to my misjudgment."

"Laramie, Edward said you would be tough on this but I seriously want to do this. We will cash you half out this year and half out next year. This will give you an opportunity to make adjustments in your tax status in the mean time. Are you on board with me?"

"Thank you for your offer. Do you want me to finalize the documents while I'm here?"

"If you can do it, then absolutely. I don't want to say it was a bad investment because ultimately you had your eye on a piece of paradise but with the economy the way it is, my company needs to stick to what we do best and down the line we can go into another venture."

"Consider it done, Frank. I will contact the owner this week and let him know he hit the lottery. I will keep you posted via email on the current hotel construction. Take care, Frank. Bye now."

How many times can you be taxed on the same money? Just ask Laramie Holden, poor businesswoman. In reality, this worked out perfectly for Laramie. This voided lease was her apology to Akihiro. Laramie called Mr. Cheung and asked him to meet her at the hotel tomorrow morning; he said he would. *Well, where else can you make two million dollars for four months of doing nothing? Thank goodness no one I know has swamp land in Florida.*

She decided to go out that evening since it was probably the safest. Once Akihiro finds out she is in country, her whereabouts would no longer be secret. In her last trip, she missed a visit to Little India. She felt odd going by herself and decided to stick to the main streets. *Safety in numbers, right?*

Laramie took a taxi to Serangoon Road. The driver insisted this is where she needed to begin. As she walked down the road, she smelled an overwhelming amount of curry. Normally, she didn't like the smell but it was different now that she was pregnant. She loved all the color on the buildings, yellow, teal, orange. The combination surprisingly looked nice together. She entered the Little India Arcade, browsing the small shops. She chatted with a few owners who asked where she was from. *Funny, they all have relatives in the States.* She picked up a few ethnic bracelets and even contemplated a silk sari. *Beautiful, but where would I actually wear it?* They had beautiful handmade dolls she thought were adorable. She patted her belly and wondered the sex of the baby. *If you're a boy, I bet a doll won't be your first choice for a toy.*

As her stomach growled, she knew she needed to eat something. She asked one shopkeeper to recommend a nice spot for dinner. He told her to try Madras New Woodlands Restaurant on Upper Dickson Road. He said it was a great mix of tourists and locals. A little skeptical, Laramie took his advice. When she arrived at the restaurant, the mix pleasantly surprised her. She sat at a table and waited for the waiter to bring a menu. She noticed it was a pleasant décor, nothing too bold. As she browsed the tables, she noticed the place was family friendly. Laramie, who knew nothing about Indian cuisine, looked at the menu and then asked the waiter what he recommended for someone new. He smiled and told her he would bring a few local favorites. She sipped some tea while she waited for her meal. *This isn't so bad. Pat yourself on the back Lara. You went out on your own in a foreign country.*

After dinner, she felt she saw enough of Little India and headed back to Raffles. With the time change, she tired easily. She went to her room and put together her clothes for the next day. Her outfit was easy, a floral baby doll style blouse and a navy knit skirt. *It looks nice and it does scream pregnant at all.* When she turned on the news, she completely forgot about Christina. As she looked up, it all came flooding back, the emotions and heartbreak. She tried not to get upset and quickly turned the television off. *Next time, choose a different channel.*

Chapter 36

LARAMIE WAITED IN the lobby for Mr. Cheung to arrive. Once he entered, they greeted each other, then moved their meeting to a quieter spot in the hotel. *The grin on his face tells the story right there.* Laramie described the circumstance with DemCorp and recovered the terms of the contract. Since they never broke ground and had no intention to do so within the year, it voided the lease agreement. Both parties agreed it was better to end it now than to wait the full year, which they had as an option. Mr. Cheung brought a copy of the lease and Laramie attached her documents that stated the agreement was invalid. She asked the hotel clerk to make her two copies of the original. When it was completed, she thanked Mr. Cheung for his time and cooperation. *Whew, that's done. Onto the next step...*

It was shortly after ten o'clock in the morning when Laramie walked into the Bank of Singapore. She remembered the receptionist and greeted her warmly. She asked to see Rhys if he was available. The receptionist informed him that Laramie was waiting in the lobby, which brought quite a shock.

"Laramie, it is so wonderful to see you. No one told me you were coming. I would've planned my day better."

"It's always great to see you too, Rhys. Actually, the trip was last minute. I hardly had anytime to forewarn anyone. As you might imagine, I need to review the contracts with you and reinterpret the language so we both understand the direction and flow of the disbursements. It has already impeded the construction and quite frankly, DemCorp is upset with the bank's performance in handling the situation."

They continued their discussion as they walked back to Rhys' office. Laramie sat in a chair opposing him. His office was similar to the many cubicles outside the door, very plain except for one personal memento. He had a picture of Akihiro and him at a soccer match. *Bingo! Now it all fits together. That is how he met me at Raffles that night. I never put the two together. How did I miss this? I didn't notice the picture last time I was here. Rhys is the British friend that Aki spoke about. I have to watch my step carefully now.* Laramie was conscious to place her laptop and documents across her front when they spoke to camouflage the baby bump.

"Laramie, first let me apologize on behalf of the bank. It was an oversight on my part and I should've corrected it. However, and this is no excuse, we have some new employees in that department who are not fully trained. Let's redo some of the language so there can't be further misinterpretations. Sometimes, how things are spoken here are not the same as the United States."

"Rhys, I hope I'm not keeping you from anything. I know this was sudden and I don't know what your schedule is like so I hope I am not creating a conflict for you."

"No, my word, no. Everything can wait. So, how long are you in Singapore this time? Added another vacation?"

"No I'm afraid vacation time is over; this is all business. I'm here until Thursday. So you can see the need to complete this quickly." *I know where you're going with that this time, very clever.*

They worked through the documents page by page, stipulating dates and payment amounts. Occasionally, Rhys called the contractors to update them and inform them of payment to enable construction to continue. Laramie made many notes in the margins of her papers and typed them in as they went. Rhys watched her work, still amazed by her abilities. She was less emotional and completely professional. She seemed to have complete focus on her project. However, he wondered if he would have a chance to contact Akihiro. He was sure that Aki didn't know Laramie was in country.

"Laramie, I meant to ask you what plans you had with the old Cheung property. Any plans in development?" *Nice try Rhys, I'm not going to slip up this time.*

"Cheung property? Oh, the beachfront property. Well, there are drawings on the board, though, I'm not sure of their completion. I would hope soon since we need to build on there in less than seven months time."

"That's right, the terms of the deal were pretty aggressive if I remember."

"Yes they were. Let's get back to this deal for now unless you want to break for lunch. You know, let's break. I have a few errands to run so let's meet back here in about an hour. Sound good?"

"Absolutely. You don't mind if I don't walk you out. I have a few calls to make."

"No problem whatsoever. See you in a bit."

Laramie walked casually out of the office and headed for Cross Street. She knew to go to somewhere new just in case. Laramie laughed to herself. *I can't believe he forgot about his picture with Akihiro. It is so obvious. I wonder when he'll catch on.*

Rhys quickly picked up the phone, dialing the Tanjong. He had to reach Akihiro. Laramie Holden was back in Singapore for three more days.

"Hello, the Tanjong Beach Hotel and Spa. This is Kat, may I help you?"

"For Christ's sake Kat, is Akihiro in his office?"

"No Rhys, he's out for a few days looking at land in Batam with Shinji. Why? What's the matter?"

"You'll never bloody believe this. Guess who walked into my office this morning? Well, guess. Never mind, you won't get it. Laramie Holden," he spoke hurriedly.

"*What?* Laramie is here in Singapore. This isn't a joke, is it?"

"Wouldn't be a funny one, now would it? She flew in yesterday. I was expecting a conference call. I wasn't told she was coming so you could imagine my surprise to see her. She said she's in town until Thursday. She's out at lunch for the moment. I called as fast as I could. Can't you reach him via cell phone?"

"I'll try. Keep me posted. Bye."

Kat dialed Akihiro's cell phone. The first try received a voice mail message, as did several others. She was nervous to the point that she kept misdialing the phone. She continued until he finally took her call.

"Damn Kat, what is so important that you called eight times? Is everything all right at the hotel?"

"Yes, everything here is fine. Rhys just called. Apparently, Laramie is in town."

"*What?* You're not kidding are you?"

"No, no joke. He thought he had a conference call with her and just before that time, the receptionist said he had a guest. He came to the front and she was standing there. He wanted to call earlier but didn't have the opportunity until she went out at lunch."

'Do you know where she is staying?"

"No."

"Well, what do you know?"

"She leaves on Thursday. Are you coming back here?"

"Damn it. I can't be back there until tomorrow morning. I have papers to sign here on a property we found. We told the listing agent we would stay until we had a solid price and closing terms. Will she be at his office tomorrow?"

"I don't know. You have to call Rhys on that. If I hear anything else, I'll call you."

Akihiro and Shinji stood in an open field along the beach in Batam. Akihiro was visibly angry. He held his cell phone in his hand and tensed his face and fists. He wanted to see her and to know she was so close was torture. Shinji listened in on half the conversation but didn't understand the subject.

"Akihiro, what's up? Everything okay?"

"*NO*. Laramie is in Singapore. I guess she flew in yesterday. She completely blind-sided Rhys. He was under the assumption they were to have a conference call. I don't know where she is staying but I do know she leaves on Thursday."

"What would you do if you saw her? What would you say?"

"I don't even know right now. I can't get her out of my head. It's not the land, well yes, I'm angry over that. There's more to it, more to her."

"You're still in love with her aren't you? You have got it bad."

"Yes, I am. I should've never let her walk away. I should've gone after her."

"I don't get it. If you love her then why didn't you go to the States to see her?"

Akihiro stood looking at the ocean. "It seemed more complicated than that at the time. Then the hotel took up so much time and then new finding property. I just never went back to that thought."

"Well my brother, let's get through this deal and head back," Shinji said as he slapped his brother on the back.

* * *

Laramie knocked on Rhys' door when she arrived back from lunch.

"Back so soon? Did you have time to eat?"

"Yes, I did, thanks. I went to a little shop up Cross Street. How about you? Did you have time to eat or have you been here the whole time?"

She sat back in her chair across from Rhys. She waited to see what his next move was; it didn't take long.

"I meant to ask you, where are you staying this visit? Back at Raffles?"

"As a matter of act, I am back at Raffles. It's such an exquisite building, so rich in history that I love walking around looking at the paraphernalia." She looked over his shoulder at the picture and felt it was time to put him on the spot instead. "Rhys, I didn't realize that you and Akihiro were such close friends."

Rhys stumbled over her statement. "What…what's that?" She pointed over his shoulder to the photograph. "Oh… yes. I thought I'd mentioned it before." Laramie shook her head no with a slight grin. "Well, yes, we go back quite a few years. We met in England when he went to Oxford. After I finished there, I moved to Singapore. He's a trusted mate."

"How would you define 'trusted'? 'Trusted' as in, Laramie went shopping before going back to the hotel? Or 'trusted' as in, Laramie is in town until Thursday?"

"Oh, for Christ's sake. How long have you known?"

"This morning and your photograph confirmed it. Thank you for the additional help. So, did you reach him over lunch? Was he too busy to ambush me again? Or should I be looking over my shoulder for the next few days?" Laramie slammed her statements firmly back at Rhys.

"Laramie, it really isn't like that at all. I really didn't want to get his personal life caught in my business. You stuck me with the Cheung property by including me in the room. You knew I couldn't say anything about it. I must say it did devastate him but not nearly as much as you leaving Singapore did. I don't know whether you are aware of it, but he was madly in love with you, probably still is. He won't bring up the subject."

"Rhys, if I thought for a moment we could work things out, I'd never leave. I still think about him everyday but we have some serious trust issues. Don't get me wrong, I brought my fair share to the table. Some things I'm trying to correct."

"Why don't you just talk with him? I can't be that difficult."

"Oh but it is. It took me a long while to get over the heartbreak, and I'm still not over it. I function. If I see him, it'll all come back again then what if we can't work things out? I can't go back to those feelings again." Laramie became misty eyed during the conversation. "I just can't do it."

"Look I am sorry, don't get upset. I made you bloody cry. Come on now, please stop it." He handed her a tissue. Rhys never handled crying women very well.

"I'm sorry. It's a touchy subject. Let's just finish this work and stop for the day. It won't take long." Laramie took a deep breath and calmed herself. "Now, show me the rest of the issues."

They worked without a break until four o'clock. Laramie had small piles scattered on the floor. She picked up each one in the order to which they discussed, very methodically. A few times, he asked her for the wording on a certain clauses and she spoke them word for word. Rhys glanced at his sheet and was stunned to see her accuracy. Her personality intrigued him. He viewed her as a legal powerhouse who had strong instincts and knowledge but mention Akihiro's name, she was an emotional wreck.

"Actually, I think tomorrow will be a short day. In reality, I don't know why this couldn't be done over the phone. However, this way there are less mistakes or interpretations to be made."

"I can't thank you enough for the clarification of your contract and terminology. You are a tremendous help."

"Anything else before I leave?" she said as she held her briefcase and laptop.

"Do you have plans for dinner? If not, we could stop for a bite."

"Thank you for the offer. However, I have more work to finish. The caseload doesn't lessen just because I'm not sitting at my desk. About tomorrow, please don't surprise me with any guests. Please."

"I won't and I wouldn't. See you tomorrow."

Laramie went back to Raffles for a quick dinner and then to her room. When the phone rang, it worried her. She debated whether to answer it. There was no way to tell who was on the line. She took a deep breath and picked up the receiver.

"Hello?"

"Laramie, it's Edward. How is everything going there? Have you finished the contract? I spoke to Frank and he told me about the beachfront property. I'm sorry."

"I'm fine Edward, though the time change is harder this time. The DemCorp contract will be finished in the morning. I have already met with Mr. Cheung. That contract has been voided. I have the signed release forms. Anything else?"

"You do have a message for your ultrasound. It's next Wednesday at four. I'm having your calls sent to me for screening while you're away. I hope you don't mind."

"No, I don't mind. I can't wait for that test. I'm not sure if I want to know the sex or not."

"One other thing, have you seen Akihiro?"

"No. I haven't. But I do know someone tried to reach him this afternoon to tell him I was here. I really don't think I will see him at all, but thanks for asking."

"Laramie, will you just listen to reason?"

"No, Edward. Now if that's all you have then we are done. Good night." She ended the call almost sounding melodious.

Laramie knew he was bullheaded and she learned from the master. She smiled as she walked away from the phone. Then it rang again.

"What did you forget this time, Edward?"

"Laramie? Is that you?"

"Kat? How are you? You shocked me with your call. I wasn't aware *everyone* knew I was in Singapore."

"Well you know this is a small country. How have you been? It's hard to believe four months have passed. Anyway, I called to tell you, if you feel up to it, we would love to see you again, all of us. I'd be happy to meet you out if you didn't want to come here. How does Karaoke sound?"

Laramie laughed aloud. She started with her rendition of Bette Midler's *Wind Beneath My Wings*, of course, completely off key. Kat doubled over with laughter. Somehow, she forgot just how bad Laramie sang.

"Are you crazy? No more singing for me. I am just thankful that no one recorded that awful sound. Actually, I'm doing okay, you know, some days better than others. I've already inquired about Akihiro with Rhys. He told me he is in Batam with Shinji looking for property." Laramie paused a moment. "Kat? You know I feel terrible regarding the Cheung property. I was out of hand and when I regained my senses, it was too late. I owe you an apology too. You work hard there and my immaturity and selfishness affected you as well. I am sorry."

"Thanks Laramie, I appreciate your apology. I see you are aware that Rhys and Akihiro have been friends for many years. I know he wants to see you. I don't think he's mad anymore. He feels partly to blame on that. The both of you need to be together you know."

"You may be right but I'm not over my own guilt yet. I don't think it would be wise to see each other until then. I still love him, Kat. You can tell him so." She let out a deep sigh. "Will this ever get any better?" Laramie knew she would be emotional but never to this degree. She truly felt the obstetrician underestimated her.

"It will, I promise. If you change your mind, you know where to find me. Take care, Laramie."

Laramie was certain this trip was avoidable if it were not up to Edward. She knew he set her up in hopes she would tell Akihiro about the baby. He went out of his way to put her front and center. However, she was determined to hold out until she was ready to tell Akihiro the news.

Chapter 37

AS SOON AS the first ferry arrived back in Singapore, Akihiro raced to the hotel. He had very little sleep the night before and was on an adrenal rush that morning.

"Kat. Any news? Did Rhys call back?"

"Actually, I called her last night. We spoke for a few minutes, that was all."

"How did she seem? Good, bad, mad? What did she say?'

"She caught onto you and Rhys. She wasn't mad, if anything I would say humbled. She still feels terribly about the land. So much so, she doesn't think she could face you. I tried to talk her out of it but she wouldn't listen. I told her she was welcome to stop in if she felt like it and that we all would love to see her." Akihiro simply nodded as if he was absorbing everything he heard.

"Anything else?"

"Yes, she still loves you."

"Did she say that or are you saying it?"

"No, she said it and not only that but she said it was okay to tell you too."

Akihiro slumped back in the chair across from Kat's desk. He felt deflated by the news. He desperately wanted to see her. He knew he couldn't push her; it would only drive her away. *But, what am I supposed to do and for how long?*

"Look Aki, she's here and she will be here again. If you want to move on then do so, however, if you want her then you have to stick it out. She will come around."

"You're right. She knows where to find me." He sat and stared at the ceiling. He knew Kat was right, she was always right. *Laramie, you are driving me mad.*

* * *

Laramie met with Rhys to finalize the contract. She was quieter than normal. She had so many thoughts and emotions racing in her head. The baby was her first concern, then Akihiro and then work. Rhys noticed her daydreaming.

"Everything all right this morning?"

"Yes. I'm fine. Just a lot of things in my head. I'm not looking forward to flying home tomorrow. I just get used to the time change and now its time to change again. It was far easier when I had three weeks to adjust."

"Do you have any plans to return soon?"

"Well, I want to be here for the grand opening. Whenever that date is, I'll be back then. You realize you are just as welcome to come to San Francisco and visit me. I am not the only one who should experience jet lag."

Rhys laughed, "You are absolutely correct."

They worked together for a few more hours and sat back to relax while they waited for the secretary to make copies. Rhys told her stories of him and Akihiro in college. They were quite the scoundrels. She asked if he dated presently and he said no. He claimed no woman wants a man who wants to be married. They want to change the confirmed bachelors instead. She laughed but agreed. He asked what she did with her spare time. She confessed she didn't have any. Laramie told him her work came first, then friends and family. He counseled her on the pitfalls of her priorities and that she should play more. She assured him she would make time in the near future. A few moments later, the secretary came in with the copies. Laramie placed her set in her briefcase. He tried to talk her into a pint at lunch but she declined. Rhys said he wanted to walk her out to the lobby.

"Laramie, I will miss you. Try not to surprise me the next time; a ring before hand is quite sufficient. Have a safe trip home and if you change your mind about him, I know he'd love to see you."

"Thank you Rhys. The hardest part of leaving is missing all of you as well. Bye."

He watched her walk out the door and returned to his office. *A truly remarkable woman.*

Laramie went directly back to her hotel. She was exhausted and desperately wanted a nap. She hoped there would not be any guests at the hotel when she arrived. Luckily enough, she was alone. She kicked off her shoes and partly undressed before she lay on the bed. Her clothes pressed against her belly, which made her uncomfortable. *Now I know why these pregnant women wear baggy clothes. This feels so much better. Ahhh!* It wasn't long before she was asleep.

When she woke, she ordered room service for dinner. She thought about dinner out but she wanted to stay in, relax and rest. She had a few things on her agenda such as a note to Akihiro and the copy of the cancelled lease agreement. She labored as she sought to find the right words for her note.

After dinner, she watched a foreign film on the television. *Thank goodness for subtitles.* She stayed clear of romance movies, she was emotional enough already. She slowly packed her things in her suitcase. *Well new friend, you have traveled twice and both times to San Francisco. Good thing you're roomy, soon I will be packing for two in you. It's only nine o'clock but that's good enough for bedtime for me.*

Chapter 38

AKIHIRO SAT RESTLESS at his desk. He wanted to find Laramie but knew it wasn't a good decision. *She is so close and I can't even see her. This is madness, she should be here, be with me. Doesn't she see the land doesn't matter? If I could just see her, talk to her. I could explain everything and tell her how sorry I am.* Occasionally, Kat heard the sound of a ball as it bounced off the wall. She sat outside his closed door and understood his frustration. She hoped Laramie would change her mind but it seemed unlikely.

She buzzed his phone. "Aki, Ahmed is out here. He wants to know if you plan on going to the market with him."

They went to the market every Thursday morning. He knew Ahmed would be fine on his own but the silence annoyed him.

Akihiro walked out of his office. "Let's go. Sitting here won't do me any good. Keep an eye on things, Kat."

Shortly after Akihiro left the hotel, Laramie walked in. She quietly strolled near Kat's desk before she said anything.

"*Did I ever tell you you're my hero*… Good morning Kat."

Kat let out a howl. "Oh my God, Laramie. Why didn't you call? Akihiro isn't here, he went — "

"— To the market with Ahmed. I know I remember. I thought it was safer this way. How are you? You look great."

"You look great too. You always look great. So you go home today, leh?"

"Yes. It's been a hard trip. I don't mean coming here, I mean the time changing so closely. I always felt good being here. Before I forget, can I drop this on Akihiro's desk?"

"Sure, go ahead."

"Has he had any luck finding property? As if it really is my business."

"Yes, he and Shinji have been working hard on that. He will be upset when he finds out you were here and he didn't see you. You know that, right?"

"I do. I wish it could be different. I know he may be ready but I'm not yet. I don't expect him to pine over me, I never did. I thought when I went back home it would all go back to normal. It will never be normal not until this is resolved, at least for me. Anyway, I have to be going. They want you at the airport two hours early so we can spend one hour bored. Hopefully next time I'm in Singapore, the circumstances will be better."

Kat stood up to hug her. Laramie thought quickly and leaned over so Kat would only meet with her upper chest. *Whew! Last the last thing I need is to expose this baby.*

"Good luck and have a safe flight. I look forward to you coming back and staying longer so we can go out next time. No excuses!"

"Bye, Kat."

A car waited for Laramie as she chatted with Kat. It made for a quick and easy escape if needed. Laramie drove off and sat back into her seat. *I am leaving him once again. Will this ever stop?* She rubbed her belly as the car traveled down the road. She knew she had a long flight ahead and dreaded it. The only consolation was the baby tired her more so she had better odds of sleeping. It wasn't long before they reached Changi Airport. This time she flew out of the brand new Terminal 3. One benefit was many of the stores were new to her. *At least I can shop until leave. That's always fun.* She recalled the last time she flew out when Akihiro called out to her. *I hope that this time won't be a repeat.*

* * *

A few hours into the morning, Akihiro arrived back at the Tanjong. He seemed to be in better spirits until he inquired about the morning. Kat didn't have any intention to lie. She knew he deserved the truth.

"Laramie stopped here while you were gone. She sang an entrance song horribly I might add." Kat still chuckled over the horrifying sound.

"*What?* Why didn't you call me? I would've come right back. You know that Kat."

"I do know that and so did she. She knew you went to the market on Thursdays."

"Well, what did she say?"

"After she told me I was her hero?" Kat saw that Akihiro found no humor in her statement. "Sorry, I couldn't help it. Anyway, she hopes for a resolution between the two of you but can't put forth that effort until she gets over the guilt of buying the Cheung property."

"Did you tell her that I don't care about that?"

"Yes, but *she* cares about it. It's hard when you do something out of anger and fear especially if that isn't who you really are. I think she scared herself. By the way, she left a large envelope on your desk."

Akihiro went into his office and picked up the envelope. He pulled out a stack of papers that had a handwritten note attached to the front.

> *Dear Akihiro,*
>
> *This is the best I can do for now. I know I owe you these words in person but I haven't the courage to do so yet. I wanted to talk with you at the airport but I was so ashamed. I am truly sorry I took and shattered your dream. I had no right and I am trying my best to mend it, that's the least I can do.*
>
> *I have to do what I think is right before I can come to terms with my feelings for you. I regret walking away at Raffles but I knew I made the right choice for that time. If I saw you today, I would want things as they were. It seemed so perfect but we had twisted that perfection to meet our own needs and not that of each other. I wish I could say everything would be better next week or next month but I don't know when it will be.*
>
> *My love, Laramie*

He stood numb in his office after he finished the note. He realized the problem wasn't him alone. She needed to find herself again. She wouldn't be comfortable with him until she did. *Does this mean she'll come back? When? How long can I wait? But the secrets are gone, we exposed that last time.* He pulled the note off the top and read the document on top. The letter terminated the lease between Mr. Cheung, DemCorp and Laramie because the lessee would not meet the said terms of the contract. As a result, the land was free for Mr. Cheung to sell or lease to another entity. In agreement to the initial terms, regarding the signing bonus of two million US dollars, all funds stated remain as the sole possession of Mr. Cheung. It finished with the signatures of Mr. Cheung and Laramie as an interested party and on behalf of DemCorp. Below that letter was a copy of the voided lease. He stood shocked, just shaking his head in disbelief.

"Kat. Get in here and see this. I don't believe it."

Kat grabbed it and read it slightly aloud. When she finished, she was in shock just as Akihiro.

"It means the land next door is free to purchase. Wow. I can't believe it. She said she wanted to fix everything and she meant it. Of course, she created the mess but… Holy cow! She lost two million dollar for a four month deal. I can't even comprehend that amount of money and then to lose it. Did I say 'wow' yet?"

He sat against the front of his desk in disbelief. *She gave it back. I can make the expansion happen again. You turned everything back around. You found a way to back out. Laramie, I just wish you were here. We can make it work. I'm not giving up.*

"Kat, can you get Mr. Cheung on the phone? We have some business to discuss."

Akihiro spoke with Mr. Cheung to renew their verbal contract and write it to paper. Akihiro knew better this time; Laramie taught him that lesson. After his call ended with Mr. Cheung, he called Shinji. He explained about Laramie dropping off the terminated contract and that he had a new appointment with the owner the next morning. The news quickly spread in the Amori household. While they were ecstatic the expansion was on again, they all wondered about the money. In normal reality, no one had the ability to comprehend losing two million dollars, yet, Laramie did it with such grace. *This starts a new chapter between us Laramie. I am not over you yet.*

Chapter 39

WARMER WIND BLEW across the bay as it signaled the coming of Spring. Laramie walked to her second ultrasound appointment. The first pictures of the baby brought her to tears. She saw the face of her precious little miracle. Unfortunately, the baby didn't cooperate with displaying his or her sex. Laramie was eager to know because she wanted to paint the nursery. She didn't want yellow and green for everything. She looked down at her expanded belly and smiled. She loved being pregnant. She loved the movement and kicks. She knew this was an active little person and she would have her hands full in the future.

A few times over the past months, she picked up the phone to call Akihiro but at the last minute, she hung up. Part of her wanted to tell him and share this but the opposite part told her to wait until the baby was born. This confusion caused her to remember his dilemma regarding Christina. *Sometimes the opportunity doesn't present itself. But I'm just not ready.* She learned a lot from their mistakes in Singapore.

Laramie slowly poured herself onto the examination table. At twenty-eight weeks of pregnancy, her belly grew at a more rapid pace. She had no way to disguise her condition anymore. The technician prepped her belly with clear gel and tested in some spots.

"Are you ready, Laramie? I believe we will be able to know the sex this time if you are interested."

"I can't tell you how hard that decision has been. I want to know but I also want to be surprised."

"Well, whether you learn it now or then, it's going to be a surprise." The tech ran the wand over her lower abdomen. "Here's the head. Say hi to

Mommy, little one." As the tech moved further up , she asked Laramie if she wanted to know. Laramie nodded yes. "Let's get a good look to be sure. Sometimes on boys, their legs hide the penis. Nothing hidden this time. You are having a daughter. Congratulations."

The news brought her to tears. "Oh my God, a little girl. I haven't even picked out a name yet. She is so beautiful in there." After she gained her composure, she added, "Well this will make the colors of the room easier, and the baby shower."

When Laramie returned to the office, she went to Edward's office first. Her face beamed with excitement.

"Your face says the appointment went well. That is great to hear."

"Yes, but that's not the best part. It's a girl, Edward. I'm having a daughter."

He stood and hugged her. He knew this baby was what got her through the day. Her work performance was always exemplary but she had better focus with the baby coming.

"I want you to know this one thing, okay? Outside of the fact that you will make a great mom, she will cause you so much grief but stay focused because the love on the other end makes it worth it."

"Thank you for supporting me. I know it hasn't been easy. I know I haven't been easy. But I love you Grandpa."

"*Grandpa*! You make me old."

Laramie walked into her office. She wasn't there long before the ladies of the office showed up at her door. They wanted to know every small detail of the ultrasound. They asked if she found out the sex. Laramie told them a girl and they responded with *oohs* and *ahs*. After the commotion settled, Linda walked in with a package.

"I didn't want to give this to you with everyone around. It came in this morning from Singapore."

Laramie held out her hand and looked at the label. It was Akihiro's handwriting. She hesitated to open it. She rubbed her palm over his writing and smiled. *Akihiro, you're going to be a daddy. I will tell you soon, I promise. Hmmm... I can't believe he sent me something. Whatever it is, it's hard. I didn't forget anything there, did I?* She pulled the packing paper off and turned it over. It was a book of prints from the Botanic Gardens. Inside was a note.

> *Dear Laramie,*
>
> *I thought you might like this book since you forgot your camera that day. Just to let you know, it holds some amazing memories for me. I hope you enjoy it.*
>
> *Love, Akihiro*

Laramie loved the book. She leafed through some of the pages and had her inspiration. She would have the baby's room painted with images from the gardens. She loved the white bandstand, orchids and heliconias. She remembered Akihiro as he studied the Bonsai. It was a good day for them both.

She called Lian later that afternoon and told her the baby news. Manny and Lian were a great support for her, not just with the baby but her relationship with Akihiro as well.

"Lian, I wanted to ask you if you would be my birthing coach. I know some people are queasy about it and I completely understand if you don't want to do it."

"Laramie, I would love it. Besides, it lets me know what to expect when my turn comes. Have you decided where you're going to have her?"

"The hospital, why?"

"No, I mean, in a birthing unit or bath. You would not believe the places where you can give birth now. Some hospitals have these rooms to play soothing music and low lights. Are you going to go natural?"

"Wow, I didn't know there were so many choices. I'd like to say natural but at the first sign of pain I want the meds." Laramie had a high tolerance for pain however, the baby stories she heard at work concerned her. "Oh yeah, I almost forgot. I got a book in from Akihiro today."

"He's sending gifts now? That's interesting," Lian teased.

"Stop it. We went to the Botanic Gardens one day and it was so beautiful. It wasn't until we walked around I realized I forgot my camera. He said he remembered that and thought to send the book. That's all."

"So there was a note too. How'd he sign it?" asked Lian teasingly.

"Love, Akihiro. Don't read into this."

"Don't read into it, huh? As long as he didn't sign it 'later, bitch' then I would say there is still hope. Don't get me started on that. You and I completely disagree regarding him. That's all I have to say."

"Good. Anyway, I will check into classes and get back with you. Bye."

Laramie had so many choices whether it was Lamaze or Bradley, or spiritual and hypnotic. *What did women do before all the classes? Everything is a science now.* She decided to call the doctor's office for a recommendation. However, the women's opinions differed. *That didn't help. What am I doing? I'll just call Liz.*

"Laramie Holden, I have been waitin' for your call. You're lucky I'm not local. So tell me how the ultrasound went. I loved having those done; seeing the little hands and face."

"It's a girl, Liz. I saw her then I cried like a baby myself. All I do is cry over the strangest things too."

"A baby girl. Oh honey, I'm so happy for you. Have you called Akihiro to tell him yet?"

"No. I decided against that. I thought I would wait until she was born."

"Laramie, you said you would when you had the first ultrasound, then you said the second, now you know the sex and you want to wait until birth. You *have* to tell him. You're not being fair about this at all."

"I will. I promise." Laramie continued, "Anyway, I want to know the best way to give birth."

"With plenty of medication. I'd add a vodka martini to that if the alcohol weren't such a problem. Are you lookin' into all those classes? I went to those with Amanda. Let me give you a piece of advice, which I know you won't take. The classes help you breathe during the contractions. However, I screamed and swore at Randy instead and felt much better." Laramie chuckled. She always loved Liz's sense of humor. "Who's doing the class with you? Manny?" Liz laughed.

"No way. Actually, Lian is going with me."

The women chatted for a while as they discussed the ins and outs of pregnancy and delivery. Laramie missed her girlfriends and their conversations. Laramie loved to hear them talk about the new things and people in their lives. It was hard for Laramie to be so far away from them but she had Manny and Lian so close.

Soon, Edward knocked on her doorway. Laramie knew the conversation was over and it was time to get back to work. Edward shut the door behind him and sat across from Laramie.

"It seems we have a slight problem. Let me think of the best way to breach it."

"Is it one of my cases or one of my clients? What's wrong?"

"I'm afraid there have been a few complaints by staff members regarding you."

"*What*? You're joking?"

"No, Laramie, this isn't a joke. I'm trying to find the easiest and nicest way to put this because I don't want to upset you. The complaints are that you have been curt with a few people and not as tolerant as normal."

"So you're telling me I have been a bitch lately. Is that it?"

"Yes, exactly. Before you go off on a tirade, let me finish. You are a partner at this firm; you became one at an early age, and deserved it completely. If you weren't a partner, you would still be an owner due to your parents. Some people find it difficult to see your legal mind first before your birthright. As such, you have to be more tolerant of others. With the economy being down, people will jump at anything to make a dollar. There is a fine line on harassment. People are not afraid to litigate anything anymore. Do you see where this is going?"

"You're telling me to be nice and not bitchy. I understand but in my own defense, I shouldn't have to tell an associate to remain current on their billing. I shouldn't have to tell a paralegal how to research a case for me step by step. I shouldn't have to play a babysitter at my place of employment either." Her anger elevated.

"This is exactly what I mean. You have jumped completely on the defensive. I realize you have hormone issues but *you* need to realize you have legal issues. You cannot, I repeat, cannot lose your temper. If you find yourself in that predicament, walk into my office and shut the door. You can swear at me all you want, but not an employee."

"I apologize. I did become angry and I didn't mean it. You are correct. I have to mind my speech better."

"I am telling you this now because your feelings will become greater. I will not settle a harassment suit. This is warning number one. If there is a number two, I will have no other choice but to send you on maternity leave early. Am I understood?"

Laramie cowered like a child. She knew her patience waned, as did her ability to keep her mouth shut. "Yes. Edward, I understand."

"Good, now go about your day. I believe you were about to call Gillian when I came in." He walked over and kissed the top of her head. She felt no different had he been her parent. *How do they always make you feel like a little kid so easily? Next, he'll probably try to ground me.*

She stared out the window for a few minutes before she resolved her thoughts. She turned to her computer and wrote an email to Akihiro. *This is my first step at contact, please don't blow it.*

> *Dear Akihiro,*
>
> *I received the book today. It meant a lot coming from you. I have warm memories of the gardens and of you as well. Thank you for thinking of me.*
>
> *My love, Laramie*

She contemplated whether she should hit send or not. She pushed the mouse up to the delete button and then she hesitantly moved it and clicked on 'send.' *It's too late now, no way to undo it. It should be late afternoon in Singapore.*

* * *

Akihiro sat at his desk as he reviewed the architectural drawings for the expansion. He estimated they had a few weeks before they closed on the land next door. He already purchased the land in Batam and was unsure which property needed construction first. His clients from the Americas dropped off due to their economy but the Aussies have increased their visitation. He called Shinji and asked him if he knew what sales had been in Singapore versus Indonesia. Shinji said Batam had higher sales due to their property costs being lower. Their tourism increased because of that also. He said to check his email for the file regarding the conversation. Akihiro opened up his account on the hotel website and noticed an email from Laramie. He opened it quickly and read it. *It seems she has decided to make contact after all and accept the peace offering. This is a great start. Let's see if we can keep this going.*

Chapter 40

By MID-APRIL, LARAMIE and the baby grew faster. All of her OB appointments were normal and that gave her added confidence. The baby kicked and squirmed all the time. It was hard for Laramie to sleep at night, causing her moods to swing a bit more. *I don't know how anyone can sleep with a huge belly. I can barely stand straight without tipping. I thought girls were calmer. This little spitfire runs a marathon daily.*

She hired an artist to paint the baby's room. Laramie pasted together copies from the Botanic book to show the artist the panorama she wanted. She and Lian went to childbirth classes every Wednesday evenings at the hospital. There were more single parents there than at Lamaze and Bradley classes. Laramie felt weird as the couples stared at her. At first she thought it was because she was a single parent but later discovered they thought she and Lian were a couple. *This is San Francisco.* They both had a good laugh over that.

She continued to work as much as she could without napping at lunch. Her caseload dropped with the impending baby. However, she maintained the DemCorp project completely. She worked too hard on it to hand it over to someone else. They regained their momentum on the building since the contract updates. She spoke to Rhys every few weeks. He always asked when she planned to return. She always gave him the same answer 'when construction is complete.' She asked about Akihiro and Rhys confided that he hadn't seen him much since he started construction on the hotel in Batam. She was happy for Akihiro and hoped she didn't damage things too badly for him. She checked her email frequently to see if she received any contact from him, there wasn't any. *Throw me a bone here, Aki.*

* * *

The following week was unusually stressful. Andrew wanted her to close out stagnant files. Edward wanted her to give the work she did have to an associate. This was very difficult for Laramie to do. She treated each client like her baby. No one knew more about any of the cases than she did. However, it all came to a head in the lunchroom one afternoon after an employee birthday. Laramie stood by the back wall and finished her cake, when a new intern stood beside her. He noticed she was pregnant, obviously and tried to make small conversation.

"I bet you and Mr. Holden are excited about the pending birth."

"Excuse me? Did you say Mr. Holden? What makes you think here is a Mr. Holden? Did you miss the part on the building directory that said *Miss* Laramie Holden?"

"Oh, I didn't know. I assumed since you were pregnant that you were married."

Unfortunately, for the poor soul, he chose the wrong words. Everyone in the lunchroom turned to the conversation. Luckily enough, someone ran to get Edward.

"I do not need to be married to have a child. This is *my* baby and I am perfectly capable of raising her on my own. Why does everyone think I need the father involved? I don't."

Just then Edward walked inside the room.

"Laramie, get in my office. *NOW*."

His loud deep voice broke her speech. She knew she went too far but it was too late. She walked into Edward's office and was about to sit when he stopped her.

Edward shouted, "I told you I would not tolerate harassment among the employees. I warned you. I want you to pack up the few files you have remaining and you can take them home, leave everything else on your desk and someone will take care of it. You are officially starting maternity leave but not before you apologize to the young man."

"But Edward—"

"No buts, do it, and do it now."

She never saw him so livid. There was no way she would argue back. She agreed and went to the young man's office first. She apologized for being so rude. He knew it was heartfelt and accepted her apology. He stated he only wanted to make conversation because he was new. She knew that and hoped this incident didn't change his impression of her. Afterward, she went into her office and packed. A few women came by and tried to cheer her up by telling her stories of their own pregnancies. It helped. The IT manager stopped by to tell her he would have her set up on the network so she had the ability to access it at home. She thanked him. A few moments later, Andrew walked in her office.

"Laramie, we know it was an accident. I hope you can see this from our perspective." She nodded yes. "We love you dearly and believe it or not, we are looking out for your best interest as well. If there is anything you need call me or call Violet, all right?"

She hugged him. He still had that uncanny ability to read people. She knew they all supported her. She was afraid this might strain her relationship with Edward. She said goodbye to everyone as she passed them. She wanted to say goodbye to Edward but felt the timing wasn't good. She really angered him. When she reached the elevators, Manny greeted her. It was apparent he knew what happened. *That didn't take long.* She gave one last hug to Linda before she entered the elevator.

"So the shit hit the fan, eh? I'm really surprised it took you this long. We should've started a pool as to when you would explode." Manny found it all amusing.

"It's not funny. I've never seen Edward so mad. That scared the hell out of me. I would never forgive myself if he had a stroke or something from that."

"Don't take this wrong but usually there are two people together getting ready for a baby. They split things up to relieve the pressure. You are on your own through this. We help where we can but you are such a control freak that you hoard everything. Did you expect it to be different?"

"I don't know what I expected. Have I been spiteful with you too?"

"If you were I didn't notice but then I have the ability to blow you off easier. Don't sweat this, Lara, you'll get through it. What are you going to do now that you have some time off work?"

"Time off? I never even thought of that. This gives me time to work in the baby's room, shop for clothes, and get plenty of sleep. What I would give for a full night of sleep. It's been so long."

"Don't shop too much. Lian has your shower planned in a few weeks. You'll really tick her off if you buy the same things."

Manny, who carried her belongings, placed them in the trunk of the limo. He opened her door next and she sat back in her seat. After Manny entered the car, she knocked for him to put the privacy window down. She hated when he drove her around. It made her uncomfortable like he was some indentured servant.

"You know Laramie, this would be a great time to call Akihiro since you will be home for awhile. I'm sure if he knew he'd be on the next plane to be with you. You can't push him off too long before he finally decides to walk."

"Did you not hear the reason for my rant? Do you really think it's necessary to discuss this now?"

"Yeah, I've got you captive. Your women friends let you off the hook but maybe it's time you heard it from a man. The guy obviously still loves you. But for how long? You're not around and that makes it easier for him to forget you. You have his child; you will never forget him. You keep cutting him out of your life then don't be surprised when he's gone. Then it'll be too late for the 'I'm not ready yet' statements. Is that what you want?"

"No. I do want him in my life but I can't just call and say 'hello, how are you and by the way, I'm seven months pregnant.' How swell do you think that will go over?" she retorted sarcastically.

"I think he'd *love* to know, love to be a part of it. You are being so selfish about this and you don't even see it. Lian told me about him wanting to see you in Singapore. She told me about the book too. If he even remotely hated you over the land deal, he would never have attempted to see you or contact you. You'd be dead to him."

"Are you finished lecturing me?"

"NO, not even close, Babe. Men don't hold out for the touchy feely stuff. We want gratification instantly. Did he screw up not telling you about the other chick? Yeah. It was a mistake. You ever make any? Oh wait let's see. You're pregnant by a man you knew for a week. You got pissed off at him and tried to destroy his dream, then you go back to Singapore and won't see him because you feel bad. Give me a break, Sweetheart. You are in a league of your own."

"I think that's enough Manny," she said seething.

"I'm not done. Do you want this child to grow up not knowing her father? Or do you want him a part of her life? How did you feel losing your Dad? Can you imagine if you never knew him at all because your mom was being a bitch about it? Don't screw up her life because you can't get your own put together."

"Shut up, just shut up," she yelled. "You made your point. Don't you think I've thought of those things? I plan to have him a part of her life but I just don't know how to do it yet. Get off my back. Everyone thinks I just simply need to call him and that would make everything better. It won't. I won't be better. I haven't healed from the first time and you expect me to jump right in again. Well, I can't do it. You weren't there every night that I cried alone. I just physically can not do it yet," she sobbed.

She finally released her truths, not to her friend but to herself. She was afraid to fall in love that deep again. She didn't talk about her pain but they all knew it existed. No one wanted to be the person to push her to see the truth but it was necessary. Now she had the ability to heal herself.

Chapter 41

LARAMIE HAPPILY WAITED for her baby shower. She loved to look in the stores and see the tiny pink dresses, little white shoes and adorable hats. She struggled not to buy anything. She waited for this day with much anticipation. They decided to hold the shower at Edward's since his home was the largest. When the guests started to arrive, he excused himself to a date of golf and cards at the country club.

Lian and Linda decorated the living room in pink carnations and baby's breath. They scattered baby style confetti on the dining table. Her cake was in the center of the table and shaped like a pink baby carriage, with the head of the Merlion as the hinge. They had the caterer make the typical finger sandwiches and salads. Around the two rooms, plates were stacked with pink petit fours. Balloons and streamers hung everywhere and off everything. The house transformed amazingly from stodgy old man to adorable baby girl.

Laramie arrived right on time. Manny agreed to get her there and bring her home but was firm in the fact he would not stay. The décor surprised her completely. Everything looked so beautiful. *How long did they work on this? It is amazing.* Laramie hugged all the guests. Most of the women were from the firm aside from Lian. Lian announced that it was time to start the party and asked Laramie to sit in the side chair next to the sofa.

"I have a quick announcement to make before we start. We have a few last minute guests that I would like to introduce." This caught Laramie by surprise. *Who could Lian have come here? Please don't let it be anyone from Singapore.* "Would our guests please come in the room?"

From around the corner hall, Liz and Gillian walked into the living room. Laramie jumped up and screamed. Her two best friends from college were there to celebrate the baby with her. They ran to each other and hugged just as if they were still in school. She asked whose idea the surprise was and they told her Lian planned it all. Laramie turned to Lian, thanked her and hugged her too. The girls felt Laramie's belly and told her how excited they were. They didn't want to miss this and refused to allow a four hour plane flight be the reason.

After they played the usual shower games and dined, the small conversations began.

Liz asked her, "Well Lara, what names have you picked out for this beautiful baby?"

Many people asked her but she didn't have real solid names yet.

"I never realized how difficult that would be. This baby has that name the rest of her life. So, I have decided on Akiko Audrey; Akiko after her father and Audrey after my mother."

This was quite a surprise for most to hear since Laramie never spoke of the father at work. Her close friends knew the story and remained quiet about it. This bit of information was enough to start rumors in the office.

"Akiko?" Gillian questioned. "Does it mean anything specific?"

"Yes, it means light and bright in Japanese," Laramie responded.

Liz sensed the lull and chimed in quickly, "Just like her mother I might add."

The next stage of her party was to open gifts. The stack of presents overwhelmed her. Lian sat with a pen and paper to take notes. Gillian passed the gifts to Laramie. Liz repacked the gifts then Linda cleared the wrapping paper. They had a very efficient assembly line formed. Laramie received plenty of diapers and wipes. The women without kids brought clothes in newborn sizes while the experienced moms brought the larger sizes. They knew how fast a child grew and compensated for it. She received baby blankets, toys, gates, bottles, etc. She wondered if the limo was big enough to get this stuff home and how many trips it would take to get it in the flat. As the last gift, Linda handed her an envelope and told her it was from Edward. *What could this be?* She read the card and became misty. The first item was a savings account in her name for the baby with ten thousand dollars. *Oh, Edward, this is too generous.* The second item pushed her to straight trailing tears. He gave her a gift certificate for Singapore Airlines. She knew he wanted her to take the baby to Akihiro after she was born. She knew he was correct but didn't expect him to be so direct about it. Gillian handed her a tissue.

"Honey, he is just looking out for your best interest. Edward's subtlety was never his best asset. Anyway, we all know you don't need an airline ticket for the baby until they reach two years old. You have this to keep until after she turns two," replied Gillian.

Laramie perked back up with Gillian's support. Laramie didn't know the airline rules so Gillian made it sound as though Edward did.

After Manny arrived, the pile of gifts astounded him. He also wondered whether the limo had enough room to haul everything to her place. Laramie hugged and thanked the women for coming to the party and for the gifts. She really enjoyed her time with everyone. Gillian and Liz planned to go to Laramie's place for the evening and help her unload and store her things. Lian decided to ride up front with Manny then go home with him. Laramie hugged Linda for planning the party with Lian. Laramie volunteered to stay and clean but Linda insisted she leave. Laramie wondered if there was something romantic happening between Linda and Edward.

After they stored the gifts, Laramie, Liz and Gillian sat in the living room to relax. Liz decided they should order Chinese delivery so they could stay in. Laramie thought the idea was perfect.

"So, Akiko, huh? It seems by the whispering, some of the women hadn't heard about the father, let alone he is half Japanese. Wouldn't you like to be a fly on the lunchroom wall tomorrow?" Gillian supposed.

"I really don't care anymore. The longer I've been home, the less I've thought about work. Tell me, what did you think of the nursery? The artist just finished a few days ago."

Liz interjected, "I think the room is beautiful for anybody, let alone a baby girl. I find it rather ironic that her name reflects her father and her room reflects her father yet the mother hasn't told the father."

"Liz, don't go there," Laramie asked.

"No, I am truly sorry but you have to talk about this. What do you plan to tell your daughter? As she starts to play with other children, she will see they all have a Daddy. She will ask about her own, Laramie. How long do you plan to cut him out of this? I know Manny ticked you off with his thoughts but he was absolutely right."

"Why is this so important to everyone? Lots of women have children without fathers and no one seems to care."

"Well, they're probably not still in love with the guy. You are due to go to a grand opening in Singapore in August. Are you going to bring the baby with you? You promised to tell him after she was born. Is that true or are you bullshittin' us too?"

"Look, I did have contact with him. When he sent the book, I emailed him and thanked him for it. Please let me do this at my pace."

Gillian decided it was her turn next. "An email? You are doing the exact thing Sam used to do to you. You are stringing him along until you see fit to allow him into your life. I remember the day you finally had it and walked out. Do you want Akihiro to do that to you?"

"No, no, no. What makes you think he wants to be a father? What makes you think he wants me? You want me to go to him with everything and lay my heart out there. I can deal with the fact he doesn't want me but I cannot deal with rejection for his daughter. Do you get it? How am I to explain that later in life? Gee, I'm sorry, I love you but he doesn't? I refuse to do that. Let's just drop it."

Liz had to have the last word. "Fine, I will drop it but you will regret this decision. It will come back to bite you in the butt."

After a short while, the tension eased in the room. The women laughed about old college stories and the losers they dated. Gillian said she hadn't been to Vanderbilt since they graduated. Laramie and Liz confessed to the same. Liz told stories about her children, which caused Laramie to question her own sanity. She talked about Randy and life in South Carolina. Liz had her roots there and she planned always to be there. Gillian was the same way with her home in New Jersey. For Laramie, it was different. She lived back and forth across the country and didn't have roots in one particular spot. She never gave it much thought until her friends brought it up.

After dinner, they hugged and kissed goodbye before Liz and Gillian took a cab back to their hotel. Normally, they stayed at Laramie's but since the guest room was now the nursery, she started to wonder about a larger home. *Do I need one extra room? But how many times do I get visitors?* Laramie decided to go to bed early since she didn't nap during the day. *I think tomorrow would be a great day to sleep in.*

* * *

Laramie was sad when her girlfriends flew back to the East Coast. She didn't realize how quiet things were at home. She kept busy with work and birthing classes but the evening silence was unbearable. She began the motherhood rituals as described in her books. She spent evenings with children's book and read to the baby. *Eight different creams. You'd think one of these has to prevent stretch marks.* She was fortunate enough to carry the baby long and small. Only when she turned to the side was it obvious that she was pregnant. She thanked her parents for those genes. One benefit was her breasts grew larger. She wondered about implants and this gave her the option to view without the surgery.

Laramie finished her thank you cards and placed stamps on the envelopes. Each card had a seal with a pink baby's rattle. As she stood, she felt a sharp pain below the baby. She sat for a moment before she tried to stand again. This time when she stood, a warm rush of fluid poured between her legs.

Laramie realized her water broke. *This isn't supposed to happen for another month.* She called the doctor who told her to get to the hospital and she would meet her there. Laramie then called Lian and told her that her water broke. Lian told her to call 911 for the ambulance to get her. Within minutes, the paramedics knocked at her door. They helped her on the gurney and told her to relax. The hospital was further than she thought and seemed like an eternity before they arrived. Lian and Dr. Post were already there when they wheeled Laramie inside. Her contractions were at three-minute intervals. The doctor told her that she had some time but the baby was on her way. By the time they admitted her and rushed Laramie up to a birthing room, her contractions were just minutes apart. The excruciating pain in her lower back made her realize she wanted the meds as Liz told her. However, when the doctor checked her out, the baby's crown showed through the cervix.

"Laramie, listen to me. The baby doesn't want to wait for you to have the epidural. She appears as stubborn as you and decided to come today. Let Lian coach you through breathing and I will tell you when to push. Okay?"

Laramie did her series of breathing sounds and nodded to the doctor too. She squeezed the heck out of poor Lian's hand. Lian wiped Laramie's brow as she breathed.

"Laramie, remember what we did in class, short inhales, long exhales. You're doing great."

Laramie yelled out in pain. She never anticipated this agony. The doctor told her to push and keep pushing. Laramie listened. Then the doctor told her to stop pushing.

"You've got to be kidding me. I want this kid out of me now," she shrieked.

Lian tried to calm her, but Laramie didn't want to hear it. She wanted the baby out.

After a few more pushes and screams, the baby appeared all covered in a white paste and blood. The nurse suctioned Akiko's throat and Laramie heard her cry. Akiko arrived in time for Cinco de Mayo. Lian cut the umbilical cord and the nurse took Akiko to be cleaned off. They wrapped her and placed her on Laramie's chest. Laramie sobbed holding her new daughter. She was the most beautiful baby, so tiny. Akiko had the same dark eyes and jet black hair as her father however, she cried just like her mom. She weighed barely over five pounds and was eighteen inches long.

The nurse took the baby to the nursery and told Laramie to rest. She didn't want them to take Akiko. She waited so long to have her. Lian hugged Laramie and congratulated her. She told Laramie she did a fantastic job considering Akiko was a month early. Lian said she had to go into the waiting area to tell everyone but would be back shortly.

Laramie lay in bed totally wiped out by the ordeal. *I have a daughter. Oh God, thank you. She is so beautiful. Mom, she's finally here. I just wish you were too. I need you so bad right now. I'm so afraid..* When Lian arrived back in the room, she told Laramie that Manny and Edward were there. Laramie told her to let them in. She didn't care that she was full of sweat and a total mess. After the interns came into to see her give birth, she didn't have much modesty left.

"Well, congratulations, Dear. You have one beautiful daughter. How are you feeling now? Do you need anything?"

"No, Grandpa but thank you. Oh actually, I would love something to drink, juice or water."

Manny laughed at hearing Edward called Grandpa. He seemed so perfect for that title. Manny hugged Laramie and kissed her.

"Lian told me you did a great job. I'm not surprised. I don't know how to tell you but she looks nothing like you."

Laramie smirked. "I know, I saw that too. Don't stand too close or they'll think she's yours."

"Geez, I didn't think about that either. I am innocent I swear. Lian stay close." Lian laughed with them.

A few moments later, a nurse came in to review the paperwork for Akiko's birth certificate.

"Miss Holden, I have her name as Akiko Audrey but I need you to tell me the last name. Will it be Holden or something else?" Manny and Lian looked at Laramie as they waited for a response. Laramie never thought about the last name. *Do I give her my name or his? If she stays Holden now, will I have to change it later? Do I deny the fact of her father? Can I deny it?*

Laramie took a deep breathe and held it a moment before she exhaled. "Her last name is Amori. The father is to be listed as Akihiro Amori. A-K-I-H-I-R-O A-M-O-R-I . His place of birth is Singapore, Singapore."

"Thank you. I will get this typed for you to review. Congratulations too." The nurse walked out of her room.

"Well, I for one am very proud of you. You did the right thing by having Akihiro listed as her father," replied Manny. Lian completely agreed with him. "All that is left is to tell him."

"I will, I promise." Changing the subject Laramie continued, "She is the most beautiful baby. She is so tiny. I was really scared about being in labor. I wasn't sure if she was big enough. I can tell you if she would've been any bigger and I would've screamed for a c-section."

Lian added, "Laramie you did great. You followed your breathing though you about took off my hand."

"Thank you both for being here for me. I don't now what I would've done without you."

Edward walked in with her juice. Manny turned to him, shook his hand goodbye and said he and Lian were going home. Lian told Laramie she would stop in later in the morning.

"Well Lara, you did it. You have brought a beautiful daughter into this world. I know your parents would be so proud of you just as I am."

"Thank you Edward, that means a lot to me. By the way, I put Akihiro's name on the birth certificate. He may not here but he is still her father. Besides, she looks just like him."

"That was the right thing. I know you will continue to do so but don't wait too long. Get your rest because soon you won't have anymore."

Laramie kissed him goodbye and laid in bed. She knew she gave birth but it had not sunk in yet. She knew tomorrow brought motherhood classes in swaddling and bathing. *Get some sleep now because it's all over at home.*

Chapter 42

LARAMIE WAS FORTUNATE to have a wonderful nurse stay the first month after she arrived home with Akiko. She thought she could do it on her own but sleeping was a luxury. Finally, Edward had enough and called in a nurse to help. Laramie initially fought him but after the first night of continual sleep, she called to thank him. Akiko had grown another inch and gained a pound. Laramie wanted to breast feed and tried several times since Akiko was always hungry. However, Akiko had a problem latching on and when she did, it was painful. The nurse suggested doing both, formula and pumping, instead of latching. That idea seemed to work well for mother and daughter.

Akiko's black hair stood up on her head like spikes. Laramie tried to wet it to stay flat but it didn't work. She loved to bathe her and dress her. Akiko was like a tiny doll. She was a happy baby and cried very little unless she was hungry which was all of the time. When naptime and bedtime came, Akiko went right to sleep without a fuss. Laramie talked to her everywhere they went and Akiko gurgled. Strangers stopped Laramie to tell her how beautiful her daughter was. This was no surprise to Mommy.

Laramie hated to think she would leave her to return to work. Laramie wanted to stay home but she also missed being around other adults during the day. She called friends but many of them worked and didn't have time to chat. Manny, Lian and Edward visited often but they had lives of their own. Laramie stopped in the office to show everyone her daughter. They all huddled around Akiko. Laramie thought it was funny to see all these professional adults talk like a baby.

"Laramie, I want to tell you something in confidential if you don't mind," said Linda.

"Sure, that sounds rather mysterious."

"We had a slip up here at the office a few days ago."

"What kind of slip up?" Laramie became nervous.

"I went to lunch and a temp answered phones. I'd just walked back when someone called for you. She didn't know all the details and told them you were on maternity leave."

"*What*? Who was on the phone, Linda?" Laramie panicked.

"I grabbed the phone and asked them to repeat who they were calling. She said your name again and I corrected the temp's answer saying she read the wrong line. Harris was on maternity leave and Holden was in Chicago for a meeting."

"Did they say who they were?"

"No, but I believe they bought the story. They seemed content with that answer. However, it was an overseas call because the number comes across the switchboard. I am so sorry. I hope we didn't blow this for you."

"No, it's okay Linda. I'm sorry I put you in the position to lie for me. Eventually someone will slip, even me. Thanks for telling me."

Laramie went home worried who may have called her. *It could've been someone at the bank for Rhys. No need to panic. Let me fire off an email to Rhys just in case. I'll just say I've been in meetings in Chicago and the temporary receptionist hadn't been sending messages to the right people. It sounds believable enough. Heck. It's happened on more than one occasion.* She sent her message and figured he might respond tomorrow depending on the time. Sure enough, Rhys was in the office, though he said he didn't call her. Now she worried about the caller even more. *Pick up the phone and tell him. This won't get any easier. No, I can't do it. What do I say? Hey Aki, sorry I haven't called, been pregnant for the last several months, had a baby and I forgot I didn't tell you. I don't know how it slipped my mind. Yeah, that'll go over in a big way.*

* * *

Laramie spent the next few days interviewing nannies. She had women of all ages and nationalities apply for the position. She narrowed her list down to three women, all equally experienced. However, Francesca Sanchez had the best demeanor with Akiko. When Francesca held the baby, Akiko didn't squirm or fuss as she did with the others.

Francesca adored Akiko. She sang lullabies to her in Spanish. *Now that's someone who can sing, completely unlike Mommy.* Francesca browsed around Akiko's room and stopped by the bedside table.

"Quién es esto? Sorry. Who is this?" Francesca asked in broken English regarding the man in the picture.

"That is Akiko's father. He doesn't live here. We've had some problems. But I want her to know who he is."

"That is very nice. El hombre es muy guapo… very handsome."

"Francesca, I would like to hire you if you want the job. But I need to know if transportation is an issue as well as immigration."

"La immigración no es problema. I born here, Señora."

Laramie checked all references, credit reports, and police records. She checked anything she had access to or anyone who did. She was uneasy about leaving Akiko with a stranger. She decided to have Francesca start the following week while Laramie was on her last week of maternity leave. Laramie felt she could watch Francesca with the baby to build up a comfort level. Laramie wrote out the feeding and nap schedule. She listed all the contacts and their phone numbers, especially the pediatrician. When Laramie had too many pages written, she decided a dry erase board was a better solution. She had Akiko on a strict schedule and wanted Francesca to follow it. Francesca assured her she was okay with the baby since she had two grown children of her own. That was a partial comfort but this was Laramie's only child and she wanted everything perfect for her. Laramie showed her where all the baby's toys were located. She opened every drawer, closet and chest.

The weekend went faster than Laramie expected. She showered and dressed early so she had time to feed Akiko. Francesca arrived right on time and took over the feeding. She assured Laramie everything was okay. Laramie knew the first day back to work would be hard. She hated to leave her daughter and cried as she locked the door behind herself.

Laramie spent most of the morning answering questions everyone had regarding Akiko. Being the doting mother, Laramie was happy to talk about her daughter. Edward squashed all the chit chat and handed Laramie a few new cases.

"You'll need to keep busy the first week otherwise I'll never get you back to work. By the way, what's the status on the DemCorp building?"

"Its about a month away from completion. I'm sure Frank will be happy when it's open and has guests booking rooms."

"Speaking of that. You'll need to book a flight and a room for the opening as well."

"Edward, Akiko is only two months old and you want me to fly thirteen hours with her. That's a little unreasonable."

"Yes it would be but you are going alone and leaving her with Francesca during the day and Lian overnight."

"No. I'm not going. You pushed me into it last time and I didn't need to be there, Now you're doing it again. It's not fair."

"Life isn't fair Laramie or I'd be retired by now. We all do things we don't like and now you have another one. As soon as the hotel is ready, book the flights."

She wanted to fight this out but she knew Edward won. She hated to be away from Akiko. *It's my first week back and already he has me flying off for business. He forgets I can always retire myself and live off my trust. What would that teach Akiko about hard work and earning satisfaction? This will be the third trip to Singapore. Where can I hide this time? I've been to almost every cultural area. I will see Rhys, that's definite. Rhys will call Akihiro the minute I touch down. I can't keep hiding from Akihiro. I am bound to run into him sooner or later.*

* * *

Over the next few months, Akiko, known as Kiki to Mommy, grew and matched her target weights and lengths even though she ranged in the lower ten percentile. Her pediatrician told her that the charts were just a guide. He said Akiko's height and weight were great for her being premature which made Laramie feel better about their conversation. It seemed every other mom's baby was a super sized kid, all in sizes that doubled their age. Akiko was a petite little girl however very strong. She laughed a lot since she was very ticklish. She repeated her sounds of 'baba' and 'dada'. Laramie worried over everything, but at least Francesca calmed her. She knew the nanny loved her daughter very much and took great care of her.

* * *

As Laramie packed for Singapore, she felt proud to fit in her normal clothes. She didn't have much weight to lose but it was the shape that needed to change. She noticed she was curvier than before and her breasts stayed slightly larger. Since breast-feeding was over, she didn't worry about leaks anymore. She wondered if she was a good mother, normal for a first time parent. She hated to leave Akiko in San Francisco and desperately wanted to take her. However, she knew the flight was too long for a newborn. She felt confident in the skills of Francesca and Lian to care for her daughter knowing they loved Kiki as their own.

She cried at the airport when she gave the baby to Lian. She couldn't let go. She was with Akiko everyday since birth and to leave for a week was a mix of guilt and loneliness. She also told Edward this was her last trip without the baby. Her fears from her parents' death became a concern for her. She refused to leave her daughter an orphan. Of course, he tried to explain the difference but Laramie didn't see it.

She boarded her flight, the same one she took twice before. She was more optimistic this time. She felt comfortable in her skin and knew what she wanted. Motherhood gave her a quick lesson in reality and priorities. She knew no one and especially no man was more important than her daughter was. *Isn't that surprising? Still the same flight crew.*

Chapter 43

AS LARAMIE WALKED around the open lobby, she knew she would see Akihiro this time. There was no way to stay hidden with the grand opening of The Democracy. She stayed by Frank's side for most of the preliminary festivities. Frank Paradise was tall, medium built, and quite handsome. His hair was dark with just the right amount of gray over his ears. He stayed fit by running and weight lifting. Laramie always had a crush on him since she went through puberty. Now she viewed him more like Edward, a father figure. When they stood side by side, they made an attractive couple. They appeared as the typical established older man and his trophy girlfriend, which was what many thought at a first meeting.

Laramie walked around the hotel and browsed the small boutiques. She had a sense of pride and accomplishment as if this building was her baby too. As she passed the baby clothes, her heart sank, she missed her daughter. *As soon as I get to the hotel, I can call her, listen to that little coo, and gurgle.* She walked back into the lobby area and saw Rhys with his staff from the bank.

"Laramie, you look wonderful. Our conversations have been great but I miss seeing your face, Love."

"I miss that accent too, Rhys." Laramie hugged and kissed him hello. "I've always been a sucker for foreign men."

"Right and you tell me know. I could've had you to myself for the past year."

"I believe you are flirting with me. Tell me anything, just do it with an accent."

"Actually, I need to congratulate the owner. The Democracy is a stunning building and hotel. For a while, I wasn't sure we'd pull it off."

"Come with me, I'll introduce you to Frank."

Laramie took Rhys' arm and walked to Frank. She introduced him as the sole responsible party for his hotel's completion. Rhys' modesty pushed the credit to Laramie. They were able to laugh at their problems now that the project ended.

Frank excused himself and went to the podium set up in the lobby.

"I would like to say a few things before the party begins. I want to thank all the trades for their commitment to excellence in building this hotel. This is our first endeavor in Singapore and we hope to continue in this area. So many people are responsible for seeing this to completion, our title company, insurance company, and …" Frank listed many companies and individuals. "… I do apologize if I leave someone out. I want to thank the Bank of Singapore and the Singapore government for welcoming us to your country. Lastly, I want to thank my right hand over here, Laramie Holden. Sweetheart, I know I really extended you in this project, but your dedication to your task, even now, as I speak, remains my biggest pride. Thank you."

Laramie waved back to him and blew a kiss for the beautiful words he shared. She knew she just did her job. She knew she had the ability to do it better had she not met Akihiro. She knew her relationship with him clouded her judgment in the beginning, however, now she felt more stabile in this environment.

"Congratulations, Laramie. You did an outstanding job."

She didn't have to turn around to know who it was. She knew the voice and the smell. His presence was not cause for surprise. With her champagne glass in hand, she turned to face him. There wasn't anywhere to hide and she no longer wanted to do so.

"Hello, Akihiro. I wondered when you would be here."

She looked him in the eye for the first time in a year. He still was gorgeous and still had the most unbelievable eyes. Her heart still fluttered and her body still burned, even now. *Don't screw this up Laramie. You played this scenario in your head over and over again. Keep your cool. But, does he have to look so hot?*

"You knew I was coming and still chose to stay? I'm surprised."

"Don't be. I've grown a lot in the past months. I'm still the same woman, just better."

He was stunned to hear speak so clear-cut. *This isn't her normal stance.* He was still attracted to her. He wanted to pick up where they left off and pull her into his arms.

"You look wonderful, you always did. I don't know… something seems different. I can't put my finger on it."

Change the subject Laramie. You don't need him to start a guessing game.

"How are Kat and the rest of the crew? It's been a while since I've seen them as well."

"Kat is doing great, so is everybody else. Shinji asks about you. Though we both know Rhys is the one with the answers."

"And your hotel? I assume you bought the Cheung property. By the way, I really apologize for that. My anger got the best of me and I responded inappropriately. I had no right to lash out at you in that manner. I am truly sorry."

Wow, she finally apologized. That was quite an accomplishment for her and still she kept it simple. She looks great, too great. Why didn't I go after her? What was I thinking?

"Thank you, but I was partly responsible for that, too. Besides, it's in the past. Let's talk about now. I've missed you over the past year. Many times I thought of coming to San Francisco but work and construction always seemed to get in the way."

"I missed you too. I've wanted to call many times but I never found the right words."

"Laramie, have dinner with me tomorrow. We can talk about all of it; get it all in the open. You know we can't do that right here. This isn't the place for it either. Will you do that?"

She knew she couldn't say no and so did he. *Dinner is harmless, right?*

"I'm staying at Raffles. Why don't you pick me up at six? Does that work for you? We can go to Boat Quay or Clarke Quay. It doesn't matter."

He smiled. He knew this was his chance to win her back. Unbeknownst to him, she never left. They stared into each other's eyes without a spoken word. They blocked out everyone around them. They still had the same raw desire for each other. He leaned closer to her and brushed his hand across her cheek. She closed her eyes and absorbed that feeling of passion.

"Six is perfect. I can meet you at your room. What's the number?"

She knew what he had in mind and stopped him in full stride.

"I think it's better to meet you in the lobby." *Whew! That could end without ever leaving the hotel.*

He smiled and agreed. She excused herself and mingled with the other guests at the party. They maintained eye contact throughout the evening, which just intensified their thoughts and passions. Rhys stood by Akihiro and watched this obvious mating ritual.

"Why don't the two of you get a bloody room already?"

"What do you mean?"

"Right. You can't take your eyes off each other. I'm not sure which one of you is more pathetic. I'll say you since you're the man. Get a hold of yourself, mate. She'll be here for a few days. Slow it down."

As the evening wound down, Laramie and Frank thanked their guests and left together for the hotel.

"So that's the man, huh, Laramie? Akiko looks just like him."

"What Frank?" His statement caught her off guard.

"The man you stared at all evening? Is he not Akiko's father?"

"Edward told you, didn't he? He just won't give up."

"Let me give you a bit of advice from an old man. A man doesn't look at a woman the way he looks at you and not feel something. He can't tear himself away from you and he won't when you tell him about his daughter."

"I can't do that just yet. However, we're having dinner tomorrow night. I'm going to see how things progress before I say anything. Also, you'd better not bring up the subject. No one at the Bank of Singapore knows I have a daughter. The man you met this evening, Rhys, is his best friend. One slip and the phone will ring. Please do that for me, Frank. And when you talk to Edward tell him his push didn't work either."

Frank chuckled since he knew she was correct. Edward and he did have a discussion before they left. Frank was the watchful eye over Laramie this trip.

Laramie entered her room. She checked the clock and counted back to San Francisco time. She wanted to call Akiko and just hear her coo or say anything. She missed her daughter terribly. *I will not go anywhere without her next time. How did I let Edward talk me into that? She could be with me and she could meet her Daddy. What was I thinking?*

"Francesca, yes, it's Laramie. Is Akiko awake? Can I talk to her?"

"Sí, Senora. Let me put the telephone by her ear. I will say when to talk."

Francesca put the phone near Akiko's ear. Laramie talked to her daughter and told her she missed and loved her very much. When Akiko heard Mommy's voice, she repeated 'ba' over and over. The nanny told Laramie the baby was excited to hear her voice. She thanked Francesca and said she would be home in a few more days then she blew kisses to her daughter over the phone. *How will I make it two more days without her?*

Laramie hung her clothes neatly in the closet. She lay in bed with her arms behind her head and her legs crossed, she thought about Akihiro's touch and yearned for him to touch her again. After all, she was a woman before she was a mother. She knew she couldn't push him off too long nor did she want that. She waited for this time since Akiko was born; she wanted to tell him all about his daughter. *He said he missed me but does he love me? Will he love her too?*

Chapter 44

LARAMIE HAD BREAKFAST with Frank. They discussed the events of the previous evening and the various people they met. Frank was hesitant to breach the subject but still went forward anyway.

"Laramie, I've known you since you were little. I've watched you grow up to a beautiful, smart, and fascinating woman. I'm sure in conversation you and this fellow have talked about your family, friends, and work to a degree. Does he know everything about you, excluding Akiko? Where I am going with this is… did anyone ever question you about the land lease? You lost two million dollars over four months and while the money doesn't mean much to you, it is a motivator for others."

"Are you asking if he is interested in me for my money? I'd never believe that. I'm sure some people questioned that deal but I don't think anyone looked further into it. My judgment was awarded many years ago. Of course, if someone really wanted to investigate me, they might find something but the amount was sealed from the public. There is only speculation and that really is mainly back home. Besides you know people, something is news until the next tragedy comes along."

"I'm just looking out for you, that's all. You are a beautiful young woman, if only I were twenty years younger," he said with a grin.

"Even if you were, my heart is for another. But I do love you." *Frank, I would've been all over you if you were twenty years younger and before Singapore.*

After breakfast, Laramie sunbathed at the pool. She ordered an ice tea while she read a magazine. *Oh, look in the past year, Christina married. At least it was to someone besides Akihiro.* She thought of Shinji, Kat and Rhys. *I've never met his parents. I wonder what they're like. I just can't picture a half British-half Spanish woman with a Japanese man but whatever they look like; they've produced two very attractive sons.* The more she thought about his friends, she wondered what their thoughts were of her. *Do they even like me? Is Rhys nice to my face but slamming me behind my back? I just assumed since everyone was pleasant that they liked me. They could be telling him to lose the crazy American and I would never know.* She tried not to be so paranoid but these questions were important to her. *If I gave up everything in California, would I be happy here? Would I have any friends?*

She rolled over in her bathing suit, thankful it was one piece but still fashionable. She still had light toning to do and sit-ups were the only way to firm it back up. Laramie loathed exercising but did it to stay healthy. She could not afford to get sick around the baby however, she didn't mind if she missed a day or two of work now that Akiko was there. *Where is my sun? Geez. I thought I pulled this chair in full sun? Now I'm going to have to get up and find a new spot. This never fails.*

"Excuse me, Madam. I wondered if you would like to start your day earlier?"

"I believe you are in my sun, Sir. Would you kindly move?" *Crap, I'm in a bathing suit and looking a bit flabby. I'm a mess. Hair in a clip and no makeup. Really cool.*

Akihiro sat on the edge of her chair. Laramie pulled her pareo on top as she rolled to her back. She was nervous with him so close to her.

"What brings you here so early? I thought we were going to meet at six?"

"I had a meeting in the city and thought I would see you afterwards. Why? Do you want me to leave?"

"No, no. I'm just surprised. I assumed you were busy with construction and wouldn't have free time, that's all." *As if I'd want you to leave. Hello?*

"Come here. Sit up a minute."

He pulled her to him by her shoulders and kissed her. She melted in his arms. She wanted that moment to never stop. He ran his fingers through her hair and held her close as he kept plunging his tongue to meet hers. He never lost that effect on her. She ran her hands along the side of his face as she greeted every kiss. *This has been one long year without him. Maybe dinner in my room would be better.* When he stopped, he looked into her eyes they way he used to with passion and desire.

"As much as I want to continue this, I think you need to get dressed if you want to go for a ride and dinner." *She still drives me wild. I can't let her go this time.*

Laramie worried about him coming to her room. If he saw her undressed, it would force her to disclose everything about Akiko. She didn't know how to stop him. She couldn't think of anything to say.

"Lara, get dressed and I will meet you out front. I have a few calls to make and I can't get a signal inside the building. Don't take too long."

Whew! That was extremely close. I've got to keep my wits about me. She dressed quickly in a sundress that was form fitting in the top but loose in the waist. *Thank goodness, the styles are camouflaging right now.* She grabbed her purse and slid on shoes then went downstairs. Akihiro sat in his car and motioned her over when he saw her. Laramie sat in the car and put on her sunglasses.

"Where are we going?"

"It's a surprise, at least for a minute." He smiled at her.

Laramie watched as they drove toward Sentosa Island, unsure where he planned to stop. Of course, when he pulled into the Tanjong, she knew. *However, are we seeing friends or bungalows?* Laramie greeted Samad and shouted for Kat when she saw her. Kat called out Laramie's name and hugged her. It was like visiting old friends. *Why did I ever worry?*

"I can't tell you how happy I was to hear you were back in town and that you agreed to see Aki. When I get you alone, I'll fill you in on how miserable he has been without you. How long are you here visiting? Don't tell me you go home tomorrow."

"No, sorry but the day after that. How have you been? You know if he ever lets you leave this place, I'd love to have you in San Francisco."

"I was almost there once but they said you were in Chicago." *So it was Kat that called. I hope I don't look pregnant now.*

"Enough, today you are mine." He grabbed her hand and led her out the back of the hotel. Handing her a hard hat, he said, "You need to wear this."

They walked between the bungalows and passed what used to be a privacy wall. He wanted her to see the new hotel addition. His dream was a reality again. She was ecstatic for him. Seeing his face light up was worth losing the two million dollars.

"Akihiro, it's magnificent. I'm just in awe. When do you expect to be finished?"

"I'm hoping in another four months depending on the work pace and supplies. You *really* like it?"

"No, I love it. I am so happy for you. I'm speechless."

Laramie felt a pang of guilt looking at the new building. She knew the construction would be over if not for her. Her eyes became teary and she turned back to the Tanjong. He grabbed her hand and pulled he back.

"Don't go. Walk around with me," he asked sincerely.

"But I feel so bad. This would've been complete if not for me."

"That's true but because of you, the terms were easier to negotiate. Since you left Mr. Cheung such a windfall and the economy on new construction lessened, I was able to buy the land for less money. So, I may have lost time, but I saved in the end."

"Are you making that up to make me feel better?"

"No, not at all." He shook his head as he grinned.

He walked Laramie around the new area set up for a larger spa, the larger kitchen area and to the top floor where the junior suites will be. She asked him questions about every aspect of the building and décor. She asked him about his plans for the old spa and kitchen, and if he was going to build more bungalows like the one she booked. Akihiro rambled on as he told her every detail he planned. Obviously, his pride and heart went into this structure.

Afterwards, he took her hand, walked her to the beach area, and sat on a lounge chair. She sat with her back against him, between his legs.

"This is so beautiful. I missed the views on the beach. Somehow, I forgot about the humidity," she laughed.

"I still love you, Lara. I missed you. It will be so hard to watch you leave again. Can't you stay here?"

"I wish I could but I have a few responsibilities in San Francisco that I need to attend to first. I promise I'll be back sooner next time. For the record, I love you too. You can't imagine how much I've missed you and needed you."

Just then, a construction worker interrupted their conversation to ask a question and review a drawing. Akihiro excused himself for a moment. Laramie sat on the chair alone staring at the sea. *Those waves are still mesmerizing. I wonder if he would want me to stay if he knew it was a two-person package. We have so many things to discuss.* Laramie sat alone for a short while before Kat walked down to join her.

"Laramie, how are you really doing? I mean you haven't seen him in a year. Do you care more or less now?"

"Kat, I feel as though it was yesterday when I saw him last. He asked me to stay but I'm not sure he's ready for that. He seems busy with construction and I wouldn't want to be in his way or compete for his time."

"He goes home every night. Are evenings enough for you?"

"Yes. I'm not trying to make excuses for either of us but my life is a little more complicated now. He wouldn't just be dealing with me, but all the baggage. It's a package deal."

"Well I'm not following you one bit. However, I can tell you he loves you and thinks about you all the time. If it wasn't for the construction to take up his time, I don't know how he would've handled you being gone. He may sugar coat things but if you want the straight answers, come to me."

"Thanks for telling me. I've never loved a man more than him; I don't think I ever will. There's a connection I can't put into words that will be there forever." *Yeah, the word is Akiko.*

Akihiro returned to see the women chatting on the beach.

"Can I get either of you ladies a drink? Oh wait, I believe I employ one of you. Miss Tan, break time is over."

"See you, Laramie. Maybe we can talk more when the boss isn't around."

"What were you talking about?" He sat behind her again.

"You. Then we got onto a new subject and talked about you."

"You are hilarious, Holden. I missed your sense of humor, your smile, your eyes, your lips, and your body." He spoke between kisses.

"I wondered how long it was going to take you to get to my body. It certainly wasn't going to be my brains."

"No, I love your brains, but I love your body more."

"Well, what else have you planned? Do you have an itinerary I can review?"

"I can say it doesn't involve boats, heights or karaoke, especially the karaoke. Do you have any requests?"

"How about a quiet evening together?" she poised.

"I thought you wanted to go out the quays? So you *want* to be alone with me. Any particular reason?" He nibbled at her ear and neck.

"I hate to end that thought but it isn't a convenient time for me."

"I don't care. You want to visit your old bungalow?" *He called that bluff.*

"You are so tempting and so hard to push away."

He took her hand and walked to her old bungalow. He opened the door and walked into the bedroom. He pulled the covers down and went to her. She wanted him and at first, she felt apprehensive since the baby. The doctor told her she was very susceptible to another pregnancy since she just gave birth. She knew she needed to have some contraceptive. She decided to take her chances. *Not my most responsible move but damn, he looks so good. I can't say no.*

As he lay on the bed, he pulled her close to him. He kissed her passionately and rubbed his hands over her body. Her desires started her breathing to increase and deepen. She wanted him even more now. It was so long ago since she felt his touch.

"Tell me how much you missed me," she asked.

He pulled his lips from her neck. He started to unzip her dress.

"I have missed you so much. No one has been able to make me feel the way you do. I need you here with me." *Hold it. Hold everything.*

"Akihiro, did you just say no one has been able to make you feel as I do?"

"Semantics, Laramie. What difference does it make? It's you that I want," he continued as he started to lift her dress.

She stopped him. He rolled off to her side.

"How many have there been, Aki?" her voice became agitated.

"It doesn't matter, Lara."

"It matters to me. I sat in San Francisco trying to work through everything so we could be together without any reservations. It seems like life went on fine for you without me."

"You were gone for a year. *A year,* Laramie. What did you expect me to do? Wait for you? How long was I supposed to do that? Moreover, if you never came back, then what? Think about it. Look at the reality of the situation."

This was a hard pill for her to swallow but he was right. They weren't together any longer. She did refuse to see him last time she was in country. However, it hurt to hear he was with someone else.

He continued, "Look, I'm sorry if that hurts you but see it from my perspective."

"You're right. I don't know what I was thinking. I don't know what I expected. I'm sorry, I just can't do this right now. The mood is gone."

She stood up, pulled her dress down and zipped the back. She grabbed her purse and walked out of the bungalow. Akihiro ran to catch up with her.

"What is your problem, Lara ? Why can't you just talk to me? Why do you run away every time?"

"Because, I don't know how I should react. I run away because it hurts and I don't want anyone to see me hurt. Are you satisfied with that answer? Do you need a better explanation?"

"Stop, please. Talk with me."

She stopped and turned to him. "I love you and that won't change, ever. I don't have the experience in relationships you do. I didn't have that example growing up so I have no basis. All I know is when I hurt I need to get away from the hurt. Is there another pathetic tale to my life you want to know? Let me go to the next one." She wiped the tears that ran down her face. "My first boyfriend didn't happen until college. *College.* He cheated repeatedly on me. I heard him with another girl through the dorm room door. I was too afraid to confront him and be alone, so I stayed with that loser for months until I built up enough self-esteem to leave. What another one? The list doesn't end. You would've known that had you cared enough to learn something about *me.*"

She turned back and continued to walk away from Akihiro. He stood there stunned. He had no idea. So many pieces began to fit. *She's right. I've never asked her about her life, her personal life. I've always wanted her to conform to my life and surrounding.* He ran to catch her, which he did in the lobby.

"Laramie, wait. I didn't know. You are right, I've never asked about you.

I am so sorry." He held her close and hugged her as she sobbed. "Let's go in my office and talk, okay?" She nodded yes.

She paced his office. "You have no idea how lucky you are. You have your parents and your brother. I've been alone since I was twelve. My grandparents tried to take care of me until they died and I was sent to Edwards. While I love Edward, he wasn't the most nurturing person. Work is all he knows so that was all I learned. I am one hell of an attorney, you'd really be surprised. Ask me anything about the law, I can recite it. So I learned to study people and how they interact with each other but that doesn't make you friends, it teaches you who the liars are. I have four friends that I've told you about because that's all I have. I know hundreds of people but have only *four* friends." She stopped to take a breather, still sobbing.

Akihiro sat speechless. He didn't know what to say to her or how to make her feel better. At first all he could mutter was her name.

"Laramie, don't assume you have only four friends. I love you. I've loved you since the first day we met. I think you're amazing. Rhys thinks you're fantastic. Kat adores you and Shinji would throw me in front of a bus to take my place." She tried not to laugh about Shinji but it still slipped. "I don't think you give yourself enough credit in the number of people who love you." He took a tissue and wiped her tears. He kissed her forehead and just held her tight. "Let's go to the condo. We can be alone and just talk all night, okay?"

She sniffled a little as she tried to gain her composure, again. She liked the idea. She grabbed her things and they drove to The Berth. She remembered the last time she was there, so was Christina. *At least that's old news. However, I still don't want to see her on TV.* He held the door to the elevator for her. When she stepped into the foyer, everything was the same as before. Nothing out of place. Akihiro sat on the sofa and propped his feet on the table. He placed a pillow on his lap and told her to lie down. Laramie lay on her back with the pillow beneath her head.

"Okay Miss Holden, I want to hear everything about you. Tell me about your parents first. I'm sure they loved you more than anything."

Laramie told him what she remembered of her parents and how alive their home was. She remembered people coming over all the time for parties. She remembered her father's sense of humor and her mother's southern drawl. She told him how they read to her all the time especially at bedtime. Laramie continued how they went away for their anniversary and never came back. She recalled how quiet the other homes were compared to hers, the laughing was gone, the parties never happened.

"Laramie, you knew your parents loved you, right?"

"Yes, they told me all the time. There was never a question about that. What about you? What was it like in the Amori household?"

"I'm told I was happy until Shinji came home. I asked my mother to return him for a puppy." Laramie laughed. "As you can see we kept him. I grew up normal. We visited family on holidays, spent weekends in the park, played sports after school. My mother is wonderful. She is the peacekeeper. My father is strict. He grew up with the old values and work ethic, which isn't bad, just out dated some. He wanted me to work for him after University but I wanted to go out on my own, as you know. We had many arguments regarding that. My mother finally stepped in and demanded a trial period. I haven't work for him yet. Shinji will tell you he hates to work for him, he doesn't. He lives for the arguments so he can make a point."

"I may regret this but what about you? I mean I've told you about the only other guy. I'm assuming by your knowledge you've known many women. If you don't want to answer, that's okay too."

"I dated a few girls in high school but I was more interested in karate because I was so shy."

"*Shy?* You? Really?"

"Yes, I was shy. I went to Oxford and you know I met Rhys there. I missed Singapore and came back after two years. I met Kat at the University but we are just friends. While I worked for the bank, I met Christina. Her father was on the board of directors, she came in often. We dated for two years and became engaged. We both thought it was the natural progression; it's what our parents did. Eventually, we realized we didn't love each other that way. We let it continue as a support instead of ending as we should. Then, came you. We know how that went."

"What's your opinion on marriage and family now?" Laramie felt as though she was on a witch-hunt. She hated to set him up but she wanted to know his true thoughts without any outside influences.

"I haven't given it much thought. I always seem to have something else happening. Do I want to get married? Yes, someday. Do I want children? It would depend on the marriage. Why? What about you?" *Marriage then children, I don't have that option.*

"I suppose I'm old fashioned in a way, but I want both. I think it takes two people to raise a child but I've seen a lot of single parenting as well." *Just speaking from experience.*

"This has been an educational night. Are we to continue or are we finished for the night?"

"I think we've had a great start. We can pick this up another time. What next?"

He bent over and kissed her lightly. "I do love you, Lara."

"I love you too." She smiled back at him.

"Do you want to go out and eat? Or we can order anything you want from the hotel and have it delivered."

"Actually, I'd like to stay in if you don't mind."

Akihiro went into the kitchen for the phone. Laramie walked onto the deck and looked at the boats moving through the channel. She wanted to call Akiko but knew it was near naptime. She missed her baby so much. She missed playing with her and holding her. She didn't want to miss anything. She already felt she was by working.

"What are you thinking about?"

"Believe me you don't want to know." She shook her head with a halfhearted laugh.

"Sure I do. Tell me." He stood behind her and placed his arms around her.

"Since you asked… babies." She winced.

"Okay, you're right, I don't want to know." *That's what I was afraid of, but he doesn't know he has one and it is different when it's your own. Change the subject. Not a hot topic.*

"Did you order something good?"

"Yes, it should be here in twenty minutes."

Akihiro kept his hands on her. She didn't mind but knew she was in dangerous territory. Talking wasn't the only thing on his mind nor hers. He sat in the patio chair and pulled her close. He lifted her dress so she could straddle him. She held his face as she kissed him. Their movements became rapid and intense. Their kisses left the other breathless. His hand moved behind her, pushing her hips over his. He moved one hand, pulling down the straps of her dress, and kissing the upper parts of her breasts and cleavage. He drove her wild. She didn't care anymore and wanted to remove her clothes. She wanted him desperately. He lifted her and carried her into the bedroom for the privacy. He unfastened his pants, dropping them to the floor. He climbed on the bed and began to lift her dress. Suddenly, the phone rang. He assumed it was their food and decided to have them leave it. However, the phone continued to ring. He became frustrated and finally answered it. Laramie knew something was wrong but couldn't make out the conversation..

"Laramie, I have to go. One of the concrete posts has cracks and they feel it may affect the structure."

"Do you want me to go with you?" She noted his concern.

"No stay here, the food should be on its way. I shouldn't be long."

Laramie hung out at the condo. This wasn't how she imagined the night. Shortly after Akihiro left, their food arrived. She sat in front of the television and watched old American reruns. When she tired of that, she browsed the place looking for a book to read. She felt queer as she looked through his things, almost like a spy. *This is really innocent. I just hope I don't find something weird*. She went into the office, just as orderly as her last visit. She opened the closet doors and saw he had books on an upper shelf. Most of them were on architecture and minimalist design. *Well this is obviously the influence for his hotel*. When she pulled out an additional book, a picture fell to the floor. It was a family portrait. Akihiro appeared to be around eighteen. He looked similar except now with a thicker beard and fine lines. Shinji was adorable though chubbier. *He must've started working out after that picture*. She looked at his father. He was tall and thin, somewhat stoic. She wondered if that was more of his culture than his personality. He was a handsome man. However when she saw his mother, she realized Akihiro resembled her the most. She was a stunning woman, very European with the same smoldering eyes. *Kiki has many of the same features. This is so cool to see a history of family for her. I may be jumping the gun there. He hasn't exactly been endearing toward the mention of children. I may love him but my first duty is to her.*

She watched the clock. Akihiro still was gone. He didn't contact her with any news. She worried that something terrible happened to his hotel. *I wonder if this will cause further delay? I know this is extremely important to him. Just keep your fingers crossed.*

Laramie thought about him wanting her to move there. It seemed sudden but it didn't surprise her. *We haven't talked about where I would live, what I would do for employment. I'm not qualified to practice Singapore law without studying their bar. I really don't want to have to do that again. Money isn't an issue. Would he still want me knowing Akiko would be with me? How will that affect us? How do I break that news to Edward and Andrew? They are my family. What about the corporation and the firm? What about my friends? Well, they do have their own lives and when they all have children their time will wane. I haven't given this as much thought as I need. It isn't a simple move after all. I do love him and I want to be with him. How much time will there be for family after the other two hotels are built? Assuming he wants a family.*

The time passed still without notice from him. She worried about the damage and wanted to call him. *If I call I may be interrupting something. Don't call him*. She was a prisoner there, without conversation or entertainment. She finally decided to go to sleep. She was out of other options. *Do I sleep with clothes on or off? I'm taking a big risk if I go bare*. She climbed onto the bed with her clothes on and pulled the comforter over her. *Duh? That was an easy answer.*

Shortly past midnight, Akihiro arrived at the condo. He called her name, no response. He looked to see if she was on the deck but it was dark. He looked into his bedroom and she was sound asleep. *Not much of an exciting night for you? All this way only to be left alone. Believe me, this isn't how I planned the night.* He didn't want to wake her so he left the comforter turned on her. He undressed and crawled in next to her. He leaned on his side and played with her hair. *Laramie, you have turned my world upside down. I can't imagine you leaving me again. You have to come back and stay this time. The hardest part is behind us.* Akihiro rested his arm over her and went to sleep.

Chapter 45

LARAMIE ROLLED ONTO her back and stretched her arms out. She slept soundly and appeared to be alone. *Did he ever come to bed? What time did he come back?* She sat on the edge of the bed a moment before she went to find him. She walked out of the master and found him on the deck with his phone. She quietly went into the kitchen to see if there was fresh coffee or tea. Nothing. *Well, I can get that at the hotel, no biggie.* She walked onto the deck and sat at the table. She knew better than to interrupt him on the phone especially in a heated conversation. He finally turned and acknowledged her. He held his finger up to say one more moment. He ended his conversation shortly after that.

"How are you this morning?" he asked, as he kissed the top of her head. "I'm sorry I got back so late. You were asleep and I didn't want to wake you."

"I'm fine. I can handle being alone. Tell me what's happened at the hotel?"

"One of the concrete support columns cracked. It wasn't deep but it went long. I had to have x-ray equipment brought in and a structural engineer review the slides to make sure the column was safe to bear a load. He felt the column would be fine but we used a special epoxy resin to fill the groove. This would allow for expansion and contraction. It wasn't really technical as it was time consuming."

"So everything is fine and construction can still commence?"

"Yes. Just another day in building. You missed most of this since you had a general contractor who assumed those responsibilities."

"Why don't you hire someone to oversee the addition and new hotel? Wouldn't that relieve some of the stress off you?"

"Yes, but I would also lose the control I have on the project like quality, times, deliveries. I would be at the mercy of the contractors instead of pushing them."

"It's hard to delegate duties when you're a perfectionist. Been there, done that. Anyway, what's the plan for today? I know you're busy but what about later?"

He walked beside her and rubbed her shoulders. "What about now? You didn't ask me that?" He kissed the back of her neck. She moved her head side to side accommodating him.

"There's a flaw in that plan. I have a meeting with Frank this morning to sign off some papers for the bank. He also wants to do a walk-through in some areas at the hotel. I'm going along to help him."

"Don't you want to help me?" he said running his hand over her chest.

"Is your mind ever out of the bedroom?" She smiled.

"Not with you. We keep starting and never finishing."

"Well Tiger, I hate to be the bearer of bad news, but you're not getting lucky this morning either. I need you to drive me to the hotel so I can shower and change."

"You can shower here."

"Sure that'll take forty minutes. I still don't have clothes or my toiletries. Our schedules just aren't meshing well this time. What about tonight? You haven't answered that."

"Tonight is fine. Let's get your things together and get you off to work."

Their drive into the city was smooth. He agreed to pick her up later in the afternoon for a quick boat ride and dinner. She loved to be on the water except when wake jumping. As they pulled in front of Raffles, his cell phone rang. He told her to go inside and he would meet her there. As Laramie walked through the lobby, she ran into Frank.

"Are you just getting in?" He seemed agitated by her morning arrival.

"I might be. Are you my father?" Laramie shot back.

"No, but we are supposed to meet in thirty minutes and you're not ready yet. Are you going to make us late?"

"No, Frank, I will run upstairs in a moment. I have to wait for Akihiro."

"I suppose since you were out all night you must've told him. How did he take the news?"

Laramie became angry. She was fed up with everyone directing her on this issue. They began to quarrel in the lobby. They didn't make a lot of noise but their movements were animated. Since Edward wasn't there to take up the cause, Frank took his place.

"When do you plan to tell him?"

Just then Akihiro walked up and said, "Tell me what?"

Laramie leered at Frank. He put her on the spot and she need to recover quickly.

"We've already talked. I told him we were working this afternoon. He has to work as well so it worked out for everyone."

"Sorry, let me introduce myself. I'm Frank Paradise. You must be Akihiro. I've heard a lot about you. Great to meet you finally. Sorry you had to pick up on our quarreling. I've known Laramie she was a child and sometimes I find myself playing the overbearing father-type instead of client."

"It's a pleasure to meet you as well. I attended your grand opening of The Democracy. Really a remarkable new hotel. I'm sure it will do well here in Singapore."

Laramie asked if Akihiro was coming up but he had to beg off. He told her he would see her later and kissed her goodbye. He turned, shook Frank's hand and politely excused himself.

She glowered at Frank. "Don't do that to me. You can tell Edward the same. I will not be bullied or blackmailed into telling him. Now, if you'll excuse me, I need to get dressed."

Laramie was livid as she walked away. Frank knew she needed to tell him. He also knew it wasn't his responsibility to do it either. Everyone seemed against Laramie and the choice she made. *Won't everyone just give me a break. I can handle this in my own way.*

After she showered and changed, she met Frank in the lobby. She carried her laptop and purse. She dressed more casual than normal for a meeting. She decided on jeans and a satin blouse. She knew Frank was very particular in his walk-through and the possibility of climbing a ladder or crawling under counters was not uncommon. She didn't understand why he did not have someone better educated to do this type of work, like his architect. Perhaps it was pride of ownership that made Frank inspect everything. They entered the limousine and headed to the bank.

"Laramie, I apologize for arguing with you earlier. I know it is none of my business but since I know you so well I couldn't help it."

"I understand. I understand everyone's concern. However, this really is a matter between Akihiro and me. He's asked me to move to Singapore, and quite frankly, I am tempted to do so."

"And do *what*? Your family, friends and your career are in San Francisco. I can't imagine you leaving the firm after becoming partner. Who would run the place? Have you given that thought? What about Cummings Corporation? Are you just going to leave that on Edward?"

"I'm not saying this hasn't been difficult. I have thought about housing, work and care for Akiko. If I wanted to practice law, I probably would have to go back to college and sit the bar. I've thought of staying home and taking care of my daughter. It's not like there isn't money in the bank. But first and foremost, I want to be sure he loves me and understands what is involved in this relationship."

"Does that mean you plan to tell him tonight?"

"Maybe… yes, if we can get that far. He has two construction projects going and they seem to interrupt our time. Please understand the difference. I am not hiding Akiko from him. All he would have to do is check newspapers on-line. I am trying to find the calmest time to tell him he has a daughter. He isn't exactly keen on being a parent right now and I don't want to push him away when he finds out. Does that make sense?"

"The problem with your thought process is he may not want a child now but it doesn't negate the fact that he has one. It isn't some hypothetical. I don't know of any man who has told his wife or girlfriend, 'hey I would really love a kid about now.' It is something we adjust to having. We don't have your maternal feelings or ticking clock."

"Nevertheless, the child is mine and so is the timing."

"True. Have you said anything about moving to Edward? I know he won't take it well. He has grown so close to you as if you were his actual daughter."

"No, not yet. I didn't want to jump the gun until I saw how things went here. There's no telling how this will end up." Laramie looked out the window and realized they were at the bank. "Let's go finish our business."

* * *

Akihiro worked most of the day via cell phone. Every time he sat in his office, another worker came to ask a question. When he walked to the job site, his phone rang from workers in Batam with questions also. Kat tried to get him to delegate some responsibility but he wanted to maintain complete control. She knew these projects overwhelmed him and caused much of his stress. He controlled his temper and comments but Kat knew it was a matter of time before he lost it. She called Rhys and Shinji to volunteer to help but Akihiro brushed off their efforts.

The late morning's Sumatra hindered any progress. Akihiro scheduled the concrete work for the morning, which he called and canceled. Between the support post last night and the concrete today, his aggravation exceeded his limit. The plastic sheeting that covered the pour area blew off during the storm and filled the formed area with water. He checked around for unused pumps but many of the businesses already rented them the night before to remove any water that could hamper tourism. He walked back to his office disgusted by the morning events.

"Hey Kat, what's on the remaining agenda?"

"Which agenda do you mean? Tanjong Hotel, Tanjong addition or Tanjong Batam?"

"Is that a joke? Because it's not funny," he retorted.

"No, no joke. We have three agendas we follow everyday. So, it makes it difficult to know which one you are speaking about."

"I really don't need the sarcasm."

"Sarcasm?" Kat shut his office door behind her. " Look, we are all trying our best to get through this. You aren't making it any easier by thinking you are some superman. You couldn't control the weather. It's the same at Batam. Unfortunately, that causes delays in construction but it's not our fault. Don't take it out on us."

"Then let me have the hotel's agenda so I can work."

"Here." She threw the papers on his desk. "Oh and thanks for the great apology too."

Kat stayed level headed unless someone singled her out for their problems. She normally walked away from Akihiro until he calmed down but everyone felt miserable from the weather. She knew he needed space to vent but had no intention of being the target.

"Kat, I'm sorry. I don't mean to take it out on you. It is just aggravating."

"Then hire someone to assist you. Let them field the calls. How much do you know about concrete? There are experts for that. Let them do their job. You cannot handle the construction of two hotels while running a third all at once."

"I'll look into it."

"Which means you won't do it. I will tell you right now. I am not going to sit here and let you shout at me because you have no other way to vent your anger. I will leave. Look, you can't do much here because of the rain. Why don't you meet Laramie since she leaves tomorrow?"

* * *

Laramie struggled to finish with Frank. After she walked each banquet room and conference room, she no longer cared if the GFCI outlets were installed properly. She was tired. She never paid attention to the number of restrooms in a building and now felt there were too many. This was beyond her realm and whether Frank wanted to stop or not, Laramie boycotted any more work.

"Frank, this is ridiculous. Neither one of us are general contractors. Even if we found something wrong we don't have the knowledge or tools to address it. You've paid good money for other people to do this. Besides, many of the bugs won't be detected until the building is in full service. So, you can stay and finish this madness but I'm going to the hotel and getting ready for my evening."

"Where's he taking you? Anywhere nice?"

"You know, I don't even care if we stay indoors. I'm tired of walking in heels even if they're low."

"Wait, I'll go back with you. I still have some papers to leaf through and I can reach the States finally with the time difference."

When Laramie entered Raffles, she checked for messages at the desk. She had one from Akihiro that said he would be there earlier than he thought. As she walked through the lobby area, he came out of Harry's Bar and called for her.

"Laramie, slow down. I'm already here."

"Well, hello. How did construction go today? Did the storms affect you very much?"

"Let's not discuss it. The whole day was a waste."

She kissed him. "I'm sorry to hear that. However, it still had to be better than being with Inspector Frank. Come on up. I really need to change my shoes."

"I know we talked about going out on the Kisaki but the waves are high and rough especially in the Straits. I thought we'd walk the Riverfest down at Clarke Quay."

"*Walk*? Did you just miss the last comment about shoes?"

As they entered her room, Laramie kicked her shoes off in her closet. *Ah, relief!* She pulled off her blouse and put on a black knit shirt. She wanted relaxation at any cost. After she freshened up in the rest room, she sat next to Akihiro on the sofa.

"I figured construction was on the back burner with the weather. That was a hell of a thunderstorm. Does that happen often? I don't remember any last year," she asked.

"Sometimes, only today was the wrong day. However it should be a few weeks before another comes. Most of the concrete work should be done by then."

"See... there is a positive." She ran her fingertip through his hair, along his ear and down his neck.

He grabbed her hand and kissed the top. "Are you ready? Let's go."

They walked down along the river. The steps were bright with neon lights. The decorated bumboats formed a parade along the water. He walked Laramie inside of Ma Maison Restaurant in The Central. Laramie expected French cuisine based on the name but quickly learned it was a Japanese version of European dishes. It was small inside but quite cozy. The décor seemed European cottage with fringed curtains and empty bottles on the sills. The tables each displayed a floral cloth similar to the restaurants of Burgundy. The place offered a great view of the Singapore River without the humidity.

The waiters, mainly Japanese, spoke with heavy accents. Laramie opted to use Akihiro to order for her. She thought to order something different and opted for the *tonkatsu*, unknown to her, it was a breaded pork cutlet with brown rice. Akihiro ordered the seafood paella.

"Don't you think that's cheating on your mother's recipe?"

"How will she know? Are you going to call her?" he asked testing her follow-though.

"No. You called my bluff. I didn't have a thing," she laughed.

"What time is you flight tomorrow?"

"It's the same as always, nine fifteen. Too early to be there two hours before departure I might add. I've most of my things packed so the morning should be easy."

Laramie felt saddened by the conversation. She hated the thought of leaving him again. The terms never went positive. She hoped this time might be different. They didn't have any outstanding disagreements. They seemed more relaxed around each other. Dinner conversation centered around her day mainly. A few times she inquired about the hotels and he changed the subject. She asked how Kat and Shinji were. His answers were short and to the point. She tried to brush off his curtness but the longer into the night the more evident it became. Finally, she chose silence. *If he has something to say, I can wait.*

After dinner, they walked along the river. *This is a big commitment to make. Am I really ready for this? There are so many questions that need answers first.* They sat on a bench near Riverside Point and people watched for a bit before Laramie decided to strike up a conversation.

"Akihiro, I know we've touched on the subject but we never set any details. You want me to come here and be with you but where am I supposed to live? What am I to do for employment?"

He looked at her through the side of his eyes as if the subject wasn't a priority. *Not now Laramie. Is this really necessary?*

"I assumed you would move in with me. I want to be able to wake up with you by my side. As for work, I figured you would continue to practice law."

"Well, the problem with that is I don't have reciprocity between countries. They haven't agreed on those terms in the foreign trade agreement. While I could establish a joint venture with a Singapore firm, but as such, I can only practice US law. I don't see much demand in that. However, I suppose going back to law school and sitting the bar for Singapore is another option. I don't know if I could qualify for that position not being a citizen. I haven't looked into that option as much."

"I guess that gives you something to look into when you get back." *Again short and curt. Hmmm…*

"Akihiro, come to San Francisco. I know you're busy here but you can take a week and help me with this move. There are so many things I need you to see. Would you do that?"

"Lara, you know I can't leave right now. You have heard the phone calls. I'm too busy."

"Okay. What about three days? Please come for at least three days. I wouldn't ask if it wasn't extremely important. Three days… for me. Please, I am begging you."

Laramie pleaded with him to agree. She wanted him to meet his daughter. Akihiro was firm in his choice.

"No. I can't go," he replied agitated.

"Can't or won't?" she retorted.

"Do not start this. You have seen the work I have. I can't leave it right now."

"I also know Kat, Rhys and Shinji can cover you for three days. Why can't you let them help out?"

"Because this is *my* life and *I* control it. I know what I want and they don't." His temper elevated.

"Yes, you're right because you are so qualified at the pouring of concrete. God forbid it shouldn't cure on your time schedule." Her mockery just began. "You know, I can't believe I am having this conversation. I am listed second in priority to a building, a damn building."

"You are taking this the wrong way and overreacting."

"*Overreacting?* You should've chosen your words better. Let me tell you something and see if I'm still overreacting. You want me to leave my company, my career, my family and friends, everything that I know to come here so you can have someone there when you wake up. I am supposed to give up everything and you won't even give me three days of your time."

"Laramie, it really isn't the time for this."

"When is it time? I leave tomorrow. What about commitment? Is this a trial period or are you in this for the duration? Do you even want to marry me? Do you even plan on it?"

"Yes, eventually."

"*Eventually?*" Laramie let out a disgusted laugh. "You know what? I deserve better than this. I have loved you for a year and I've tried to make things better between us. But you won't make a single effort for me. You don't see that as selfish? You don't even recognize what I am giving up. You just expect it." Laramie stood up in front of him. "I am so glad I asked before I did anything. I saved myself from a big mistake."

"What does that mean? Are you saying you're not coming back?" Akihiro was visibly angered as he sat on the bench.

"That's exactly what I'm saying. I refuse to be second in your life. I refuse to be treated like I'm second-class. You are obviously not the man I thought you were and that's pretty sad. Moreover, you know what else? You will *never* know what you are missing. You will *never* know what I had to offer. Good bye, Akihiro."

Laramie turned around and walked away incensed.

"I'm not in the mood to chase you, Lara."

"That's even better."

Laramie walked until she was out of view. She didn't cry mainly due to shock. He angered her more than anything. *It's your loss buddy. My daughter and I refuse to take a back seat to anything or anyone. I can get on that plane without any guilt. I can't believe I begged him. Begged. Just someone to wake up next to him? You've got to be kidding me. Such a fool I was. I won't make that mistake again.* She hailed a cab back to Raffles. Once she entered her room, she started to pack her remaining things.

Akihiro sat on the bench and waited for her to return. She didn't. After a few more minutes of waiting, he walked toward his car. He assumed she would be there. She wasn't. *She'll call me feeling bad and we'll go on just as before. She's overreacting and she'll see that.* He drove back to Sentosa Island. A few times, he thought to turn around and go to Raffles but his stubbornness prevented it. *She leaves tomorrow. When does she think we have time to make up?* He refused to give it anymore thought and viewed it as a normal spat.

When he entered the condo, he checked to see if she left a message. There weren't any. He sat on his sofa and watched television. Occasionally, he checked the time as he expected a last minute phone call. The evening stayed silent.

Chapter 46

LARAMIE REALIZED THE finality of the love affair. Her heart was broken not because they didn't reconcile but because he valued her so little. She knew she walked away with a clear conscious. He made his choice and it wasn't her. Unfortunately, his choice also excluded his daughter.

She met Frank in the lobby.

"Well, how was last night?" He assumed she told him about Akiko.

"Over before it happened. I'm really not in the mood to discuss it but let's just say I won't be leaving San Francisco anytime soon."

They entered the limousine and drove to the airport. Laramie remained quiet during the ride, just staring out the window. She knew she wasn't coming back and that fact saddened her. She truly loved Singapore. Frank watched her in silence. He knew sometime between Singapore and San Francisco, she would open up.

They checked in at the ticketing counter and proceeded to Immigration. Laramie remembered a previous time she was in that location. She felt awful about the land deal and avoiding him on the second trip. This time, she felt as though she made her restitution. She didn't expect him to be there and he wasn't. Frank and she checked their bags and breezed through Security. He asked her if she was interested in having a Bloody Mary for breakfast. She smiled and agreed.

"Tell me Laramie, any plans when you get home?"

"Absolutely. I can't wait to get my daughter. I have really missed her. She means everything to me. I was so unsure about being a single parent but I have much easier than so many. She's four months old and I can't imagine life before her. I never thought I'd feel that way about kids. What about you Frank? Your new hotel is complete. What's next for DemCorp?"

"That's a good question. I really need to watch the economy. People are vacationing less right now. That means lower revenue for me. The highs and lows are all a part of business. Let's make a toast." They lifted their glasses. "To the new Democracy."

"Cheers. To lost loves," Laramie added. He seconded.

"Laramie, I'm surprised you're not more upset about this. You loved him enough to give up everything. Yet, you seem so relaxed about it being over. If you don't want to discuss it, just say so."

Laramie told Frank of the previous night's conversation. She told him how she walked away and how he refused to come after her.

"Frank, this wasn't some chasing game. I didn't expect that. He didn't acknowledge what I was sacrificing. In that sense, he wasn't acknowledging me. I'm sure I will have many nights of crying to get over him, but I will get over him. It's a true shame because he doesn't realize what he lost."

"Will you ever tell him about Akiko?"

"Yeah, some day when she inquires about him. For now, it'll be just her and me."

The hour before boarding passed quickly. Laramie said goodbye to Singapore as the plane took off. Her eyes welled up but not a tear fell. Her life was ahead of her in San Francisco.

* * *

Akihiro walked into his office and slumped in his chair. He never heard a word from Laramie. He truly believed she would call before she left. *She could not have been serious. She does get emotional and cry easy. Though she wasn't crying last night, at least in front of me. She does have the tendency to be childish. Besides, she went through this with DemCorp. She knows what it takes to build a hotel. It's impossible to just drop everything and go to San Francisco. How could she ask that knowing how unreasonable it is?* He browsed his agendas and tried to find ways to reschedule some trades. He called Ahmed only to learn he left for the market already. No matter what he did, his thoughts returned to her.

Kat knocked on the door and entered.

"I see you're here early. Catching up from yesterday, I bet. You only lost one day due to the rains. Nothing but sunshine for the next week so you have plenty of time to have the concrete poured."

"I'm sorry Kat, I didn't hear what you said. You said something about the rain." Akihiro looked withdrawn. Kat sat opposite in a chair.

"Tell me when Laramie is moving? You must be excited. You two are finally together after all the chaos." Kat waited with excitement to hear the good news.

"She's not."

"*What?* I thought it was all set. She said she looked forward to being in Singapore. Do you think she had second thoughts of leaving everyone in the States? Some people are afraid of change."

"No, I don't think that was it." He sat in his chair with his elbows on the armrests and finger woven together.

"She must've said something. She wouldn't just leave quietly."

"She did. She wanted to know what type of commitment I was making, if I planned to marry her. I said eventually."

"*Eventually?* You're kidding right? You didn't expect her to move here on a trial basis?" She looked at his face when he didn't respond. "Oh my God, you did."

"What if we didn't work out? Then what? She wanted to know about marriage and family. I don't have answers for that. I wanted her to be with me. Then she had all these questions about work and moving in. Those were all things that we could accommodate. Then she wanted me to meet her in San Francisco. I told her it was impossible. I have two hotels under construction and one to run."

"How long did she want you there? A long time?"

"No, three days, plus two for travel. I can't lose a week of time at this point."

"Three days? And you told her no? You are such a *char tau*, such an idiot."

"That's right. You're going to side with her. You're here every day. You know the demands I have right now. It wasn't realistic." Kat stood and walked out of his office. "What? Where are you going?"

She sat at her desk and began her work. She tried many times to stay out of their relationship. However, she knew he made a huge mistake. He didn't see it and if he did, he didn't acknowledge it.

He walked up to her desk, bent over and braced himself on the edge.

"You think I was wrong. I can't believe this. How can I make it any clearer?"

"You don't need to make it clearer. And, yes, I get it. But you don't, not even remotely. She loved you. She was willing to walk away from her own existence and start over just to be with you. And I might add, in exchange for three days of your time. Would you have done that for her? Obviously not.

I have to say she opened her eyes at the last minute, good for her. I wish her luck because I'm sure she is truly hurt right now." She stood and started to walk away. "If you'll excuse me, I have inventory to take in the spa."

Akihiro refused to believe he was wrong. He went into his office and threw himself into his work. *I can't be bothered by this now. There is too much at stake. If this were her investment she would realize that. She knows what's involved.*

Chapter 47

THE NEXT THREE months brought many changes in Akiko. She cut more teeth, which brought slight fevers. Laramie felt awful when Akiko's gums were red and too sore for her bottle. She gave her cold formula even though she knew Akiko disliked it. Akiko learned to crawl and Laramie found herself constantly on the move behind her. However, Laramie's favorite experience was when Akiko called Mama when she walked into a room. Laramie doted on her constantly, bringing Akiko to the office on Saturdays if she had work. They mostly spent their weekends at the park on the swings. Outside of normal business hours, Laramie was never without Akiko.

Laramie continued to cry many nights over Akihiro. She hoped he would see things from her perspective and come to the States but he never did. There wasn't any contact, not even so much as an email. She convinced herself she was better without him, *they* were better without him. She continued her life right where she left off before the grand opening in Singapore.

Edward grew concerned over her. He knew her silence wasn't healthy and tried to have her fly out to South Carolina and see Liz or New Jersey for a weekend visit with Gillian. Laramie always had an excuse why she couldn't leave. Other than a few adult nights out with Manny and Lian, she was a complete homebody. Lian tried to fix her up on a blind date. Laramie agreed to go but it was disastrous. The man was good looking and well educated however his favorite topic of discussion was himself. She agonized three hours before she found a gap for oxygen. *I need a sign that says please don't resuscitate. Does this guy ever stop? His best date would be a mirror.* She thanked Lian for thinking of her but from that time forward she handled her own dates.

Despite seeing Akihiro's face in her daughters, she was on a slow road of heart recovery. She knew she loved him and always would however, she came to terms with living without him.

* * *

The Tanjong Hotel ran smoothly. Kat backed up Akihiro when he traveled to Batam to oversee the new hotel. They never mentioned Laramie to each other again. Kat knew he was wrong. She believed he realized his mistakes but would not admit them. Akihiro spent most of his time on the job site or at his condo. Occasionally, he took the Kisaki out for a run. Though as the rainy season began in November, the timeline on construction met with many delays. Many items for his hotels came in via sea containers but when the seas got high, it slowed the ships from coming into port. As with any construction project, upgrades and change orders cost more money.

Akihiro decided to sell his office building near Orchard Street. He had paying tenants which made the building self supportive. Shinji agreed to sell the building without any commission. Akihiro needed the capital to continue on his current projects and the banks felt he extended himself already. Rhys tried to assist by renegotiating the terms of the construction loan and that bought Akihiro an extension. However by the second month, there still wasn't any activity for the office building. Shinji knew the building had to sell otherwise all construction would stop and Akihiro would be left with the payments for both buildings without enough revenue. It was possible to continue the addition only if the construction on the Batam property ceased.

The Amori Real Estate Company was located in a small building off Orchard Road. Akihiro's father, Tadashi employed several realtors including Shinji. Most of the employees completed residential listings. Tadashi and Shinji kept busy with commercial sales and leases. However, as the U.S. economy slowed, it affected foreign markets as well. Some Aussies still traded leases for lower payments but the sales portion was sluggish. Shinji called many clients to offer them a chance at a commercial sale at a price below market value. Many buyers shied from large purchases until the economy made a slow upswing.

Shinji sat in his office looking out the window to the street below. He knew real estate suffered more than most industries. The news speculated about Singapore's ties to U.S. banking. Even tourism felt a decline, which created a new set of problems for Akihiro. *I have to find a buyer. I have six to eight weeks left before money runs out. I can't believe this is happening. Aki worked so hard to build this company and to watch it fall to ruins would kill him. So much of this could've been avoided if he would've let go some of the control and not been so demanding.* Shinji exhausted all of his Singapore contacts, that only left international. Many business owners in Kuala Lumpur felt the same pinch as Singapore and Indonesia. *What about the U.S.? Laramie represented DemCorp, I wonder if she knows anyone else? At this point, it's worth a try.*

Linda paged Laramie when she didn't answer her phone.

"Yeah, Linda. I'm in Andrew's office. I can take the call here if you want to transfer it."

"Actually, Laramie, I believe you might want the privacy of your office. It's a Mr. Shinji Amori from Singapore.

"You're absolutely correct. Transfer the call in a minute, let me get there first. Thanks."

Laramie quickly walked to her office. *Shinji? Why would he call? I hope everything is okay with Akihiro.* Her mind wandered to every worse case scenario. *I would never forgive myself if something happened to him before meeting Akiko.* Her heart raced as she picked up the phone.

"Hello, Shinji? I hope everyone is okay. There's nothing wrong, is there? Your call caught me by surprise." Her breathing increased.

"Hello, Laramie. Sorry to catch you off guard but everyone here is doing fine. I'm actually calling on business. But how are you doing first? We miss seeing you here."

"Who do mean by 'we'? Because I'm certain it's not Akihiro."

"Laramie, he won't discuss what happened but the rest of us were so disappointed when Kat told us you weren't moving here. I know its none of my business but what changed your mind?"

"The condensed version is I asked him to visit me for three days in San Francisco to help me move and he wouldn't do it. He couldn't understand the ties I had to cut here before I could leave. I *begged* him but he said he was too busy with his hotel. I realized then we didn't feel the same way about each other. Our priorities weren't the same. That was our last discussion."

"Wow, I had no idea. I can't believe he wouldn't go with you."

"Yeah, well, me too. His hotel was tops on the list and I wasn't going to compete with that. Anyway, how are you? It has to be rainy season right now. Wasting your days in the office?"

"Laramie, do you still love him? I mean there used to be a chance. Is it totally gone?"

"I will always love him but I do believe the chances are gone. I can't imagine him changing. Still a touchy subject." She let out a deep breath. "Lets get to the reason for your call. What kind of business?"

"It's Akihiro's business. He has a office building for sale in the Orchard

District. I'm trying to find a buyer. The Singapore market is flat so I thought I would try the international markets. Indochina isn't much better. I thought I'd call you to see if you had any clients looking for a great investment."

His statement confused her. "I don't understand. If it's such a great investment then why is he selling it?"

Shinji stood and closed his office door. "Do I have your word of silence? He would kill me if he knew I was talking to you."

"Yes, Shinji. What's going on?"

"The hotel addition and Batam new construction have hit their delays, of course the rain doesn't help. Anyway, he's had cost overruns, like all builders, but the bank won't lend any more money. They feel without more capital, he's a risk. So, the building is for sale."

"No takers, I see. How much time does he have left?"

"Another six to eight weeks max then it will all come to a complete halt."

"Shinji, you're talking about a free hold sale. Even if I could find you a buyer, they'd have to be a Singapore citizen to make that sale. Any foreigner would be subjected to the Singapore Land Authority permitting chaos, and SLA would take longer than eight weeks."

"I never considered that. I don't know how I overlooked it. Damn, this just keeps getting worse. You're absolutely right. Well, let me see if I can come up with another plan. Hey, it was great talking to you. If you ever change your mind about Amori men, I'd see you for three days for the same deal." He brought a much needed smile to her face.

"Just wait a minute, Shinji. Do you have the specs on the property? Could you email them to me? Before you do anything, give me a couple hours, okay?"

"Anything you want, Laramie. I'll kiss you if you can make this work."

"I'll hold you to it. Wait for my call. Bye."

In a few moments, the email popped up on her terminal. She downloaded all the information, gave it a quick glance and then headed for Edward's office. She called into Andrew's to have him follow her.

"Edward, I have a investment I need to pass by you. Andrew take a seat because this will involve you too." Laramie brainstormed as she read through the papers.

"Lara, what are you involved in this time?" A valid question by Edward.

"Hear me out. It's a forty-three thousand square foot office building. Close to the city center and a short distance from three subway stops. Near great schools, restaurants and shopping. The building has central air, additional meeting rooms and off-street parking."

Andrew cut in. "What's the price per square foot?"

"Andrew, it is… seven hundred sixty-six. A little high— "

"That's about thirty three million dollars. What's the occupancy?"

"Occupancy is at ninety percent. Also, the thirty three million is a negotiable figure."

Edward watched her expression. He knew she was excited by this property. Her sudden mood swing pleased him greatly. "I assume by this meeting you are interested in buying this building by withdrawing funds from your trust."

"Actually, yes. That is why I called you both in here. I don't want to have to repeat this twice."

Edward asked, "What year was it built?"

"1990. Also, it is a brick and concrete structure. What do you think? It sounds great, huh? A friend of mine called me with it."

Edward sat back in his chair and was silent for a minute. His eyes narrowed as he looked at her, trying to figure out what else she wasn't telling him. "Laramie, there is more to this story. I can tell by your actions. Come clean with all of it, every detail."

Edward knew her quite well. She could sell snow to an Eskimo but she couldn't fool Edward. He taught her many of her tools of the trade. She inhaled deeply. He cornered her.

"Okay. What if I said the building was worth twenty-one million US dollars?"

"US dollars? Where is the building Laramie?" voiced Edward.

"Singapore. Now wait. You thought it was a great investment. What difference does it make if it's here or there?" Laramie posed.

"All the info, down to every last detail. I knew you were up to something." Edward shook his head in disbelief.

"Okay, okay. I got a call from Shinji Amori. He is Akihiro's younger brother and a commercial realtor. He is selling the building on Akihiro's behalf. Aki doesn't know anything about this. I am not trying to steal it from under him. Anyway, Akihiro has some high debts with the hotels and needs to sell the building to raise more capital to finish construction."

"For crying out loud Laramie, I thought this was over between you two. Is this a new standard? Are you going to bail out every ex-lover?" retorted Edward.

Laramie remained calm. "Edward, I am not bailing him out. I am looking at it as an investment for my daughter who also happens to be *his* daughter. Actually, I would purchase the building in her name with me as her guardian."

Next was Andrew's turn for interrogation. "Why can't you buy it in your name?"

"Time. The sale has to be completed in six to eight weeks. If I wanted to buy the land I have to submit applications for permits to the Singapore government. That'll exceed the time limit. However, Akiko is a citizen by descent of Singapore. She can purchase the building outright. She doesn't have to declare citizenship for either country until she is eighteen. Her birth certificate already shows her father as Singaporean."

Edward wasn't comfortable with this arrangement. "I understand where you are going with this, though I'm not sure why. What do you think will happen when he sees she bought the building?"

"I've thought of that. It will have to be done covertly. He won't know. If it wasn't a great investment, I would pass. But you both sat here and thought it was great until I said Singapore. Admit it. With the economy in a slump here, a global investment is less riskier."

Andrew looked at Edward with a 'she's right' expression. It was in Edward's hands now. She had the two signatures she needed, hers and Andrew's, but she wanted his blessing.

"Let me make my opinion heard first. If you choose to do this, do not cry to us when he finds out. You are walking behind his back already. No man wants to find out that it was a woman who bailed him out. It can be debilitating for his ego."

"Thank you, Edward."

"Wait a minute, Laramie. There is a bigger question at the heart of this. In order for you to buy this in Akiko's name you will have to tell Mr. Amori about his niece." Laramie hadn't thought about that. She had to tell Shinji about her, there wasn't any other way. "Are you sure he won't tell his brother?"

"Well, I guess that'll be my bargaining chip, won't it? He tells Akihiro and all bets are off." Andrew snorted when he laughed. She was shrewd and she learned that from Edward, too.

Laramie rushed to her office. She dialed Shinji and waited for his pick up.

"Amori Real Estate, Shinji speaking."

"Shinji, it's Laramie. I may have solved your problem. However, there is one requirement, none of this transaction can be known to Akihiro. You have total silence on my half. You have to swear you won't ever bring this up, ever, or the deal is off."

"Laramie, I can't tell him any of this anyway. You found a buyer? A Singaporean that fast in San Francisco? I can't tell you how much I love you for this. Is it some old retired businessman?"

"No, actually, she is an eight month old baby named Akiko."

"What the... how did you manage that?" Shinji's confusion was obvious.

"She's my daughter, and your niece," Laramie admitted genuinely.

"Are you joking? Come on. What?... How?"

"About four months after I came home from Singapore the first time, I thought I had the flu. It turned out I was pregnant. Imagine my surprise especially after the land fiasco."

"Why didn't you tell him? He would've wanted to know." His concern grew.

"I wanted to when I was there in January. I knew if he saw me he would know immediately since I was starting to show. I wasn't sure how he would take it so I avoided him that trip. Lucky for me, no one picked up on it. Anyway, she was born a month early in May. Oh Shinji, she is so beautiful. Everything about her is beautiful. She really is my miracle. She is what got me through all the heartbreak."

"So she was... what?... four or five months old when you were here? Why didn't you tell Aki then? You were back together."

"I know. I tried. I hedged around the subject for three days. He made it clear he didn't want to be married or have children anytime soon. I begged him to come to San Francisco because I wanted him to meet her before I flew her halfway around the world." Laramie became upset. "His hotel meant more to him than I did. As far as I was concerned that meant Akiko too."

"Laramie, I am so sorry. You shouldn't have had to be alone through this. I would've helped you anyway I could have."

"Thank you, I know you would have. My friends and family here have gotten me through all of it. Believe me, so many times I wanted to call him but I kept remembering our last conversation. We were over." She cleared her throat and continued. "I mean it Shinji, you tell him and I will pull out completely. Promise me."

"Laramie, I promise I won't say a thing. I can't believe this. I can't believe you have the money to do this. How are you going to do this?"

"There's more to my story, don't worry about it."

"Laramie, could you email a picture? I'd love to see her."

"Yeah, that's kind of funny because every new mother has thousands of pictures of their baby." She selected a few pictures with Akiko at different ages and sent them. "They should show in a minute."

Shinji opened the email. "She looks just like Akihiro. She is beautiful. I get it... Akihiro ... Akiko. I bet you're a great mum, Laramie."

"I can't tell you how hard it was being away from her for a week. I called Kiki every night except one, your brother was there. Anyway, getting back to the sale. I will send a notarized copy of her birth certificate. It lists Akihiro as her father and his place of birth. Also I will send a document stating guardianship, along with a DNA sample. If there is any question on paternity, you need to get his toothbrush or spit or something to confirm it. I don't think it will be necessary but, having back up won't hurt."

"Wow, I am still in shock. I cannot believe I am an uncle. Is she talking? Crawling?"

His questions pleased Laramie. She felt some relief letting the secret out partly.

"She is crawling everywhere and says a few words, mama, baba, dada."

"Dada? You lost me."

"She has his picture in her room. She points to it and says Dada. Just because he doesn't know about her doesn't mean I cut him from her life."

"You really are amazing. I don't think I could've done that if I were in your shoes. Do me a favor, when you get a chance, send me updated pictures of her. Would you do that?"

Laramie smiled. "Of course, Uncle Shinji. Anyway, send me the contract by second-day-air. I will list our account number on it so you aren't showing any foreign billing. I don't know how involved your father is in the office."

"Don't worry Laramie, I won't say a thing. And, thank you."

Laramie sat in her chair and let out a huge exhale. She prayed they maintained their concealment. She was happy to share Akiko with her uncle. It was a slow start but nevertheless, a start. *Whew! That went better than I thought.*

Chapter 48

SHINJI MAINTAINED HIS secrecy. He told Akihiro he had a buyer for the building and everything would close as normal. An added benefit for his task, a DNA test wasn't required. He checked with an attorney in the city who validated the birth certificate and guardianship. Shinji's only remaining task was to keep their identity secret. A few times Aki asked questions about the buyer like if they were local or if they would be at closing. Shinji assured him the buyer was local but traveled extensively. If the closing fell on an out of town date, he would overnight the packet for signing. Lucky for Laramie and Shinji, Akihiro was so busy with his construction that he had little interest in the details of the sale. After all, he trusted his little brother.

Within six weeks, Shinji had Akihiro in his office to sign the contract and deed. He told Akihiro the buyer was out of town but would have the papers signed and back within a few days. Shinji contacted Laramie and told her she would have the hard copy in a day or two. It seemed they pulled their caper off after all. A few days later, Laramie wired the funds to a title company, which in turn wired them into Akihiro's account. The sale of the building was complete.

"Laramie, I have to say, you made this so easy. I can't thank you enough for all your help. I will thank you on Akihiro's behalf as well since he can't speak for himself. Also, I love the new pictures of Akiko. I see she is standing on her own."

"Standing? She's walking at nine months. Unfortunately, she ignores the word 'no' really well. She can be so stubborn."

"Like her parents."

"Not me. Shinji… has he said anything about me at all?" She knew this could hurt but wanted to know.

"No, Laramie, not a word. Kat seems to think he saw your point of view but felt it was too late to do anything. I can tell you he works nonstop. He used to take the Kisaki out but now she stays covered in her berth. He's become reclusive since you left. He knows how we feel and I think that's mainly why he avoids the subject. I can drop a random question if you really want to know."

"No, that's okay. I'm just glad I was able to help and keep it in the family. I'm glad I have you to share this with Shinji. You can't imagine how hard this has been. I know eventually I will come back to Singapore with her but not right now. Take care. Bye."

* * *

A few weeks later, Akihiro, Rhys and Shinji went to a soccer match. Rhys tired of Aki's excuses and pulled him off the job site. He needed the escape. After the match, they went to the Highlander for a few pints. Akihiro lightened up and began to laugh again. He hadn't done that since Laramie left.

Shinji made a few whistles as young women walked by. Rhys found his brunette in the group and asked Aki if was interested in the third woman.

"No, but if you want to chase them go ahead. Besides the third one isn't my type."

Rhys replied, "That's because she isn't Laramie. What the hell happened anyway?"

Shinji knew but pretended ignorance. "Kat said you two talked. What happened? I thought she was moving here?"

"I made a mistake. By the time I realized it, she was long gone. She had a lot to say and she was right. I wasn't fair to her. Now she's there and I'm here."

Rhys countered, "Well, call her now. You still love her?"

"Yes, but it's too late. I haven't heard from her in months."

"That's why I just said for you to call her. Did you miss that?"

Shinji chimed in. "I agree with Rhys, better late than never. Isn't that what the Americans say? That's it. She was so into you. Why can't I find a woman like that?"

"No, I'm not calling. I wouldn't even know what to say at this point. That's assuming she would take my call."

Shinji pressed him. "Aki, you have to do something, you're like some hermit at that hotel. You have more than enough money to finish now. Take a break. Go to San Francisco. Now that would make an impression."

Rhys slurred, "Shit, that would impress me too. Let's all go. I'm not into blondes but she had a great pair of uh… legs."

"Can we talk about something else besides Laramie Holden?" Akihiro asked. *Enough.*

Rhys continued his rant. "Well, you are one lucky son of a bitch to find a buyer last minute. How'd you pull that off?"

"Shinji did it. He found some wealthy Asian woman."

"Really, well, find me one too," Rhys begged.

"See you all laugh at me but it pays to talk with the ladies. Tell them what you are looking for upfront."

"Damn, I should listen to my little brother more. Was this woman married?"

"No, I don't think so. Hey, how about a round of shots?" Shinji quickly covered himself.

Both Amori brothers assisted Rhys in going home. Shinji agreed to get him home on the MRT if Akihiro agreed to help walk him there. After he left the men, he walked back to his car. He tried not to think of Laramie. However, recent conversations brought that memory back. *I was so wrong. I should have listened to her. She asked for three days, that was it. Why couldn't I see that at the time? Maybe I didn't want her to come after all. No, she was right, I owed her a commitment with the move. I miss her. I miss everything about her. I miss her smile, her laugh, her snoring, and I even miss her horrific singing. She's everywhere to me. My head. My dreams. Why did I have to screw this time up so badly? Would she even believe me if I said I changed? If I said I was wrong?* He finally admitted he was wrong, unfortunately he did so to his friends and not Laramie.

He stood on the deck of the condo remembering their visit to Bintan, the snorkeling and then the playing around on the swim platform. He remembered her expression when she realized she had no where to run. He missed her touch, her kiss. The reminiscing ate at him until he couldn't stand it anymore. He picked up his telephone and dialed her cell phone. *It should be Saturday morning in San Francisco.* It rang a few times before she finally answered.

"*Hello? Hello? Is anybody there? It must be a wrong number.*"

He felt even worse after hearing her voice. He was still in love with her. He didn't deny it. He just didn't know what to do about it.

Chapter 49

SUNDAY MORNINGS WERE always lazy at the Holden residence. It wasn't uncommon for Akiko to sleep in which allowed Laramie the same. Laramie woke up and made her coffee while she prepared Akiko's breakfast. Akiko was a great eater. Her word behind Mama and Dada was 'more.' She loved fruit and vegetables, completely unlike Laramie at that age. Laramie went into Akiko's room to wake her and she seemed slow moving. Her first thought was a cold. She decided to let it go for the day and if she wasn't better by morning, she would take her to Dr. Crawford, her pediatrician.

Akiko remained cranky all day. Laramie wasn't sure if it was a cold or teething that accounted for that. She fed her daughter then put her on the floor to play. Akiko sat in place without walking into her room. Laramie picked her up and looked closer at her. *Her eyes don't look as bright and her hands and feet are cold. I don't think this a regular virus.*

Laramie dialed Edward's home, waiting until he answered. She told him she felt something was wrong with Akiko. Her plan was to take her to her pediatrician first thing in the morning. He asked her to call in if she thought she would be out all day.

Early morning, Laramie called Dr. Crawford. She explained Akiko's appearance and behavior. The receptionist told her to come right in.

Laramie arrived at the doctors office around nine o'clock. Akiko sat with her mother instead of going to the playcenter, which she loved. After twenty minutes, their names were called. She carried Akiko to the examination room where they took her temperature, height and weight. Within minutes, her doctor entered the room. He was an elderly gentleman of average height and weight. His hair was white with years of experience. His demeanor was that of a child still which explained why the kids all loved him.

"How you holding up, Mom?"

"I'm fine but Kiki has me worried. She hasn't been herself lately. Also, her hands and feet are cold. She's been tired and her eyes don't look bright as normal."

He placed Akiko in her mother's lap. He listened to her heart and then laid her on the exam table. He pressed around different parts of her body. He used his light and examined her eyes. Her chart showed her body temperature to be normal but indeed her hands and feet were cold. He asked Laramie the types of food Akiko ate. She told him she drank formula and ate strained fruits and veggies.

"Laramie, I don't think it's anything to be alarmed about. I believe she is slightly jaundice. While it's more common at birth than now, it is treatable. But…" He looked over the top of his bifocals at her. "I want you to see a specialist that works specifically in this area. If it is jaundice like I think, it could be as simple as dietary changes for a while and she'll be fine."

"A specialist? What kind of specialist? She's not in any danger is she?" Laramie panicked. "This is my baby. Tell me she's fine."

"Laramie calm down. I've seen kids with jaundice for many years. It isn't anything to worry about. Get her dressed and meet me in my office. I'll give you a name of a reputable doctor who's great with kids."

Laramie followed Dr. Crawford's advice and called Dr. Patel immediately. He was a pediatric hematologist as the Medical Center. He worked in the Children's Hospital and was very well known and highly recommended. His office informed Laramie they had an afternoon cancellation if she was free to come in that soon. Laramie jumped on the appointment.

They entered the San Francisco Medical Center shortly after lunch. Laramie filled out the numerous forms they required. Unfortunately, the forms asked for family medical history. She didn't know anything about Akihiro's side. She knew her side from her grandparents and old medical records of her parents. *If this isn't a sign to tell him, I don't know what is. It never occurred to me I needed to know about his medical history.* She turned in her driver's license and insurance card as well. She sat with Akiko on the floor and waited for their name to be called once again.

Quickly, a medical tech escorted them to an examination room. Once inside, the woman took Akiko's temperature, weight and height. She went through a list of standard questions about bowel movement, appetite and behavior. She told Laramie that Dr. Patel would be in shortly. Laramie looked around the room, the doctor had his degrees framed on the wall. *Wow, John Hopkins Children's Center…Rainbow Babies and Children's Hospital. He has some impressive credentials but that doesn't mean a thing if he doesn't make my daughter well.*

The door opened and an middle-aged Indian doctor came inside. He wore his lab coat over his dress clothes. He held his hand out to shake Laramie's.

"Very nice to meet you Miss Holden. I understand Dr. Crawford has some concerns regarding your daughter. I know he has done this already but I need to exam her. Just leave her diaper on." He spoke with a Punjab accent.

Laramie complied once again. She watched the doctor poke and prod Akiko. He listened to her heart and checked her eyes and limbs. Afterward, he had Laramie dress her and join him in his office. *The same ritual again.*

"Miss Holden, I want to have some tests run on Akiko. They are standard and other than the blood draw and an bone aspiration, which are painful, the rest are not painful for her."

"Tests? Why? What do you think is the problem?" Laramie panicked once again.

"The first test is a CBC or Complete Blood Count. This checks the hemoglobin and hematocrit levels."

Laramie interrupted, "I don't know what you are saying. Those terms mean nothing to me."

He continued, "They measure the red cells, white cells and platelets in the blood. Sometimes changes in these counts can explain what the problem is or can be. Also , I am requesting a Reticulocyte Count. This shows the number of young red blood cells. I want them to check her B12 and Folate levels as well. Lastly, I'd like to do a bone marrow aspiration."

"Bone marrow? What exactly is wrong with my daughter?" Laramie was afraid to hear his answer.

"Actually, I think she has anemia. I'm not sure what type but these tests can help us narrow them down."

"Anemia, isn't that just iron poor blood? I heard the OB talk about it when I was pregnant."

"Sometimes it can be that simple of a more iron rich diet. I don't want to scare you but I won't know where Akiko lies until I have the test results."

"So it could be worse?"

"Miss Holden, I don't want to cause you undue anxiety. Let's just wait to see what the results are, okay? The receptionist will give you a form with the tests marked on it. Take it to the lab inside the hospital and they will take care of everything. I should have the results in a few days and I will call you them. Until then, keep Akiko away from sick children and adults, keep her hands clean, the normal antibacterial behavior. Everything will be fine."

Laramie took Akiko to the hospital lab and they drew vials of blood. Akiko screamed. Laramie, with tears in her eyes, felt awful to have to hold her still. The worse by far was the bone aspiration. It took Laramie and two other workers to hold Akiko still.

When they finished, Laramie sat in her chair, crying as she held Akiko. The whole experience upset them both. *I can't bear to see her in that pain. I pray to God everything is fine. I can't put her through more tests like that.* Laramie called Edward when she got home and explained the trials of their day. Edward was deeply hurt by their experience. He tried his best to convince Laramie that everything was fine and what they did was routine. She didn't believe him.

The next few days were awful for everyone. No one wanted to call Laramie for news but they sat on edge. Akiko stayed the same with her behavior and eating. She still was sore on the spots where the needles entered her. Laramie opted to stay home those days with her, the office would only make her feel guilty.

Thursday morning, Dr. Patel called Laramie at home and asked her and Akiko to meet him in his office. He had the test results. Laramie asked over the phone for any information but he would not disclose anything.

Laramie sat in the doctor's guest chair with Akiko on her lap. Her heart pounded out of her chest and sweat dripped at her brow. Dr. Patel sat in his chair and opened Akiko's medical record.

"Miss Holden, I don't mean to be invasive but is Akiko's father Asian?"

Laramie was fine with that but found it odd since Akiko looked Asian. "Yes, he's half Japanese. Does that mean something?"

"It will in a moment. Akiko's red blood cell count is very low. The new cells from her bone marrow aren't enough to sustain her at a healthy level. Her white blood cell are fine and her platelets are low. Her corpuscular volume or MCV, is also low but not enough to narrow anything. It is my diagnosis that she has Aplastic Anemia. The chances are about eight in a million for a child to have it but for someone of Asian descent the odds are doubled."

"So what does this mean? I'm not following you. She has anemia, that's treatable right?"

"Yes to a degree. There are a few treatments available but understand some cases depending on severity may not be curable."

Laramie began to tear. "Are you telling me my daughter is going to die? Because you can't say that to me. I can't believe that." Laramie, stunned by the news, held Akiko and kept kissing her head.

"No, actually I don't think she is that severe but she is serious. I can not determine if there is a contributing toxin in your house that could be lowering her count. First, I want to admit her to the Children's Hospital. While she is there, we can order more intensive tests of her kidneys and liver. However, I believe it to be treatable through stem cell transplants in the worst case scenario but mainly through anabolic steroid treatment. There are some risks associated with steroid use but I feel coupled with a transplant, she may be curable. My main concern is finding a donor match. You are not a match."

"But I'm her mother. She's half me."

"Exactly, not the right half. I'm sorry. I have to ask this but are you in contact with her father? The odds are he is a match to her. It's his stem cells we would need since there is no sibling."

Oh my God. Akihiro. I have to call Akihiro. "Yes, I can reach her father. But what if he isn't a match either? Then what?"

"Then she will be added to a donor list and wait for a match. You can also check blood relatives. It is very simple for a test to be done and it could save you months of waiting."

"Months? Just say we find a match, how long before we have results that she's okay?"

"That's could take months as well if the other treatments don't work. I don't want to paint the picture completely negative. She's very young and her body may respond to treatment without a cell transfusion. She may respond to basic vitamin treatments. If it should be a toxin, my nurse practitioner will give you a list of all toxins found in the home. Eliminate those things now."

"I understand. I will call her father tonight. Do I take her over to the hospital now?"

"Miss Holden, I feel positive about this but it does take time and you caught this early. Also, the nurses at the hospital are great with kids. You are welcome to stay the night there in her room as well."

"Thank you, Dr. Patel."

Laramie received the list of toxins in the house from the nurse. She was too upset to look at it. Akiko's health concerns scared ever part of her being far more than calling Akihiro. She was in a daze as she admitted her daughter into the hospital. She didn't want to leave her daughter's side but the nurses reassured her Akiko was fine. They told her to go home and pack up some of her favorite items to make the transition easier. Laramie agreed. She kissed her daughter and told her Mommy would be back later.

Laramie sat in her apartment stunned. She called Edward first, who came over immediately. Then, she called Manny and Lian who also joined them. They asked all sorts of questions. Laramie had answers for most and the one she didn't know Edward wrote down for an additional specialist to answer. He wasn't about to rely on one physician's opinion. Laramie told him of Dr. Patel's credentials. While they were admirable, he wanted every available pediatric hematologist on her case. This was *his* granddaughter.

"He also said to contact her father about being a stem cell donor. I wasn't a match. He said that Asians had double the risk as Europeans. I filled out papers. They asked for medical history on the father's side and I didn't know any. My God, what have I done? This is my baby."

Lian was first to her defense. "Laramie, this isn't anything you have done. There wasn't any way for anyone to know this. Don't beat up yourself over it. You are a great mom. You really are."

She sobbed on the floor holding Akiko's teddy bear. "I don't want to think about anything bad but I can't lose her. She is my life."

Lian hugged her, sobbing along with her. "Laramie, I promise she will be fine. I know it in my heart. Truly I do."

Lian held her and let her cry. She had to release these emotions. "Cry now Laramie because tomorrow you have to be strong for Akiko. Okay? Just get it all out."

Not many things brought a tear to Manny but this was one time that wore on him as much as Edward. A few times he walked into the kitchen under the pretense of getting a drink so he could wipe his eyes.

Laramie looked at the clock. She knew it was time to call Singapore.

"I hope you don't mind if I make this call in my room"

Everyone told her to keep her privacy. They knew she didn't want to call Akihiro, not under these circumstances. They told her they would remain in the living room for support. Laramie sat on her bed and dialed the Tanjong Beach Hotel. Kat answered. Laramie tried not to cry and become emotional but her voice cracked a bit.

"Kat, It's Laramie. I need to speak with Akihiro. Is he in?"

Kat knew something was wrong by her voice. "Laramie, are you okay? Do you want to talk about it?"

She sniffled a little. "No, I really need to talk to Akihiro first. Please."

"Sure, hold on a minute." Kat rang Akihiro's phone. She told him Laramie was on the line but she was obviously upset over something. She asked him to think before he spoke since no one knew what the call regarded.

"Laramie? Are you okay? Kat said you sounded upset."

"Yes. I'm fine. Let me just say I'm so sorry right now before I say anything further. I never planned for this to happen."

"Laramie, tell me, what is it?" he asked quizzically.

She took a few deep breaths before she continued. "Ten months ago, I gave birth to your daughter."

"*Daughter?* I have a daughter?" The news stunned Akihiro.

"Yes, her name is Akiko. I never meant to keep it from you. Honestly. I kept wanting to tell you but when I was pregnant, I was trying to make up for the Cheung deal. I didn't know how you felt about me and I didn't want to make it worse."

"You should've told me. I can't believe you would keep something that important away from me." Agitated by the discussion, he remained calm until she finished. "I would've been there for you and her. You know I loved you. Why couldn't you tell me?"

"I tried when we were together this past September. I asked you all those questions about family and children for that reason. But you made it obvious I wasn't important enough to you. And I felt if you didn't want me that meant Akiko too." She kept sniffling. "That's why it was so important for you to come to San Francisco. I wanted you to meet her before I moved to Singapore. I didn't know how you would react if I showed up with a baby."

"Oh my God." Akihiro sat with disbelief. He leaned forward with his hand at his brow. "This is my daughter too. I deserved to know. I deserved to know when you were pregnant. You've cut me out of that experience. I can never get that back. Do you realize what you've done?" His anger began to rise.

"I'm sorry. If I could do it again, believe me, I would. I can't tell you how many times I picked up the phone."

"But you still hung up. I don't know if I can get past this. I don't know what to tell you. This is a lot of information at one time. It's a lot for me to think about. Damn it. What about the talk on trust? You said you trusted me. Was that all a lie? Everything you said you stood for is over, it's gone. You lectured me about a girlfriend. You couldn't be honest enough to tell me I have a daughter."

"I know. I admit this was a mistake. I trusted you. I didn't trust myself."

"I'm speechless. I don't even have words to say."

She continued with her conversation. "Akihiro, there's more to it. I don't even know how to say this. It's still so new to me."

The fury in his voice was evident. "How much more? What else is there, Laramie?"

Laramie cried into the phone. Akihiro told her to calm down and finish.

"I took Akiko to the doctor because she wasn't feeling well. I thought it was a cold, but it wasn't. He had me bring her to a specialist and they ran all these tests. Dr. Patel said she has Aplastic Anemia. I didn't even know what that was."

"What is it, Laramie? Keep going." Akihiro felt his stress level rise.

"Her red blood cells aren't producing what they should. They are going to try some kind of vitamin treatment but if that and the medication don't work..." She started to cry.

"Laramie finish what you were saying. Stop crying."

"If that doesn't work, she needs stem cell transplants. I can't be a donor, but you can."

"What happens without the donor?" He was afraid to hear her.

"Then, she would go on a national donor list. If a donor isn't found, she could…" She sobbed into the phone. "… die."

He closed his eyes. He was speechless. This was his worst nightmare. His heart sank with that news. His stomach felt sour.

"So you want me to come to San Francisco and help her?"

"Yes." She waited for his answer.

"Let me see if I understand you correctly. You call me to tell me I have a daughter, which you have kept secret for at least a year and a half. Now, she could possibly be terminally ill without my help. If she did not get sick, how long were you going to wait until you told me? How old was she going to be by then? How much of her life was I going to miss?"

"I don't know that answer. I'm sorry."

"*I'm sorry?* That's all you have to say is *I'm sorry*?"

"If you hate me, I can deal with that. But she is my life. I am nothing without her. She is the only family I have and I don't want to lose her. Will you please do this for her?"

"I can't believe I'm hearing this. It's not just about her, is it Laramie? I can't even deal with you right now. You fucking bitch." Akihiro slammed the phone down. He was livid. He stood in his office and threw everything off his desk. He slammed his fists on the desktop until they were numb.

Kat sat outside the office and waited until it quieted. She never heard him lose his temper to that degree. *Whatever Laramie told him must've been really awful.* She didn't know if she should knock or wait until he came out.

After about fifteen minutes, Akihiro opened the door. Kat saw his eyes had tears in them. She never saw him so upset.

"Akihiro? Are you all right?" Kat asked cautiously.

He looked at Kat with a dazed expression. "Did you know about this?"

Kat shook her head side to side. "What are you talking about, Aki? Why don't you sit down? You don't look good."

"Laramie just informed me that I am a father."

"*What?*"

"Yes. I have a daughter that is ten months old."

"Why did she wait to tell you now?" Kat asked with hesitation.

"Oh that's the best part. Apparently Akiko, that's her name, has some rare anemia. If I don't go to San Francisco and do some type of transfusion she could die."

"Oh my God. I had no idea. I speculated a few times. Once when she was here while you were at the market. I thought she just gained weight. Her office said she was on maternity leave but corrected themselves to say it was a different employee. I just thought they were common mistakes. I never gave it anymore thought. But it all fits. What are you going to do? What did you tell her?"

"I don't know what to do. It hasn't sank in yet. Laramie? I hung up on her. Let her suffer a while. She deserves it."

"Aki, you need to go there. The baby is still your daughter, you need to be there for her and for you. Don't make the mistake of not going."

"Look Kat, I'm leaving for the rest of the day. Just take messages."

"Don't worry about anything here. We'll be fine."

* * *

Laramie walked out of her bedroom. Edward, Manny and Lian waited for her to respond. They overheard her crying but weren't able to make out the conversation.

"Laramie? How did he take the news?" Lian asked.

Laramie sat on the end of her sofa, still sobbing from hearing his voice and hate for her.

"I know I should've told him sooner. I really meant to do that. He was surprised to learn of Akiko. Then he became so angry. I know that was my fault and I deserve it."

Edward quietly spoke next. "Laramie, did you tell him she is in the hospital? Is he coming here?"

She no longer held in her emotions, she bawled uncontrollably. "I don't know. He was so furious he hung up on me. What if he doesn't come here? I'm the one responsible for this. Anything that happens to her is my fault. This is all my fault." She was on the verge of hysteria. Edward had Lian console her while he made a quick call. They all felt helpless.

Lian walked Laramie into her room and told her to lie down. She sat beside her stroking her hair while Laramie cried. Manny stood at her window and shook his head in disbelief. *How can this happen? This is such an innocent child. This family goes out of their way to help others. It's not fair for this to happen to them. It's not fair to Akiko.*

About fifteen minutes later, there came a buzz from the lobby. Edward pressed the button to release the door. Within minutes, there was a knock at the door. Edward opened it and greeted the physician. He was Edward's doctor and dear friend. Edward explained the circumstance to him to which the doctor was happy to help. He went into Laramie's room and spoke with her. He sympathized with her ordeal but stressed she need to be strong for her daughter. He gave her a sedative to calm her and help her sleep. Lian volunteered to stay the night at the hospital with Akiko. The doctor gave Lian a bottle of Valium and told her how often Laramie could take a pill. Based on her distress, he warned Lian not to leave them in Laramie's possession. Lian understood. Slowly, Laramie tired and fell asleep.

The doctor and Lian left her room. Lian felt awful.

"She is my friend and I can't even help her. This is so sad."

Manny rushed to Lian's side to comfort her. "Lian, you are helping her. You are here for her. And you're going to be there for Akiko. There isn't anything more we can do besides support her."

The doctor interrupted, "There is something more you can do. Go to your community and asked for donors. It's an easy procedure. Just a cotton swab in the mouth. Even if you can't help Akiko, you may save the life of another person."

They all agreed to be donors. Edward decided to send an email to all employees stressing the importance of this cause and urged them to contribute. Manny told Lian he would make calls as soon as he went home and also post a sign in the door of the market. Lian was concerned to leave Laramie alone however, the doctor said she would remain asleep until morning. Lian grabbed the small suitcase for Akiko and they all left together.

* * *

Akihiro walked into his mother's kitchen and sat beside her at the table. She looked at her son and knew something horrible occurred. She saw he had cried and this behavior was totally abnormal.

"Akihiro, what's wrong? What's going on? Are you okay?"

"I'm fine, I think. I can't feel anything right now, just numb."

She placed her hands on his arm and spoke to him calmly. "Just start anywhere. We can put the pieces together after."

"The American woman I was seeing called me today."

"Is she okay?"

He got angry. "Oh yes, *she's* fine. She called to tell me I have a child and that the baby is very sick."

"What, you have a child? How old is the baby?"

"Ten months. She said she needs me to come to San Francisco. She feels I can help the baby."

Just then, Shinji walked into the kitchen. He looked at his mother's and Akihiro's faces and discerned that something was wrong. "What's going on? What's wrong?"

"Your brother just found out about his child. But the child is very sick in San Francisco."

Shinji, shocked by the news, questioned them. "Is she going to be all right?"

Akihiro heard his brother clearly. *She? She!* He jumped up from his chair knocking it on the ground. He lunged at his brother forcing him against the wall. He held him there with his forearm against Shinji's throat.

"*She*? How did you know it was a she? I never said if it was a boy or girl. But you knew. How did you know?" he yelled in his brother's face.

Lucia, confused by this sight, asked, "Shinji, is this true? Did you know about the little girl?"

"Yes. I've known for a few months. I wanted to tell you but she made me promise."

"You took her side about *my* daughter? How could you betray me like that?"

"*Betray you? I saved you.*" Shinji pushed back.

"What is that supposed to mean? Saved me?" Akihiro said still furious. Lucia calmed Aki and told him to let go of Shinji. She questioned why Shinji would do such a thing. She told Akihiro to let his brother explain.

"You were going to lose the hotels. I couldn't stand to see you lose everything you worked so hard to build. Time was running out. I called everywhere looking for a buyer. I called Laramie in San Francisco to see if she knew of any buyers. First, she said no, but then she reminded me about a foreigner buying a free hold property. I realized I didn't have enough time for a foreigner. She asked to give her a few hours to work on something. When she called me back. She said she had a buyer." Akihiro leered at him but wanted to see where this conversation led. "She said she had a Singapore citizen as the buyer. She made me promise not to say a word or she would pull out of the deal. So I promised."

Lucia wondered why he went to such lengths. "Shinji when this happened, why didn't you come to your family first? Your father and I would've helped Akihiro."

"I wasn't thinking about you. *I* wanted to help him. *Me.* After all he's done for me, I wanted to be the person to give back. I had no way of knowing what she was going to say." Shinji continued with the story. "She told me then she had Akiko. I asked all the same questions you are. She just never found the right time. She tried to tell Aki when she was here but he refused her begging to go back with her. They broke up over him not giving her three days of his time. She wanted him to meet their daughter."

"Is this true, Akihiro? She asked you to go back with her for three days and you told her no?"

"It wasn't that simple. I was in the middle of two construction projects.

I couldn't just leave. She wouldn't understand that." His mother closed her eyes in disbelief.

Shinji continued, "Anyway, Laramie bought the building in Akiko's name. Akiko's a Singapore citizen since Akihiro was listed as such on the birth certificate."

Akihiro looked shocked at his brother. "She listed me on the birth certificate?"

Shinji nodded yes. "Laramie used her own money to buy the building in Akiko's name. She said she knew Aki wouldn't take her money, so this was her way to have Akiko help her father."

"Where did she get that much money?" asked Lucia.

"I asked but she wouldn't say. Anyway, Akiko is the owner of the property. It was the only way I found to end this mess." Akihiro closed his eyes. He didn't want to look at his brother. "You asked about the buyer. I told you it was an Asian female. That was true. You never would've allowed this if I told you. I just didn't want to let you down. But, I had no idea Akiko was ill. I am so sorry Akihiro. I didn't mean to keep this from you. No one did."

"I can not believe this is happening to me. Did anyone else here know about the baby?"

"No, no one else knew."

Akihiro knew Shinji did this out of love and desperation. His brother never lied to him before. He understood the position Shinji was caught in. He knew he wouldn't allow Laramie to help him, he would've turned her down flatly. It was his pride that stood in the way. Akihiro stood up and held his hand out to his brother. Shinji grasped it and stood beside him. Akihiro wrapped his arm around him and firmly patted his back. This display relieved Lucia's concerns between her sons.

"Don't ever hide the truth from me, about anything."

"You may not want to know this but she still loves you. She asks about you all the time. She wanted you to succeed as much as I did."

"You're right. I don't want to hear about her right now. I don't know where anger stops and hate starts."

"Are you going to go? I'll help you anyway I can. Just ask me."

"I haven't told her if I was coming yet or not. I was so furious, I wanted her to suffer for awhile with the unknown."

Lucia stepped in quickly. "Akihiro, you will go there and you will help that child. You need to tell her you are coming. She is the baby's mother and you cannot imagine the suffering she is experiencing. This is the most horrendous thing for a parent. You can find another way to retaliate."

"I'll keep that in mind. First, I need to contact a hematologist here and find out what I can do now and hear a better explanation of what Akiko's illness is before I fly. She said the doctor's name was Patel. So at least I know who to contact."

Lucia hugged her son. She knew he planned to do the right thing.

Shinji added, "Aki, before you leave…" Shinji swallowed hard. "… do you want to see her picture?"

This surprised him. He hadn't thought about what his daughter looked like yet. Through all the mayhem, his mind didn't reach that far. *My daughter.*

Shinji brought in his laptop. He sat at the table and opened the file with all the pictures Laramie sent. When he had it ready, he moved so his brother could sit. Akihiro sat nervously in the chair. *Am I ready for this?*

Lucia was the first to comment. "Oh my, she is the image of you, Akihiro. Look at that hair and those eyes. My granddaughter is beautiful. Shinji, you send those pictures to the photo shop. I want them printed."

"She does look like me. I never expected that. I guess I thought she would look like us both but she doesn't. Look how small she was when she was born. I wish I could've been there. She is so happy." Akihiro beamed with pride. She hooked him with her first smile. *I can't believe I'm a father.*

"That's because she is so loved. You may hate the mother right now but she has been a good mother to her. You can see it in the baby's face."

"What else do you know Shinji?"

"She named her Akiko Amori after you. She just started to walk and Laramie said she is very stubborn."

Lucia added, "Also like you." He smiled.

The anger in the household subsided to happiness yet concern for Akiko. Akihiro began his phone calls and appointment to see a doctor. He arranged his flights to San Francisco. He would arrive in four days, still unknown to Laramie.

After he met with the specialist, he asked that the results not be sent to Dr. Patel until after he landed in the States. He still wanted to punish her for withholding Akiko from him. However, his doctor was far more optimistic regarding Akiko than Laramie felt. Still until both doctors spoke to each other, there wasn't any way to confirm that.

Chapter 50

AFTER LARAMIE SHOWERED and dressed, she headed for the hospital. She told Lian how much she appreciated her for being there for Akiko. Lian, of course, blew her off saying she was happy to be there and it wasn't any trouble. Laramie called and thanked Edward for sending his physician. She knew she never would've slept after last night. She still felt hurt from the conversation. *I know I was wrong not to tell him. But it seemed like the right thing at the time. I just hope he doesn't use that against her to get back at me. What do I tell Dr. Patel? He'll want to know if Akihiro is coming here. How do I say no because I'm a bitch and never told him? What sort of person does that make me now?*

Laramie stopped at the nurse's station to talk to the shift nurse in charge.

"Good morning, I'm Laramie Holden, Akiko Amori's mother. I was wondering if Dr. Patel has been here yet."

The nurse looked at Akiko's chart and told her that he had not. "Sometimes they see the patients that are worse off early in the morning. He'll be here later I'm sure."

Worse off? That made Laramie feel a little better to think Akiko wasn't in any immediate danger. Laramie went into Akiko's room. Already flowers and stuffed animals came in for her daughter. She walked over to Akiko and picked her up. She hugged her daughter dearly. She played a kissing game all over her face as Akiko tried to cover herself while giggling. She saw Lian had put the teddy bear in her crib, and pajamas in the drawer. Laramie walked over to the bedside table and picked up the picture frame with Akihiro in it.

"Dada. Dada." Akiko pointed to the picture.

"Yes, Kiki, that is Daddy. I know he loves you and wants to be here. Mommy doesn't know when that will be." She knew Akiko understood none of it, she didn't herself. But, Laramie maintained hope. She wanted to call him and hear his answer but after the way he hung up, she felt it safer to give him time to come to terms with the information. *I know it had to be a shock. I don't know how long to wait before I try again. How much time do I have? I'll have to ask Dr. Patel that question.* Laramie brought Akiko's favorite book, *Good night, Moon*. She sat Akiko on her lap and read her the story. The baby, still fatigued, listened to her mother's voice. Every so often, she stuck her finger in Laramie's mouth and laughed.

"You are one crazy girl, you know that?" Laramie would suck it in as Akiko tried to pull it out. "Mommy loves you very much, Kiki."

Akiko pointed to Mommy and said, "Mama... Mama... Mama."

She sat with Laramie for quite a while before Dr. Patel came in.

"Good morning, Laramie. Are you better today? I know yesterday was a lot of information to take into consideration. We are going to run blood cell counts every few days to check production. In the mean time, I am going to start her on low doses of iron and B12."

"I called a contractor to check for lead paint in the flat. If they find any, they will remove it immediately. Also, I have an insecticide expert going through every bottle and cleaning agent looking for the ingredients you had on the list."

"That's great. Sometimes the smallest thing can cause the most damage. Have you contacted her father yet?"

She knew this was coming. "Yes, I spoke to him on the phone last night. It was quite a shock." She hated to continue but the doctor needed to know the circumstance behind her opinions. "He didn't know he had a daughter. I had never told him. As I said, it was a shock. I can't say when or if he will be here. I'm sure once he absorbs it all, he will come."

"Oh, I thought the situation was different. I'm sorry."

"No, don't be. It's not as bad as you think. He lives in Singapore, so the travel is a small obstacle, that's all. Will the delay harm Akiko?"

"No, not really. We aren't at that point in treatment yet. When you do hear from him, have him contact my office."

He tickled at Akiko, who just smiled back. Laramie was thankful her doctor was a very friendly man. Shortly after the doctor left, Nurse Charisse came in with an IV and a bag of liquid. She asked Laramie to hold Akiko very still to get the IV in her arm. Laramie hated to do this to her daughter. Akiko screamed at the needle prick. *Oh Baby, I am so sorry to hurt you.* Once it was in, the nurse taped and bandaged up her arm to prevent Akiko from removing it. The nurse asked Laramie to hold Akiko while she received the medicine. Laramie wasn't sure when Akiko woke up this morning but she knew as she laid in mom's lap, her eyes grew heavy. *This will make taking the medicine far easier.*

Charisse was an ample woman of African descent. She spoke with a dialect, almost Dominican, that made it difficult for Laramie to understand. She was a caring woman and loved the children on the floor which was evident by the children's reactions when seeing her. She somewhat reminded Laramie of Kat with her directness.

Later that afternoon, Edward called Laramie to check on Akiko. He asked if she heard back from Akihiro and she sadly said no. He asked if she wanted him to call Akihiro and talk to him. Laramie said no again. She told Edward to give him a few days to absorb it, Edward agreed. He informed her that he sent an email to all of the employees informing them of Akiko's condition and stated that anyone who wanted to donate marrow would be excused from work *paid.* She knew that was generous of Edward especially since Andrew worked the numbers. Edward laughed when she asked what Andy had to say. He told Laramie how Andy came running in the office with the numbers of hours and the amount of loss. They both got a great chuckle from the story.

Later that night, Manny and Lian stopped in the see the baby and Laramie. Lian made signs to post in Chinatown and at the market. Laramie thanked them both for their grass roots effort. However, she remained hopeful that Akihiro would come. After a few hours, everyone was gone from Akiko's room except for mother and daughter. Laramie decided to spend the night with her and not just for Akiko's sake. Laramie hated being in the flat by herself. The loneliness was unbearable.

Chapter 51

THE WEEKEND BROUGHT more flowers and teddy bears. Akiko played in the crib as Laramie fielded visitors. The outpouring concern over her daughter astounded her. Even the local news became involved. They filmed a segment on children with anemia and its causes. They talked about treatment and recovery. She was surprised they even cornered Dr. Patel for a quick interview. He politely told the crew that many times things in your own home could be the cause. He listed several items that are common but dangerous for children. As her case became more public, well-wishers appeared out of thin air and sent gifts. Eventually, Laramie donated the toys to other kids in the hospital. This was truly more than she expected.

Still there wasn't any word from Akihiro. She thought by now he would at least call back. The waiting ate at her. Her friends kept positive telling her that he would come around. Liz and Gillian called everyday to check on Mom too. Liz warned her to take care of herself as well. Akiko needed her mother to be healthy. Laramie knew that to be very true. Any illness would prevent Laramie's presence around her daughter since Akiko could not risk any infection.

Chapter 52

LARAMIE RACED HOME in the morning to pack another overnight bag. She spoke to the contractor who found lead paint on the baseboards and window moldings. He told her they removed them all and would replace them with trim in nontoxic paint. The inspector found a few chemicals in the bathroom and removed them from the premises as well. She felt better about bringing Akiko home to a safer house. Before she left, she grabbed her laptop, figuring she might as well work with all her time just sitting there.

Laramie said her good mornings to the nurses. She knew most of them by face without looking at their nametags. She stayed positive as best she could. She knew today was another day of needles for Akiko. She dreaded that, the guilt just consumed her. Charisse told her she would be in shortly to draw blood.

When Laramie entered Akiko's room, more flowers, plants and stuffed animals filled the tabletops and windowsills. She walked around reading some of the cards. She cried when she came to one animal, a lion sent by Grandmum and Grandpapa Amori. She knew he told his family about Akiko. She knew her daughter had family. Family was all that mattered to Laramie. Still there wasn't any word from Akihiro. *Does this mean they embrace her but he doesn't? I thought I'd hear from him by now.* She tried to make sense of his silence. Eventually, she asked someone to come, disperse the toys throughout the hospital, and give the flowers and plants to the elderly patients except the ones from family and friends.

Shortly, the nurse came in with her tray of needles and tubes. Laramie tried to keep Akiko's attention on her face but it didn't work. Her daughter knew what was about to happen and she cried. Laramie held her firm while he nurse drew the blood. *This never gets easier. How can they hurt these tiny bodies? You would think someone would come up with a better way.* Dr. Patel arrived after the nurse. He asked Laramie if Akiko was eating any better. She said no. He asked if there was any news regarding her father. Laramie, already depressed, again replied no. He tried to encourage her to be hopeful of the situation. He told her he saw many miraculous healings in his career and sometimes you need faith.

Faith? I have never been a religious person. I've never really thought about God. It's always been just and expression or a cry of desperation. It doesn't mean I don't believe I just never pursued it. It's at times like this I wonder about a higher being controlling my life like this for a reason. She stood at the window as she looked toward the park. Religion - the subject intrigued her. Her grandparents went to church regularly. She knew their beliefs were strong.

Laramie looked around quickly when Manny knocked on the door. She was happy to see him. It was lonely in the hospital all day even if she was busy with work.

"Laramie, you can't believe the frenzy over Akiko."

"What are you talking about? What frenzy?"

"I just came from the building for marrow donors. There was a line outside with people wanting to donate. I haven't seen so many Chinese people in one spot since New Year." He laughed at his slight joke.

"Are you serious? People are really doing that for my daughter?" His news amazed her.

He grabbed the television remote and turned it on. "Look, the news will be on in a few minutes. It's got to be part of it. There were all kinds of news crews outside. The woman I spoke with said it had been like that since they opened in the morning. They weren't staffed for such a response. Some people they asked to return in a few days because they couldn't accommodate them."

Laramie watched the television station. Sure enough, they had a quick blurb about the marrow donors but would be back later with the story. "Oh, my God." *That's it, my God. He said to have faith and look what everyone's faith has brought.* "You weren't kidding. Manny you can't imagine the cards and gifts people have sent. Oh wait... you need to see this." She picked up the card from Akihiro's parents and handed it to him.

"Wow, that's a step in the right direction. Has there been any word yet?"

She shook her head no. "I don't know when I should even call him back. I don't know if he'd even take my call."

"Lara, you got to have faith, girl. He loved you very much once, he still may. You don't know what he's thinking. You still have time."

"Thanks. Faith seems to be the word of the day."

Just then, the story regarding marrow donors came on. People cheered for Akiko and for all the sick children who can benefit from their donations. The director for the local foundation thanked the community for their outpouring concern for those in need, stressing the ability to cure those of any age, race or creed. Akiko's sudden stardom astounded Laramie. *All these people donating a gift of life because of my daughter. I never realized how truly blessed I am to have her.* Her eyes teared thinking about it. Manny put his arm around her for support.

A few minutes later, Lian walked in. "Geez, it's like a media whirlwind outside. I could hardly get inside the door."

"What?" Laramie responded.

"You haven't left the building yet, have you? Well I can tell you right now, it's madness. Total madness. You need to go down there and speak with the hospital director or someone. Call a press conference or something."

"You're kidding, right?"

"Not at all. Laramie, you need to do something. It's a zoo outside. Go on. We'll stay here with Akiko."

Laramie took the elevator down to the first floor. She looked out the front doors to see photographers set up and news teams. A second later, the Hospital Director touched her arm. He asked she join him at the podium for a public statement. Laramie wasn't comfortable being in the spotlight like that. *No. I can't do this. It's too many people.* Dr. Patel came up to her and urged her to say something short. He explained how this benefits more than anemia patients; all the marrow donations help people with leukemia, HIV, genetic disorders and lymphoma. Laramie walked outside with the director. The flashes from the cameras blinded her. After the director spoke, he asked Laramie to say a few words.

She was very nervous and stuttered a bit when she began. "I want to thank the community for their outpouring generosity toward my daughter, Akiko. Your thoughts and prayers are very much appreciated. We continue with hope and vision for a full recovery. However, there are so many others who can benefit from your care. Please keep in mind all the families who are suffering with a loved one who can benefit by a single donor match. These people need your support too. Call your families and friends, here and across the states to join in this admirable cause. You might not save the life of someone you know but what better way to help your neighbor. Thank you once again."

The cameras flashed like hundreds of strobe lights. Laramie was happy to leave the crowd. She returned to Akiko's room and joined Manny and

Lian. Manny and Lian watched Laramie's speech on TV. Since Akiko's room faced opposite the main entrance, Laramie had no idea of the commotion downstairs.

Manny expressed his opinion. "You know Laramie, you do a lot for this city and it's nice to see some of it given back. But I have to tell you, that almost brought a tear to my eye. Do you have a tissue for your neighbor?" Lian elbowed him in the ribs.

"Ignore him. I know how you feel about public speaking and I thought it was sincere and poignant. Don't be surprised if the mayhem picks up. How did everything go with Akiko today?"

"No, no tissues for you, Manchu." Laramie shoved his shoulder. "They took more blood from Akiko. I hate that. I feel so awful for her. I know it hurts. I hate having to hold her as she cries. I want to comfort her. She already caught on by seeing the tray. I'm hoping today's tests show an improvement from last week. But Dr. Patel said it was too early to see conclusive results."

"Any news from Akihiro?"

Laramie breathed heavy. "No, but I did receive a toy and card from his parents. That really surprised me. You know, I can probably email Shinji to thank them. It's sort of like an olive branch. Though if Akihiro doesn't forgive me, what are the odds of his parents?"

"Quit carrying the guilt. Are you sure you're not Catholic?" Lian said. "This can be worked out over time. Let it happen naturally."

As Lian and Manny gathered their things, Laramie thanked them for coming. She said it wasn't necessary for them to be there daily. They told her to allow them to make that choice. Laramie knew there were no better people than Manny and Lian. She couldn't wait until the time came when she could pay them back for all the care and support.

Chapter 53

LARAMIE SHOWERED IN the attached bathroom. She felt better to have a good night's sleep at Akiko's side. She sat in her rocking chair and held Akiko while she drank her bottle. She looked for any sign of improvement but didn't notice any. She decided to go to the hospital chapel when she took a break. She wanted to talk to someone about faith and how it would fit in her life. She had many questions about the different sects since theology wasn't her strong suit.

More cards, balloons and gifts poured into their room. Laramie was at her wits end in what to do with all of these things. She packed bags for the homeless shelters and hospice centers. *At least the crowd at the main entrance dispersed.* She was apologetic to cause such an inconvenience for the other families.

Laramie worked some on her cases, mainly research. She emailed her associates with directions and locations for their work. She became the Laramie they used to know, giving, happy-go-lucky, friendly. The experience truly humbled her. She stood up and stretched her legs. Akiko sat quietly in her crib and played wither teddy bear. She walked to the nurse's station to talk with Charisse, nothing case related, just girl talk to pass the time.

"How are my favorite nurses today?" she asked cheerfully.

"Well, you know girlfriend, I saw you on TV last night. And I must say you don't look so skinny on camera." The other nurses laughed as did Laramie. She adored Charisse's humor. "You might want to touch up those roots before your next interview." The women were howling.

Laramie replied, "Come on. I really am a natural blonde?"

The humorous quips continued until Charisse halted the conversation.

"Mmm-mmm-mmm. Now that's a fine looking man and I hope he's walking right to me."

Her statement caused the women to look down the hall. Laramie gasped before she murmured his name aloud. It was Akihiro. Charisse looked at Laramie to see her face turn pale, realizing it was Akiko's father. Laramie froze in position. She had no idea he would be there, let alone today. She swallowed hard. As he neared the nurse's station, he saw Laramie standing there. As he gave her a stare so cold with those steel black eyes, she looked down ashamed to face him. He never said a word as he walked past her. Charisse looked at Laramie and asked if she was okay. Visibly shaken, she nodded yes. She excused herself to go to Akiko.

When Akihiro walked into his daughter's room, Akiko looked up and called out, "Dada, Dada, Dada."

Akihiro stopped in his step, frozen. He wasn't sure if he heard her correctly.

Again, Akiko called out, "Dada, Dada, Dada." This time she raised her arms for Daddy to pick her up.

He slowly walked beside her crib and picked her up. Laramie cried as she witnessed this event. It was far more emotional than she expected. He looked toward Laramie questioning his daughter's words.

"She knows you're her Daddy," Laramie said with tears streaming down her face.

"But how?"

Laramie walked beside the bedside table and picked up the picture frame. She showed it to Akihiro.

"Just because she wasn't a part of your life doesn't mean you weren't a part of hers."

His eyes welled up holding his daughter. He just hugged and swayed her. He did not expect to become so emotional. Laramie continued to cry silently before she excused herself from the room. She knew her daughter couldn't be any safer than with him. She walked down to the waiting room and called Edward. She couldn't get a word out before she cried into the phone.

Edward called out to her, "Laramie, is everything okay? Can you talk, Dear? Try to calm down and speak slowly."

"He's here, Edward. Akihiro is here. Oh God, I was so wrong. Why didn't I listen to you? To everyone? How could I have done this to him? She called out to him when he entered the room. He picked her up and hugged her as if they never missed a day. He had tears in his eyes. What did I do? What kind of evil monster am I?"

"Laramie, you are no such thing. You were simply hurt and reacted to the hurt. Listen to me, we've talked about this. We all make mistakes. Some are bigger than others. You have the opportunity to correct things but do it slowly. Has he said anything to you?"

"No, but if looks could kill… Edward, I don't even know what to say to him. How do I start the conversation?"

"You start the conversation by turning around and talking to me directly," Akihiro said firmly.

Laramie jumped at his voice. Edward told her to hang up and talk to him. She said her goodbye and turned to face him.

"I… I'm sorry. I thought you were with Kiki. I was trying… trying to give you privacy." She stammered quite noticeably. "Do you want to sit?"

He watched her carefully. He knew his presence caught her off guard, which is what he wanted. She sat and squirmed in her seat before she spoke again. He sat across from her, his arms stretched along the arms of the chair, leaning back with a look of detest.

"I spoke with her doctor yesterday. He was waiting on the results of her blood work to come back. He started her on iron and vitamin treatments." She rubbed her hands nervously as she spoke. Most of the time she stared at the floor. "He asked to have a meeting with both of us when you arrived. I didn't know you were coming."

"I notified him this morning. He was faxed all my test results this morning as well." He sat cool and emotionless. His eyes bored deep into her soul.

"So, you didn't want me to know you were coming. I see. I deserve that and more."

"You're right. You do deserve it, but Akiko doesn't."

He was stern in his voice. He felt some vengeance by this meeting.

"She looks just like you."

"I saw that."

His short responses made it difficult for her to speak, fearing she would say the wrong thing.

"I don't know how this would be received but thank your parents for the beautiful card and toy they sent her." He wasn't aware his mother did this but not at all surprised.

"I will," he replied unemotionally.

This method of conversation became excruciating for Laramie to continue. He watched her stir. It surprised him that she stayed in the room this long. Normally, she ran from their confrontation.

"Are you here long?"

"As long as I need to be." *Another brief answer.*

"Okay. Um… do you need a place to stay?"

"Not with you." The words hit her core and stung.

She took a deep breath and continued, "I've been staying here. My flat was inspected for any toxins in paint and cleaning solvents so it's pretty torn up for now. Just as a safety precaution for Akiko. Do you need a hotel room?"

"I'm staying at the Westin St. Francis."

"Very nice place. Do you need a car or anything?"

"No. I'm fine," he responded, still callous.

"Do you have any questions?" she asked.

"Yes, one. Why, Laramie?"

She meant about Akiko but it was too late to take it back. She looked up at the ceiling and quivered as she breathed. Her tears streamed down her face in rapid succession.

"I was hurt which isn't a reason but an excuse. I wasn't trying to hurt you back, not with her. I tried to find the perfect time but that never came. I realize now there is no such thing. When I left the last time, I felt so hurt that I didn't mean more to you. I assumed by our conversation that included Akiko too. So I thought I could just continue our lives as before and eventually a time would come that I would bring her to you when I felt I wasn't hurt any longer."

He sat stoically. She turned to the table for a tissue and dried her eyes. He took a long look at her. She seemed tired and worn. He knew this experience took a toll on her. He didn't blame her for the sickness; she had no control over that. He blamed her for robbing him of his time with his daughter.

"Then you kept her from me for purely selfish reasons?"

"No… and yes. Yes, I kept her from you but because I thought you didn't love me and she is a part of me. I was afraid you wouldn't want her and I couldn't bear to see her rejected." Laramie crouched by his feet. "I am sorry. There are no words to express how awful I feel about this."

She put her hand on his and he quickly moved it off him. She couldn't take it any longer and tried to walk out of the room. He stood up and pulled her back inside.

"You are not running away this time. You are going to face this."

"What do you want me to say? I can tell you I'm sorry a hundred times over and it doesn't make a difference. I can't change this. It's all too late. I wish I could go back and do this differently but I can't. You can hate me for the rest of your life, I can accept that, but right now she is my first concern." She cried uncontrollably as she sat in the chair. "*I'm sorry…* I'm sorry… I'm sorry."

He didn't mean to torture her to this degree. She asked him to leave her.

"No. So you can sit and wallow in self pity? I don't think so. You are going to have to face me for a while and you had better get used to it. Now get up and walk back to her room with me. Get you act together so you don't upset her."

He pulled her up by her arm and forced her to walk beside him. The nurses watched in silence, guessing about their conversation. As soon as they entered Akiko's room, their daughter called their names repeatedly. Laramie picked her up and sat Akiko in her lap on the rocker. She talked with her about her teddy bear and walked her fingers up Akiko's belly. Laramie did not look in Akihiro's direction. Being in the same room was difficult enough. When the phone rang, Akihiro answered it. He took Akiko off Laramie's lap and held her as he passed the phone to Laramie.

"Lara, who was that? Was that Akihiro? He came after all. Are you okay?"

"Hi Lian, yes, everything is fine. How's everything at the market?"

"Boy, he has you on edge. You never ask me that, ever. I realize you can't talk and he'll catch on with yes and no questions. Have you heard from the doctor?"

"No, but he should show up this afternoon. He sees the cancer kids first. I'll pass on any information as I get it. Thanks. Bye Lian."

Laramie hung up the phone. She watched as Akihiro bounced Akiko on his knee. Akiko giggled as he moved her around. It was the first time her face lit up in days.

"You must have a secret. She hasn't been that alert in days."

"No, she just loves her father."

Touché. I don't know if I can do this for long. Days of insulting quips. Look at it this way; at least he cared enough to come. Laramie asked if he minded if she worked some. He said no. She emailed Edward, told him she was fine and that they shared the same room. He told Laramie to stay at his house when she needed to get away since her place was in upheaval. She thanked him but said she planned to stay at the hospital with Akiko. She would breakaway when she could. She emailed Liz and Gillian with the newest news. This enabled her to converse in privacy. She worked quietly for a while as Akihiro rocked Akiko in his arms. She handed him the baby bottle and said Akiko was probably hungry. He took to it like a pro. *I was right. There isn't anything he can't do perfectly.*

Dr. Patel arrived in the room shortly after two o'clock. He was surprised to meet Akihiro. He had been to his office and received the faxes but didn't realize Akihiro was in town as well. Akihiro stayed seated, with Akiko in his lap, as he shook the doctor's hand.

"Well, this is a wonderful surprise. I'm sure Akiko is enjoying having both her parents to dote on her. I received your faxes from your physician in Singapore. I am very pleased with the extent he followed in assisting me, very pleased. He was more familiar with these cases dealing with a much higher Asian population. You're results show you are a healthy match, which

I expected. I hope your aspiration wasn't too painful." Akihiro nodded no. "I can not say for sure we will need the stem cell transplant but having you close is a great benefit."

Laramie asked about the test results and if there was any news.

Dr. Patel continued. "The tests are inconclusive at this point." Laramie looked bothered by the news. "However, let me stress this, her red blood count has not lowered any. That is positive news. The vitamin and iron mix may have stabilized her some. I still want blood drawn every three days for testing. If there still isn't any progress after this week, we will begin steroids to force the increase in production. We will see if she can hold her own at that point. She could be in the need of a jumpstart in production. She is otherwise a healthy child whose body can do miraculous things at speeds we would love to have."

Akihiro thanked Dr. Patel for the meeting. He felt optimistic after his statements. When he looked down, he saw that Akiko fell asleep in his arms. Laramie offered to take her but he said he wanted to hold her.

Laramie attempted to make conversation. "She's lucky to have you, I mean as a match."

She fumbled those words. *Crap, that's not how I meant it.* It didn't matter, he ignored her. *Oh this will be a joy, won't it. How long will the punishment last? What price do I have to pay?*

"Akihiro, do mind staying with her for a bit? I have an appointment with the chaplain downstairs."

"I never you knew you were religious."

"Yeah, well, I guess I'm full of surprises. Oh, crap. That's not what I meant. I—"

"I know what you meant. Go ahead."

Laramie met the chaplain in his office near the chapel. She explained her circumstances with her parents, Akihiro and Akiko. They discussed many religions and their basis such as Judaism, Christianity, Buddhism, and Hinduism. They laughed some, she cried some. His words of advice were to accept God and not to question his work. He told her to keep faith and pray, eventually, God will answer her. She thanked him for his time and support before she returned upstairs.

When she walked down the hall, Charisse pulled her aside.

"Laramie, you all right, girlfriend? You were very upset before. He didn't hurt you or anything, did he?"

"No, Charisse, but thank you for your concern. We had a very intense conversation. We have always had a lot of intensity, that's part of the problem. I'm okay, really." Laramie hugged her for her concern.

When Laramie entered Akiko's room, she found Akihiro asleep with

Akiko in his arms. She slowly walked over and gently picked her up and placed her in her bed. She grabbed a blanket from the closet and covered Akihiro with it. *Finally, for once, someone else experiences jet lag and time change.* She sent a quick email to Shinji to notify him of Akihiro's arrival, as well as Kat and Rhys. She figured they were concerned and would want to know. She watched him sleep on and off while she worked. As everyone reported to work in Singapore, they emailed her back thanking her for notifying them. *Still handsome as ever. And of course I look like hell. Faith? What about fairness?* No one asked any details except for Kat. She asked if the first meeting went well. She expressed her concerns regarding Aki and asked how Akiko was doing. Laramie told her she was holding her own.

Akihiro woke up and looked around for Akiko.

"She's in her bed. I know my arms fall asleep holding her. I thought you would be more comfortable. I hope I didn't do anything to offend you."

"No. Thanks for the blanket." *That was the first nice thing he has said today, I should consider myself honored.*

"It's the time change. You'll get used to it after a few days. Sleep as much as you can at first. If you're interested you can use my laptop to email home. The hospital has WiFi set up. I'm sure everyone is concerned about you and the baby."

"I may later. Is there any place decent to eat?"

"Not in the hospital. I don't think your body could handle the cafeteria food. Your best bet is Chinatown or North Point. You can catch a cab in the main lobby area." She spoke to him as if he was a stranger asking for directions.

"Aren't you going to eat?" Laramie correctly assumed it was a simple question and not an invitation.

"Actually, my body is deadened by the food here already and I'm not very hungry." She continued to type without missing a beat. She wasn't callous just merely answering his question. "Akihiro, she's fine here if you want to go back to your hotel and rest."

"I may do that." He walked over to Akiko and kissed her head before he left.

Whew! These are going to be long days with two word question and answers. I have to say I am happy to see him. I'm sure this is the calm before the storm. We don't do anything the easy way.

Chapter 54

AKIHIRO WAS GLAD he took Laramie's advice and went back to the hotel. He slept soundly through the night. He wasn't familiar with the city or its neighborhoods. However, he remembered Laramie mentioned something about Chinatown. The doorman at the St. Francis told him to walk about eight blocks north and he'd be in the heart of Chinatown. When he stepped out from the building, the bitter wind blew up from the bay. Akihiro wasn't prepared for such cold temperatures. He wore a light jacket but quickly purchased a leather coat along the way.

As he walked along Washington Street, he noticed posters in all the windows. When he stepped closer, he realized they were pictures of Akiko. He stood there, reading the text regarding bone marrow donations. He grasped the fact that when he hung up on Laramie, she petitioned the city looking for donors. *Wow, I am impressed by her initiative. She wasn't going to wait on me. I can't take away the fact she is a good mother. She loves Akiko completely.* He walked into a market on Grant Street and asked the girl where their teas were located. Lian nearly fell on the floor to see Akihiro. She recognized him immediately from the pictures in Laramie's flat. She found this meeting to be good karma. She handed him a variety of teas. She asked him if he was looking for something specific. She told him they had a great mix of fruits in from Asia. He found that statement odd and looked puzzled at Lian. She told him she heard his accent and assumed he wasn't local. He bought the tea and longan berries then left.

"Holy cow Laramie, you won't believe this, not in a million years. Akihiro was just in here buying tea and fruit. Out of all the markets in Chinatown! I almost passed out. I didn't introduce myself, safer that way. He checked out the posters of Akiko as well. Better looking in person, I have to admit. How are you holding up? How is our angel?"

"That's really interesting news. Thank you. I'm doing fine. Though it is rather nerve wracking having three word conversations but I'm fine. Akiko slept through the night, which I am thankful. Nothing new from Dr. Patel. I'll keep you all posted via email since I have more privacy that way. Let me go and feed Akiko."

Later in the morning, Akihiro arrived in Akiko's room. Laramie said hello and continued with her work. She let some time pass before she decided to make her move.

"So, was the tea and fruit what you were looking for?"

"Yes." Akihiro suddenly caught what she said. "How did you know I bought tea and longan berries?"

"Oh, don't be so surprised, San Francisco is a small town." *Ha! How does it feel to be in the hot seat?*

"Let me ask you about this then." He pulled out one of the posters from the window. "How many of these are floating around this *small* town?"

"Huh. I can't honestly say for sure. My best guess… hundreds." She nonchalantly continued with her work.

"Why did you do it?"

"I think you know that answer better than I do."

"What's that supposed to mean?" he asked agitated by her coolness.

Laramie took a deep breath and looked him in the eye. "I didn't know you were coming to San Francisco. I didn't have the luxury to wait for a donor to knock on my door so we went looking for one. Luckily in the end, it wasn't necessary."

He kept his eye on her and stared her down. *She's rather brave today.* His adversary built up her defenses overnight. "Yes, I suppose it was clever move."

Charisse knocked on the door. Laramie's heart sank. She knew what was next.

"Charisse, I know we have to do this but I can't take it anymore. This tears at me."

He looked at Laramie trying to deduce the conversation. *What tears at her?*

"I know, Laramie, but you know it has to be done. I wish there was another way."

"What is she talking about Laramie?" inquired Akihiro.

"She is here to drawn blood from Akiko. I have to ask you to leave, Akihiro. Believe me you don't want to be in here." She looked at him with tears. "Please, I am asking you."

He agreed to leave the room. As he stood outside the doorway, he heard Akiko scream. It sent chills down him. He never saw this portion of the treatment. He found it unbearable to hear her in pain. He listened to Laramie as she tried to console her daughter. She kept telling her she was sorry and it was okay, Mommy was there. He walked back in after Charisse left the room.

Laramie stood in front of the window rocking her daughter and wiping Akiko's tears. Now he understood what tore at her so bad.

"How many times have they done that?"

"This is her third time and it doesn't get any better for her or you." She tried to hush Akiko. "The first time was the worst. It devastated me to hold her still knowing she was in pain. She doesn't deserve this. No baby does."

"I had no idea."

"Neither did I. Do you want to hold her?"

He nodded yes and took her from Mom's arms. *Laramie is right, no baby deserves this.*

"How long before they have results?"

"Saturday, but we wont know the results until Dr. Patel reviews them. I don't know if he'll be in on a Saturday. On Sunday, it's time for another draw."

Akiko calmed down, as her father held her and kissed her lightly all over her head and face. There was no doubt he loved her.

"Laramie can you take her? Do you mind if I use your laptop. I want to send some emails home."

"Oh sure, go right ahead."

Akihiro logged onto the server at the hotel. He checked his construction log and it seemed Shinji covered well for him. His mother asked how everyone was too. He told her the baby is more beautiful in person. He never imagined her could love someone so fast and hard. He gave her as much detail as he felt she needed. Lucia asked if he and Laramie resolved their differences. He didn't answer that question. He emailed Kat concerning the baby. She told him the hotel was fine and not to worry about anything. She and Shinji were in control. Lastly, he had an email from Rhys. It contained the name and number of a Richard Barnes. Akihiro wrote it down and placed the paper in his pocket. He deleted the unimportant things and saved the rest. Before he gave it back, he deleted any history and cookies linking to his website.

"Thanks, it helped a lot. I'll take her back if you don't mind." Laramie leaned forward and placed Akiko in his arms. Their faces were close as they tried to finagle the hand over. Laramie looked into his eyes and he into hers. She turned her head and backed away. She excused herself from the room. *Damn all those old feelings. Why do they come back? Is there a solution to this?*

No. If anything happens to her, he will never forgive me. How long can we go on like this?

He wasn't sure what she felt or what he felt. *It seems so natural being around her and the baby. Why is that? We haven't really argued yet and I'm sure we will.* When Laramie entered the room he asked if she was okay, she replied she was fine. He knew she lied but left it alone.

She had a few business calls that she conducted without her laptop. He watched her during the conversations. As he listened to her speak, it sounded like someone reading a contract, almost a foreign language. She quoted legal cases and told associates where to find them in the books down to the page number. Watching her mind work fascinated him. He never saw this side of her. Rhys told him she was an amazing attorney but he didn't put much weight into it. Her last phone conversation was with Frank Paradise. Akihiro was able to pick out that much from the conversation. He knew they were arguing over money but he didn't know why. Finally, she raised her voice and told him she refused to bill over their last project, something about Andy and an overage of funds. Aki figured he must've given in because she thanked him before she hung up.

"Laramie, is everything okay?"

She turned without missing a beat and relied, "Yeah, why?"

"You raised your voice and I was just asking that's all."

"Oh, you mean Frank. Sometimes, we don't agree and argue. But after I explain things the way they are, he usually folds."

"Just like at Raffles that morning when he asked if you told me about Akiko and you said no. That was the argument, wasn't it?"

What difference is the truth at this point? The pieces will fall together for him. "Yes, that was the argument."

"Laramie, how many people knew?"

"Everyone here." She swallowed hard. He had her on the spot. She knew even if the truth was hard, it was best to say it.

"What did they say you should do about Akiko?"

"Why are you doing this? You know the answer." She paused a moment. "*Everyone*, yes, *everyone* said I needed to tell you. Yes, I argued with every one of them. It was a continuous battleground. The only peace I had was in Singapore, except Edward told Frank and I had him on my back the whole time."

"Why is it so easy for you to tell the truth now?"

"Because I have nothing left to lose. Can we finish this now? Please."

She became restless. He knew he got to her. He wanted to push her just a little farther.

"What did you lose?"

She licked her lips and shook her head. She sniffle a minute. "You, okay? I lost you." She turned and walked into the restroom and shut the door. That was what he wanted to hear. In her mind, 'they' were over but she wasn't over him. Laramie pulled herself together and returned into the room. She avoided eye contact. She felt he interrogated her enough for one day. *How many times do we have to rehash this? He knows how I felt. He knows the truth.*

The tight quarters of the room added its own pressure. A young girl with a delivery cart stopped in front of Akiko's room, dropping off more toys, flowers and cards. Akihiro looked at all the gifts in amazement.

"Do you know all these people?"

"No. This is a result of the posters. So many strangers took up her cause, pray for her, and donate things on her behalf. It has tapered off some, thank goodness. I was running out of places to pass them onto. The only thing is I read the cards in case it's someone I know."

"What are you doing with today's delivery?"

"That's a good question. Maybe I'll have them taken to one of the children's homes. I'm running out of ideas and it's too early in the year for *Toys For Tots.*" Laramie looked over all the numerous gifts astounded by the generosity.

"Do you want to take a break and have a late lunch?" He tried to make a good will gesture.

"With you?" she questioned his surprising offer.

"Yes, why not?"

"I don't think it would be a good idea. Besides, one of us needs to be with Akiko. You go on ahead, I'll stay with her."

"That's right, you can't take confrontation. Fine, I'll go alone," he snapped.

"You're such a jerk." He really found the buttons that set her off.

"Why am I the jerk? I asked you nicely if you want to eat with me. Where's the harm in that?"

"I think you get off on upsetting me. I think you completely love to watch me squirm under your command. No matter where we would go, I would be forced to participate in your guilt ridden games, unable to do anything because of public bystanders. If I walk away, it calls attention to us. I can't yell, cry or scream. I am a prisoner. No thanks, I'll pass."

"I don't do that."

"Oh my God, you do it everyday. You have to keep pushing the envelope. *Gee Laramie, what did you lose?* What the hell was that? You know the answers but you don't feel better unless you make me miserable admitting it to you. Go ahead, pull out more pitiful things in my life to make me feel inadequate.

God knows I'm not emotional enough already. Let's just send Laramie over the edge. Is that when you'll stop?"

"You always overreact."

"That's right, it's always Laramie's fault. I overreact too much. I cry too much. I lie too much. I run away too much. Tell me Akihiro, what exactly was it that you loved about me? You know what, just forget it. You stay with Akiko. I need a breath of fresh air. And by the way, I'm running away again, just so we both understand it."

She grabbed her coat and stormed down the hall. The nurse's station across the hall remained a buzz with the excitement. Charisse told her girlfriends about Laramie and Akihiro and said they were better than any soap opera. Most of them called her at the end of her shift for an update.

Laramie walked the grounds of the Medical Center. She was furious with the conversation. *I was stupid. I should've just said no thank you. But now we have a fiasco over my words. I have to start thinking faster. I can't allow that upper hand. He screws me on it every time. I need to be the lawyer more and the woman less. I work so much better when I'm mad. Like the land deal. That went smooth until I got sucked in by his card. They need a school to teach woman to be better bitches. Maybe that's my calling. Ha, where's Liz when I need her. She is so great at that. Randy crumbles. Maybe it's a southern thing.* She ranted in her head for quite a while before she felt in control again. *What do I say when I go back to her room? How do I cover myself? I don't. That's the ticket. Let it end without another word. Why backtrack? Show you've moved forward and the conversation is finished. Enough said.* After an hour passed, she went back to relieve Akihiro to lunch.

He watched her carefully as she entered the room. She remained calm and casually made eye contact. She grabbed a magazine and sat in the rocker. Laramie looked up and told Akihiro he was free to go eat. *Something is up. She is way too composed. She always comes back with more fight in her or an apology for losing her temper.*

Laramie called Liz. She needed her friend's help. Liz always knew how to put a man in his place. Laramie hoped this was a learned trait and not instinctive.

"Laramie darlin', I was hoping to hear from y'all. How is Akiko?"

"She hasn't changed any, but I see that as a positive because it isn't any worse. We'll know more in another week. Hey, Liz, I have a question for you. I'm hoping you can help with this."

"Well, tell me your troubles. I'll help any way I can."

"How do you control men? I mean you always seem to have them eating out of your hand. Where as I am the blubbering fool, apologizing and crying."

"I don't need to ask that this has to do with Akihiro. I wondered how you were handlin' him. Not so well I see. Baby, he knows you love him and he can twist his words as easily as he twists you. You fall into his trap, I saw you do it with Sam. Not to bring up any bad memories. You are too eager to please others. You need to make others please you. If they don't give the answer you want, don't ask for it, just ignore the one they gave you. It forces them to try and find another way to satisfy your question. They will question the silence in your reaction. Haven't you Yankees ever seen *Gone with the Wind*?"

"Yes. But when I ask him a question, he answers with another question."

"*Stop* asking him questions. You are setting yourself up. If you can't think of a good answer, just answer with 'huh' as if you are contemplatin' the question. If you don't answer it, he may rephrase it and ask again. Let your responses silence him. Do you understand what I'm sayin', Lara, dear?"

"Huh."

"Exactly. Now how is that dear angel baby of mine? Any word yet? I must say that your daughter has made national news as well as you. I'm sure the good Lord has a plan for you. Be patient and have faith."

"Faith. I've heard that word a lot lately. I've been doing a lot of praying too."

"It never hurts. I heard a saying once that you can never have too many people love your children. It is so true. We all love her. She will get through this and so will you. When you get home and settled, we will chat more. We need another girls only night. I love you both, darlin' and take care."

Laramie knew Liz and her abilities to stay in control. She was correct, she did put herself out there to be manipulated. *Well, not anymore Mr. Amori. Now it's my turn.* Laramie picked up Akiko and they looked out the window. *It has been so long since we went to a park and played. Soon, baby, soon.* She couldn't wait until her daughter was a child again and not a patient. She sat down in the rocker and they played patty cake when Akihiro walked in. Laramie looked up to acknowledged his entrance but didn't mutter a word. He watched them play for a few minutes. He kicked his feet up on the edge of the bed. She thought about what she wanted to say. Laramie waited until just the right moment before she spoke. He just closed his eyes.

"You can easily go back to your hotel if you want. I'm used to being here all day. Most of the mothers are here while the fathers are working." She paused. "Speaking of working, how are your hotels coming along?"

"They're fine. The addition is almost complete. The Batam location has the exterior finished. They should start the contractors inside shortly. Why do you ask?"

Oh God, you make this too easy. "Well, I remember how important they are to you, that's all." *Bingo, you jerk! How's the guilt trip now?*

Akihiro remembered their last conversation. It was a long while before he realized his mistake. He never apologized to her for that. Had he gone to San Francisco when she asked, he would have had all those months with her and Akiko.

"Laramie, I did call you once."

"Huh. I don't recall that." *There's my 'huh' just like Liz told me.*

"I hung up after you answered."

"But why? Why would you call that far away and then hang up?"

"I wasn't sure what to say."

"About what?" He started to feel the pressure. It was uncomfortable being on the receiving side.

"You were right. I didn't appreciate you or what you were giving up to be with me. I was too consumed with work. I—"

"You know, it's all water under the bridge as they say here. Why revisit the past? It can't be changed." Laramie cut him off. She didn't want his apology now. His work decimated their relationship.

Laramie went back to playing with Akiko. She grabbed a book and read to her. Akiko fell asleep half way through the book. Laramie picked her up and lay her in the crib. When she stood up, she walked out of the room. She didn't say a word to Akihiro, not even to excuse herself. She stood at the nurse's station and chatted with Patty, the evening nurse. They compared baby stories and laughed over them. Patty was the grandmother type. She had a few more years of working before retirement. She was divorced and completely aware of the Laramie-Akihiro saga.

Laramie went back into Akiko's room. Akihiro sat and daydreamed.

"I'm sorry, did I startle you?"

"No, I was just thinking. I'm surprised I haven't seen any of your friends here."

"Well, if you were here at seven a.m., then you would. Edward, Manny and Lian stop in the morning before work. They keep Kiki busy so I can shower and dress. It's far easier than making the ride after an exhausting day at work."

"Speaking of morning, I'll be running late tomorrow. Just so you know."

"Okay, that's fine."

After Akiko woke up, Laramie sat and fed her. *She ate half her plate. Which is better than nothing.* Akihiro knew something was going on. He watched her closely but couldn't pin point it. Laramie acted so calm, almost professional. *Why? There is a change in her whole demeanor. This is not like her.*

She is going somewhere with this and I will catch her on it. She can't control her emotions. And eventually, she will burst.

Laramie sat in the chair as she caressed her daughter. Akiko laid back against Laramie's chest with her head on Mom's shoulder. Laramie closed her eyes for a moment and continued to rub Akiko. The boredom of sitting in a hospital room every day somehow exhausted her. At least during the day she kept busy with phone calls and emails but the evenings were long. Laramie turned the television on and tuned into Sesame Street for Akiko. Akihiro sat across from them, fidgeting. It was obvious, the evening bored him too.

Laramie closed her eyes. "Why don't you go? Watching you fidget makes being here even worse. There must be something you can do in the city. If you want to know where good bars, good food and good shopping are, just ask."

"So, I don't have the privilege of a tour guide then?" Laramie dismissed his comment. She knew what he meant.

"If I can think of someone, I'll send them over. My tours are booked for the moment."

"Just as well. I have some things I need to go over at the hotel. Remember I won't be here until later."

"Yes, I heard you the first time."

Akihiro walked over to her chair and leaned over bracing his hands on the arms. He bumped Laramie's leg when he moved causing her to open her eyes. As he pulled his face away from Akiko's, he found himself staring into Laramie's eyes. They stared at each other for a moment as they waited to see who made the next move. Nevertheless, their cat and mouse game was interrupted by the evening nurse.

"Good night, Laramie."

"Good night." *Why get so close? What the hell was the point in that? Was he waiting for me to reach out to him? I refuse. If he feels something then he should say it. I'm not going to assume anything and look like the idiot when I'm wrong.*

Chapter 55

AKIHIRO ENTERED A small office building on Turk Street. He went to the fourth floor and opened the door to the office of Richard Barnes, attorney. He got the name from Rhys as a great reference for counsel. The elderly secretary announced his arrival by phone when she clearly could have said it out loud. She told Akihiro that Richard expected him and to enter. Akihiro looked around the old office. Though maintained decently, the age of the building was obvious. A room air-conditioner was in the window. Stacks of papers covered the gentleman's desk. The attorney stood up, buttoned his jacket and shook Aki's hand. Akihiro figured Richard to be the same age as his father, around sixty-five. He was thin with thick wavy white hair that parted in the center.

"A pleasure to meet you Mr. Amori. Please sit down and tell me your concerns." *Rhys must've known him from London because he speaks with the same heavy British accent.*

"Yes, but call me Akihiro. Rhys Davis recommended you. I'd like you to represent me in a custody and visitation case. It seems my ex-girlfriend had a child and has just now informed me of her existence. As you may know, I live in Singapore but I'd like to be able to have summers and such with her."

"Obviously, paternity has been established."

"Yes."

"Well, father's rights are becoming increasingly more in demand. A benefit for you. A judge is always pleased to see a father involved in raising their child. I assume the mother lives here in San Francisco."

"Yes, she does. I have all her personal information written down for you."

Akihiro handed the attorney his sheet. The attorney reviewed it, and peered at Akihiro over his reading glasses.

"Come now, are you trying to make merry with me? Did Rhys put you up to this?"

"I don't understand. What's the problem?"

"You've listed Laramie Holden as the defendant. Blimey, that's rich."

The attorney's statements confused Akihiro. He didn't understand the joke.

"I'm sorry but I don't understand what you're talking about. This isn't any kind of joke. We are talking about my daughter."

The attorney's expression changed to one of concern, as he cocked his head sideways. He eyed Akihiro a moment before he responded.

"You're not kidding, are you? So, you're the bloke. You're Akiko's father. I do apologize. I had no idea you wanted to sue Laramie. By the way, how is little Akiko doing? We all feel awful to hear of her condition."

"You... you know my daughter? And Laramie? But how? Was it the posters?"

"Come now, this the San Francisco, who doesn't know Laramie Holden? Ha." Again, the attorney looked at Aki's expression. His confusion was obvious.

"You have me completely confused, Mr. Barnes."

"Oh dear, you don't know about her, do you? Well, before we go further, let me give you a bit of a history lesson. Get comfortable and try not to be too stunned at what you're about to hear." Richard cleared his throat before he began. " Tom and Audrey Holden, her parents, were wonderful, brilliant attorneys. They had some very lucrative cases, of few of them precedent setting. Their careers, along with Edward Graham and Andrew Mathers, exploded in the early eighties. They won this landmark case for a Chinese family. As a result, every minority in the city rushed to their doors. Laramie, cute as a button, grew up in this environment. She played with the children of judges and politicians. They were among the city's most prominent families. Are you following me so far?"

"Yes."

"When her parents were killed, it was devastating news in the legal community. She became the adopted child of almost everyone. Edward Graham represented Laramie in her parent's wrongful death suit. Of course, they won the twenty million dollar judgment but the real secret was the amount they collected in a punitive damage settlement. Outside of Edward, Andrew and Laramie, only the senior execs at the paper company know the amount. They agreed to pay it as long as it remained sealed to keep their stocks from plummeting. Everyone has their guess, mine is an additional twenty million."

"I had no idea." *Twenty million dollars, that explains some things.*

"Apparently. Anyway, the firm never took a dime for their fee. Edward refused to profit off the death of his best friends. People everywhere felt awful for Laramie. She was such a happy child back then. She became very introverted and unemotional after their death."

"Unemotional? Are we talking about the same woman?"

"Let me finish. She spent a year with grandparents until they died. Her maternal grandparents had a long lineage in the South, dating way past the civil war and held property from then. Her grandfather was a shrewd businessman and accumulated quite a bit of wealth. When they passed, Laramie was the sole heir. Naturally, she inherited his holdings."

"She never mentioned any of that."

"Not a bit surprising. At that time, Edward took over Cummings Corporation. He still oversees that part of the business. Clever attorney but an even more astute businessman. A King Midas, so to speak. Anyway, she went to live with Edward then. He taught her the law and business from such a young age. She went onto college and law school. She was in the top ten in her class at Harvard. I mean top ten students not percentile. Do you have any idea how brilliant you have to be to get to that academia?"

"No, I've heard talk that she was smart."

"*Wrong.* I'm smart, she's brilliant. She recites case law as sports announcers recite baseball statistics. I've never seen such a thing."

"I have, yesterday."

"Anyway, after graduation she worked for the firm. She did not make partner because of her parents but because of her achievements. She is in a league beyond anything you could imagine. She does it because she loves it. She is on the board of her own companies and that of several more in the city."

"How does she have time?"

"Isn't that the question? She donates most of her salary to civic organizations. She, along with Edward, has funded theater restorations, public park equipment, constructed shelters for the homeless and if you're quick, you can catch her at the mission serving the homeless on Sunday mornings."

The news stunned Akihiro. He didn't know what to say, let alone think. He just sat there as Richard continued.

"There was much speculation regarding the father of Akiko. It was uncharacteristic of her to be an unwed mother. Though when would she have time to date, right?"

"Sure, right." Akihiro never knew any of this about her. *Who is this woman? Why didn't she ever mention any of this?*

"When Akiko's case made national news, we were all surprised to see her speak publicly."

"National news? Why?"

"Haven't you been listening? She is a very powerful woman. She spends her free time with the wealthy and politically connected. She is an icon in this city. As I said, she made a speech on the news. This city went into an uproar over Akiko. The lines at marrow donor clinics stayed busy for hours. Across the country. Here, wait a moment."

Richard leafed through some papers on the floor. He handed the newspaper to Akihiro. Aki looked at the headlines. It was about Akiko. *It's front-page news.* The article went on to mention several of Laramie's contributions to the city. This astonished him. He knew nothing of this side of her.

"I thought she was just a lawyer in the U.S. I didn't know any of this."

"Why would you? She would never brag about herself, not her style."

"Are you saying you won't take the case?"

"Not at all. I relish the thought of opposing her. You, Mr. Amori, have the law on your side. It comes down to timing. If she gets wind of your suit, don't be surprised if she tries to have you deported."

"But, I have a ninety day visa."

"Dear Lord, my young man, wake up. There isn't a soul she doesn't know. Surprise is the issue. We need a judge in the Unified Family Court. Who's on the outs with Edward right now?" Richard tapped his fingers on the desk and called out to his secretary for an answer. "Yes, Judge Gallagher, brilliant. We will send out the summons the same time we request an emergency hearing due to your visa limitation and the defendant."

"Are you sure this will work?"

"The one thing I know about Laramie Holden is she can't tolerate confrontation. Jammy for us, that's why she isn't a trial attorney. A word of warning before you go, steer clear when she is served. All hell will break loose. I will contact you at your hotel if I have any other questions. Again, a pleasure to meet you."

"Thank you, Mr. Barnes. I appreciate this."

As Akihiro walked out, he heard Richard's excitement over the case. *Afraid of confrontation, yes, that is the same Laramie Holden.*

* * *

Laramie waited for Akihiro to show up. She wanted to grab something to eat and hated to leave Akiko alone. As he walked through the door, she quickly asked him to watch Akiko. He said he didn't mind then asked to use her laptop. She said sure as she disappeared through the doorway.

Akihiro was on a hunt to find out who this woman was. He went through some of her files and found one listed as 'Cummings Holdings.' He needed a password for access. *Damn.* Another file called 'Banks' also required a password. He decided to try the WiFi and see what that brought him. He did a search on Laramie's name and Cummings Corporation. *Aha, a company website. Let's see what this shows.* It showed a globe with circular arrows encompassing it, at the top were the headings: Locations, Companies, Financials, Executives, and Careers. He chose Executives first. Her picture appeared at the top, then other board members below her. *Laramie, why didn't you ever say anything? And this is Edward Graham. Too hard to get a good look with that picture.* The Location heading listed companies all over the world, every continent. *How can she work at this and have time for law? Better yet, how does she have time for Akiko?*

He searched other articles in her name alone. One of the first images showed her looking over her parents caskets. Akihiro couldn't bear to look at it. *It had to be incredibly sad for her.* Many of the items showed her half smiling. *Apparently, she shied from the camera too. That's why the news conference surprised everyone. It was confrontation. It's the same reason why she runs away when we argue.* Akihiro remember their last conversation in Singapore just before she walked away. *She said I would never know what she was giving up for me. She was going to walk away from all of this.* Suddenly, his two hotels seemed miniscule compared to her corporation. *The land deal, the building sale… this is how she had the money to make the transactions. How much money does she have?* Learning her history stunned him. Then, it scared him. *How am I to compete with her? On her home ground? If she is as powerful as Richard says, she won't take being served happily.*

He sent a few emails to Kat and asked why she never found any of this information. He emailed Rhys to find out his extent of information. Lastly, he sent the hyperlinks to Shinji. He told his brother briefly about his history lesson. He needed to talk to someone and Laramie wasn't the person. Once again, he cleared his footprints on her laptop and removed the risk.

A short time later, Laramie came into the room. She thanked him for taking over for her.

"Don't misunderstand me, I am not saying the food is good, I was just that hungry." She sat in her chair and picked up a magazine. "Hey, did you take care of the business you needed to do?"

"As a matter of fact, yes. You sound in a good mood, any reason?"

"Yes, my flat is finally back together. All lead paint has been removed and replaced by new wood. All chemicals are gone, only environment friendly solvents are there. That is such a relief to know when we go back home."

He remembered her home was thousands of miles from his home. *Will they ever be the same? Probably not after the court date. Unemotional? How could he say that? She is the most emotional person I've ever met.*

"Laramie, is it hard for you to go to work and take care of Akiko?"

"That's an odd question. No. She has a nanny at the flat while I'm at work. The hardest part is being away from her. Travel is agonizing." She stopped there when she remembered the last time away was Singapore.

"Would you be able to work from home?" *He's asking a lot of questions. Why?*

"I would love to but I have so many calls in a day, the phone would wake her. I couldn't have clients there; I wouldn't feel right having a stranger near her. Besides, with all of her toys, everyone would be tripping. Why all of the questions? Why do you want to know?"

"No reason. I was just trying to imagine an average day for her. Is she on a schedule? What does she do with the nanny?"

"Francesca comes in about seven in the morning. By then, I've already fed Akiko. I get ready for work and then leave. She plays with her toys, has snacks, and eats lunch. Depending on the weather, Francesca takes her to Moscone Recreation Center. It's a block away and it has a great playground. Lots of kids. Kiki loves the swings. She would stay on them all day. Though she's not sure yet about the slide."

"What about the weekends?"

"On the weekends, she and I go to the park and sometimes shop. A few weeks ago, we spent the afternoon with friends. We go to the zoo, I let her run at Golden Gate Park, and we walk the Japanese Tea Gardens."

"Japanese Tea Gardens? Where's that?"

"Next door, inside Golden Gate Park, next to the Botanical Gardens. I'd say it's about a half mile from here. It's not Singapore but it is very beautiful." She gestured over her shoulder.

"I'll have to see it sometime. What brings you there?"

She wondered why the long line of questions. "My daughter is part Japanese if you weren't aware of that."

"Really. I heard she looks just like her father. Must be a good looking guy," he grinned.

"I guess if you like that type. Lucky for her, she has her mother's brains."

"Don't be fooled, even smart people make dumb mistakes." *This is no longer funny. If he wants to rip into me fine, don't play games.*

"*Everyone* makes mistakes." She refused to continue this bantering.

I must have hit a nerve. She almost lost her temper. She is so sexy when she's fired up.

They sat in silence for a few hours. She worked on her laptop. She sent a few emails to her friends. The girls had questions regarding Akihiro. She replied by sending a phrase about cold temperatures in the room. He played with Akiko when she woke from her nap.

"You asked about parenting earlier. How much do you want to learn?"

He wasn't sure where this was going. "All of it, but not in one lesson."

"Great. It's your turn to change her diaper." She handed him a new diaper, wipes and a garbage bag.

"Come on, this is not what I meant. I don't know how to do this."

"No time better to learn than the present. Go on the other side of the bed and I'll help you." She set the garbage bag at the foot of the bed. She pulled three or four wipes out first before she pulled the tabs open on Akiko's diaper.

"Oh no, that's awful. Close it back up." The contents repulsed Akihiro.

"No, you're doing this. Use the diaper to remove most of it and place it in the garbage bag. Take the wipes and go front to back. You have to do it that way or she could get a urinary infection." Laramie laughed as she watched Akihiro clean Akiko.

"Next time, I'd prefer mixing formula."

"Pull the tabs tighter so it doesn't fall off her. Not bad for your first time. By the end of the weekend, you'll be a pro."

She found the lesson humorous. He walked toward his chair at the same time she tried to reach the rocker. It became a game of sidestepping. Finally, he grabbed her hands and pretended they were dancing. She laughed along. *Ah! A moment of harmony.*

"Lara, can I ask a favor?"

Still coming off the humorous dancing, she responded, "Sure, what is it?"

"Do you think you could have someone watch Akiko tomorrow night?"

"I suppose, why?"

"Would you show me around San Francisco? I hate to be here and not see anything. Just for a few hours. That's all. Besides, I think we can use a break from the hospital."

His question surprised her. She wanted to say no but hesitated. *If I say yes, I'm asking for trouble. If I say no, I'll be the cold bitch. This is why Liz said to stay in control of the conversation. Huh, isn't going to work this time. Though, I could sure use a change of scenery.*

"Sure. Let me call Lian right now to see if she can come here."

"Thanks." He knew it was a hard question.

Laramie dialed Lian. She asked Lian if she would watch Akiko for a few hours Saturday night. Lian jumped at the chance to spend time with the baby. She asked Laramie what she planned to do. Laramie said she needed to play tour guide for Akihiro. She reminded Laramie that was how she fell for him in the first place. Laramie responded in the affirmative. Lian knew Akihiro was close by Laramie's responses. Laramie asked her to be there by five. Lian agreed.

"Well, that was easy. I have a few things to drop off at my office, which is right around the corner from you. It would be easier to meet you in your hotel lobby. Is that okay with you?"

"Sure, I'm fine with that."

Laramie faced some risks with this date. However, if she kept them in the public eye, she could maintain a more platonic role. Laramie knew she loved him, she knew she wanted to be with him but she also knew this wasn't the time. Since he came to town, the tumultuous days haven't stopped. One minute, they threw barbs at each other, the next minute, they laughed together. Keenly aware of that fact, Laramie stood guarded.

Great, now what? Small talk about the weather, maybe? I wish I knew what he was thinking. I don't know which direction to take now. Who would've thought being nice would be so difficult?

"I noticed you walked in with a heavier jacket. I'm guessing you bought it after your arrival."

"Oh, yes. I hit a breeze the other morning. I didn't realize it was so cold here."

"The bay area is nothing like Singapore. In the mornings, we have fog, but in the afternoon, after the fog burns off, it can be really nice out. In the summer, the city's warmer. If you want Singapore weather, you'd need to go further inland, toward wine country."

"That's right. I forgot this was a big area for wineries. Have you been to many?"

"A few. It's great for a day trip, the countryside is beautiful. Watching the hot air balloons fly overhead on some weekends is breathtaking. I guess I spend too many weekends in the office to enjoy it. Well, not lately at least."

"I have to guess with your fear of heights that you've never been up in a balloon."

"No, actually, I did many years ago with my parents. I almost forgot about that until now." Laramie raised her eyebrows and smiled a bit as she remembered the nostalgia.

"It sounds like you did a lot of things with your parents. They must've been a lot of fun."

"They were." Laramie leaned back in her chair and crossed her legs. She looked out of the corner of her eyes as she recalled her favorite memories. "My father was a bit of a daredevil which was fine with Mom as long as it didn't involve me. He took me out for a ride on an ATV once and we flipped it. We both had helmets on, luckily, we were only scratched up. My mother was furious with him. Another time we went sled riding near Lake Tahoe. I fell off and it wasn't until my father reached the bottom that he realized I wasn't still behind him." Laramie chuckled to herself. "I must've been about seven or eight years old."

"I don't mean to bring up any bad memories but how did you feel when you lost them. Do you even remember?"

"Of course, I remember. I was shocked at first. I felt lost without them. Days I sat at the door waiting for them to come home, but they never did. Then there were days when I wished I was dead too, just so I could be with them." She wiped her eyes. "The grownups kept telling me it would get better with time but it never did. That's really when my childhood ended. When I moved to my grandparents, the kids at my new school asked where my parents were and why they didn't come to the school activities. To avoid that, I just stopped doing anything after school. I just came home and read. That was my biggest escape." She pulled herself back from the past. "I don't give that part of the past much thought, mainly because it was so empty. Though I do wish they were alive to see Akiko. That is probably my biggest disappointment."

"I suppose I take for granted that mine are there."

"Show them you appreciate them while you have the time. It can change in an instant. I hope you don't mind if we change the subject. Not exactly a conversation I want to continue with in the hospital."

"Oh, yes, you're right."

"Hey, how are Kat, Rhys and Shinji?"

"Um, Kat is doing good. She's been working hard maintaining the Tanjong while I'm involved in construction. Once everything is done, I want to move her to a higher position. I thought about as a manager for the Batam location but I know she won't leave her friends and family."

"At least give her the option. You'd show her that you appreciated her dedication and knowledge. She has the qualifications."

"Okay, so you are a big Kat supporter. I'll take it under advisement."

"I know what that means," Laramie retorted.

"What? I agree with you. She's great. She's been there since the beginning and knows every aspect. She could probably run the place better than me."

"I'm sure she could."

"You're saying that because you're a woman," he argued.

"No, I'm saying it as an employer. Her sex has nothing to do with it. But you jumped on that reason. She has to do her work well but then contribute even more to be noticed. That's sexist."

"Are you saying I'm sexist?"

Laramie teetered her head a moment, "Yes."

"You are kidding, right? I'm the least sexist person I know."

"Well if you're the least then I'd hate to see the rest of your group."

"Lara, do you *really* believe that?"

"Yes. I'm not saying you can help it. You obviously don't recognize it. However, you feel women are lesser opponents in business because we are more emotional. Just because you can internalize it doesn't make you better. For example. Have all your business decisions been a financial gain?"

"No, not all of them, most though."

"Okay, now, has Kat stopped you before making any bad ones?"

"Well, yes, but so what?"

"*So what?* Not only are you both looking at the same decision process but she saw potential failure before you did. Does that not constitute her the better decision maker?"

"But some of those decisions —"

"No, stop. It was a yes or no question."

"I'm not answering that."

"*Ha!* You won't answer because you know I'm right."

"I'm not answering it because it's a loaded question. What makes you think all of her decisions have been correct? Didn't you stop to think she also makes mistakes?"

"Now you're changing the arena. I used your business decisions. I compared her with you, in your capacity. You just answered my question but now you won't admit it to yourself that she has made better decisions than you have and that my dear, is sexist. Thank you very much."

"Well, Rhys has been really busy at the bank."

Laramie cracked up as he changed the subject. *Maybe I should've been a trial attorney after all. Nah.*

"I haven't seen him much." Akihiro started to laugh with her. He knew she nailed him and he found no escape.

"I miss his conversations sometimes. I have the perfect brunette for him in New Jersey. She might even be able to go pint for pint with him. I love that British accent. They always sound so polite even swearing. It's kind of sexy."

"Really? That's what it takes, an accent?"

"Yeah but it has to be the right accent. Like Irish or French, not Russian or German. Asian doesn't do it for me."

"Thanks a lot."

"No, no, no, I didn't mean you. I meant I hear that in Chinatown. It doesn't sound foreign, not when it's here."

"Keep back pedaling."

"So, how has Shinji been?" Laramie laughed. This time, he entrapped her.

"He's fine. He's looking over the construction for me. Real estate has been slow so he has the free time."

"It's probably a good break, trying something different."

He waited to see if she would touch on her property purchase but she changed the subject. *At what point will you tell me about that deal? It will come out.*

"Is there anything in particular you want to see tomorrow?"

"No. I thought I'd leave that up to you."

"Do you want to have dinner first or just sight-see?"

"Are you sure you want to have dinner with me? The other day you said you felt like you were a hostage. I don't want you to do anything that will make you feel uncomfortable."

"Yes, I'm willing if you agree to be civil about it."

Civil? When haven't I been civil? Don't fight her, just let it go.

"Yes, I agree."

Their conversation ended with the ring from Laramie's cell phone. As usual, an associate had questions regarding an upcoming trial. Laramie spoke on the phone for quite a while as she told the attorney what to expect from opposing counsel. Once she finished her guidance, she asked questions to see if the associate prepared properly. Satisfied by the response, she hung up. Akihiro watched her closely this time after learning about her background from his attorney. He didn't know anyone in that profession so he had no basis in which to measure her knowledge.

"How do you do that?"

"Do what?"

"On all your phone calls you sound as if you're reading from a book yet, you don't pick up your laptop or have anything in your hands. How do you know what you are telling that person is correct?"

"I remember things well, I guess." She answered modestly. "Besides, a lot of people remember facts and figures for their job. Mine isn't any different. Most cases are not precedent setting so most of the law you use is repetitious."

"What do you mean precedent setting?"

"That means the case is the first of its kind or the facts go beyond the existing ruling enough to change the law. Most people don't realize that the legal field is just as specialized as the medical field. You wouldn't go to a patent attorney for a divorce. Or a real estate attorney for medical negligence. It makes as much sense as going to a podiatrist for a broken arm."

"Well then, what type of law do you practice?"

"I mainly stay with contracts and corporate business. That's where my interest lies. But I also love research. I love to find old cases that can be used in new settings. You can break boundaries that way." The subject excited her causing her face to light up.

"You are confusing."

"How so?"

"You speak on the phone in a language only you understand. You read law books for their content. Yet, the only things I've seen you pick up and read are entertainment tabloids."

"Yeah, I know the rags are addicting. If it weren't for them, I'd be at a loss in conversation. I work so much that I don't watch television so I don't know who half the actors are anymore. Now with Kiki, I have less time for that unless it's naptime. It's hard cramming a world of information in a two hour nap."

"I know it's unfair but I'm going to take off early. I want to get some work done at the hotel. I have a few hours before they arrive to work. Do you think Dr. Patel will be in an earlier than nine?"

"He hasn't yet. Go ahead I have things covered here. Besides, it's almost dinner for her. Unless you want another lesson?"

"Ah, no, but thanks for the offer. I'll see you tomorrow." Akihiro walked over to Akiko who played quietly in her crib and kissed her good bye.

After he walked out, Laramie called Gillian. She brought her girlfriend up to speed including the plans for Saturday night.

"Laramie, I know you want to believe you can do this as a friend but it's not realistic. What do you do if he starts talking about a relationship again? Do you even know if that's what you want? Are you prepared for that heartache again?"

"I know, Gillian. I understand everything you are saying but I still need to stay on good terms. He will always be the father of my daughter. My main objective is to stay public, the restaurant, the pier, and busy clubs. Besides, it's only for a few hours. I don't want to be away from Akiko too long."

"So, how does he look?"

"Hot. I have to admit I do have good taste in picking them."

"Yes, but bad taste in long term plans. Get your head out of the clouds. It's not a first date. You need to keep on your toes. Remember he is the same person who omitted an engagement. On top of that, he left you hanging about coming there to help Akiko." Before Laramie spoke, Gillian continued. "I know you are going to try and take blame for it but stop. You did what you thought was right and what was right for you. Don't apologize for that."

"Do you rehearse these speeches with Liz ahead of time? Anyway, I am going to run. The staff just brought her dinner and I need both hands. I'll keep you posted. Bye."

Chapter 56

LARAMIE DRESSED EARLY. She knew Manny and Lian would be there to visit shortly and she didn't want to lose time talking by showering. Akiko slept in late that morning which made it easier for Laramie to prepare herself. She looked out the hospital window and wondered what the night would bring. She tried to decipher her feelings for him. She still loved him, but their love was also combative. *Is there any stability in that?*

"Good morning baby doll!" Lian called out. "I miss seeing you play in your room. We have to get you better so you can go home. Hi, Lara. I didn't mean to cut you out."

"Hey, I don't blame you. I'd pass you by for her any day. How you both doing? That's was crazy that he went in the market."

Manny wondered what they meant. "What market? What are you talking about?"

Lian turned to him and said, "The other morning Akihiro walked in the market looking for tea. I recognized him from the photos and called Laramie after he left. Talk about a coincidence."

"Oh, too funny. When he came here, I asked if he was happy that he found his tea and fruit. That brought a million dollar expression. He asked how I knew and I told him this is just a small town. I was on the ball that day."

Lian asked, "Yeah, but what happened yesterday? How on Earth did you end up on a date?"

"A date?" Manny interjected, raising his eyebrows.

"It's not a date. We are having dinner and I'm showing him the wharf and pier. Totally, above board. That still has me on edge. But I am looking forward to getting out of here for a few hours. Thanks for watching her for me by the way. I couldn't say much on the phone since he's here most of the time."

"Speaking of which, where is he now? I thought this would be the grand meeting."

Manny shook his head. "You women make a big deal out of nothing. He's a guy. You make it seem like he's a celebrity or something." Manny picked up Akiko and spoke as if she understood him. "I will break you of that habit, Sweetie. That's why Uncle Manny is here."

"I don't know actually. He went to the hotel early yesterday to work. It may have taken him into the night. I know he plans to be here to see if Dr. Patel comes here. We haven't heard any news on her blood count since they drew it on Thursday. I'm hoping no news is good news. Though she has been in a better mood the past few days."

"Anything is a positive. So, you need me here around five. I suppose I will meet him then."

"Actually, I'm meeting him at the hotel."

"Hotel? Yeah that's a safe place. What are you thinking? You'll never get out of his room?"

"Let me clarify that, the hotel *lobby*. I have a few things to drop and switch at the office so that location became central." Laramie defended her position despite Lian's raised eyebrows.

After Lian and Manny took turns holding and playing with Akiko, they left for work at the market. Edward called Laramie and told her he wouldn't be in that morning because he had a long standing golf game. It didn't bother her since, there wasn't anything he could do anyway. *Better that he be on the golf course than lecturing me.*

Laramie thought about her wardrobe. She wanted the night to be casual. She needed to run home, repack her suitcase and drop off her laundry to be cleaned. *Hmm... maybe I can leave at lunch to do that. My dark jeans and black cashmere sweater is fine. I'll bring my boots with me and change them before I leave here.* Laramie remembered their first date in Singapore and cringed at the part regarding the bumboat. She remember the progression each evening brought and it's tragedy. She laughed to herself as the thought about singing karaoke.

"What's so funny?" She looked up and Akihiro walked into the room.

"I was thinking about singing karaoke."

"You don't plan on doing it right now because the dogs in the neighborhood deserve fair warning." He picked up Akiko and kissed her, his first priority. He loved to hold her and smell that baby scent of a fresh bath. "If Mummy wants to torture us I will sacrifice my own hearing to protect yours."

"I wasn't planning to sing. I was just thinking about the last time I did. Besides, she hears me sing all the time and doesn't cry a tear."

"That's because she doesn't have anything to compare." He faced Akiko and said, "I was a witness to the awful scene. If she sings anymore you tell Chichi. Oops, sorry, I mean Daddy. Your Daddy will make her stop. Daddy will do anything Akiko wants." He continued to place kisses all over her face.

Laramie loved the interaction. Seeing his love for their daughter brought enormous relief.

"By the way, just a casual night. Lian said five worked well. Actually, you just missed them. You'll have to meet them sometime."

A knock against the door frame startled their conversation. It was Dr. Patel.

"Good morning." He walked to Akiko and stroked his fingers across her cheek. "Good morning, Akiko. The news is she is still holding her own. I am going to continue with the vitamin therapy but I want to give her a very low dose of steroids. Don't worry, let me continue. I've talked to other colleagues at John Hopkins regarding her case. There isn't one particular item that seems to cause the lack in cell production. Before I decide to go with a full steroid treatment, I want to try a short term boost. Similar to a jump start. I want to see if we assist her body if it will continue once the drug is out of her system."

"Will we lose anything but doing this experiment? It is an experiment, isn't it? Would it not be better to go with the stem cell treatment?" Akihiro inquired.

"The stem cell treatment is a procedure I only want to use as a last resort. There are complications associated with that as well such as infection and graph rejection. However, I will give her a shot today. It should show an increase in tomorrow's blood count. Then another shot on Monday, which should increase the count for Tuesday draw. Then stop. When we take the next draw on …"

"Saturday." Laramie stated.

"Yes, Saturday. If her body regenerated her own cells, we will know by the following Tuesday. I truly don't want her to have any extreme treatment if we can prevent it. Is this acceptable to you both?"

Laramie nodded in agreement. Akihiro didn't see much choice in the matter. He planned to send all this information to the hematologist in Singapore for his opinion as well.

After the doctor left, they looked at each other waiting to see who would speak first.

"Well. It's a small step. If it works, it makes it worth it than over treating the problem. We did the right thing, right?" Laramie asked, upset that the news wasn't more positive. "How long will this take? Why isn't she getting better? This isn't fair."

Akihiro walked beside her and put his arms around her. "Laramie, it's only been a week. All he is asking for is another week. I'm sure she will pull through this, she is strong like her mother."

His concern was just as great but he knew she needed support right now. He risked rejection when he touched her but she allowed him to get closer. It was a big step for them both.

"Ha. Her mother isn't so strong right now. But thanks for trying to make me feel better."

He kissed the top of her head before he let go and turned around to sit. It was the first time he held her since Singapore. He didn't want to let go but it wasn't about them, that time was about her and the fact she needed him. It felt so natural to Laramie that she didn't realize it until after he let go. *Could we finally be getting along? Are we finally putting our differences behind us? Does this mean he'll forgive me for not telling him about Akiko?*

The day dragged. Laramie fed Akiko lunch and Akihiro played with her. He carried her down the halls to give her a change of scenery. He didn't know how he felt about fatherhood when Laramie first told him the news. However, after the last four days, he didn't want to be without his daughter. He emailed everyone at home how beautiful and happy she was. He knew her happiness would increase once her illness disappeared. He told them she knew him as her father and she called him by name. She said Dada, along with Mama, no and bye. His mother was ecstatic to be a new grandmother and told all of their families and friends. Akihiro kept them current on any medical treatment. His family asked for new pictures and he promised to send more.

"Aki, why don't you take off? I'll meet you at the hotel. Lian will be here shortly and I'm running home for a minute before the office. I'd say to expect me around six."

"That's fine. It gives me a minute to walk around Union Square."

"Did you need to pick up something in particular?"

"No, no. Don't worry about it. I'll see you later." He kissed Akiko before he left.

Laramie waited for Lian to arrive. She stepped out to the nurse's station to chat with Charisse. Laramie loved her stories and advice, even if she didn't take it.

"Hello, girlfriend. I see Daddy has left already. You keeping the late shift?"

"Actually no, I am meeting him out for dinner then I'll be back to spend the night."

"Aha. Just how did that happen? You were fighting the last time I was here."

"Yeah, we do that a lot. When we agree, everything is great. When we disagree, we're ready to kill each other. I haven't found the happy medium yet. I know we have to for the baby's sake."

"You know Laramie, I truly believe your baby will be fine. At that time, you'll need to think of her future and yours. What happens after he goes back home?"

"I have no idea. Right now, my main concern is getting Akiko healthy again. There is no chance for us without her."

Lian walked down the corridor to relieve Laramie. She had books and toys at hand.

"I see you came prepared. Still I can't thank you enough for doing this."

"Shut up and go already. We have a private party and no moms allowed. Lara… be careful." She smiled and hugged her friend. Laramie knew despite the mess she caused, she always had Lian to support her.

Laramie raced home and repacked her suitcase. After she left Akihiro, she planned to pick it up. She threw together her laundry to drop off along the way. As she pulled on her dark jeans, she noticed they were loose. *Woohoo! I fit into my skinny jeans. I thought they might be a little tight but I guess from all the stress, I lost a few pounds. Damn, I look hot. Wait, I don't want to look too hot. On second thought, let him see what he's been missing.* She grabbed her brief case, laptop and laundry and took off.

She stopped at the firm first to synchronize her laptop. While she waited, Edward knocked on the door.

"So what brings you in on a Saturday evening? I'm surprised you left the hospital."

"Before you say a word, don't. I don't want a lecture. I am actually just passing through. I'm meeting Akihiro out for dinner and a walk along the wharf. Then, I'm going back to the hospital."

"Dinner and a walk, huh? Whose idea was it?"

"His."

"Then, enjoy yourself," Edward smiled.

"Oh no. What does it matter whose idea it was?"

"I know how you feel about him. I didn't want you to be chasing him. If he wants to be a part of this, let him do it on his own time frame. You've had over a year to adjust to the baby, he's had a week."

"You're right. What would I ever do without you? How did you get to be so smart?" Laramie hugged Edward.

"I helped raise a girl. Sometimes I still am. Enjoy yourself."

Laramie finished in her office. She grabbed her suitcase and left the laptop and briefcase. She felt safe enough to store her luggage at his hotel but not the cases and computer.

When Laramie entered the St. Francis, she walked to the house phone and asked to be connected to Akihiro's room. After he answered, she told him she was in the lobby. Within minutes, he joined her.

"Where are you taking me for dinner?"

"Actually, I thought for your first tour that we'd take a boat ride. If you can survive it, then we'll go onto dinner."

He laughed. "Don't you think the circumstance is a bit different? It was twenty nine degrees Celsius out for you. What's it here, maybe four degrees?"

"No, we're going to try a restaurant for the first time. La Mar Cebicheria. It's Peruvian. And I've heard a lot of great reviews. It's down on the Embarcadero on one of the piers. Then we can take a ride to Pier 39 afterwards if you're interested."

They exited the hotel and hailed a cab to drive down to the restaurant. By the time they arrived, the restaurant's lighting was bright against the night sky. The light blue awning and wide open windows gave an airy feel. Akihiro held the door for Laramie as they entered the lobby area. The décor, reminiscent of Rio De Janeiro, was in bright blues and yellowish greens; orange pillows accented throughout. It's dark floors were a true contrast to the white walls and ceiling. The volume inside surprised Laramie. The hostess asked if they cared to wait at the bar while they prepared their table. Laramie walked over to the bar, which stood adjacent to the open kitchen. The aromas in the air added to the customers hunger. The bartender asked for Laramie's order first; she opted for one of the house's specialties, a Pisco Sour. Akihiro stuck with his signature, Grey Goose straight up. The commotion made it easy to forget the hospital. Laramie sat on a bar stool as Akihiro stood beside her.

Once their cocktails arrived, Akihiro made a toast. "To Family."

He quickly surprised Laramie with his statement. *Whose family? Hell, go with it.* They started off with small talk, covering her office work, errands and his free time to shop.

"Shopping, that's right. What were you looking for anyway?"

"A gift for my daughter. Everything she has is from you, your friends or family. Though I should've asked what size she wore before I went. Holding my hands out a few feet didn't help the store clerk." Laramie laughed at his story.

"I was going to ask why you didn't call but I forgot the whole cell phone issue. Never mind. Will I get to see whatever it is that you purchased?"

"Maybe. I did go a little crazy. I never bought anything for a baby before but the boys have better toys." Laramie rolled her eyes.

The hostess greeted them and asked them to follow her to their table. She sat them at a table for four next to the window. It had a clear vista of the water since all the outdoor seating wasn't in place, due to the cold weather. It was very similar to Boat Quay but indoors. They sat side by side to both enjoy the view. Fortunately, the noise level was lower away from the bar. They both perused the menu and remained undecided until the waiter arrived to review the dishes.

Laramie shared her dilemma first. "What are you getting? Because I'm not sure what I want."

"Why don't we get something different and then split it?"

Laramie laughed and said, "But what if I don't like the half you order? Then I only have half of mine."

He turned, with a grin, to see if she was serious. "That can go both ways. What do you want to do, pick both? What if I don't like your choices?"

"Then you'd be hungry." He shook his head. *She's insane.*

Eventually they both opted for seafood dishes, one with a linguine base and the other a stew. When their meals arrived, they actually like the others better and traded. During the dinner, conversation roamed around Akiko, each other's work and friends. Laramie ordered a second cocktail but remembered that was her limit, since she still had to go back to the hospital. Akihiro pointed out the ferries that passed. Laramie told him the ferries go to different cities along the coast; some as day trips and some as commuters. She offered to show him Sausalito if that interested him. He asked where she lived in respect to where they were. She told him in the Marina District closer by the Wharf on the northern side of the city. They enjoyed each other's company, listened to each other's thoughts, laughed at the stories that were retold. When they finished she asked if he cared to walk some. Since he had a heavier jacket, the idea sounded great.

After a short walk, they hopped a cab ride up the Embarcadero to Pier 39. The place was open only for a few more hours since it was off season. A Giant crab sculpture in a planter guarded the entrance. Across from the Hard Rock Café, a musician treated the tourists to his one man jazz band, as he belted out tunes on his saxophone. They walked past Boudin's Bakery, picking up the scent of the sourdough bread as it baked. Laramie looked in the windows as she slowly walked along, careful not to lose her heel between the wooden planks. There wasn't much for her to see since she was there recently with Akiko. In the rear of the pier, a carousel spun with it's vibrant painting, lights and calliope music.

"This is Akiko's favorite spot. She loves to ride the carousel, especially the tiger. I get dizzy before she tires of it."

"This is an exciting spot with the restaurants and shops. I have to ask. What is that horrendous noise?"

Laramie laughed and took his hand. He followed her through a set of double doors. After they passed them, the sound amplified.

"It's the sea lions. They're here everyday. I loved coming here as a kid to watch them wrestle each other off the decks. Once in a while, you find a real character among the crowd."

Akihiro noticed her face lit up watching the animals play. It was obvious *she* still loved to see them. As more tourists arrived beside them, Akihiro got her attention to go back inside. He gripped her hand and she followed behind him. Once it was quieter, they continued their conversation.

"It seems to be popular with the tourists. I have to say a few shops are interesting."

"In the summer, the place is packed with tourists from here to Fisherman's Wharf. If you want to walk a few blocks we can head that way or make our way back into the city."

"What's back in the city?"

"A lounge. That's if you want to stop for another drink. It can't be long because I still need to grab my suitcase from the hotel storage and relieve Lian at the hospital."

"That's fine. There's three different lounges inside the hotel. You can have your pick."

Akihiro hailed a taxi to go back to Union Square. As they made their way down Stockton Street, Akihiro told the driver to stop on the far side of the square. Laramie wasn't sure the reasoning. Nevertheless, they both exited the car. As they strolled through the park, Akihiro grabbed onto Laramie's hand. They held hands on and off during the night but his grasp was firmer this time. Akihiro looked around and wondered how the palm trees survived the cold. The park was busy with shoppers and people out for the evening. Some street mimes performed while others remained statuesque. On the outskirts of the park were homeless people that waited for a handout and didn't solicit for one. As they neared the steps in front of The St. Francis, Akihiro stopped against the rail. His quick halt jerked at Laramie's arm.

"What are —" she began to ask.

He drew her close, wrapping one arm around her waist and the other behind her head. He pulled her mouth to meet his. His kiss was open and moist. Then he placed his other hand behind her head and kept her from pulling away. He paused for a moment to look into her eyes and plunged his tongue to meet hers once again. Laramie met him half way as she placed her hands atop his shoulders. He lowered his arm to pull her hips against his as his body hardened.

His lips pulled at her ear as he whispered, "You don't know how much I've missed you. You feel so good, so close."

"I've missed you too."

"Come to my room with me… just for awhile. I want you so bad." His breathing picked up and his kisses grew intense. "Tell me you want me, too."

She closed her eyes tight as her body burned. She wanted to go upstairs. "I do want you. God, I've always wanted you."

As he trailed his kisses to the other side of her neck, he continued to taunt and excite her. "Tell me what else you want."

Laramie knew she had to stop or else she would land in his bed. She pulled away to put her hands on the sides of his face. "Aki, I want you, you have no idea how bad I want you but I can't. I can't do this yet. Not until Akiko is out of the hospital. Not until she's better."

Noticeably displeased, he questioned her motives. "What difference would it make if it were now or week from now?"

"I can't fall into this again, not yet. If I went with you now, all my wants and needs would return. You don't know how hard it has been without you or how long it took to go a day without crying over you. If I went now and something happened to her, you would hate me, not for being sick but because of the lost time. I can't survive through that again. I just can't do it."

"I could never hate you. Be angry, yes, but not hate."

"I can't. I have to put her first right now. I'm sorry."

"No, I'm the one who's sorry," he answered back angry.

He let go of her and they walked side by side across the street. As they went into the building, Laramie said she wasn't going to stay, just pick up her suitcase and go directly to the hospital. He leaned in, kissed good bye on the cheek and walked toward the elevators. *I didn't lead him on. I wasn't the one who started it. A tease? No. We have one great evening and he gets ticked off because I won't sleep with him. God, do I ever want to sleep with him. He has no idea how hard it was to stop him. I could've ripped his clothes off on the steps. But, I have to stand by this conviction.*

Akihiro tossed his jacket on the chair in his room. He emptied his pockets and threw the contents across the dresser. After he kicked off his shoes, he jumped onto the bed. He turned the television on and flipped through the channels. Eventually, he tossed the remote onto the bed. *What goes through her mind? I have never seen a woman put such ridiculous thought into a scenario. Why would you even think that far ahead?* He tried to determine where his frustration laid, with her sexually or with her mentally. *So close. I just wanted to touch her, feel her. I needed that closeness. I need her. What is wrong with just sex without any other commitments? No, she has to feel just right. Come on. I think she does this to me on purpose. Of all the crazy women in this city…*

Laramie walked briskly down the hall to Akiko's room. Lian sat on the rocker as the baby slept. She quietly rolled her suitcase against the wall. Lian looked at Laramie as she searched for a clue about the evening.

"Well? You made it back in under four hours. That alone is surprising."

"Oh, please. Everything was great except for the last ten minutes. Dinner was fabulous. La Mar. You have to try it. Then we walked around Pier 39. That was fun in a touristy way. We get near the hotel and he wants to walk through Union Square. What could go wrong? Right? He gave me this kiss that was to die for and wanted me to go to his room."

"Did you?"

"Noooo. I told him I wasn't ready for that and I needed to get back here."

"I'm sure that went over well. Manny just loves it when I push him away," Lian said sarcastically.

"For crying out loud, of course I wanted to go upstairs. I'm freaking human. I haven't had sex since I got pregnant. It was so tempting. Five more minutes and I would've been naked in the square."

"Did you ever think of causal sex? Just for the release."

"Yes, but not with him. I can't. I have too many emotional attachments. One night would suck me back in."

"Laramie, you're already sucked back in. You think you have some strategy. You don't. The only thing you control is the timing. Sooner or later , you'll lose that too. What exactly was your reasoning? Just out of curiosity."

"Akiko. If anything happened to her, he'd never forgive me. I am the responsible person for cutting him out of her life. Who do you think he'd blame? And, here I stand."

"Nice thought. However, if that reasoning actually worked, he'd be blaming you now. He seems to have gotten over that fact. So tonight, you screwed yourself. How'd it feel?"

"Funny. End of subject. So, how was she? Cranky at all?"

"Not one bit. She is still an angel. We played and read. You'd never know she was sick. She did call out for both of you at bedtime. She's very attached to him."

"That goes both ways. He said he went shopping for her today. He talked about her all night. He just adores her."

"You couldn't ask for more Laramie. Now a days, guys run at the mention of fatherhood. Here is one who is embracing it. Anyway, I'm headed home. Take care."

"Thanks again. I owe you. Oh, by the way, here's taxi money."

"I'm not taking your money. Good night."

Laramie shoved the cash into her coat pocket as she passed. She didn't want her to take public transit since it was dark already.

Chapter 57

LARAMIE DREADED THIS day. The only thing she was thankful for was Charisse worked today, she was the best nurse for drawing blood. By nine o'clock, the nurse knocked on the side of the doorframe.

"Laramie, it's that time again. You know I have to do this, Sweetie."

"I know, Charisse. It just doesn't get any better."

Laramie picked up Akiko and held her on her lap. It was torture for mother and daughter. Akiko screamed at the prick of the needle. Her poor little leg had bruises on it from all the needle marks. Afterward, Laramie cradled her in her arms and rocked her to calm her. *God, please heal my baby. I can't bear to watch this happen anymore.* Slowly, Akiko stopped crying. She called out for Mama several times which filled Laramie with incredible guilt.

A short while later, Akihiro showed up in the room. After he sat down a package, he walked directly to Akiko and picked her up. As she started to cry, he realized they drew blood and he bumped her sore spot. He held her and rocked her back and forth. He pulled a camera out of his packet and took a few pictures. He turned the camera around to show the photos to Akiko which seemed to interest her enough to forget about her leg. After he placed her in her crib, he retrieved the package he brought, a wind up music player with the Sesame Street characters. He wound the knob for her and handed it her. She smiled and giggled as she watched the figures disappear into the side, searching the back to find the missing Elmo.

"It seems you found something she likes. Sesame Street is her favorite show."

"I guess I got lucky," he said coolly.

Akihiro was distant to Laramie, which bothered her. She wanted to say something but wasn't sure how to approach the subject of last night. *Just forget it. He doesn't see things from my perspective. Remember I overreact. It just confirms I made the right choice.* She leafed through the pages of her magazine. When she finished, she excused herself. *I might as well find a book. The magazines are too short to cover the day. I wonder if they have Tolstoy's Love and War. That rather defines us, doesn't it?* She browsed the gift shop as she thought more about the previous evening. *I can't believe he is being so angry over this. If he went to his room frustrated, it's was his own fault. I'm not some frigid bitch. I can't have sex for the sake of it. I need that attachment. It means something to me. That's his problem, not mine.* She looked over the best seller list in hard covers. *Another Grisham legal story, pass. A book about three sisters, can't identify. A book by Dr. Denis Leary? Perfect.* She picked it up and walked to the checkout where she grabbed a pack of mints. She paid for her items and went back to Akiko's room.

She walked in to see Akiko by herself, then she realized he was in the restroom. She sat in her usual rocker and began to read her book. *I'm hoping somewhere in here it will tell me why men suck. By the title, it seems we all suck.* She sat quietly and sucked on a mint. She didn't pay any attention to him as he walked out and sat in the other chair. He seemed disturbed that she left, at least that was what she assumed. She wondered how long the silence would remain. He said something that she missed.

"I'm sorry, what did you say? I was in the middle of a sentence."

"I said I'm surprised to see you read a normal book."

"Yeah, well, I've read all the tabloids and work doesn't interest me right now. Your free to use the laptop. Wait, never mind, I left it in my office last night. I can get it if you want it."

"No, I'm fine without it. Thanks."

Short and curt. She rolled her eyes after his comment.

"What's with the eyes?"

She looked up at him. "Huh? What are you talking about?"

"You rolled your eyes at me. Why?" His annoyance was obvious.

"I'll tell you. You come in here and don't even say hello or good morning. Act as if I don't exist. I try to accommodate you and you answer me with a few short words. I figure if you're ticked off with me then so be it. That's why I rolled my eyes."

"You don't make things any easier," he retorted.

"What did I do wrong because I don't see it? If your still mad because I wouldn't sleep with you then get over it. I gave my reasons. I didn't even owe you an explanation. I don't owe you anything."

"You're right Laramie, you're always right."

"You know, forget it. I don't even care why your mad this time. I am so exhausted trying to please you and it's never enough. Even if I slept with you, you'd have a reason to be mad by morning. I apologize if I frustrated you last night, it wasn't my intention."

"I can't sit here right now," he replied snidely.

"Then leave. I was fine before you came."

"Good." Akihiro stood and left in a huff.

Damn him. What is his problem? I didn't dress provocative. I didn't insinuate at any time I wanted to sleep with him. He took that initiative. Laramie cleared her head. She knew he'd be back. She didn't care whether he was mad still or not. She began her new book with a few much needed laughs. Occasionally, she set the book down and played with Akiko. She felt the need to stretch her legs so she picked up Akiko from the crib and set her on the floor. The baby quickly walked out the door. Laramie pursued her just as fast. The baby laughed as she saw Mommy get closer. Laramie slowed her, held her hand and let her walk up and down the halls.

A few hours passed and Akihiro was still gone. Laramie questioned herself and her choices. She tried to see if she went wrong somewhere but never saw it. *I am not blaming myself. Not this time.*

When the phone rang, Laramie answered it. Lian called to hear the outcome of the previous night. Laramie explained he came in mad and took off mad. She stood her ground and didn't make any apologies. They talked about the early morning and Akiko. Laramie said she was fine and even walked around some. Eventually, they hung up and Laramie went back to her book. Every so often, she stood up and wound the toy that Akihiro bought.

When lunch came, Laramie fed Akiko. She held her while the baby drank her bottle. Laramie hummed as she rocked her until Akiko fell asleep. She placed her in her crib. Laramie pulled the other chair over and used it as a foot rest. *This is an excellent time for my own nap.*

When she opened her eyes, Laramie found Akihiro watching her. "What the hell are you doing?" Laramie jumped in her chair. "You scared the daylights out of me."

"Sorry."

"Here's you chair back." Laramie crossed her legs and closed her eyes.

"Is that all you have to say?"

Laramie opened her eyes. She could feel her face redden. "You have got to be kidding me. Is this a conversation or a fight? Because I need to know what position I should take. You evidently expect an apology from me but I don't know why. Are you going to tell me or do I have to play twenty questions?"

"Are you done with the sarcasm? How would you know what anyone else is thinking? It would require you to think of that other person and not yourself."

"This is still about last night. You're mad because I wouldn't sleep with you. What do you want from me?" She slammed her hands down on the chair arms.

"Compassion. Could you once think of my needs? The world doesn't revolve around just you. Other people are affected by this." He held his arms out to mean the illness and hospital. "I needed you last night. I reached out for you and you left."

"How was I to know that? It's not what you said. There's a difference between want and need. I can't read your mind to know which one you mean." The conversation heated up.

"Really? The same person who reads people for a living. The same person so in tune with her surroundings. I thought you knew me better than that."

"I thought I did too. I am not going to apologize for my ignorance. What you expect isn't fair." She stood up and faced the window to stretch.

"What if I said I needed you now?" He asked with a softened tone.

Laramie felt a rush of warmth come over her. She placed her hands over her eyes to stop the tears.

She turned to face him and said, "Then, I'd be there for you."

She walked up to him and put her arms around him. He held back his emotions as best he could as he embraced her tightly. Akiko's fate scared him. He didn't want to lose this precious gift after so little time. Laramie rubbed her hands up and down his back. She never saw this side to him. She didn't know how to react or what to say. She took his hand and walked him to the clinical sofa in the back of Akiko's room, where she slept at night.

"I am so sorry I didn't pick up on it. I had no idea. Truly."

"I don't know how you face this every day. For the past few days I just felt numb. I sit here everyday helpless and it eats at me. It wasn't about the sex. I wanted to feel something real. I don't have that with anybody but you. When I kissed you, I felt it and I wanted more."

"Why didn't you just say that? We are in this together. I would've never turned my back on you. Look, Akiko will make it. I know it. We will see improvement. I can't afford to lose faith. It's what keeps me going. I'm not a religious person but I do know I can't give up on her. She needs us both. And we need each other. Yes, it's hell to get through the day but we don't have a choice."

"You're right. I can't expect you to know what I feel. I apologize for that."

"I can't forget the first time I met Kat. She told me we needed to talk more and smile less. She was right. We don't communicate the way we should.

We assume the other knows what's in our heads. And we don't. We have to work through that."

"I know. I hate it when she's right." He laughed and she joined him.

Laramie looked into his eyes, she wanted to kiss him, to taste him again but she knew this wasn't the place. If she took that step forward, there was no turning back. It was all or nothing. Akihiro sat back against the wall as he looked across the room, watching his daughter sleep.

"She is beautiful. We may do a lot of things wrong, but we do make a beautiful child. She hasn't started to sing yet, has she?"

"No and you can't imagine all the times I prayed she doesn't have my voice."

"You and me both." His statement warranted a shove from Laramie.

After her nap ended, Akiko played with her father until her dinner arrived. Laramie informed Aki it was time for another parenting lesson. It was his turn to feed Akiko.

"I don't know why you think this is hard. You need to make this fun. She'll go for it."

Laramie laughed at the statement. "You go on and believe that. It looks like strained peas for tonight. She hates peas. How much do you want to bet she won't eat them?"

"Give me a second the think of something. It has to be good. Something you're not willing to part with easily. Um,... never mind, let me think of something else."

"No, wait a minute. What were you thinking?"

"Sex."

"Just wait a minute. If I agree to that, then I get to pick something you're not willing to lose either."

"Go ahead because I'm confident I'm going to win. Besides, there is much I'm not willing to bet."

"Okay, if I win, you have to call Kat and offer her the job in Batam."

"No, that's my company. You can't use that. You have to pick something else. It has to be between us."

"All right. If I win, you have to spend the evening and overnight shift with Akiko. Wait... before you think you have the edge, that includes diaper changing, feeding and bathing."

"You're on, Holden."

Akihiro placed Akiko in her high chair. He started off with a few spoonfuls of fruit and meat. She watched her father as her made the spoon take an imaginary trail in the air to her mouth. She smiled and accommodated the new regime. He tried a spoonful of the peas. It made it to her tongue before she spit out the food. She wiped her mouth to remove any leftovers.

"I told you. She hates peas."

"Hold on, I'm not done yet."

He tried to hide the peas under a layer of mixed fruit. Once again, he led a playful trail to her mouth. Akiko opened and then spit out again. In another attempt, he used more fruit and less peas. Still, the baby refused to eat it. By the fourth attempt, Akiko refused to open her mouth. He leaned over and whispered in her ear a bribery of toys. Unfortunately, Akiko could not be bribed to eat peas.

"Well, Amori, what night is good for you?" Laramie laughed. "I can't tell you how I look forward to sleeping in my overstuffed bed, with thick down pillows and soft sheets caressing my naked body. Oooh. That will feel soooo good. Too bad you won't be there. I'll leave my blanket for you." Laramie gloated on her win.

He shot up next to her and embraced her. He kissed her neck and slowly made his way up near her lips. He streamed his fingers along her throat and lips. Laramie threw her head back and ran her fingers through his hair. He worked his lips around her face and just as she went to kiss him, he broke away and sat back in his chair.

"Yes, you're right, it is too bad I won't be there," he said over his latest triumph.

"You cheat. That is so unfair." Laramie let out a huff. "Just like a man to start something and never finish." She walked over to her rocker and started to sit down.

He pulled her back and pressed his lips firmly against hers. He planned to continue what he started. He ran his hands over her breasts and down between her legs. Laramie breathed heavily as he moved his hands over her. He took her hand, yanking her into the restroom. It became a frenzy as they tried to remove their clothes. He lowered his pants to his knees as they struggled to take off Laramie's jeans. He grabbed her face and thrust his tongue in her mouth as it meandered to find hers. She finally got her jeans down and began to lower her panties.

A hard sound echoed through the other side of the door.

"Miss Holden, it's Patty. I just wanted to make sure you were in there since the baby was out here alone." Akihiro cringed at the interruption.

"Yes, Patty, I'm fine. I'll be out in just a moment." Laramie looked at Akihiro and mouthed they needed to go out there. He nodded no. It became a silent argument where there wasn't a winner. Laramie quickly dressed and fixed her hair then exited the restroom. A minute later, Akihiro left the restroom as well.

She looked at him from her chair and tried not to giggle. She did want him but not with the embarrassment of being caught by the evening nurse.

"You're two for two, Laramie."

"Oh, no, no. You can't blame me for that. That was out of my control." She stooped low and squatted in front of him.

"Where was your theory on emotional attachment that time?" He had a valid question.

"It was lost somewhere between your hands and mouth. Apparently, all reasoning left me at that moment. But it would've been worth it." Laramie stood bent at the waist and kissed him gently. "You don't face these women every day. For crying out loud, Patty looks like my grandmother. It doesn't get more uncomfortable than that."

Akihiro sat frustrated, semi-pouting, "You have the worst luck of anyone I know."

"You know, I've given that thought and I realized my luck is fine until I'm with you. So, back to the bet. I will withdraw my win due to the present circumstances. We'll pick up where we left off soon. I promise."

"I'm going to hold you to it."

Laramie smiled at him. She knew he would not forget. Akihiro couldn't sit any longer. The constant waiting day in and day out wore at his patience. *How do families that stay here for weeks handle this monotony? I've been here for five days and I've got to find an outlet somewhere.* He watched Laramie read her book.

"Can you at least talk to me?"

She put her book down and looked at him. "Are you feeling a bit restless? I was there last weekend. It doesn't get any better but you do have to find something to burn off the stress. What about a gym? You know, I don't even know that about you. Do you exercise or anything?"

"I used to work out every other day but when the hotel opened, I lost time for that."

"I have a great idea. I know there is a Karate studio on Van Ness. I see it on my way to work. Why don't you go down there and talk to the owner. See if you can work out with them? Maybe you can help out with the kids."

"That would help me relieve the stress plus get back in shape. Great idea. I'll call the Sensei tomorrow."

"See, I do have great ideas. You just don't give me enough credit." Laramie picked up her book and opened the page to where she left off. She situated herself in her rocker to get comfortable. She started to get into her new book. She could appreciate any humor right now and certainly, Denis Leary had the ability to help.

"Are you still going to read?"

Laramie grinned and closed her book. She knew he wouldn't give up until she focused her attention on him.

"Tell me your suggestions? What do you want to talk about? What burning questions do you have?"

"Don't patronize me. I just think we should talk instead of remaining silent. Tell me a story no one else knows about you. You must've done something you've hidden from people."

Laramie ran her hands through her hair as she tried to think of something. She was a great student, and responsible kid. She followed the law and authority.

"I don't think I've ever done anything wicked. I've been fairly responsible. Oh, there was this time I went to Singapore and met this guy. Oh, but you probably don't want to hear about another man." He grinned. "Geez, what a boring life I've led. I did get stoned once in college with Liz and Gillian. We were so high that all we did was giggle and eat cereal all night. We made better drunks, at least that's what we heard after the frat parties."

"Really. I never knew you did that. What would the California Bar Association think of that?" He teased her.

"They will never know. I will vehemently deny all of it. You have no evidence or witness. Besides, alcohol is legal."

"What did you do at these parties? Let's compare how different your college days were from mine."

"First, we all drank too much. Then the games started, *quarters, beer pong, kings* and *flip, sip or strip*. Of course we always showed up with extra clothes on just in case. Liz, Gillian and I started the night with a bet to see who was sick first. I usually lost. Even as a college student, I couldn't hold my liquor."

"Explain this flip, sip or strip game.

"The more people the better. The rules are simple. Flip a coin and call it when it's in the air. If you guess right, pass the coin to your right and you're safe. If you guess wrong, pass the coin to your left and either take one piece of clothing off or drink a shot. That's the general rundown. Like I said, the more people the better. The longer your clothes stayed on."

He leaned back in his chair, looking her up and down. "How many times did you lose that game?"

"That will remain unknown since a pact was formed at graduation. However, I can tell you my girlfriend Liz lost far more times than I did. Randy had the benefit to see exactly what he was getting before he married Liz." Laramie grinned as she recalled the old stories.

"Well, what about you? Up at Oxford with Rhys. Now there's someone who is fond of their pints. I'm just glad he wasn't at Vanderbilt."

"We weren't too different from the States. We had one called *depth charge*. You had to float a shot glass in the top of a beer. Each person poured a bit of beer into the shot glass. Who ever sank the glass drank the beer. What do you say I bring a case of beer and a quarter for tomorrow night? You against me, flip, sip or strip."

"Get out of here. We can't do that. Did you forget we're in a public hospital? We were caught in the restroom earlier, now you want to drink and strip."

"Get a sitter and let's go to your flat. You're not afraid are you?"

"Of course, I'm not afraid. I've been naked with you. You have to play the game in a group."

"Fine. Call Manny and Lian to join us."

"No. N-O. They'd never believe I did that. Manny would do it but not Lian. I really don't want to see them naked. Well, maybe Manny. No, I'm just kidding."

"Let me see, I can't get you drunk and see you naked. What about sober?"

"Now we're hitting what you really want. It has nothing to do with beer."

"You are the quick one. Is your car in the lot?"

"No, it's at the flat. I already thought of that when we were busted in the bathroom."

He stood up and walked over to the window. He stretched out his arms and let out a big sign. It was still dark out early. He wondered how the people in this town survived the depressing colors of winter. He missed the greenery of Singapore, he also missed the warmth. He looked down at Laramie beside him. *This is torture to be this close and still apart.* He rested his hand on her shoulder. *At what point will we settle our differences and reconnect?* He looked behind him at a drowsy eyed Akiko. *If it wasn't for her, who knows if we'd ever meet again. I should've done things differently. I should've been there for her. I should've come to California after her. What was I thinking? Yet, we still hold back. It doesn't make sense anymore. What is it between us that isn't working right? How do I find it and get rid of it?*

"What has you so perplexed, Aki?" She looked up at him.

He exhaled deeply. "What is it indeed? I don't know the answer if I can't find the question. We are connected, permanently now. What happens after this?"

Laramie swallowed hard. She faced the same questions without solutions. "I've wondered the same things. I guess we won't know until we face it. First is to get through this."

"But why do we have to do it alone? Why aren't we together? Why are you in your flat and me in the hotel? What prevents us from being together?"

"Me. I'm the reason for all those things. I'm afraid of making the same mistake as Singapore. I don't want there to be any more chances of either of us walking away from the other. I suppose I'm at the point of all or nothing. At what point are you?"

She knew it put him on the spot but ultimately they had to answer that question.

"I don't know. I haven't thought it about it in those terms. I can't answer that yet."

Laramie stood up to cover Akiko, asleep in her crib. She lightly pushed her daughter bangs to the side. Akiko looked so peaceful asleep. Laramie loved Akihiro but first in her heart was her baby. *Sleep my angel. Get all the rest you need, anything to make you better.* Laramie turned around. Akihiro still stood at the window. She leaned on his arm and stared outside beside him. He pulled her around and kissed her gently. He wasn't looking for anything, just her support. She embraced him and laid her head against his chest. She heard his heart beat, and felt the warmth of his body. There was a sense of security in that for her.

"Aki, why don't you go back to the hotel and get some rest? If you go to the business center, you could probably reach home right now. It should be morning in Singapore."

"You're right. I think I will. I'm going to call the Karate studio in the morning so I may be late."

"That's fine. Besides, I'm sure Edward will stop. He hasn't been here all weekend. Be careful going back."

"I will." He leaned over Akiko, kissed his fingers and rubbed her cheek with them. He turned to Laramie and kissed her again, just lightly. As he left the room, he lifted his hand and waved.

Laramie felt as though they made a break-through. They communicated finally. She was glad to have the humor since it broke up the day. She thought about their escapade in the bathroom and silently laughed to herself. *Only five more minutes, why couldn't we have five more minutes?*

Chapter 58

LARAMIE STARED OUT the window. She watched the dawn emerge as if the sun brought answers for the new day. She wanted to give Akihiro the attention he deserved but she knew Akiko came first. She believed he knew that too.

Edward tapped on the door. "Am I interrupting anything?"

"No, not at all." Laramie walked over to him and hugged him tightly.

"Well, I haven't had a hug like that since you had your first crush. Don't tell me that boy's back in town?"

Laramie smiled at him. "I don't know what you mean. Good morning. Where have you been all weekend? I missed seeing you here."

"I had a lousy golf game on Saturday and played cards yesterday. I figured I'd give you some time alone, as adults and parents. How was the date?"

"Great then argumentative. I never know what he's thinking therefore I don't know how to respond. It's a huge guessing game and I'm afraid to guess the wrong answer."

"So, no answer is better than the wrong one. I see. Laramie, you're almost thirty one years old. Why are you guessing at all? You're a grown woman, if you have a question, ask it. You know, you surprise me. For all the brilliance you have in your career, you don't use it a damn bit in your personal life. I never understood that."

"I don't either. I'm fine in the beginning, especially over the phone. The minute we are face to face, I get flustered and stumble over my words. I'm the damn bull in the china shop. I've played it in my head numerous times. I don't know how to get past that."

"I have a suggestion. First, don't put your heart out there. Use your head and keep questioning until you find the answer you want. You are allowing your emotions to cloud your judgment and you're not ready for your heart to lead you yet. Second, establish your expectations and his. Tell him what you want in your future. If it's going back to Singapore, then say that. If you want to stay here, then tell him. Make no mistake, you have only until Akiko gets better to make those decisions. Once she is released, he will leave again."

"I know everything you're saying is correct. If only I had you to speak for me. I think about Singapore and him. It was easy to give everything up the last time but I don't know about that anymore."

"Laramie, look at me and listen to me clearly. If you love him and he loves you, be with him. You won't get any comfort at night from a corporation. The only things it gives you are money and stress. I've spent enough years to know that. Don't make the same mistake. I am so fortunate to have you as my family but you are all I have, no one to sit and reminisce with or laugh with at night. I'm telling you this because your daughter will grow up and leave home. What will you have left at that time?"

"I understand, I really do. I'm not sure if he even wants me anymore as far as anything long term. That would be a hard fact to face." She looked at Edward. "Yes, I know, then ask questions. I will."

"Well, Dear, I am off to the office. Call me if you need anything."

"Oh, could you have someone send over my laptop?"

"Sure. Bye." Edward kissed her forehead and patted Akiko lightly so she wouldn't wake up.

Laramie knew he was correct. *How could he be wrong with those years of experience? I need to look further into what we both want and expect. Eventually, I will have to tell everything about me. It's not some secret but I don't want him to be intimidated by me either. Would he care? Would it matter? Is he secure enough in himself to accept a woman like me? Some men need to be that bread winner. Geez, then I have to tell him about the office building with Shinji. How do I break the news on that one? Oh, by the way, your brother, daughter and I saved you from financial ruin. There has to be an easier way to break that news.*

Akiko laid in her crib kicking and clapping. She was happy this morning, which was a great sign. She seemed energetic. *Let's hope she's hungry, too.* Laramie changed Akiko's diaper first before she put her into the high chair. Akiko wanted to play patty cake before breakfast and it seemed reasonable request to Laramie.

A hospital worker stopped inside to drop off Akiko's breakfast. Laramie felt the fact that Akiko ate anything was good news, especially since it was hospital food. *Broccoli, beef and mixed fruit, gross.* Laramie sympathized with Akiko. The foods served as breakfast were awful to see, much less taste. Laramie wanted to speak with the dietician later for alternative items for

Akiko. As Laramie fed her daughter, she did notice an increase in her appetite. She made a note on a pad of paper to tell Dr. Patel when he visited.

"Well, Mommy is so proud of Kiki. You ate everything. Won't Daddy be happy too. You are such a big girl." Laramie went through a slew of baby talk with her. It didn't matter what Laramie said as long as the tone was happy. Laramie clapped her hands then Kiki clapped her hands. After she cleaned up the baby, she put her on the floor. Akiko didn't mind sitting; she had her toys all around her. Laramie thought a walk had to be better than sitting in the crib all day.

After a few laps around the floor, Laramie guided her back to the room. She wound up Akiko's toy and sat it in front of her. Laramie was about to pick up her book when she noticed a message on the phone. She dialed for the message. It was Akihiro. He reminded her he planned to call the karate studio, which he did. He arranged to go to a late morning session. *Good, he needed that. Maybe now he can burn off his frustrations, all of them.* Laramie went back to reading until Dr. Patel came in to visit.

"Well, Laramie, good morning. Another long weekend here, I presume."

"Good morning, Dr. Patel. Yes, the weekends are monotonous. I'm waiting for good news from you one of these days."

"Well, that is why I am here. The steroid treatment has established new healthy red blood cells. This is very good, so now we know she is responding to treatment. She has one more treatment tomorrow and a blood draw the next day. If it shows the same promising news, then we will stop for a few days and see if her body will produce them on her own."

"Oh, that's great. Are we sure it is the treatment and not the removal from a bad environment or diet?"

"She did not respond as well as we thought on diet alone. As with anything, the body needs time to heal itself even if it was a bad environment. We are in the right direction I feel."

"I just wondered. By the way, she ate everything this morning and seemed to have more energy when she awakened."

"That is wonderful as well. I will make a note of that in her records. If there is anything else be sure to call me. Also, please inform Mr. Amori as well."

"Thank you so much. I will be sure to tell him." *Yes! Let's just keep this going. Oh wait until I tell Aki, he will be thrilled.*

A few moments later, a courier knocked at the door and dropped her laptop. *Perfect timing! I can email everyone and let them know we made some progress. I don't know if I should email Kat or let him do that. I'm sure he wants to tell them the good news.* Laramie typed out her blanket email and sent it. She knew the East Coast would be up and moving already. Instantly, she received and email from Liz. She stated she would continue the prayers. A few minutes later, an email arrived from Gillian, that stated much the same thing. She called Edward instead. He told her it wasn't over yet but don't lose faith. *Faith, again. It is obvious there is more to it than I perceive. Keep the faith, Laramie.*

Laramie continued to play with Akiko and read her books when time permitted. Every so often, she looked at her watch, waiting to see Akihiro walk through the door. Her cell phone rang shortly before noon. She didn't recognize the number but answered it anyway.

"Laramie, is that you?"

"Yes, Akihiro? I wondered where you were. Are you coming in soon?"

"No, that's why I'm calling. Remember when I said it had been a while since I exercised?"

"Yeah…"

"Well, even stretching wasn't enough. After I worked with the younger kids, I did some small sparring with the Sensei. I was in the middle of a Mawashi Geri when I pulled a muscle."

"You were in a *what*? I don't speak that language. English terms please."

"I was in the middle of a…uh… roundhouse kick and I pulled a muscle. Anyway, I can't walk really well right now. I am going back to the hotel."

"Wait a sec. You did some sort of kick and pulled a muscle. That's all. I don't understand why you won't be here."

"Laramie, it was a groin muscle. Do you understand now? I have to go back to the hotel and lie down with an ice pack. Not exactly something I can do in Akiko's room."

Laramie tried to contain the laughter but found it too difficult. "I'm sorry but I think the nurses here would treat you better. I'm sure we can find you a room down the hall."

Akihiro responded with sarcasm. "You are amusing. I'm in pain and you're laughing at me."

"I am not really laughing *at* you. I'm sure you're in pain. I find it unbelievable that a grown man would work out with children then consider himself fit enough to spar with conditioned adults. Do you not see something wrong with that?"

"No. I am so pleased to have your support." Akihiro found no humor in his situation.

"Ok, fine, two different perspectives. Go back to the hotel and rest. If you thought you were going crazy here, your room will be worse. I'll pick up some supplies, books, whatever and bring them to you. What are you going to do about eating?"

"I'll just order room service, unless you want to bring something with you."

"I'll bring you something to eat, too. Just relax. As soon as I have someone cover for me here, I'll leave. What room are you in? Can you get up to open the door at least?"

"I'm in room 702. I'll have them make you a key, just pick it up at the front desk." He paused a moment. "Laramie, thank you."

She smirked. "You're welcome."

Laramie quickly hung up and called Manny's cell phone. *Damn, right to voice mail.* Next, she tried Lian's cell phone.

"Hey, Laramie. How's everything going there?"

"Actually, I have good news regarding Kiki. The steroids have increased her blood count. We're going to continue with this for the weekend then stop to see if her body will produce her own. Keep your fingers crossed. But there was another reason I was calling…" Laramie closed her eyes tightly, anticipating a lecture, before she continued. "Do you think it's possible for you to relieve me an hour this afternoon?"

"I suppose I could. It's slow here. Can't Akihiro cover you?"

"See, therein lies the problem, Akihiro. I made the suggestion to spend time at a Karate studio to break up his day from sitting here. Well, he took my suggestion and apparently injured himself doing some kick."

"Is he okay? Does he need to go to the hospital?" Lian asked concerned.

"Well, I think he'll be fine. He pulled a groin muscle and can barely walk. Played with the kids and he was fine but when he got to the big boys, he overdid it. Don't say a word. I am working hard enough not to laugh. Anyway, I wanted to run some compresses, books and food over to his room."

Lian laughed through the phone which in turn caused Laramie to laugh again.

"Well, Lara, this is probably the one time you can go to his room and be safe. Do you want me to bring you anything?"

"Sure, if you're offering. Can you bring some hot and cold compresses? That would save me time. Thank you."

Laramie fed Akiko lunch. *Great, another meal almost completely eaten. Come on baby, you can do this. Wait until I tell Daddy. He'll be so happy.* About thirty minutes later, Akiko took her afternoon nap. She tired quickly with a full belly. Lian arrived shortly after the nap began. She handed Laramie a bag full of teas and herbs, instant-hot body pads and some fresh fruit from the market. Laramie thanked her again and promised to be back quickly.

On her way to the hotel, Laramie stopped and picked up a pizza and a tossed salad from Scala's on Powell Street around the corner from the hotel. *Hopefully, this'll still be hot when I get there. Super, there's a Walgreen's across the street. I can get his magazines there. It doesn't get any more convenient than that and I'm only a block away.*

She finally made it to the St. Francis. As she walked into the lobby, she noticed the beauty of the grand hotel, a landmark in San Francisco. She went past the boutiques and wine shop to the registration desk. Laramie walked with her hands full; the smell of the pizza was right at her nose. The desk clerk had a key waiting for her and placed it in her hands so she didn't have to put anything down. She turned behind her to the hallway with the elevators. Someone was kind enough to hold the door and select the floor for her. Ding, she was at the seventh floor. She turned left and followed the hallway to his room. She placed the magnetic key in the slot and she entered.

"Don't worry, no need to get up. I've got everything," she jested.

"I wasn't planning on it. I am in pain and this is funny to you. I don't understand it," he replied from the center of his bed.

After she placed everything on his table, she walked over to the bed. "I really am not laughing at your pain just at your circumstance. You just don't see any humor in this, do you?"

"I see foolishness and poor judgment. Maybe a small amount of humor." Akihiro lightened up his mood. "What do you have in all the bags?"

Laramie picked up the food first and laid the boxes next to him on the bed. "First, you have a plain pizza because I wasn't sure what you'd eat. Also a tossed salad." She picked up the other bags and carried them to the bed. "Second, Lian brought herbs, teas and fruit for you."

"That was my next question, who was with Akiko. What's in the last bag?"

"Oh, some tabloid magazines." He responded with a perplexed look. "No, not really. They're some men's magazines. I wasn't sure what you read so I grabbed a few. Any other requests?"

"Yes, come here, please." Laramie walked to his bed and sat on the side. "Thank you. I really appreciate you doing this. I know it wasn't anything you expected. And, I know it was difficult for you find someone to sit with Kiki."

"Well, you're very welcome. So, you finally got me in your room and you can't do anything about it. Isn't that a shame?"

He smirked. "I've already thought of that. You seem to get luckier as my luck worsens. How did you manage that?"

Laramie lay next to him on the bed and placed a pillow behind her head. "Oh, wait, I don't know how I forgot this. Dr. Patel came in and the steroids are working. Akiko's red blood count is up. He is going to continue treatment to the weekend and then stop. Her appetite has increased. And she was very energetic this morning."

"That's the best news yet. I feel awful I won't see her today. Hopefully, tomorrow the pain will subside enough and I can be there. Still, great news."

Laramie rolled over on to her stomach. She propped herself onto her elbows and faced Akihiro. Her eyes flickered as she looked at him. She wanted to ask him to stay at her flat but hesitated. He wasn't going anywhere for a few days anyway, so she passed on the subject. He followed her eyes and wondered what danced inside her head. Laramie slowly crept up closer to him. She placed her hands on his cheeks and kissed him very gently. She teased him with her lips until he opened his mouth. She knew this compromised her convictions but she wanted to feel closer. He embraced her tightly, surprised by her boldness, yet, seduced by it. He met her kisses gladly.

She stopped and looked into his eyes. "I'm not trying to work you up. That's not my intention. I just… I just needed to do that." Her eyes teared just once. Something about that moment completely confused her. "I guess I just needed you to know I still cared. That's all." She turned off the bed and stood up wrought with emotion. "I have to be going. If I hear anything else, I'll call you."

"Laramie?" he called out.

""Yes?"

"This will all work out. You, me and Akiko."

She smiled halfheartedly. She picked up her purse and said goodbye.

Laramie made it back to the hospital before Akiko awakened. Her feelings for Akihiro intensified since he arrived in the city. She realized how much she missed him and missed being together. She cautiously thought about having him move into the flat. *Even if it was temporary, how would he perceive it? It's just an offer, nothing more. Unless, of course, he wants to make it more.* She thought about her conversation with Edward. She believed in his experience and wisdom.

"Well? How was he?"

"He seemed to be in real pain. He was appreciative for your help and supplies. The next few days will be tough sitting in a hotel room. If he has an ounce ambition, he should go online in the business center. I don't think I could watch television all day."

"I could. I would love a vacation from the market. Once Manny makes a little more money and we have our house, I can't wait to quit the market. Don't get me wrong I love my in-laws but I don't like the market. The smells are getting to me."

"Thanks for standing in for me. I do appreciate you and Manny and all the help you give me. I don't know what I'd do without you."

"What else are friends for than to bail each other out, right?! Anyway, I'm on my way back to work. If Manny calls, let him know I left. Bye."

"Bye."

Laramie valued Lian more as a sister than a friend. They confided with each other often. Lian knew the heartache Laramie felt for Akihiro. She told her the truth whether Laramie wanted to hear it or not.

Laramie stood over Akiko and watched her daughter slowly wake up. She had the blackest eyes that squinted closed when she smiled big. Her few teeth made her smile adorable. *That poker straight black hair, you drive me crazy! I know it will lay flat as it gets longer.* She looked so much like her father but she had Laramie's bounce at that age. *I can't believe you will be one year old in seven weeks. Where did all the time go, my precious baby? I certainly hope my stubbornness and your father's cancel each other out and you are more flexible.* Laramie had many wishes for her daughter and she knew she was no different than any other parent.

Laramie wasted the day with Akiko with walks and toys. Laramie picked up her laptop after the baby went to bed. She no longer wanted to be there. She wanted to take her daughter home where they belonged. Laramie wanted her life to have order again. She tried to envision it without Akihiro and couldn't. *It was so much easier before he came. Having him in front of me makes me want him to stay with us. Of course, who knows what he wants. I'm so tired of dancing around the subject. We really need to have this conversation sooner. Edward is so correct about everything. I act like a kid when I'm a grown woman. So what is it that I want? What is most important to me? My family. But who is my family? Do I want him as my family or is he just a part of Akiko's? What does he want? I need to know that too. Well if he's in tomorrow, I believe we need to discuss this. I've already learned there is no perfect time for anything, the hard way no less.*

Chapter 59

LARAMIE LOOKED AT her calendar. *Day 12. Twelve days too many.* She noted today was a steroid shot day. She was thankful that it wasn't a blood draw day. She quickly scanned her emails and noticed one from Shinji. She was hesitant to open it but did so anyway. He wrote to ask about Akiko's condition. He remained busy with Akihiro's hotel but finally found a minute to relax. He said Akihiro's emails were few but informative. Laramie thought Aki would've said more to his family. She didn't want to take the accolades for good news but felt that Shinji deserved to know. She responded by telling him of yesterday's news with the medication. She mentioned that Akihiro injured himself at the local Karate Studio but did not elaborate how. She said they have barely talked about themselves as a couple but went on to say they are on friendly terms. She inquired about his hotels, family and friends. She finally ended the email with a brief statement that she hoped it worked out for the best.

Laramie waited for Akihiro to come in but the day just passed by without him. After lunch, Akiko had her shot, which was painful. Laramie took her on a walk immediately after to work the muscle from soreness. Akiko's appetite increased, as did her disposition. The progress was thanked with a prayer by Laramie. She had many years of anger toward God for the death of her parents. She realized the anger never solved the loss and was wasteful over all the years.

Shortly after dinner, the room phone rang. Laramie wondered if it was Akihiro.

"Hello?"

"Hello, Laramie. How is my daughter today?"

"She's doing well, Aki. They gave her the last steroid shot. She took it really well for being ten months old. I'm surprised you haven't called earlier. Are you up walking any?"

"Yes, barely. I'll be there tomorrow at least by noon. I had some business to take care of today and I lost track of the time. The hot and cold pads worked great too. Thanks."

"Your welcome. I'm glad you're feeling better. If you don't mind tomorrow, could you watch her while I go home and repack clothes? I'm running low here. There are a few errands I want to run as well."

"Sure, take your time. I won't be going anywhere."

"Great, thanks. Was that it or were you in a talkative mood?"

"Actually, I've been on and off the phone and computer all day so I really plan to grab dinner and go to bed early. You don't mind, do you?"

Laramie did mind. "No, go ahead. Get your rest. I'll see you tomorrow. Bye."

After she hung up, her email from Shinji confused her. *He said he hadn't heard much from Akihiro, so what's he been doing with his time? Maybe he's just resting in his room. It was obvious the other day that he couldn't walk. Quit being the detective Laramie and cut the guy some slack.*

Laramie picked up her book and continued to be amused by Denis Leary. She valued his humor at this time. A few times she tried to convince herself she didn't find him very funny, she knew better. *If I could be a comedian for a day and say all the things I want to without being socially or politically correct. They have that keen ability to push the limit in society without any repercussion. Maybe that's the stand I need to take, just a little less vulgar.*

Chapter 60

LARAMIE WOKE UP stiff from her night's sleep. She showered quickly and dressed only to find Akiko awake in her crib. Her alertness returned. She no longer slept through Laramie's showers. *Great baby! You are doing so well.* Laramie opened her laptop. *Ugh! Hospital day 13. Unlucky thirteen is a blood draw day as well.* Laramie tried not to think about it. *At least Akihiro will be here today. That'll be nice to have company. I forgot how quiet it was here before he arrived. Maybe it is time for a small surprise. I can stock the refrigerator and see if he wants to stay at the flat from now on. A big step for me, yes. It doesn't make sense to pay for the hotel especially at three hundred dollars a night. I wonder if he'll accept the offer. Will he want to do this or will it pressure him into making a decision? Just ask the question, Laramie, don't second-guess yourself.*

After breakfast, Charisse knocked on the door right on schedule. Akiko saw her and cried. The baby even knew what would happen next. Laramie felt horrible when she took her out of the crib and had to restrain her. *Hopefully baby, only one more time after this. Mommy hates this too.* As always, Akiko screamed and Laramie teared. She rocked her daughter until she no longer cried. Afterwards, Laramie played on the sofa with her. She bounced her on her lap like a pony. She pretended to dance with her around the room. She wound her toys for music and shot out of the room quickly to the vending machine for a coffee. She needed the boost of caffeine.

On her way back to Akiko's room, a gentleman stopped her in the hall. Laramie thought he needed directions. He asked if she was Laramie Holden and she replied yes. He handed her an envelope and told her she 'was served' a summons to court. *What? That can't be correct.* She opened up the envelope quickly and read the letter. *That son of a bitch!* She felt her face become warm with anger. *This can't be true. He wouldn't do this to me. Edward, I need to call Edward.* Laramie ran to the room, picked up the phone, and dialed Edward.

"Edward, he did it again. I hate him. I hate him." Laramie became upset as her anger grew. "He is suing me for visitation and partial custody of Akiko. You have to stop him. He can't do this to me. Please."

"Well, I have to say this does surprise me. Laramie, listen to me. I can't do a thing and neither can you," Edward answered calmly.

"*What?* No, Edward you must know someone who can stop him. I will not let him take my daughter. She is all I have."

Edward hollered into the phone. "*Laramie.* Laramie, listen to me. Akiko's condition brought national news coverage. You cannot afford the negative press on this. Father's will come out of the woodwork in his support. The best thing for you to do is stay quiet. You are emotional right now and I completely understand that. However, use your education and experience. He is battling you on your ground. Do not let your emotions control you. You can't risk that right now. Are you listening to me?"

She sobbed into the phone. "I hate him. I wish he never came here."

"Laramie, do you hear me?"

"Yes, Edward. I hear you. Believe me as soon as I hang up I will be looking into child custody cases. He will never leave here with my daughter. Please assign someone to this for further research in the office. Have Andy bill the hours to me. Will you do that?"

"Yes, I will, Dear. Please remember what I said, use your head."

Laramie hung up and sat in her rocker. She pulled up her laptop and began to search Westlaw and LexisNexis. She wanted actual cases, decisions and legal opinions. She refused to let him win this time. This time was war. As far as she was concerned, their relationship ended the moment the summons hit her hand. She no longer trusted him. *Ha. I was going to ask him to move in the flat. How long had he planned this? What a fool I was to believe him. I won't make that mistake again. Things aren't any different from Christina in Singapore. Is this why he wasn't here yesterday? Was this supposed to happen then? I went to his hotel to help him. Friday. That was it. That was the reason he was late. Moreover, the phone calls yesterday, he was talking with his attorney. It all falls into place.* Laramie replaced her sorrow with anger. She knew she fought better that way. *I won't soon forget this betrayal. God, give me the strength not to kill him because I really could right now.* Every time she found something that pertained to international custody, she flagged it and emailed it to herself and the office. *How am I supposed to sit in this room with him? I'm not. He'll have to be here another time. I don't want to see his face.*

Laramie stood up to stretch her legs and get another cup of coffee. She knew long nights of research were ahead. She stopped at the nurse's station for a moment on her way back from the vending machine. Just before she entered Akiko's room, she heard her name called. She felt her temper boil and her muscles tighten.

"Laramie, slow down. I can't walk that fast," called Akihiro.

She seethed as she turned around. The expression on her face warned Akihiro not to come too close.

"You son of a bitch. Don't even talk to me. Don't even come near me," she spoke with her teeth gritted.

"What now?" Then he paused, he knew what happened as soon as she raised the paper. "Laramie, let me explain that."

She walked toward him and shoved him with her hands. He tried to grab them but she pulled them free. She shoved again.

"You may think you are smarter right now but you are *so* mistaken."

Quickly, Charisse jumped between them. "You are on *my* floor and you are disturbing *my* patients. I know you both and I am telling you right now, either you be quiet or take it outside."

Laramie strode to the elevator with her fists clenched. Akihiro caught up and tried to talk to her but a hospital visitor entered the elevator car. They rode downstairs in silence. When they reached the parking lot, Laramie's temper exploded.

"How dare you sue me. You are nothing but a liar. I trusted you. You planned this and waited for me to be served. Did you ever think to ask me for visitation or custody? No, you found an attorney, on Friday, wasn't it?"

"Yes, but that was when I first got here. I was angry over you hiding Akiko from me."

"Fine, but you had the entire weekend to tell me. You never ever mentioned it. You wanted to talk about needing me and missing me. So, this is how you missed me, you son of —" Laramie caught herself as a family with small children passed them. "You lied, every day you lied. I went out of my way to show you around, help you when you were hurt. I didn't deserve this. I am too good for this. You never did appreciate me. Let me tell you a few things."

Akihiro jumped in. "Laramie, I never thought you'd get this upset over this. You, out of all people, know this is a tool to insure my rights as her father."

"*Rights?* You don't deserve any rights. Where have you been for the last week? Sleeping in your hotel. You're not the one here when she wakes up crying at night. You fed her once and changed her once. Now you want to tell me about your rights. What makes you think you'd be a good father? You were a lousy boyfriend, you weren't even honest then."

Angered by her, Akihiro retorted, "Boyfriend? I didn't know we were at those terms. What makes you think you were any better as a girlfriend? Huh? You couldn't keep your emotions controlled for a single day. You did nothing but cry and feel sorry for yourself."

His words stung her severely. She had tears in her eyes but refused to let them fall. She remembered Edwards's words. "At least I made an effort which is more than you can say. How foolish of me to trust you again. Let me give you some advice. You are in my town, on my playing field. Your attorney may have beaten me to this point but this is where it stops. If you don't think I won't pull out all stops to beat you, then you are sadly mistaken."

"You don't intimidate me, Laramie. You may be a good lawyer but I have the law on my side."

She laughed hard in his face, which caught him off guard. "Oh, that is too humorous. One too many television shows. First, I'm an exceptional lawyer. Second, the law is open to interpretation and no one in this city does it better than me. I will do anything it takes."

"She is our daughter, Laramie. 'Our' meaning half mine."

"Half? Wrong. She is *my* daughter, you were merely the sperm donor. You will never be anything more than that." Her attacks were vicious.

Akihiro grabbed her by the arm, pulling her close. "I don't recall you ever putting up a fight against those donations. I remember a night when you asked for it. *Please?* What does that make you?"

She remembered when she asked him to make love to her. She quivered as she breathed. She was on the verge of losing her emotional restraint. She pulled her arm away and looked him in the eyes.

"I hate you. I have never hated anyone so much as I hate you right now. I can't believe I could have ever loved you even for a minute." She started to turn and quickly turned back and slapped him across the face. "Never come near me again. Find a time for visiting Akiko, you will have unsupervised time alone and then stay away. If you don't, I will have a restraining order brought against you."

"I plan to see her right now," he announced.

She smiled. "No, you can't. You don't have approved visitation or custody. From here on out, you have no rights unless I agree to them. Your attorney should've advised you better on that. Your summons only confirms the rights you don't possess. Call my office. I have an attorney there that will schedule your times of visitation. We are through and I mean in every way possible, Mr. Amori."

She walked away visibly shaken by this sudden argument. She was furious. Even though she shied away from confrontation on a regular basis, this was her daughter, and she became the lioness that protected her cub. *How can this be? This morning I was going to ask him to stay with me. How much of this was part of his lie? It proves the theory of keeping your enemies close to monitor their actions. I allowed it happen again. I fell for him only to be betrayed. Why haven't I learned anything from this? Why do I keep going back? I am smarter than this.* Laramie tried to keep her mind on the hearing and the cases she needed to locate. She knew the next few weeks were critical to her case. *Keep my mind on my business. Apparently, my heart overlooks everything.*

Akihiro knew he spoke without thought. He didn't mean to hurt her intentionally. She angered him so quickly that he responded on instinct. He rubbed his cheek where she slapped him. She hit harder than he imagined. *This went nothing like I envisioned. I assumed she'd be angry. I never anticipated her to react so strongly. Visitation schedule? Before I ignore her, I should call Richard to confirm what she said.* Akihiro went inside to the lobby of the hospital and walked to the pay phones. He dialed his attorney.

"Richard, its Akihiro Amori. Laramie was served about an hour ago. Let me tell you, she didn't take it well."

"Well, Akihiro, I didn't suspect she would. Has she addressed any of the legal issues?"

"No. She told me I'd never win and I should coordinate a time for visitation through an attorney at her firm. Is that correct? I don't have any visitation rights?"

"Actually, you do but there are limitations. You don't need an uproar inside the hospital. To force confrontation would be risky. I would advise you to call and choose the hours you want to spend with your daughter. At least we can show you have been tolerant to her demands at the hearing."

"I can do that. If today was any example of her anger, the hearing could be very explosive."

"Yes, indeed. You, Sir, have just awakened the sleeping giant. You can be sure she has already started to prepare her case, as I must mine. If you have any questions, call me. If she says or does anything make a note of it and let me know. I will be in contact as we go. Keep your guard up, Akihiro. Do not underestimate her. Bye for now."

"Bye," he replied wearily.

Akihiro wanted to go up and see Akiko. He knew that was no longer an option. He called the firm and spoke to Kevin Brown, her legal associate. Akihiro scheduled his visitation with Akiko daily between noon and six o'clock. He hated that she limited his time but followed his attorney's instructions. *What am I going to do with my time every day? Should I have talked with her first then sought an attorney? Too late for that thought now. Sperm donor? I hardly think that's all it was. How much did she mean and how much was said in anger? What happens after the hearing? Will we still be bitter enemies? She's come around before, she will again.* Akihiro left the hospital and returned to his hotel. He hoped he had enough work to keep him busy through the next week.

Laramie sat stunned in Akiko's room. She tried to recall her words but many came out so fast she reacted without thought. *It's too late now. He doesn't understand what he's up against. Not a clue. His attorney was clever enough to make the first jump however it's now my turn.* Laramie pulled up her laptop and began more research. *Let's go beyond U.S. Federal law and supersede him by using the Hague Convention. He cannot trump that.* She sent an email to Kevin to research the cases that used Hague as part of their argument. Kevin emailed her back, writing that Akihiro called and scheduled his visitation for six hours daily beginning at noon. *Still playing the part-time father. If he was serious, he could've gone for half the hours. Why put yourself out for your child? He'll probably hire someone to change her and feed her. Jerk.*

The room phone rang and Laramie hesitated to answer it. *He wouldn't dare call here.*

"Laramie, it's Lian. Are you okay? Manny just called me with the news."

"I'm fine. Numb. Foolish. Gullible. Many things. He's suing me Lian. I never saw it coming."

"No, Lara, none of us did. It's not you, Sweetie. Don't blame yourself. You went out of your way for him. It was Akihiro who turned his back on you."

"Lian… I fell for him again. And it really hurts this time, far more than the others. We said some terrible things to each other. I guess it shows how he really felt. It was all a charade. He never wanted me, just Akiko. But, I will not let him take her, ever."

"I know you must be so hurt but remember your daughter loves you and needs you. So do we. Don't lose sight of those who care for you. You lean on us for anything. Do you hear me?"

"Yes, thank you so being so supportive. I don't think I could get through this alone right now." Laramie sniffled in the background. "I love you both. Bye."

Laramie's life turned into a labyrinth, each path led to nowhere. She needed focus on her next task but emotions occasionally surged through. She looked at Akiko who played quietly in front of her on the floor. *I tried to make this work Kiki for the three of us. He wanted just you this time. I don't know how to move forward. You are all I have and I won't let you go. Mommy will always be here to protect you. I will make sure he can't ever hurt you or take you from your home.* Laramie knew trials brought out the worst in people. She saw it too many times however this time she was on the inside. She planned to retain her composure and professionalism. She planned to refrain from snide comments or jabs. She felt she could handle being in a room with him for five minutes in passing.

Laramie sat in her rocker with her computer on her lap. *Damn it! Singapore is not a signatory with the Hague Convention. They don't participate in that child advocacy. Why? Who do they work with? The United Nations, excellent.* She downloaded the *U.N. Convention of the Rights of the Child 1989* document for further review. *Let's see what else we can find. What about custody laws of Singapore? It seems they have three they use for most cases, the English Children Act 1989, Child Custody Law 2005 and the Women's Charter.* Between the Singapore Laws and international cases, Laramie's reading list was full. She planned to make her brief impregnable.

* * *

Akihiro sat in his hotel room unsure of his next move. The silence of being in the city alone eroded his resolve. He was without a guide and a companion. He recalled two days prior when Laramie was in his room. She wanted to be with him, near him. Now, that vanished. Each day would contain the same loneliness until the date of the hearing. He wanted to believe he made the right choice in the lawsuit. He knew from the Cheung deal that a contract was necessary to insure his interests. Laramie taught him that lesson. *What lesson will be hidden in this? Do I stand a chance in winning?*

Chapter 61

AFTER TENDING TO Akiko's breakfast, Laramie contacted Kevin to update him on her research. She listed all the files she found which surpassed Kevin's research. She wanted each case and law printed so she could highlight the areas pertinent to her case. She wanted them delivered directly to her and not left for her in the room at the hospital. She made sure Kevin completely understood her demands. She redirected him to work on child custody and visitation laws in California. She told him to look for laws in other states that set a new precedent and the effects such laws had in additional states. She wanted anything that was groundbreaking.

By lunchtime, Laramie's headache throbbed continually. She knew it was from stress and the computer screen. She tried to remember the last time she spent an entire day researching. It was difficult for her to recall anytime before Akiko's admission in the hospital. She lived there for two straight weeks and tried to anticipate the future length of time. *Only two more days until the next blood draw. The results of that test will give us a sign of what we can expect. God willing, it will be positive.*

Right on queue, Akihiro walked into the room without even a knock. Laramie closed her research and shut down her laptop without a word toward the plaintiff. She stood up and placed her belongings on the chair behind her. She picked up Akiko, hugged, and kissed her. After she placed her daughter in the crib, she picked up her things and started out of the room.

"That's it? You can't even say hello or goodbye? You're not going to speak to me at all?" he asked as he blocked the passage out of the room.

"Excuse me, but you are in my way." She looked directly into his eyes without as much as a flinch.

Akihiro stepped side, waiting to see if she would say anymore. She didn't. Laramie walked out as though he was just another stranger.

She thought about her short-term freedom from the hospital and how to best utilize it. She planned to stay out of the office for now unless she absolutely had to guide Kevin. She needed this time for herself. First on her agenda, exchange her clothes for clean ones. She dropped by Marina Cleaners on Buchanan Street, a block away from her flat. She exchanged pleasantries with the clerk when she picked up her order. They inquired about Akiko and Laramie just briefly explained she had an illness. The next item on her list was home. The smell of fresh paint faded during the week which pleased Laramie. She wanted Akiko to come home without the smell of paint or cleaners. She was desperate for a nap on a real mattress with real pillows. Laramie placed her pressed clothing in her closet and jumped on her bed. *Aw! This feels awesome. No odd springs or lumpy filling. Soon, my glorious bed, I will be here nightly.* She set her alarm for a hour nap with the plan on having a real shower to follow.

Akihiro played with Akiko for quite a while until he realized she needed to be changed. He remembered the steps Laramie showed him with the garbage bag and wipes. He knew to be prepared before he opened the vessel of toxic waste. *Oh, this can't be coming from my daughter. Breathe through your mouth, Aki. Damn, I need more wipes. Wipe front to back, good, I remembered that.* Within a few minutes, he had a clean diaper on his daughter. *Now that is great work. What's the big deal with this? I can handle it.*

He asked Akiko if she wanted to walk and understood her squeal to mean yes. He held her tiny hand in his as the departed down the hall. The nurses whispered amongst themselves at his new training in fatherhood. He wasn't sure what followed next. Laramie didn't leave any notes or instructions. On his way back to Akiko's room, he asked Charisse if there was anything particular that needed to be done. She told him that as long as the baby smiled, he accomplished his mission. He appreciated her vote of confidence. *See that, Laramie? I'm doing just fine without you here.*

He sat on the floor with his daughter to play with her toys. Akiko took her music player and swung it in the air. Unfortunately, she didn't see the direction of her swinging and she knocked herself in the head. At first, she was silent with her mouth open. Next, she let out a loud scream. Akihiro panicked and scooped her into his arms. He tried to talk quietly to calm her but that didn't work. He rubbed her head and luckily, no bumped formed. He held her in his arms, rocking her. Slowly, her tears subsided. *Whew! That was close. How would I explain a knot on the side of her head?* Charisse stepped into the room to check on Akiko. After Akihiro explained the situation, the nurse laughed and welcomed him to parenthood.

Laramie woke to the sound of her alarm buzzer. *I forgot how annoying that sound was. But, that nap felt excellent.* She went into her shower and stayed there until the water ran cool. She lazily dressed and dried her hair. She appreciated the open space in which to move; a luxury not found at the hospital. She called her favorite salon, Bamboo Nails, on Union Street. She needed a pedicure and manicure and surprisingly, they had an opening. Laramie quickly packed fresh clothes in her suitcase and rushed out the door. Within minutes, she sat in a massaging chair while her feet soaked. *I could go right back to sleep.* The kneading of her feet and leg muscles felt relaxing. After her pedicure, she sat at the table of one of the nail techs for a manicure. *You just never know how bad you need this until someone touches you. The baby wipes have taken all the moisture out of my skin. At least they'll look great for a few hours.* Laramie sat with her hands and feet under the ultraviolet light for drying. Laramie remained undisturbed in her chair. She was happy that she had some freedom from the hospital. *Less than a few hours left. I better stop and eat before I go back. I can't take anything from the cafeteria anymore. I can take a sandwich back with me so I'm not late. Wait a minute. Who would suffer if I was late? Akihiro. Well too bad for him. He could stand to be there a while longer. Part-time parent. Full-time jerk.*

Laramie walked next door to Rose's Café for a light dinner. She hated to dine alone. It always brought some weird company, usually elderly men looking for a young girlfriend. She sat by the window and placed her order. *Real food. Will my body recognize the difference anymore? I can hardly contain my hunger at this point. This day turned out to be better than I expected.* She waved to a few women she knew from the playground. *Apparently, I am not the only person to get a break. Mom's are out in full force without their children.* She dined quietly. She contemplated taking a container for leftovers but passed since she was off to the hospital next. *Those six hours surely passed too quickly. At least I can do this until the hearing.*

Akihiro pulled his chair adjacent to Akiko's high chair to feed her dinner. He noticed the peas again and decided against trying to slip them in. *How can a child eat this? It looks horrible.* Akiko ate all of her chicken and mixed fruit however, she brushed the beans off her tongue onto her chair. Once she finished her dinner, he removed her bib to find more food underneath the cloth. *What? Where did this come from? I watched her. How could she get food everywhere?* He cleaned her face and hands and put her on the floor to play while he moved the high chair out of the way. He sat near her on the floor and became her mountain to climb. He enjoyed his one on one time with his daughter. He learned he was capable to take care of her alone, at least for six hours. He knew Laramie would return shortly and wondered how that encounter would be.

Laramie walked into Akiko's room, appearing refreshed. Her face had a glow from her nap and a little bit of makeup. Akihiro noticed she didn't look as tired anymore. Despite their differences, he was happy to see her. She placed her laptop on the rocker and her suitcase in the corner. She dreaded the idea that she wouldn't be sleeping in her bed. *Well, the nap felt great.* Akihiro stood up and picked up Akiko for a hug and kiss goodbye.

"Do you want to know how the afternoon went?" he asked.

Laramie replied rather flippant. "No, not really."

She held her hands out for Akiko to come to her. Akihiro placed his daughter into her mother's arms.

"Are we going to discuss anything about Akiko? Or, are you just going to ignore me? I'm right in front of you, Laramie. Will you acknowledge me?" Akihiro became miffed.

"Please direct anything you have to say through our attorneys. I'm not going to say anything that can be misconstrued and used against me."

Laramie turned her attention to Akiko. She knew she infuriated Akihiro. She didn't care. The more she ignored him the angrier he became.

"*Fine.* I'll be sure to do that. I'll be here the same time tomorrow."

He banged his fist against the doorframe on the way out. He thought about ways to up the stakes. He knew her weaknesses were confrontation and emotions. He thought about baited arguments. *If I say something slighted regarding her emotions she should argue back. She has that fiery side to her. Actually, it might be fun to see that sexiness.* As he reflected back to their nights in Singapore, it brought a grin to his face. Many of his thoughts revolved around their sexual escapades. *Well, we are a far cry from that scenario now. I don't believe she hates me the way she said. I'll give her mad as hell but I don't think she has ever hated anyone in her life.*

When Akihiro arrived back at the hotel, he went to the business center to send an email update to his family and friends regarding Akiko. He mentioned that since he served Laramie with a summons, she won't speak to him and that it wasn't a surprise. He asked Shinji to send him pictures of the construction progression. He asked Kat to email the budgets and accounting information for his review. He told Rhys to have a few pints for him. In a separate email to his mother, he confided that his daughter was the best child, with personal bias. He told her how he fed her and changed her on his own. His mother was the only person who knew his true feelings for Laramie and Akiko, though many could easily guess it. He said her silence toward him was painful. He didn't want to lose her over this hearing but he felt his presence as Akiko's father was more important. He dreaded the days to come with Laramie but remained hopeful of Akiko's health. Finally, he said he loved her and his father and missed them. He signed off and ventured up to his room. His interest in dinner diminished from his depression.

Chapter 62

THE FOLLOWING DAY played out similar to the first day of tag team sitting. Laramie remained curt with her few word responses. She felt no remorse for her behavior and viewed it as a calculated strategy. She delved further into her casework. She knew no one had more at stake than she did. She read all of the cases she planned to cite in her brief and tried to think of an impressive beginning. She played different ideas in her head but none of them had the 'wow' factor. She had time to work on that.

Akihiro tolerated Laramie's antisocial behavior. He remained angry that she would not communicate regarding the welfare of Akiko. He felt that anything about Akiko took priority over their legal trials. Laramie's lack of speech proved she didn't view things the same way.

He looked forward to his time alone with Akiko. He was better the second day when he fed her. He watched when her hands disappeared and looked under her bib for the missing food. He detested changing her diaper, at least the noxious ones. Though, he loved the smile on her face once a new diaper was on.

At the end of the day, Laramie and Akihiro reflected on happier times. They both maintained their steadfast course to the trial and winning.

Chapter 63

AFTER FEEDING AKIKO, Laramie looked at her calendar. She saw it marked as another blood draw day. She dreaded that procedure and its effect on Akiko. Laramie went to the nurse's station to inquire the time for the draw. They told her Charisse was not in and that any of the nurses would do it whenever a convenient time arose. Laramie asked them if they could schedule it in the afternoon when Akiko's father watched her. She expressed her guilt in being the one always to hold their daughter and just couldn't bear it any longer. In reality, the nurse's knew the story behind the pleading and agreed to accommodate Laramie. She thanked them profusely.

Laramie played all morning with Akiko. It was fun to be the good parent for once. *Ha. Let him have a taste of the pain and guilt. He wants to be there for her so let him learn what it feels like. Yes, it is a bit vindictive but why am I always the bad guy? Fair is fair.*

Laramie hoped for a miracle with this draw. She knew this sample would tell them if Akiko's body produced her own healthy red blood cells. *Please dear God, give me back my healthy baby.*

This afternoon, Akihiro knocked on the door before he walked inside. He felt he could be pleasant even though Laramie was not.

"How was your morning, Laramie? Oh me? I'm fine, thanks for asking. Akiko? Yes, she looks great today. Did she eat well at breakfast? Really. Thanks so much for all your helpful insights," Akihiro remained sarcastic.

Laramie glanced in his direction with a look of displeasure. She knew what he attempted but it didn't sway her. She left without a word or warning.

Wait until he receives his surprise. How sarcastic will he be then? Mr. Humorous won't be smiling.

During mid-afternoon, a nurse walked in with a tray and vials for the blood draw. Akihiro caught sight of it and questioned why it wasn't done earlier. They told him Laramie just couldn't accept doing it any longer and asked it be done later in the day. Akihiro felt the tension in his shoulders tighten. *She specifically set me up. That bitch. I'm sure Akiko and I can get through this. How bad could it really be?* The nurse instructed him to hold the baby's upper body down and her legs. When she inserted the needle, Akiko screamed with such pain. Akihiro found it excruciating to hold her and force the pain onto her. He held her in his arms and rocked her as soon as the nurse finished. *Baby, baby. It's okay. Daddy is here. I will make it better. Hush, hush, hush. Come on now, no more crying.* Slowly, Akiko stopped. He wiped the tears from her face and kissed her.

Laramie finished her nap and shower. She cleaned what little there was in her flat. The afternoon getaways gave her a sense of rebirth from the sadness of the hospital. She wondered how Akihiro's afternoon went and his struggle with guilt. She knew he would have something to say when she arrived back. Even though she dreaded a lecture from him, she felt relieved it was his experience and not hers. *So much has changed in a week. Last Saturday we went out for dinner and sightseeing. Now, we are battling over our daughter. Every time I think I found happiness something comes along and strips it away. Why is everything so complicated? Eventually, we will have to get along for Akiko's sake. But right now isn't eventually.*

When Laramie arrived back at the hospital, she was correct in her assumption. Akihiro waited for her without any intention of leaving quickly. He let her set her things down and hold the baby before he spoke. She anticipated his words and anger.

"It was quite the experience you set up for me. There wasn't any real reason why you couldn't have them draw blood while you were here. The nurse told me about your plea to do it on my time. Does that make us even in your mind?"

"It isn't a matter of being even. It's a matter of shared responsibilities. You asked for it, now you got it. I only accommodated you. You should thank me."

That statement incited his temper. "*Thank you?* I could wring ... I'm not going to finish that because that's what you want. I can deal with my responsibilities."

Laramie placed Akiko in her crib. When she turned, Akihiro blocked her with both of his arms flanking her sides. As he leaned in closer, the further she bent backwards almost losing her balance.

"I shouldn't have to be the bad guy all the time. Why should I carry the burden of guilt? Why can't you?"

Laramie was nervous. He was close enough that she could smell his cologne. She swallowed hard and waited for him to back away. He stood still for a few moments knowing he flustered her. He kept a straight face as he peered into her eyes. He secured the confrontation she disliked.

"I'll take what you're too emotional to handle. Bring it on." It was his turn to put on the pressure. He knew she would react to that statement.

"*Emotional?* I hardly think so. I have dealt with every episode in her life and I've done it alone. I don't need you to help me. But, since you are so eager to break into our lives, then take on the duties that come with it."

"I believe I have already agreed to that. You are repeating yourself. Feeling a little anxious? Not so sure in your convictions? Do I tempt you? You seem a bit… agitated."

"Get out. Your visitation is over. There is nothing more to say."

Akihiro smiled right at her. They both knew he got to her. As hard as she tried to maintain control, he pushed her to the very edge.

"By the way, thanks for the conversation."

Laramie turned her back to him. She allowed him to bait her and she despised that. After he left, she talked to herself in anger. *How could I let him do that? The minute he starts talking to me, I need to leave, ignore him or something. He has that uncanny way of pushing me to where he wants and making me squirm. I need to bite my tongue from speaking. He hates the silence and that's what I need to follow.*

Akihiro smiled to himself. Yesterday was her turn to grin but today was his. He didn't mind going back to the hotel alone tonight. He planned to have a few drinks at the bar and listen to the music. *I know she is stewing right now. She is so predictable. Where's her brilliant legal strategy now? I don't have to have her mind, just her emotions. I have to think that levels the playing field a bit.*

Laramie allowed herself this one slip but vowed to maintain control from that moment forward. She needed additional work space and planned to go to the office during her relief tomorrow. She intended to call Kevin but remembered it was Saturday night. His face time in the office was over. Anything she had considered would have to wait until Monday. She shut down her computer and played with Akiko for an hour before bedtime. The baby's energy increased and that made it harder to put her to bed after two naps during the day. Slowly, Akiko fell asleep. Laramie changed the channel on the television. She flipped through the channels and found nothing interesting to watch. *I might as well go to sleep too. I've got a big afternoon in the office and a lot of typing to complete.*

Akihiro sat at the bar inside his hotel with his Grey Goose cocktail. It wasn't long before an attractive woman sat beside him. She was tall, curvy and had deep dark auburn hair. Her fair complexion made him wonder if she was Irish. It was hard to determine under the heavy makeup. She put her hand out to shake his and introduced herself as Erin. He introduced himself and offered to buy her a drink. He wasn't surprised to see she drank a Cosmopolitan, a trendy drink for those unfamiliar with the actual taste of spirits. They sat for a few hours as they discussed their reasons for being in the city. She claimed to be there on medical business. She may have said surgery techniques but he was sure she was there for plastic surgery. After getting a better look, he assumed a boob job. He didn't discuss anything about Akiko due to all the attention. He wanted to stay off the grid.

The more they drank, the friendlier they became. She asked him to join her in her hotel room. He didn't see the harm in it and followed her up to her floor. While she went into the bathroom, he made himself comfortable on her bed. When she reappeared out of the bathroom, she wore a robe that remained untied. It was obvious then, it was a boob job. He thought they looked okay, somewhat bigger for his taste. She dropped her robe and climbed onto of his lap and slowly began to undress him. As she kissed him, he closed his eyes and called out Laramie's name. That brought the games to an abrupt halt. She inquired who Laramie was. His wife? He said no, the mother of his daughter. Apparently, that was acceptable. However, after he brought up Laramie's name, he wasn't able to continue. Despite his current fight, he was in love with her and didn't want to be with anyone else. He apologized then left.

He sat in his room frustrated once again. *Even the mention of her name brings bad luck. What kind of control does she have over me? I can't even get laid without guilt now. How long are we going to torment one another? We have to get past this. Something has to give.*

Chapter 64

LARAMIE WAITED FOR Akihiro to show. She had a list of items she needed to cover for her brief. She occupied Akiko with Patty Cake and other nursery rhymes to pass the time. Slowly, Akihiro appeared around the corner of the doorway. He looked ragged. She wondered if he had a hangover.

"Sorry, I didn't mean to be late," he remained apologetic.

"Don't you think it's too early for a victory celebration?" Laramie asked in her usual sarcasm.

He held his head and laughed. "Yeah, that's what she said. Oh, sorry."

Laramie's face reddened. She didn't know how to respond. She needed to let it go casually. "That's okay, no apologies necessary. I hope you enjoyed your date."

"Again, that's what Erin said. Sorry. Just go. I'm fine here with Akiko. When she takes a nap, so will I."

Laramie fumed as she gathered her things. She wasn't sure if he angered her or hurt her more, it was a toss up. She wanted to tell him she hated him even more but knew that would admit her feelings. She bit her tongue until she walked out of the door. *He went out with another woman. I can't believe it. I guess it really is over. There isn't anything more.* She was jealous, hurt and a myriad of other emotions. *It's for the best I'm sure. It had to happen, but so soon? I guess it isn't so soon when the past days have all been a lie.*

Akihiro knew he got to her this time. There wasn't any way for her to hide her emotions despite the things she said. He ran down the hall that over looked the parking lot and saw her cross the asphalt to her car. She wiped her face, which meant tears. Then he questioned whether he did the right thing or not. *She wouldn't believe the truth anyway.*

Laramie sat in her office. Weeks passed since she actually worked there. She opened her laptop and printed out her list of documents. She organized them by relevance, then by date.

Her first recourse was to define the visitation schedule. She didn't have any objections to that as long as all visits remained in the United States. *Of course that will bring the first argument. Why does it have to be here?* She cited the Hague Convention and it's protection under civil law of children since 1996, stating their main objective is to protect the child and impose measures concerning parental responsibility of protection and care. She also used this international agreement to show cause for her daughter to remain in the United States since Singapore has not agreed to the laws regarding children and their abduction. She stated she has no recourse to bring her child home if Akihiro took her to Singapore. *The Singapore laws don't force the parent to remove the child from that country.*

She went on to cite the case of *AB v. AC* and *ANOR Application*. In that case, the mother took her sons from Norway to Singapore away from the father. The father petitioned Singapore to give back custody to him in his country of residence. The high court in Singapore ruled that the proper forum for custody was in Norway and gave custody back to the father. She cited another case, *D2538/1997*, where as a parent abducted the child from Texas to Singapore. Once again, the high court determined that the location of care and concern, new terminology replacing the word custody, was in Texas and sent the child back. In addition to the Singapore laws she mentioned, she added text from the *English Child Act of 1989* and the *Women's Charter*, both that supported her side of custody.

She went on to list that while there were four cases in which Singapore gave custody back to the other parent, there were twenty-two more cases where the court remained uninvolved. Her argument was that since Singapore was not a signatory to Hague, there wasn't any guarantee that should Akihiro abduct Akiko, that Laramie would have a safe return of her child. She further went to discuss that under Singapore's Child Custody Law of 2005, custody remains with the parent responsible for the care and concern of the child, meaning the mother. Her additional argument reaffirms that even though his own country views custody to be with the primary care giver, the mother.

She felt that should any custody be granted that it should be a joint *legal* custody not a joint *physical* custody. She stated that she wanted to remain as sole physical custody. She used the Hong Kong Law Commission as her example of legal custody. This law states that if a parent plans to remove the child from their residence for more than one month that the other parent be notified. It stipulated that change of domicile or nationality required further notification. Laramie agreed to the terms of advance notification regarding medical procedures, unless an emergency; change of residence and alterations to the visitation schedule.

Now let's get to the U.S. laws. He just can't see he doesn't stand a chance. I am using our laws, international laws and even Singapore's laws against him. He can never bring her out of the country without my knowledge or consent. And he never will.

Her first course of action here was to include the *Uniform Child Custody Jurisdiction and Enforcement Act.* This was established by the Federal Government to determine where custody lies between the States. However, custody by international location is addressed by the same rules. During Akiko's last six months of birth, she spent with Laramie in California therefore determines that California is her state of residency and holds jurisdiction over custody proceedings. *I know he will bring up the fact I never notified him of her birth until recently. However, he cannot prove he would have been here the past six months had he known either.*

Pleased by her progress, she left a note for Kevin to do the research for the states custody laws. She sent him a copy of her brief so he could follow the same direction. She leafed through the beginning of her brief, amazed that she already typed a dozen pages.

I can't believe that he went out with someone else. I realize we are at odds but didn't I ever mean anything to him? A stupid question as I type up a ambushed custody defense. It was nothing more than a ploy to keep me off guard while he stepped in to take Akiko. He lies far better than I gave him credit. He won't get past me anymore. I have to stay focused.

She placed her papers on her desk and shut off her equipment. She wasn't sure what to do with her left over time. She called Edward to see if he was home. *Crazy thought on a Sunday afternoon. He's at the country club, I'm sure.* She hung up the phone after a few rings. She grabbed her laptop and decided to sit at Golden Gate Park for the remainder of her time.

The weather seemed cool but the wind was low which made her feel warmer. She sat on a bench by herself and watched a young couple try to teach their dog to catch a Frisbee. It was humorous as the dog had a mind of his own and Frisbee wasn't a part of it. She watched other couples roller blade past her with their iPods attached to them. She missed her days of pushing Akiko's stroller throughout the area. She hoped it wasn't long before they did it again. *Soon she'll be talking and I won't get a word in edgewise.* She glanced at her watch and noticed it was time to return to the hospital.

When Laramie entered the room, it was empty. She sat in her rocker and waited for them to arrive. She didn't want to see him especially since their last encounter. She knew it was time to put on the happy face as if everything was okay. He didn't need to know how upset and hurt she really felt. *He'd probably use it against me.*

Moments later, Akihiro and Akiko walked through the door. He looked surprised to see her back already. He looked at his watch, realizing his visitation ended.

"I didn't realize the time. I hope you weren't waiting long."

"I wasn't." She sat quiet and unemotional.

He let go of Akiko's hand and she walked directly to Mommy. Laramie picked her up and hugged her. She needed that little face of sunshine.

"Did you enjoy your afternoon?" he asked as he tried to determine her mood.

She shrugged her shoulders as if the day was uneventful. It didn't warrant any words. He apologized for being late again and she didn't respond. She no longer wanted to hear his voice, or see his face. She wanted this hearing to be over so she could continue her life without him. She no longer wanted the memories of Singapore to haunt her dreams. She just wanted to finally let go.

"Laramie?" He waited for her to look up, she didn't. "I'm going. Same time tomorrow." He leaned over Laramie's knees to kiss Akiko goodbye. Laramie wouldn't even look at him. She seemed despondent to the whole conversation.

After he left, she sat in her chair numb to her surroundings. She played with Akiko but her mind was elsewhere. *He obviously found it easier to move on. Now it's my turn. It's hard to believe after all these months nothing came out of it. The only good thing good is Akiko.* Tears flowed down her cheeks and her shoulders bounced as she cried silently in the rocking chair.

"Laramie, are you all right?"

She looked up and found Akihiro staring at her. *Oh, great. How do I explain this? You know what, I don't have to explain anything to him anymore.*

"I'm fine." She shook her head in disbelief that he came back and caught her emotional display.

"I just forgot my jacket, that's all. Sorry to disturb you."

He walked out of the hospital and felt guilty for making her believe he was out on a date. Though, he couldn't be sure that was what made her upset. For all he knew, it could've been Akiko's condition. *Maybe I shouldn't have pushed her. Stupid statement, no maybes.*

Chapter 65

LARAMIE SPENT MOST of the morning on the phone with Kevin. He received her email and prepared domestic cases for her to review. She didn't feel like being at the firm with everyone at work. She truly appreciated their support but knew she would have to repeat Akiko's condition a dozen times. She knew the test results were at Dr. Patel's office but he wasn't there to review them. He had an emergency earlier in the morning and that prevented him from coming in for rounds. *I don't have a choice to wait another day. Please just make the news worth it.*

Akihiro walked into the room with another toy for Akiko. He found it hard not to spoil her. Every time he saw something cute, he bought it. This time he purchased a Tickle Me Elmo. He thought ahead and bought batteries at the same time. He showed Akiko how it worked and she giggled. He took her hand, placed it on Elmo and made the toy laugh. Akiko squealed with excitement. *Great, isn't he the perfect parent? He sucks. Add him to your book, Denis.*

Once again, Laramie gathered her laptop and suitcase. It was time to change out her wardrobe again. She crouched down near Akiko and kissed her good bye.

"Are you feeling better today? You seemed upset yesterday."

Laramie rolled her eyes and walked out of the room. *Lying bastard, I know you could give a crap less. I know there is some stupid saying about things that don't kill us makes us stronger. Whoever said that was a jerk too. Perhaps, they know each other.*

Akihiro ran down the hall to catch her. "I meant to ask what Dr. Patel said. Any news?"

"He was called away to an emergency. No news." She turned and entered the elevator. *Call him yourself. I'm not your messenger.*

She ran her errands and then went to her office to meet with Kevin. She already heard the whispers as she walked by. She sat in her office to begin her work when Linda knocked at the door.

"Do you feel like talking at all?" Linda asked.

"There isn't much to talk about. I'm sure Edward told you about the hearing. I got a memo that it's this Friday due to Akihiro's limited time in the States. His attorney must know Judge Gallagher as well."

"How are you, Laramie? Not Akiko or the court case, you."

"I think I'll survive." She placed her hands over her face and cried into them. "He's already moved ahead. I thought we'd be able to work this out but there isn't any more hope."

Linda walked beside Laramie and rubbed her back. "Laramie, I've known you for many years. I've never seen you lose a fight yet. I know love can be disconcerting but we all feel it and survive it. You will, too."

"I just can't take it anymore. The pressure with Akiko, the hearing and now he went on a date. I believed all his lies from last week and fell for him again. He never cared about anything except for Akiko. I question that, too. Is he in it for her or for the win over me?"

Linda handed her a tissue. Laramie wiped her eyes and nose.

"Lara, you know this business better than most attorneys. You see the lies and deceit all the time. You give your clients support and hope. You need to have that for yourself as well. I know it doesn't help right now but everything works out for a reason. It may not have the ending we want but the end gives us a lesson to learn. You are a strong young woman and you will get through this. I know you will."

Laramie sniffled a bit and regained her composure. She didn't want anyone in the office to see her breakdown. She had an image to uphold among the younger attorneys.

"I know I will get through this but it really hurts right now. I need to stay strong and focused. My emotions are my weakness and Akihiro knows that. He may have broken my heart but I wont let him break my spirit."

Linda smiled. "Now, that's the Laramie Holden I know. Remember what is at stake here, your daughter. She depends on you to do the right thing. Don't lose sight of that, Dear."

"Thank you, Linda. Your support has always meant a great deal to me. And, you're right, I need to do this for Akiko, not me. Thank you."

Linda left Laramie's office and shut the door behind her. *She's right. I have to do what's best for Akiko, not me or Akihiro. Somewhere in this chaos I lost sight of that. Well, not anymore.* Laramie buzzed Kevin's extension and asked him to come to her office with his materials.

A few minutes later, Kevin entered Laramie's office and sat in the chair across from her. He showed her the California Family Code that empowers the court to make an order for custody. It basically duplicated the Hong Kong Law Commission and the Child Custody Law in Singapore except it was California law and that held support for her being the home state. Laramie stated in her brief that due to Akiko's age, health and emotional connection to her mother that sole custody be granted. Her recommendations to the court were based on statutory law, in addition to the precedent international laws. She made sure Kevin had copies of all the cases, statutes and regulations cited. She placed them with her copies of the international laws. She printed out two copies of her brief so they both could make any necessary changes. They mainly made changes to typos since Laramie was not a proficient typist.

By the end of their time, she was satisfied by her documentation. Her work impressed Kevin. Her depth into the laws, local and international, amazed him. They briefly discussed their positions at the hearing. Laramie decided to let Kevin represent her. She had the information spelled out for him, all he needed to do was present it. She told him she would offer assistance if warranted. She smiled, they were ready. *Let's see his attorney beat that. He doesn't stand a chance. It's unfortunate he isn't smart enough to realize it.*

Laramie stopped in Edward's office before she left the firm for the hospital. He was on a call but motioned for her to sit and wait. She sat and tapped her feet. Edward hung up quickly.

"Well, I haven't seen you in days. How are you holding up?"

"Ups and downs, you know. Each day depends on the circumstance. Dr. Patel was called away on emergency so I won't know the test results until tomorrow. That alone has me on edge."

"Linda told me she spoke with you earlier. She said you were upset over Akihiro. Is that true?"

"Yes, but it doesn't affect my work. Actually Kevin and I are finished. I have to say that outside of a few typing errors, my case is very solid. I don't believe he has a chance."

"You will have to come to terms with your feelings for him. You two are forever connected. He will come and go and not always alone."

"So, she told you about the date. Edward, that was crushing. I never expected him to do that here. Not so blatantly. I think once he leaves I will get over him easier."

"Let me ask you a question. Have you told him you were still in love with him since he came here? I don't recall you saying that. You have tapped around the subject more than anything. Could it be he moved on because he thinks you did? Just a thought."

"No, I never told him how I felt. Yes, I have tapped dance a bit too. I wanted to be sure about the whole package before I let my feelings out. I'm afraid our time has already come and gone."

"You'll be fine. You're a fighter. Just do me a favor and stay alert. I just feel unsettled about all of this and I can't figure out why. I know what he's said to you and what you feel to be true. But still something isn't clicking right about this mess. I'll figure it out soon."

"I bet you will. Nothing gets past you. Anyway, I am back off to the hospital. It does feel great to get away from there." Laramie walked over to Edward who sat in his office chair. "You are nothing more than a big softie. Too bad more people don't know it like I do. I love you."

"I love you too, Lara. Kisses and hugs for Akiko, okay?" She nodded agreement.

When Laramie entered the hospital room, she found daughter and Dad asleep on the rocker. Laramie slowly picked up Akiko. She needed to wake her slowly to ensure a good mood. She didn't want the baby to sleep yet or she wouldn't sleep at night. She carried Akiko in her arms and whispered silly things to her. The baby slowly smiled for her Mommy. Laramie knew she was lucky to have such a good baby. She saw too many screamers at the park. Akiko motioned to be put down. She hurried over to Elmo and tickled him. Akiko found her toy very amusing.

Akihiro woke up to the noise. Somewhat startled at first until he saw Laramie in the room. He stood, stretched his arms and yawned.

"I didn't realize it was that time already. We rocked for a while and I guess we both fell asleep. Oh, for your information, everything here was fine. She played and ate everything."

Laramie twirled with Akiko in her arms almost oblivious to his words.

"Well, I hope she will sleep tonight when I lay her down." She sounded annoyed but that wasn't her intention.

"Lara, it was an accident. You don't have to be snide."

"I wasn't trying to be mean. I was merely making a statement."

"Right."

"Look who's being snide now." She raised her hand in a stop motion. "Forget it. You are not going to bait me into one of your arguments. You can interpret it any way you want."

"Bait you? Really now, that is amusing. Everything is an argument to you. I can't have a normal conversation with you because you wont participate in one."

"You're right. Everything you say is right. Look, no fight. I really mean it. From this point on, I won't say anything if it isn't nice."

She sat in her chair and picked up her book. With her brief completed, she enjoyed the free time to read humorous items and not legal. Akihiro watched her. He knew he baited her and now so did she. He kissed and hugged Akiko before he left. Neither spoke another word to each other.

When Akihiro returned to his hotel, he had a voice message from his attorney, Richard Barnes. Richard told him their hearing date was the coming Friday at eleven o'clock. He asked Akihiro to be a little early in case either of them had questions. *That is quick. I wasn't prepared for four days from now. I wonder how he worked out that time frame. Laramie is the wildcard in this arena. I have no idea what she will come in with and I don't think Richard knows either.*

Laramie sat in the darkness of Akiko's room unable to sleep. She wondered what news Dr. Patel had tomorrow. She prayed for something positive. Amid the mess in her personal life, she wanted Akiko to be healthy more than anything. Nothing else mattered more to her than her daughter. She thought Akiko seemed better in her eating and behavior especially compared to two and a half weeks ago. *I don't want to guess. I just want to know. I don't want to think past that point. It serves no purpose.*

Akihiro laid on his bed and stared at the ceiling. He knew Dr. Patel would be there tomorrow morning. He wished he could be there to hear the news. He wasn't sure if Laramie would relay the information considering their current status. *Akiko. I've never wanted anything more than to have you healthy. You have to pull through this, Baby. Which way do things go from there?*

Chapter 66

LARAMIE SAT ANXIOUSLY in her chair as she waited for Dr. Patel to come. She had little to no sleep the previous night. She ran completely on adrenalin. She prayed all night long that the news would be good. At first, she stared out the window and waited, then paced Akiko's room. Akiko was a delight as she played with Elmo. It was hard to tell the child had any illness at all. Laramie checked her watch. *Only five minutes since the last time I looked. I can't take this waiting. It's excruciating.*

The telephone ring caused her to jump. She hoped it wasn't the doctor's office with more emergencies. She quickly picked it up. It was Lian.

"Hello?"

"Hey Lara, any news yet?"

"No. I just keep pacing around the room waiting for him to come through the door. I have never prayed so much in my entire life as I have for today."

"I know you must feel nervous. Manny keeps calling me asking if I know anything. I hate to call you because you are even more on edge. I thought we could keep each other company to try and pass the time."

"Great idea. I can't take looking at my watch every five minutes. How are things at the store?"

"Quiet right now. Once the old people leave their homes it'll pick up. I have to tell you the smell today makes me want to throw up. All the dried fish really is disgusting."

"I don't know how you go in everyday. I couldn't look at that stuff without getting sick. I'm sure there is a miracle cure in there but I won't be the one to find it."

"Hey, what's the latest with Akihiro? Has he been showing up for his visitation?"

"Yes, though he was hung-over the other morning. He said he was on a date the night before. Someone named Erin. Believe me that was a knife to the heart. I don't know how I ever trusted him. I believe he never intended to work things out with me. It was all a pretense to get Akiko."

"A date? And he told you about it? That's kind of nervy."

"I asked if he was out celebrating his victory early. He slipped with his statement. To make matters worse, I sat crying over it after he left. Then I hear his voice. He forgot his coat so now he finds me upset. I couldn't recover fast enough."

"Don't beat yourself up over it. You could very easily be upset over numerous things, not just him. You know he didn't have to lie over the past few weeks to fight over Akiko. You wouldn't have known anything until you were served that day. Why go through the trouble of deceiving you? What purpose did it serve? I don't get it."

"Me, neither. How's Manny's new job going? He seemed excited to start. I remember the years of schooling. I didn't think they were ever going to end."

"He seems to like it so far. Thanks for the recommendation by the way. This puts us near our own house sooner."

"I tried to get him to work at the firm but he wanted a fresh start. I suppose I don't blame him. I would've —" Laramie turned to the knock at the door. "Lian, I have to go. Dr. Patel is here."

"Call me."

Laramie hung up the phone as the doctor sat in Akihiro's usual chair. She sat in the rocker across from him. The doctor reviewed Akiko's record for a moment before he began the conversation.

"Good morning, Miss Holden. I am so sorry to put this off but I had an emergency that I needed to tend to yesterday. I realize how anxious you must feel at this point. Will Mr. Amori be joining us?"

"No, he won't be in until noon." Laramie squirmed in her chair. "I told him I would relay all the information to him. Is everything okay with Akiko? Please just tell me."

"Yes, your daughter is fine and getting healthier."

Laramie bent over in her chair, sobbing harder than she ever had before. She thanked God repeatedly. Dr. Patel handed her a tissue.

"I'm sorry but that is the best news I have ever heard. Please tell me you are sure."

"Yes, I am very sure. Her red blood cell count has increased as well as the size of her cells. I have to believe at this point that her illness was toxin related since we already ruled out dietary. She has been away from whatever the source was and that alone can increase her numbers. You did mention you had your home stripped of all lead paint and chemicals, correct?"

"Yes, I even had someone come through and take random samples to make sure it was safe for her. They didn't find any traces of any contaminants."

"That is encouraging news. I want to do a small blood sample today and confirm the results. I will be sending them to an outside laboratory for same day results. I do not wish to put your family in any further torment. I assure you, we do not appreciate the wait anymore than you do."

"That's fine. When do you think she can come home?"

"I would say by Friday if she improves as I suspect she has."

"Oh my, that is great news. I can't thank you enough for all the help you've given us. Oh, I can't stop crying. I am just so happy." She hugged him so tight.

He chuckled over her emotional display. She held Akiko for the last time in the hospital for blood work. She hated the screams but saw the finality of the situation.

"Once again Miss Holden, the lab will have the results today and I will call here as soon as I receive them. Enjoy the rest of your day."

"Thank you again, Dr. Patel." Laramie twirled around with Akiko in her arms. Their nightmare was over, finally over. Laramie placed Akiko on the floor and wound up her musical toy. Akiko sat happily for her.

Laramie ran to the phone and called Edward first. Unfortunately, she cried with tears of joy and poor Edward couldn't understand her.

"Laramie, just tell me good or bad. I can't make out what you are saying."

"Good. It's all good. She's going to be fine," she said between her gasps for air.

Even Edward's eyes welled up with the news. Laramie heard him blow into his handkerchief.

"Edward Graham, do I detect emotions from you? You are not the stoic old man you try to be. Let me catch my breath a minute… whew! Dr. Patel said if her numbers increase, as he thought, from today's test, then she could go home by Friday."

"Laramie, that's the best news you've ever given me. Nothing could make me happier. Have you told everyone else yet?"

"No, you were the first. I have to call Lian and the girls yet. I plan to do that as soon as we hang up."

"You haven't told Akihiro yet?"

"No, he should be leaving to come here about now. Yes, I will tell him."

They exchanged their goodbyes. Laramie was delirious with joy and relief.

She dialed the girls first and passed the news. It created a long line of jubilation among her friends. The wait was finally over. Next, Laramie called Lian. Once again, she could hardly talk she cried so hard. Lian tried to determine what Laramie said. Finally, Laramie said it was good news. Lian screamed so loud that Laramie removed the phone from her ear. Her back was to the door as she, still crying, spoke to Lian. They both heard Akihiro's voice in the background. Lian said to hang up, they would talk later.

Laramie turned around with tears flowing down her face. Akihiro tried to read her expression but couldn't. He panicked when she couldn't speak clearly. He held her arms in his hands and told her to speak slowly.

"Dr. Patel… he said… she was good." That was all she said before crying again. "It's over, finally over."

Akihiro sat down and trembled with his hands over his face. He took the news so emotionally. Laramie never saw him this way, it clearly surprised her. She squatted down in front of him and put her hands on his forearms.

"It's okay. Everything is okay. She is going to be fine. Dr. Patel did one more test today and he will call this afternoon with the results to confirm everything. He doesn't doubt she is healthier. He just wants to have that piece of mind."

"You're sure?" he asked as he wiped his face.

"Yes. I'm sure." She looked at him sincerely and smiled.

He stood up and hugged Laramie tightly. She felt his breathing relax and then his arms. She felt so safe there that she didn't want to let go.

"Was there anything else?"

"He said if everything is fine she should be released to go home on Friday."

"That's great news. I couldn't have asked for anything better. You had me scared at first when I saw you upset. It didn't cross my mind that you were happy. Wow, Friday."

Laramie let go and pulled away. *Friday. I forgot all about Friday. This is over for Akiko but now our battle begins.* She kissed Akiko and grabbed her jacket and purse. She tried to make a fast exit but he caught her arm.

"Why are you running out so soon?"

She pulled her arm free. "I have to leave now. I just have to."

Akihiro wondered what caused the quick departure. *What has her on edge? Damn it, it was Friday. Same day as the hearing. It's not over. We still have to deal with that.* Akihiro sat and wondered about that situation. He wasn't sure what his next step was. Her emotional roller coaster made it difficult to know where she stood and what she felt. He knew his own antics didn't help the situation. Nevertheless, that was three days from now. And right now, his happiness for his daughter's recovery came first. He wanted to go to his hotel and email everyone the good news but knew that had to wait. His afternoon would pass quickly as always.

Laramie caught her breath as soon as she stood outside. *Why did he have to touch me? Why did I try to console him? What was I thinking? I have to keep my distance. This isn't over yet. It won't be over on Friday either. There won't be an end until he leaves to go home.* Laramie took a cab to Union Square. With her legal brief completed, she didn't need to be at work. *I know I will sleep soundly tonight. A first in three weeks.* She felt as though her life was back in motion. *What is my favorite cure for the blues? Shopping! Time for the summer wardrobe-shopping excursion. I've seen so many commercials but let's see what the stores have.*

She started her therapy at Saks Fifth Avenue first. She shopped there infrequently but loved their sales. She found a few cardigan sweaters by Juicy Couture. *Jeans, great. I need a new pair. What cut? Cali Boot Cut, and… yes, in my size.* She tried on her garments. It was a pleasure to shop without Akiko's stroller in the changing room. She knew those days were numbered and she gladly wanted her daughter with her anywhere. She changed back into her clothes and paid for her items.

As she walked toward Neiman Marcus across the square from Saks, she browsed the windows of Tiffany's and William Sonoma. While in the square, she remembered their night on the steps when Akihiro asked her back to his room. She very much wanted to go with him but now in hindsight she knew she made the right decision. *If I slept with him, would he ever have told me about the lawsuit? I wish I knew the separation of lies and truths. Unfortunately, I have to see it as all lies. Why did I have to be in love with him? Why couldn't he be a one-night stand or something? It certainly would make my life easier.*

Once inside Neiman Marcus, she forgot about Akihiro. This was Mecca for a shopper. She noticed, despite the economy, people carried bags full of items. She knew she was luckier than most. She carried more responsibility than most as well. *Oh, a good sale in Ralph Lauren, my favorite.* She browsed the racks. *Have. Have. Have. Ooh, don't have.* She picked up a short double-breasted trench coat in black. She chose his styles because they were classics and always fit her perfectly. She grabbed a navy double-breasted cardigan. *Navy. Great choice here, besides the weather will warm and I can wear it soon. Cute cashmere nightshirt. It's mine.* She strolled into the other designer areas. She added a Calvin Klein wrap blouse and a Burberry belted jacket. She was on her way out when she passed the shoe department. *I need to get with Manny again and hit the old Chinese guy's store. That man had the best selection of shoe I've ever seen.* She spotted a Gucci ankle boot in black. *Half off… it's so mine. I need to get out of here before I do anymore damage.*

She caught a cab outside and had him drive her home. She didn't want to walk around carrying all her shopping bags. With more time on her hands, she tried to think of things to occupy her time. *I could visit Lian at the market. Though, I hate to interrupt her at work. I don't know how I would've gotten through this with out her help. Manny better know how lucky he is to have her.* She entered her flat and placed the coats in her closet. She took off the tags on the clothes she wanted to drop off at the cleaners. *I don't even remember if I have stuff there. I can ask when I get there.* Laramie put her jacket on and walked her new clothes around the corner to Marina Cleaners. She did have garments there so she picked them up and walked back to the flat to hang them up as well. *Okay, that took a half hour, now what? I could stop and eat but I'm not really hungry. I'm bored.* When she neared Moscone Rec. Center, she hailed a cab to take her back to the hospital. *I guess being a few minutes early won't hurt.*

She saw Charisse at the nurse's station and stopped there first. Charisse read the chart and saw the good news regarding Akiko. She was happy for Laramie and her family. Charisse inquired about Akihiro and the lawsuit. Laramie told her the hearing was in three days. Charisse confided in Laramie to accept some of the needs of the father. She said a child needed two parents to succeed in the world and not to slight Akiko because the adults can't agree. Laramie understood what she meant and told her she would take it to heart.

Laramie knocked on the door as she entered as not to startle anyone. Akihiro looked up as she came in. He sat on the floor with Akiko.

"You don't mind giving me a hand to get up, do you?" Laramie shook her head and held her hand out to pull him up. "Thanks."

"Has Dr. Patel called in yet?"

Akihiro smiled at her with a huge grin. "Yes, she is cleared. She can go home at the end of the week."

Laramie placed her hand over her mouth and smiled back. Tears escaped from the corner of her eyes and she didn't bother to wipe them.

"It's real. It is finally over. That's some of the best news I've heard in a while."

"It's very real," Akihiro replied, backing up her statement.

Awkwardness took over in the room. They both wanted to embrace the other yet each was afraid to make the move.

"Laramie, I have a proposition to make you." His statement peaked her curiosity. "If you choose not to accept it, that's fine. Anyway, tomorrow when I come in, why don't you let me stay the night with Akiko? You can go home and get a solid night's sleep. You can sleep in if you want."

Laramie was skeptical by this sudden offer of generosity. "Why the sudden kindness? Why would you offer that?"

"I thought about it today while I was here. I thought it would only be a fair gesture after all the nights you've spent here on that bed. Let's face it; it's not even comfortable to sit on."

"I don't know. I don't know if it's a good idea." She pulled back from the offer.

"You don't trust me, do you?" he asked genuinely.

"No… not anymore. I really don't want to discuss that today." She remained calm even though internally her emotions began to stir.

"At least think about it tonight. If you change your mind, you can tell me tomorrow at noon. Is that fair?" She nodded in agreement.

Akihiro knew the conversation was over. He doubted she would accept his offer. *At least she was honest. It's been two weeks and we are still at odds.* He kissed Akiko goodbye and turned back around to say goodbye to Laramie. Surprisingly, she said goodbye back to him. *That was civil. How much of her mood has been controlled by this atmosphere? Will she loosen up now that the threat is over?*

Akihiro's first order of business was to email his family and friends the tremendous news regarding Akiko. He sent the first email to his parents. He told them Akiko was healing from her illness and would be released on Friday. He also wrote that was the same day as the hearing. He didn't mention anything regarding Laramie; he wasn't sure what to state. He regretted his actions and felt that contributed to her lack of trust in him. He knew he had to work on that in the future. He emailed Rhys, Kat and Shinji together. It was easier than separate emails all with the same words. Not surprising, his first response back was from Kat.

> Dear Akihiro:
>
> I am so happy and relieved for Laramie and you. I could only imagine how difficult this has been for you both. By the way, you never mentioned anything about Laramie. Is she doing okay? Better yet, are you two speaking? Of course, it is none of my business but… You were meant to be together and you need to work it out before you come back. Seriously. Anyway, I'll chat later since I have a business to run!
>
> Sayonara, Kat

Kat, you are a pain. It's even worse when you're right. The relief from Akiko's diagnosis lightened his mood dramatically. Akihiro knew everything from this point forward was his responsibility. If he wanted a relationship with Laramie then he needed to do the work. *If I pursue her now she can't use*

Akiko's illness as an excuse. What excuse would she say next? How do I beat her to that point? It has to be her. I can't be with another woman without thinking of her or speaking her name. That makes it more difficult to get laid. She'll come around, she always does. I just need to be witty and charming.

Laramie thought about Akihiro's offer as she lay on the hard bed. She wanted to except it but felt there was a hidden agenda behind the offer. *Was he being nice because he was in a good mood? Does he have a reason to keep me away overnight? Does he plan to use this at trial? It would make him look concerned and giving before the judge. However, one time out of two weeks doesn't make you the ideal parent. No, I just feel there is more to this. He has given me more than my share of reasons not to trust him. As much as I crave to sleep in my bed, my answer is no. I can't afford to take a chance.* Laramie looked forward to a good night's sleep. She knew Friday night would be her nirvana.

Chapter 67

LARAMIE PASSED ON Akihiro's offer to stay the night at home, she didn't trust him. Also, she didn't feel as though she owed him anything for the offer. It was too close to the hearing for her to let her guard down.

Akihiro accepted her answer even though the offer was sincere. He didn't know how to regain her trust. The hearing only added to the pressure of their situation. However, he planned to fight for his rights as Akiko's father. He felt certain his rights under the law held a higher place than her ability to twist the law. He hoped Richard prepared well for the upcoming conflict. All of the hype of Laramie's career and education caused internal anguish for Akihiro.

Laramie called Kevin to refresh him on the strategy for the hearing. Kevin assured her that he knew what to do and reviewed their papers thoroughly each day. Nevertheless, Laramie knew she did her best work. It was impossible for Kevin to screw it up with her there to coach him. Her nerves tensed with anticipation. She was the subject of the trial not some stranger. This hearing affected her life. Even in the wrongful death trial of her parents, Laramie was the plaintiff not the defendant. She never sat in that seat before and found it unsettling.

Chapter 68

LARAMIE FINISHED HER book by Denis Leary just before Akihiro arrived. *I really need to read more books like this. It lightens my thoughts. The tabloids have far less entertainment than a comedian does. Maybe my problem has been too much career and less fun. Love my time with Akiko but after bedtime, I need to do something else besides work. Laramie Lila Holden, I can't believe you are having those thoughts. Less work. Geez, that would give Edward a coronary for sure.* She chuckled to herself over her new outlook.

Akihiro walked into the room always with her having to explain herself. "Did I miss something funny?"

"Actually, you did. I just finished a book that was exceptionally funny and witty." She stood and handed him the book. "Here, you now have something to read on your flight home."

She walked over to Akiko and kissed her goodbye for the afternoon. Akihiro found her statement unsettling not by the words but by her delivery. She left in such an uplifted mood it surprised Akihiro. *Something is different. She hasn't been like that since our dinner out. I hardly believe it was the book. No, there has to be more to this.*

Laramie almost felt liberated. She had a renewed sense of happiness with Akiko's change in health. Not everything seemed bleak anymore. Good health, good humor and good friends and family seemed to be what she needed to fulfill her. Laramie needed this new outlook. She felt in control of her being again. She saw a bright future again with or without Akihiro. Of course, she preferred a future with him, but if he wasn't in it, she knew she could survive.

Akihiro looked at the book she handed him. *Who is Denis Leary? He turned over the book jacket and saw the picture. I thought he was an actor. I didn't realize he was a comedian too. She doesn't realize American humor is different than Singaporean.* He tossed the book back onto the windowsill where it sat most of the week while he was there. He found it odd that Laramie's mood was so cheerful since the hearing was a day away. *The past two days she left without a word. Today she's happy. What changed? Is she trying to hustle me? Is this some plan to set me off course?*

Laramie stopped in the office to see Edward. She said hello to Linda and Andrew before she knocked on Edward's door. She closed it behind her and sat across from him.

"Well, to what do I owe this honor? You look radiant this afternoon."

"You know Edward, I feel really good. Despite the hearing tomorrow, I feel like I have a new lease on life with Akiko. Everything was so grim and now it's over. I don't have the same pressures anymore. My daughter is getting healthier every day. Soon, she and I will be back home in our beds. Life will continue with or without Akihiro. Don't misunderstand me. My feelings haven't changed regarding him. Though now that he knows about Akiko, I don't have any secrets, I have nothing to hide and I don't have the guilt anymore either."

"Well, it's about time. Lara, I have waited a long time to see this side of you again. It's been almost two years since you first went to Singapore and you haven't been the same since then. Now I don't mean you've been worse but just not yourself. It's time you started to enjoy your life not work it. You have a beautiful daughter who adores you. Worry about making her happy. When that happens, yours will fall into place. Only you can find your own happiness."

"It's funny you should say that Edward. I've thought about this subject for quite a while and I think it's time we address it."

"You are feeling brave if you are willing to confront me on an issue. What do you have?" He smiled at her tenacity.

"What exactly is the story between Linda and you? Now, I've watched you talk with her many times. She has been at your home several times even when I lived there. She respects you and genuinely seems happier when you're around. So what gives?"

Edward choked a moment at her directness. She caught him completely off guard. He didn't know how to respond to her.

"Laramie, for Pete's sake, are you trying to kill me?"

"No, Edward and don't avoid the question. You know there have been whispers in the office for years. I've actually contributed to them a few times myself."

"Lara, I don't think I need to address this." Edward tried to build up his stoic persona.

"Yes, you really do. I'll tell you why. You gave me the lecture on happiness and family. You said you were too attached to the firm and it doesn't give back comfort of companionship. There has always been some eyes made between you both but neither of you pursued it. Why are you waiting? Your womanizing days are over. Why would you want to spend the rest of your life at a country club with a bunch of stodgy old men?"

"Hey, I am one of those stodgy old men. I'm too old for that now."

"No, nice try. Ask her out. Take her to dinner. Where is the harm?"

"Lara, why must you push this?"

"Because, I don't want you to be alone anymore. We have great careers but there is so much more than work. I get to see life grow in Akiko's eyes. Maybe you need to see companionship through a woman's eyes."

"I'll make you a deal. You show me growth in your life and I don't mean with Akiko. Then, I will follow your advice."

"But this isn't about me."

"Yes my dear, it is. I've watched you grow as a child. I've seen you mature into a woman. Somewhere, you let the lawyer in you take over. You need to be the woman again. I think you're on the right path but you have a little farther to go."

"I'm not sure what you mean."

"Think about it. It will come to you. Now, out of my office. I have plenty of work and you are distracting me." He stood and walked her to the door. He kissed her on the forehead and pretended to boot her out.

Laramie left the office and walked about three blocks down Grant Avenue to the market Manny's parents owned in Chinatown. She wanted to see Lian and talk a little before going back to the hospital. She hated to bother her at work especially since the smell of dried fish and other creatures disgusted her. *Maybe I can get her out for a coffee or something.* As Laramie stood in front of the store greeted by wooden barrels of dried shrimp, dried mushrooms, exotic fruits and vegetables. She caught the durian out of the corner of her eye. She remembered the Esplanade in Singapore with the same spikes in the architecture. That was her first night out with Akihiro when the oncoming bumboat soaked her dress. It was the first time she thought of it in a while. She fell in love with him that same night.

She walked into the store and said hello to Mrs. Tién, Manny's mother, who smiled and nodded to her. *I swear she can speak English but doesn't. She probably knows everything we say and laughs at us.* Laramie asked if Lian was at work when she didn't find her. Mrs. Tién motioned Lian felt ill and went upstairs to sleep. Laramie didn't want to disturb her so she said goodbye and left.

I suppose I could go back early again. I don't have anything to read. Well, that's not true. I do have my brief. I doubt another run through will hurt. That is the last piece of depressing news left. Once that is over, my life can move on. Laramie hailed a cab to take her back.

Akihiro fed Akiko whose appetite grew, of course not enough to eat peas. He cleaned her face and hands. He felt proud of his accomplishments as a father in such a short time. *I can feed her and change her. We play together and nap together. I think I have the hang of this. Kat would never believe it. I'd have to have it on video.*

Laramie walked in the room. "I see I came back at the right time. Dinner is over. Did she eat well?"

"Yes, she did great." Akihiro noticed her good mood was still intact. He was hesitant to say much. *Why the sudden conversation? I've tried to discuss this with her for the past week and every time she rebuffed me. If she's on some medication, she needed it the past two weeks.*

"Great. I thought I'd relieve you early today. I'm not kicking you out. I can leave if you still want to stay."

He watched her closely. "Sure, I can use the extra hour." He almost said he'd see her tomorrow but caught himself. "Well, then have a good night."

He picked up Akiko, kissed her, and bit at her until she giggled. Laramie watched their interaction. She knew he loved Akiko that was undisputed. *Why does he make this so difficult? This could've been worked out.* He waved as he left the room.

Laramie played with Akiko for a while before she sat in her rocker and grabbed her laptop. She allowed her benevolence to get the best of her. She typed away for a solid hour. She cut and pasted pieces of her brief until she had a solid, yet fair contract. She asked the nurses if she could use their printer, and they obliged. When she finished, she clipped the pages together and sat them by her coat and purse. *Now all I have to do is wait for Akiko to fall asleep. Edward wanted to see growth, it doest come any faster than this. I m actually proud of myself, either that or I have lost my mind.*

Akihiro was partly dressed. He had his pants on, waistband open and belt unbuckled, but no shirt. He walked around his hotel room with his electric razor as he watched the news. The extra hour given by Laramie helped greatly since he didn't have to rush before dinner. He had a dinner meeting with Richard to review their plans for tomorrow's hearing. He was nervous. He hoped they had enough to win.

Shortly after seven o'clock, Akihiro heard a knock on his door. He assumed it was the turn down service. It surprised him to find Laramie there.

"Well, this is surprising. What brings you here?"

Laramie, still a bit nervous, swallowed hard before she answered. "I thought maybe we could talk and perhaps settle this issue before the hearing tomorrow."

He smirked. "I really shouldn't be surprised after all. I should've expected it."

Confused, Laramie asked, "What? What do you mean?"

"Come on, Lara. You were being so nice when I came in. Then, you happily offer to take over early. You inquire how my afternoon went. All the things you never did the past week since being served."

"I'm not following you."

Akihiro shook his head. "So this was your plan. Be nice to me and try to settle the night before. Unfortunately, I don't buy it. Why are you really here?"

Laramie became slightly angered. "I'm here to make a settlement with you. If we go to the hearing you don't stand a chance at winning anything more than visitation."

Laramie watched him walk in and out of the bathroom. He still had a muscular build and great naturally toned abs. She tried not to think of what he felt like. Seeing him half dressed brought back so many memories of Singapore. She tried to find something else to focus on in the room. He saw her look away. He felt her reason dealt with her inability to confront people.

"I think you're here because you won't win tomorrow. I think this is your last chance effort to come to an agreement before the judge rules in my favor."

Laramie accidentally laughed aloud. "Oh, you can't honestly believe that." She looked at the arrogance in his expression. "Oh my God, you do believe that. Akihiro, I tried to tell you the other day that this was out of your reach. We don't even compete in the same league. I came here because I am done fighting. I can't do it anymore. I am willing to give you visitation here, whenever you want and as much as you want."

"And what about custody? Where do you stand on that?"

"You can have joint legal custody meaning I would consult with you on any major change in her life, like residence, schools, and healthcare."

"What about Singapore? Can I take her to Singapore with me?"

"No. I can't give you that. There are too many variables to that. I can't chance it."

"Then, we don't have a deal. You're wasting your time and my time." He was abrupt.

"This is more than what you will be granted tomorrow. I am willing to give you everything but I cannot let you take her out of the country." She was adamant about that.

"Laramie, I am tired of your attempts to screw me."

"Screw you? I am giving more rights to my daughter than anyone would give you. If anything, I am screwing myself," she replied in a factual manner.

"Your daughter? You seem to forget she is also *my* daughter. On top of that, my rights are not yours to give. I don't think we anything further to discuss. Now I have to get ready for my date. So if you don't mind…"

Date? He's going on another date? Those words infuriated her. She tried to remain calm during their conversation but those words incensed and tore at her.

"You know what? *Fine.* I was trying to be nice but you don't want nice, you want a fight. Well, I'll give you that fight." She picked up her papers and stood with her finger pointed at him as she began to lecture. "Let me tell you how this will play out. You will get visitation by schedule only, nothing more. As far as custody goes, forget about it. It will never be granted. You will lose your ass. You will wish you had signed these papers but it will all be too late."

"You can threaten all you want. I don't believe you," he yelled back.

Laramie gritted her teeth as she turned toward the door.

"Mark my words, she will never set foot in Singapore. *Never.* That would require a passport and guess who has to sign that application? Damn right, it's me and I'll never do it. You will never get her."

She tried to pull open the door but Akihiro ran up behind her and slammed it closed. He grabbed her shoulder and spun her to face him. He held her against the wall and brought his face close to hers.

"You are not the only person that can get her a passport. She is also a Singapore citizen which means I can do it."

At first, he startled her but she quickly regained her position. She laughed in his face.

"You think that will make a difference? You are so naïve. You have no idea who you're fighting. The minute you have her, I will be posting her name up on immigration alert. You won't be able to get past them. Your embassy can't even help you. It'll be my face you see last before you board your plane… *alone.*"

She meant every word. She was vicious when backed into a corner especially when it came to Akiko. His ignorance to her laws saved any comfort he had. He stood silent for a moment and stared into her eyes. He didn't know if she had that ability. He didn't care. *Damn, she is sexy when she's mad. She is so fired up.* He leaned in and kissed her passionately. Laramie didn't respond and stood emotionless. As he pulled back to see her expression, she spat in his face.

"Save it for you new girlfriend."

She pushed him back. As he wiped his face, she quickly grabbed the doorknob and made her exit. He shut the door behind her and laughed. *She is getting better at confrontation but she can't hold her temper. I probably shouldn't have pushed her but she wouldn't be here if she were going to win.*

Laramie stormed out of the hotel and made her way to the square across the street before she stopped. She sat on the concrete steps and wept into her hands. She hated the fact that he upset her and she allowed it. She went there with the best intentions. She couldn't understand why he didn't see that. She truly wanted the fighting to end. *I just can't do this anymore. It has to stop. I gave him my best offer. What choices do I have left now? She's my daughter. I can't let him take her from me, at least not to Singapore. It's so far away.* She thought about her earlier conversation with Edward. She tried to imagine his expression if he knew she went to settle a case. *He'd never believe it. I am trying so hard to move forward but it's one block after the other. I don't know what to do next. I really don't want to face him tomorrow. I don't want to see his reaction when he loses.* She stood up and slowly started her walk across the square.

Akihiro came down the stairs in front of the St. Francis to hail a cab for his dinner with Richard. As he entered the car, he looked across the road. He was certain he saw Laramie there. He tried to look again after a small crowd walked by but the person was gone. *It must be my imagination. I'm sure she's back at the hospital trying to find a way to win. Not this time.*

It was a short ride to Harris's Restaurant on the corner of Van Ness and Pacifica Avenues. As he entered the stucco building, it surprised him how well lit the restaurant was. He looked around the room to see if Richard arrived. He found him in a horseshoe booth in the rear corner surrounded by raised wood paneling. Akihiro walked past the booths filled with couples and businessmen. When he reached Richard, he shook his hand then sat.

"Right, I see you found the place easy enough. Best to put your order in first then we can discuss your case."

Richard seemed more casual in this setting than in his office. He dressed simply in a pair of dark slacks and an oxford shirt sans the tie. His gray hair, parted in the center, gave him a distinguished look. Akihiro browsed the menu quickly and made his choices. He also put in his drink order for his usual. Richard held his Tanqueray and tonic as he ordered. Akihiro wondered how much of this meeting he would be billed. *All of it.*

"Well, I had an interesting night already. Just before I left for here, Laramie stopped by my room. She claimed to want to settle the case."

"Oh go on," Richard said in almost a Cockney style. "Laramie settle? I hardly believe such a story."

"Oh, it's quite true. I don't know if she really meant to settle or throw me off guard. Either way, I declined. She didn't take it well."

"Well if that doesn't take the biscuits," replied Richard in disbelief.

"Excuse me? I don't understand."

"Pardon me. I meant to say, if that isn't a shocking surprise. It would be a first if she actually meant it. Though she has never approached opposing counsel out of the courtroom either. I find it interesting how her behavior is quite uncharacteristic with you. You truly paint a picture of her we never see. I wonder if she is representing herself tomorrow or bringing in another attorney from her firm."

"I don't know. She hasn't mentioned anyone, not that she would. You have me a bit nervous with your knowledge of her being so different than mine. I suspect there isn't any way to tell what tomorrow brings."

"I'm afraid not. If there is some ancient obscure law that should've been removed from the books centuries ago, you can bet she could find it. That is the person I am most fearful to meet."

"What do you think my chances are, realistically?"

"On visitation, you will have a one hundred percent chance of winning. On custody, I predict about a fifty percent chance. Much of that will be decided by the judge. I don't know how he will rule based on the fact you live in a different country than your daughter."

"Well, I have to take a chance and push it. Based on what you've just said, that's about all Laramie offered. However, she claims tomorrow will be no custody whatsoever."

"Really? She offered that much? Quite surprising. There is obviously a hidden agenda we aren't aware of existing."

The men bantered back and forth regarding what to expect inside the judges chambers, the flow of the proceeding, proper etiquette and so forth. Akihiro felt prepared for the morning. Richard coached him through the questions he posed for the plaintiff and hypothetical questions from Laramie's attorney. As they dined, the conversation switched from their current dilemma to a more casual one. They conversed about their favorite soccer teams. Akihiro questioned how Richard came to know Rhys. Richard explained that Rhys' father and he grew up on the same neighborhood as children and often dated the same girls. Aki spoke of his college days with Rhys and the predicaments they got into regularly. They both had an enjoyable evening.

Afterwards, they bid each other goodbye until the next morning. Akihiro took a cab back to his hotel and prepped his clothes for the next morning. His nerves tensed thinking about it. *She really did come with an offer to settle, she wasn't trying to cheat me. However, if that's what she is offering, I have to think the judge would do the same.* He felt guilty for letting her believe he had another date. He knew that was what incinerated her temper.

Laramie sat in the hospital room for what she hoped was her last night. She tried to think of her next move. She thought Akihiro would want to settle. *Apparently, his arrogance got in his way. Did he have to bring up the fact he had another date? I could see he was going out, why rub it in. That was just cruel. And, what was with the kiss? One minute he's pushing me against the wall then he confuses me with that?* She thought about each step she took. Unable to find her mistake, she passed it off as just tension in the room.

She watched Akiko sleep peacefully. She remembered to have faith and she prayed for her daughter. She believed there was a deity who answered her prayers. She didn't know the particulars of a higher being or God, but she believed one existed. She thought of her parents and what she would ask them if they were alive. She tried to view her dilemma from their perspective. *How would've my parents fought over me? What would they have done? How would it be decided? As I grew older, I can't say that one parent was more important than the other. I loved them both. I couldn't imagine being in that tug of war. They both wanted the best for me. They both loved me. I would've resented one if I was held away from the other. Eventually, each side has to let go. I know my daughter and she loves us both. Is it fair to her to keep her from him? I know he would never hurt her. We are only hurting each other to keep her. I don't trust him but she does. God, help me, but I have to find a way to let go. Do I love her enough put aside my fears and trust his love for her?*

Chapter 69

LARAMIE SAT ON the sofa, staring out the window. She slept restless due to the anticipation of the pending hearing. She tossed scenarios through her head all night. Still, she found no conclusion to her dilemma. She knew there were three choices; fight, conceded or let the judge decide. If she chose to fight, he stood no chance of winning. He would never let go of his anger toward her and any relationship with Akihiro would be over. She knew that wasn't a good choice because it created tensions that Akiko would grow up to recognize. If she conceded, she risked being wrong and the possibility of fighting the Singaporean court system to get Akiko back. If she let the judge decide, it created the fairest deal between them. However, Akihiro would think she manipulated the system and the people for a decision in her favor. He would never see it as fair.

She fed Akiko whose hunger grew daily. She found it very pleasant considering where they were three weeks ago. Her daughter held to the railings of the crib and jumped until her legs buckled beneath her. Laramie placed her toys inside the crib and showed Akiko how to wind the music player.

While Akiko occupied herself, Laramie sat and picked up her laptop. She worked diligently for thirty minutes. When she finished, she called Kevin at the firm. She told him to check his email because she had a document for him to deliver to opposing counsel. He questioned the validity of her signature since it was electronic. She told him to pass it by Linda who could authenticate it for him. He asked her if she was sure in her decision. She replied yes.

The judge's chambers were small, smaller than Akihiro imagined. As he looked around the office, he read the various degrees and positions of prestige the judge held. Barrister bookcases, stuffed full with different books pertaining to law, covered every wall. Sitting at the conference table flanking the judge's desk was his attorney, Richard Barnes. Richard seemed ready for his showdown against Laramie. Akihiro wasn't sure about this visitation and custody hearing. After last night, he wasn't sure this was the right approach in seeing Laramie again. *What if she was right? What if I'm chasing a losing battle?* His cockiness overpowered her confrontation. He knew she worked hard to muster up that courage. However, he would not let her control every aspect of Akiko's life. He was a part of that and he wanted time with his daughter as well. He deserved it.

The raised panel door opened right on queue. A bailiff walked in and said, "All rise. This hearing is now in session, Judge William T. Gallagher presiding."

Everyone stood up. Akihiro saw enough of U.S. television to know to follow his attorney's actions. Judge Gallagher entered the office with his court reporter and bailiff. The judge was short and rather round. His red hair receded and his mustache grayed. He glanced around the room and greeted Akihiro and Richard.

"You may be seated. "Does anyone know where opposing council is?" Judge Gallagher asked.

"No, Sir. I imagine they will be here any minute. If I can answer any question in the brief before we begin, please, feel free to ask," replied an over zealous Richard.

Everyone sat quietly. As they read their papers, they heard time tick away from the wall clock. By then, ten minutes elapsed. The doors quickly opened and Laramie's assisting counsel, Kevin Brown rushed in. In all honesty, this was the first actual case he represented and he expected Laramie to be at his side to guide him. He looked a bit disheveled and clutched his briefcase extremely tight.

"I truly apologize, your Honor. We had a last minute change in our case. I believed I had enough time to present our decision with the defense council. However, they had already left for your chambers," Kevin replied.

Akihiro looked over to the young attorney with a confused look. *What could Laramie be up to this time? Is this another trick? Why would she have a young inexperienced attorney represent her? Richard spent almost the entire evening talking about Laramie's prowess and legal intellect. This seems odd in comparison.*

"Let me read this, Mr. Brown. Why isn't Lara… pardon me, Miss Holden with you?" said Judge Gallagher as he snatched the paper from Kevin's hand. *Apparently Laramie knows the judge as well.* Judge Gallagher glanced it over and said, "It appears opposing council has conceded on all matters in the visitation and custody arrangement. Is this correct?"

"Your Honor, Miss Holden was unable to attend due to a sudden illness. I am sure she regrets this and extends her apologies. Yes, she has agreed to all the terms in Mr. Amori's visitation and custody agreement regarding their daughter, Akiko Audrey Amori," replied Kevin, almost breathless.

Akihiro leaned into Richard and asked what was happening. *Why isn't Laramie here? What sudden illness would keep her from appearing especially regarding our daughter?* Richard explained quietly that Laramie agreed to and signed the original agreement. Richard released a sign of relief. He was an above average attorney but not in the league of Laramie Holden.

Judge Gallagher hammered his gavel to quiet the loud whispers. "It appears we did not need to be here after all. However, in light of the new documentation and the original agreement set forth by defense council, this hearing moves in favor of Mr. Akihiro Amori. This judgment shall be recorded and be put in effect within the next two weeks. This hearing is adjourned." The judge, pounding his gavel down, said, "Congratulations, Mr. Amori. It is always a pleasure to see a father show interest and involvement in the upbringing of his child."

"Thank you, Sir," Akihiro replied.

Once again, the bailiff said, "All rise." As they watched the judge exit the room, the bailiff continued, "This court is now dismissed."

Richard shook Akihiro's hand and congratulated him. He told Akihiro he would send him a copy of the judgment as soon as the documents became of record. In addition, he would advise him the start date of the visitation agreement.

Akihiro looked at Kevin's expression. He seemed defeated.

"Mr. Brown, I don't understand most of the court proceedings here. However, I am surprised there wasn't any counter to the suit. Was she just not prepared with all the pressure of Akiko's illness?"

Kevin chuckled openly, "You've obviously never seen Laramie in action. She is the most feminine pitbull. She can charm you at the same time she has her teeth in your seat. Oh, she was more than prepared. She finished her brief days ago. If she hadn't changed her mind this morning, you wouldn't have stood a chance in the hearing."

"You're just saying that because it's over." Akihiro questioned Kevin's integrity.

"No, I have the brief. It reads like a book. Don't tell her I showed you, but you at least deserve to know what you were up against."

Kevin pulled the brief out of his portfolio. It contained three sections, international law, Singapore law and California law. Richard asked to view it, realizing by her table of contents alone that she had prepared herself to win. He quickly browsed the pages and read her cites.

"Blimey, you are absolutely correct. The woman is bloody brilliant."

Akihiro seemed confused. "I don't understand. How would she have won?"

Kevin began to discuss the details in layman's terms.

"She pretty much had California law on her side since she was the only parent to Akiko since birth, regardless of the fact you didn't know. From there she went into international law. She had information on custody issues between parents from foreign countries. Most all sided with the custodial parent. She covered her bases on child abduction."

"Child abduction? I wasn't taking Akiko anywhere."

"You're right and you never would. There are international laws about taking children into other countries and not sending them back. Singapore wasn't one of them. Therefore, you did have an option to abduct her. She used that in her favor to keep your daughter here. To go one-step further, she cited Singapore law to back up her requests stating they didn't always support the case of sending the child back. Even when enough evidence was presented in their court and Singapore ruled in favor of the mother, that still wasn't a guarantee based on other outstanding cases."

"She was telling the truth last night. I thought she was bluffing." Akihiro sat stunned.

Richard quickly chimed in, "Laramie Holden doesn't bluff. She doesn't have reason to do that. I told you she was brilliant. I never thought to use Singapore's law to support my case. She played both sides in her favor. Bloody brilliant."

Kevin interjected, "So, now you see my plight. My first case with her and she concedes. I never thought that would happen for a second."

"Did she say why she changed her mind?" asked Akihiro.

"No, and I wasn't about to ask her."

The men cleared up their belongings. Richard accepted it as a false win but a win nonetheless. Richard offered Akihiro to join him for lunch as a celebration of their case though Akihiro politely declined. He already planned to visit Akiko in the hospital.

Akihiro was bewildered. He couldn't imagine that Laramie would just give in to his demands. *She would've won just as she said. She told the truth and I laughed in her face. Why didn't she fight? Why was this any different?* He grabbed his jacket and walked out of the judges chambers. The closer he got to the elevator the more excited he became. *Wow, my daughter. Akiko is now a permanent part of my life.* The last few weeks were a whirlwind. Akihiro entered the elevator with a big grin. This time, he won, even though it was bittersweet.

Akihiro walked through the marble halls of American justice toward the sunshine. A day he thought covered in gloom turned unexpectedly bright. His black hair blew in the wind and his jacket opened. He stopped to button it as he headed down the stairs.

A young man raced up the stairs and blocked Akihiro's way. "Excuse me, Sir. Are you Akihiro Amori?"

Caught a bit off guard, Akihiro cautiously answered, "Yes, I am. Can I help you in some way?"

"We've never met but I have heard all about you. My name is Manchu Tién. However, most of my friends call me Manny." Manny extended his hand out to shake.

"Manny, I've heard Laramie mention quite a bit about you as well. Did she send you here?" Aki's curiosity began to peak. *Is this another trick played by Laramie? Does she now have her friends trying to manipulate me?* Akihiro's demeanor was a bit guarded. He didn't fully grasped the twists and turns of the day's hearing and now to have Laramie's dearest friend show up at the courthouse, it all seemed calculated.

"No, and please don't tell her I was here. She would be furious. There are things that go on behind the scenes that you don't know. As much as she has tried to hide her emotions and thoughts, we all compare the info on the phone. But, before I get to that part, how can I convince you to have lunch with me right now?" Manny continued to plead, "It really is very important."

Intrigued by Manny's statements, Akihiro agreed. "I was on my way to see Akiko, but I am interested in hearing what you have to say."

"Great. There's a small place just down the street. We can walk there if you don't mind"

Both men walked down McAllister Street not really conversing. Manny tried to play things out in his head. Akihiro was taller and more muscular than he expected. They started to talk about all the safe subjects, sports and weather. As they entered the City Grille, Manny saw Edward at a table in the rear. They continued to walk to the rear of the place. Edward stood and offered his hand out to Akihiro.

"I'm Edward Graham. It is a pleasure to meet you, Mr. Amori. We all have heard so much about you, some good, some not so good," he chuckled. "Sit down. Get comfortable, there is a lot to discuss."

This is Edward Graham. I pictured him smaller built. I never expected a towering older man. He could easily have been a rugby player.

"Sir, I must say, I have wanted to meet you but please call me Akihiro or Aki. I didn't think our paths would cross while I was in town. I am glad to meet you. Laramie has spoken highly of you both. Though, I am confused by this ambush." Akihiro sat in the chair between both men. He knew he must keep a keen ear to the conversation ahead. "Is there anyone coming to join us?"

"No Son, just the three of us," Edward replied in his burly voice. He chuckled again. "*Ambush*? I guess I would feel the same if I were you. We want to talk to you about Laramie."

The waitress came to the table and asked for their drink preference. Edward ordered a Crown and Sprite. Manny asks for a Grey Goose straight up. Akihiro, still trying to get a feel for his surroundings, decides that alcohol might be in his best interest. He looked to the waitress and doubled Manny's order.

"Good, good. I'm glad to see you order a drink. You can tell a lot about a man by the company he keeps and the booze he chooses. I really don't want to tap around this so I'm going to the point. It is obvious you love Akiko, we all do. However, what are your feelings for Laramie?" *Bam!* Edward jumped with both feet.

"Wow, you were serious. I can't say for sure you're going to like my answer. She has really gone out of her way to make my life hell. She left Singapore without giving me a chance to explain myself. She has tried to destroy my business. Coming very close to succeeding. She has kept the news that I have a daughter from me for a year and a half. She finally tells me about Akiko when she is in grim health. Then she comes to my hotel last night to settle the case before the hearing."

"Wait a minute. Did you say settle?" Edward thought he misheard Akihiro.

"Yes, those were her words. She said she didn't want to fight and said I had no chance to win. Of course, I didn't believe her."

"That is interesting news. Laramie has never settled a case," Edward said.

"That's what I hear today. Then, she doesn't show up at the hearing to fight but concedes to all my requests. Taking it all inconsideration, I would have to say I really don't know how I feel right now. Though, I am completely confused by her actions."

Edward stated he was as well. "We knew about the concession early this morning but she wouldn't say why she changed her mind. She also never mentioned going to the hotel last night either. You realize had she fought you, you would have lost."

"Sure, I do now after listening to all the legal minds discuss it."

During this conversation, the waitress placed their drinks on the table and asked if they were ready to order. Edward motioned his hand as if he was dismissing her.

"I can't say that I don't blame you. We have seen changes in Laramie so out of character since she came back from Singapore. She was never an emotional girl. She worked through her problems logically. She didn't give up on anything. I never saw her truly cry until she came back from Singapore. We thought she was going to have a breakdown. If it weren't for Akiko, she probably would have. So, let us fill you in on what happened on this side of the Pacific."

Edward began with the slow progression at the firm. He described how Laramie came back from Singapore and poured herself in her cases. At first, he was proud to see her become extremely serious about her career, not that she wasn't before. No matter what case came in, she worked many nights and weekends with her legal team of associates. Laramie slowly became more demanding and less tolerant to excuses. Edward thought this was odd but dismissed her actions knowing she worked so many hours. Sleep was a luxury. It wasn't until she began to feel ill on a regular basis, did he have concerns. It was then Laramie found out she was pregnant. The mood swings became more frequent. Her tolerance at work deteriorated. It all came to a head at a company birthday lunch when a young intern made mention of a Mr. Holden. Laramie came unglued. She berated the poor fellow about the need for a man in her life when she was perfectly able to raise her child on her own. At that point, Edward stepped in. He demanded Laramie go on maternity leave over a month early.

The men ordered another round of cocktails, and then Manny took over the conversation.

"I can stop here if you have had enough but I think you will want to know what happened after Akiko was born."

Akihiro agreed. He listened very attentively. He began to see where the correlation was between her visits to Singapore and not wanting to be seen by anyone. *Of course, she was pregnant.*

Manny began his side of the story showing the Laramie everyone truly knew. While she was home, she began to get excited about the baby. She went to every baby boutique in the Bay area. At last minute, she didn't want the usual neutral colors for gender, so when the opportunity came to determine the sex, Laramie wanted to know. She was elated to know she would become the mother of a baby girl. All of her friends, including those at work, all volunteered to help wherever she needed. Manny went on to describe Akiko's birth and that Lian was there to coach her. He told Aki they were surprised when Laramie added Akihiro's name to the birth certificate, however glad she did. It was upsetting to Laramie to go back to work. At first, when maternity leave was over, Laramie seemed happy to be in an adult environment again. Regardless of her personal thoughts when she returned from Singapore, her description of Akihiro to Akiko was always in the most positive light.

Laramie's stories always had Akihiro working hard and far away. Nevertheless, she told her that her father loved her very much and would see her as soon as he could. Laramie told her never to forget that Daddy will always love her.

As the story continued, Akihiro connected the correlation between Laramie's work, mood and questions regarding children and commitment during her last visit to Singapore. In one sense, he felt awful and wished she had told him of the baby so that he could help. On the other hand, he was angry that she took her frustrations out on him. Slowly, with every story Manny told, Akihiro began to wear.

"I don't excuse her for what she has done. She brought much of this upon herself. Lara had many opportunities to call me and tell me, she chose not to do so." Akihiro leaned back into his chair, running his hand through his hair. "So, what is it exactly that you want from me?"

Manny began, "I don't want to pry but is it possible for you and Laramie to have a relationship again?"

"Again, no punches pulled. You Americans are so different. Anything is acceptable to discuss."

"Whoa, dude. Men are men regardless of your country. I really don't get into the touchy feely stuff. There is a reason for all the questions and I'll get to that," Manny interjected.

After a few rounds of cocktails, the men began to develop a comfortable friendship. Akihiro began to feel as if he knew them for years. Maybe that is why he felt comfortable to continue with the conversation.

"I know this can be strange to hear but, I fell in love with Laramie the first time I saw her at the bar. Yes, very cliché, but it's true. My engagement to Christine was genuine in the beginning. We knew it wouldn't last but promised to be there for each other in face until one of us found someone new. I had no idea Lara was going to be at that dinner. That night after the party when she walked out of the bungalow, I felt as if my world was crashing down around me. I called her several times at Raffles, but no calls were returned. I went to the hotel to talk and gave her an ultimatum, which I regret. A few times, I went over there planning to knock the door down until she listened to me but I held back. When she convinced DEMCOR to buy the land, adjacent to my hotel, out from under me, I did want to strangle her. I tried to reach her at Raffles but they told me she just left for the airport. I was too late to get to her, she was already past Immigration. I tried to get her to come back through but she refused."

"Then we had our fight the last time she visited. She went through all the same problems I did with hotel construction. However, mine were on a personal basis. I couldn't just hand things off to a general contractor. She just couldn't understand that. Of course, I wasn't aware of her situation either.

She told me I would never know what I would be missing. I didn't put any weight into the statement until she called me about Akiko. Now... now I understand the magnitude."

Akihiro went on to tell Manny and Edward that he learned of the office building purchase right before he left for the States. He was furious his brother contacted her, but more so, that he kept Akiko secret. They told him Laramie really put the pressure on Shinji regarding that deal. Shinji didn't stand a chance. Aki told them Laramie was not aware that he knew about the sale. He asked them not tell her since it no longer made a difference.

"I have to tell you Akihiro, the night she called you to tell you about Akiko, I was there. She did not want to make that phone call. We had to convince her, even though she knew it was the right thing. She agreed this had gone on too far and for too long. When she hung up the phone, she was hysterical. I think hearing your voice and not knowing if you would come to San Francisco scared her the most. Nothing matters more to her than Akiko. She kept sobbing and saying, 'My daughter can die and it's all because I was too afraid to tell him about her. Too afraid to say I still loved him. Too afraid of everything.' Man, she's been in love with you since her first visit to Singapore. It crushed her when you hung up. Anyway, we tried to quiet her but it didn't work. We eventually had to call her physician to come and sedate her. I don't mean to get *sensitive* on you gentlemen, but that point just about sent me over the edge."

Edward stepped in to say, "We were so relieved the day Lara told us you had showed up at the hospital. I must say, I personally was going to fly to Singapore and plead with you to help Akiko. Those girls are the only family I have. Nothing would have stopped me."

Akihiro set his drink on the table and bent forward, with his elbows on the table and his face planted in his hands. He covered his emotions, yet he felt so much of the heartache return. *So many twists and turns. Why do women make it all so complicated? Why did I have to bait her into arguments? Or make her jealous? We've both behaved like school kids. I should have just been direct with my feelings.* Manny patted him on the back and told him it could still be fixed, it wasn't too late. Akihiro raised his head and wiped his hand over his mouth.

He sighed heavily, looked directly at Edward and then Manny and said, "What do I have to do?"

"Well, all right! We were hoping you would feel that way. God knows what we would have done if you said 'no' We put everything into this long shot. Yesterday, she made mention her feelings haven't changed for you but she wouldn't elaborate what they were. Though when she said she signed the petition and conceded on all items, it only confirmed our thoughts."

Edward, in an attempt to lighten the mood, proclaims, "Well, I don't know about you men, but I am ready to eat." Manny agreed. Akihiro nodded his head, not certain if he had the stomach to hold down food.

How can so much transpire in twenty-four hours? He was certain this morning that Laramie was out to get him one more time. He thought he had her figured out. He was prepared to out-maneuver her. *What did I miss between last night and this morning? I was too bullheaded to listen to her.* He didn't count on the fact that they still loved each other despite the fights. *Where there signals at the hotel that I missed? Yes, when she said she was tired of the fight.* He was so sure she was there for a fight. *Why didn't she tell me how she really felt? Did I really give her the chance? No. I basically kicked her out of the room after I ticked her off one more time.* He wanted to be with her and Akiko.

As the men ate, Manchu discussed the plan they devised. It seemed everyone had a hand in this except for Laramie and him. Elizabeth was the most devious overall. The young men questioned her ability to get Laramie to follow.

"Apparently, you have underestimated the power of a Southern woman." Edward smiled.

Manchu and Edward vowed they would not misjudge her again. Liz constructed the plan at the courthouse, flawlessly.

Manny decided they should call Elizabeth and put her on speakerphone. No one could describe the plan in better detail than she could.

"Hello, Manchu darlin'. I was wonderin' when y'all would get back to me. Did everything go as planned at the courthouse?" she said in a heavy southern drawl.

"As a matter of fact, it did," Akihiro interrupted.

"Well, it is so nice to finally meet you, Akihiro. I've been waitin' a long time, honey. I am terribly sorry this meetin' was not under better circumstances. I love Laramie to death but sometimes that ole gal needs a southern kick in the drawers to get her moving," she laughed. "Y'all need to be really discreet or she *will* catch on. I believe Lian has a birthday coming up, does she not?"

"This weekend, you are correct," Manny tried to say under his breath, "as always."

"I heard that Mr. Chinaman. I may be an old horse but I ain't a deaf one," Lizzie quickly retorted.

By now, Akihiro can't help but laugh. These new friends seemed as though they have been his for years. He understood why Laramie smiled when she spoke of them. So many different backgrounds yet, they all had the same sense of humor. He knew they would be there for Laramie no matter the circumstance. They were her family.

"Tell me what you need from me," Akihiro volunteered.

"Now that's what I love to hear, a man who knows his place. You other two can learn something from this foreigner. God, Akihiro, I love you myself. Actually darlin', all you need to do is show up early. Edward, sugar, you need to arrange the suite at the hotel for Friday night. Manny, most of the work is yours. Tell Laramie, you are having a party for Lian's birthday. Since you Chinese have so many relatives, your place is too small. You need space for all the people so you need the hospitality suite."

"Yes, Elizabeth. I can relay this to Lian. I have never seen anyone keep a straight face better than my wife."

Akihiro sat in amazement as he listened to all the planning. *How does such a woman come up with these bits and pieces and yet, do it so far away?* As the table continued to plan, Akihiro faded out of the conversation. *Am I doing the right thing? What do I say to her when I see her? How do I act?* He knew he might see Laramie at the hospital this afternoon. *Can I keep this hidden for a week? Will she suspect anything?* Aki knew this was a chance worth taking. For Akiko's sake, he needed it to work. He came so far to meet his daughter and fall in love with her mother all over again. The years of fighting and anger released from his heart. *There is no mistake, I will be with her again.*

"Akihiro? Akihiro, are you with us? Eventually, it all comes down to you. We can place you in the perfect scenario, but when Laramie walks through that door, you are on your own, darlin'. If you don't tell her the truth, it may be over for good. She will be angry with us but we can handle that."

"I know that, Elizabeth. I don't even know how to thank you for what you're doing. I would not have thought this possible a week ago. I still love her …her and Akiko. No mistakes."

Manny put his hand up to high five and Aki met it. They said their goodbyes and ended the call with Elizabeth. Manny looked at his watch and say, "Damn, we got to get going. Edward, I'll drive you back to your office before I go to mine. Akihiro, I'd give you a lift but I don't want anyone seeing us together. You understand, right, Brother?"

Edward grabbed the check and threw the cash down on the table. He stood up and met Akihiro next to him. Aki put his hand out to shake it and Edward grabbed it. Edward put his other arm around Aki and patted him on the back. "My Son, we will get this back on track. Otherwise, I will have you both locked in a room until it's settled. Now get to that hospital and kiss my little angel for me."

Edward sat in his office and looked out the window. He felt rather smug about the plan they hatched. If all went as planned, he wouldn't hear from Laramie until Saturday afternoon. He picked up the phone and dialed the receptionist. "Linda, I need you to reserve the penthouse suite at the Grand

Hyatt for Friday night. Yes, next Friday," he repeated. "Put the reservation in the name of Manchu Tién. Make sure it's stocked and put the charges on my credit card also."

Akihiro exited the elevator on the children's floor. The nurses all shuffled to get a glimpse. After numerous visits, he still found their attention unsettling. He brushed it off since they treated his daughter excellently. Even the doctors on her case were generous with their time. He found it hard to comprehend he had been there three weeks already. Akihiro wanted this to work out. However, Laramie was a cause of great concern. *Are Manny and Edward sure this is how she really feels? Elizabeth is her best friend. Surely, she would be aware of Laramie's true thoughts. She made herself clear after she was served and again last night. But that was also out of anger.*

As Aki walked into the hospital room, Laramie startled him. He didn't expect to see her in the room alone. It was time for 'his' half day. She looked up to meet his eyes and didn't move.

"I'm sorry but I didn't expect to see you here. I mean, at the hearing they said you felt too ill to be there. I thought you would be at home or something."

"Yes, the hearing. I'm sure Kevin covered me well."

"Why Laramie? Why did you concede?" he asked earnestly.

"I have my reasons, nothing more. Now that you have what you wanted, does this mean you will be returning to Singapore soon?" She sat emotionless.

"Actually, I'm not really sure. Everyone seems to be maintaining the business well. I was hoping to spend some time with Akiko outside of the hospital. That is if Dr. Patel feels she's up to it."

"I'm sure he doesn't have a problem. They plan to release her later today. She will still need rest. I suppose if you want to see her, some type of arrangements can be made. Call ahead first though." Laramie did her best to maintain her composure. *He succeeded in court, what more does he want? Gee, months ago you couldn't leave your hotel for three days. Now you are in no hurry back. Don't let him fluster you.* Laramie pulled out a business card from her purse and inscribed something on it. "Here, this is our address on the back. My cell phone number is on the front." As she handed him the card, his hand brushed against hers. Even through her anger, her heart raced as she felt that sensation of his touch. Just then, Akiko came into the room.

"Mama. Dada. Bye bye." exclaimed Akiko.

"Hi Sweetie. I am so happy to take you home today." said Laramie as she picked Akiko up from under her arms. She kissed her all over her face and nibbled on her neck. Akiko squirmed and giggled, as she tried to make her mother stop.

"Akiko, I will come and see you tomorrow. If that works out for you, Lara," he said as he posed the question to Laramie.

Without thinking, Laramie blurted, "I suppose it is inevitable."

He walked toward Laramie and Akiko, and bent over to kiss Akiko. "I'll come over tomorrow and we can play then. I love you." He kissed her again and ran his hand around the sides of her face. He looked at Laramie and said, "I'll call in the morning."

Akihiro walked back out of the room and headed for the elevator. *Whew! That could've gone wrong.*

* * *

Akihiro exited the main doors of the Children's Hospital. He raised his hand and hailed a cab. Slowly through the traffic, a yellow taxi emerged. Aki opened the door and asked the driver to take him to the Japanese Tea Garden in Golden Gate Park, only a few blocks away. As they entered the park, he felt a sense of peacefulness within. He glanced out the windows and watched a tight group of bikes expand on the roadway. People ran and walked down the asphalt paths. The large trees overhead provided a blanket of shade with bits of sun flickering through the holes. He missed the greenery of Singapore. While San Francisco was beautiful in its own right, nothing matched a person's comfort of their homeland. He paid the cab driver and exited the car.

Looking up at the main gate, it reminded him of being in Japan with his family visiting his father's relatives. Akihiro walked up the steps, entered inside the gate, then stopped and paid his admission. As he looked around, the scenery was quite peaceful. Purple irises grew along the edge of the pond. The water was still except for the Koi fish that swam below, eager for someone to throw them a morsel of food. Aki walked along the path and climbed the steps of the Drum Bridge. The panorama stunned him, making it hard to believe he was in a busy city. Topiaries leaned over the pond. The maple trees brimmed with new buds that anticipated the day they would open to maturity. To the rear of the view was a cherry tree covered in delicate white blossoms. Aki left the bridge, heading for the Tea House. As he turned the corner, he greatly admired the Hagiwara Gate, in its Shinto architecture.

Akihiro needed this oasis. He knew there were so many things that needed to happen in the next week. He ordered a tea from the salesperson inside. She was short and petite, and reminded him of his Aunt Matsuko. She delicately poured the cup and handed it to Akihiro. He bowed respectfully at the waist and thanked the woman. He walked over to an outdoor wooden table and sat, admiring the view. He began to think ahead anxiously. *What do I say to Laramie tomorrow morning? How long do I stay there? Do I try to talk with her or wait for the party night? What seemed so easy in the hospital now appears more challenging.* There were too many variables for Aki to control. He sipped his tea slowly as he basked in the warmth of the sunlight.

As the Tea House became crowded with tourists, Akihiro took it as his queue to walk the garden. He strolled over to the Buddha. With his hands together, he bowed his head and asked for guidance and wisdom. The tranquility of the garden reminded him of the botanical park at home. He walked past the pagoda and through the temple gate. The smell of wisteria blew in the gentle breeze. Ahead was a bench and Akihiro decided to sit and people watch. *How funny Americans can be with cameras. They take pictures in front everything.* An elderly woman yelled across the water to her companion. Akihiro wondered which of them was deaf. *Why do they speak so loud?* Obviously, there was no peace available when the tour busses came.

* * *

The evening sky cleared and dusk settled in. Laramie buckled Akiko in her safety seat and closed her door. Laramie sat in her car and fastened her safety belt. She smiled in her child mirror, so happy to see Akiko back in her familiar spot. *We are going home.* The long days and nights at the hospital were finally over. *Life can get back to normal. Normal? What am I going to do when Akihiro calls in the morning? I can't face him in a private setting yet. I wonder what else he has hidden. How am I ever to trust that?*

As the car rolled over the hill on Fillmore Street, Laramie was happy to be only a few blocks from home. She picked up her cell phone and dialed Francesca's number.

"Hola, Francesca. Bueños dias. ¿Cómo esta usted?"

"Aha, hola Señora Holden. ¿Cómo es mi ángel, Akiko?" Francesca replied.

"She is healing great. In fact, we are on our way home. Francesca, do you think you can start taking care of Akiko tomorrow? I know this is short notice. I really need to have you there. Her father is coming to visit in the morning and I really don't want to be there."

"Akiko's Papa? Aquí? De Singapur? You say mañana, sí?"

"Si, mañana. ¿Puede venir usted aquí?" Laramie responded with desperation. *Please, please, say yes you will be there.*

"Sí, sí, mañana. Bueños noches, Senora."

Yes! Francesca can greet Akihiro in the morning. Laramie's face showed the relief she felt inside. She needed to remember this when payday arrived and add something extra in the check.

After the car turned onto North Point, Laramie saw her flat. She was fortunate tonight to have a parking space right in front of the doors. She knew that any property in the city was a hot commodity and that included parking spaces.

"Yeah, we are home!" exclaimed Laramie.

Laramie carried Akiko on her hip while she tried to get her keys out of her purse. The flat was so quiet without Akiko running around. She truly missed the giggling and cuddling. She placed her daughter in her high chair with a few of her toys so she could run downstairs and retrieve the rest of her things from the hospital.

Laramie hurried down to the car and ran into Manny and Lian. "What brings you two out tonight?"

"Lian wanted to come by and see Akiko. Actually I did too," admitted Manny. "Laramie, why don't you let me take this up for you?" He grabbed the suitcase out of her hand and shut the trunk of her car. "Let's go."

Laramie opened the door and entered first, Lian followed behind her. Manny walked directly to the counter and placed the suitcase nearby. He headed to the refrigerator and grabbed a water. "Lian, you want water too?" She nodded yes.

Lian moved to the edge of the sofa, hugging Akiko tightly. "We missed seeing you at home. I know you were tired of the hospital too."

"We all needed to escape that place," Laramie added. "Unfortunately, my past is still haunting me."

Manny and Lian turned their heads back to Laramie. "Why's that?" Lian was first to ask.

"Well, Akihiro was at the hospital earlier today. You would've thought he'd be out celebrating his big win. Anyway, he asked to come over tomorrow to spend time with Akiko. Nothing like putting me on the spot. When does he go back to Singapore anyway?"

"Well that can be a good thing. It would give you a chance to talk," Manny suggested.

"No way, not after the hearing. I don't want to talk about the concession. I don't need him pressing me."

"*Concession*? You didn't fight him? Why the change of mind?" Manny inquired.

"Yes, I conceded. I went to settle with him last night—"

Lian jumped in. "What do you mean *settle*? You tried to settle this with him?"

"Long story. Anyway, he refused to settle. He would've lost but he was too arrogant to see that. Anyway, after I left, I tried to think fairly, which was difficult. I didn't want to fight anymore. Kiki deserves both parents. I felt I kept her away from him and his family long enough. I have to trust him to take care of her and he has to trust me on this."

"I have to say I am really proud of you. I know that had to be difficult for you to do," Manny said.

"Nevertheless, I have Francesca here tomorrow. I figure I can leave before he gets here and go to the office for a while. Francesca can call me when he's gone."

"Laramie, eventually you need to talk. Akiko needs some stability right now. She knows he's here and she's bonding so well with him. You have painted him a prince to her. She needs to see the interaction to believe it." Lian was always the most levelheaded of the group.

"She's right, Lara. You can't keep going at this rate. I know the hearing was totally emotional for you but see it from another prospective. He has a daughter. He loves her and wants to be a part of her life. That includes you whether you like it or not. You will always have a connection no matter how hard you try to run from him."

"*Run?* You have to be kidding. I'm not running. I just don't feel the need to converse with him. His visit is with Akiko, not me. So, that's who will be here when he comes," Laramie jumped to respond. "Now he wants to spend as much time as he can with her until he leaves. Why should I have to accommodate his daily schedule?"

"You know Laramie, you are my friend and I generally agree with most of your ideas, but not now. He is her father and he does have rights," Manny jabbed back.

"Rights, oh yes, he has rights. The right to lie to me. The right to sue me behind me back. What are you on his side now?" retorted Laramie.

"Both of you stop it," Lian jumped in. "Enough. You don't want Akiko to hear you. You're both adults, so just stop it. It is obvious we all have issues to work out. Manny sit down. Laramie calm down. It amazes me that you aren't true siblings sometimes."

"You're right. Laramie, I'm sorry. Really." Manny walked over to her and hugged her.

"I'm sorry too Manny. So many things going on, I guess the stress is just getting to me," she said as she hugged him back.

"Well then, I have a solution. I have convinced Manny to have my birthday at the Grand Hyatt, in one of the suites no less. Our place is too small for our family. Besides, I want it to be great. I won't have time for any big celebrations once the baby comes."

"*Baby?* Lian, are you pregnant? Oh my God, why didn't you tell me?"

Laramie asked. "You have to be so excited. I am so excited for you. You both will be so great at parenting. Look how well you take care of me!"

"Well now you know the reason for the big celebration. I can't drink but the party will be fun."

"Oh wait, I'm not sure I can make it with Akiko and all. I couldn't leave her."

"Too late, Lara. You have already said you are leaving her with Francesca tomorrow. There is no reason you can't have her baby sit Friday night too. No excuses," Lian pressed.

"You caught me. I don't think I can talk my way out of this one," Laramie accepted.

"Good. Then we will see you Friday night around eight o'clock. Oh yeah, I'll give you a call tomorrow night to see how visitation went. Manny, are you ready to go?" Lian knew she trapped Laramie this time. *So far, everything is going smooth. Let's hope we're all friends after this.*

Manny and Lian walked over to Akiko's door. "Come here, Sweetie. We have to get going and I want a kiss and hug before I leave." Akiko walked over to the door holding her Teddy and stood on her tiptoes.

"I'll walk you to the door," said Laramie politely.

Chapter 70

RIGHT ON CUE, the house phone rang at eight o'clock, just as Laramie served Akiko breakfast. Hesitantly, Laramie picked up the phone. The St. Francis Hotel's phone number showed up on the caller I.D.

"Hello?" she said in a cheery voice, as she pretended she didn't know who called.

"Laramie, its Akihiro. I was wondering if it was acceptable to come over around ten. If not just let me know, I can make it later." Akihiro stood in his hotel room. He knew Laramie wanted to cancel the whole thing but he remained firm.

Trying to be ever so nonchalant, she replied, "Oh that's right, you have a play date today. Sure, I think ten o'clock is fine. Akiko is just eating breakfast now. I will have her cleaned up and ready to play when you get here."

"That sounds great. Bye," responded Aki. *I know she's mad, she can't act that well.*

Laramie realized she needed to rush and shower. She put Akiko in her high chair and wheeled it into the bathroom. She gave her a few toys to play with and hoped she found that acceptable. *Ah, my own shower. This feels so good. I missed the comforts of my home.*

"Señora Holden, estoy aquí," said Francesca in her broken English.

"I'm just about done dressing. I will be out in a moment." *Great, she is here early.* Laramie threw on her dark denim jeans with a long sleeve sweater, and ankle boots. She tied her hair up, though a few tendrils fell off to the side. She gazed at herself in the mirror. *Wow! I look damn good, ready to face the public. I look alive again. I missed sleeping in my own bed.*

"Francesca, I am so glad you could make it. Gracias. Muchas gracias,"

Laramie responded with a hug. "Akiko has already eaten breakfast. I've already given her vitamins. Mr. Amori should be here around ten o'clock. Call me when he leaves, por favor. Also, there is food en el refrigerador. I shopped yesterday morning." *Eventually, my Spanish will get better.* "Otherwise, call me if you need me." Laramie leaned over and kissed Akiko. "You have a fun day, Baby, and I will see you later. I love you."

Laramie grabbed her purse and a jacket and ran out the door. *Whew, I made it. Now, I can have some quiet time at work.*

Akihiro jumped out of a cab in front of Laramie's building. He looked up at the structure. *This is where she lives. It doesn't have the same style as Singapore. Rather plain.* He wondered what it looked like inside, and how the décor reflected the woman. *Let's see if it tells a story about her.* He was nervous. With all the history they shared, it still flustered him when he saw her. He no longer doubted his love for her. His worry was the contempt and curtness she had toward him. *Why should I be worried? I haven't done anything wrong. I only asked for my rights as a father. She's the emotional one. She can't be mad about this forever.* Feeling some new found strength, he rang the doorbell promptly at ten. Akihiro waited for the buzzer, and then opened the door.

He knocked on the door prepared to greet Laramie. When Francesca answered the door, it surprised him. *She must be the nanny.*

"Good day, Señor …I mean Mr. Amori. Please come in." Francesca stood to the side of the door and Aki passed her.

"Is Miss Holden here?" He looked around the place. It had a softer feel to it, yet still traditional. The mix of baby toys on the floor made the space smaller. He noticed Laramie painted the pictures on the wall. *I didn't know that she had that talent. Though I've found there are many things I didn't know about her. I've learned so much this trip.*

"Dada, Dada." Akiko held her arms up. He picked her up and hugged her tightly. He wondered how he could love her more each time he saw her. He showered her with kisses, and spun her around.

"Hello, my little love. Just a minute though." Akiko was eager to play. "Is Miss Holden home?" Aki looked around, then out the windows, out to the bay. *What a beautiful view with the fog slowly burning off.*

"I am sorry Mr. Amori, but the Señora has gone into the office," explained Francesca. "Can I help you?"

"No, no, it's okay."

So, this is how Laramie wants to handle conflict, always on the run. It is one thing for her to avoid me, but Akiko just got out of the hospital last night. Her place is here with her daughter. He began to question the plan on Saturday night. *Are they sure that she is still in love with me? I am doubting their knowledge some and hate is looking really strong. Is she still so mad that she couldn't be in the same room?*

Akiko walked him into her room. *This looks like the Botanic Gardens.* He looked around at the bandstand painted behind her crib. One wall had the bonsai plants he loved. Another wall had the heliconias and orchids Laramie loved. Butterflies were on the wall and hung from the ceiling. *She gave Akiko a piece of Singapore in her room.* He glanced at her nightstand and recognized the picture of him from the hospital. *It's right where Manny said it would be.* It confused him that she went out of her way to keep him alive for Akiko but she won't meet him face to face. *I know… confrontation.*

They played on the floor for quite a while before Akihiro settled in the chair in Akiko's room. His arm was around Akiko as she nestled closer to her father. As Akiko pointed out the different animals in the book, he felt content with *his* daughter next to him. It felt so natural. He never gave fatherhood any thought before this trip. Now, he couldn't imagine life without Akiko.

The house phone rang. Akihiro heard Francesca answer it in Spanish. He figured it was Laramie checking up on the visit. He wished she were there. *She needs to see we are a family. I'm not out to take Kiki away.* After a few minutes, she hung up.

"That's right. I need to finish reading the story." He grabbed her around her waist and held her over his head. "What kind of animal are you? A fish? A bear?"

She giggled.

He picked up one more book, *Goodnight Moon.* He knew it was Laramie's and Akiko's favorite from the hospital. Halfway through the book, Akiko yawned. He laid her flat in her crib with her head on the pillow. He sat on the floor to finish reading. When he glanced up, he saw she was asleep. He placed the book on her nightstand and kissed her.

"I love you my sweet," he spoke quietly as not to awaken her. She fidgeted a little than fell asleep.

Akihiro walked quietly out of Akiko's room. He glanced into Laramie's bedroom and noticed she had the same great view of the bay from her windows. *This seems more like the Laramie I know, softer, similar to the living area but more feminine.* He saw a photograph on the wall of Laramie cradling Akiko as a newborn. Laramie looked so beautiful and peaceful. Her happiness was obvious. Akiko was so tiny, so precious. *I would've been there if only she asked me. Though why would she ask? I was too wrapped up in my hotels to give her any of my time.*

"Are you leaving Señor?" asked Francesca.

Akihiro turned around to answer her and realized that she watched him.

"Yes, and quietly too. When Señora Holden calls, you can tell her I left. It's safe for her to come home now."

Francesca smiled at him. She knew he caught on to the phone calls. She walked him to the door, said good-bye and locked the door behind him. *What a crazy woman, Miss Holden is. He is a good man and loves their daughter too.* Francesca believed she needed to tell her what love means. *No one knows love more than a Latino woman.* Francesca picked up the phone and called Laramie. The coast was clear.

Laramie made it home without any confrontation. She didn't want him to pressure her for a reason for the concession. She felt it was over and the decision was granted. That was enough for her to continue with her future. She wondered when he would ask for Akiko's first visit to Singapore. *Well, at least she has a passport. Though he doesn't know that. That could buy me time on his schedule. How do we even work that? Do I travel to Singapore with her? Does he travel here to get her? Damn, I'll have to talk with him eventually to establish that.*

Laramie thanked Francesca for coming on short notice. She asked her to be there for the following week as well for Akihiro's visitation.

"Senora, he is a very nice man. You can see he loves Akiko mucho. I must say he loves you too."

"Francesca, I know he loves Akiko. As for me, I believe you are mistaken. Maybe a long time ago but not anymore. We've had muchos problemas más de muchos años."

"No. No mistake. I see the way he looks at you in photos. I hear the way he describes you to Akiko. That is not hate. Latino women know all about love."

Laramie smiled at her persistence. She no longer believed that after the hearing. The lawsuit carried all the misery of a fictitious divorce.

"Either way, it will all be the past when he goes back to Singapore. I'm fairly sure he'll stop a few more times before then and I really don't want to speak with him. It would be easier on me to have you here. We'll just do the same thing as today and call me when he leaves."

"I will do that, Señora. See you on Monday."

"Gracias, Francesca."

Laramie walked her to the door. She sat on her sofa and relaxed a while since Akiko was asleep. *Love? I really believed in that at one time. Now I wonder if he ever really felt that way. He certainly moved on easily enough. I don't know what hurts more the fact he let go of us or that he found someone else. This isn't how imagined my life to be with him. Either way, I don't know how to move ahead. I'll see him every few months. How do I get past that constant reminder?* Laramie blotted her tears away. She went into the kitchen to prepare lunch for Akiko. She knew her daughter would awaken soon.

Chapter 71

AKIHIRO SPENT HIS morning at the Karate studio. He stretched out better and did not attempt any moves that could injure him. The exercise and meditation helped relieve the stress of the situation with Laramie.

When Akihiro arrived back at his hotel, he noticed he had a phone message. He assumed it was Laramie but was mistaken.

"*Hey, Akihiro. It's Manny. I have to think you have a lot of time on your hands and wondered if you wanted to meet out for a few beers on Tuesday night. Call me on my cell phone, the number is …*"

Akihiro wrote the number down. He was glad to hear from him. *This week will be tough not seeing Akiko or Laramie every day.* He figured he would schedule visits every other day. *Of course, I have to call Laramie regarding that. Will she take the calls or have the nanny do that too?* He called Manny back and agreed to meet out on Tuesday. He felt better with the camaraderie of another guy in town. He planned to ask Manny of things to do alone in the city since his tour guide left him.

Later in the afternoon, he decided to call Laramie to schedule visits. He planned to avoid the subject of her not being at the flat. He decided to discuss that on Friday night.

"Hello?"

"Laramie, it's Akihiro. I wanted to talk to you about seeing Akiko this week if you have a minute."

She anticipated this and prepared herself for the call.

"Sure. Do you want ten o'clock on Monday, Wednesday and Friday? Like yesterday." She didn't mean to mention yesterday. She didn't want to hear his thoughts on her leaving Akiko with Francesca.

"That's fine. Do you mind if I take her to the park? I didn't know how you felt about her leaving your home."

"Um…" She paused. "She can go but please make sure she is bundled up. I'll have her coat and mittens out. Is there anything else?"

Yes! Why are you being so difficult? Why can't you just stay home and talk with me?

"No, that's all I have. Thanks."

Gee, that'll free up your nights for dating. Maybe she'll find you aren't her type and dump you. I really shouldn't think that, it isn't very nice. Besides, it always comes back to bite me. Let's face it, my luck is awful when it comes to him. I don't need the added grief.

Laramie called Lian afterwards. She needed to vent to someone who understood the situation.

"Lian, I don't know how much more I can take of this. I am being pleasant even if it kills me. I told him to visit Kiki every other day. Though, I am surprised he didn't mention Francesca. I thought I'd hear a lecture for that. His new girlfriend must be alleviating his frustrations."

"Lara, you don't know that. I'm telling you, there is something going on. I haven't figured it out yet. But if he were seeing someone else, he wouldn't be pleasant to you, in fact, the opposite because he wouldn't care how mad you got. Come on, you're the specialist and you don't see red flags up anywhere?"

"I know what you're saying but when it comes to him, I don't think straight. He flusters me too much. How did I become this emotional wreck?"

"Love, my dear. We all go through it pretty much the same way. Manny and I bickered quite a bit after we became engaged. First, it was over the wedding, then where we would live. I was never fond of working at the market, even more so now that I'm pregnant. The smell disgusts me."

"Well, the smell disgusts me and I'm not pregnant." They laughed. "Since I have you on the phone, I need some ideas for a birthday gift," Laramie asked.

"That goes both ways. I didn't forget yours is on the first. And your gifts have to be the most difficult to buy."

"Easy answer, don't buy me anything," Laramie answered.

"Lara… you know that won't work. Come on, there must be something you've been eyeing."

"I've got a great idea. Why don't we go out Wednesday night and you can buy me dinner? This way we get to see each other and talk about the baby."

"Great, that works for me. I'll come up with a few ideas and you do the same. We'll compare them and pick whatever sounds the best."

"You should be a referee. I don't know if Manny could ever win an argument with the straight sense you speak. You'd be a great closer at a trial."

"I'll pass. I have all the headaches I need. I'll chat with you later. Kiss Akiko for me."

Laramie knew Lian was a stabile force in her life. If she wanted revenge, she would call Elizabeth. If she wanted to party without guilt, call Gillian. If she wanted a good drag out fight, call Manny. She relied on each of their characteristic differences and subtleties. That kept her balanced. *They all thought I was this completely together person before Singapore, now look at me. I'm an emotional mess.*

Chapter 72

MONDAY MORNING RIGHT at ten, Akihiro arrived at the flat and once again, Francesca greeted him at the door.

"I'm not going to ask if she's here. I already know the answer."

"Lo siento, Señor. I am so sorry. Miss Holden is not at home. I try to talk with her but she is stubborn woman."

"Thank you Francesca. I know she is stubborn. Please do not risk your job over this. It really isn't important. Is Akiko ready to go?"

"Sí. She needs her coat. Her stroller is in the first floor storage room. It is near the side door. I will be here if you need anything. I have a bag with a bottle for her and snacks."

"Gracias. I didn't think of a bottle. I can find the stroller on my own." Akihiro picked up Akiko and kissed her playfully. "We will be back in a short while."

He carried her down the elevator and found the storage room. After a few trials and errors, he figured out how to fasten her in the stroller. *This is a foreign concept for me. No one I know has children. Why won't it push forward?* After a short investigation, he realized the stroller had foot brakes on it. *I suppose with all the hills here that brakes are a necessary thing.*

He pushed Akiko in the shady side of the street; he didn't want the sun in her eyes. As they reached the playground at Moscone Rec. Center, Akiko began to squeal with delight. She saw her swings and wanted to climb out of the stroller. *I see why they fasten kids in now. Calm down, Akiko. We are almost there.* He parked her stroller near the swings and began the process to free her. After he set her inside the seat, he noticed how loose it was. Afraid she'd fall out, he looked around for something to place inside. One of the regular mother's watched from the bench. She recognized Akiko and noticed how alike they looked together. She introduced herself and told Akihiro she often spoke with Francesca at the park. He explained that he was Akiko's father in town for a visit. She offered a blanket to stuff behind his daughter on the swing. He thanked her graciously. *It seems that works perfectly.*

Laramie was correct when she said Akiko loved the swings. Every time he stopped to pull her out, she cried. *Eventually, you will have to come out of there. I will have to take you home and it won't be hanging from a swing. I could picture Laramie's face right now.* He felt brave and quickly removed her from the swing. Akiko moaned at first. He carried her off to the slide to see if she would go down it. The first time he held her tightly. *So far, so good.* Akiko wasn't sure what to think about this new ride. After the second time, he gradually lessened the hold on her. She rapidly became aware of her speed and didn't like it, in addition to the bump on her head at the bottom when she fell back. He picked her up and admitted Laramie was correct on this ride too. *She must've tried them all with the same results.*

After an hour or so, Akihiro arrived back at the flat with Akiko. She slowly began to nod out on the stroll home and he talked to her to keep her awake. He carried her up to her room and placed her in her crib not before he kissed her goodbye. He hated to leave her but he knew Laramie would call soon to see if he left. *I really hope we work this out. Two hours a day, every other day isn't going to cut it.* He didn't want to think about going back to Singapore without Akiko or Laramie.

He said his goodbyes to Francesca and told her he would be back on Wednesday. She extended her normal courtesies. Once he was gone, she called Laramie and told her Akihiro left. Laramie inquired how the visit went. Her nanny said she didn't see them until they came back from the park. But she said, it must've been fun since Akiko was so tired and fell asleep quickly.

Chapter 73

EARLIER IN THE day, Manny called Akihiro to meet him at the 21st Amendment Brewery on 2nd Street, in the Financial District. They planned on dinner and a few beers to break up the workweek.

Akihiro arrived first at the joint. He noticed the architecture was reminiscent of the shop houses in Singapore. However, the name of the brewery escaped his knowledge to understand that it represented the amendment having to do with prohibition. When he walked inside, it was crowded with patrons. The u-shape bar greeted him first. He walked around it to the hostess podium and asked for a table. She happily walked him along the left wall to the second booth. All the furniture was made from wood and the center benches were similar to old church pews. The high ceiling held globe style fixtures, which provided enough light for Akihiro to see Manny arrive. He waved Manny over to the booth. The men shook hands before Manny sat completely down.

"How's it going? You didn't have any trouble finding the place, did you?"

"No, your directions were on the mark. I got here a few minutes ago. I haven't even ordered a beer yet. Which ones are the best here?"

"I, myself, like the I.P.A. It's one of their most popular. Unless you really like Guinness, then stay off the darker ones. Heavy."

"Do you work near here?"

"Yeah, I started a new job at a company down the road. It does a lot of business with GMH. Actually, Laramie got me in the door. That's the toughest part in this city. Very competitive."

"Your background is in finance, so what exactly do you do there?"

"I manage preferred customer accounts. I started at GMH right out of high school in the mail room. That's how I met Laramie. She spent her summers and vacations as an intern to Edward and Andrew. Anyway, we became really good friends over that time. When I was able to go to college full time, I became the driver for them so my days were flexible for classes."

"Did you date or anything?"

"Oh, no way. She's like a sister to me. Besides, I met Lian early my freshman year and we got married the following summer."

"She's the last hold out, besides Andrew, that I haven't met."

"Well, I hate to inform you but you did meet her. Actually, she was the first one you met. You were fortunate enough to walk into my parents market in Chinatown. I believe she sold you fruit and tea."

Akihiro laughed as he pounded his fist on the table. "You're joking? Well, that explains how Laramie knew what I bought that day. She claimed it was a 'small' town. I remember her now that you bring up the location. I'm going to have to pay more attention to the people around me."

"Don't be fooled by that statement. Laramie knows a ton of people in this city and even more know her. You've never walked the city with her. She knows half the homeless by first name, every judge, the mayor and his cabinet, and most every politician and all their families. She's probably the safest person to have at your side."

"That's what I hear. I have to say it was a shock to learn who she really was after I got here. I thought she was just another lawyer." Manny laughed out loud at that statement.

The waitress showed up and both men ordered the 21st I.P.A. She asked if they were ready to order but both men said they needed more time.

"Yeah, I can see how you would think that. I did too when I first met her. I thought she was staff at the firm. I didn't know she was *the* Holden. We hung out together, ate lunch often and partied on the weekends before an associate pulled my aside to hand me the lowdown. I couldn't believe it. Hey, don't let that throw you off. She isn't the type for all the hype you hear. She stays away from that as much as she can."

"My attorney thought it was a joke when I told him who I was suing. I had no idea. He gave me quite the history lesson. Between her parents, her career and her assets, I was amazed."

"Assets, yeah, don't bring that up to her. She gets furious about that. I think you were the only reason she took a draw on that. I don't mean to bring up bad blood."

"No, it worked out for the best. Just on a different timeline. I have a hard time believing she is the same woman I met in Singapore. She is so different from the stories I hear now."

"Really, how so? She never talked much about Singapore when she came back. We knew about you but not a great deal. She'd get upset so we didn't want to push it. And believe me, it had to take a lot for Laramie to get upset. She doesn't show her emotions easily."

Akihiro laughed. "You haven't seen the side I have. Did she say anything about the beginning when we first met?'

"No, at least not to me. Lian tried to get her to open up but she wouldn't."

Akihiro began with the bumboat ride and the water dousing. Then, he continued with the Singapore Flyer. Manny knew she was afraid of heights and couldn't believe she actually went inside the car. Then, Aki continued with trip to sing Karaoke.

"Oh man, say you didn't. She is the worst singer by far. The seals bark at Pier 39 when she gets near. I refused to let her sing in the limo unless the privacy window's closed."

"I never thought of the seals. That is so accurate."

Akihiro spoke about the beer nose spray at Brewerkz and the fight at the Moon Festival. He continued with the boat trip and her drunken stupor but not in detail. Manny roared at the stories.

"Laramie was afraid to do anything in Singapore for fear of what came next. My brother Shinji never laughed so hard. I never laughed so hard. Her luck was better the third time around. She has a great sense of humor. But, damn, that woman can snore."

"Ask her about camping sometime when this is over. She came with a group of us up to Tahoe. She was the first to fall asleep. Within minutes, we were scared to death that we had rabid animals around the camp. It was *her*. We growled around her for months before Lian ratted us out."

Akihiro held his stomach as he laughed. He needed this break and this laughter to get him through the next few days. He carried a lot of tension as he anticipated their hotel meeting.

A waitress came by and took their orders. Manny ordered the tortilla soup and fish tacos. Akihiro decided to play it safe with the Southern Steak salad. He was amazed at how much American food was fried. Accustomed to a leaner, healthier diet, some of his menu choices brought adverse reactions to his body.

"Manny, I have to say I'm glad you called. I was going crazy in my hotel room. Outside of going to the Karate studio in the mornings, I don't know what to do with my time. I don't know what areas to see."

"Well the first thing I would suggest is getting a ticket to see the Giants play. Home opener isn't until next week but they have three training games in a row on Wednesday thru Friday. Actually, Friday is out for you."

"The Giants?"

"Baseball. Good old American baseball. The stadium is right down 3rd Street a few blocks off the square. They have the best hotdogs and beer. Take my word on that."

"Thanks, that's a great start. Had Laramie and I settled our differences, I could've seen a lot more in the area. We talked about some things but I wanted to see them with her."

"Hey, one other thing before I forget. Tomorrow is Laramie's birthday. One way to make bonus points is to remember it. I know you're stopping there for visitation tomorrow. Lian seems to think I need to know everyone's schedules."

"No, that's great to know. She'll assume Kat sent me the info anyway. I'll have to stop by the florists before I go over there."

The waitress brought out their dinners and placed them on the table. She asked if they needed anything else and Manny replied they were set. The men ate their dinners and spoke of sports and cars. They compared stories of their youths both being from Asian backgrounds. Akihiro invited Manny and Lian to come to Singapore anytime and stay as his guest. He was so appreciative just to have company. Akihiro thanked him again for calling him and helping with Laramie.

After dinner, they shared a cab up to Union Square. Manny agreed to pass on any information he picked up from Laramie prior to the Friday night debate. As Akihiro exited the car, they shook hands and said goodbye.

Akihiro sat in his room pleased with the way the night flowed. He knew Laramie would be furious to know Manny and he were out together. She would view it as a sign of betrayal at this point. *She's has great friends who care a lot about her. Let's just hope they know her better than she knows herself. Hmm... so she has a birthday tomorrow. I have to think of something amazing to catch her emotions favorably. Orchids? She loved them enough to put them in Akiko's room. What about a lotus blossom? It looks like I have some quick shopping to do in the morning before I visit Akiko.*

Chapter 74

AKIHIRO SLEPT LONGER than he planned. He searched the Internet late last night for a florist and a jeweler nearby for specific items for Laramie. Unfortunately, this put him behind schedule for his visitation time with Akiko. He knew he had to call Laramie and ask to change the hours slightly. He dialed her cell phone and anticipated her mood change.

"Hello?"

"Laramie, its Akihiro. I wanted to ask if I could change my hours slightly today."

"Are you serious or is that a joke?"

"What? Why would I be making a joke?"

"It's April first, April Fool's Day. I'm guessing by your reaction that you don't have a clue what I am saying. Obviously, not a Singapore thing. Never mind. What time do you think you will be here?"

"I plan to be there by eleven o'clock, noon at the latest. Is that all right with you? I just have a few stops to make before I get there and I don't know how long that will take in this city."

"The time is fine. I don't need to know your itinerary." Laramie assumed he was late due to another possible date. She planned to pass right over the subject without losing her temper. After all, it was her birthday. *What a glorious day. The sun is shining and the temperature will be nice. A perfect Spring day in the bay.*

"Great… and thank you for being understanding. I appreciate it." *Why is he sucking up to me today? Is there anything left he could sue me over now?*

"Well, I have to run. I'll pass on your time change to Francesca. Bye."

He remembered in England they had a day for pranks. He didn't remember what the exact date was but now he knew this was a custom in the U.S. as well. *I hope she doesn't view my gift as a prank too.*

He walked up Powell Street until he reached Sutter Street. His first stop was the San Francisco Museum of Craft and Design. He found a specific pendant for her and hoped it would bring back friendly memories. After he entered the building, he felt the rooms were similar to that of a modern museum of art. He noticed the many graphic forms of advertisement and art; however, he was there to locate a specific piece of jewelry. He found an Internet site of an artist whose work was sold there. He inquired where he might find Thea Izzi's jewelry. The store clerk showed him a display case and in the center was the sterling silver and gold lotus flower pendant with a hanging pearl. It was more beautiful in person than in the website photo. The gold inside of the petals reflected the light softly. Its contrast to the outside of the petal in silver added a luminescent quality. The pearl dangling below dressed it up with simplicity. *This is perfect. I hope she likes it.* He purchased the item quickly since his errands weren't finished.

As he continued to walk another block down Sutter Street, he stopped in Jane's Roses flower shop. He wanted an arrangement with orchids and heliconias if it were possible. He inquired if the owner had such flowers in stock. She asked him to wait a moment while she pulled out a photograph of an arrangement. The photo stunned Akihiro since it contained both flowers just as they were painted on Akiko's walls. He asked if he could wait for it to be made and he smiled when she said yes. *I can't believe I am this lucky today. It certainly isn't April Fools for me.* He signed a card to Laramie to be placed in the flowers. The arrangement was taller than he imagined. The storeowner hailed a cab for him since his hands were full and he thanked her graciously.

He buzzed the doorbell for Francesca to let him in. It was quite the juggling act at first. He managed to reach the door but had difficulty when he attempted to knock. He tapped the door with his foot and Francesca opened it quickly.

"Oh Señor, the flowers are beautiful. Miss Holden will be so jealous you brought them for me." She laughed.

He laughed with her. "Actually, today is her birthday. I wanted to surprise her."

He looked around the room unsure where to put them down. Francesca pointed to the granite bar between the dining area and kitchen. Next to the vase, he placed the box with the pendant.

After the chaos settled, he searched for Akiko who played quietly in her room. However, her silence quickly ended when she caught a glimpse of her father. She ran to him with her arms up. She wanted him to pick her up and twirl her by the noise she tried to describe. He kissed her a few times first before he spun her around in circles. He loved every moment he spent with his daughter. He knew it was close to her lunchtime and offered to feed whatever Francesca prepared. After his time with her at the hospital, he knew the tricks to feeding her. Akiko gladly sat in her high chair and waited for Akihiro to create random sounds of the food coming near her. Her appetite increased dramatically since the days of sickness. *I wonder when her follow-up appointment will be with Dr. Patel. I'll have to ask Laramie next time we speak. When will that be?*

After another hour of playtime, Akihiro sadly put Akiko down for her nap. He wished he had more time with her but today wasn't one of those days. After running late, he knew Laramie would be calling soon to see if he left. *I wish this meeting was over. Only two more days. I want to be with her for these occasions not finding out reactions secondhand.*

Shortly after two o'clock, Laramie came home. She assumed Akihiro would be gone. She dropped her things off on her bed and walked out of her room before she noticed the flowers. *Oh my gosh, are they beautiful. It looks like the painting on Akiko's walls. Oh, how I love these flowers.* She looked for a card first. She had a sneaking feeling who sent them.

Dear Laramie,

I really hope you enjoy your birthday.
This all spoke your name.

Love, Akihiro

Laramie smelled the flowers and their sweet scent. His remembrance of her birthday truly surprised her along with her favorite flowers in Singapore. She picked up the square box beside the vase and opened it. *Oh my, I am speechless. This is gorgeous. A lotus flower. How did he find this? Where did he find this? This is why he was late. I really am speechless. Geez, what am I going to do with him? Why did he do this?*

"Qué linda, Señora. That is from him. So beautiful. Here, let me help you."

"Would you? Thanks. I can't believe he did this. I can't believe he remembered any of this. I feel so bad after being snippy on the phone this morning."

Francesca slid together the clasp for Laramie and turned her around. The nanny gasped and smiled. Laramie quickly ran into the bathroom to look into the mirror. *This is exquisite.* Her eyes misted as she stared into the mirror. *He gave me something that represented both of us. Why? Especially after I've been such a bitch. Why would he do this if he's seeing someone else? Why did he have to go and do something so thoughtful and intimate? I have to call him and thank him. I'm afraid to but I know I have to do this.*

"Don't say a word Francesca. I know I have to thank him. I already feel bad enough."

Francesca pretended to zip her lips in response. Laramie knew Francesca's feelings regarding Akihiro. She knew everyone's feelings. *I know I am the last holdout but I have reason to be.*

Laramie's hand shook as she dialed the St. Francis and asked for Akihiro's room. She walked into her bedroom and closed the door behind her. Luckily, she was sent to the message center and didn't have to speak to him directly.

"Oh gosh, Akihiro. I don't even know what to say. I am just speechless. The gifts are breathtaking. I don't know if thank you is enough. A card would've been plenty. I see the memories in your thoughts. I… um… I remember them too. Thank you. It was extremely thoughtful. Bye."

She felt torn by his gifts. She loved the thoughtfulness in his choices and knew he had to search for these items himself. No one else would know the meaning behind the items to be able to find just the right thing. She knew he still cared enough for her to go on such a hunt. However, she didn't want to fall into the same trap only to be hurt again. She still felt deceived by the hearing, not to mention his dating. Her thoughts and emotions conflicted in her body.

She looked into the mirror again to see the beauty of his gift before she opened her door and joined Francesca in the living area.

"He wasn't in but I did leave a message. I will thank him again if he calls."

"His gift has meaning? Not many men would do such a thing even for their wives. He must care muy mucho."

As they spoke, Akiko called out for her mother. Her nap ended just in time for Laramie to end her conversation with Francesca. However, Laramie remembered to ask Francesca to baby-sit Friday night for Lian's party. Laramie didn't need her for the morning because Akiko had a follow up appointment with Dr. Patel. Laramie thanked her as always for coming to sit with Akiko. *The follow up appointment. I forgot to call Akihiro regarding that. I guess can do it again and leave a message since he's out.*

Once again, she dialed his hotel and waited for the message center to answer. However, this time her luck ran out.

"Hello?"

"Akihiro? I… I didn't realize you were back. I called a short time ago and got the recording."

His voice flustered her. She was on the spot for everything now. He noticed by the way she stumbled over her words that she really expected to get voice mail.

"Actually, I just walked in a few minutes ago. I haven't heard my messages yet."

"Oh, well, one of them is from me. Thank you for the gifts. And, for remembering my birthday. I don't know what to say. Both of them are stunning. I'm, uh, quite speechless. You really shouldn't have gone to the trouble but I am touched by your thoughtfulness."

"Lara, you're welcome. I just wanted to do something nice for you, for a change. It reminded me of a time when we were both happy."

Why does he do this to me? Crap, now I'm all choked up.

"We were then. I remember." He could hear her sniffle even though she tried to cover it. "Anyway, the reason for this call was to let you know Kiki has a doctor's appointment Friday morning. I thought you might want to be there. It's at Dr. Patel's office in the medical building next to the hospital. Oh, at nine o'clock."

"I do want to be there. Thanks for telling me. And Lara, happy birthday."

"Thank you again. Bye."

She broke into tears after she hung up. She remembered too clearly the happy times they shared. *I miss him so much. I feel as if someone is tearing out my heart. I can never stay mad at him. But why did this have to become so complicated? Why did we have that hearing? It ruined everything.* She sat on the floor with her elbow on her sofa and cried into her hand. *I'm so confused. I can't stand the thought of him with anyone else.* She caught herself and stopped crying when her phone rang.

"Hello?" She sniffled.

"Hey, it's me. I wondered what your thoughts were for a restaurant tonight."

"Oh, Lian…" Laramie burst into tears. She tried to control herself but was too emotional.

"Lara, what's wrong? Is it Akiko?" Lian inquired rapidly.

"No, she's fine. It's Akihiro." She held the phone away and asked Lian to hold a moment. "I just spoke to Akihiro and he…"

"He what? Did he hurt you again?" Lian's concern grew.

"No. He gave me the most thoughtful present. It reminded me of being in Singapore with him. God, I miss him, Lian. This is just eating at me. I know he'll be going back to Singapore soon and it will all be over then."

"Laramie, listen to me. You need to pull yourself together first. Just calm down. Let's talk, okay?"

Laramie's emotions ran the gamut. For so many years, no one saw that side of her. She was a happy-go-lucky person. Her trip home from Singapore sent her into a new realm she wasn't accustomed to feeling. She truly didn't know how to control herself. Lian knew to proceed slowly.

"Okay." She blew her nose and wiped her face.

"You need to tell him how you feel. You can't keep this inside. That's what's eating at you. Honey, you love him and there isn't anything wrong in that."

"But he doesn't love me."

"You don't know that. Have you asked him directly?"

"No, but he's dating. Isn't that enough?"

"No, it's not. I don't believe the date thing. It all came about too conveniently. And now, he sends you a gift. Lara, you will regret not telling him after he goes home. Please take my advice on this if for no other reason than I'm begging you. Please. I'm your friend and I can't bear to see you hurt like this any longer."

"I will. I promise. I'm supposed to see him at Akiko's doctor appointment on Friday morning. I'll talk with him then." She dried her tears. "Thank you for being my friend. I don't know what I'd do without you and Manny."

"Now just stop it. No more of that. This is what we do. Now, straighten up. We need to decide on dinner. What do you have a taste for?"

"Margaritas." Laramie laughed.

"Well, that's a great start. How about Mercedes on Commercial Street? It's close for Manny to meet us there after work. We can get there early, grab a table, and start sipping. Of course, mine will have to be virgins. Does that work for you?"

"Absolutely. I'll take a cab that way I can sip a few for you. Do you want to meet there at four-thirty?"

"Sounds great. I'll call Manny. Come on now." Lian broke into song. "*They say it's your birthday. We're gonna have a good time…*"

"Don't start or I may have to join you."

"Oh no, please don't sing. Remember I'm pregnant. Think of the baby."

"Okay, okay, I get the hint. I'll see you later."

Laramie laughed with her friend. Laramie finally agreed to tell Akihiro how she really felt. She planned to do it sometime before the doctor's appointment or right after. *How am I going to find that courage? I am such a wus. I can't be afraid of confrontation forever. I have to do this. How else will I teach my daughter to have a voice? I don't want her like me. She needs that self confidence. I want her to be stronger than I am.*

Shortly after Lian and Laramie's conversation, Manny called Akihiro at the hotel at Lian's urging.

"Hey dude, what's up? I hear you brought Lara to tears with your gift."

"Tears? I thought she got a little choked up but I wouldn't go that far."

"Yeah, well, Lian just called and she had to console her over the phone. She made me call you to say take it easy. I really hate getting in the middle of all this chick stuff. I don't want to be in touch with my feminine side."

Akihiro laughed. "I didn't realize you had a feminine side. All I did was leave a gift that had some meaning between us. You know, just to start the ball rolling."

"Apparently, it was more like a boulder. Now, what's the story with this woman you've been dating?"

"Now that… that was a mistake on my part. I met this woman in the bar. Nothing happened but I led Lara to believe something did. She ticked me off in the parking lot when we fought over Akiko on the day she was served. I was so mad at her after that. I made her believe I was with someone else. Same thing the night she came to settle. I had a date but it was with my attorney."

"That explains a lot. One reason she has avoided you is that she thinks you have someone new and she's out of the picture. She told Lian that's why she won't confront you. That plan went down in flames, Dude. Heads up, she supposed to call you in the next few days to talk. Enough said, no more 'feelings' talk. This is so out of my norm. If Lian asks, I did my part."

"I follow you. Anyway, I think I'm going to go to the Giants game tomorrow night. Let me know if you want to do something *manly.* Outside of that, make sure she has a great birthday for me."

"Later Dude."

Akihiro knew the new girlfriend idea could backfire and it did. He needed to make sure, when he saw her on Friday morning, he would be polite and agreeable. That could buy him points at the planned meeting on Friday night. He hoped they talked before then. *I know she will feel trapped and that could really anger her. How do I keep her from walking out? How do I make her listen to me? That's going to be tough.*

Right at five o'clock Manny met Lian and Laramie at the restaurant. It was a great choice for Laramie because the interior was bright and cheerful. The walls were painted in vibrant colors and had Mexican folk art hanging on them. The place had a festive quality inside and the musical beat added to the ambiance. Laramie had a tall margarita in front of her. Next to her, Akiko sat in a highchair and nibbled on her Cheerios. Lian sat across from Laramie so Manny opted to sit next to his wife. Before he sat, he leaned over, kissed Laramie on the cheek, and wished her a happy birthday.

"Man, the food smells so good and I am starving." Lian handed Manny a menu.

As he perused the menu, their waitress came for his drink order. Since they were onto a theme, he opted for a Corona with a lime. Laramie ordered another Margarita, frozen and no salt.

"Any celebrations at the office?"

"Yes, Linda had a cake for me. Triple chocolate, my favorite. Everyone sang *Happy Birthday*. You know, the usual. It was nice."

"What did Edward do this year? Another theatrical performance?"

"Actually, he stayed very subdued. He gave me a gold charm of a baby shoe with Akiko's name engraved on it. I'm going to add it to my bracelet. It really was adorable. I'm sure Linda picked it out." Laramie laughed.

"You're not joking there. Good thing she's around or we'd be admiring your cigar humidor." Manny always cracked himself up. This characteristic of his usually made everyone else laugh at his laughter, not the joke itself.

Lian cut in. "Leave him alone, raising Laramie was hard enough. Besides, he's not here to defend himself."

"He did great by me for many years. He taught me the law. Well, actually, he had to since I had no coordination for sports." Laramie sipped her drink and continued. "Aha! That is the one thing worse than my singing."

"Nice try, no go. Your singing still tops the list as worst ever by a human," Manny said as he trumped her.

The waitress returned and everyone placed their orders. After eating a bowl of chips and salsa, Laramie ordered a salad thinking it wouldn't be as filling. Poor Lian, who desperately wanted more of the chips that Laramie hogged, ordered the chimichanga. Manny asked for another bowl of chips before he ordered. His appetite was as large as Lian's. Occasionally, one of them played with Akiko who sat happily, as she watched all the people in the restaurant. One of the staff brought her a maraca to play with. She shook it around and banged it on the table. Quickly, Laramie substituted it with her Elmo music player.

"So, how old are you now? Thirty-five?" Manny asked.

Lian elbowed him in the ribs and told him to be polite.

"Gee, I'm sorry Laramie, you don't look a day over twenty one." He faced Lian and said, "See, just how believable was that? Who cares? It's just a number and I was curious. Don't tell me. Just hand me your driver's license under the table so other people won't see it."

"You are pathetic. *Who cares?* Then why ask the question? Duh?" Lian replied as she rolled her eyes.

"Both of you stop. I am thirty-one today and proud to say it. However, in nine more years don't ask me that question."

Another bowl of chips made it to the table and Lian grabbed them. She claimed her stake and warned others to keep away. It wasn't much longer before their meals arrived. Full mouths made conversing harder. Laramie fed refried beans to Akiko as a test that didn't pass. She made a mental note to add that to the list with peas. Lian fed Akiko some rice. Akiko liked it so much she tried to pull the plate closer but not before Laramie stopped her.

"She likes rice, huh? Must be the Asian in her." Manny laughed. "Hey, speaking of which… how has visitation gone with Akihiro? You getting along better now?"

"Actually, I haven't seen him. He comes to visit while I'm at work. So, he's greeted by Francesca. I guess it's working out for him. I never asked. Though, I will see him on Friday morning when Akiko sees Dr. Patel."

Lian interjected, "Yes, but he did leave her a present and flowers for her birthday."

"Yeah, I'm trying to figure out the motive for that."

Manny asked, "What makes you think there is a motive? See, that's where guys differ. We buy stuff because we like it. You women put too much thought into things." He continued in a women's voice. "*Oh, he bought me a CD. He must think I'm fat and wants me to exercise.* No, he bought the CD because he thinks you like music. If he thought you were fat, he'd buy an exercise bike or a gym membership."

"Yes, but his gift carried a lot of sentiment in it, Manny"

"Were they things you liked?"

"Yes, but—"

"No buts. That's all there is. He bought it because he thought you would like it. Period. I see your face, Lara. You're trying to put that chick factor in it. Stop. When you thank him, don't get all mushy. *How did you know my inner most personal feelings? It had my favorite colors of periwinkle, sage, and taupe.* Just say thanks."

Laramie laughed at his female impersonation, as did Lian.

"I already thanked him this afternoon. I could've used your alter ego then."

Lian looked at her watch. "It's six thirty already. That went fast. I know you need to go Lara and put my little angel in bed soon. Manchu, wait for the check."

Lian stood up and helped Laramie pull Akiko from the highchair. Laramie packed up her diaper bag and hugged Lian and Manny for her birthday dinner. She took Akiko from Lian's arms and waved goodbye to her friends.

Lian sat with Manny as he waited for the check.

"Whew. That was a close call. Did you talk with Akihiro yet?"

"Yes. I said everything you told me, Dear. For the record, can you call him about that kind of thing yourself? It freaks me out to talk about all the chick stuff."

"Thank you. We have two days left. I am crossing my fingers that he can get her to open up. His gift really got to her. She was a wreck. Nice cover. I'm going to have to watch you more closely. By the way, don't ever buy me a gym membership."

The waitress returned with the bill and Manny's credit card. He signed off, stood up and held his hand out for Lian. They began their walk home to Chinatown, hand in hand.

Chapter 75

LARAMIE SPENT HER morning in the office as usual. She had a few files she wanted to clear out and others she wanted to organize. Edward stopped by to check on her previous evening.

"Who all went? More importantly, did you have a nice birthday?"

"Actually, it was very nice. Akiko, Manny, Lian and I went out for Mexican food. I made it home with enough time to bathe Akiko and put her to bed. I had a few margaritas so I went to bed early as well."

"How is everything else at home?"

"I know what you are eluding to Edward. So far, things are running smooth. He stops by every other day to visit with Kiki. No, I haven't seen him. I will tomorrow at Dr. Patel's."

"That week surely passed quickly. How has Akiko been at home?"

"Great. She is back on schedule and eating well. I have a feeling they will do a blood test to be sure. I am confidant she is getting stronger and healthier."

Edward walked into her office and shut the door behind him. He sat across from Laramie and looked at her.

"Laramie, I have thought about what you said to me last week regarding Linda. You have some valid points and I have to agree with you. I don't plan to work much longer and I don't want to be old alone. So, I have asked Linda if she would care to make our relationship more personal."

"And…"

"She agreed. I don't know what she sees in this old bear but I am willing to move ahead. Now, I have taken your advice. We had a deal. Have you taken mine? Have you told Akihiro how you really feel?"

"No, but… don't interrupt me. Let me finish. I've had the same talk with Lian yesterday. I plan to call and meet with him, maybe tomorrow after the doctor appointment to talk. Edward, I have a confession to make. I don't want you to be surprised either."

"There isn't a whole lot for you to surprise me with anymore." He chuckled.

"The night before the hearing, I went to Akihiro's hotel to try and settle our case. I tried so hard but he didn't believe my intentions and fought me over the issues."

"Laramie, settle? That does surprise me after all. What made you consider that avenue?"

"Our talk actually. I didn't want to fight anymore. I wanted to make peace with him but it didn't work. When I left, I made some really awful threats, which I regret. Anyway, that's why I conceded the next morning. He has just as much right to be in Akiko's life as I do."

"That has to be one of the most mature things I seen you do in a long time. I have to say I am very proud of you. Even though you were discouraged and hurt, you did the right thing. That isn't always easy but you know that now."

"I know it's not over yet but I'm working on it. I really am trying."

Edward stood and walked behind Laramie's desk. He bent over and kissed her forehead. He patted her hand resting on the desk.

"Dear, I know you are. You'll make it yet."

Edward opened the door and walked out.

Laramie felt relieved in expressing her reasons behind the settlement and concession. She knew it was hard for her to take those steps but she took them despite the obstacles. She had one left, Akihiro. She thought about that conversation and feared the rejection. *Could Lian be right? Could he still care? Was that the reason for the gifts? The only way to know is to ask.*

After lunch, Laramie went home to spend time with Akiko. She wondered how visitation would work tomorrow since the doctor's appointment is near the same time. *Will he still want to play with her? Will he have time to talk afterwards? Will he want to talk?* She reminded Francesca that she doesn't work in the morning, only in the evening tomorrow. She asked her to be there by seven o'clock. Francesca agreed, smiled and said goodbye. As she walked back into the living room, Laramie stopped to admire the flowers sent by Akihiro. *All of my favorites. I wonder if Kat called him and told him. She knew so much about me as part of her job. But the lotus flower. That had to be Aki's idea. He had to find it somewhere here in the city, right? I wonder how much he played in the finding of the gift.* She adored the necklace. It was such a custom look. Laramie rarely wore jewelry. She never wanted to look flashy or opulent. Most of her items were simple hoop earrings and her watch. She glanced at her wrist. Her watch, a Patek Philippe Twenty-4, was a law school graduation gift from Edward. It was a simple stainless design with diamonds flanking the bezel. It was nice since it was both casual and dressy. However, she noticed it needed a good polishing. She took great care when she first received it but with years of wearing and now the baby, it looked worn. *I really need to drop this off at the jewelers for a good cleaning and polishing.*

Akiko broke her concentration by pulling at her leg. When Laramie looked down, Akiko raised her arms. *I am sorry Baby. I got lost in thought and forgot about you.* She picked her up and kissed her face. Even Laramie found her resemblance to Akihiro astounding. *There is no denying who your Daddy is.* She walked into Akiko's room and looked around for a toy. She spotted the Tickle Me Elmo in the corner and pulled it out. Laramie imitated Akiko's movements and poked her every time Akiko poked Elmo. Her daughter found this pattern very humorous and began to poke Laramie as well.

After Akiko found toys to occupy her time, Laramie walked into the living area and checked her voice messages. Both of them were from Gillian and Elizabeth inquiring about her birthday. She picked up the phone and dialed Gillian first. Laramie filled her in on the dinner with Manny and Lian, Edward's gift and the office party. She did not disclose information regarding Akihiro's gift. Laramie knew Gillian would ask questions that she didn't want to answer. The conversation stayed pleasant and upbeat, what Laramie needed. They laughed at stories of the birthdays of their youth. As they ended their call, each promised to visit the other soon.

Now it's time to call Elizabeth. This won't be as smooth as Gillian's call. She knows how to move in and nab me all the time. She dialed Liz and noted the time change. It was evening in Charleston. Elizabeth answered the phone still yelling at her kids before she acknowledged the caller.

"Liz, stop yelling at those angels."

"You forget, even Satan was an angel at one time. My Baptist upbringin' won't allow me to say what I'd like to right now."

"Oh my God, you liar. You aren't even Baptist. Is that lightning I hear outside your house? Do you forget to whom you are speaking?"

"Well, if it isn't our birthday girl. Did you have a great time, Sugar? I see you got my message. So tell me about your presents. Did Edward get a chorus line to sing for you again?"

"No, thankfully. I'm hoping that was a one-time thing for turning thirty last year. Manny asked the same question. I got a charm of a baby shoe from Edward."

"Don't you mean Linda?"

"Yes, I should have said from Edward via Linda. Manny and Lian took me out for Mexican. I was stuffed afterwards."

"What was this Mexican fellow's name that stuffed you?"

"Ha. Ha. Ha. Food, Mexican food. I was home early to get Kiki to bed. Actually, I got myself to bed early as well."

They chatted about Akiko's health. Laramie spoke of the pending doctor's appointment. She told Liz that Lian was pregnant. She told her friend about Manny's new job. Laramie thought she covered everything until Liz made her inquiries.

"You have kept the best news for last I assume. So how is Akihiro? Are you speaking? And why wasn't he at your birthday dinner?"

"I just knew you wouldn't let go of that. I thought about inviting him, especially after he left flowers and a necklace for me. I have to say his gift was spectacular. I was stunned."

Laramie proceeded to describe the gifts.

"Let me see if I have this correct. This man, who happens to be the Daddy to your daughter, buys you a thoughtful gift and you didn't even extend an invitation? Where are the southern manners I taught you? For Pete's sake, Lara, that man is crazy about you and you don't even see it. Do I need to fly out there to straighten things out for y'all?"

"*No.* I have a better chance of controlling him than I do of you. I will see him tomorrow at the doctors. I already told Lian I would sit and talk with him. No lectures. I gave in at the hearing; let me take small steps first."

"*No*, back at you. You don't have time for small steps. That man will be goin' home soon. How much time do you think you have? Seriously. Laramie Lila Holden, you need my foot up your sweet behind to get you movin'. I have never witnessed such a tragic case of love in all my life. Y'all better get together and fix this for your daughter's sake, and I truly mean that."

"I know you do. I am working on it, really. In fact, I will call him after dinner and ask to talk tomorrow after the appointment. Are you satisfied?"

"I won't be satisfied unless I am in on that phone call. That is the only way I know you did it."

"Oh, you can forget that. I may be hardheaded but I am not stupid. You would take the conversation over in a heartbeat."

"Are you tryin' to say I'm pushy?"

"Exactly."

"Well, in the south we like to call it being helpful to our friends and kin. Though I am impressed with your new ability to stand up to me. You must be gettin' over your fear of confrontation."

"Not really. You're 3000 miles away and we're on the phone. Upfront is a completely new ball game. Anyway, I hate to cut you short but my daughter needs her dinner. So, this conversation will continue another time. Give my best to Randy and the kids. I love you, Dear."

"Call me with *good* news next time, Sugar."

Laramie shook her head as she hung up. No one could pass anything by Elizabeth. She had keen senses and a quick wit. Laramie knew it was far better to have her on your side than against you. She pulled out jars of baby food and heated them in the microwave. Once everything was ready, she placed Akiko in her highchair. Laramie gave her daughter a break with eating green beans, mixed fruit and turkey; all her favorites. Mom wiped her down and checked under the bib before she let her down to play. After she finished the dishes, Laramie drew a bath for Akiko. *Sure, this is the one time her hair lays flat.* Akiko played with her squeaker toys and rubber ducks while Laramie washed her. Laramie knew Akiko liked the water and splashed quite a bit. She always laid towels around the tub to catch the tidal waves. Bath time was a favorite of Laramie's. Afterwards, Lara dried her baby off and wiped her down with baby lotion. *I love that baby smell.*

Laramie placed Akiko in her footed pajamas. Once her hair dried, she rocked her in the chair in Akiko's room. As the baby grew tired, Laramie slowly placed her in her crib. *Whew! That was an easy night.* It's hard to believe it's already after seven o'clock. She picked up the phone to speak with Akihiro. *This is going to be so hard. I can do this. How can I be so confident in my work and such a chicken with him? Every time I talk to him, I get flustered. In two years, this hasn't changed one bit.* As she listened to the phone continue to ring, she realized he was out. *I hope it's not a date. Please let it be something else. Maybe he is in the business center working. That would explain all of this.*

"Akihiro, it's Laramie. I called to see if you felt like talking. You must be busy and I don't want to interrupt you. I guess we can do this tomorrow as well. Anyway, have a good night. Bye."

Her first attempt went better than she anticipated due to the fact no one answered. *It was an attempt. I asked to talk. That is a first step, right?* She reclined on the sofa and watched television, a luxury at night. Slowly, she dozed off. Around midnight, she walked into her bedroom and climbed into bed.

* * *

Around the same time of her message, Akihiro sat in a field club seat between home and third base at AT&T Park. This was his first American baseball game. He knew the basics but obviously none of the players. He looked around and saw a giant Coke bottle and a huge catcher's glove. The advertising was normal compared to Singapore. He placed his beer in the cup holder in front of him. The green of the grass surprised him in the cold weather. He understood why many fans came with blankets, especially for a night game. He placed the t-shirts that he bought for Rhys and Shinji at the souvenir stand, on his legs to keep warm.

Moments later, a short, burly, elderly man with gray hair sat in the seat beside him. He placed his beer in his cup holder and unfolded his blanket. He wore a heavy stadium jacket and a Giants baseball cap. After he situated himself, he turned to Akihiro and greeted him with a 'hello' and 'how you doing.' Akihiro nodded and replied he was fine.

"You here for the single game or all season?" the man asked.

"Actually, just for tonight. I've never been to an American baseball game so I wanted to see one before I go home."

"So, where's home?" he asked with his lower husky voice.

"Singapore." Akihiro put his hand out to shake. "I'm Akihiro."

The man shook his hand with a firm grip. His fingers, slightly bent from arthritis, looked like stuffed sausages.

"Well Akihiro, I'm Henry Bledsoe but most people call me Hank. So, your first game, eh? If you have any questions, I'm the guy to ask. I've been coming here since I was a young man stationed at the naval base. Since I retired, I bought season tickets and this is where I hang out."

"Nice to meet you Hank." This man seemed like a colorful character to Akihiro. He assumed he carried many tales in his years of experience.

"What brings to here from Singapore?"

"I'm visiting my daughter and her mother."

"What'd she divorce you and move here?" This stranger's questions into his personal life shocked Aki. Then, he remembered Americans knew no limits.

"No, we never married. We haven't gotten to that point."

"Let me give you a bit of advice from an old fool. Do what she wants. In the end, you'll get what you want. I lost my wife a few years ago and there isn't a day that I don't miss her. She was a hell of a woman. Stubborn and fiery, and I loved her like that."

"Sounds like we both know similar women. She can go from hardheaded to emotional in a flash."

"Like I always say… keep the beer cold and the women hot."

Akihiro picked up his beer and toasted with Hank. "I have to say, I completely agree. So how long have you been here?"

"I was stationed on the USS Coral Sea in the late sixties and early seventies. Alameda was our homeport. We were at Yankee Station, just off the coast of Da Nang, Viet Nam. I worked on deck when the A6's flew in. Anyway, San

Francisco was different back then. You didn't see much of the gays but the hippies were everywhere. I met my wife down on the wharf during shore leave. She was a looker."

They pause briefly for the National Anthem. Akihiro stood along Hank as s sign of respect to the home country.

"Did your wife come to the games with you?"

"No, this was my time as a man. Back then, the Giant's played at Candlestick Park, further down the bay. That's when the players made it on their own merit not all pumped up on steroids. I watched Bobby Bonds, Willie Mays and Gaylord Perry. They were a great team. Too bad the Cincinnati Red's won the pennant that year. Perry had one hell of a spitball back then. A few years earlier, he pitched a no hitter. Boy, I would've loved to see that. *Is that a new kind of call Ump! What do you call the strike zone!* Sorry. As I was saying… eventually, they traded him to the Cleveland Indians. Stupid move. We got Sam McDowell who couldn't throw a ball worth a damn."

"It sounds like you have had some great years, Hank."

"Yeah, if I weren't me, I'd be jealous. I've had a good job, a great wife and beautiful kids. Now, I see my grandchildren twice a week. Their parents spoil them too much. They walk around with their radios and cell phones to their heads. Can't even have a conversation. Once in a while, I bring one with me. The younger ones like the sports before the older ones corrupt them." Akihiro chuckled with his statements. "*Yes, a homerun. All right Chavez. Run those bases.*"

As they watched the game, Hank pointed out and explained the happenings on the field. Akihiro learned there was more to the game than swinging the bat. He got a lesson in strategy and risk, a very similar situation as with Laramie. He bought Hank another beer and each of them a hotdog.

"*That's the way to do it, Sandoval. Way to go. Nice triple,*" Hank cheered.

He admitted he enjoyed this experience mainly due to meeting Hank. *Americans can certainly be overbearing and loud. This guy tells me, a complete stranger, his whole life story in an evening. But, what a story he has. It has made the game so much more interesting. All of the history. Yet, we are similar in our taste of women and values. Amazing.*

"You must be good luck, Akihiro. Giants win over the A's seven to four. Plus you got to see some great pitching by Lincecum."

Akihiro stood with Frank as the stadium emptied. He pulled a business card out of his wallet and handed it to Hank.

"If you ever come to Singapore, call me. I own hotels there and I'd love to have you as my guest. Bring the kids with you if you want. This has been one of the best evenings I've had. Thank you, Hank."

"Well, Akihiro, I might just take you up on that offer. Is it warmer there?"

Aki nodded yes. "That's enough reason for me. It has been a pleasure meeting you. Anytime you are in town and want to see a game, you call me, Henry Bledsoe."

Both men shook hands and slapped the back of the other. Akihiro stood behind the man as he climbed up the steps. He wanted his new friend to be safe. *What a great time. I have to thank Manny for the suggestion.* After spending this time with Hank, Akihiro realized how homesick he was and wanted more time with his own father. *Not much longer.*

When Akihiro returned to his room, he noticed he had a message. As he played it, he smiled. *Laramie is finally wanting to talk and not too soon either. It's too late to call her back. We can talk tomorrow. What a great night all around.*

Chapter 76

LARAMIE SAT IN the doctor's office, watching Akiko play with the toys on the floor. She noticed the place lent itself to children exclusively. All the chairs were a smaller scale, not to mention the maze toys in the corner. Akiko played with a wallboard that changed colors when her hand touched it. It enthralled her. Laramie looked at her watch and wondered where Akihiro was. *Probably another date and he overslept. Don't get angry, I don't know that for sure. I have to give him a chance. I have to talk with him especially after leaving a message. Oh, why didn't I just hang up? Now I'm locked.*

Akihiro came through the door out of breath. He kissed his daughter first before he sat beside Laramie.

"Whew! Sorry I'm late. I forgot to set my alarm last night and I overslept."

"You haven't missed anything so don't worry. Another date?" Laramie had to ask, her curiosity ate at her.

"No, not at all. I went to a Giants game last night and met the most interesting guy there. We talked on and off during the game. He told some of the most amazing stories. What a rich life he has…"

As Akihiro continued to discuss details of the night, Laramie watched in surprise. *Who ever this man was, he surely captivated Akihiro.*

"Is he married?"

"No, a widower. Why?"

She smiled. "Because it sounds like you're in love with him."

"If he was forty years younger and a woman, I would be." He laughed. "Hey, I got your message last night. I wanted to call back but it was late and I didn't want to wake Akiko. What did you want to discuss?"

"Nothing in particular. We can do it later." Laramie was nervous.

"Sounds great. I don't have any plans."

He didn't want her to backpedal out of this discussion. He knew if she did, they would still meet tonight.

Laramie leaned over and kissed Akihiro on the cheek. He turned to her with astonishment.

"Thank you for the birthday gift. That's all."

He smiled back and patted her hand on the armrest. *So far, so good.*

Moments later the medical tech walked them back to an examination room. She had Laramie undress Akiko down to her diaper. The tech did her usual routine, temperature, weight and asked about any concerns. Laramie said all was fine. The worker said the doctor would be in shortly. Akihiro watched Laramie across the room. He thought about the words Hank said regarding beer and women. He smiled. *She is one hot woman.* The knock on the door startled Akihiro.

"Good day. How is everyone? Good to see you all under happier times."

Laramie said, "I completely agree. It's been wonderful to be back home again."

"I am going to have someone draw a vial of blood, just one this time. This way I can see the counts and how Akiko is healing. Everything fine at home? Eating? Sleeping? Playing?"

"Yes, all of it. She has a great appetite and is full of energy."

"That is good news."

After a minute, a young nurse walked in with a needle and vial. She asked Laramie and Akihiro to hold Akiko very still which they complied. Akiko shrieked at the pinch of the needle. Laramie's eyes welled up. She hated this part. Akihiro kissed Laramie's head and told her to be calm for Akiko since they were almost finished. Once done, Laramie cradled her daughter and tried to play with her to distract her from the pain.

"Are there any questions you have for me?"

"When will you have the results from this test?" Laramie asked.

"Since the lab is in the building, I should know later this afternoon. I will have someone from the office call you with those results."

"Actually, I have one question as well." Laramie looked over at Akihiro. "How long will it be until Akiko is healthy enough to travel?"

"She is ready to travel now. As long as she is kept away from the ill, she should be fine. Keep her current on her diet and vitamins and there shouldn't be any problems."

"Thank you Dr. Patel."

Laramie grew angry. *Why? Why now? Couldn't he have waited to ask that? No, he wanted to see how fast he could travel to Singapore with her. Do the wonders ever cease?* She quickly dressed Akiko and walked to the front office to schedule her next checkup. Akihiro waited in the hallway for Laramie to come out.

"Lara, where do you want to go and talk? Do you want to grab a coffee or tea?"

"No."

"No what? No you don't want coffee or tea or no, you don't want to talk?"

"Both." She walked with Akiko on her hip. He knew she was angry but didn't know the reason.

"Wait a second. What's going on? What did I miss? One minute you were happy, everything was great, and now you're mad at me. What did I do?"

"Why didn't you just ask if you could buy the ticket to Singapore for her today? Why wait?" She remained sarcastic.

"Hold it." Akihiro pulled at Laramie's free arm. "You are not going to twist my words. That is not what I asked. I wanted to know when she could travel, period. If he said two weeks, fine. If he said six months, then fine too. I didn't ask for a date just her health status. Don't put words in my mouth that I didn't say."

"Well, that's not how it sounded." She continued to walk thru the parking lot.

"Then you misunderstood my position. I wasn't trying to steal her away from you. Do you understand me? Look at me, Lara. I want to be sure we are clear on this."

Laramie stopped walking and turned around. "Yes, I do understand you. I apologize for my words. I am sorry I didn't know what you meant." She was sincere. "Did you still want to have Akiko today?"

"Well, yes, but how?"

"I can drive you to your hotel and give you her diaper bag. It has her lunch and extra bottle in it. Her stroller is in the trunk in case you wanted to go somewhere."

"Did you want to stay with us? I wouldn't mind. It would give us time to talk."

"I can't. I have a party tonight and I need to find a gift. Normally this would be easy but I haven't any ideas."

He knew she wanted to back out. He needed time to convince her to stay with them.

"Well, I'll take the ride just the same."

He walked with Laramie to the parking lot. *I knew she had a car from the hospital lot but I couldn't see what it was. I just assumed she took public transit for everything here in the city.* They stopped in front of a black 2007 BMW 328i Coupe. Laramie pulled her remote out of her purse and unlocked the doors.

"It was a great car when I bought it. Though now with Kiki, the two doors make it hard getting her in and out."

"Let me give you a hand. I'll hold her and pass her to you when you're ready."

He held his daughter under the arms. Laramie made the motion to hand her over. She got Akiko in her seat and buckled safely. She put the seat back and sat behind the wheel. Akihiro opened the door and sat beside her. *It's a nice car. I don't know if I would've guessed a BMW, a Porsche maybe.*

Laramie pulled out and cut through the side streets as she made her way to Market Street.

"I'm surprised you have an automatic."

"Well, I'm thankful I do. The hills are hard to stop on and it really is difficult to shift when your feeling for a baby bottle on the floor." Occasionally she glanced into the baby mirror to check on Akiko.

"Do you want to talk now?" he asked in a soft voice as not to put on any pressure.

Laramie knew she was targeted. She had nowhere to run inside the car. She never anticipated this scenario. She attempted to cover herself.

"Actually, it wasn't anything important. I, uh, felt a little … um, it was just a mood thing. That's all."

He knew she lied. She was afraid to take the first step. The fact she made it into a car with him surprised Akihiro.

"Do you want to talk about us, Lara?" he replied calmly.

"What 'us'? There is no 'us'? There are you, me and the daughter we share." *Oh, crap. I can feel the anxiety attack starting. I'm not ready for this.*

"Do you want there to be an 'us'?"

"No... maybe, I don't know. I don't want to talk about that right now."

"When do you? I have one week until I leave for Singapore. One week."

"God, stop pressuring me. I said I don't know," she snapped.

Her grip on the steering wheel tightened. Her anger was a sign of retreat. She felt encaged. Akihiro left her alone since the discussion would continue later at night.

"I won't say another word. Will you at least help me set up the stroller when we get to the hotel?"

"Yes. It's easy."

Laramie kept twisting her hair. She was nervous. She felt claustrophobic in the car. However, she remained quiet on the drive. Akihiro sensed her restlessness and decided to change the subject for her.

"Have you ever been to a Giant's game?"

"Yes. They're a lot of fun in a group too. The firm has had sponsored events there for the employees too. I like going in the summer when it's warmer."

"Yeah, it was pretty cold last night. That didn't keep the fans from showing up."

Laramie turned up Grant Street to make her way around the square.

"Footballs games are even colder. The 49er's fans are some crazy, die-hard people too. I've seen them play a few times at Candlestick Park but I prefer to see the games from inside a sports bar."

"I didn't know you were such a sports fan."

"I'm not. I go for the fun and the beer. I couldn't hit a ball or throw a pass if my life depended on it. No coordination. Even worse than my singing."

"I find that hard to believe since I've heard you sing." He didn't mean to say it so loud. He quickly apologized. "Maybe you just needed a better coach."

"Nice cover, too late. Anyway, here you go. Front door service."

Laramie exited the car and released her trunk. Akihiro pulled out the stroller and she showed him how it popped open. She went back for Akiko and carried her around to the sidewalk. She kissed her a half dozen times then handed her to Akihiro. He assured her they would be fine. Laramie said she would be back in a few hours and waved goodbye. Akiko placed Akiko in the stroller and wheeled her into the hotel.

Damn, I should've just told him when he asked. But he didn't say that he wanted an 'us' either. I don't have time to think about that right now. I have to find something for Lian. She found a parking spot further down Powell Street and walked back toward the square. *If the square doesn't have something then it doesn't exist. It has to be something girlie, something personal.* Her problem was the fact that Lian was pregnant so clothing would not be a good choice. *If it's too small, she will feel fat from the baby weight. If it's too big, she will think we viewed her bigger. Hmm… what about a purse? No, I would hate that. Nothing for the house, that's too impersonal. I've got it… it's perfect… a Spa day!* She stopped at Starbucks for a latte and thought about where to get the spa certificate. She wanted somewhere nice but close to Chinatown. *What about 77 Maiden Lane Salon? I've heard great things about it from the girls at work.* It was a simple fix to her problem. She grabbed her coffee and headed back out the opposite direction from her car. *Well, I can shop for me after I pick up something for Lian. I say that until I pass a children's store and get sucked in the place. The last think Kiki needs is more clothing… but she does need new shoes.*

Akihiro sat in his hotel room and attempted to feed Akiko sitting in a chair. Every time she had a mouthful of food, she tried to get down. It was a true game of cat and mouse. Eventually, he put her into her stroller and fed her from there. *Now I have the idea. You can't take off from there. I don't know how you eat this stuff, it looks terrible.* He smelled the jar. *Well, it doesn't smell bad but I'm still not going to taste it.* He continued to feed her until she ate everything. He noticed the increase in her appetite since her release a week ago.

After she finished eating, he pulled her out of the stroller and played with her on the floor. She quickly decided the knobs on the drawers were her favorite new toy. Determined to open the drawer, she pulled hard until she released and fell on her butt. *You have the tenacity of your mother. She was so close today. I think if we'd been outside she would've done better. She's going to be mad. She's out shopping for the perfect gift for a party that doesn't exist.* He lay flat on the floor and allowed Akiko to climb him. She found that easier than the drawer pulls. After a few times to the summit, Akiko began to yawn. *I know what that means. Where do I put you? Should I call downstairs for a crib? How long would that take? Maybe I should call your mother.* Akihiro picked up the phone and dialed Laramie.

"Hello, Akihiro. Is everything okay?"

"How did you know?"

"Caller ID on my phone. You're the only person I know at the St. Francis."

"Akiko is getting sleepy and I don't have a crib. What should I do? Do I leave her on the floor?"

"No, grab all the pillows off the bed and put her in the middle. Then lay the pillows around her. She won't roll off. I forgot she would want a nap after eating."

"No, that's fine I just didn't know what to do. That's all. Everything else is fine. Finish shopping. Thanks."

"No problem. See you shortly."

Laramie hung up and smiled. She knew he wanted to be a good father but common sense dictated in most cases. *Why would you leave a child on the floor, especially a hotel room? Disgusting.* She shuddered to think about it.

She just entered the salon and asked the receptionist for their list of services. She liked the Deluxe Day Package. *Ooh! A massage, facial, pedicure, lunch, hair and makeup. That's sounds perfect for her. Maybe Manny could take her out for dinner after and make a whole day of it. Well, I think I found the perfect gift.* She purchased her gift and browsed the product lines on display. *No more Laramie, you spent enough. Besides, aren't shoes more fun? Speaking of shoes, I want Manny to take me back to the Chinese guy with the Jimmy Choo's.*

Akihiro played the proud father and took massive pictures of Akiko asleep. She looked adorable in the center of his bed. *She sucks her thumb?* He pulled it out and within seconds, it was right back in her mouth. He tried it a few times and she repeated it. He didn't know if that was a bad thing or not. He made note to ask Laramie about it.

A half hour later, Laramie knocked at his door. He opened it quietly and told her Akiko was still asleep. She walked in quietly and smiled. Akihiro placed every pillow and cushion he got his hands on around her. It was impossible for her to fall off the bed even if she tried.

"Did you know she sucked her thumb? Is that okay?"

"She's fine. It's the only trait of mine that she got. Besides, I never gave her a pacifier. I never liked them. If she is any more like me, she'll need braces too."

"You wore braces? I never knew that."

"Why would you? Let me guess, your teeth came in perfect?" He nodded yes. "I should've known." She seemed disgusted by that fact.

"Why?"

"Have you ever experienced any hardships at all? You weren't skinny or fat, your teeth are perfect and so is your hair. It must've been hard growing up as Akihiro Amori."

"Stop. I had hardships." She looked at him and waited for a response. "I just can't think of any off hand." She rolled her eyes.

"Mama, Mama." Akiko cried out as she tried to stand inside the walls of the fortress.

Laramie picked her up, kissing her hello. She asked Akihiro to hold the baby while she packed up her things. He had everything strewn across the room. Once she had it all, she held her hands out for Akiko. She placed the baby in the stroller and started to head out. Akihiro held the door open for her to navigate. He walked them to the elevator.

"Lara, I know we are doing this every other day but since I'm leaving in a week, do you think I can see her tomorrow and Sunday too?"

She hated the fact he would be leaving soon. She didn't want him to go. The only way to stop him was to talk with him.

"We'll both be home tomorrow. Francesca is off on weekends. You're welcome to come to the house and visit."

She meant while she was there as well and he understood that. The offer wasn't going to get any better. That was the best Laramie could do based on her character flaws. She knew it was a chance she had to take.

"Thanks. I really appreciate that."

"Oh, by the way, Dr, Patel called. Everything is great. Her numbers are in the normal range," Laramie added.

"Great news. I'll call you in the morning."

The elevator doors opened and Mom and daughter entered. Akiko said bye-bye over and over. He waved them off.

Now for a shower, for tonight. She is going to be furious everyone hid this from her. If she'd opened up on her own, it wouldn't have been necessary. Akihiro pulled out his clothes and laid them on the bed. He took his time as he got ready and casually shaved. He looked over his face in the mirror. *Perfect hair? She's crazy.* He rubbed his cologne in his hands and wiped his face. He noticed his nerves were on edge as well. *I hope Edward has a stocked bar. The only thing left is to grab a bite to eat and walk a block to the Grand Hyatt.*

* * *

Francesca showed up on time to baby-sit Akiko. Laramie showered and already dried her hair. She asked Francesca to finish feeding Akiko while she finished getting ready. The nanny happily obliged. *This is so hectic but what a way to spend a birthday before the baby arrives. Lian truly deserves this night out. A penthouse suite, no less. Manny gets his first paycheck and blows it on Lian. What a good husband!* She put her hair into hot rollers. *I don't even remember the last time I used these. I'm surprised they still work.* Laramie applied her makeup as her hair cooled. She normally wore her makeup light but since the occasion was in the evening and it was a party, she added a little extra. She pulled out her black gabardine dress slacks. She put on her new white Calvin Klein wrap blouse and tied the ribbon around into the front over the black lace looking cummerbund. It looked better on her than on the hanger. She put her new ankle boots on and walked to the mirror. *I look better than I thought. Well, except for the rollers.* She reentered the bathroom, took the rollers out and brushed through her hair to make soft curls. *Not bad, Laramie.*

When she walked out of her room, Francesca told her she looked beautiful. Laramie thanked her. She walked into her kitchen and grabbed paper and a pen to write the hotel information for the nanny in case of emergency. Laramie hugged and kissed Akiko before she left her flat.

She grew more excited the closer she got to the hotel. *Ooh, a party. I haven't been to one since the baby shower. This is just what I needed.* She stopped by the front desk to inquire about access to the penthouse since most hotels had special elevator keys to allow entry. The desk clerk handed her a key and pointed to the location of the elevators. She told Laramie that the suite is on the thirty-fourth floor. *Great… heights.* She walked to the elevators, pressed the button and waited for the doors to open. She primped last minute in her reflection in the elevator car.

Laramie walked down the hall to the Penthouse Suite. She opened the door and thought it odd the room was so quiet. As she passed through the small entry, she saw the back of a man as he stood at the window looking outside at the bay and downtown skyline. It was Akihiro. He turned around, and stood still with a drink in his hand. He looked calm as if he expected her. Laramie's face expressed complete confusion. Stunned to see they were the only people in the room, she looked around for a familiar face.

"What… what are you doing here, Akihiro? I don't understand. This is supposed to be a party for Lian," she asked inquisitively. She slowly walked toward the bedroom area to see if they were just hiding, as if this was some twisted trick.

"They won't be here Laramie, none of them." Akihiro looked at her straight-faced waiting for her reaction. "Why don't you sit down?" Akihiro gestured his hand toward a chair.

"I don't know if I'm staying yet. Did you put them up to this? What more do you want from me?" Laramie said heatedly. She walked over to the chair and set down the gift bag and her purse. As much as she wanted to leave, she was curious to know what Akihiro planned. "What kind of game are you playing?"

"Glad you decided to stay. Can I get you a drink?" he spoke in a calm monotone voice and tried not to upset her. She shook her head from side to side and watched his every move. *Calm yourself, Laramie. Don't let him get the best of you.*

"So whose idea was this? Whom do I get to thank? Edward? Manny? Lian?" she asked sternly.

"All of them and don't forget Elizabeth too," replied as he looked directly into her eyes. "It was a joint effort of many." He walked slowly back to the window, leaned with one hand bracing himself on the wall and gazed at the city lights.

It was apparent this trick stunned her. She walked over to the bar and decided she wanted a drink after all. *A conspiracy by all of my friends and family? They know what's going on, why would they do this? They don't trust me to have this talk on my own, do they?* She looked across the granite countertop to see what alcohol choices she had, nothing that she would normally drink. At this point she figured, the stronger the liquor, the quicker it would work. She poured herself a Crown and Sprite then took a sip. *God, is this awful! I just hope it works fast.* The warmth of the liquor created a tingling in her body.

"What are you doing, Laramie? You don't drink that."

"I do today," she replied with a halfhearted grin. She raised her glass as if she was toasting the occasion. "How did you get involved in this? And what's the purpose?" With each sip, she shuddered at the taste.

"I'll get to that in a minute. Are you sure you don't want to sit down?" She nodded no again. "It was at your friends and family's mandatory request that we sit down and talk everything out, at least for the sake of Akiko."

"No, there has to be more. We've already agreed as to what happens with Kiki."

"No, Laramie, nothing has been settled. We have too many lies and unknowns between us. This is our time to be honest with each other and ourselves in order to move past this." Laramie walked over to the window adjacent to where Akihiro stood. Her eyes glared at him, as she tapped her foot on the floor nervously.

"Completely honest? What other lies are there? How much more can you possibly be hiding?" she retorted, in the manner of a cross-examination.

"Don't look at me that way, you are just as guilty as I am," he countered. Akihiro took a deep breath and tried to calm himself again, wiped his face with his hand. "Look, I am not trying to point fingers or place blame. I just want you to be honest with me and I will be honest with you. Can you do that?"

Laramie walked over to the Asian inspired chair that faced the window, sat and flipped her hair over her shoulder. She attempted to look relaxed even though she felt uncomfortable. She took another drink before she placed the glass on the table. Her hand trembled as the glass touched the table, which created a short ringing sound. Akihiro caught the action out of the corner of his eye. He realized she was nervous and wasn't sure if that was good or bad.

"So, where does this begin? Who goes first? You seem to have this planned. What's the next step?" Laramie didn't meet his eyes; she just looked out the window. With each gulp of her cocktail, the room felt warmer. She felt a bit lightheaded and placed both hands on the armrests. "You know, let me go first, if that's okay with you?"

She looked to Akihiro. He took a sip of his drink and nodded yes. This move surprised him. He was ready to pour his heart out to her. However, now that Laramie decided to be first, it gave him the opportunity to see how the mood went and how to phrase the things he wanted to say.

Laramie took a deep breath and exhaled in an exaggerated way. *You can do this Lara. There is nothing to lose at this point. The truth is the truth, nothing fearful.*

"How far do you want to go back? All the way to Singapore? The hospital? I've already apologized for not telling you about Akiko. You did deserve to know about her. I don't suppose you will ever forgive that."

"If I didn't forgive you, I wouldn't have asked you out." He replied as if the dinner out erased all the ill feelings.

"You make it sound as if I think too deeply but that's only because of you.

Every time I give in to you, I get hurt. Every time. Yes, I agreed to show you around town and I did that. You couldn't leave it at that. You wanted me to sleep with you. I wanted to. You don't know how bad I wanted to but I didn't want to take that risk. There's no such thing as casual sex with you, at least not for me. If I gave into you there, I would've given into everything."

"It's not casual sex. I wanted you, I needed you, not just a screw. I told you that the next day."

"Yes, that's what you said, however I questioned myself the next two days over that. Was it just want? Or need? What about love?" Laramie's tears fell. "I loved you, I wanted to be with you. I'd planned a night alone, just the two of us, at my flat. If all you wanted was sex, I was fine to accept that over nothing at all." She wiped her eyes and continued. "Then, I questioned even that when you had me served with papers." She took another sip of her drink. "I wanted to believe you still loved me but that destroyed any hope I had. You came here for your daughter and now you have her. You've won. So, why can't you go back to Singapore and leave me alone?"

Akihiro's face was expressionless at first until she mentioned she was in love with him. "Laramie, I ..." Akihiro began.

Laramie took another large sip from her glass and still stared at the window in front of her. "I just can't continue to have you in my life like this. It's destroying me."

Laramie stood up, grabbed her glass and walked toward the window. The tears dripped down her cheeks and created a path down her neck and chest. Laramie wiped her eyes and sniffed to clear her nose. She walked to the bar for another drink. The next drink, stronger than the last, became her elixir of courage. Laramie walked back to the window still looking away from Akihiro's face.

"I came to your room to settle. I've *never* done that in my life. You've no idea how hard that was for me. I didn't want to fight you anymore. But, you just wouldn't except that. You were so sure I was out to deceive you. Then, you had your *date*. I was so jealous and hurt that you moved on so easily."

"Laramie, let me talk about that."

"No, just let me finish. I wanted to hurt you back and the only thing I could do was fight you. After I left, I realized I didn't mean the things I said. I was just angry. As I walked around, I thought about you and Kiki and how much you love her. I know both my parents would have fought for me. I realized we were both fighting for the same thing, her love." She stopped for a minute to catch her breath. "I had no right to keep you from her or her from you or your family. That is why I conceded at the hearing. Because you did have rights. More importantly, Akiko has rights to both parents." She turned to face him with a helpless look. "I am trusting you on that."

Now it became Akihiro's turn. He knew she meant everything in her statements and feelings. Akihiro walked over to her and placed his hand on her arm to try to show some comfort. She jumped at the touch not revealing if that was good or bad. Akihiro refilled his glass, just pouring vodka over the remnants of ice. After a few minutes, Laramie calmed down and wiped the tears off her face. Akihiro cleared his throat. He was unsure how to begin. He learned going second wasn't easier after all. He walked back to the window, looked out, and took a big gulp of vodka. *Thank God, Edward stocked this bar. I don't think I could do this without a few drinks.*

"I believed you forgot a section in your confession."

She looked at him strangely, tilting her head, unsure of what he meant. "What did I forget?"

"An office building?" Her eyes widened and her mouth opened with the realization of his knowledge.

"You know? For how long?"

"The same day you told me about Akiko. Shinji slipped in conversation. You told my brother and blackmailed him from telling me. Clever. Feel any guilt about that?"

"No. I was trying to help you. We all were trying to help you. I'm sorry I had to do that to Shinji but I wasn't ready for you to know. Besides you wouldn't have taken the money if I offered it," she explained with complete sincerity.

"Money, that's another one," he said throwing his arms in the air. "You can't imagine the history lesson I've had since coming here. You never said a thing about your settlement or corporation. Why?"

Laramie became defensive. She hated to be associated with her wealth.

"Because the money isn't who I am, it's what I have. Don't you think I'd give back that settlement if it brought my parents back? Apparently, someone has told you all about me. Tell me, what figure did they come up with?" She watched him shrewdly.

"What do you mean?"

"Oh, come on… they all have speculated for years. What was the number?" she asked sternly.

"Forty million."

"Ha. That's pathetic. The jury despised that company so bad for the lies and cover-ups. They tried to make it look as though my parents drove into that truck. Thank God Edward exposed it all. No, the lawsuit was for twenty million. The punitive damages were set at another eighty million dollars." Laramie's response floored him. *One hundred million dollars*. "The Cheung property was the first time I ever touched that money and the second being the office building. Once to hurt you and once to help."

"Do you think that squares you?" he vented.

"I never said that. I did it to help you, not hold it over your head."

"Anyway, you're right, I hated you when I came here. I wanted revenge. I could not conceive how you could justify keeping Akiko from me. But, I believed you when you said you meant to tell me, otherwise I would've been a stranger to her. After the Cheung deal, you taught me all about having a written contract. I believed it was necessary to see an attorney here. I didn't know the state of our relationship, friendship or whatever you want to call it. I wanted to make sure you couldn't prevent me from seeing her."

"I would've never done that if you would've been honest."

"I never anticipated you losing you mind over that."

Laramie added her sarcasm. "Oh right, everyone takes being sued so lightly."

"Don't interrupt me. You had your say, please respect mine," he snapped. "The night at the hotel, you were no surprise. I did have a date but it was more like a business dinner with my attorney, Richard."

"But, you said you were with a woman before and you led me to believe you were going out with her again. Why? Why would you say that?" Her tone became calmer, almost hurt.

"I got the name from a woman I met at the hotel bar a few nights after you were served. I'm not going to lie. I went to her room but I couldn't stop thinking of you so I left. Nothing happened."

"Am I supposed to thank you or feel relieved by that?" she asked confused.

"No. I'm not saying it was the right thing. It wasn't. I kept up the charade because I wanted you to be jealous and mad. You can't control your temper when you're angry. I figured if I got you mad enough you would say why you were really there. You would slip."

"But I didn't slip. You pushed me back into a fight. A fight I didn't want."

"There was no way for me to know that. All I heard about was the barracuda attorney you were. The *brilliant* Laramie Holden. I thought there was something more to your story and I tried to prepare for it. I kept waiting for some sly maneuver because you just couldn't view this from my perspective. What I had not counted on was you acquiescing to all demands in the agreement. Still, I didn't want to underestimate you. I was waiting for your next step. Then I was met by Manny outside the courthouse. He asked me to lunch where I met Edward. We drank and talked. I really believe they care about what is best, not just for Akiko but you and I as well. That's when Elizabeth rang in and disclosed her plan. After hearing the stories on what

I missed here, I realized we needed to discuss everything from beginning to end."

"So, all of you hid this from me. What made you think I would stay and not walk out when confronted?"

"We weren't sure how you would react. I didn't mean to deceive you but I wasn't sure you would see me if I just asked. I assumed you wouldn't. I planned to talk with you at the flat following Akiko's release but Francesca greeted me. The woman barely speaks English. How could you leave our daughter after just arriving home? What if there was an emergency? What was a Spanish-speaking nanny going to do? What kind of mother are you, Laramie? I would've been fine if you didn't want to talk to me but to leave Akiko because you couldn't face me. Three times, three times you left her." He baited her anger. He needed to get her to open up.

Laramie, irritated by his remarks, found it necessary to defend her position. She pointed her finger at Akihiro and declared, "You seemed fine with those arrangements on the phone. Besides, I spoke with Dr. Patel before you came over. I wouldn't have left her if I didn't feel she was safe. She is my first concern and don't you dare lecture me on parenting. I am her mother and I can decide what is best for my child."

Akihiro walked in front of her, acting angrily by the confrontation, and looked down at her. "Well, damn it, act like it then. Quit running all the time and be the adult. Don't you have it in you or is running all you do?" he fired back.

Laramie raised her hand to slap him but he caught her by the wrist. "I was wrong to stay here. All you want to do is berate me on my actions. I won't fight you anymore. This solved nothing," she shouted in his face. She tried to turn but Akihiro would not release her wrist. "Let go of me," she spoke with her teeth clenched.

Akihiro knew he had her in control. As much as she tried to contain her anger, she exposed her position. He held both of her wrists. She couldn't pull away.

"Why? So you can run again? Admit it Laramie, you're afraid of this. You're afraid of the confrontation. You're afraid when you're not the one in control. You're afraid of being alone with me. You're afraid to tell me you still love me."

She tensed her arms and faced downward to his chest, avoiding eye contact. "No. That's not true."

Akihiro grabbed the back of her hair in his hand and pulled her head back, and forced her to look at him. "Look me in the eye and tell me you don't love me. Look at me, Laramie."

She kept her eyes closed and begged him to stop. Once again, Akihiro demanded, "Look me in the eyes. I won't let you walk out on me again, not unless you don't love me."

"You don't understand. I can't do it. I can't take that pain again. It still hurts. Please, please don't do this to me." The alcohol certainly took effect; her strength weakened.

Akihiro whispered, "Then tell me, Laramie. Tell me you love me because I still love you and I can't bear to go back to Singapore never knowing the truth. Please, tell me the truth."

Laramie slowly opened her eyes, stared at Akihiro for a moment, and then closed them, tears running down. Her arms became limp, no longer able to fight him. "I still love you. I have never stopped loving you. … I never stopped."

Akihiro let loose her hair and raised his hand to wipe away her tears. He kissed her, at first slow pecks around her face and neck. Laramie opened her eyes and met his. He held both sides of her face, cupped in his hands, and kissed her hard with his lips apart.

"That's all I wanted to know. My God, I love you Laramie" Akihiro he plunged his tongue between her lips, kissing her deeply and passionately. He wrapped his arms around her, not willing to let go. She began to place her arms around him, and greeted his kisses with her lips. Her body burned at his touch as it did every time. His lips trailed slowly down her neck. With their every touch, she gasped for a breath. He untied the bow, then unbuttoned her blouse before she stopped him.

"I can't. I have to get home to Akiko."

"No Laramie, Akiko is staying at Manny and Lian's house. There is no where you need to be other than right here."

He continued to unbutton her blouse, exposing her satin bra and uncovered her shoulders. He kissed her left shoulder, around the front of her neck to the right shoulder, as her chest bellowed. Akihiro placed her arms around his neck. He bent and lifted her into his arms and carried her to the bedroom.

While she sat on the edge of the bed, he undressed. As each button freed, her eyes followed his hands to the next one. He removed his shirt, which exposed his chest and rippled abs. He unbuckled his belt, then the clasp of his trousers. His pants fell to the ground. Next, he removed his briefs, enabling him to stand in front of her completely bare. Laramie noticed his erection and her eyes slowly followed his body up to his face. There she met his eyes, which stayed locked on her face the entire time. Akihiro knelt in front of her and continued to undress her slowly. First, he removed her blouse, and then he unfastened her pants. He tilted her back, pulled off her shoes, then her pants to the floor. Even though she lay there half-naked, the room felt so warm to her. He took off her lace panties and pulled her up to a sitting position. When he pulled her bra away, her breasts lowered just slightly. Maintaining their gaze, he moved forward to kiss her. She placed her hands upon his shoulders, rubbing the muscles and feeling their definition. Akihiro rose to pick her up and move further back on the bed. As they lay there with their legs intertwined, his kisses were harder and deeper, his tongue controlling her, teasing her.

Looking into her eyes, Akihiro asked, "Tell me you love me."

Laramie's breathing increased, not wanting to stop, she answered, "I love you."

Akihiro moved over top of her. He placed his legs between hers. "Tell me you love me again," he whispered while showering her with sensuous pecks.

Laramie ran her hands across his back and stopped them on his shoulders while she looked him in the eyes. She repeated, "I love you. I have always loved you."

"Now, tell me you want me," he whispered in a deep, sexy tone into her ear.

""Of course, I want you. Don't make me beg," she replied hurriedly.

"But would you?" he asked while biting at her neck.

"Yes."

At that moment, he penetrated her slowly but deeply. Laramie arched her back to meet him and took a short gasp. Each time he thrusted, a small moan escaped her lips. She moved her hands to his arms and squeezed with each plunge. Their lovemaking became heated and tense. His rhythm started to speed, going deep and hard. Laramie pressed her nails into his arms and moved her hips upward to meet his force.

She wanted him, all of him. She missed his touch and feel. Too much time passed between them and they were going to make up for it. All their emotions channeled into complete desire. Laramie's moans became louder and closer together. Akihiro knew she was close by her hands tightening around his arms.

"Oh God… yes… Don't stop. Oh my God, yes… yes," she screamed out, tears trailing from her eyes. Her body met him at every thrust, her legs trembling against him, wanting more.

Akihiro maintained the same cadence until she no longer moved with him. He pumped harder and faster. Damn, she felt so good, so warm. He missed their lovemaking. After several more thrusts, he stopped. He groaned as he arched his back and pushed his pelvis into her one last time. He stayed over her, very still, a few more minutes until he rolled off to the side, pulling her beside him.

"My God, you are so beautiful," he said kissing her forehead. "I didn't realize how much I missed you, how much I loved you."

Looking up at his face, Laramie smiled and kissed him. "I missed you too." She nuzzled her head into his chest. She was happy to lay there in his arms, running her fingers over his skin. She no longer needed to imagine how he felt, how he smelled or how he tasted. Their night repeated until neither had the strength to continue.

Akihiro rolled onto his side with Laramie's face toward him. She was sound asleep and breathed slowly. He gently caressed her face and placed her blonde tresses behind her. She intoxicated him now just as she did when they first met. *How is it that I am so fortunate to have you in my life again? How do I keep you there?* Akihiro knew he must leave for Singapore in a week. He couldn't accept leaving her and Akiko here in the States. *We both have responsibilities at home and a long distance relationship won't work out.* He refused to continue thinking about it. It was a long evening and morning would arrive soon enough. He bowed his head to kiss her once more when Laramie let out a loud, deep snore. He smiled to himself. *This is the Laramie I know and love.* He kissed her softly and closed his eyes.

Chapter 77

LARAMIE AWAKENED ALONE. She looked around the room for Akihiro but didn't see him. She knew he was there; his clothes were on the floor. She smiled as she thought of the previous night. They were together again and nothing else mattered to her. Still naked, she stood from the bed and walked into the bathroom where she put on a robe. She looked at herself in the mirror. *Not great but not bad*. The alcohol left a horrible taste in her mouth. She grabbed a capful of mouthwash to rid the taste. She took a washcloth and wetted it. She ran it over the soap and washed the left over makeup off her face. *Better*. As she walked back into the bedroom, Akihiro stood in the door between the bedroom and living room. His grin from ear to ear made her slightly shy.

"What is it?" she asked. He walked up to her and placed his arms around her.

"Good morning. I didn't want to wake you. You were snoring so peacefully." She smacked his arm. "I ordered breakfast. I thought we'd eat in bed."

"That sounds great. I'm starving. When will it be here?" She began to kiss him repeatedly.

"Before we have time to finish anything." Laramie pouted. "Come back on the bed with me. I want to talk with you."

"I don't like the way that sounds. Don't tell me you're taking back what you said last night. Don't do that to me," she said almost alarmed.

"No, I wouldn't do that to you."

They lay on the bed and faced each other. Laramie's head was on the pillow and Akihiro propped his head up on his hand. Laramie ran her finger over his face. She started around his eyes, down the sides of his cheek, over his whiskers then down his nose. When she reached his lips, he kissed her finger, which brought a smile from her.

"Lara, I want you to know you mean everything to me, you and Akiko both."

"But…?"

"No, buts. I love you. I fell in love with you the first day at the hotel. It took me longer to realize it. The last time you left Singapore, I was lost without you. For months, I regretted not coming after you. I put my business before you and I never should've done that."

"I understand..."

"Shh. No excuses. It was wrong. We've had so many ups and downs. We get pretty volatile together. I realized after I came here that I couldn't let you walk out of my life again. You and Akiko are my family. I don't have the right to ask you to leave your home and friends. It wouldn't be fair but I have to ask anyway. They have a saying in Japanese that encompasses it what I mean perfectly. *Aishiteru. Choshoku-ni miso-shiruo tsukuttekureru?*"

She wasn't sure exactly where this conversation headed but wondered.

"What does that mean in English?" she asked with a curious expression as she looked into his eyes.

"It means I love you and will make my miso soup for breakfast?"

His eyes flickered side to side as he waited for her reaction.

"*Will I make you miso soup for breakfast?* You have completely lost me now," Laramie answered. He found her expression priceless.

"Maybe I should explain that," Akihiro laughed. Laramie nodded yes. "It is an old expression in Japanese that roughly means… will you marry me?"

Tears welled in her eyes and ran down her face.

"How do you say *yes* in Japanese?"

"*Hai*"

"Then my answer is *Hai*."

He kissed her and wrapped their arms around each other. Between each breathe, she repeated her answer over again. When they stopped kissing, Laramie still cried.

"Was my offer that bad that you need to still cry?" She laughed and wiped her face.

"No. I waited so long to hear you say that. With all the troubles we've had, I didn't think it would ever happen. I love you so much." She tried to hold emotions but couldn't. She cried again. "You are giving me the one thing I've wanted most in my life. A family."

She wrapped her arms around him and cried into his shoulder. He held her tight and just let her release her feelings.

"It's okay, Lara. Everything will be okay. I will always be here for you. I love you."

He exhaled deeply. She pulled back some to look at him. His eyes had tears in them, which made her cry all over again. He pushed her onto her back and wiped her face.

"You have to stop this now. You're making me emotional. One of us has to support the other."

She blew out in an exaggerated manner. She turned to him and smiled. He stood up from the bed and went to get her tissues. She sat up as he handed them to her.

"Wow! This has been one hell of date. Mr. Amori, you certainly have surprised me. I can honestly say I didn't see that coming. But I am so happy it did." Laramie chuckled. "Miso Soup. Never would've guessed that." *Whew!*

The knock on the door brought a disruption to their conversation. Akihiro opened the door and the hotel staffer wheeled in their breakfast and placed it on the dining table. Before he took away the cart away, he removed the stainless dome covers. Akihiro thanked and tipped him. After the worker left, he walked back into the bedroom where Laramie sat on the bed. He asked if she wanted to eat in bed or in the other room. She said she wanted to eat at the table.

As she sat down, she looked over her choices of food. He ordered scrambled eggs, bacon, assorted breads, fresh fruit, coffee and tea. Laramie poured herself a coffee and motioned to Akihiro for the same. He passed and opted for the tea.

"It all looks great. I don't normally eat breakfast but… after the workout last night, I am very hungry."

She made a plate with a cheese Danish and fresh fruit. Akihiro sat beside her and took the eggs and fruit.

"So, was that the rest of our conversation?" she asked as she sipped her coffee.

"No, but it was the start. You haven't answered me regarding the Cummings Corporation or your firm. Will you and Akiko be going back to Singapore with me?"

"As far as the corporation and firm, I, no, *we* need to discuss that with Edward. There is more to that than just leaving it. As for Singapore, you bet we're going back with you."

"Wait, we have a problem. Can we get Akiko a passport in a week?"

"Yes, we can get one in three days but we won't be doing that since she already has one."

"But you told me she didn't that night at the hotel."

"Seems we both lied that night. Sorry. She's had a passport since the time

I came in country for the grand opening of The Democracy. I almost brought her but I was afraid the flight was too long for her."

He glanced at her over the edge of his teacup as he took a sip. "Is there anything else?"

She smiled. "You know, I don't think there is but I am giving my disclaimer right now in case I forgot something."

He pulled her chair closer to him, pulling her off the seat. She sat straddling him.

"My breakfast is going to get cold." He glanced at her plate.

"Lara, everything on your plate is cold already."

"Oh." She smiled.

"So tell me, Miss Holden, when do you want to get married?"

"Hmm... Monday, no wait, Tuesday. I want to get married on Tuesday."

"*This* Tuesday? Are you sure? Can you do that?"

"Yes. You're not backing out are you?" she asked holding his robe collar tight.

"No, not at all. I just thought you'd want the whole thing with the dress, party and reception. I never expected you to say in three days."

"I used to when I was younger. However, the idea of me in a white gown with a daughter pretty much blows the virgin theory." He laughed. There was credence in that statement. "If it's something you want, we can do it again in Singapore. I don't need a huge celebration to validate my marriage." He smiled at her reasoning.

He stood up with her on his lap and carried her to the bedroom.

"What about my breakfast? I was hungry." She held her hand out as she tried to reach for her Danish.

"Yeah, well, I'm hungrier. Just have a bigger lunch."

After they made love, they both dressed and went to Akihiro's hotel first. Laramie watched TV as he showered. He invited her in but she declined, she didn't want to put the same clothes back on, again. Once he was out, Laramie asked him what he wanted to do.

"Go get Akiko at Lian and Manny's."

"No. I mean you're going to check out of here right? And come back to the flat?"

"Only if we shop first. I've seen the inside of your refrigerator and you have nothing outside of baby food. How do you eat?"

"I order out a lot. I probably should've told you this before you proposed but I don't know how to cook."

"Oh well then forget it. The wedding's off." He smiled as he dressed. "I don't figure you to be working right away and with my family, my mother will probably take up much of your day to see Akiko. Not that she won't love you but she's dreamed of a grandchild. I'm sure she would be happy to teach you how to cook."

"You don't mind paella a few nights a week, do you? I can always get lessons from Ahmed, and your mother." She sat on his bed with her legs Indian style. "Wow, I'm going to have a Mom and Dad again. That is so awesome."

"Don't forget Shinji."

"How could I? He offered to take your place." She cringed after she said it.

"*Really?* Just when was this?" He sat beside her on the bed. "Another secret?"

She laughed. "No, it was when I bought the office building. It was a pretty standup offer." She continued in a manner of hypothetical theory. "I must say, it was rather generous. Since he was the *love 'em and leave 'em* type, I chose not to pursue that option."

He teased back. "Was that the *only* reason?"

"Well, since I've never had him in bed, I couldn't compare him against anything. I didn't want to assume he was just like you. However, now that I think about it, he could've been better, huh?"

He tackled her on the bed and straddled over her as he held her arms over her head.

"And, you will *never* find that out."

She pulled her arms free and pulled him down closer. She lifted her head and kissed him as she put her hands behind his head, trying to pull him closer.

"Again?"

"Yes. Again and again and again." She started to unbutton his shirt.

"We don't have to make up for it in one day. Besides, we need to pick up our daughter."

"Are you blowing me off? So quickly?" She grinned slyly.

"No. We have naptime to continue. Besides, don't you want to tell Lian you're getting married?"

"Oh yeah. Good one. I'll let it go this time but not so easy the next."

Laramie walked around his room and looked for anything he missed when he packed. She was happy he would be staying with her and Akiko. It was where he needed to be. She wondered about her flat and asked his opinion on what she should do. He said to keep it since she would travel back and forth to see her friends and family. It made great sense since she owned it and it was more comfortable than staying in a hotel.

After he checked out, they picked up her car at the valet. She drove down

Grant Street to Lian and Manny's place above the market. They knocked on the door of the second floor apartment. Lian was the first to greet them and welcome them.

"Well, this is a great sign. You both are together and smiling. I am assuming you settled your differences and were honest about your feelings toward one another."

Laramie hugged her. "Speaking of honesty, I have a birthday gift for you. It seems you were unable to attend your own party last night. Such a shame since you missed the excitement of the morning."

"Laramie, I don't need to know the details of your sex life."

"No. I believe that part came later. I meant the part where Akihiro asked me to marry him and I said yes." Both girls hugged and screamed like children.

"No way." Lian looked at Akihiro. "You never said a word about doing that. Oh my God, I can't believe it. That is great news. I am so happy for you both. Manny did you hear that?"

"Not clearly over the screaming." He extended his hand to Akihiro. "Congratulations. So when's the big day?"

"Thank you. Laramie has picked Tuesday."

"This Tuesday? No, not this Tuesday?"

"Yes, this Tuesday. Apparently, she wants to make good on my word as soon as possible."

Lian looked at her in shock. "Lara, you're going to need a dress, flowers and a place to eat. Can you do that in such a short time?"

Manny grinned widely. "Dude, that means a bachelor party. How awesome. There's you, Edward, me and I have a few married guys who can give you some tips."

Laramie jumped in. "No way. I know your friends and I don't want them near him."

"Excuse me a minute. I need to quiet my adopted sister from speaking." He turned to her and teased her to an extreme. "Lara, you are so out of this. You won't even know where we are going. Too bad. So sad, sister. You should be thankful he was into old spinsters."

Laramie lunged at him. Akihiro held her back as Manny hid behind Lian.

"You'll have to excuse their juvenile ways. They're always like this," Lian stated toward Akihiro. "That's enough from both of you. Come on. There is a lot to do if you plan to marry in a few days."

Lian always had the better judgment of the group and this was no exception. Akihiro watched at the humorous display. They reminded him so much of Shinji and himself.

He added, "You know, Laramie, you tell me how you wish you had a brother or sister. You do. You have a brother when he taunts you and a sister when he hides behind Lian."

"Low blow, Dude. I got to rethink my plan now." Laramie laughed, as did Lian.

"Akihiro, you will fit in just fine," Lian admitted. "Wait a minute. Does this mean you're going back to Singapore with him?" Laramie nodded yes. "Have you told Edward yet?"

"No, but there is some news on that front. I called him out about being alone the same day when I asked you to settle. Anyway, I was feeling brave that day. I lectured him on being alone and asked about Linda. Well, the other day he stopped in my office and told me they have officially begun to move forward with a relationship."

"That's great but he will be so sad to see you leave. He and Andrew both. They practically raised you."

"I know that will be hard for me as well. I'm going to miss my giant teddy bear."

"Giant teddy bear? You have to be kidding. He is the size of half the rugby team in Singapore. Talk about intimidation."

"Yes, but I know his buttons like you know mine. He's definitely a man's man but little girls make him crumble."

Akihiro interjected, "Speaking of little girls, where is ours?"

Lian told him she was running around the market with Manny's mother. Laramie hoped she didn't eat anything dried. The thought made her cringe. The men and women separated in the living room. The men discussed the starting the night at the 21st Amendment like the other night. Unfortunately, Laramie caught wind of their discussion.

"Did I hear you say *the 21st Amendment like the other night*? Am I to understand the two of you have been out together through this week?"

They froze, not knowing how to answer. Finally, Akihiro proved brave enough to take the heat.

"Yes, we had a guy's night out the day before your birthday. I was going crazy in the hotel and Manny called me for a beer. We didn't have the issues like you and I did. Sorry, Lara."

"Oh no. I am saving this for later. Manchu Tién, I can't believe you did that behind my back."

"So, sue me. Oh, damn! Wrong choice of words." That statement brought on fear by Manny.

Akihiro threw his hands in the air. "Sorry Manny, I can't help you on this one."

Laramie turned to him and bit her tongue. "I will let that go since I am a better person but buddy when you need a ticket fixed, don't call me."

"Ha. I can't. What good will you be in Singapore?"

Laramie realized the one-liners would be nonstop. It was easier to let him say anything than to get involved. She returned to her conversation with Lian and ignored anything the men said. Lian asked her how Akihiro proposed. She told her that he declared his feelings then asked her to marry him in Japanese. They laughed over the literal translation. She said he surprised her so much but not enough so as not to answer yes. She told Lian how she sobbed like a baby. Lian confided in her that Manny sobbed, too, when she accepted his proposal.

Manny and Akihiro decided that Monday night provided a good amount of time for the bachelor party. Manny called a few buddies to let them know to meet out Monday night. He figured Akihiro could invite Edward and Andrew once Laramie told them she was leaving. Akihiro told Manny about Hank Bledsoe that he met at the Giant's game and said they had to invite him. The process ran smoother than Aki anticipated.

Lian and Laramie decided to meet out tomorrow to go shopping for a dress for her and one for Akiko. Lian made the suggestion to have their daughter be apart of the ceremony. Laramie couldn't agree more. Laramie knew they could get their marriage license and marry in the same day but didn't want to rush to that extreme.

"Laramie, I just want to apologize from hiding this from you. I knew you would lose nerve in telling him. We all knew how you felt about him. After the hearing. he told us how he felt about you. You two had to be set apart from everything else to reconcile. I didn't want to lie to you but it was the only way."

"It almost didn't happen. After I walked in, we talked but neither of us said how we felt. It wasn't until he baited me into an argument that I finally admitted to him how I felt. I should've seen it coming but he makes me so mad that I can't be rational. Anyway, he pushed me into a corner and I had to tell him. I'm glad I did. I wasted so much time over that. So much could've been avoided. I actually need to thank you for what you all did. Though I must say the proposal caught me by surprise."

"Me too. I think it's great though. He loves you so much. You can see it in the way he looks at you. You finally have your family. I don't know what we'll do without you here."

"Oh gosh, you're killing me. I will be back in time for the shower and the baby too. You can bet on that. I haven't even told Liz yet. The main conspirator. I owe her for that big time. She is so bad."

After their talks, Laramie and Akihiro thanked Manny and Lian for all their help in their conspiracy as well as watching Akiko for them. They packed up Akiko's things and went downstairs. The new couple walked around the aisles until they found their daughter. Laramie thanked Mrs. Tién for taking care of Akiko. The elderly woman just smiled and nodded. After they left, Laramie disclosed her true thoughts about Manny's parents' knowledge of English. He laughed at her theories. *I don't mind being the last hold out. I know they speak English. I feel it.*

Laramie drove back to her flat so Akihiro could drop off his bags before grocery shopping. Once they entered the dwelling, Laramie felt is was better to put Akiko down for a nap first. As they sat together on the sofa, Laramie asked if he wanted to call home and give them an update. He thought the least he could do was call his mother. Her concern over the three of them troubled her, which in turn troubled Akihiro. He realized based on the time difference he couldn't call until seven o'clock.

"Well, so I guess this means we have some free time." Laramie straddled his lap and placed kisses randomly over his face. "What do you suppose we should do?"

"Break in your bed?"

"Why go that far?" she posed.

As he rapidly turned her onto her back on the sofa, Laramie let out a short scream. He proceeded to undress her once again. They took their time and made love at a slower pace than normal. So many times he brought her to her peak that this day she didn't care about her needs, only his. They had all afternoon until they heard noises from Akiko's bedroom. Akihiro quickly finished since he could look directly into his daughter's room. There was something disturbing about your child seeing you with their mother that didn't settle well with him. Laramie laughed at his embarrassment but still found it cute.

She showered while he fed Akiko lunch. It was a relief to Laramie to have him there to share some of the responsibilities. She thought about the day and all it held so far. She began to cry again with tears of happiness as she stood under the water. *Faith. It always comes down to faith. If my parents aren't looking over me then I don't know who is. I have never loved so much where it hurts but I love him. A family. My very own family.* Laramie dried her hair and dressed. She finished the same time Akihiro cleaned up Akiko.

She walked out of her bedroom. "Are we ready to go grocery shopping? Our first family experience. You would think it would've been more exciting."

"Seeing you in a market is shock enough."

"Ha. At least I know how to eat the foods without direction."

"But I found that so attractive about you. That's what drew me in, that and the lychee tofu."

"The lychee tofu. That was so awful," she shuddered. "Are we ready?"

The trio headed off to Safeway Market on Marina Street. This was a new experience for Laramie. She wondered what things Akihiro liked. *Will he grab things for the cart like Akiko tries to do?* As they entered the store, they followed the normal pattern of produce, meats then dairy. She noticed the items he put in the cart were far healthier than what she placed. *Why is he so sexy even shopping? I will never stop wanting to sleep with him. I'm going to end up like those women with eighteen kids, I know it. I don't know if I'm ready to be barefoot and pregnant for the next fifteen years.* She passed on the Ho-Ho's and opted for granola bars. *Well, at least I'll be healthier.* After they finished shopping, they stood at checkout. The cashier noticed Akiko and commented on how beautiful she was. Akihiro thanked her and Laramie stood there humored by the idea as if she had nothing to do with it. When it came time to pay, an argument ensued. Laramie wanted to pay as she normally did but Akihiro insisted he should. Finally, Laramie let him pay so they didn't hold up the line. As they left the store, Laramie needed to clarify a few things.

"You realize you have to let me spend my money as well. In essence, it all becomes our money. Are you going to have a problem with that?"

"No. I figure if mine runs out we'll move onto yours. Just try and control your spending habits." She laughed.

They returned to the flat and placed the food in the refrigerator. They let Akiko run around the house as usual. When she wanted her parents, she looked for them. Laramie found the entire experience surreal. She dreamed of this but never imagined it would become reality. She found the grin on her face hard to remove. Occasionally, Akihiro pulled her aside, told her that he loved her and kissed her passionately. She was open to every kiss and touch he offered. *This is what it must feel like to be newlyweds. I still have to call Edward and Liz.*

After dinner, Akihiro called his parents house. He informed his mother and father that Laramie and he were to be married on Tuesday. While it shocked his father, it was no surprise to his mother. She informed them both that they would have to renew the ceremony in Singapore for his side to which they both agreed. His mother sounded just like Laramie imagined. Though, she forgot about the British accent. Laramie's excitement to meet her future in-laws was overflowing. Shinji informed them of Laramie's background while Akihiro was gone. Lucia felt awful for Laramie's loss of family and vowed to make her feel completely at home with them. She knew her son and future bride really loved each other despite their stubbornness and it made her ecstatic to know a new family would soon arrive.

After they hung up with Singapore, Laramie called Edward. He finally returned from the country club in Palo Alto. He told Lara that he wondered all day what the outcome of their meeting was. Laramie told him that Akihiro proposed and she accepted. She hesitated to tell him she planned to move to

Singapore. He already guessed it. He told her to go and that it was time for her to build a family of her own. He asked them to stop by the office on Monday after they received their marriage license. They both agreed.

"Well, the first step is done. We have told our families. Since we are keeping the flat, I won't have to pack anything other than summer clothes. However, I do have quite a bit for Akiko. You will have to help me on that."

"We'll make it in the condo for a few months but we'll need Shinji to look for a bigger house for us. Do you want to stay on Sentosa or move to the Orchard?"

"Oh geez, I can't even think that far in advance. Do I have to decide right now?"

"No, you have time."

Laramie bathed Akiko as Akihiro sat on the commode and watched. *What a change in lifestyle this will be from being the bachelor.* After her bath, Akihiro asked to read her a bedtime story. Laramie pulled out *Goodnight Moon*. By the time he reached the end, Akiko slept soundly in his arms. He slowly laid her in the crib and covered her with her blanket. He kissed her good night, partially closed the door and left her room.

Laramie sat on the sofa and waited for him. He laid down with his head on her lap. She played with his hair as he talked with her.

"This has been a great day. The woman I love agreed to marry me and my daughter is sleeping soundly nearby. I have my family around me."

"What will you say on the days we argue?"

"That's easy. I will tell you how sexy I find your temper and pull you close like this and make love to you."

"Really? What if I don't want to make love? Then what?"

Akihiro sat up and leaned over Laramie.

"Then I'll have to hold you like this." He placed his arms around her. "Kiss you like this." He ran his lips from her mouth, over to her ear and then down her neck. Laramie jumped at the attention.

"Okay, I give up. I don't care what you want, it's yours. Just don't stop there."

He stood and grabbed her hand. He pulled her to him and guided her to the bedroom. They both undressed and crawled underneath the covers. She loved the feel of him next to her. She followed his lead until they both achieved their pinnacle of pleasure. She noticed it was never the same way twice. It was always slightly different. She wondered about their future lovemaking and what would happen next. *How much more could he know?* It was just as experimental for him as it was for her. He just had more confidence in the bedroom than she did.

Chapter 78

LARAMIE SAT ON the bed next to Akihiro. She nudged him a few times before he woke up. Once he got a better view, he noticed she was in jeans, t-shirt and tennis shoes. She wore her hair pulled back in a large clip behind her head.

"Why are you dressed so early? Are you going somewhere?"

She kissed him good morning and he sat up. "Actually, yes. It's Sunday morning and I have to go to Martin's for breakfast. You have the option of going with me or staying here and taking care of Kiki. Though if you want peace, I can take her with me, I usually do."

He rubbed his eyes for better focus.

"Who is Martin?"

"It's not a who, it's a what. It's where I go to serve breakfast on Sundays. I've missed so many with Akiko in the hospital that I wanted to go in one last time. So, what do you want to do?"

"No, I'll go with you. I can help or watch Kiki for you. Give me a minute to get ready."

He remembered this part of Richard's history lesson, Laramie the Philanthropist. He wanted to see this part of her. He already knew she made people comfortable around her and didn't think this experience would be much different. However, this was one more thing she would be leaving. He wondered if she was ready to give up her lifestyle in San Francisco to be a stay-at-home mom in Singapore.

As they drove down Van Ness Avenue, Akihiro thought more about her existing life.

"Lara, you seem to be so connected to this city. Are you sure you can walk away from it all? Will you be happy in Singapore without this?"

"Will you be in Singapore?"

"Yes."

"Then yes, I'll be happy. Don't miss understand me, I'll miss my friends here, along with other things I'm involved in, but my happiness lies within our family, not my community."

He picked her hand up off the shifter and kissed it. *She has always been amazing to me. Why should today be any different?* Her answer satisfied his question.

As they neared the center on Potrero Avenue, Akihiro saw a line of people outside. They seemed so cold and wondered how they survived in the frigid temperatures living on the street.

Laramie parked the car a few doors down. She went to the back and retrieved the stroller. Akihiro handed her Akiko and they made their way to the door. As they passed the people in line, the strangers gave their pleasantries to Laramie and Akiko by name. Laramie smiled back, greeting them by name as well.

"You know all their names? That can't be easy."

"It's important. People walk past them as if the homeless are invisible. When you say someone's name, you are acknowledging him or her as a person. They have just as much self-worth as we do." As always, she found another way to impress him without trying.

Once inside, he followed her to the kitchen area. Many of the volunteers were happy to see her and Akiko; many expressed their prayers for her recovery. When Laramie got a word in, she introduced Akihiro to the crowd as Akiko's father and her future husband. Well-wishers walked over and shook his hand but most of the elderly women hugged him. *Americans are so different, yet so amazing.* The younger girls from a nearby church offered to give up their position in line to watch the baby. Akihiro put on an apron and followed the direction of the old timers. Occasionally, Laramie glanced over and smiled at him.

The breakfast crowd lasted until ten-thirty. Akihiro assisted in cleaning up once the line was gone. Laramie stood over a commercial sink and washed dishes in an assembly line format. The amount of work needed to run the place surprised Akihiro. He swept the floors and took out the trash. By eleven-thirty, the place was clean and ready for the next day's volunteers. Many of the people thanked him for his help but most wished them happiness on their pending marriage. Laramie thanked the girls for watching Akiko and placed her daughter on her hip to carry her outside. Akihiro pushed the empty stroller back to the car and loaded it in the trunk. After everyone fastened their seatbelts, Akihiro leaned into Laramie and turned her head to face him.

After he kissed her, he said, "You are the most amazing woman I have ever met and I love you."

Laramie smiled. "You were pretty incredible in there yourself. It's always appreciated when you have another person helping. And yes, I love you, too."

They made their way back to the flat to shower and change into clean clothes. Laramie's excitement to find a dress radiated from her. She hoped she would find something that day and not be at the wire tomorrow night. Manny planned to hang out at the flat with Akihiro and watch Akiko while the women shopped. The plan seemed to work for all involved.

It wasn't long before the Tién's arrived. Manny placed the beer in the refrigerator.

"Lian look at this. There is real food in her refrigerator. I don't even see one Chinese container. Damn, we're in the wrong house. We better get out before the owner gets home."

Laramie, dismissing his joke, said, "Thank Akihiro for that, otherwise you'd be sipping on nothing but beer."

"Laramie, I don't know where you want to start. Do you know what you want? Any ideas at all? Do you want a bridal shop or a department store? Who would have an off-the-rack dress?"

"I have no idea. Let's start with department stores first. I have a better chance in finding something there. I don't think there's enough time for off-the-rack bridal shop though we can save that as a last resort."

The women left in a rush to hit as many stores as they had time for on a Sunday. Manny and Akihiro sat on the sofa and watched sports on TV. Akiko ran around the place with her baby carriage and teddy bear inside. She was happy to be on her own and in her own world.

"Aki, I've called around and we are lined up for tomorrow night. Edward will be there but Andrew won't. No surprise there, Violet controls everything. This is a big step, you ready?"

Akihiro sipped his beer and answered, "Yes, I am. I should've done this a while ago but the timing was wrong. I'm not leaving anything to chance, not this time. My concern is her leaving all of you. This is her home, friends and family. She has the firm and corporation. It has to be hard."

"She'll be fine. When she was on maternity leave, she was happy to spend her day with Akiko. She felt guilty going back to work so soon. My guess is she will step into her new life without any hesitations. I'll miss her and of course, so will Lian. She's like my sister. But it's not like she won't be here to visit." Manny sipped at his beer. "Hey, did you ever get a hold of the old timer?"

"I did. Hank will meet us there. The guy's a great storyteller. You'll like him."

"How's your family with this?"

"Great. My Mum is thrilled to be a grandmother so much that the marriage is second. They can't wait to meet Akiko and Laramie. Shinji has already met Laramie so that isn't a problem. He probably loves her as much as I do. We'll be doing the ceremony for a second time once we're back in Singapore."

"At least it's small scale here. You're getting off lucky with the number of people she knows."

"I hadn't even thought about that. You're right. I brought a suit with me for the hearing. I suppose I'll wear that."

"If Lara wants you in a tux, she'll let you know. You can rent one easily enough. What about rings? Have you looked at any yet?"

"Damn, no. I never even thought about that. We'll have to go after we get the license. I don't know how she's going to pull this off in three days."

"She will. I am so sure she will." Manny grinned.

Laramie and Lian ran into Saks first. Laramie looked through the formal dresses and some were beautiful if you didn't mind wearing a peacock blue gown. She didn't want white but not a bold color either. Lian held up ivory and champagne colored dresses and Laramie nodded against them. After they went through the stock, Laramie looked at the couture dresses. She didn't find anything that didn't require a small amount of tailoring. They decided to head across the street to Neiman Marcus next. She did find a white dress by Mark Bouwer. It wasn't what she wanted but kept it in mind as a backup. They shopped at Macy's then Bloomingdales. Still, Laramie didn't locate a dress. She knew tomorrow that she would be under the wire since she still had to go to a florist. She thought about the rings and wondered if Akihiro would share her thoughts on that. She planned to ask him later. After six hours of shopping, the women and the stores shut down for the night.

The women returned with Chinese food in hand. When asked if she found a dress, Laramie replied no but she had faith in a few off-the-rack bridal shops. Everyone sat on the floor around the coffee table. Occasionally, Akiko came along for rice and baby food. Laramie tried to get her to sit in her lap to eat but her daughter's interest was only playtime. Lian inquired regarding the bachelor party. The men finalized their plans for Monday night with the first stop at the 21st Amendment. The conversation revolved around the wedding with ideas for dinner, location, flowers and photography. Laramie cancelled the thought of an outdoor ceremony since it was so cold out, especially at night. Akihiro thanked her for that news. Of course, Manny knew a photographer. Laramie asked about his quality of work and Lian replied the guy did their wedding. Laramie remembered their photo album and the guy's work was impressive. That became Manny's task. Flowers were an easy decision for Laramie as long as they were in season and matched her dress. *How hard is neutral?* Edward volunteered to have the judge available since he golfed with most of them. He also suggested Laramie have the ceremony at his home. She remembered how beautiful it was for her baby shower but that had weeks of planning. *Can we still get the same look in two days? I'll cross my fingers.*

After Lian and Manny left, Akihiro helped Laramie clean up in the kitchen. Once she finished the dishes, Laramie grabbed Akiko for a bath before bedtime. Akihiro stopped her and told her to relax; he would bathe Akiko. She didn't turn down this generous gift. Laramie laid on the sofa while she thought about any other details. She heard the giggling from the bathroom and wondered who the real child was. After Akihiro placed Akiko in her pajamas, he brought her out to say goodnight to Mommy. Laramie kissed her goodnight and listened to Akihiro read a bedtime story.

Akihiro came into the living room. Laramie sat up on the sofa so he had room. Once seated, he pulled her back down to rest her head in his lap. Laramie looked him over and noticed several wet spots on his shirt. *It seems they both got baths.*

"Aki, I wanted to talk about rings."

"I'm glad you brought that up since we don't have a lot of time. We'll need to shop tomorrow after we get the license and before we see Edward."

"Actually, I wanted to ask if you would mind if we used my parent's rings. I know that can weird out someone because of their death. We can do something new, too. Do you have a preference? Really, either way will be fine with me."

"Do you have them here? Why don't you get them and let's see first."

Laramie went into her room to the bottom drawer of her dresser. She opened the jewelry box and pulled out her parent's rings. Tom's was a simple yellow gold band with beading on the top and bottom. Audrey's band matched Tom's. Her engagement ring was a one and a half carat brilliant cut diamond with the same matching band. Laramie carried them into the living room and sat next to Akihiro.

"Well, first, I'm glad they're plain. Let's see if it fits."

Akihiro placed the ring on his finger. It was a tiny bit tight but still wearable. He knew it could be sized to fit. *It's not bad looking.* Laramie tried on her mother's ring; it fit perfectly. Throughout her youth, she tried it on many times.

"Lara, I don't care if I have a ring or not. I'm more interested in your thoughts. If this means a lot to you, then we'll use your parent's rings. At least your Dad did well in picking one out."

Laramie laughed. "You didn't know my parents. My Mom picked them out and did everything short of buying them herself. My Dad's contribution was that he went to the store and paid for them. She'd never risk that. Anyway, I just feel by using their rings it's like they're with us, a part of the ceremony. Does that make sense?"

"Yes. Are you sure this is what you want?" She nodded yes. "You're letting me off easy with this. Then, I would be honored to wear your father's ring. I know it holds a lot of sentiment for you."

She jumped into his lap, squeezing him tightly. He couldn't say no to her if her tried. He really felt privileged by her request.

"I love you, Mr. Amori. However, we should stop at the jewelers to have them cleaned and polished. Just another thing to add to the list."

"Are you sure want to do this on Tuesday? I'm not backing out. It seems as though you have a lot to do in one day."

"The hard part is getting the license. If nothing else comes together, then I don't care if I'm in jeans at the wedding and we eat dinner at the wharf. None of the other stuff will matter."

He kissed her softly. His hands caressed the sides of her face as he looked at her, his eyes moving all around. He kissed her again. She stood and pulled his hand to her until he stood. He followed her into the bedroom. The choice to go to bed early was easy but to go to sleep wouldn't come until later.

Chapter 79

LARAMIE, AKIKO AND Akihiro arrived at the City Hall shortly after eight o'clock. Normally, a marriage license required an appointment but Laramie's connections in the system helped greatly. They walked up near the plaza area with Akihiro holding Akiko. Not a lot of the architecture in San Francisco impressed him however; the gold leaf on the spire and the size of the rotunda changed that. He looked at the carving into the limestone and clearly saw the magnificence of the skilled workers who built the structure. They climbed up the steps and through the center of the three palladium doors. Before they fully entered the building, they passed through security. Akihiro let Akiko walk through after Laramie before he passed the guard. As they entered the lobby area, he didn't know which way to go inside. Laramie walked over to the information desk where a woman told them to follow around the stairs and when they reached a long hall turn right; the office for marriage licenses was down that hall. It was easy to spot with a sign and a large arrow attached to a brass post.

After they walked into Room 168, they stood in line behind velvet roping and waited to get to the front desk. When they reached the desk, a young woman took their passports for birth information and asked for their occupations, if there were any previous marriages and education in years. After she gathered the information, she made sure the document was free of any typos. Laramie and Akihiro looked it over and all the information was correct. The woman assigned a registration number and handed them the certificate. She explained the types of people certified to perform the ceremony and that the certificate was valid for ninety days. Laramie and

Akihiro smiled since their wedding would be the next day. As they left the office, Akihiro and Laramie giggled with excitement.

"That was the hardest part and we are finished. Now, we need to meet with Edward. Are you ready for that?"

"I'm not sure. It depends on what he has to say."

They grabbed a cab in front of the City Hall plaza. The car circled around City Hall and up Van Ness Avenue. When the cab reached California Street, it turned right. The former Bank of America building was easy to spot. This was the first time Akihiro saw where Laramie worked. It surprised him that she worked in a building so high knowing her fear of heights. The geometric design of the building seemed small compared to the use of granite. They climbed the stairs and passed through the revolving doors. Laramie waved to the security guard at the desk as she walked to the elevators. Akihiro, holding Akiko, followed her. As they entered the elevator, Laramie pushed the button for her floor.

Once they exited the elevator, they walked up to the front desk where Linda sat. She was in her mid fifties and an elegant woman. Her blonde hair complimented her light skin tone. She stood to walk around the reception desk. Her height surprised Akihiro, she stood taller than Laramie. *So, this is the woman for Edward. Teddy Bear, right.* Linda came around first to pick up Akiko. She extended her hand to shake Akihiro's hand. She expressed pleasure in meeting him finally and congratulations on the nuptials.

"Laramie, I have a cellist for the ceremony but I need to confirm a time. Have you chosen one?"

"Good question. I'd say five-thirty." She looked to Akihiro for support. He remarked the time was fine. "Is Edward in his office? He asked we stop."

"He's been waiting for you to show. Go ahead."

They walked down the hallway to Edward's office. Akihiro noticed it was quite large. He agreed with Laramie the antiques were beautiful but not his style either. They sat in the wing chairs across from Edward. Akiko ran around the desk to see her Grandpa. As he picked her up and bounced her on his knee, Akihiro saw the 'teddy bear' part of Edward. It amused him.

"Well, congratulations. You both are finally together and no worse for the wear. Did you get your marriage license?"

Laramie answered first. "Yes. We just left there. Did you find a judge?"

"Yes, I did. Judge Robertson will be officiating. I'll call him back with a time. Have you given one to Linda?"

"Yes, five thirty. Now, what did you want to discuss?" Laramie already knew but it pushed Edward to speak faster. She needed to leave as quickly as possible to complete her many errands.

"GMH and Cummings Corporation. We need to discuss your plans for your seat on the board at Cummings. My opinion is that you should remain there. They meet quarterly and you can hold the meeting wherever you like. This still gives you an income without having to do any of the work."

The conversation made Akihiro uneasy to be speaking of *her* income. He had no idea what her salary was let alone her pay from the corporation. All he knew was that she donated most of it.

"Edward, that's fine. It gives everyone else a trip to Singapore and a chance to stay at a fabulous hotel on Sentosa Island." Akihiro smiled at her. She looked at Akihiro to explain some. "Graham, Mathers and Holden is run mainly by Andrew and a few other officers. Is he going to continue to do that without me here?" She posed the last question back to Edward.

"Yes, for now. I think you should open a small office in Singapore to keep your license active. Why waste all that education? Frank can send you enough small jobs to give you hours. As for the corporation management, I'd like to retire in a few years as CEO and pass that job onto someone else. It seems my stepdaughter wants me out doing more socially. You already know the requirements for establishing a satellite branch in Singapore. Why not take that portion with you?"

"Edward, I can't run a small law office and a corporation and still spend time at home with Akiko. That's too much."

"I wasn't meaning you. I meant for Akihiro. That is if he wants to do that."

Edward posed the statement and expected a response. Akihiro sat up in his chair shocked at the statement.

"Edward, I don't know anything about running a global corporation. Besides, I have two hotels to run."

"Son, the money for the stockholders is determined by the board of directors. We have some top-notch men running those subsidiaries. All you do is read the reports and conference with the individual presidents. They do the work and report to you. They are required to send in monthly reports on their financials. All you would need is a good accountant."

Laramie smiled and added, "What about Rhys? He has many years of experience at the bank in finance. Then, all you would need is an excellent tax accountant. That could work."

"But what about the Tanjong?" Akihiro looked at Laramie. "You're asking me to give up my hotels."

"No. I'm not asking you anything. I just want you to think about the offer. But, if you choose to take over the corporation, Kat would be a great choice to replace you. You know she is more than qualified to run the hotels. She knows your expectations. Akihiro, this would give you normal business hours and more time to spend at home. I think it would be a great fit. Besides, I can help out if you need it."

"I don't know. The responsibility is immense. You're talking about a huge difference in gross revenue and employees. I'm not qualified to run a business like that."

"Akihiro, how much experience did you have in running a hotel?" asked Edward.

"Well, none but the investment was my own."

"You realize the corporation is yours as well, don't you?" Edward poised.

"No, it's Laramie's. This is all hers."

Laramie interjected, "Actually, Edward's right. After tomorrow, it becomes half yours. There is no prenuptial agreement. Under California Law, once we are married, you're entitled to half of my estate. That means the corporation, the firm and the settlement, everything."

Akihiro turned to her quickly. He never thought about her assets since he thought she planned to leave it all behind.

"No…no, I can't take that. It's not right. You and her family built this up yourselves. I can't take any entitlement to that. It would be wrong."

Laramie sensed his reluctance. "Aki, do you love me?"

"Yes."

"Do you trust me?"

"Yes."

"Then trust me now. If I didn't trust you and love you then I wouldn't put any of this out there for you to access. Will the Kisaki be *ours*? Will the condo be *ours*? What about the hotel? Will that not be *ours* too?"

"Yes, but Laramie this is different. It's a huge responsibility. A huge investment."

"Yes. But your hotel started off the same way. It's all a part of you. You built the Tanjong, you purchased the condo and the Kisaki. These are things you worked for, things that are important to you. Do they not hold more than a dollar amount to you?"

"Yes, they do but—"

"But they are the same. The dollar amount doesn't matter. It's the sweat and pride and sentiment that make them important, not the money."

He knew she was right as much as he didn't want to admit it. *This is too much to comprehend at one time. How can they be so casual about this? This is a fortune, many people's fortunes.*

"Do I have time to think about it?" asked Akihiro slightly sweating.

"Yes, you have until Thursday. We would need to have the papers drawn and notarize your signature here before you travel. Lara is correct. The money shouldn't be the determining factor. We all know there are some things more important. Think carefully and let me know your answer."

Laramie and Akihiro stood up and said goodbye to Edward. Aki knew he planned to talk more in depth with Laramie tonight. *Damn, I can't. Tonight's the bachelor party. Maybe I can talk with Manny about it. He knows all about her and the firm as well.* After they said goodbye to Linda, they went into the elevator.

"Akihiro, I know this seems enormous to you right now. We've never talked about finances but that comes as part of the package. If you prefer to stay at the hotel, I understand that and I am perfectly fine with that choice. However, I trust very few people. You need to realize whether or not you take over, you will still have a stake in all the assets. How well do you trust a stranger to monitor that? Would you trust a stranger to manage your hotels?"

"No, but it's just such short notice." He pulled Akiko from her arms and kissed Laramie. "I never gave any of this a thought until now. You have to admit it's overwhelming."

"It is today but it won't be tomorrow." She kissed him back. "Now, let's stop at a jeweler to have the rings polished. We can have lunch together or split up, it's up to you."

"Lunch together since after tonight I don't know how much I'll see you before the ceremony."

"Good call. Do you want Mexican? The place we went for my birthday is over a block."

"That's fine. Why don't you give me the rings? I can have that done while you shop with Akiko. What else do have planned?"

"I have to find a dress, then a florist. The dress will be the hardest. There's a place around the corner on Columbus that I want to see. Maybe I'll get lucky."

"What do you want me to wear? Have you thought about that?"

She grinned. "I would say nothing but… Did you pack a suit? What color?"

"Yes, I wore a suit for the hearing. It's black."

"Hold out on a tie until you hear from me then I can tell you a color. I'm sure you will be the handsomest man there."

After they had lunch, they kissed goodbye and separated. Laramie went to an off-the-rack bridal shop on Columbus. Once inside, she asked the sales lady where the dresses were in a size eight. The woman told Laramie she figured her size for a six. *Ha! Never, especially since the baby.* Laramie looked at the dresses. Many were too overdone for her taste and ceremony. She wanted something formal but maybe less bridal. The lady went to the size six area and pulled out a simple dress in ivory and light gold. Laramie liked the colors but felt the size was too small. Reluctantly, she tried it on. Akiko played quietly in the changing area as Laramie stood on a raised platform encircled in mirrors. She liked the light gold sash around her waist and the simple lacework with crystals and beads. When she stood up straight, Laramie became misty.

"This is the one. I cannot believe it. It's so beautiful. It has everything I wanted, lace, nonwhite, simple but elegant. It fits beautifully."

"It suits you perfectly. You're tall enough to wear almost any shoe. I'd recommend a sandy color that matches the sash. I've seen many women try on this Maggie Sottero dress but it never fit them as it fits you. The coloring is perfect on you. I knew you were a size six, too," the sales lady added.

"Well, it must be a *large* size six. No more compliments, I'm sold. What's the best way to transport this?"

"Depends on the date of your wedding, but I'd say on hanger."

"Well, the wedding is tomorrow."

"My, you cut it close. Good thing you don't need tailoring. Let me take it in back and steam it quickly before I bag it up."

Laramie dressed as soon the lady took the dress off. *It is so perfect.* Laramie glanced around the shop at the accessories. *Do I need a veil? Nah. I'm not the veil type. Besides, it makes it more formal.* The sales lady came out with the gown and placed it on a hook at the register.

"Do you need any hair accessories? A veil? I'm throwing in the blue garter. You have beautiful long hair; let me show you something you can do with it on your own. A real no fuss style."

She had Laramie stand in front of the mirror and came behind her with hair combs covered in beads and sequins. She pulled her hair up loosely behind her ears and held it place with the combs. She left Laramie's length stay long behind it. She told her to imagine it with loose curls on the sides and back with waves up front. *She's right. That does look nice.* Laramie had her add it to her bill. *I am shocked this is done. I have all afternoon to play. Ooh, first, I need to get flowers, and then I can play.* Laramie loved the centerpiece she received from Akihiro so much she decided to go back to that florist, Jane's Roses. She loaded everything and everyone in the cab and headed up to Sutter Street. She found it easily with the small flower cart located outside.

Once inside, Laramie asked if there was somewhere she could hang her dress while they discussed flowers. The store clerk found a spot near the back work area. Laramie sat Akiko on her lap as she browsed through photos of bouquets. She explained the wedding was the next day and she needed three boutonnières and two bouquets for Lian and Akiko, in addition to the bridal bouquet. Then she also needed a few centerpieces and garland for inside Edwards home. Laramie wanted to be sure that they could provide all of this on such short notice. The woman said if the flowers were in season, it was a tight schedule but they could manage it. She asked Laramie how she found the store and she told her of Akihiro's centerpiece for her birthday. The woman remembered him. Laramie explained he proposed a few days later. She didn't blame Laramie for the rush; she would've done the same if he asked her too.

The clerk brought out a few different flowers to show Laramie the many combinations. She knew she wanted simple and traditional. She loved gardenias, orchids, and roses. *Why are there so many choices? This is harder than the dress.* Finally, Laramie asked what flowers were in season now. The store clerk said they had all the ones Laramie mentioned. *Argh!* The clerk did an experiment with gardenias, greenish and white hydrangea and stephanotis, and then she added loops of antique white lace throughout. Laramie loved it and said it was perfect. She explained to Laramie that the arrangements would match and the boutonnieres would be gardenias with the ribbon.

Laramie paid her in advance, not something she normally would do but since she would be busy tomorrow, she didn't have much of a choice. She held onto Akiko and grabbed her dress. She hailed a cab and went home.

When she walked inside, Akihiro sat on the sofa as he watched TV. He saw the long bag and knew she found a dress.

"What color tie do I need?"

"Beige with a speck of green."

"Oh that'll be so easy to find," he said facetiously. She smirked at his response.

"Do your best to find off white and you're done. I ordered the flowers. They will be delivered to Edwards's tomorrow afternoon. I found my dress. It was the first one I tried on. It took longer to pick out the flowers. All that is left is shoes and a dress for Akiko. Oh, wait. We need to find somewhere to eat after the ceremony. Any thoughts?"

He tilted his head to the side and stared at her. "Am I really the most qualified person in the city to answer that?"

"I didn't mean for a restaurant but a specific food. International cuisine? Pacific Rim? Asian Fusion?"

"Food. I pick a place that serves food." He teased. She jumped into his lap and blocked his view of the television.

"I am fine with taking care of this but don't blame me if you don't like something because I am asking for your input. This all will be your turn in Singapore."

"No, it won't. Between you and my Mum, I will be doing the exact same thing, showing up and paying the bill." She knew he was right, at least partly. She assumed she would cover this cost and he could pick up Singapore.

"What time is the bachelor party?"

"I'm waiting for Manny now. He should be here any minute."

"Aren't you starting early? It's only five o'clock. Please make sure you take a cab everywhere. No one needs to drive."

Laramie called Bamboo Nail Salon for an appointment tomorrow morning. She needed a manicure, pedicure and waxing. Akihiro commented from afar regarding the waxing. Laramie shook her head in disbelief and ignored him. She sat Akiko in her high chair and proceeded to feed her dinner. She heard the buzzer and knew it was Manny. Akihiro opened the door in the lobby and waited for him to come upstairs. When he opened the door to the flat, Lian was with Manny with Chinese food containers.

"I know it's two days in a row but I didn't know what else to bring."

"Oh, I am so glad you're here. I can't wait to show you my dress. It is beautiful. Oh, do you want to go to the salon with me tomorrow? I can change the appointment to two people."

"I'd love to join you. What are you doing with Akiko?"

"Francesca is coming to watch her for most of the day. I need a pair of shoes and a dress for her tomorrow. I did get all the flowers ordered and they will be at Edwards in the afternoon. I ordered you a matching bouquet."

"What for?"

"I'd like you to be my maid of honor. Would you?"

"I would love to be your maid of honor. You'll need to show me the dress so I can find something to coordinate well with it. What about the dinner? Have you given that thought? We are running low on time." Lian hugged Laramie. The guys rolled their eyes.

"Actually, I was thinking about the Ritz Carlton. Then I could reserve the suite for my wedding night."

"Cake. What about a cake?"

"I can ask the chef at the Ritz. I'm sure they have something small. I'll call after they leave. By the way, Aki, I ordered an extra boutonniere."

Akihiro knew what she meant; he didn't need the hint. The men reacted with exaggeration.

"Manny, would you be my best man?"

"Oh, dude, I never thought you'd ask. What are you wearing so we match?"

"Leather pants and a studded jacket."

"Oh, so you're going for that Castro look. I like the dominator style, so retro yet brutish."

The women watched in disgust. They saw no humor in the male juvenile behavior. Manny asked if Laramie had any hard liquor. She said she had vodka in the cupboard over the refrigerator in the kitchen. It was Stolichnaya. Akihiro commented that she needed to switch to his favorite.

"I know Grey Goose. It's always Grey Goose."

The men high-fived each other. Manny explained it was a Bay City tradition of doing a shot before they leave. Laramie called him on the lie. He quickly rephrased it that it was a new tradition. After their shots, the men kissed their mates and left. As the men walked down the hallway, Laramie told him to hit the buzzer when he got back and she'd help him inside.

Laramie called the Ritz and spoke to the manager of the dining room. He suggested the small dining area for privacy; she agreed. She told him there would be eight people and that she needed a small type of cake as well. He offered an amaretto, vanilla and berry torte in a butter cream icing which they could decorate to suit a wedding. She loved the idea. She told him they should be there sometime near six o'clock. *Whew, that part is done*!

"Lian, I think we're actually pulling this off. Did you get a hold of your photographer friend?"

"Yes, I gave him Edward's address and he will be there then follow to the reception dinner. I can't believe you are getting married. I know it's real but it also seems so surreal. What are you getting Akihiro as a wedding gift?"

"A bride." She laughed. "I never gave that any thought. I would have to find something tomorrow. That's short notice."

"If I know you, you'll find something special. Okay, so show me the dress."

Laramie had Lian follow her into her bedroom. She opened the closet and pulled out the garment bag. Lian loved her dress, especially the color. She couldn't wait to see Laramie in it. She helped Laramie lace the corset back and waited for her to turn around.

"Lara, it is stunning on you. You managed to find the perfect dress in one day. I can't believe it. I'm ready to cry right now."

"Don't even get me started. That's another thing I need… waterproof mascara."

The women stayed in and talked about Edward's offer to Akihiro. Lian saw both sides but agreed with Laramie, he should take the position within the family company. He didn't need to forego his own business just promote Kat to run it. Laramie talked about packing up their things to send to Singapore. Lian suggested a moving company that could transport the crates to the airport for shipping instead of waiting on cargo ships. Laramie loved the idea. *We could hire a delivery company to take our belongings to the condo at that point.*

Shortly after Akiko went to bed, Lian said she planned to go home and get a good night's sleep as well. She planned to meet Laramie at the spa in the morning and wanted to be ready. She told Laramie if Manny was too drunk to keep him there until morning. They said their goodbyes and Lian left. *A wedding gift? He's Buddhist and Japanese. There has to be something in Japantown that would be a great gift.*

* * *

Manny and Akihiro arrived at the 21st Amendment. Toward the rear of the establishment, Edward sat with Hank at a group of tables. The older gentlemen seemed to hit it off well. Edward stood up to get their attention and waved them over. When Aki arrived, Hank stood up to congratulate him on the wedding.

"Hank, I'm glad you could make it on short notice. I see you met Edward and this is my best man, Manchu, but everyone calls him their 'bitch.' Damn, I wasn't supposed to say that in front of him." Edward about spit his drink out. Hank shook Manny's hand.

"Hell, son, do they have any men where you're from? You shake hands like a pussy," Hank replied. Edward couldn't contain his laughter; neither could Akihiro.

"Aw, come on. I don't need this from all of you. I planned this. Cut me some slack, old dude."

This was what they needed to break the ice for the evening. They ordered appetizers for the tables and shortly before six o'clock; another four young men arrived for the party. Beer bottles and old fashion glasses covered their table and plates of food sat in the empty spots. The conversation became rowdy several times which brought on looks and laughs from neighboring tables.

Manny stood to make a toast to Akihiro. "I want to say best of luck with Laramie. We couldn't have found a bigger sap to fall for her crap, though I'm not surprised it took a foreigner. Here's to a pecker that stays up and a wife that goes down."

Akihiro laughed hysterically. His new friends and family let loose of all their inhibitions tonight. He wished Shinji and Rhys could be there. The drinks kept coming. Akihiro felt a little weird with Edward listening to this since he raised Laramie; she was practically his daughter. That was until Edward stood to make his speech.

"To Akihiro. Welcome, my son, to this crazy family. Remember this… a good woman is like a good bar...liquor in the front and poker in the rear."

The one-liners continued for a while as did the booze. All the men became louder the more they drank and the jokes became funnier and raunchier. Edward choked on his Crown and Sprite a few times. It wasn't long before Manny announced the next adventure in the night, a mermaid cruise. Akihiro had no idea what that was, but at that point, he just followed. Once they reached the Embarcadero, they walked over to the dock where the boat was. Manny spoke with the manager and all the men boarded.

Once inside, they noticed two brass poles in the middle of the floor. The men sat around on the seats and gave their drink orders. Once the boat left the dock, two scantily dressed young women came out and began to dance on the poles. The men were loud but not obnoxious. Manny checked on Edward and Hank to make sure they weren't in cardiac arrest. The women asked who the groom was and they all pointed to themselves. Eventually, they admitted it was Akihiro.

The first woman, a thin brunette, began her lap dance. She placed her rear on his lap and shook it with a vibrating motion. Akihiro kept his hands up but his eyes down. Edward pulled a wad of cash out of his pocket and stuck a ten in the dancer's g-string. The second dancer was a redhead with a more athletic build. She seemed taken with Manny but moved around and worked the crowd. The noise level grew and drowned out the music inside. The more Edward drank, the more lap dances he bought the crowd and the more money he spent.

Further into the cruise, the women's tops came off which brought cheers and whistles by the men. While the scenery was nice, Akihiro knew they didn't have anything on Laramie. When redhead did her shimmy in his face, her implants could've knocked out Akihiro.

Manny came out with a tray of shots. He passed them around and held the last one for himself. He held his glass up in the air.

"Cheers."

Akihiro wondered how much Laramie knew about this side of Manny. He found him hilarious, the jokes never stopped. The two women stood up and put Akihiro between them. They began to bump and grind until he moved along with them. The hoots and hollers started all over again.

Edward and Hank went outside on the deck to smoke a few cigars. They reminisced about their own youth as they looked inside to the next generation. Edward couldn't remember the last time he laughed so hard. Being a man that night had its perks.

As of yet, no one became sick with excessive alcohol. The boat began to return to the dock. Akihiro took a break and went outside by Edward and Hank. He needed the fresh air to sober a bit. The cold air against his face woke him quickly.

"I have to tell you, this has been a hilarious night. One of the best I've had in ages. Manny is a riot."

"That's why we pawned him off on a client instead of keeping him. Could you imagine the firm if he were around daily?" They chuckled. "Too bad Violet had to be her usual bitch, Andrew would've loved this," Edward continued as he blew out a puff of smoke from his Fuente cigar. "Have you considered the offer any more?"

"I want to call Rhys tomorrow morning and get his input. Of course, that's if I can wake up in time."

Manny came out and yelled for the men to join them inside for one last toast before they docked. Akihiro and Hank went inside behind Manny; Edward took one more puff off his cigar before he threw it into the bay. They stood in a circle and held their drinks.

Manny raised his glass and said, "I want to thank you all for coming, especially my parents twenty eight years ago." It took a minute for the joke to sink in. "Here's to panties, not the best thing in the world, but damn close to it. Cheers."

The men followed in their salute and slammed down their cocktails as the boat docked. Before he exited, Edward tipped the dancers generously. Many of the men parted with their cash. As the group gathered on the sidewalk, they each shook hands with Akihiro and wished him the best in his marriage. Manny's friends all lived in Chinatown and split a cab going there. Edward had his own cab to take him back to his house in Cow Hollow. Hank called his son to come and get him. He waved good-bye as he walked to the street. Manny whistled for a cab for Akihiro and him.

"Manny, that was the best party. Thanks, man. I never laughed so hard or drank so much. At first, I didn't think the strippers looked so hot but when we left, they got better looking."

"Anytime brother." The men shook hands, hugged and smacked each other on the back.

They hopped into the cab and headed to the flat in the Marina District. Akihiro jumped out and waved. Manny continued back to Chinatown. Akihiro pressed the buzzer for a long time unaware of his actions. Laramie jumped out of bed and ran into the kitchen to unlock the main door. She didn't want Akiko to wake up. *It's midnight. I thought it would be later.* She stood in the doorway and waited for him to come down the hall. After a few minutes, Laramie still waited. *Where is he?* She left the door ajar as she walked to the elevator. When she pressed the call button, the doors opened. There she found Akihiro sitting on the floor, semi-coherent. She helped him to his feet and walked back to the flat. She told him to be quiet. He spoke in an exaggerated whisper.

"That was the best party. Manny is a character. Did you know he was that funny?"

"Yes. He's hilarious. Let me get you undressed and into bed."

"He drank a lot but I watched my intake," he slurred.

"I see that." She smiled as she took off his clothes. She never saw him drunk before and found him comical. "What all did you do?"

"Well… we went to the bar and drank and ate. Then, we went on a mermaid cruise. Of course, not real mermaids. This one had poles and strippers. We drank some more then I got *two* lap dances though it could've been more. You should've been there. You have a better body." He ran his hands down her sides.

"No, I think I can forego the pole dancing. Let me get you a few aspirin and water. You'll need it before morning." She retrieved the medicine and returned to Akihiro.

"We're getting married tomorrow." He looked at her alarm clock. "No, we're getting married today. Have I told you how much I love you?" She smiled again. *He is so wasted.*

He took the aspirin and moved back on the bed so his head rested on the pillow. She wanted him to get under the covers but it was too hard to move him. She crawled back in bed beside him. He muttered a few words in what sounded like Japanese before he passed out. Laramie ran her fingers along his face and smiled. *Morning will be here before you know it. I wonder how bad you'll feel. I have to think Manny is in the same boat.* She quickly rolled over and fell asleep.

Chapter 80

LARAMIE AWOKE AROUND seven o'clock. She wanted to be up before Akiko to prepare breakfast for Akihiro's hangover. *I have the orange juice, water and bread.* She started a pot of coffee. She wanted the caffeine since she knew it would be a long day. She made oatmeal for her daughter. *Let's see if she wants something new for breakfast. Oh good, it has vitamin C and Folic Acid both things she needs.* When she walked into Akiko's room, her daughter sat in her crib and played with her teddy bear. As soon as she saw Mom, she stood with her arms up. Laramie kissed her and carried her to her high chair. Laramie sipped her coffee as she fed Akiko. *Hooray, something new for her to eat*! Afterward, she jotted down her 'to do' list. *Shoes, dress for Akiko, waterproof mascara, and a wedding gift for Akihiro. The wedding gift will be the hardest. I can't even think of something special.*

Shortly after eight o'clock, Laramie heard moaning from the bedroom. She dropped the bread in the toaster and poured a glass of juice. She carried his plate into the bedroom, setting it on the nightstand. She left the blinds closed for his benefit. Sometime during the night, he found his way under the covers. She crawled across the bed to his side and stroked his head.

"How are you feeling this morning?" He moaned again. "That bad, huh? I have to say you are rather humorous when inebriated."

"There's nothing humorous about any of this. My head is pounding and I feel awful."

"Take the aspirins on the tray and drink the juice. There's dry toast if you feel like food. Good think you monitored your intake. Manny must be feeling horrible."

"*What?*"

She laughed. He didn't recall the conversation after he came home.

"You told me all about your night drinking and the lap dances you received. You said I should've been there to pole dance. I guess that was a compliment. This was after you fell on the floor of the elevator and couldn't stand." He smiled with embarrassment.

"It was a serious party of what I remember. I couldn't stop laughing. Manny made so many foul toasts. So did Edward. It's a good thing you weren't there." He leaned over to grab the toast. He slowly propped himself against the headboard. "I sat in the elevator, for how long?"

"Just a few minutes. I went to look for you after you buzzed the door and never came down the hall. It sounds like you had the typical bachelor party. You'll feel better by lunch. Do you want me to shut the door so you can sleep?" He nodded yes. "Remember to dress before you come out. Francesca will be here to sit with Akiko. Oh, by the way, don't forget you need to pick up a tie. If I don't see you here later, I will see you tonight. Love you." She leaned over and kissed him goodbye. He just moaned back to her.

After Francesca arrived, Laramie informed her about Akihiro's hangover. She asked they try to be quiet as possible as not to disturb him. She needed him healthy for a wedding and she would make sure nothing prevented him from being there. She ran out the door in such a hurry she left her list on the table.

Laramie met Lian inside the salon.

"As my maid of honor, pick out anything and everything you want for today. This is my gift to you. I realize it barely covers all the things you have done for me in the last month. If it wasn't for you, I wouldn't be getting married today."

"Lara, stop it. You'd still be getting married just maybe not today. I am no fool so I plan to relax this morning. Definitely, I want the manicure, pedicure and European facial. What've you picked?"

"Same thing actually but I have full leg and Brazilian waxing too."

"Tell me you're not. It sounds so painful. I'll be out here when you scream."

They giggled at Lian's statement knowing there was some truth to it. Laramie never had a Brazilian wax before but she had a regular bikini wax. It was painful but worth it days later with great results. The women separated into different rooms for their facials. Laramie explained she had her wedding in the afternoon so it was very important not to have any red splotches or pimples on her face. The young woman started with a cleansing, then a toner. After, she laid a moist mask infused with botanicals on her face while she received her neck, head and shoulder massage. *Aahhh! This feels so wonderful. I can stay all day. Don't think of the wedding, think of the wedding night. Relax,*

Laramie. After the facial, Laramie received her Brazilian waxing. The hair ripped from her legs she dealt with fine. However, as they removed the hair from her entire pubic area, Laramie wanted to jump off the table. *There is something completely wrong with having to do this. We women are stupid doing this for men. It had better be worth it.* Shortly she arrived in the outside area for her pedicure.

"Well, Laramie you muffled your screams fairly well. I can't believe any of that is worth it." Lian relaxed in her massage chair as her pedicure began.

"I can't say for sure either but it still beats childbirth. I don't know if I can sit. Oh, the pain. Between the creams and powder, she said I should not have any bumps or real redness. I would hate to explain any of that on my wedding night."

"Oh, to be a fly on the wall for that. Hey, how was Akihiro last night and this morning? Manny came in totally wasted. He just kept laughing and then he passed out. He was still sleeping when I left."

Laramie described the night and the morning of Akihiro's tribulations. They both laughed at the immaturity of their actions.

"I really shouldn't laugh after what I just did. My luck, he won't notice. I just hope he remembers to get dressed before leaving the bedroom. This feels so good on my feet, and back. I need to invest in one of these chairs though I'd never get out of it."

After the spa treatments, they women headed to Nordstrom's for shoes and a dress. Laramie had a good idea of what she wanted for both. She found an adorable dress for Akiko that matched her gown along with matching Mary Jane shoes. *Great, I can mark that off my list. I need shoes, mascara and a gift for Aki. Lingerie. I need something to wear underneath the gown.* Lian went to the maternity department while Laramie looked for shoes. I can't justify a ton of money for shoes I'll wear for five hours. Eventually, she settled on a pair of Valentino pumps in gold. She quickly made her way to the Lingerie department and looked at the thongs. She wasn't a fan of that style but knew it left no lines under her dress. She bought a few styles in light champagne colors. From there, she went downstairs to cosmetics. She purchased waterproof mascara, a blush and a lipstick from Clinique. *Whew! I am almost done. Akihiro's gift is left.* She looked at her watch and saw it was only one o'clock. Her cell phone rang; it was Lian asking where she was in the store. They met at the front doors on Market Street.

"Do you want to eat lunch now? We can wait if you want," Lian suggested.

Laramie remembered Lian's pregnancy. "No, I remember when I was pregnant and I was starved all the time. Let's go eat now. All I have left is a gift for Akihiro. Maybe you can give me some ideas while we eat."

They chose to find a restaurant in Japantown since that was where Laramie planned to find something for Akihiro. The cab dropped them on Post Street and they walked the block before they decided on Mifune Noodle House. They both wanted something of substance until dinner. Laramie discussed her ideas regarding Akihiro's gift.

"Lara, you are making this harder than it needs to be. It needs to be personal and of interest to him."

"Oh yeah, like that's easy. He doesn't collect anything. His place is very simple and Zen-like. I might as well commit hara-kiri now. Oh my gosh, that's it."

"What's it? What did I miss?"

"Hara-kiri. When I was in Singapore, we went out for Karaoke one night."

"Are they crazy? You can't sing."

"Well, they didn't know that. After the song, there was a backdrop of Japanese soldiers committing hara-kiri. That has been a running joke. The knife, but not any knife, a Japanese knife. A Samurai sword. That would be perfect since he is half Japanese."

"I have to think someone in this neighborhood knows a seller. There are tons of antique stores here. I do admit, it is a great idea for him."

After lunch, Lian went home and Laramie scoured Japantown antique stores. She finally found one in a small store on Sutter Street. The gentleman described it as a Yakekuni Katana sword dated back before the 1700's. It had the original wooden case and cloth bag to cover the case. In addition, he had white cloth gloves to handle the blade. He gave each part of the word specific names, which Laramie didn't understand. She viewed the authentication documents, many of the papers were in Japanese. *But, it's beautiful. The artisanship is stunning.* Even though it was very expensive, she knew he would absolutely love it. She pulled out her American Express card and purchased the sword.

It neared three o'clock by the time she returned home. She thanked Francesca extensively for sitting for Akiko. She asked her to stay until she dressed incase Akiko woke up. As she watched her daughter, she noticed Akiko yawned a lot. *Perfect. A nap will give me time to get dressed and pack an overnight bag before going to Edward's house.* Laramie showered quickly since there wasn't anything left to shave. *I may have gone too far this time with waxing. At least there aren't any red bumps or swelling. Now, that would be embarrassing.* Lian called to see how Laramie made out on a gift and what time she wanted the limousine to pick her up. She told her Akihiro planned to dress at Edward's per info passed on by Manny.

* * *

After Akihiro woke up at ten-thirty, he went directly into the shower. The extra sleep, in addition to the juice and toast, helped him recover immensely. He tried to recall the last time he drank that much and couldn't. He stood under the hot water until it almost ran cold. He planned on dressing at Edwards but still packed up a bag for overnight. When he left the bedroom, he saw Francesca with Akiko. She inquired about his health, which led him to believe Laramie told her about the hangover. He went into the kitchen to pour a glass of juice and make more toast. *Stick to what works.* He sat at the dining table and saw Laramie's pad of paper still there. It listed all the things she needed to pick up today. Everything was fine until he read the last item, *wedding gift for Akihiro. Damn, this has to be some American tradition. What the hell do I get her, the woman who buys whatever she wants?* He quickly called Manny.

"Hello?" he replied in a moan.

"Manny, wake up. What's the story with buying gifts for each other? I mean between the bride and groom. These western traditions are completely lost on me."

"You have to buy her something specifically from you. As Lian would say, from your heart. Let me see if I get this straight, you haven't done anything and you need help."

"Come on, you're the best man, you have to help."

"I can't even help myself right now. I'm afraid to open my eyes for fear my brain would explode through them." Aki laughed. Manny drank far more than he did.

"What did you get Lian when you got married?"

"Diamond earrings. Hey, what time do I need to be at Edward's? And, what are the colors?"

"Laramie told me black suit, tan tie. You need to be at Edward's by four o'clock."

Jewelry. She hardly wears any. It has to be heartfelt too. What are those odds? I struggled on the lotus blossom. What could I possibly get now? He left the flat quickly and headed up to Union Square. He remembered seeing countless stores in that area. He assumed one had to have something unique for her. He started at the large well-known stores but found them overpriced for their name and not unique in design. He stopped in stores along Post Street and

Grant Street. The search worsened with his headache. *I can't lose the entire day looking for something, eventually I'll have to settle.* In the meantime, he found an ecru silk tie with tiny black checks in it. *It doesn't have any green but I can't take anymore shopping right now. This will have to do.*

After a half dozen jewelry stores, he made his way down Geary Street. He was near the St. Francis and stopped in another store. He asked the sales clerk for something unique and understated, just not a ring. She guided him to the case that held tennis bracelets. They all appeared nice to him but never saw anything that spoke her name. She showed him one that was very plain. It had twenty bezel set diamonds linked by platinum bars. He didn't see any distinctive qualities about it. However, it was a simple design. She went to a neighboring case and pulled out the colored stones. She explained that the last link of the bracelet held gemstone charms of precious stones, whether the date represented a birthday, anniversary or favorite color. She asked for the birth months of Laramie and he. He told her April and July. Then he added Akiko's month of May. She smiled since she knew the combination of stones. She laid the bracelet flat and placed bezel set stones of diamond, emerald and ruby near the clasp. The bracelet now represented their family. *Family, the one thing Laramie wanted most.* He leaned over, kissed the woman on her cheek, and explained the saving grace she was. Now he had the perfect gift for his bride.

Akihiro looked at his watch. *Wow, it's after three o'clock.* He quickly caught a cab back to the Marina. As he opened the door, Laramie stood on the phone with Lian. He didn't expect to see her until later. It was a pleasant surprise.

"I am so happy to see you. Thanks for the early morning remedy. I'm not a hundred percent, but close." He kissed her.

"I'm glad you're feeling better. You know you can't stay, right?" She grinned, standing in her robe.

"Yes. I came back for my clothes and bag. I have a cab waiting downstairs to take me to Edwards. I'll only be a few minutes."

He grabbed his suit, duffel bag and quickly fled the flat. Laramie sighed with relief. She could slowly get ready. She gave Francesca the dress she bought for Akiko with instructions not to dress her until the last minute before they leave. Laramie placed her hair into hot rollers again. She pulled out the hair combs, thong, garter and shoes. She laid them on the bed as her dress hung on her closet door. She nervously applied her makeup. The closer to ceremony time, the more anxious she became. A quick rap on the door almost made her jump out of her skin. It was Lian. Laramie opened the door and left it open in hopes to circulate the airflow. She asked Francesca to lower the heat.

"Lian, you look beautiful. Where did you find that dress? It matches everything perfectly."

Lian wore her jet-black hair on the side. Her shift dress made of beige silk disguised any signs of pregnancy and her sling back pumps in gold complimented Laramie's dress.

"Oh, this old thing?" She laughed. "I found this at Bloomingdales, on clearance no less. I came a little early. I thought you could use a hand. You never told me on the phone if you found a sword for Akihiro."

"I did. It's wrapped in a box already otherwise I'd show it to you. It truly is beautiful. I just hope he likes it."

"It won't matter to him. He'd like anything from you. I brought these rhinestone bobby pins incase your hair doesn't cooperate."

Laramie removed the hot rollers and brushed out each curls separately before she ran her fingers through her hair. Lian sprayed the hairspray around her head before she put the two crystal studded combs in her hair. *Perfect!*

When Laramie disrobed, Lian burst into tears of laughter.

"Holy crap, they waxed everything. Ouch, that had to hurt."

"Please, let's not go there. I wish they left a little something. I feel so weird."

Laramie put on her lace thong and then her garter. She put on her shoes since she didn't think she'd be agile enough to do so in her dress. Lian grabbed her dress off the door and pulled the corset laces further apart. Laramie slowly stepped inside her dress and pulled the straps over her shoulders. Lian asked Francesca to help her lace the back. As Lian pulled the two sides together, Francesca pulled the laces, and then tied them in a bow at Laramie's waist. It wasn't as tight as Laramie anticipated. As the bride turned around, the woman awed at how stunning she was.

"Lara, before you look in the mirror and cry. I have to tell you, you look exquisite. I'm not saying that because you're my friend. You are so beautiful. That dress is perfect on you."

"Señora, que linda. She is right. So beautiful."

Laramie stood in front of the mirror behind her door and beamed. "Oh, thank goodness for waterproof mascara. This is so surreal. I can't believe it's actually happening now. I am really getting married. We actually pulled this off in three days."

"Nothing was going to stop you. You are so much more focused when you two are together. He may make you emotional but he also gives you strength. You both are so well suited for each other. I can honestly say in the years we've known each other, I have never seen you happier than when you are with him." Laramie waved the tears dry in her eyes. "And, another thing, he loves you very much. You see it in his face. I am so happy for you both." Laramie hugged Lian.

"I can't thank you and Manny enough for wonderful friendship you've given me. You both are like my family. I love you guys so much." Laramie began to tear.

"*STOP!* Save it for the ceremony. Hurry and touch up your makeup and I'll get Akiko dressed."

After they finished with Akiko, the women went downstairs and into the black limo. First, they dropped off Francesca near her home and then made their way to Edward's home.

* * *

As the cab dropped off Akihiro in front of Edward's home, his awe of the design was clear. On top of a quiet street in Cow Hollow, sat a Mediterranean mansion in limestone with a tile roof. There was an open balcony with three arches on the top floor with windows flanking each side. The second floor had palladium windows all across the front. At street level, Akihiro walked up one set of brick stairs that went around a center raised bed of formally landscaped bushes. At the top of the stairs, a very ornate entry led into the home. Akihiro pressed the doorbell and Linda greeted him. As he walked into the ground floor, marble stairs with wrought iron railings went to the upper levels. To his right was an English pub style room where Manny and Edward waited for him.

"Come on in, Son. We've been waiting for you. Hell, you're not even dressed yet. There's a bathroom around the corner; go get ready."

Manny sat on the leather sofa with his elbow on the arm. He rested his head there with his eyes shut. His hangover remained ever so slight. Edward sat in a leather wingback chair similar to those in his office and held a Crown and Sprite in his hand. Edward gave Manny a lecture on the 'hair of the dog.' Manny swore off alcohol for life. Edward, amused by the statement, made him a Bloody Mary. He instructed the novice to drink it slowly as he explained the alcohol would thin his blood and relieve some of the headache. It wasn't much later before Akihiro joined them in the room. He, too, swore off any cocktails.

"You are getting married today. You will be drinking so a short one now won't hurt you."

"By the way Edward, I've given your offer a lot of thought. I've decided to take on the job and responsibility."

"Good news, no, great news. What changed your mind?"

"Akiko. I'm fine financially, as is Laramie, but thinking about her family history and grandfather's work into building the company, I didn't want her to lose that legacy."

"Let's toast to that."

They raised their glasses, toasting to family. They sat casually and talked about the previous night, at least what they could recall. Linda came to shut the doors as she explained that Laramie, Akiko and Lian arrived. She would open the doors once all the women were upstairs.

As Laramie walked into the house, Linda instructed them to remain quiet until upstairs. Once Laramie reached the main floor, she noticed the flowers along the railings. She peeked into the living room and saw the mantle covered in beautiful floral arrangements. Two pedestals, flanking the fireplace, had cream colored flowers and greenery draping down them. The side tables had smaller arrangements with candles burning inside cut crystal hurricane jars. The room was gorgeous just as her shower was. When she turned around to go upstairs, she noticed the dining room decorations as well. *They went beyond what I asked. This home is just elegant. Mmmm… I can smell the gardenias too.* Once inside Laramie's old bedroom, Linda asked if she needed anything.

"Yes, a drink. I'm becoming a little overwhelmed with emotion. I never pictured any of this as a young girl in this room. I never expected this was how my life would be."

"Laramie, that's what makes life so wonderful. It's the little surprises we get. I'm sure you never thought of Akiko either. Now look at you. You're a wonderful mother and she is your pride and joy. It's what's outside your work that molds you, friends and family."

"I know you're right, Linda. I am more fortunate and blessed than so many. I lose sight of that sometimes."

Lian added, "We all do that. That's why these are called special occasions."

As the women talked, Akiko pulled old dolls out of a baby crib and played. She looked adorable in her dress. Laramie put her hair into a whale spout ponytail on top of her head and a bow around it. She couldn't get it to lie flat no matter what gels or sprays she tried. Linda went downstairs to get a glass of champagne for Laramie and water for Lian. She informed the men they could carry on as usual.

"Okay, Lara, what's your something old, new, borrowed and blue?"

"Old is my mother's diamond pendant, new is the dress, blue is the garter. Oh, I don't have anything borrowed."

"You do now." Lian pulled off the diamond earrings she received from Manny. "Put these on. They were from Manny on my wedding night."

The girls sipped on their drinks as Linda went downstairs to show the cellist where to set up. They heard the music start and knew the ceremony was close. Shortly after the music began, Judge Robertson arrived. He joined the men in the pub room for a drink and a toast. Edward invited him to stay with them for the dinner as well but he declined because of previous engagements. A second knock on the door came from Andrew with his wife, Violet. Edward never liked her. *The old hag. Andy could've done so much better. Even now.* However, he let his grudge go since it was a day for Laramie. Edward suggested they go into the living room and get started since everyone was there. He continued up the stairs to Laramie's room. Once inside he asked everyone to leave except for Laramie.

"My dear, you are beautiful. I know your parents would be very proud of you just as I am." Laramie teared up. "Who would have known when you came here as a young teen that you would once again have the family of your dreams."

"I love you so much. I couldn't have had a better man become my father than you. I am going to miss you, too." Edward became quite misty as well.

"He truly loves you and I know you love him deeply. Don't ever lose that in your hearts. That's what gives you strength. Are you ready to go?" She nodded in agreement, sniffling slightly.

The cellist began the ceremony with *Prelude* by Bach. First, Lian walked in with Akiko by her side. Their daughter stood with her small bouquet and a basket of petals, and dumped them in a big pile on the floor. Lian took her hand to keep her walking. As the bride neared the bottom of the stairs, the *Wedding March* by Mozart started. Laramie and Edward stood arm in arm, taking a big breath, before they made their entrance into the living room. Everyone in the room turned to see the bride. The photographer had his tripod set up to capture Laramie's entrance.

A very nervous Akihiro faced her with his hands clasped together. *She is stunning. How is that possible to be beyond beautiful?* His smiled at her and brought his fist up to his mouth as if to clear his throat. He swallowed hard. His eyes became glassy as she neared.

Laramie held onto Edward's arm tight. She was thankful for the glass of champagne to calm her some, though not enough. She smiled huge at her future husband as her eyes welled with tears. Edward patted her hand to relax her.

When they reached Judge Robertson, the judge asked, "Who gives this woman away?"

Edward responded, "I do." He took Laramie's hand and placed it in Akihiro's. He gently kissed her on the cheek before he walked to the side.

The judge began the ceremony with the exchange of their vows. Laramie stood firm as Akihiro promised to love, honor and forsake all others for life.

However, as she repeated her vows, Akihiro's eyes welled up so much he had to wipe them. This, in turn, caused Laramie to tear and stumble on her words. The judge asked for the rings. Manny and Lian passed the respective rings to the bride and groom.

Akiko, frustrated with the silence, decided to get involved in the ceremony. She pulled at her father's pant leg. When he looked down at her, she held her arms up. Manny tried to pick her up, but she yelled 'no.' She pulled at her father's leg again and called out his name. That provided another excellent photo opportunity for the photographer as he quietly moved around the room. Akihiro looked down, rubbed her cheek, and shook his head no to her request. She finally sat on the floor and tried to pull the silk petals out of the tulle overlay on her dress.

"I, Akihiro Amori, take you, Laramie Lila Holden to be my wedded wife, to have and to hold, for richer and poorer, to love and to cherish, from this day forward."

"I, Laramie, Lila Holden, take you, Akihiro Amori, to be my wedded husband, to have and to hold, for richer and poorer, to love and to cherish, from this day forward."

They placed the rings on each other's hands and declared to wed. The judge spoke a few words of consent to wed, laws of the state and his authority to perform the ceremony before he confirmed them as husband and wife.

"You may kiss your bride."

Akihiro placed one hand behind her waist and the other along the side of her face. She smiled as she went toward him. At first, he kissed her tenderly, followed by a few pecks. Then he pulled her tight and kissed her hard and passionately. Laramie wrapped her arms around his neck. Quickly, Manny made the comment that they needed to save the rest for the wedding night, which brought smiles from the bride and groom.

The witnesses in the room came and hugged them both as they gave many blessings and good wishes. Linda passed out glasses of champagne for everyone to toast the new couple. After Manny and Lian signed the marriage license as witnesses, the Judge congratulated the bride and groom before he left. Edward informed them that the limousines were waiting. He decided the bride and groom with the matron of honor and best man would ride in the first limo. He offered to take Akiko in the second limo with the Mathers, Linda and him but Laramie stated Akiko would go with them.

The limousines made their way toward the Ritz Carlton on Stockton Street.

The laughter in the first limo started immediately.

Manny asked, "You've been married ten minutes. Aki, do you feel that added weight pulling at your ankle?"

Lian smacked him. "Ignore him. I thought the ceremony was beautiful. If I didn't keep looking at Akiko, I would've cried through the whole thing." Laramie agreed.

"Kiki definitely made her presence known. She certainly is a daddy's girl," Laramie added while she looked at her daughter on her father's lap.

Manny passed out glasses with champagne to everyone except for Akiko and toasted the new Amori family. Lian took her false sip which worked well for her since she didn't care for champagne all that much.

"I have to admit that 'hair of the dog' theory of Edward's seems to work. My headache is gone. Oh wait, I take that back, Violet is in the other car," Manny joked.

Lian asked him to behave, especially at the dinner. "At least you both have privacy tonight. Sleep in and check out late. Akiko will be fine with us. You know how Manny's mother likes to spoil her."

As they pulled up under the porte-cochere, Manny and Lian exited first. Laramie started next until Aki pulled her back, kissed her again and declared his love for her. She returned the same sentiment.

After they entered the hotel, The Maitre 'D guided them to the private dining room adjacent to the pub. Akihiro assisted Laramie in her chair due to the length of her gown. Akiko sat between her mother and Lian. Manny sat next to Akihiro, and then came Edward on the side opposite. Beside Edward, Linda sat with Andrew to her right and Violet on the end across from Lian. A lot of small talk started the evening with giggling intermixed. A young man about his mid twenties came in to collect their cocktail orders. The men ordered their normal drinks. After he left, the sommelier recommended 1996 Billecart-Salmon, Grande Cuvée, Brut, for the ladies champagne request. Lian stuck with an herbal iced tea.

The waiter returned with the cocktails and the menus under his arm. He passed out the menus to everyone's left. The sommelier returned with the champagne and a standing ice bucket. He poured Laramie's glass first, which she found to her liking. Once everyone had their drink, Manny stood to make the first toast.

"Akihiro, you are a lucky groom; you've got Laramie. She's beautiful, smart, funny, warm, and loving. Laramie, you've got .... Akihiro." His humor brought on many laughs. "Honestly, though none of us are blood relatives, we are one family. Lara has been like a sister to me and a best friend to my wife. Akihiro, in the weeks you've been here, we've gotten to know you fairly well. Speaking for everyone here, we're thrilled to have you join this family and be a long part of Laramie's life. Welcome."

Akihiro shook Manny's hand. They developed a great friendship in the short time together and, despite their manly exteriors, they would miss each other. Manny walked behind Aki to kiss Laramie congratulations. Edward stood next. Laramie hoped she wouldn't cry from anything he might say.

"Lara, you've grow so quickly before my eyes. We've had our struggles and our triumphs. However, in all the years I've known you; I have never seen you happier than right now. Akihiro, you are responsible for giving her the happiness she looked for so long. For that, I am truly indebted to you. We are proud to have you join this family, especially on your own volition. Cheers to the bride and groom!"

Once again, Laramie wiped her eyes while Akihiro and Edward shook hands. Not to be outdone by Edward, Andrew stood to say a few words. His action surprised Violet, who found it too late to pull him back into his chair.

"Lara, Edward did a fine job of raising you. We could've done better but he needed you to force him to grow up." Laramie laughed. People rarely saw this humorous side to Andrew. "We never expected you to travel half way around the world to find a husband." Andrew placed his hand beside his mouth as he pretended to speak in a whisper to Akihiro. "Did the check clear?" Akihiro almost spit out his drink while Manny choked. "Violet and I wish you many years of happiness and health. We will miss you dearly but look forward to all the emails. To the bride and groom, cheers."

Laramie wanted to stand and hug Andrew but she was a prisoner in her chair for the moment. She thanked Violet and him for their beautiful words. Lian started to clank the water glasses with her silverware. Laramie could see as everyone joined her that Akihiro was not familiar with this custom. She leaned into him and explained the noise meant for the bride and groom to kiss, which they did. He asked aloud if this was only good at weddings or could he continue it at home. Manny told him to continue the tradition. Akihiro backed his chair out behind him and grabbed his glass. Laramie didn't notice him as she faced Lian in a conversation. Akihiro cleared his throat, which caused Laramie to turn around.

"I want to thank you, as does Laramie, for being a part of our wedding celebration. We couldn't imagine the day without all of you. Personally, I want to thank Manny for being my best man, and a great new friend. You helped me get through some tough days. But in all sincerity, I would like to toast my new bride, Laramie." They looked at each other with smiles. "I hope you stand against the waves that come toward you. I hope you find new heights that you accept in your heart. I hope you always sing to your own song. I hope you roll with the punches that are thrown your way. I look forward to going through life together. Most of all, I love you."

Laramie teared lightly. She smiled at the memories behind each of his statements. He pulled her chair back so she could stand. She wrapped her arms around his neck and kissed him. Manny laughed at Akihiro's reference to the accidents she had in Singapore. Laramie realized Akihiro told him about the early days together. Manny turned to Edward and relayed the story, which brought on many snickers. Laramie shook her head in disbelief and allowed the embarrassment to continue. She told Akihiro that he owed her handsomely for his lack of discretion. After Akihiro sat, Laramie stood alone.

"Thank you, all of you. You are my family and I love each of you dearly. To my husband, I am glad you stuck it out with me. I couldn't imagine growing old without you. I love you very much. So… in honor of this special occasion, I have decided to sing you all a song."

Lian clanked the glasses as quick as she could. To stop her singing, Manny threw his napkin at her. Akihiro stood rapidly and kissed her to shut her mouth. Edward covered his ears with his hands, as did Andrew and Linda. Violet actually laughed when she realized by everyone's actions that Laramie could not sing.

"Okay, I won't sing, I promise." Her statement caused a rowdy applause by her guests and husband.

After dinner with a cleared table, the waiter brought out the wedding cake. It was small but very elegant. In the center of the cake was a small bunch of orchids. Around the edges, a swirl design replicating lace went all around. The edges had small pearls with smaller beads in between. The photographer poised himself in the center of the table across from the bride and groom. Laramie and Akihiro stood and cut the cake together. They each took a small piece, gently placed it in each other's mouth and kissed. The guests all cheered the new couple and tapped their glasses. Akihiro pulled his bride close and kissed her openly and with enthusiasm. Laramie blushed from the display.

As it neared nine o'clock, the guests slowly left, leaving only Manny, Lian and Akiko. Edward arranged for the payment to be on his credit card before Laramie or Akihiro could do anything. They expressed their appreciation to Manny and Lian again for all their support and patience. They kissed their daughter goodnight before they retreated to the Presidential Suite 910 for their wedding night.

Laramie stood in the hall alone after Akihiro entered the room. He turned to see where she was. She educated him on the tradition of carrying the bride over the threshold. He smiled, picked her up and carried into the suite. As they entered the suite, Laramie noticed the Steinway grand piano.

"Look, I can sing a song for you after all. You need to sit there and play something for me," she jested.

"I only know instrumentals," he joked back

The golden color of the furniture stayed subdued with the muted colors of the wall and rugs. Laramie walked over to the chaise lounge and laid back. She used her toes to kick off her shoes. Akihiro sat across from her on the matching sofa and tucked the striped pillows behind his head. They both looked at the ice bucket with a chilled bottle of champagne and grinned at each other. He stood, placed his suit coat on the adjacent chair and took off his shoes before he poured them a glass of the sparkling wine. *Damn, I can't sit up. The fabric has me pinned.* Laramie laughed as she asked for help up since the train of her dress held her back on the chair. He walked over to her and bent his knees to the floor. He wrapped his arms around her and lifted her to a sitting position. Her eyes flickered around his face as she smiled at him.

"I love you, Mr. Amori."

"And I love you, Mrs. Amori."

He held her face with both hands and kissed her. The aggressiveness in her kiss surprised him. She loosened his tie and began to unbutton his shirt. He unbuttoned the sleeves as she worked on his belt and trousers. He helped her stand and turned her around. She needed his assistance to undress since the laces were out of her reach. He untied the bow at the bottom of the corset and pulled the laces free. As he pulled the straps to the side, he kissed her shoulders and back of her neck. She slowly moved out of the bodice of her dress and let it fall to the ground. He ran his hands down her body to the sides of her thong. She stood still and waited for a reaction. *Oh, geez. I know he's going to say something. I am going to feel embarrassed, no less on my wedding night.* He placed one hand in front and one in the rear to push it down. Immediately, he noticed the results of the waxing then hesitated a moment before he continued to remove it. When she faced him, his grin was devilish. She smiled back but could feel the heat in her cheeks.

"What have you done, Laramie?" he teased.

"I don't know what you mean," she responded as she tried to avoid the question. *Absolutely the last time I get a Brazilian waxing.*

His kisses began at the base of her neck as he moved to her mouth. She met him with the same fervor. She had a few surprises for him tonight. The first, he obviously discovered. She loved the contact of their skin. It made her feel closer to him. As his lips pulled away, she started a trail of kisses down his chest. Her hands worked to remove the last remaining clothes on him. When her mouth reached his waist, he pulled at her arms.

"Lara, you don't have—"

"Shhh."

She didn't want him to interrupt her. This was a huge step for her in their lovemaking. She wanted to make this night different from all the others. Once she made her way to the southern hemisphere, he began to groan. She assumed this was a good sign since it was her first time. For once, it was *his* breathing that increased which improved her confidence. When the groans became closer together, he pulled her up and plunged his tongue in her mouth. She ran her fingers through his hair and down his back. He laid her back against the chaise and kneeled between her legs.

"Akihiro, tell me you love me." She half smiled after she said it.

"I love you."

"Tell me you want me." She planned to use his method against him. He knew her plan.

"I want you. I want you body and soul."

He placed one of her legs over the side arm and the other to the floor. He stared into her eyes for a few seconds, his breathing still rapid, before her entered her. Laramie held onto him as he buried his face in her hair along the side of her neck. She felt the muscles in his lower back flex with the movement.

He moved back from the chair and pulled her toward him. He lifted her up and she wrapped her legs around him. When they reached the bedroom, he pulled the comforter to the floor before he laid her down.

As he climbed to her on the bed, she demanded, "I want you and I want more."

This was a monumental evening. He knew she would always remember their first time and their wedding night. It had to be unforgettable. She was insatiable tonight and that excited him tremendously. He did things with his hands and her body she never imagined. She remained open to his moves and embraced every new feeling. When she reached her peak, she didn't moan softly or plead quietly to continue, she screamed out his name repeatedly. She learned to be a better partner as he guided her to help him in his climax. When he finished, he continued to kiss her with an intimacy she never felt before. Their lovemaking reached a new level that night.

Afterwards, she lay against his chest with their legs mingled together. They were exhausted. It remained quiet in the room as they caught their breath.

"Lara, you were amazing. Just unbelievable."

"No, *we* were amazing. You were a part of that, too. I've been lying here and all I can think is 'wow.' I can't think of another word for that."

"Love, passion, adoration, honest, raw. Or, just 'wow' works fine." She softly laughed.

"Are we done for the night?" She crossed her fingers in her mind.

"Yes."

"Oh, thank you. I don't think I can move. What about the lights?"

"Let them burn out on their own. I'm not getting up," replied a worn out Akihiro.

"Push me to the side. I'll turn them off."

Laramie rolled off the edge of the bed to stand. She walked into the living area and shut the lights off. When she entered the bedroom, she turned off the lamp on the nightstand before she returned to her spot in the bed.

"I love you, Laramie Amori," he said in the dark.

"I love you, too."

Chapter 81

AKIHIRO PROPPED HIMSELF onto his side as he watched Laramie sleep peacefully. If she snored the previous night, he wasn't aware of it. He took a lock of her hair and brushed it slowly and lightly across her face. She crinkled her nose from the irritation but still slept. By the third time, she opened her eyes. Once her bearings were set, she smiled at her husband.

"Why didn't you just wake me? It would've been easier."

"It was more fun this way. You must've been tired to sleep this late."

"What time is it?" She partially sat up to find the clock.

"Just past nine o'clock. Are you in a hurry this morning?"

She smiled and shook her head no. He asked if she wanted to eat or wait.

"Wait for what? Because I don't think I can do another session like last night without food first. I don't think I've been that exhausted since our first night together in Singapore."

"I have something for you. Do you want it now or later at home?"

"Ooh, I have something for you too. I almost forgot."

"Who goes first?"

"No, who's *on* first."

"What?"

"He's on second."

"You've lost me. Completely."

"Sorry, just a little American baseball humor. I'll explain it another time." She laughed to herself and kissed him an apology. "I want to go first. I believe the rule is that person with the newest name goes first."

"I believe you made that up."

"See, the second rule is that the person with the newest name also gets to make the rules. It's a deep rooted American tradition." Even with her best poker face, he didn't buy it.

"Good thing we leave for Singapore in three days because there you have to be a citizen to make the rules."

He climbed out of bed and went into his bag. He pulled out the small box and brought it to her. She quickly sat like a child at Christmas time, excited to open a present. He started to hand it to her and as she went to grab it, he pulled back for a kiss as an exchange. Laramie slowly ripped the paper and revealed the box. She looked in his face to see if his expression gave any clues of what was inside. *Nothing. What could it be?* She lifted the lid and gasped.

"Oh my… it's beautiful. You didn't have to do this. Ooh, I love it. I really do." She kissed and hugged him.

"Do you know what the other three stones are?"

"Yes, it's definitely a chick thing. They're my family, you, Akiko and me. You are so romantic. I just love you."

She placed the box on the bed and had him fasten the bracelet on her wrist. She held it up and watched the stones dangle on her arm. It could've been a homemade crayon picture with the three of them and she would love it the same. She told him to wait in bed while she brought out his gift. Her nerves jumped in anticipation of his reaction. The size of the box surprised him. *What could she have gotten?* She placed the box in his lap and told him to wait until she sat across from him. She wanted to see his face when he learned what the object was. He tore the paper off and opened one end of the box. Inside was a slightly smaller box. He looked at her to see if this was a trick. The next box opened on the length. He lifted the lid and pulled away the tissue paper. As soon as he saw the fabric, he knew what she bought.

"Lara, tell me you didn't." She grinned as much as if it were hers. "What have you done?"

He pulled the stand out first, then the gloves. He took a deep breath before he went any further. Next, he pulled out the wooden case and opened the end. He tilted the case and the sword slid out. He put the gloves on before he went further. Then he drew the sword from its sheath.

"A Katana Samurai sword. I'm speechless." She clapped her hands together. She knew she did well. He looked at the papers and read the maker and date. "A Yakekuni, no less. It's beautiful but you shouldn't have done this."

"It's for when we go to Karaoke!" She laughed.

He started to smirk then fought to hold it in. It wasn't possible. The visual he made of her on the stage singing was enough to burst into laughter.

"Actually, I'm going to bring it with me if we ever go camping." He laughed.

Her mouth dropped with his statement. "Manny is so dead. That rat fink. How much has he told you? I have to keep you away from him. Oh, I just can't believe him. Good thing we're moving."

"When he growled, I about fell off my chair. You have to see the humor in it."

He put the sword away as he continued to giggle.

"What I see it two grown men behaving like boys comparing Laramie stories. Each well equipped no less." She pretended to pout. "You're not supposed to pick on me."

He pulled her close so her face was near his.

"Come on, no pouting. Those stories and imperfections make you real. I love those things about you."

"I think you're just saying that so you can have sex later."

"No, I'm saying it so I can have sex right now." He grinned.

After their late morning romp, they showered and dressed. They sat at a table along the wall in the Terrace Restaurant that overlooked the grassy gardens at the hotel. Laramie ordered a fruit platter, croissants and a cappuccino. She decided to start a healthier diet since he was a better eater than she. He ordered a vegetable omelette, tea and ice water. Although he adjusted to the fare in the States, he wanted to get home where the dishes were normal to him.

"I have a moving company coming today at two to pack up all the clothes. It shouldn't take long since the bulk of my closet is cold weather clothing. Akiko's things are small and that shouldn't take more than one or two boxes."

"How long before your things reach Singapore? Any estimate on that time frame?"

"Since the boxes are lighter, even though there may be many, they gave me an estimate of two to four days."

"Faster than I thought. I can have Ahmed take the truck and pick your boxes up at Changi."

"We are going to need a crib first thing. Then a dresser for clothes..."

"Lara, calm down. It doesn't have to be done at once. Besides, Shinji already bought the crib. It almost matches the one she has."

After breakfast, they had a cab take them to the flat to drop everything off, then they drove Laramie's car to Manny and Lian's.

"Well, good morning, newlyweds. You both look well rested. Nothing else needs to be said," Manny voiced. He stayed home due to an alcohol related illness.

"As a matter of fact, there is one thing, Manchu." Laramie pinched his ear and said with her teeth clenched, "It seems someone told my husband about a camping trip."

He pulled away from her grasp and hid behind Lian. Lian shook her head and rolled her eyes at her husband's lack of self-defense.

"I'm sorry, Laramie. It slipped one night after a few beers. It's not like he hasn't heard the chain saw ripping through wood in the middle of the night. Between your snoring and singing, which I use the term loosely, you scare the hell out of everyone."

"Was there an apology in that?" She lunged around Lian and Manny continued to run.

Akihiro pulled her off the antagonist.

Akihiro looked at Lian and said, "I came here for my other child. Any idea where she's hiding?" Lian walked him to the rear bedroom where Akiko sat quietly as she played with her teddy bear. From the living area, they heard Manny beg for Laramie's forgiveness followed by a few 'ouches.' *Hmm, she must have a good hold on him. Poor excuse of a man. I'm almost embarrassed.* Akiko saw her daddy walk in and stood quickly with arms up, as if that was automatic. He picked her up and spun in a circle, which made her giggle. *I love that laugh.* He carried her bag filled with clothes and toys over his shoulder as he held her in the other arm.

"Are we ready? I have one more stop to make," Akihiro poised at Laramie.

"Yes, but where else do we need to go?"

"I'll get to that. Thank you for everything. We had a great wedding in part because of you both. And, thanks for taking care of Kiki. We'll see you out tomorrow night for a big farewell, right?"

"Absolutely, just let us know where and when," Lian replied. "You are welcome to bring her here anytime. I'm going to miss saying that."

Once they reached the car and strapped Akiko in her seat, Laramie asked him where they needed to go.

"We need to stop in and see Edward."

"Edward, for what?"

"So I can sign the papers as the new CEO of Cummings Corporation." She screamed with delight and placed small pecks over his face. He smiled back at her.

"I am so happy you decided to do this. I'll help you any way you need."

"Actually Edward is staying on another year in a consulting capacity. I spoke with Rhys and he's game to take Andrew's place with the same arrangement. Your job is to file the documents with the government to open the office in Singapore, a task you are familiar with already."

"Of course. What made you change your mind?"

"I thought about Akiko and you. This is your family's legacy. Your grandfather and parents worked hard to build it, like my hotel. You've already given up your home and friends. I wanted to give you something back. And since you've already stated this fact, Kat is more than capable of running the Tanjong."

"What did she say when you told her?"

"I haven't yet. I wanted to wait until we returned. I'm hoping she wants this promotion."

"I'm sure she does."

Before they entered Edward's office, they met Linda up front. She congratulated them again and told them how much she enjoyed the wedding. They thanked her for words of kindness. Laramie was happy that Linda was there for Edward. It made her choice to move to Singapore easier with the knowledge he had someone to care for him. Linda told Laramie she would keep Akiko with her during their meeting. She motioned them to go on in. Edward pulled out a stack of papers and set them in front of Akihiro. He described them as his contract. Laramie reviewed each page as she passed them to Akihiro. She explained briefly what each page meant. She called out the board reports, stockholders share and dividend statements, all the areas he specifically had to complete. There were incidental items on travel, housing and stock options. However when they reached the page that his listed salary and bonus package, his shock caught them off guard.

"Is something wrong? I know we didn't discuss salary and so forth so I put together a package I thought was fair to all parties," Edward inquired.

"Are you serious? I mean really serious? Don't you think it's a bit extreme?"

"Well son, then you have me somewhat confused. We can entertain a counter offer."

"No, Edward, you don't understand. This is a generous… no, a tremendous amount of money. I expected less, a lot less. I can't possibly except that. I would feel that I was taking advantage of the situation."

Edward scratched is forehead a moment. "Akihiro, let me explain American business to you. First, you never negotiate a lower amount for a salary unless you boost your bonus structure. Second, despite what you may think, the offer is a competitive amount based on the cost it would take to replace *me*. I took into consideration the cost of living in Singapore that varies slightly to San Francisco. Laramie, …" Edward looked to her for support.

"As your attorney," she said with a smile, "my expert advice would be… to take the money and run. No, just kidding. Edward isn't doing anything special for you, *believe* me, he's not that type of businessman. I see the P &

L's, so I know what the company can afford. If you run it into a higher profit, then you profit. If you don't, Edward and Andrew will call you immediately. It is a reasonable offer for the position, really."

Akihiro looked back and forth between the two, unsure of his next move. *They are talking about a base salary nearing seven figures alone. Maybe I'm not ready for this type of position. What will I have to sacrifice for that income?*

Laramie crouched down beside him. "Look at me. He isn't doing you a favor. You need to see that fact right now. By taking the position, you are doing us the favor. It would take months to find then interview the right person. I know you can do this, I've seen you work. Do this for the reasons you told me, if for no other."

She held out the pen for him to sign and waited for him to take it. He sat into the chair with his hand stretched over his mouth as he contemplated the deal. Finally, he grabbed the pen and signed his name.

"I really hope this was the right choice." Laramie kissed him and told him it was.

After they left the firm, they went back to the flat. Neither were hungry since they had a late breakfast. Once inside, Akihiro fed Akiko so Laramie could set aside the things she wants in her suitcase. It wasn't much longer when a man from the moving and storage company came in with boxes. She explained she only wanted lightweight and summer clothing packed. He loaded her closet into wardrobe boxes so her clothing would remain on hangers. When he went down to his truck for a second time for boxes, she realized she underestimated the amount of clothes she had. She packed the contents of her dresser into smaller boxes. *It's hard to believe I've been here six years. So much has changed in the last two alone. One benefit in keeping the flat is that I don't have to permanently say goodbye. Now, Akiko's room, that will be hard. How big will she be when we come back to visit? How many times will she sleep in her crib before she's too big?*

"Laramie, you need a hand?" offered Akihiro.

"Not here. I'm almost done with my room but if you want to start on Akiko's..."

"*Want to?* I was going to suggest me taking her to the park so she wasn't in her room while you packed."

"That's actually a better idea. By the time you come back, she'll be ready to nap."

He kissed her good bye after he dressed Akiko in her coat. Laramie finished her room. The moving man labeled her boxes and took the larger ones to his truck. Laramie walked into Akiko's room and looked around. She loved the mural of the Singapore Botanical Gardens. *Now she can see the real thing. I wonder if she'll notice that.* Her small clothes took minutes to pack. Laramie placed some mementos in the boxes between the layers for safety in shipping. *The picture of Akihiro has to be packed. She loves to see her Daddy.* Once she finished packing, she counted twelve boxes in all. *Oops, only six more than my estimate. Just think of all the people I keep employed with my shopping.* The man gave her a list with all the shipping numbers on the boxes so she could track them. He told her once they get loaded, which would be in a day or two, they will air-ship to Singapore. She thanked him and tipped him before he left.

She walked around the place and had a surreal feeling about the move. *I know I'm going but it still doesn't feel real to me. Being married still doesn't feel real either.* She looked at her ring and smiled. *But it is real.*

Shortly after four, Akihiro and Akiko arrived back. He told Laramie he fought all the way home to keep her awake. Their daughter whined a bit once she was inside. Laramie picked her up and carried her to bed. She tossed a few moments before she finally fell asleep. Akihiro sat on the sofa and looked outside at the bay as he held a beer in his hand. She walked over and sat beside him.

"It is a beautiful view. Will you regret leaving it?"

"No. I'm going to where there's a better one." He turned his head and kissed the top of hers, which made her smile.

Akiko slept only a short while which surprised her parents. Laramie felt it was a lucky break for them as she hoped her daughter would go to sleep better at night. By the time dinner neared, Laramie's stomach growled several times. They decided to walk a few blocks and go to the Pacific Catch on Chestnut Street. Outside Akihiro locked Akiko's stroller and carried her inside. When they opened the door, their hunger grew as they absorbed the smells of the room. Laramie sat at a small table against the windows, not usually available on the weekends. Akihiro sat across and held Akiko on his lap until their server brought a highchair. They perused the menu as they looked for the one thing to satisfy their hunger. *Ah, finally, normal food. It's almost like being in Singapore but colder.* Their server, a pleasant girl in her early twenties, came for their drink order however they were ready to place the dinner order as well. Laramie asked for the Chipotle Mahi Mahi salad with a glass of the Thai iced tea. Akihiro ordered the Tofu Teriyaki rice bowl and a Tiger beer. Laramie made a face of disgust when he mentioned the tofu.

"You will learn to like it."

"Ah, no. I tried that at your hotel even with sugar and lychee fruit and it was still bad. It's nothing but white looking Jell-O. It's gross."

The server brought their drinks and offered to heat Akiko's bottle, which was welcomed warmly by Laramie. Her iced tea was sweet and creamy in flavor.

"How's your beer? Feel like you're at home yet?"

"Close, real close."

When their food came, they seemed like starved animals. Neither took a break from eating to converse. Akihiro realized their behavior first.

"You would think we've never eaten before." Laramie couldn't answer with a mouth full of salad. "We haven't said two words to each other since our food arrived."

"Here's two words for you… I'm stuffed. I ate way too fast and my stomach hurts."

Laramie took a drink from her tea when Aki suggested they work it off later. Unfortunately, it caught her funny and she sprayed the tea out of her mouth but at least not her nose. Most of it dripped down her hand. Akihiro tossed his napkin at her and shook his head.

"Singapore. The reason is Singapore. The closer we get, the more things go wrong for you."

"That has nothing to do with it. Your statement surprised me and I found it humorous. I had a full mouth of tea. Lucky, I didn't drown from it."

When the check came, an argument ensued over who would pay it. Laramie told him that when he's in her town, she pays. Another American rule. He opted for the traditional rule of 'the man pays.' Laramie let him pay but the discussion continued all the way back to the flat. Even inside, she still ranted about equality, joint bank accounts, and personal contribution. When he couldn't stand it any longer, he kissed her to shut her up. She still tried to sneak a few words out until he held her mouth closer. Quickly, she got the message.

"We can continue my part of the discussion after Akiko goes to bed," said Akihiro as he winked.

Coming down off her high, Laramie responded, "Okay. I really didn't have anything left but I'd be glad to listen."

They rolled a ball with Akiko, read a few stories to her and danced with her. The baby seemed to have hidden energy and not tire from any activity. Laramie swore off anymore late afternoon naps. Finally, Akihiro scooped her up and brought her to her room. He sat on the rocker and read stories to her. By the second book, she yawned. He knew she was on the decline. When he reached the end of the fifth book, she repositioned herself in his arms completely asleep. He gently placed her in her crib and covered her and her teddy bear.

"Whew. I didn't think she would ever fall asleep. Can I get you something while I'm up?"

"No thanks. I poured myself a glass of wine while you were reading. I just wanted to unwind a bit. It's been another long day." She sat with her computer on her lap.

While he had the refrigerator door open he called back to her. "Do you want to have everyone here tomorrow to get rid of the food and beer?"

"No. I have Francesca coming once a month to monitor everything here. She'll go through all of that sometime on Friday."

He joined her on the sofa. "What are you doing?"

"I'm changing my billing for all the utilities and cable. Plus, I already changed my mail to the office. They can overnight my bills to me until I have everything completely changed. I have to change my address for my banking but I can do that in Singapore."

"What are you doing about your car?"

"I'm dropping it off at Edward's before the airport. He's going to drive to Palo Alto and store it in Frank Paradise's garage. I don't want the headache of trying to sell it right now."

"How much do you have left?"

She knew where his mind headed. "Just a few minutes." She quickly finished her work, made a few downloads and shut down her laptop. She picked up her glass and drank the last few sips of wine before she stood, went into the kitchen and placed the glass in the sink. When she walked back into the room, she bent down behind him and placed her arms over his shoulders as he sat. She lightly kissed his neck before she asked if he wanted to go to bed. His grin was her answer.

Chapter 82

LARAMIE RESTED ON her side and stared between the slits of the vertical blinds to view the fog on the bay. She spent most of her life in this city; those connections brought pain and joy. She hoped for a clean break but knew that was unrealistic. Her true feelings would reveal themselves when the goodbyes officially began. She thought her new beginning would overshadow her mourning the loss of her previous adventures.

Akihiro awoke and lay quietly in bed. He didn't know if Laramie awakened or lay asleep since she was so silent. He caressed her arm, which caused her to turn over. She had tears rolling from her eyes.

"Laramie, tell me what's wrong. Why so upset?" He pulled her closer.

She wiped the tears with her hand. "I thought it would be easier to leave. Now I see how wrong I was. I'm going to miss everyone so much." She cried into his shoulder.

"Lara, it'll be okay. Everything will be fine. Of course, you'll miss your friends and family. This was your home. It would be wrong if you didn't miss it. Shh. It'll be all right, I promise you. We'll get to Singapore and you will be so busy with starting the new corporation and finding a bigger house. Besides, Kat and my Mum will have you all over the city." He rubbed her back as he tried to console her. "Anytime you become homesick, you tell me and I'll help you through it. Okay?" She nodded yes. "Come on now. You have the entire flight to Singapore to cry. You don't need to start now."

She sniffled. "I know you're right. I just can't help it. I get so emotional since Akiko was born." He laughed. "What? Why are you laughing?"

"You've been emotional since we met. I can't believe you don't recognize it."

"Alright, well maybe a little." She smiled back at him. "Just hold me close."

"This is my last full day in San Francisco and after almost five weeks, I've barely seen the city. Why don't we spend the last day sightseeing? If you don't have any plans."

"No. That's a great idea. Let's see… you've seen the piers, the wharf, Chinatown, Golden Gate Park, and Union Square. We can go over to Sausalito for a few hours and have lunch there. How does that sound?"

"That sounds great. Let's get moving."

They decided to drive over despite the lack of parking since they had Akiko's stroller. This also gave Laramie the opportunity to make a few stops on their drive. The dense fog on the Golden Gate Bridge blocked the view of the top. After they pulled off the highway to Sausalito, he understood more her statements regarding an automatic shift car. Houses and roads sprang from any viable area on any steep surface. The homes along Bridgeway reminded him of the contemporary homes on Sentosa only without the privacy. They parked along the road and started their walk. Laramie popped into a two story Victorian building to browse the women's clothing. He waited outside with Akiko and watched the people walk. When she came out empty handed, they continued their walk. He noticed the Starbucks on the corner. *Just like in the city, one on every corner. Americans humor me with their habits.*

He saw a gallery, actually many, but went inside one to check out the oil paintings of boats. Laramie assumed he wanted to add to his collection. She decided to cross the street and let Akiko run in the small park. *I have to let her run a bit or she'll never sit still at lunch.* Laramie took coins out of her purse and showed Akiko how to throw them in the fountain. Her first throw made it in, however, the other coins she preferred to drop right at the edge. When her daughter ran out of money, she looked to her mother for more. *I know that look. More, Mom.* Laramie shook her purse and felt the bottom for loose change. Fortunately, she found more money. After the fountain collected her money, Akiko ran in circles on the grass until she fell from dizziness.

When Akihiro left the gallery, he looked up and down the block for them before he looked across the street. He spied the stroller and knew they were close. He sat on the concrete bench on the opposite side of the iron fence from his wife and daughter. He smiled as he watched Laramie pretend to chase Akiko. His daughter squealed with laughter as she ran past her mother. After a few minutes, Akiko recognized her father on the bench and ran toward him. Laramie stood up and walked near Akihiro. As she reached him, she informed him that it was his turn to entertain their daughter since she was out of breath. He gladly took over that duty. He held her hands and spun her like an airplane. He put her down and watched her try to walk. When she gained her equilibrium, her hands went into the air for another trip.

Laramie suggested they eat lunch before anymore playtime. They decided to walk back near the car and find a place to eat there. As they came upon Scoma's on its own pier, Akihiro thought it might be great for the view alone. They entered the walkway down the side of the Victorian style building. The place was in immaculate condition and seemed very charming with the gingerbread trim. The interior was crisp with white table linens and settings. The white walls had gray wainscoting and casually placed artwork and mirrors. They sat against a window and placed Akiko between them. They both ordered sandwiches, a bay shrimp salad and crab cake burger. Laramie had the waitress fill Akiko's bottle with warm water and shook the formula inside. Between sucks on her bottle, she eyed her parents' meals. Laramie wanted to see if she would try any of their food but since it was seafood, she knew it wasn't safe yet for her age.

"Since it's our last night here, I thought I'd surprise you with where we'll be going for dinner. I've seen the restaurant but never ready paid attention to the cuisine. Anyway, I think you'll like it."

"Another surprise? I thought we agreed not to withhold anything from each other any more," he teased.

"It's not that kind of surprise. Remind me when we get outside to call Lian, Edward and Andrew with where and when to meet. I doubt the place will be crowded on a Thursday night but you never know."

After lunch, they walked back to the car and Laramie made her calls. Everyone planned to meet at six o'clock at Straits in the San Francisco Shopping Center on Market Street. Laramie told them to go up to the fourth level, near Nordstrom's.

"Well, everyone has been informed of the time and location. Let's get Akiko home for a nap even though she'll probably sleep in the car. She'll be up late and I don't want her to become cranky at dinner."

"I'm ready for a nap as well," added Akihiro.

"No way. You need to stay up in case Akiko wakes up. I'm taking the bed."

Laramie raced back to the flat to keep Akiko from falling asleep. Akihiro talked with her along the way. The baby stayed quiet for most of the short ride but wanted the sleep her parents denied her. As they pulled in front of the building, Akiko's head began to bob.

"We made it just in time. Looks like we both can have a nap."

As they entered the dwelling, Akihiro carried Akiko to her crib and placed her down for her nap. There was very little fighting. Laramie dropped her purse on the counter and checked for messages. Andrew and Violet had to cancel their attendance to the farewell dinner. Their daughter had an emergency and needed her parents to watch the grandchildren. *Emergency, my butt. I know Violet is just being a pain. God only knows what he ever saw in her.* Laramie pulled out her laptop to check their reservations for tomorrow's flight. *I really hope Akiko travels well. That is a long time in the plane for such a young child.*

When Akihiro came out of Akiko's room, he met Laramie on the sofa.

"What are you doing now?"

"Oh, nothing. I just wanted to check our flights for tomorrow. We're at the bulkhead in business class. Since the seats fold out to a bed, we should be fine getting Akiko to sleep. We'll see how she reacts to flying tomorrow."

"Shut down the laptop and meet me in the bedroom."

"Ooh, that sounds interesting."

"Not really. I'm actually going to sleep and so are you. With the stress you have coming, you might as well get some rest in now."

She knew he was right. She didn't want to think about the things she had to accomplish until tomorrow morning. If she started now, she would never fall asleep. She set the computer on her dining table and walked into her bedroom. Akihiro already lay on the bed and patted the mattress for her to lay down next to him. She kicked her shoes off in her closet and then joined him. She started to speak when he cut her off with a hush. She tried again and he replied in the same manner. She got the hint and remained quiet.

As she spooned next to him, she wondered what life would be like in Singapore with her new husband. *Will we go out much? Will we be homebodies?* The major issues they covered but she wondered about the small things. *Does he squeeze the toothpaste from the bottom or the center? Maybe I'll just keep my own tube. I know I have to take my shoes off at the door. That's very Japanese. His car. Oh geez, Akiko won't fit in there on a regular basis. What do we do about that? I'm going to have to do laundry again. Oh, I hate that. Who's going to watch Akiko while I work? I don't know anyone well enough to trust them.* The questions compounded in her head.

"Lara, go to sleep."

"How did you know I wasn't asleep?"

"You weren't snoring. You have to snore. How else will I grow accustomed to the sound of a tugboat near my head?"

"Funny. You know, you have little idiosyncrasies too."

"Really? What are they?"

"I can't think of one since you put me on the spot. But when it comes to mind, I'll tell you." She lay there for a minute. *I know he has to have one. There's got to be at least one. Come on Lara, think. Aha!* "You eat off my plate. So there."

She felt vindicated by her statement. He wasn't the model of perfection after all. Now that she had that behind her, she could sleep easier. He smiled to himself at how she just had to make a point. *It doesn't matter what she finds about me, nothing can top her horrid singing.*

Manny and Lian arrived first at Straits. He told the hostess they had a reservation for a party of eight. Slowly up from behind, Laramie corrected him that they were a party of six. She explained that Andrew and Violet cancelled at last minute. Not a surprise to anyone there.

The hostess led them past the bar to a long table near the kitchen. The décor was in dark reds with long cream contemporary lanterns as fixtures. It was modern with obvious Asian influences, including Buddha. The hanging panels between set areas had etched glass stenciling with a Thai feel. They passed some of the conversation areas that sat lower to the ground than the tables for a more intimate atmosphere. The walls held draped golden fabric as the cover. The kitchen area was mainly in stainless steel that reflected the light into the dining area along with some unknown yet heavenly aromas. Laramie wanted a brighter spot and became happy when the hostess motioned them to their seats.

A young waitress came and took their drink orders. Shortly after that, Edward arrived with Linda. Laramie faced Lian, Manny and Linda. She had Akiko between Akihiro and herself. Edward sat at the head of the table as the patriarch. It seemed comfortable for everyone to see each other and converse. Once Akihiro opened the menu and viewed the choices he understood her surprise. The restaurant Straits stood for the Straits of Singapore. The menu contained dishes native to his home.

Akihiro leaned over to Laramie and kissed her on the cheek. "I see the surprise now. Thank you."

She smiled back at him. "I found it a week or so ago. Had I known it was here, I would've told you. I know all the American food hasn't been good for you. Besides, it gives me a head start in what I'll soon be eating."

Manny interjected, "What is some of this anyway?"

Everyone else felt relief when Manny asked that question. Akihiro explained what some of the ingredients tasted like which made their choices easier. They decided to order different items and share them around the table. When the waitress came back, they placed their orders. Laramie pulled out a jar of baby food and fed Akiko while they waited for their entrees.

Edward was the first to breach the subject. "Are you all packed and ready for your flight?"

"Yes, I checked our reservations as well. Everything is fine. The moving company is supposed to email me the tracking codes for our clothing. It should all arrive a few days after we get there."

"Laramie, what will you be doing with all of your time? I can't believe you won't be working," Lian asked.

Akihiro stepped in. "Actually, she'll be working with me."

"At the hotel?"

"No. She's going to open a satellite office for the firm and establish Cummings' Corporation's new headquarters in Singapore."

"Well, I don't follow. How is she working with you if not at the hotel?" Lian questioned, as she was unaware of his acceptance of the position.

Akihiro explained that he would be the next president of Cummings Corporation. Edward added a few statements in between pauses. Despite the surprise, the Tién's felt it was a great career move for Akihiro and Laramie. As things settled, Laramie would move into the role of Mom as her first position.

"Who's going to watch Akiko while the two of you work?" Linda said.

Akihiro commented that his mother would watch Akiko. Laramie didn't mind the suggestion or the thought, however, the offer needed further discussion. Lian caught the surprised look on Laramie's face.

Lian asked, "Aki, are you ready to make the transition from your bachelor pad to a family home?"

"Yes. It'll be tight until we find a larger home. I don't think the place is large enough to accommodate Laramie and Akiko's clothing alone." He laughed.

"Just be thankful I only packed warm weather clothing then."

Manny asked about the location of the office to the home, transportation, and language barriers. Akihiro explained the main language was English with a Singapore twist similar to the Aussies. He expressed a surety that Laramie would pick up the slang quickly. Lian noticed Akihiro had an answer for all the questions. Laramie took a backseat to him, which was uncharacteristic of her.

"Lara, are you ready to make the transition to have a man disturbing you home?" Lian joked.

"As long as he doesn't squeeze the toothpaste at the wrong end, I'll be fine."

"What's wrong with the middle?" She rolled her eyes at his statement. "Okay, tell me the rules now so I'm ready. What other things are there?" Laramie shook her head and planned on not giving a response. Akihiro pushed her. "Tell me. I can tell by your expression there are other things."

She exhaled deeply before she responded. "Well, you squeeze the tube from the end so there aren't any air pockets. Toilet paper wraps over the top. I don't know. I can't think of those things off the top of my head."

"Don't forget your closet. What about the mess in there?"

"What about my closet? It's the only part of my home that isn't organized."

"Oh, come on. Look at your kitchen. Everything is scattered all over. The reason you can't cook is because you probably can't find anything in there." Laramie began to feel uncomfortable by the conversation. "Look at the refrigerator. Until now, there was never any food inside it. It amazes me how you fed Akiko with things in that state."

Lian knew by Laramie's expression that the conversation needed to end as did everyone else at the table. Laramie took criticism well but not when it came to Akiko. She was defensive regarding her mothering skills.

"Aki, let's just drop it," she asked quietly.

"No, you have to admit living with you won't be any easier than living with me. At least now there will be two of us to take care of Akiko."

With his last statement, she stood up and excused herself from the table. She turned and walked calmly to the restroom. Everyone else at the table looked around uncomfortably with the situation. Manny was the first to break the silence.

"So, who's going to run the hotels?"

"Well, Kat will once I promote her when we get back. It was Laramie's suggestion, and a great one at that." Akihiro looked at his dinner guests and sensed something was amiss. "What is it? She didn't have to use the restroom, did she?"

Lian nodded no. He said he was going to talk to her and Lian suggested she do it. She excused herself from the table and joined Laramie in the restroom.

Lian knocked on the different doors until she reached the stall with Laramie inside.

"Lara, are you okay?"

"Yeah. I can take the fact I have faults. I just don't know how to respond when someone questions my ability to take care of my daughter. Out of all people to criticize me, why my husband?" She sniffled.

"I don't think he made the statement on purpose. Men say stupid things all the time. He knows you're a great mother to her. I think he meant to say that with two of you your parental duties will be split."

"I had to leave the table. I didn't want to cause a scene. It's too late for that now. I saw everyone's expression when I left. I know I have to go back and sit down. I just don't know a way to do it unnoticeably."

"There isn't one. Just come back with me and put this behind you. I'll keep the subject matter changed. This is our last night together and I don't want to spend it in the restroom, okay?"

Laramie opened the door and smiled at her friend. She stopped in front of the mirror and touched up her makeup before they exited. Once they made it back to the table, Laramie apologized for taking so long and didn't realized they waited on her before they ate. She smiled and said the food looked amazing. Lian agreed with her and despite her pregnancy, the food looked appealing. Laramie avoided eye contact with Akihiro at first until she felt she could contain her feelings well enough.

Everyone passed around their entrees for each to sample. They agreed the Origami Sea Bass was their favorite, then the Lemongrass beef, although no one disliked any of the dishes. The conversation stayed limited with all the full mouths. Drinks were replenished frequently. Lian reminded Manny that he worked the next day and to limit the alcohol. Linda inquired when Lian's baby was due. Lian said they estimated the due date to be in early November. Laramie expressed her excitement for the baby's arrival and her plan to be visiting at that time. Linda asked if Laramie had met Akihiro's parents. She said no but she did meet Shinji, his younger brother. As the conversation increased, the mood lightened at the table. Akiko wanted more rice and Laramie fed it to her. They all laughed as Laramie tried to show her how to hold a spoon. Most of the food flung on the floor toward the kitchen. Laramie apologized to the waitress for the mess, offering to clean it.

When the check arrived, Laramie grabbed it. Edward tried to make her give it to him but she refused. Akihiro told her to hand it to him and he would take care of it for them. Still, she refused. Akihiro let it go despite the tension it created. Manny toasted to Laramie and Akihiro and their new life together. He wished them many blessings for their home, work and life together. The rest of their friends joined in the well wishing, too.

After she paid the bill, they met outside the restaurant and took the elevator to the first floor. Once they reached the sidewalk, the women began to cry. Laramie knew she would miss Lian outside of work and Linda at work.

"Laramie Amori, you better email me all the time and send pictures of Akiko getting bigger," demanded Lian.

Laramie nodded yes since her crying impaired her ability to speak. They hugged for awhile. Manny came up to her and hugged her tightly. She knew she would miss him and his humor. Their friendship dated back to their early days at the firm. He was her first friend in the city. He maintained his honesty with her, which she always appreciated. She viewed him as a sibling with all they shared. Manny shook hands with Akihiro and welcomed him again to the family. He said he would miss his friend but knew Laramie would keep him in line. They shared a manly hug before Lian interrupted for a hug goodbye as well. Eventually, they got into a cab and went home.

Linda hugged Laramie goodbye first, then Akihiro. She thanked Laramie for pushing Edward to move ahead in his life with her. Laramie always liked

Linda and knew she was a great match for Edward. Frankly, she was the only woman who tolerated his behavior. Edward came forward toward Laramie. She knew he was the most important force in her life. She cried hard while she hugged him.

"I am going to miss you so very much. Who will keep me in tow with all those lectures? You have been my father the last eighteen years and I love you so much. How will I go on without you always by me?"

"Laramie, I will always be there for you. All you need to do is call me. Dear, you have given me more years of joy than I can tell you. I can't thank your parents enough for entrusting me with someone they loved so much. We have been a great team together. I will miss you terribly but it is time for you to move on with your new family. I know you will be happy and make the right choices ahead. It's hard to believe that little blonde girl with braces is all grown up and moving on in her life. I love you with all my heart." He had tears for her as well.

Edward shook Akihiro's hand and patted him on the back. "Please make her happy. That's all I ask from you."

"I'll do my best Edward. I promise you. Thank you for everything. I wouldn't have any of this if it weren't for you. Thank you so much."

Edward and Linda entered a cab and waved goodbye through the window. Laramie waved back before she turned into Akihiro's shoulder and cried hard. She hugged him as he held Akiko in his other arm. He knew the difficulty she faced in leaving them even though she didn't. He tried to calm her at first but felt it was better for her to get it out of her system. When she stopped to wipe her eyes, he hailed a cab. They entered in and placed Akiko between them. She pulled a tissue out of her purse and continued to wipe her eyes.

Akihiro didn't say a word until after they reached the flat. Once inside, Laramie had Akiko kiss and hug her father goodnight before she placed her in her pajamas. She read her a story and gently carried her to her crib. She kissed her daughter lightly and laid her flat. Laramie closed the door partially as she exited Akiko's room. Once she walked from the nursery, she went into her bedroom to change. She was still upset by Akihiro's words in addition to leaving her friends and family. The night became more emotional than she prepared herself to expect. Once she had her nightshirt on, she left the bedroom for the kitchen. She wanted a glass of wine to calm her and help her sleep better. After she had her glass poured, she turned to exit the kitchen. Akihiro stood in the entryway. He took the glass from her hand and placed it on the counter. He held her in his arms. She placed her arms around him but not tightly.

"Lara, I am so sorry. I never meant to insinuate you were a bad mother at all or that you needed my help in the future. You have been a great mother to Akiko and that is evident to everyone. I should've chosen my words better. Will you forgive me?" He poised the question as he held her chin up in his hand.

"I have done my very best with her and I'd like to think I've been a great mom to her so far. The last thing I expected was to hear you criticize me, especially in front of everyone. And then with the check. Why can't I pay for anything? I have an income. I am an adult. I don't understand your problem with that. Am I supposed to be subservient to you?"

"First, I didn't mean to criticize you, not at all. I am sorry if that is how it came across. Second, I know you have an income. As a matter of fact, it far exceeds mine. I'm just more traditional when it comes to finances. It's just how I was raised. I know I need to loosen up on that and I will. But most importantly, don't ever think you are subservient to me, ever. You are my partner, we are equals. You are never behind me but beside me. Will you forgive me?"

She knew she did. She could never stay mad at him. She told him she forgave him and picked up her glass of wine. She walked toward the living area to sit and relax. Akihiro watched her pass by and followed her to the room. Once she placed the glass on the table, he knelt down between her legs. She wondered what more he wanted to say.

"Laramie, you are an amazing woman. I've known that for a long time and everyday you show me more of how wonderful and giving you are. I am so lucky you want me, to the point of giving up your life here to be with me. I can only see and hear how much you love your friends and home. I can't feel what it's like for you to say goodbye. I love you, I really do."

She smiled at him. *He always finds the right words.* "I love you too."

He pulled her face to his and kissed her passionately. Her state of mind didn't matter, she melted every time he touched her. Her breathing increased with every kiss. She ran her fingers through his hair and down his back. He continued to kiss her until she finally pulled away and said she wanted him. His eyes glanced over her face as his heartbeat moved faster. He stood up and took her hand to help her stand. He pulled her behind him to the bedroom. He undressed quickly and helped remove her nightshirt. They stood together as she kissed him. She told him she wanted him now and again and always. As they lay on the bed, she continued to tell him how she wanted him. He found the talk completely erotic and aimed to please her every request. Laramie knew her words turned him on and said them specifically for that reason.

After they made love, she lay in his arms as she stroked his hand. Despite their earlier nap, they tired from their workout. Laramie made sure to set her alarm, even though they had plenty of time to get ready before their flight. They exchanged their *I love you's* before he shut the light off and went to sleep.

Chapter 83

AFTER THEY DROPPED off Laramie's car at Edward's house, they arrived at the airport with plenty of time. Laramie had her fill of the international concourse and wished she was on the flight already. She wanted this part of her new adventure to be finished. She was ready to start her new life with her family in Singapore. Akihiro sensed her restlessness and suggested she browse the shops, he'd watch Akiko. At first, she declined but as she fidgeted in her chair, she took him up on his offer. She didn't want a magazine, she read most of them at the hospital; none of the books appealed to her either. She purchased a few bottles of water for the flight and returned to her husband and daughter.

"Nothing worth buying in the shops?"

"Nothing that I had room for in my carryon. I hope Akiko fairs well with the cabin pressure and time. It'll be hard to keep her occupied."

"She'll be fine. We'll keep her occupied between the two of us."

Akihiro took his daughter's hand and walked around the concourse with her. He felt if she ran her energy off, she might sleep quicker on the flight. Akiko happily accommodated her father. He pretended to chase her and she ran away squealing. Laramie watched from her chair and couldn't help but laugh. She tried to decide who the bigger child was. *There goes my husband and daughter. I never would've imagined this a week ago. So many things happened so fast. If I would've resolved my own issues this could've occurred faster. Nevertheless, it did happen and I am so thankful for that.*

They boarded their flight first since they had a small child to situate. Laramie had a bottle prepared for Akiko for takeoff. Akihiro asked to hold her and feed her since she was less likely to squirm out of his arms. Laramie gladly agreed. As the plane ascended into the clear blue sky, Akiko sat up to see out the window though her father held her down to drink. Laramie felt melancholy as she watched the city slowly shrink and disappear from her view. As Laramie's ears plugged from the pressure, she observed her daughter's expression. *Hmm, I guess she doesn't have a problem with it. Lucky for us and everyone else on the plane.* The longer Akiko lay in her father's arms and drank, the quicker her eyes fell shut.

"How long do you think she'll sleep?" Akihiro asked. Laramie shrugged her shoulders.

"There's no way to know. I guess a few hours. I'll take a nap now so I can take her when she wakes up."

They took their shifts fairly as Akiko played. Thankfully, the airline had bassinettes that plugged into the bulkhead. When the turbulence was low, they placed their daughter there to sleep. Laramie and Akihiro reclined their seats for better sleep as well. Their first thirteen hours passed faster than Laramie imagined, partly due to Akihiro's help. As the made their descent to Incheon Airport in Korea, Laramie picked up Akiko for the landing. Without a bottle to suck on, Akiko cried from the pressure. Laramie tried to quiet her but to no avail. *I can almost feel the tension from the other passengers. Believe me, I don't want to hear her cries either.* Akihiro took the baby and played with her to occupy her attention. As they neared the ground, the pressure lifted and Akiko's mood lightened.

They debarked the plane for no other reason than to stretch their legs. The layover was long enough for Laramie to freshen up in the restroom. When she walked out, she saw her daughter take off down the concourse. Quickly on her tail, Akihiro ran behind her. Laramie pretended not to know either one of them.

"Whew! You could've given me a hand in catching her."

"You seemed to be doing a fine job on your own," laughed Laramie.

"Do you have another bottle ready for takeoff?"

"Of course."

Laramie picked up her daughter and twirled her around. She wanted to keep her busy until they boarded the plane. *We only have six more hours and we'll be home. Hang in there baby. We are almost there. Gee, can I hang in there? I'll be meeting my in-laws for the first time. What if they don't like me? It's not as if they don't have good reason. I kept their grandchild hidden for months. I blackmailed their younger son from speaking about her. I have my own virtual soap opera. Just because we're married doesn't guarantee acceptance into the family.*

The flight to Singapore went smoothly. Laramie fed Akiko on takeoff and landing, which prevented Akiko's crying. As they started their walk toward Customs and Immigration, Laramie stopped Akihiro in the walkway.

"Aki, what if they don't like me? Have you given that any thought?" Laramie grew nervous.

He smiled at her. "They are going to love you just as I do. You are nervous for no reason at all." He continued to walk with Akiko on his side. "Besides, you already have Shinji on your side." *That's true.*

They picked up their suitcases and walked them over to Immigration. Other than a few souvenirs, they had nothing to declare. *Hmm, this went smoother than when I'm alone. Must be because he's from Singapore. Either that or we look so awful they don't want us to stop.* Akihiro walked a few steps ahead of Laramie and passed through the doors before her. She struggled with the two suitcases, as their wheels seemed not to cooperate in synch. *Oh, for the love of Pete. I should've taken Akiko instead.* This only furthered the gap between her and the rest of her family.

The crowd in the waiting area stood together as they awaited the new arrivals. Shinji stood taller and looked among the people coming toward them.

"Here they come. I see Akihiro with Akiko. Laramie is a bit further behind."

As Akihiro neared his family, his grin became larger. He looked to his daughter on his side and told her that her family was up ahead. Once he reached his mother and father, his eyes teared as he introduced them to their granddaughter. Lucia had her tissue in her hand and sobbed freely. She put her arms out to hold Akiko, who went right to her. Akihiro hugged his father and told both his parents he missed and loved them very much. He was happy to be home. Shinji went up to Laramie, once she joined the crowd, and hugged his new sister-in-law. She appreciated his welcome. She knew he cared for her and that made her more comfortable.

"Mum, Dad, I want you to meet my wife, Laramie."

"Dear, we've waited awhile to meet you. Welcome to the family." *Family. That brought tears to Laramie's eyes.* "You can call me Mum or Lucia, whatever makes you comfortable. Tadashi, come closer."

Tadashi walked over to his wife's side. He held his arms out to hug Laramie. This was quite uncharacteristic for Akihiro's father. He was the traditional Japanese man that didn't display emotions, let alone in public. "Please call me Dad."

"Actually, Mum and Dad are perfect. I am so happy to meet you both, finally."

From behind the crowd, a familiar voice sang, "*...have I ever told you that you're my hero...*" Laramie looked around to find her.

"Kat. I know you're here somewhere. Come out or I'll start singing."

"Oh please, I beg you not to do that. We could be arrested for violating the noise ordinance," she laughed and stepped out from the crowd. "Laramie, I am so happy to see you. Or should I say Mrs. Amori?"

Laramie smiled and replied, "Laramie is fine. I'm still getting used to Mrs. Amori."

Rhys stood next to Shinji and waited for Akihiro to come his way. While his parents doted on Akiko, Aki walked to Rhys and shook his hand.

"It's great to see you. I'm glad everyone took off from working on my hotel to meet us here. You're off the clock, right?" joked Akihiro.

"Congratulations, mate. It's about time the two of you got it right. Though, I didn't expect you to become the family man so quickly."

"Neither did I. It took me about two minutes to adjust. Akiko is great."

"Well, what about your wife? Not one for long engagements I see."

Laramie walked up and hugged Rhys. "Actually, I wasn't going to give time to change his mind."

"So I hear. Welcome, Laramie. We've all missed you, Love. Good to have you back permanently."

"It's so good to be back. Looks like we'll be working together again, at least for a short while."

Kat interrupted. "What's this? You'll be working here too?"

Akihiro stepped in. "Actually, there are a few things we all need to talk about. Why don't we meet over at the Tanjong? I can discuss it further there."

Everyone agreed to meet at the hotel. Shinji, Rhys and Kat rode in Akihiro's car. Akihiro, Laramie and Akiko rode with his parents. Between the two cars, they barely fit their luggage inside the trunks. Laramie sat in the back seat with Akihiro and Akiko. She looked out the window as they passed through the city. She smiled when they passed the Esplanade and then the Singapore Flyer. She vowed to get over her fear of heights and do these things with her daughter. The drive seemed to pass quickly since she was familiar with it.

Once they arrived at the hotel, Samad took all the suitcases out of the cars and placed them into the hotel van for delivery later. Laramie held Akihiro's hand as they walked through the hotel lobby. Some of the employees came up to welcome them home and congratulate them on their marriage. Laramie couldn't stop smiling. Lucia held Akiko, who seemed to develop a special bond with her Grandmum. Shinji and Rhys assembled a group of tables outside for everyone to sit. Huan delivered all the drink orders. Ahmed came out of the kitchen once the news spread that Akihiro was back. He quickly returned to make some appetizers for the crowd.

Kat began first. "I can't tell you how happy I am for you both, no, you three."

"It was a lot of ups and downs but we made it," Laramie said. Akihiro kissed her hand.

"So tell me, what's the deal with the business?" Kat inquired.

Akihiro sat back in his chair. "Kat, that's something I want to talk with you about. I wanted to ask how you would feel about taking over the Tanjong for me. Are you up for the challenge?"

"Wow, absolutely, which one?"

"Both."

This caught Akihiro's family by surprise. Rhys and Laramie had the luxury to know the situation already. Akihiro's family kept turning their heads to follow the conversation.

"Both? What are you going to do?"

"Well, first, do you want the job? We can go over salary and benefits later."

"Yes. Of course. Do you know what you are saying? We are talking about the Tanjong, your baby."

"Yes. I know what I am saying. Actually, I will be busy with another business."

Shinji couldn't take the suspense. "What are you going to do?"

His parents wondered the same question and waited for his response.

"I will be taking over Laramie's corporation as CEO. We are moving the world headquarters to Singapore. That's what Laramie will be working on, setting up the new corporation in accordance with Singapore's business laws. Since she has the most experience in that, it was an easy decision."

Kat asked, "I thought you were leaving all of that behind. Then you plan to expand the firm?"

Laramie saw the confusion and spoke. "Yes, I do have the firm. And yes, I will be opening a satellite office here in Singapore for specialized cases only. However, I also have a corporation that I inherited from my grandparents, Cummings Corporation. My parents' friends that raised me, Edward and Andrew, run the corporation and are at the age where they want to retire. Edward asked Akihiro if he was interested in taking it over. After a few days of thought, he accepted. We couldn't just leave it to a stranger to run after all. Akihiro wanted to keep that legacy for Akiko."

Akihiro picked up where Laramie left off. "Since the subsidiaries are located globally, the headquarters could be anywhere. Rhys will be leaving the bank to join me in a finance capacity. Edward and Andrew are staying on for one year in a consulting role. The only thing I need to do is hire a savvy accountant. Board meetings will be easy to plan since the chairman, excuse me, chairwoman is here."

"Holy shit," slipped Shinji.

Lucia smacked him upside the head. "Watch your language around the baby and women as well."

Kat sat in awe. "Laramie, I had no idea. I mean I saw the website but I had no idea you were going to move everything here."

"Imagine my surprise after my arrival in San Francisco. I learned so much about my wife in four and a half weeks." He looked over to her. "She is so much more than an executive and attorney. I should mention what a phenomenal mother she is too." She smiled at his comment.

"I must add my thoughts to all of this news. If Laramie will be working, then I insist to care for Akiko at those times. My granddaughter is not going to be watched by some stranger."

"Absolutely. I wouldn't want it any other way," Laramie added. She thrived on her new family's acceptance of Akiko and her. "Another thing, we are in need of a good realtor to help us sell the condo and find a larger house. Anyone know one?"

Shinji interjected, "I'm on it."

"Wow. This is a lot to absorb at once. Looks like everyone will be shuffling around. Rhys, you never said a word. I call you on everything and you cut me out. I can't believe you," Kat spoke and smacked him on the arm.

"What? I've known for five days. I've been rather busy in that time. Besides, I wasn't to say a word until they arrived home. So, thank your employer." He quickly passed the blame.

Laramie was ready for that part of the conversation to end. She didn't want her friends and family to view her as a giant conglomerate. She was still the same person they met a few years ago. She looked to Akihiro to change the subject for her. He noticed her actions and complied.

"On a lighter subject. Akiko is recovering great. Dr. Patel suggested a brief visit to her hematologist here so he can familiarize himself with her better. Her records have been emailed already. They couldn't pinpoint the cause and Dr. Patel said we may never know."

That news came as a relief to everyone at the table.

"Mum, can you pass her this way? I've been waiting to hold my niece."

Shinji took to her as easy as Akihiro did. He held her on his lap for a few minutes before he realized her diaper leaked. Akihiro, Kat and Rhys laughed aloud while Laramie tried to muffle her reaction. Akihiro stood up, grabbed Akiko and the diaper bag before he headed into the hotel. Everyone looked at Laramie, shocked by his actions.

"He really is amazing with Akiko. He's been that way since his first five minutes with her. He does it all, the bath, the feeding, of course the diaper duty took a bit of convincing. He's a great father and she adores him. Of course, they seem to forget I'm around sometimes."

Laramie went on to describe how they play together and dance. She relayed the stories regarding his first diaper experience, feeding her peas, and at his hotel room when he panicked to find a place for her to sleep. Once Akihiro returned, Shinji took back his niece and bounced her on his leg. He asked to bring Akiko on the beach. Akihiro and his parents wanted to see her reaction to the sand and water. Laramie and Kat decided to stay at the tables and relax a bit.

"So... big changes are happening. I can't tell you how relieved I was that you finally reconciled," Kat expressed.

"It was your words that made the first step. *Smile less, talk more.* I never forgot that. I try not to think of the wasted time. I suppose it all happens for a reason. I can say I've never been happier."

"It shows on you both. Your daughter is beautiful. I can't believe the resemblance to Akihiro either. Tell me, how are *you* doing? I mean with the move. I know your friends and family are back in San Francisco. That had to be hard to leave."

Laramie's eyes welled with tears. "It was hard to say goodbye. I know I'll miss them as everything settles. But this is where my family is now and I try to look at that."

"If you ever need to talk with someone, please call me. I want you to know I'm here for you."

"Thanks Kat. I really do appreciate that."

"You will be busy for awhile. Not only do you have the business to start but a second wedding."

Laramie nodded in agreement. She stated that meant a second bachelor party for Akihiro. That led into a conversation regarding the first party. Kat cried with laughter regarding Akihiro on the floor of the elevator, not to mention the stripper pole. They watched the rest of the group near during their conversation. Rhys asked what the laughter regarded. Laramie mentioned Aki's bachelor party but not any specifics.

"Blimey, that's right. You lucky bloke. You get to have another party. Shinji, we need to start the planning now."

Akihiro shook his head when he remembered his recovery from the first. This also reminded his mother about the Singapore ceremony. Laramie sat attentive as she listened to her mother-in-law's ideas. *No rush this time. However, this does give me another wedding night. Now that is exciting. I wonder which night will be the better one.* Occasionally, Laramie looked at Akiko, who yawned repeatedly. She knew it was bedtime for her, for all of them. The time change slowly pulled their energy away. Akihiro was the first to end the gathering. He caught the yawns as well.

Lucia asked, "Before we leave, Laramie, would you mind if we brought Akiko home with us? I realize it is a lot to ask and if you feel it's too soon, I completely understand. I thought the two of you could use a good night's sleep. It would give you time to sleep in and unpack."

Laramie felt the offer was generous but she felt uncertain about leaving Akiko so soon. After all his parents were still strangers to Akiko. She felt torn in a response. Laramie looked to Akihiro for support. His reaction was indifference. *No help there.*

"Mum. Laramie. Why don't we let Akiko go back with my parents? If she cries, we can always drive in and get her."

That appeased both women. Laramie worried about a crib and clothing when Lucia assured her they had a full supply at their home. Laramie asked about food, once again, Lucia told her they had it all. Laramie finally handed off the diaper bag to Tadashi. Laramie and Akihiro hugged and kissed their daughter. Akihiro knew it was hard for Laramie to let go and he reassured her that their daughter was in great hands. The new Amori couple thanked everyone and expressed their goodbyes before the departed for the condo.

Samad followed them to the condo. Laramie went up first while Akihiro assisted Samad. She came off the elevator and looked around the place. *My new home. At least, for now.* She walked into Akiko's room and saw the crib set up along the wall. *Nice. They had everything prepared for our arrival.* She went into their bedroom and closed the door. She undressed, put on Akihiro's robe, and then walked out to the patio to view the harbor. She smiled when she thought of the Kisaki. As she entered the condo, Akihiro met her at the door. He appeared pleased to see she undressed.

"What do you have in mind, Laramie?"

She grinned. "I've meaning to talk to you about that."

She untied the belt around her waist and let the robe fall open. Akihiro looked down and smiled back at her.

"Are you sure we have time to talk?"

She whispered softly, "Have I told you lately how bad I want you?" She placed her arms around his waist.

"No, why don't you tell me again." He started to kiss and bite at her neck.

"Ooh, I want you. I want to taste your lips." She kissed him with small pecks. "I want to feel your touch here." She took his hand, placed it on her breast and held it there for a moment. "I want to feel your touch here." She moved his hand between her legs. She ran her hand down the front of his pants and knew she excited him. "I want to feel you slowly at first, then faster and harder."

The more she spoke, the more turned on he became. She planned on that effect.

"Anything else?" he said running his hands over her body.

"Oh yes. I want you to make me feel good. Oh, so good like only you know how." She moaned as she spoke.

"You're driving me wild," he said between kissing her

"Good because that's how I want you… wild," she replied as she seduced him.

He grabbed her close and squeezed her body against his before her pulled her to the bedroom. As he continued to kiss her, he yanked his clothes off. He couldn't peal them off fast enough. Laramie kept calling to him with her desires. He climbed on the bed between her legs and touched all the spots she led his hand.

"I want you to show me things you never have before. I want to feel you, all of you."

He plunged into her and she moaned. He started off slow as she asked and gradually moved faster and harder. He sat back on his feet and pulled her hips up to him. He moved his hand between her legs with the same rhythm. Laramie flexed her hips with him.

"Oooh, that feels so good. You make me feel so good. Don't stop. Yes, right there. "

Her words made him move harder inside her that caused her to gasp short breathes. As she began to climax, he bent forward over her and kissed her violently. She grasped the covers in her hands and pulled at them like reins. She let go quickly before she dug her fingers into his arms and yelled out. His excitement continued with her display of pleasure. He twisted her body and moved behind her. He continued to thrust. Her words wound him up to a new level. He couldn't get enough of her.

"Keep going, baby. That's exactly what I want. I want to feel you finish. Ooh, yes…"

She spoke with a soft moan. His hands moved feverishly over her as he continued. Her words were erotic. He called out her name as he groaned. His breathing was rapid as he held her tight. Slowly, his body relaxed. He turned her to face him. He stared into her eyes before he plunged his tongue between her lips.

Once his breathing slowed, he said, "Laramie, you have amazed me tonight. Incredible, just incredible." She smiled at him. "Whatever happened to that shy woman I met so many months ago?"

"She met this incredible lover and married him."

They lay together and kissed before Laramie climbed on top of him. Akihiro moaned, he wasn't ready for round two.

"What do you want this time?" he teased.

She smiled openly before she answered. "I want another baby."

He drew her close to him. His face lit up at her statement.

"Really? Are you sure?" She nodded yes. "I love you, Laramie."

"I love you, too."

Chapter 84

"LIZ, LET ME know when you have us on the screen. Akihiro said it was easy, just go to the website. We should be streaming but with the distance you might have a small delay."

"*Sugar, I can't believe you've been gone a year already. Where did all the time go?*"

"Between starting the satellite office and new headquarters, I have to say most of the time has been spent working. House hunting was the easy part and not too soon. Wait until you see the size of me. I'm huge or at least I feel huge."

"*Well, what name have you decided on? Oh wait… never mind. I thought Randy had it.*"

"Tadashi Thomas Amori. We're going to call him Tom. The order of the names is what took so long to decide."

"*Okay, I see the table and the cake but where are you? I'd say I see your big rear but I recognize it at Gillian's. Oh, I wish I was there too.*"

"I heard that Liz." Gillian interrupted.

"*Tell me what's going on with her and Rhys. Did they hit it off?*"

"They seem to be. I knew they would the minute I met him. He is such her type."

"*Oh I see y'all now. Tell Akihiro to wave. Yes, Randy has it workin' now. Now, Mrs. Amori get in front of the camera and show me your profile.*"

Laramie walked in front of the webcam and pulled her clothes tight against her body to show her protruding belly. Akihiro stepped in front of her, bent down and kissed it. He was proud to have another addition to the family coming in a few months.

"Only a few months left. Edward and Linda promised to fly in after the baby is born. I will hold him to it."

"*Well, where is the star of the hour? I haven't seen the birthday girl yet.*"

"Oh, you mean Princess Jasmine. Let me get her in the room. … Mum, can you bring Akiko in here? Thanks… Okay doll, stand on the chair. Aunt Liz wants to see how big you are. I can't believe she's two."

Akiko waved at the camera and blew kisses. She tried to stick her fingers in the frosting on the cake but Laramie quickly stopped her. Akihiro walked behind the table and dipped Laramie for a passionate kiss.

"*Tell him to save it. We have children watchin' here. Oh Lord, she has gotten so big. Look at the long hair. It see it's finally laying flat. Where's the Chinaman and Lian? I don't see them anywhere.*"

"Wait a sec. I'm going to call everyone in here to sing. Hold a sec… All right everyone, it's time to sing. We have to stand on this side of the table so we don't block the camera."

Laramie stood on one side of Akiko as Akihiro stood on the other. She was flanked by her in-laws, Shinji and Kat. On the other side of Akihiro stood Manny, Lian and their baby boy. Behind everyone was Rhys and Gillian laughing it up.

"Okay, Akiko. When we are done singing, make a wish and blow out your candles. Just wait. Mommy will tell you when. Happy birthday to you,…" This was the one time they allowed Laramie to sing. "… dear Akiko. Happy birthday to you. Make a wish and blow."

RESOURCES

Singapore

Uniquely Singapore (www.visitsingapore.com)
Sentosa Island (www.sentosa.com/sg)
Brewerkz (www.brewerkz.com)
Al Dente Trattoria (www.aldente.com.sg)
Hot Stones Restaurant (www.hotstones.com.sg)
The Clinic @ The Cannery (www.the-cannery.com)
Equinox Restaurant (www.swissotel.com)
Highlander Bar (www.highlanderasia.com)
Rogues Restaurant (www.rogues.com.sg)
St. James Power Station (www.stjamespowerstation.com)
Raffles Hotel (www.raffles.com)

San Francisco

21st Amendment Brewery (www.21st-amendment.com)
Mercedes Restaurant (www.mercedesrestaurant.com)
Pacific Catch (www.pacificcatch.com)
La Mar Cebicheria (www.lamarcebicheria.com)
Straits restaurant (www.straitsrestaurant.com)
Scoma's Restaurant (www.scomassausalito.com)
Asqew Grill (www.asqewgrill.com)
Ritz Carlton Hotels (www.ritzcarlton.com)
Westin St. Francis Hotel (www.westinstfrancis.com)
Harris Restaurant (www.harrisrestaurant.com)

Thea Izzi Designs (www.theaizzi.com)

A warm thanks to Dr. Lynn Hawkins, Linda May and Craig Compton

A special thanks to my Dad for rekindling my interest in Journey.